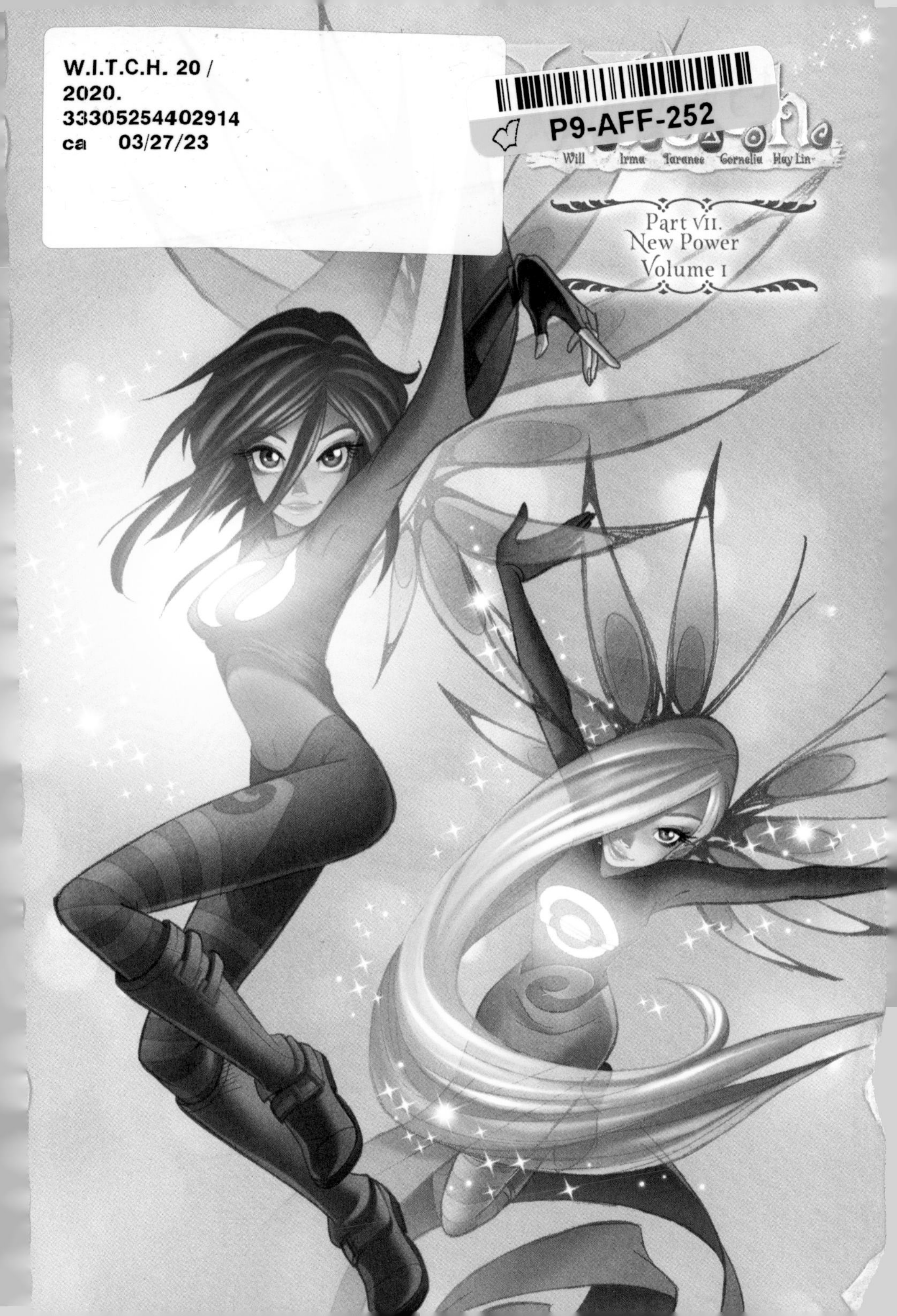
Will Irma Taranee Cornelia Hay Lin
Part VII.
New Power
Volume I

W.i.t.c.h.

Will   Irma   Taranee   Cornelia   Hay Lin

Part VII.
New Power
Volume I

CONTENTS

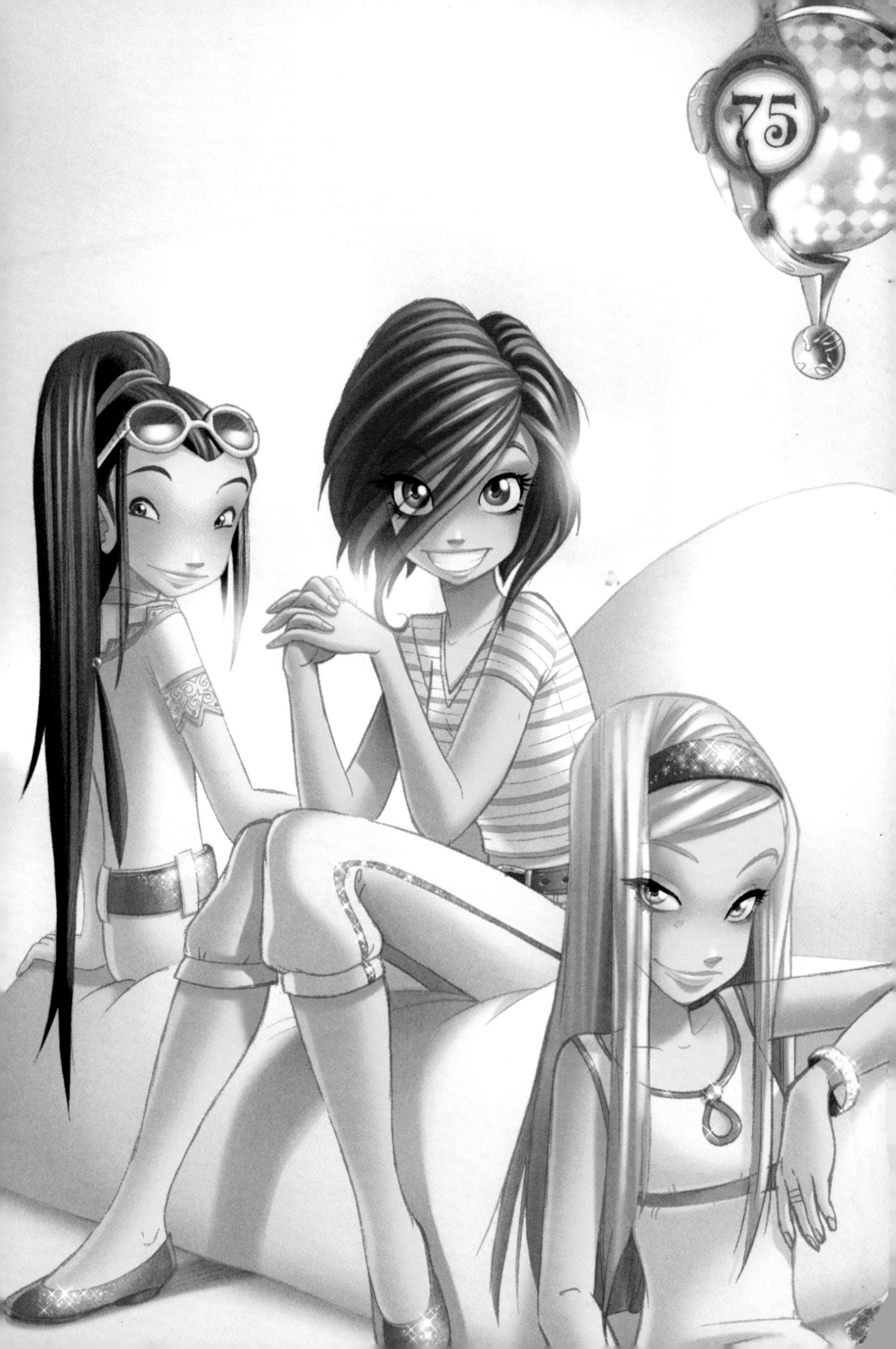
75

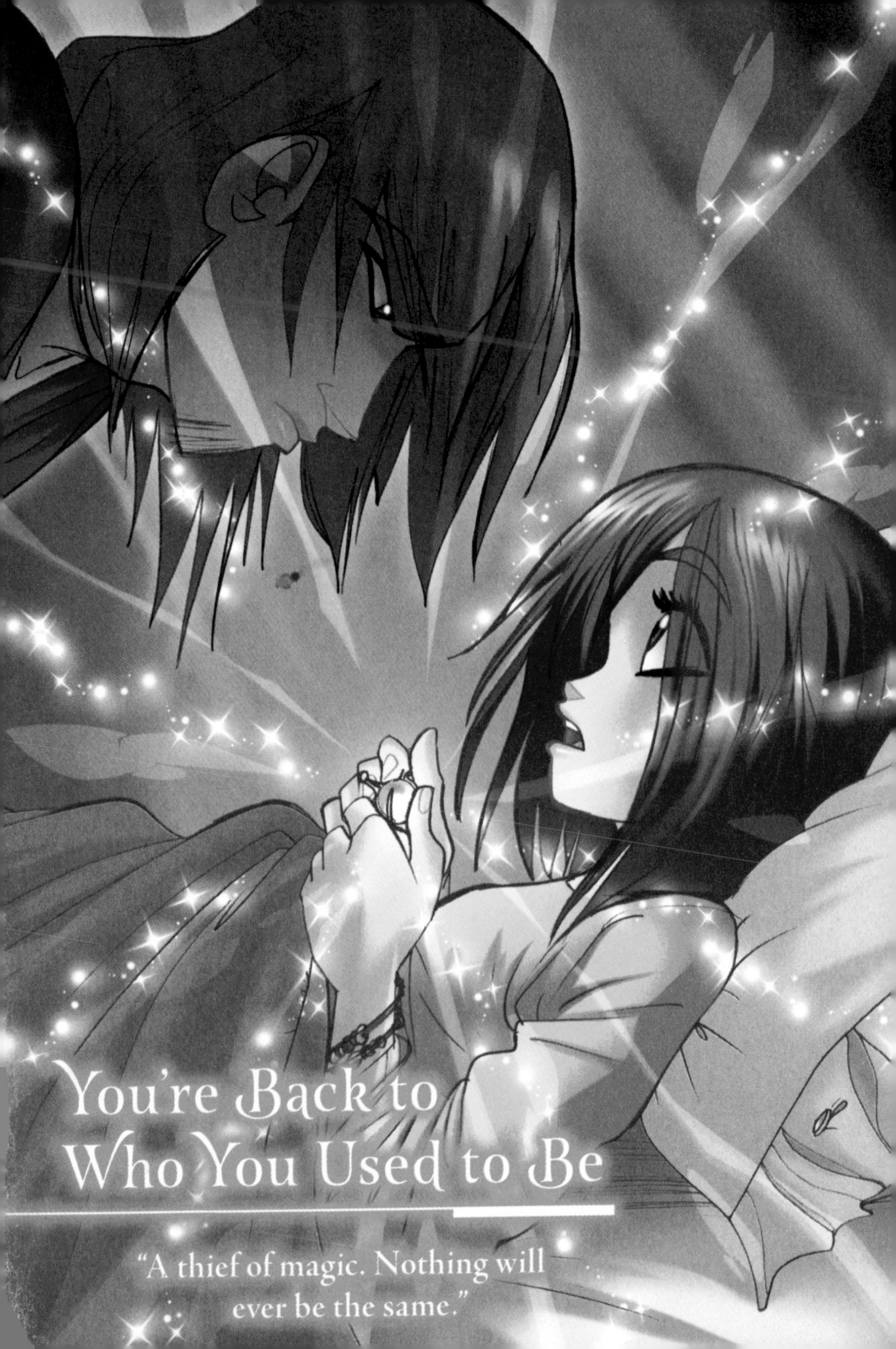
You're Back to
Who You Used to Be
"A thief of magic. Nothing will
ever be the same."

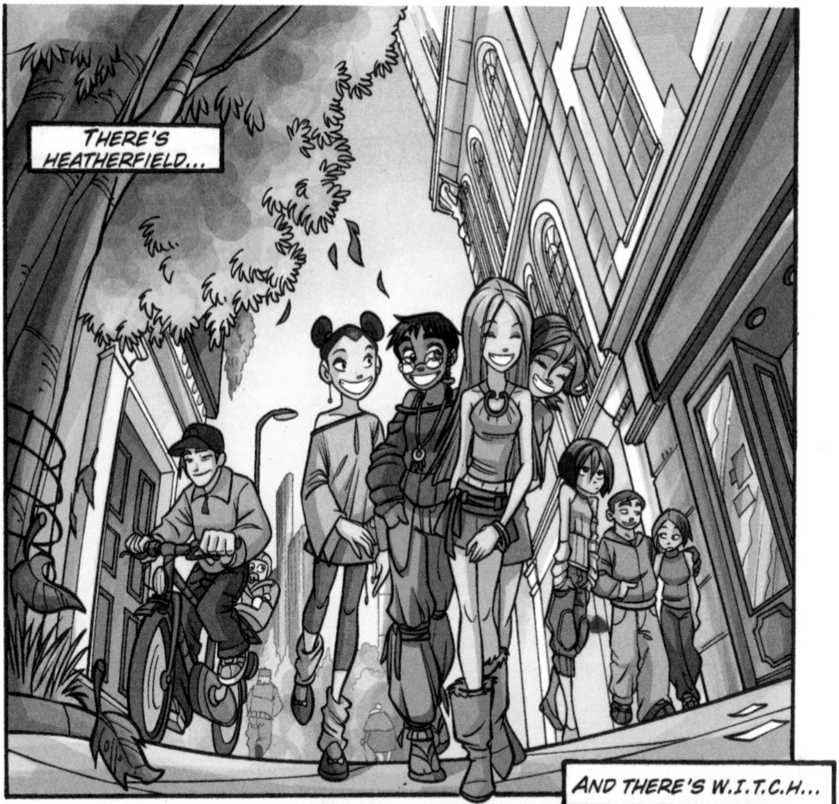
THERE'S HEATHERFIELD...
AND THERE'S W.I.T.C.H...

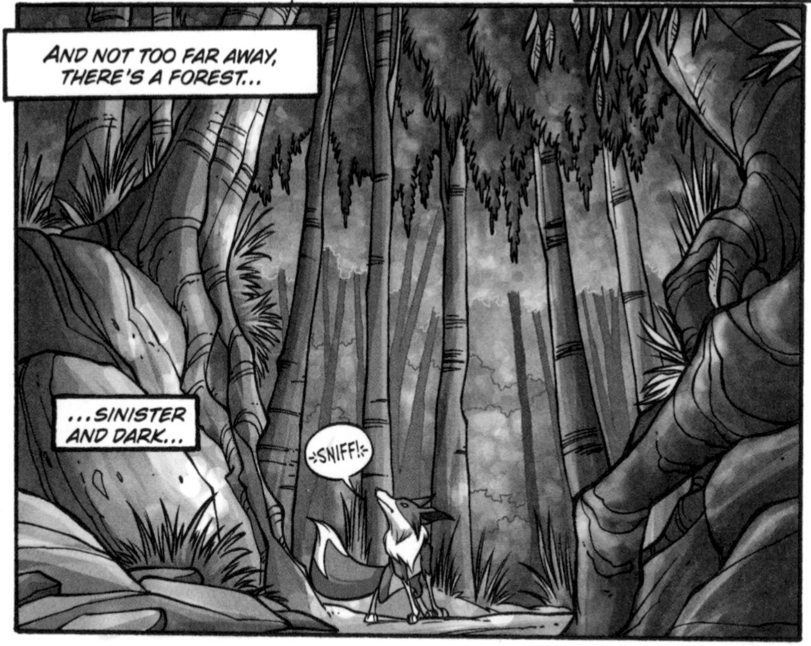
AND NOT TOO FAR AWAY, THERE'S A FOREST...
...SINISTER AND DARK...
-SNIFF!-

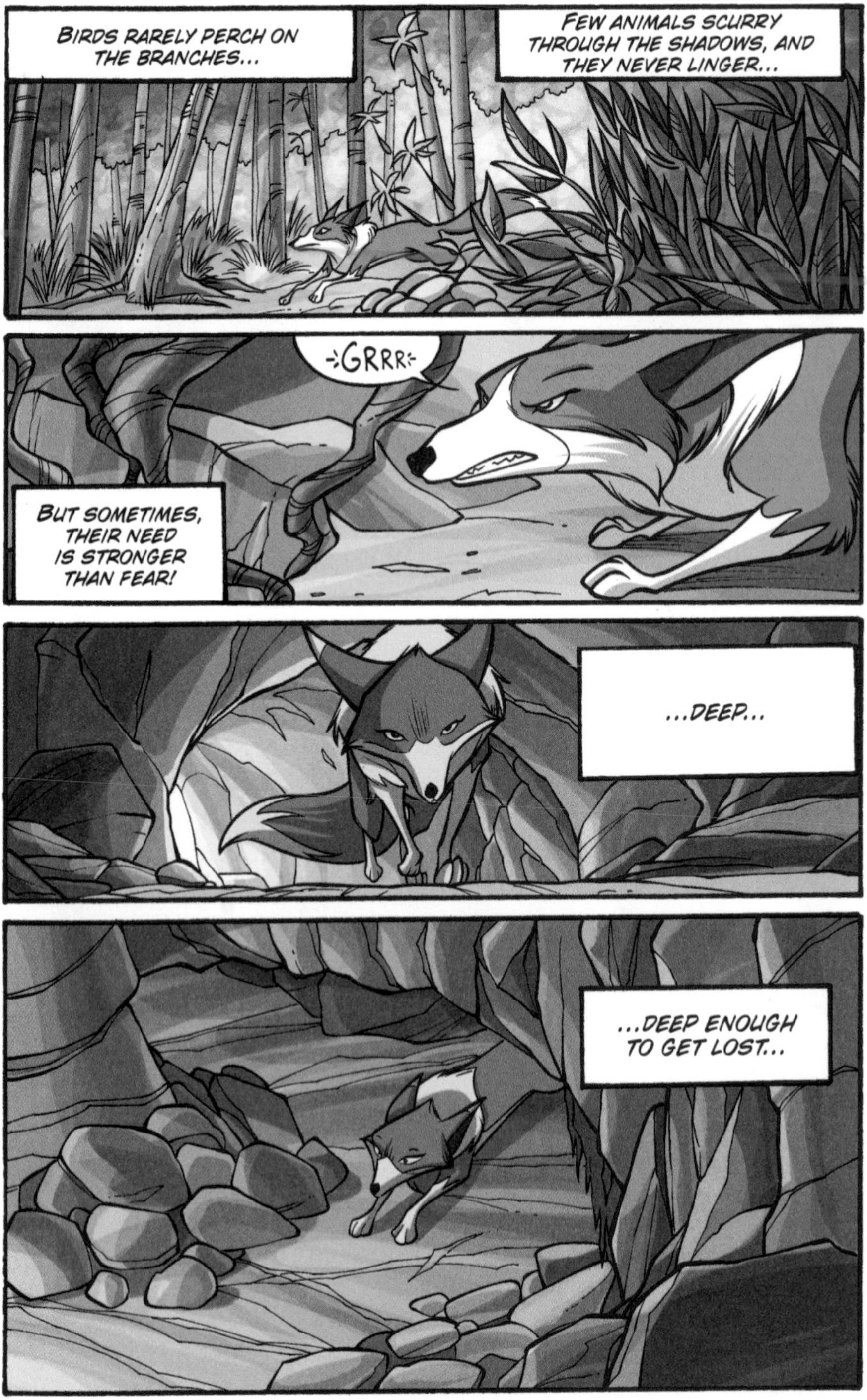
BIRDS RARELY PERCH ON THE BRANCHES...
FEW ANIMALS SCURRY THROUGH THE SHADOWS, AND THEY NEVER LINGER...
GRRR
BUT SOMETIMES, THEIR NEED IS STRONGER THAN FEAR!
...DEEP...
...DEEP ENOUGH TO GET LOST...

BUT ALSO DEEP ENOUGH TO SHELTER THEM WHEN A SUDDEN **STORM** COMES!

WOOOSHHH

FROM THE WIND THAT STIRS EVERYTHING UP, BLOWING BLACK **SEEDS** FROM THE DARK FOREST...

...TAKING THEM FAR, FAR AWAY...

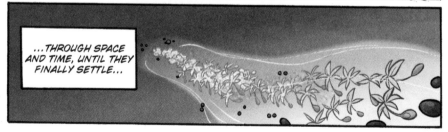

...THROUGH SPACE AND TIME, UNTIL THEY FINALLY SETTLE...

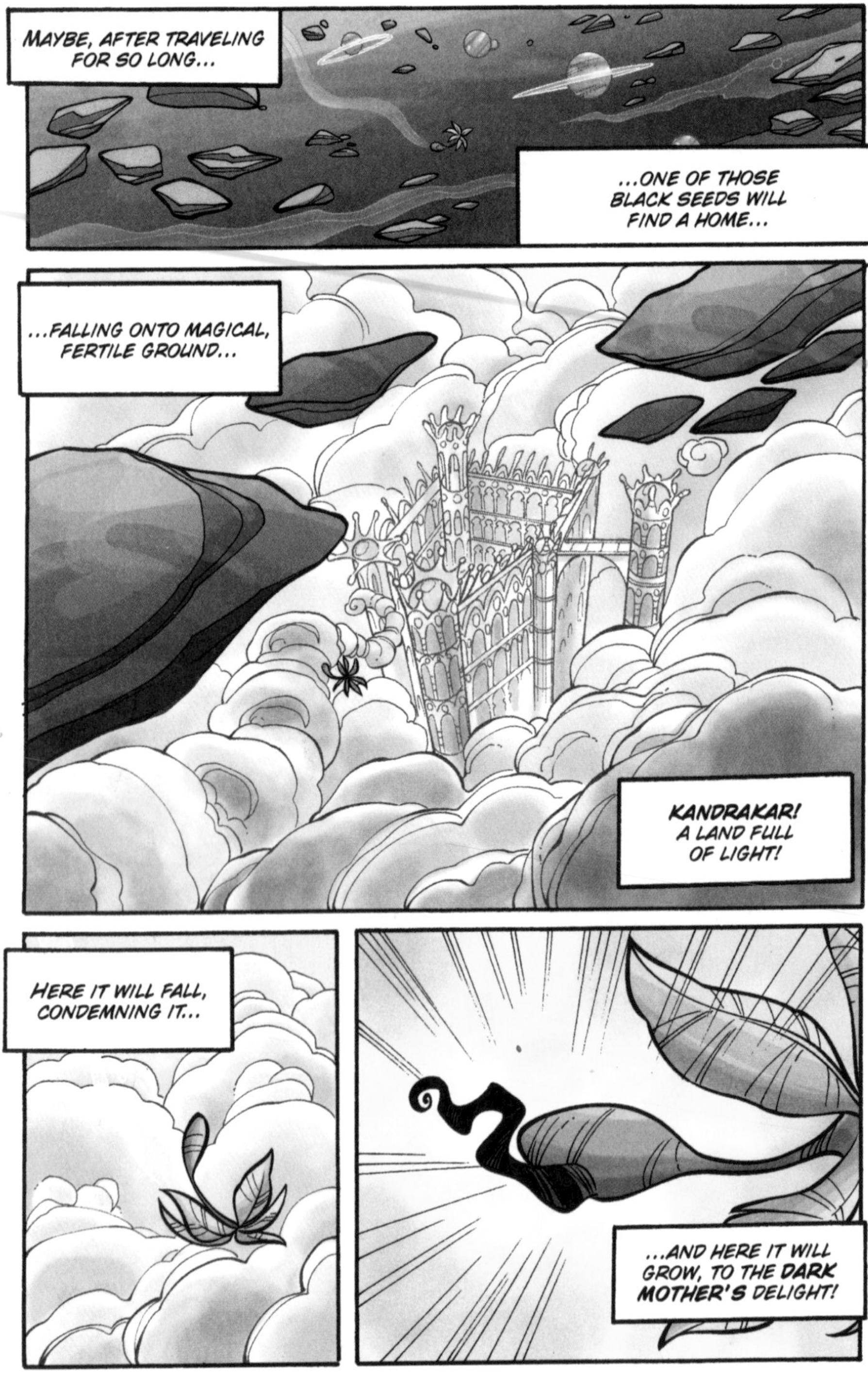
MAYBE, AFTER TRAVELING FOR SO LONG...
...ONE OF THOSE BLACK SEEDS WILL FIND A HOME...
...FALLING ONTO MAGICAL, FERTILE GROUND...
KANDRAKAR! A LAND FULL OF LIGHT!
HERE IT WILL FALL, CONDEMNING IT...
...AND HERE IT WILL GROW, TO THE DARK MOTHER'S DELIGHT!

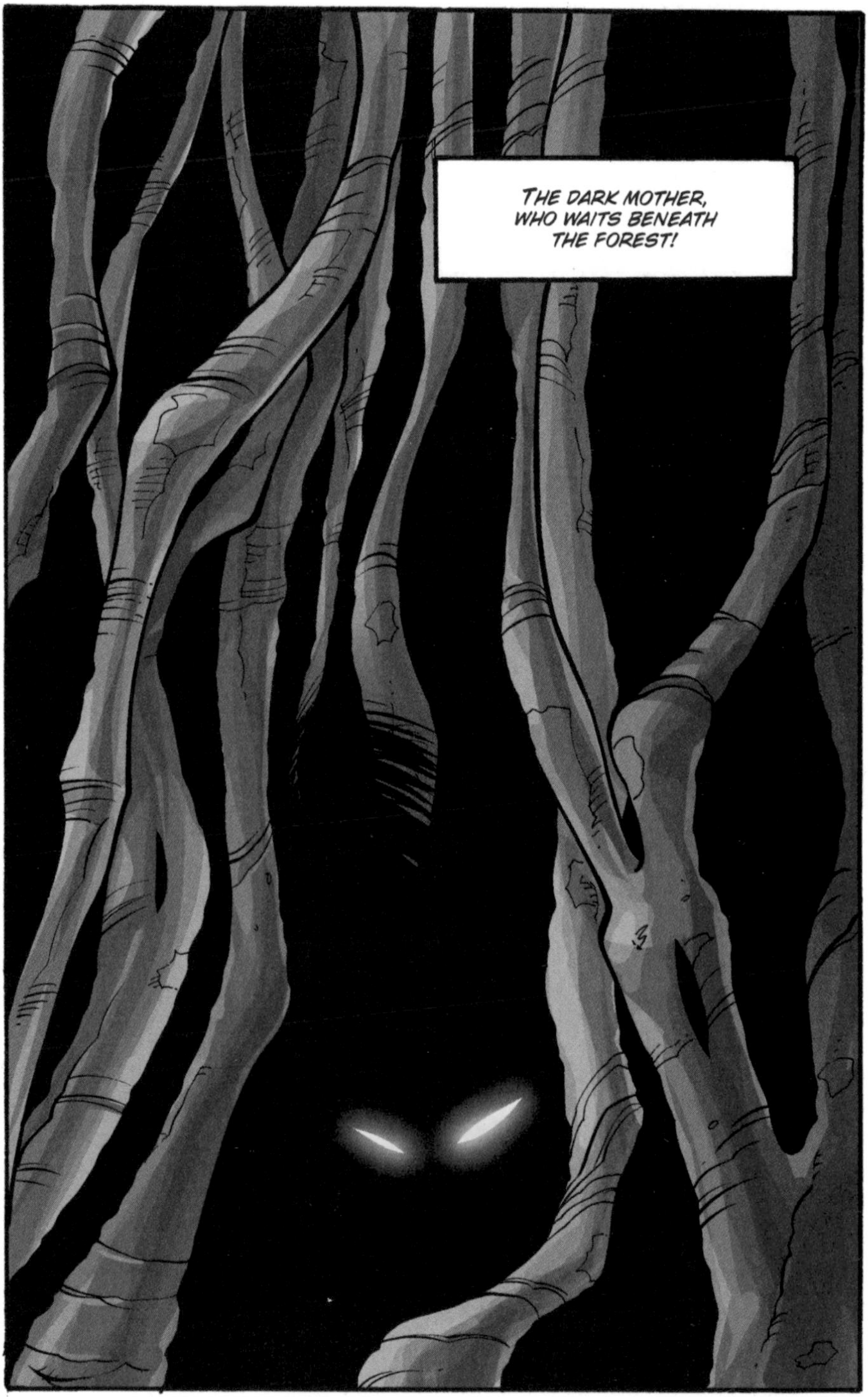
THE DARK MOTHER, WHO WAITS BENEATH THE FOREST!

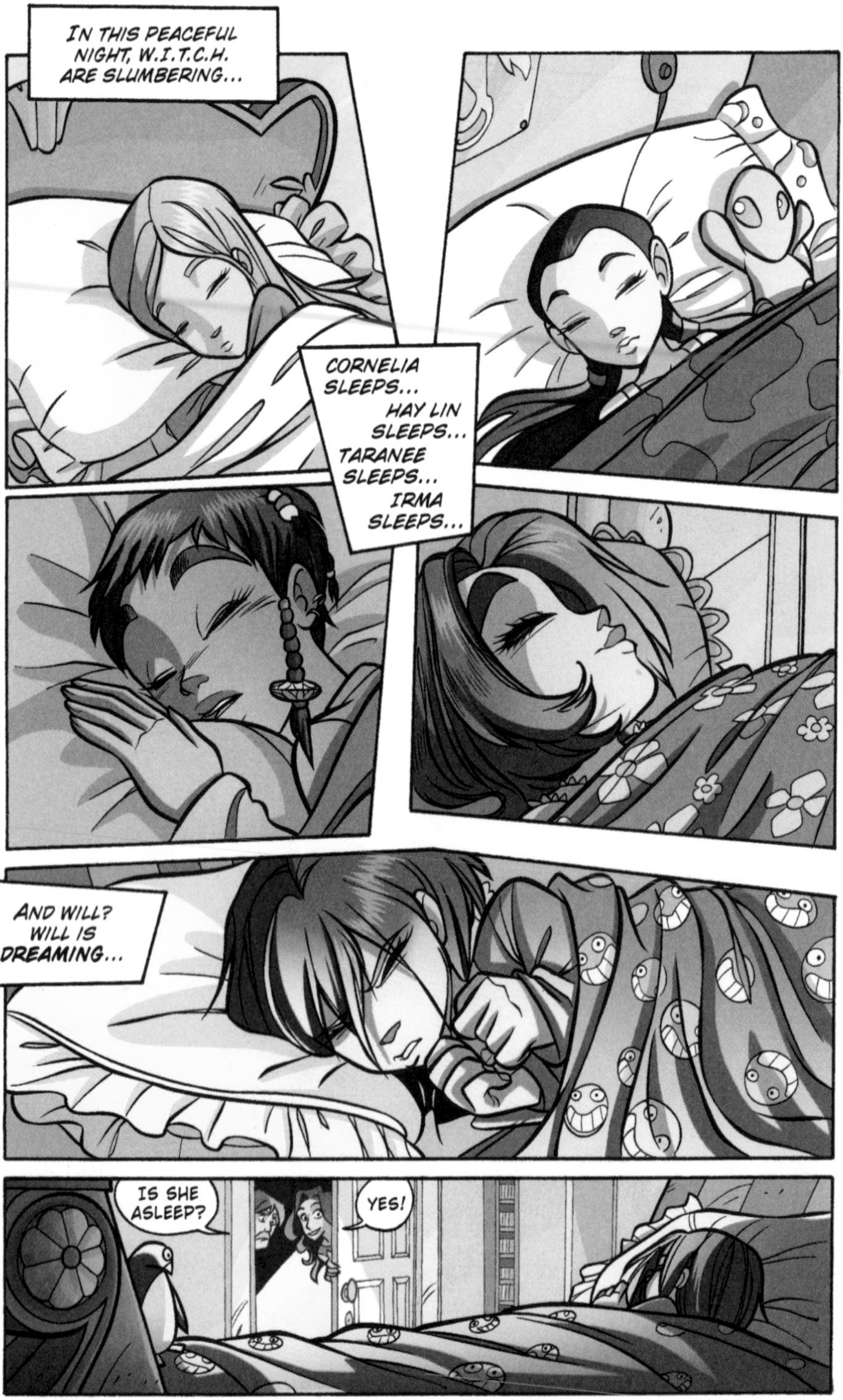
IN THIS PEACEFUL NIGHT, W.I.T.C.H. ARE SLUMBERING...
CORNELIA SLEEPS... HAY LIN SLEEPS... TARANEE SLEEPS... IRMA SLEEPS...
AND WILL? WILL IS DREAMING...
IS SHE ASLEEP?
YES!

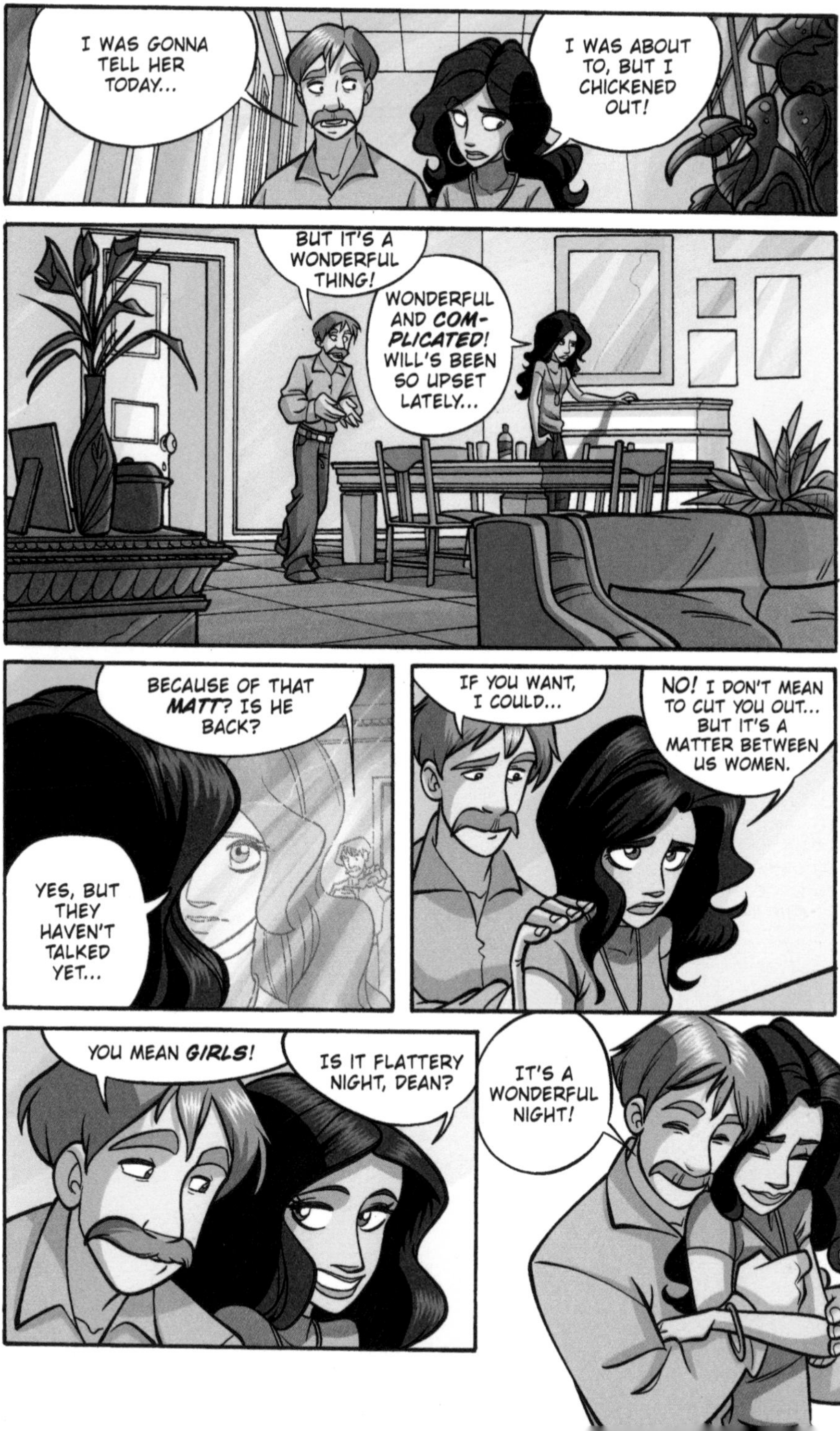

I WAS GONNA TELL HER TODAY...
I WAS ABOUT TO, BUT I CHICKENED OUT!
BUT IT'S A WONDERFUL THING!
WONDERFUL AND *COMPLICATED*! WILL'S BEEN SO UPSET LATELY...
BECAUSE OF THAT *MATT*? IS HE BACK?
YES, BUT THEY HAVEN'T TALKED YET...
IF YOU WANT, I COULD...
NO! I DON'T MEAN TO CUT YOU OUT... BUT IT'S A MATTER BETWEEN US WOMEN.
YOU MEAN *GIRLS*!
IS IT FLATTERY NIGHT, DEAN?
IT'S A WONDERFUL NIGHT!

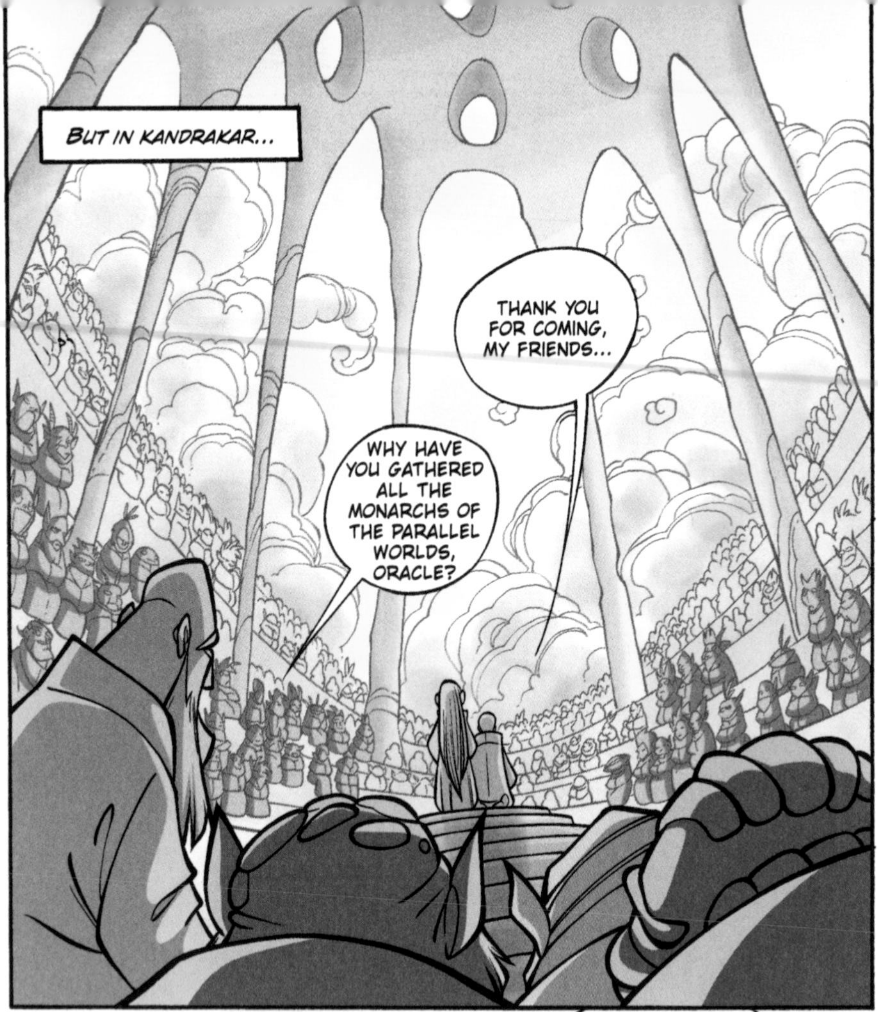

BUT IN KANDRAKAR...
WHY HAVE YOU GATHERED ALL THE MONARCHS OF THE PARALLEL WORLDS, ORACLE?
THANK YOU FOR COMING, MY FRIENDS...

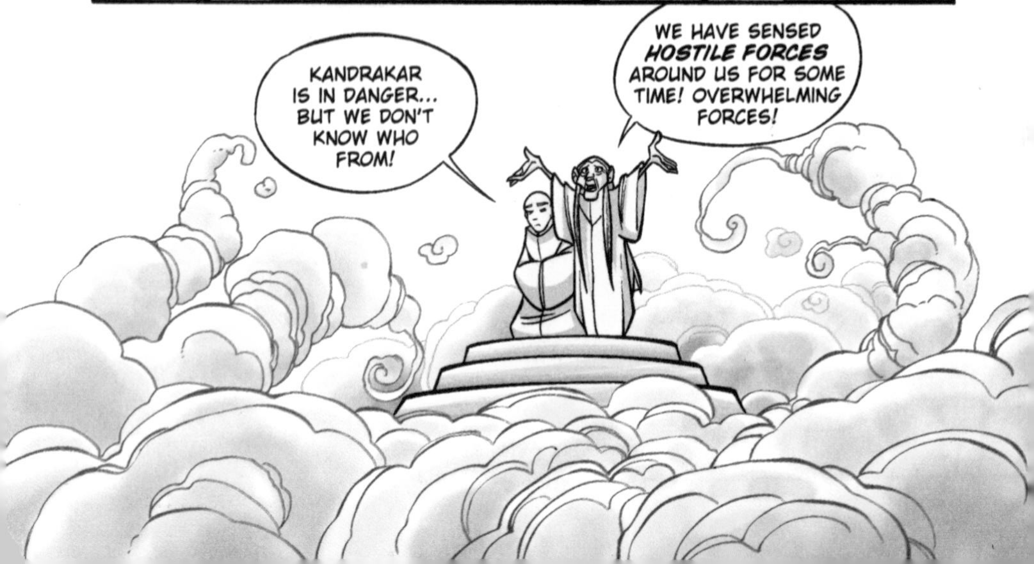

WE HAVE SENSED HOSTILE FORCES AROUND US FOR SOME TIME! OVERWHELMING FORCES!
KANDRAKAR IS IN DANGER... BUT WE DON'T KNOW WHO FROM!

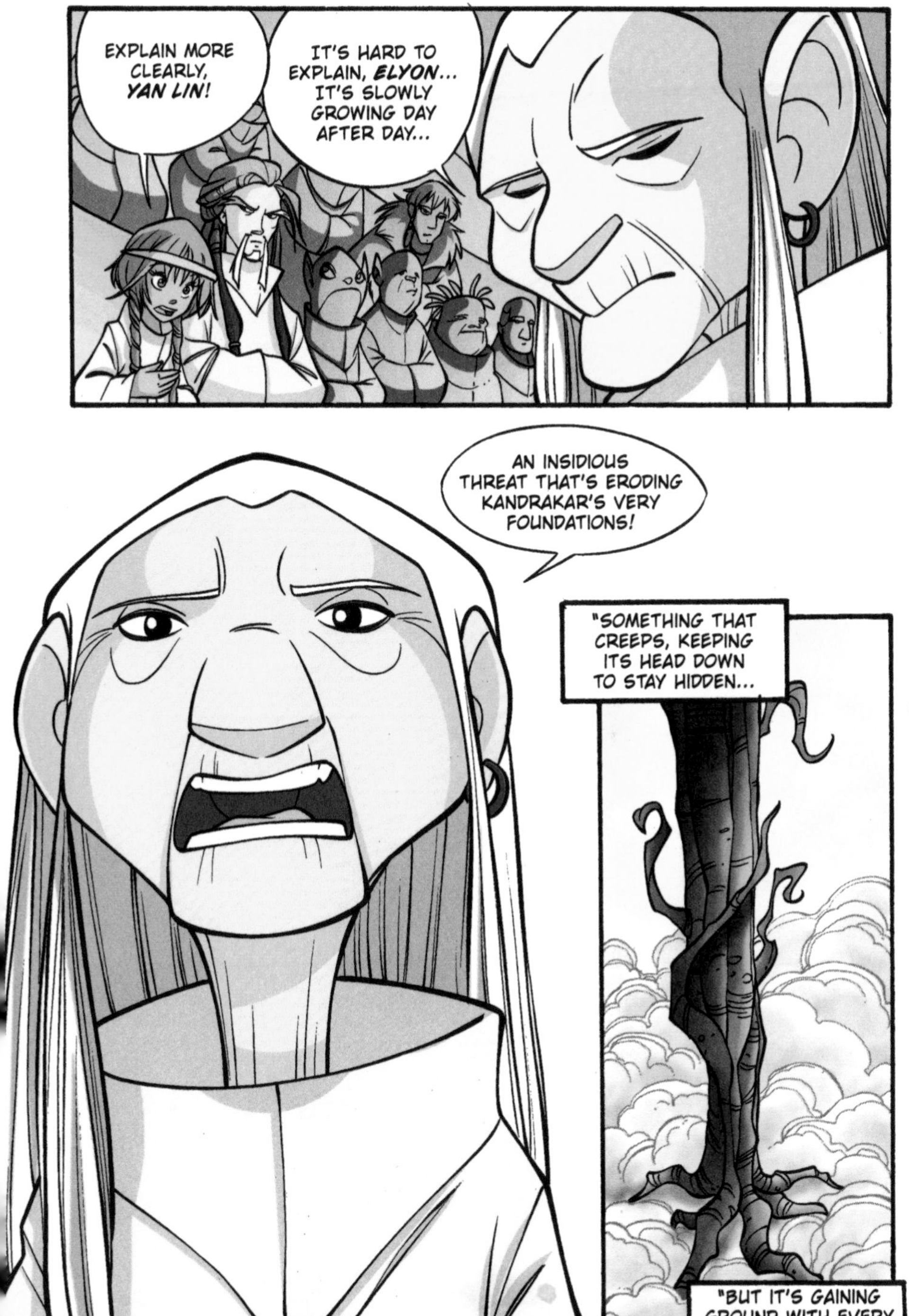
EXPLAIN MORE CLEARLY, YAN LIN!
IT'S HARD TO EXPLAIN, ELYON... IT'S SLOWLY GROWING DAY AFTER DAY...
AN INSIDIOUS THREAT THAT'S ERODING KANDRAKAR'S VERY FOUNDATIONS!
"SOMETHING THAT CREEPS, KEEPING ITS HEAD DOWN TO STAY HIDDEN...
"BUT IT'S GAINING GROUND WITH EVERY PASSING HOUR!"

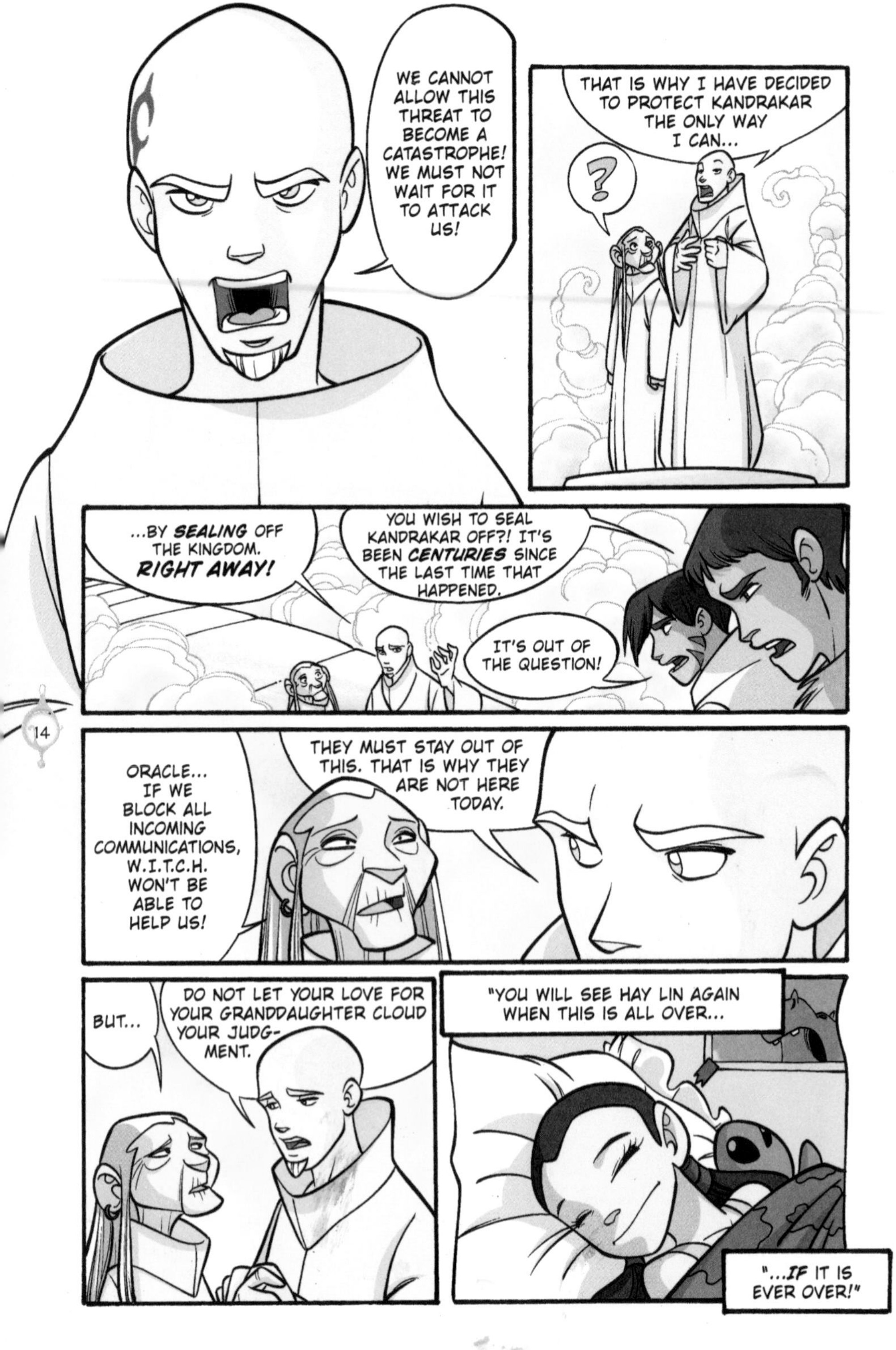

WE CANNOT ALLOW THIS THREAT TO BECOME A CATASTROPHE! WE MUST NOT WAIT FOR IT TO ATTACK US!
THAT IS WHY I HAVE DECIDED TO PROTECT KANDRAKAR THE ONLY WAY I CAN...
?
...BY SEALING OFF THE KINGDOM. RIGHT AWAY!
YOU WISH TO SEAL KANDRAKAR OFF?! IT'S BEEN CENTURIES SINCE THE LAST TIME THAT HAPPENED.
IT'S OUT OF THE QUESTION!
ORACLE... IF WE BLOCK ALL INCOMING COMMUNICATIONS, W.I.T.C.H. WON'T BE ABLE TO HELP US!
THEY MUST STAY OUT OF THIS. THAT IS WHY THEY ARE NOT HERE TODAY.
BUT...
DO NOT LET YOUR LOVE FOR YOUR GRANDDAUGHTER CLOUD YOUR JUDG- MENT.
"YOU WILL SEE HAY LIN AGAIN WHEN THIS IS ALL OVER...
"...IF IT IS EVER OVER!"

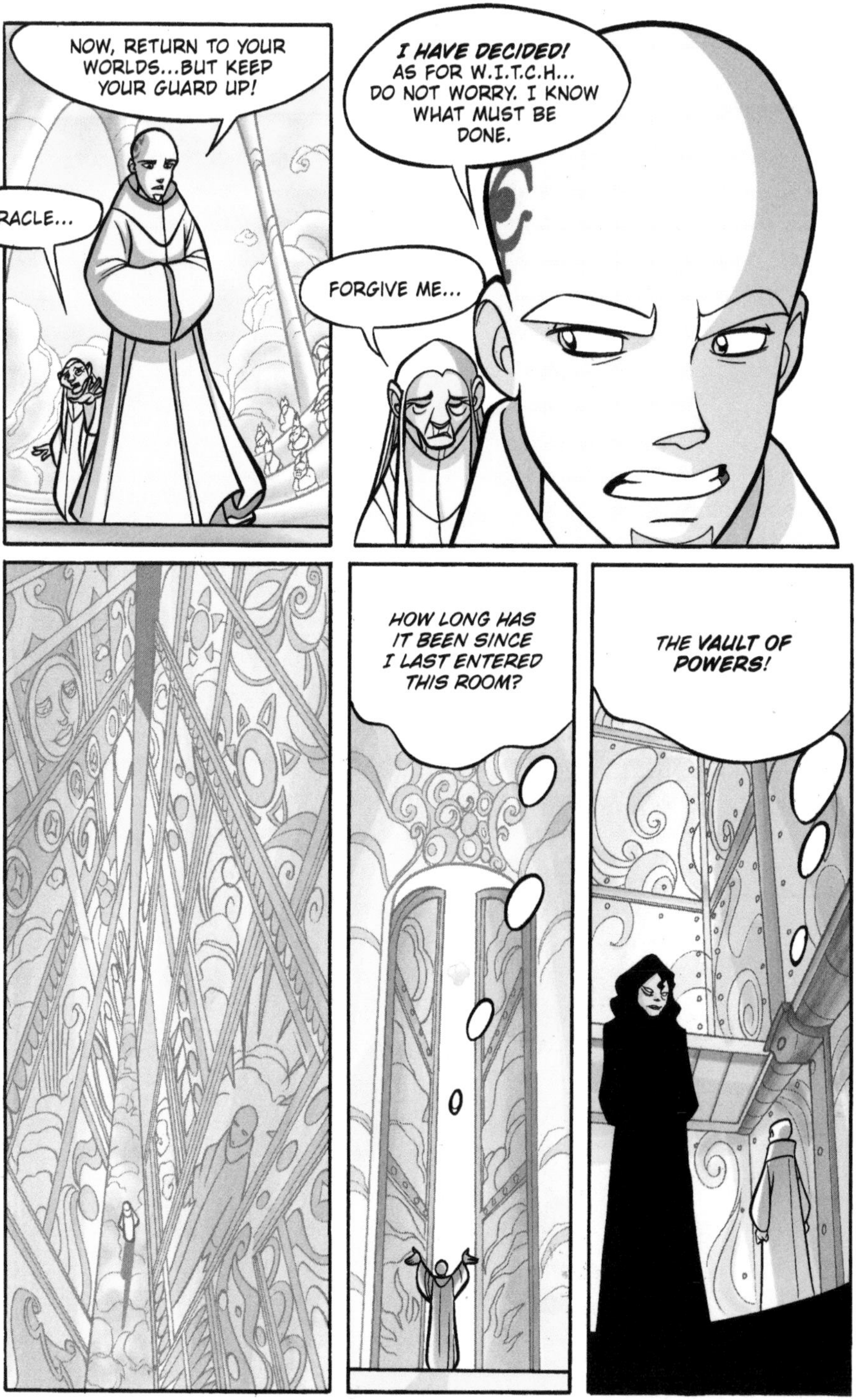
NOW, RETURN TO YOUR WORLDS...BUT KEEP YOUR GUARD UP!
ORACLE...
I HAVE DECIDED! AS FOR W.I.T.C.H... DO NOT WORRY. I KNOW WHAT MUST BE DONE.
FORGIVE ME...
HOW LONG HAS IT BEEN SINCE I LAST ENTERED THIS ROOM?
THE VAULT OF POWERS!

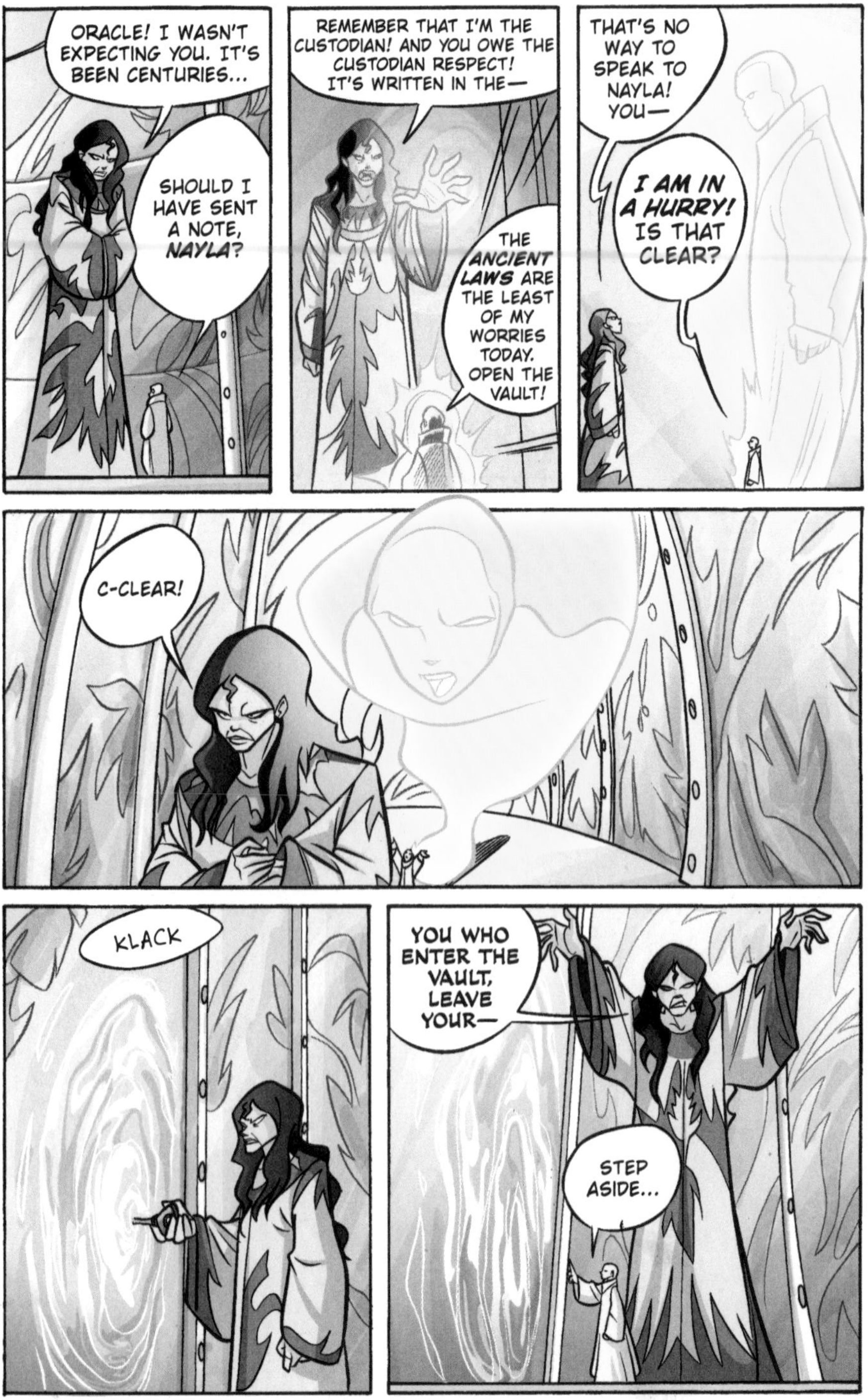
ORACLE! I WASN'T EXPECTING YOU. IT'S BEEN CENTURIES...
SHOULD I HAVE SENT A NOTE, NAYLA?
REMEMBER THAT I'M THE CUSTODIAN! AND YOU OWE THE CUSTODIAN RESPECT! IT'S WRITTEN IN THE—
THE ANCIENT LAWS ARE THE LEAST OF MY WORRIES TODAY. OPEN THE VAULT!
THAT'S NO WAY TO SPEAK TO NAYLA! YOU—
I AM IN A HURRY! IS THAT CLEAR?
C-CLEAR!
KLACK
YOU WHO ENTER THE VAULT, LEAVE YOUR—
STEP ASIDE...

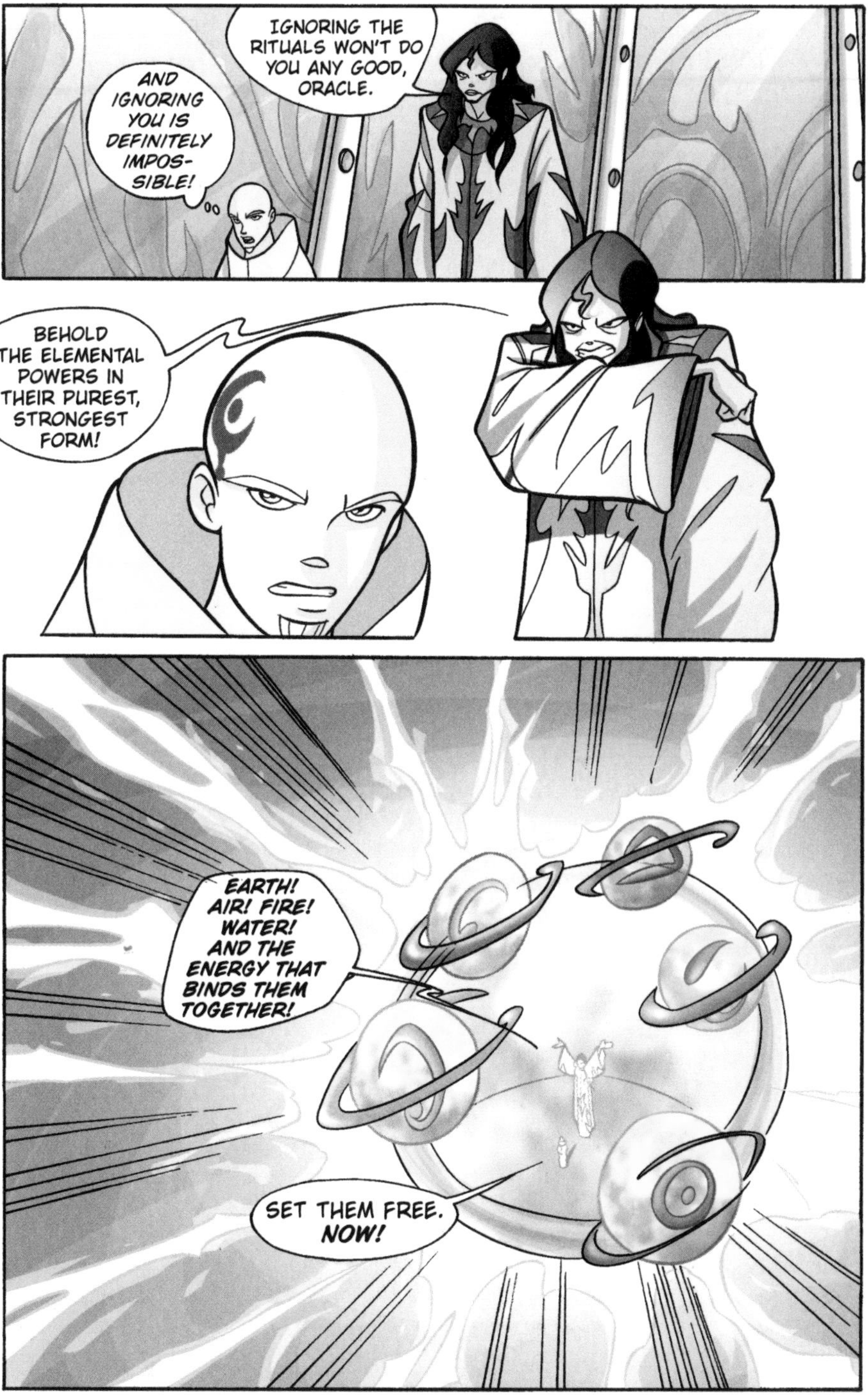
IGNORING THE RITUALS WON'T DO YOU ANY GOOD, ORACLE.
AND IGNORING YOU IS DEFINITELY IMPOS-SIBLE!
BEHOLD THE ELEMENTAL POWERS IN THEIR PUREST, STRONGEST FORM!
EARTH! AIR! FIRE! WATER! AND THE ENERGY THAT BINDS THEM TOGETHER!
SET THEM FREE. NOW!

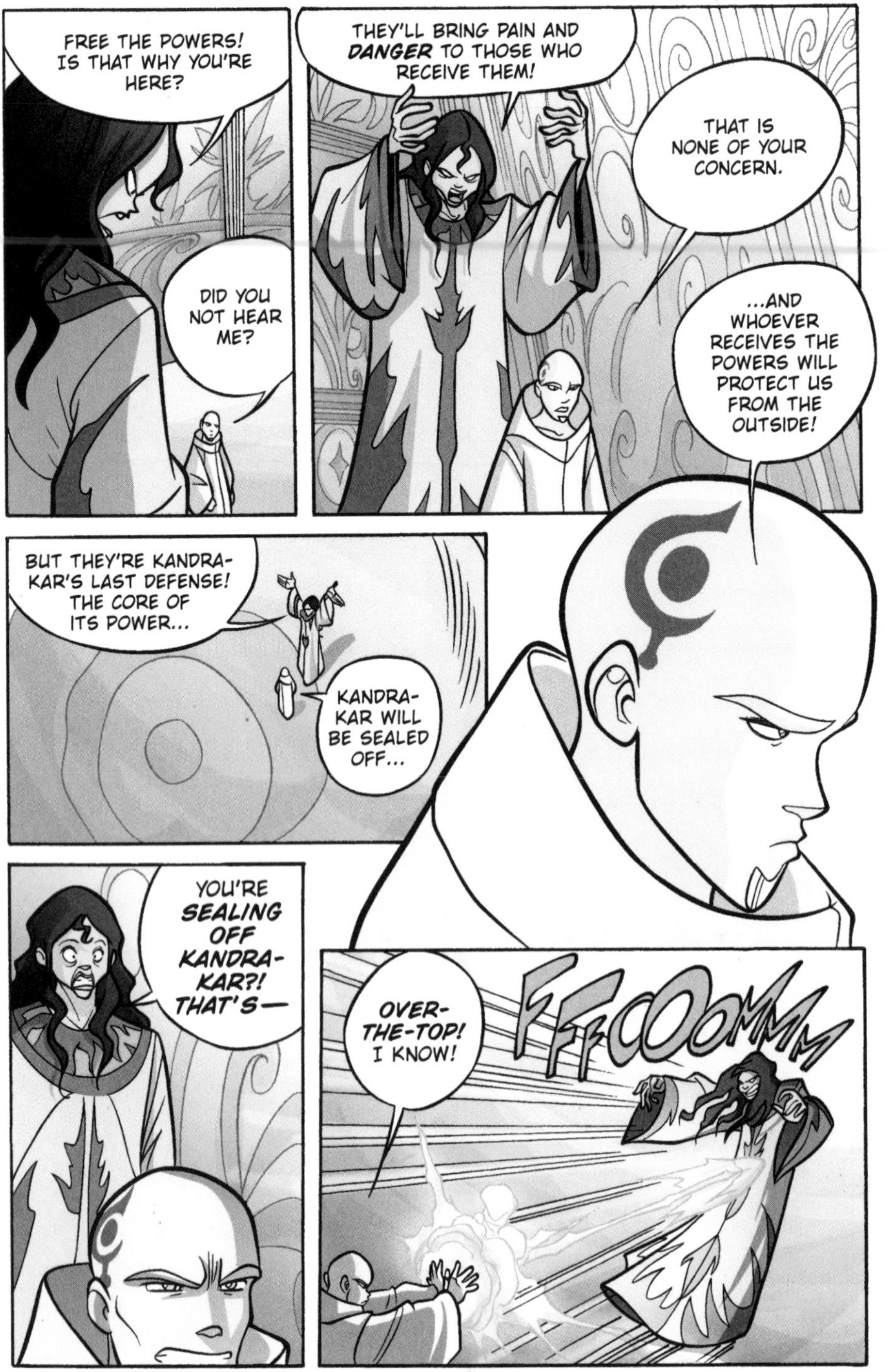
FREE THE POWERS! IS THAT WHY YOU'RE HERE?
DID YOU NOT HEAR ME?
THEY'LL BRING PAIN AND DANGER TO THOSE WHO RECEIVE THEM!
THAT IS NONE OF YOUR CONCERN.
...AND WHOEVER RECEIVES THE POWERS WILL PROTECT US FROM THE OUTSIDE!
BUT THEY'RE KANDRA-KAR'S LAST DEFENSE! THE CORE OF ITS POWER...
KANDRA-KAR WILL BE SEALED OFF...
YOU'RE SEALING OFF KANDRA-KAR?! THAT'S—
OVER-THE-TOP! I KNOW!
FFFCOOOMMM

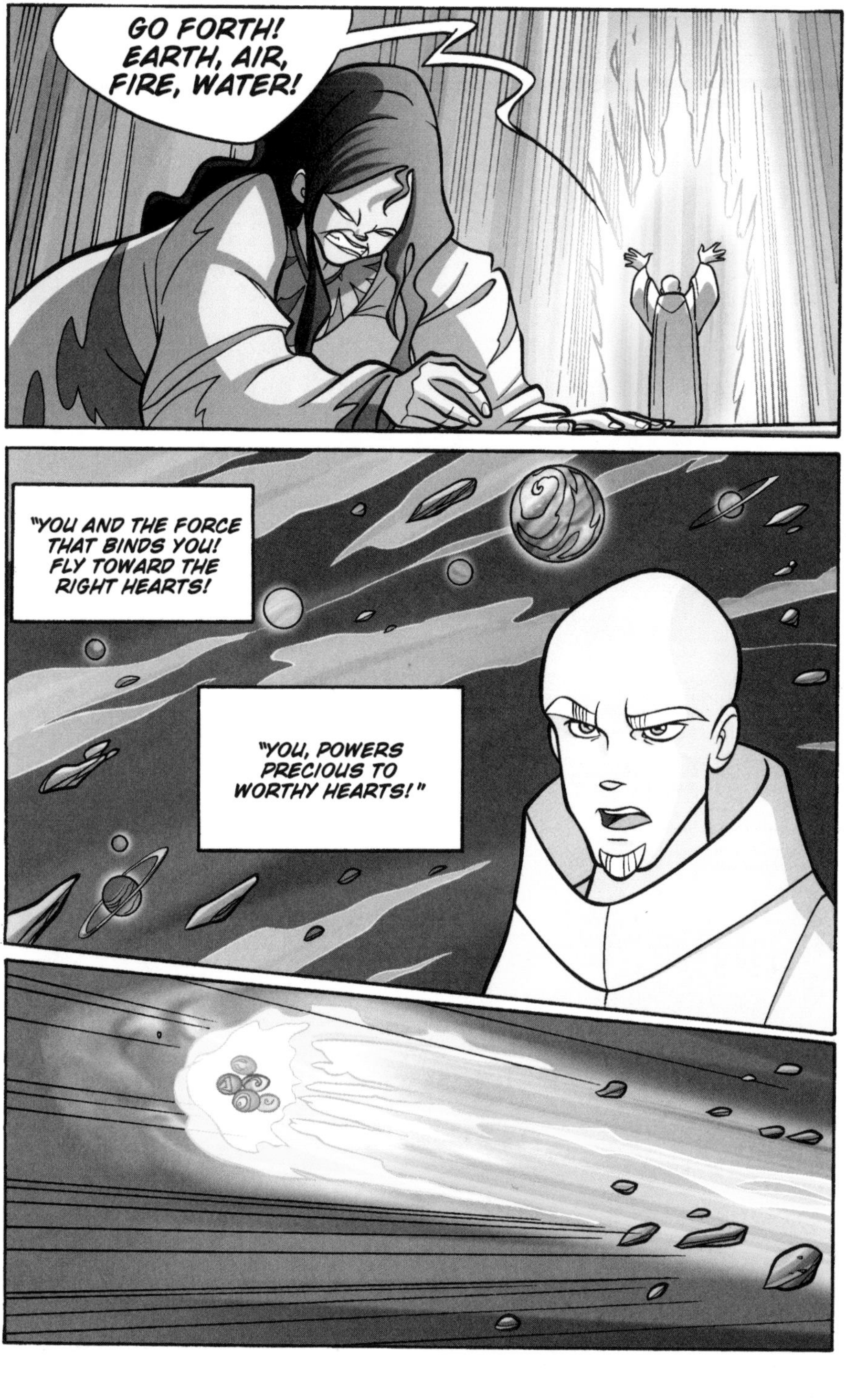
GO FORTH! EARTH, AIR, FIRE, WATER!
"YOU AND THE FORCE THAT BINDS YOU! FLY TOWARD THE RIGHT HEARTS!
"YOU, POWERS PRECIOUS TO WORTHY HEARTS!"

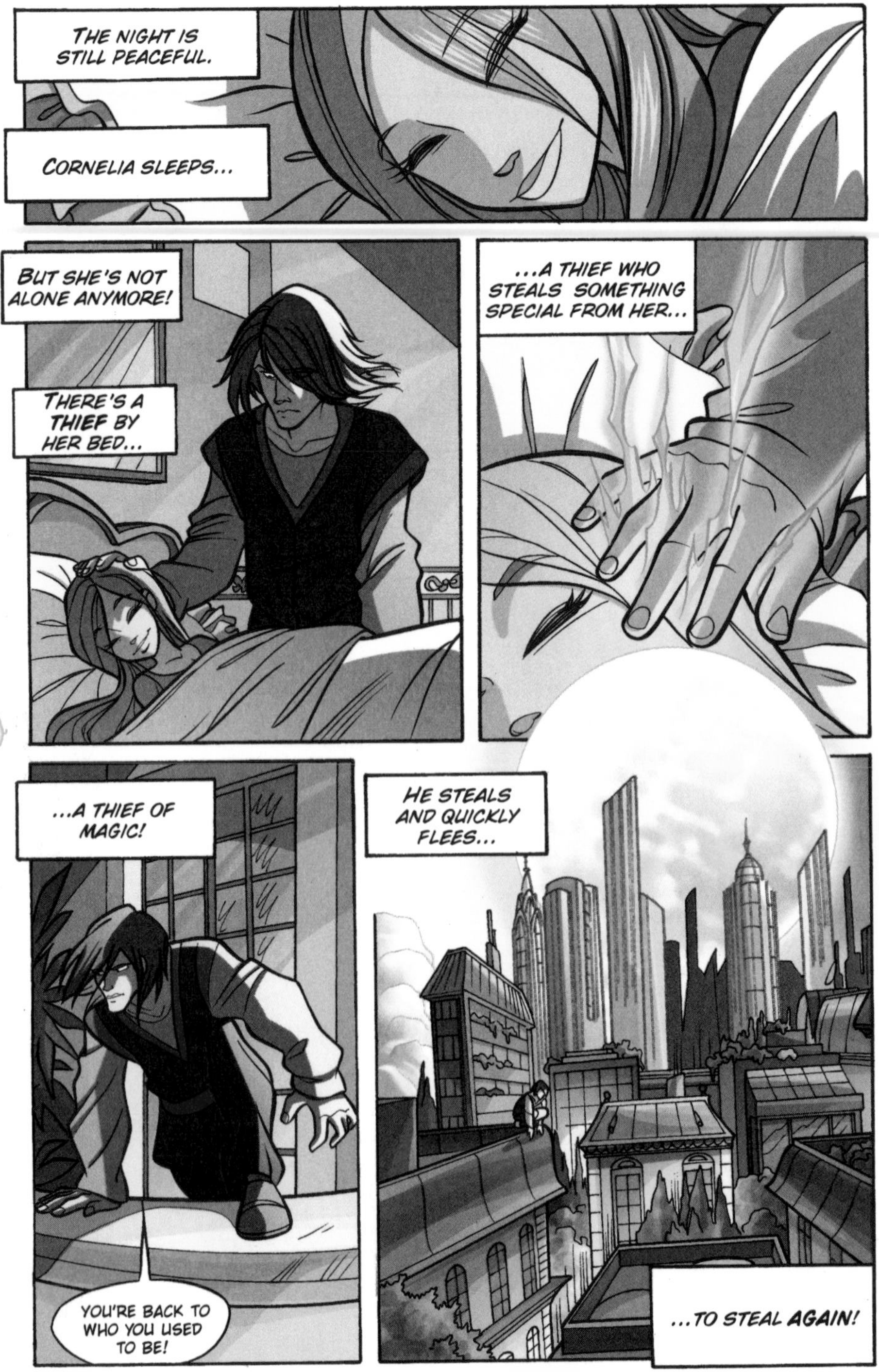
THE NIGHT IS STILL PEACEFUL.
CORNELIA SLEEPS...
BUT SHE'S NOT ALONE ANYMORE!
THERE'S A THIEF BY HER BED...
...A THIEF WHO STEALS SOMETHING SPECIAL FROM HER...
...A THIEF OF MAGIC!
YOU'RE BACK TO WHO YOU USED TO BE!
HE STEALS AND QUICKLY FLEES...
...TO STEAL AGAIN!

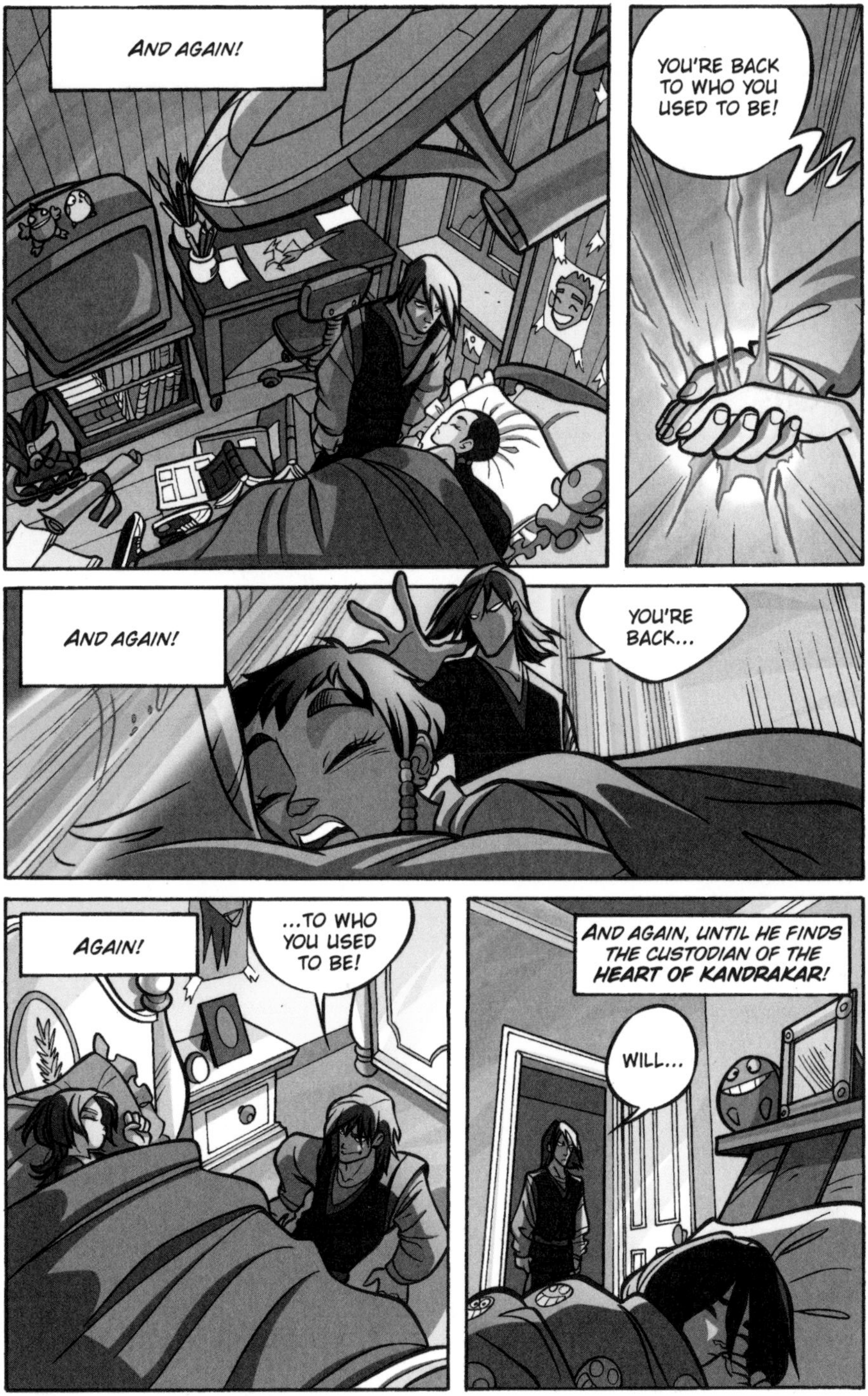

AND AGAIN!
YOU'RE BACK TO WHO YOU USED TO BE!
AND AGAIN!
YOU'RE BACK...
AGAIN!
...TO WHO YOU USED TO BE!
AND AGAIN, UNTIL HE FINDS THE CUSTODIAN OF THE **HEART OF KANDRAKAR!**
WILL...

THE **HEART!** I GOTTA TAKE IT!

STEALING THE HEART OF KANDRAKAR, THE SYMBOL THAT HOLDS ALL POWERS, ISN'T EASY!

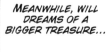
MEANWHILE, WILL DREAMS OF A BIGGER TREASURE...

MATT...

MATT! IT'S YOU!

LET'S HUG! HUG ME, PLEASE!

HUG ME!

THERE'S... THE HEART!

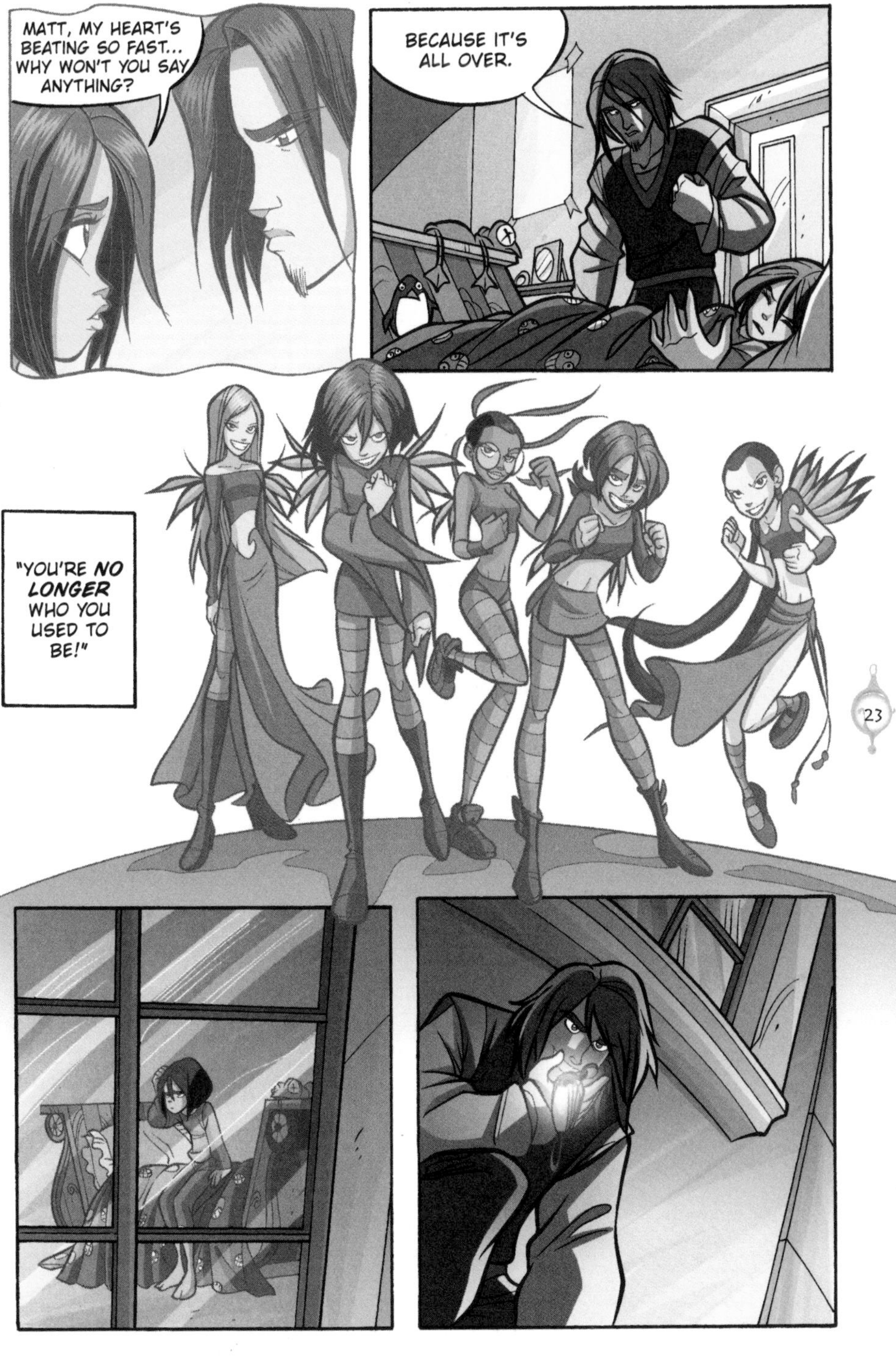

MATT, MY HEART'S BEATING SO FAST... WHY WON'T YOU SAY ANYTHING?
BECAUSE IT'S ALL OVER.
"YOU'RE **NO LONGER** WHO YOU USED TO BE!"

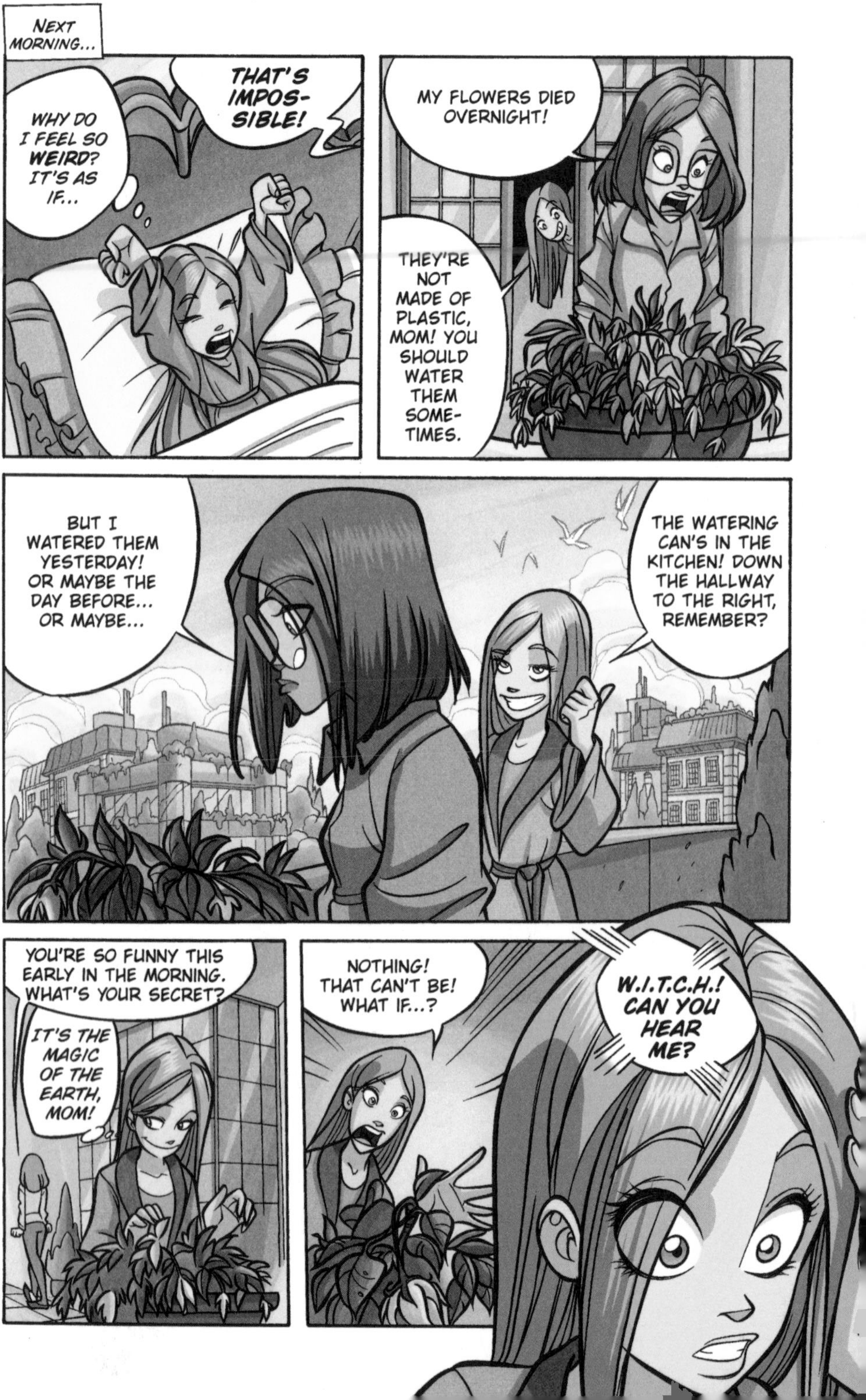
NEXT MORNING...
WHY DO I FEEL SO WEIRD? IT'S AS IF...
THAT'S IMPOSSIBLE!
MY FLOWERS DIED OVERNIGHT!
THEY'RE NOT MADE OF PLASTIC, MOM! YOU SHOULD WATER THEM SOMETIMES.
BUT I WATERED THEM YESTERDAY! OR MAYBE THE DAY BEFORE... OR MAYBE...
THE WATERING CAN'S IN THE KITCHEN! DOWN THE HALLWAY TO THE RIGHT, REMEMBER?
YOU'RE SO FUNNY THIS EARLY IN THE MORNING. WHAT'S YOUR SECRET?
IT'S THE MAGIC OF THE EARTH, MOM!
NOTHING! THAT CAN'T BE! WHAT IF...?
W.I.T.C.H.! CAN YOU HEAR ME?

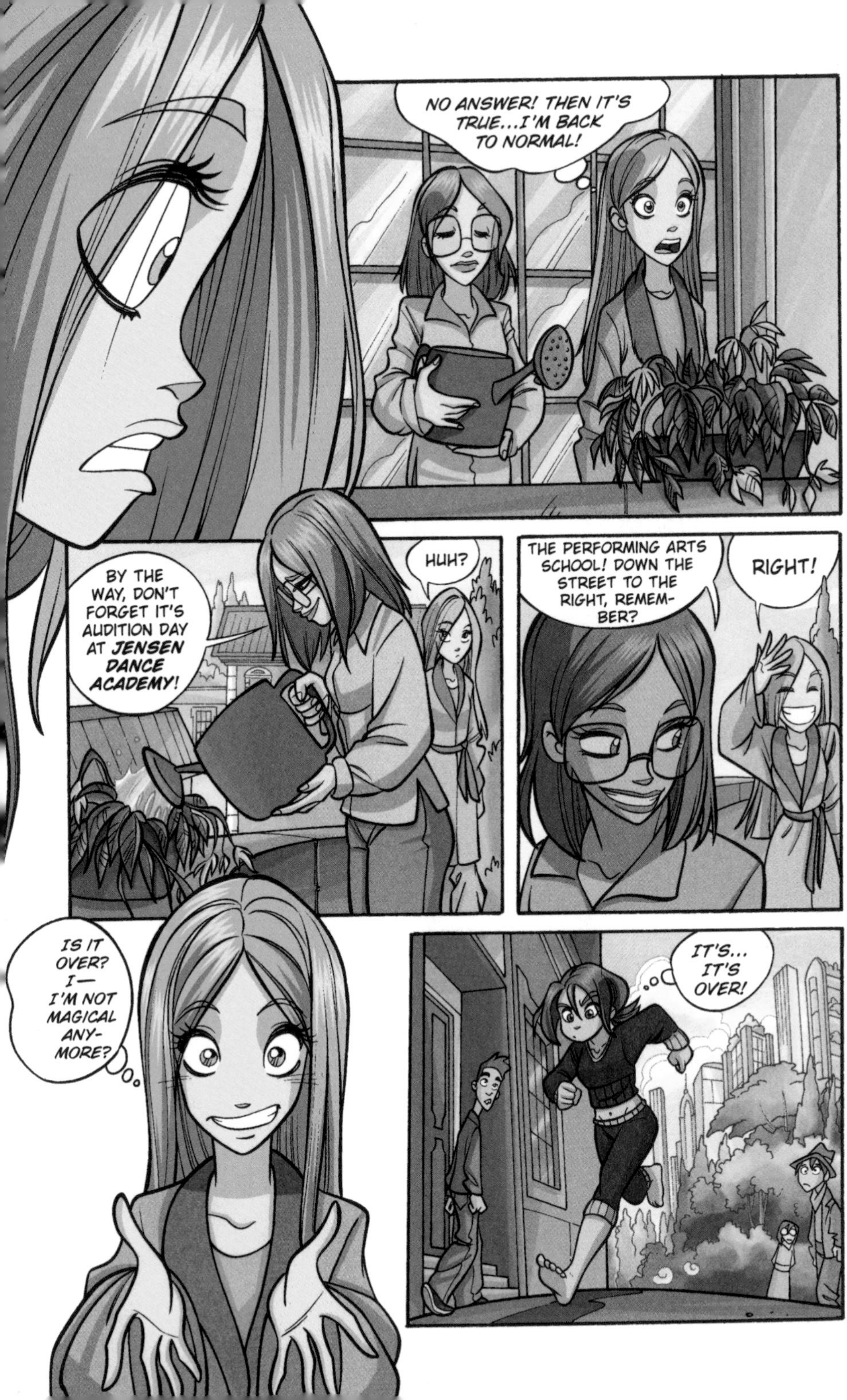

NO ANSWER! THEN IT'S TRUE...I'M BACK TO NORMAL!
BY THE WAY, DON'T FORGET IT'S AUDITION DAY AT JENSEN DANCE ACADEMY!
HUH?
THE PERFORMING ARTS SCHOOL! DOWN THE STREET TO THE RIGHT, REMEMBER?
RIGHT!
IS IT OVER? I— I'M NOT MAGICAL ANYMORE?
IT'S... IT'S OVER!

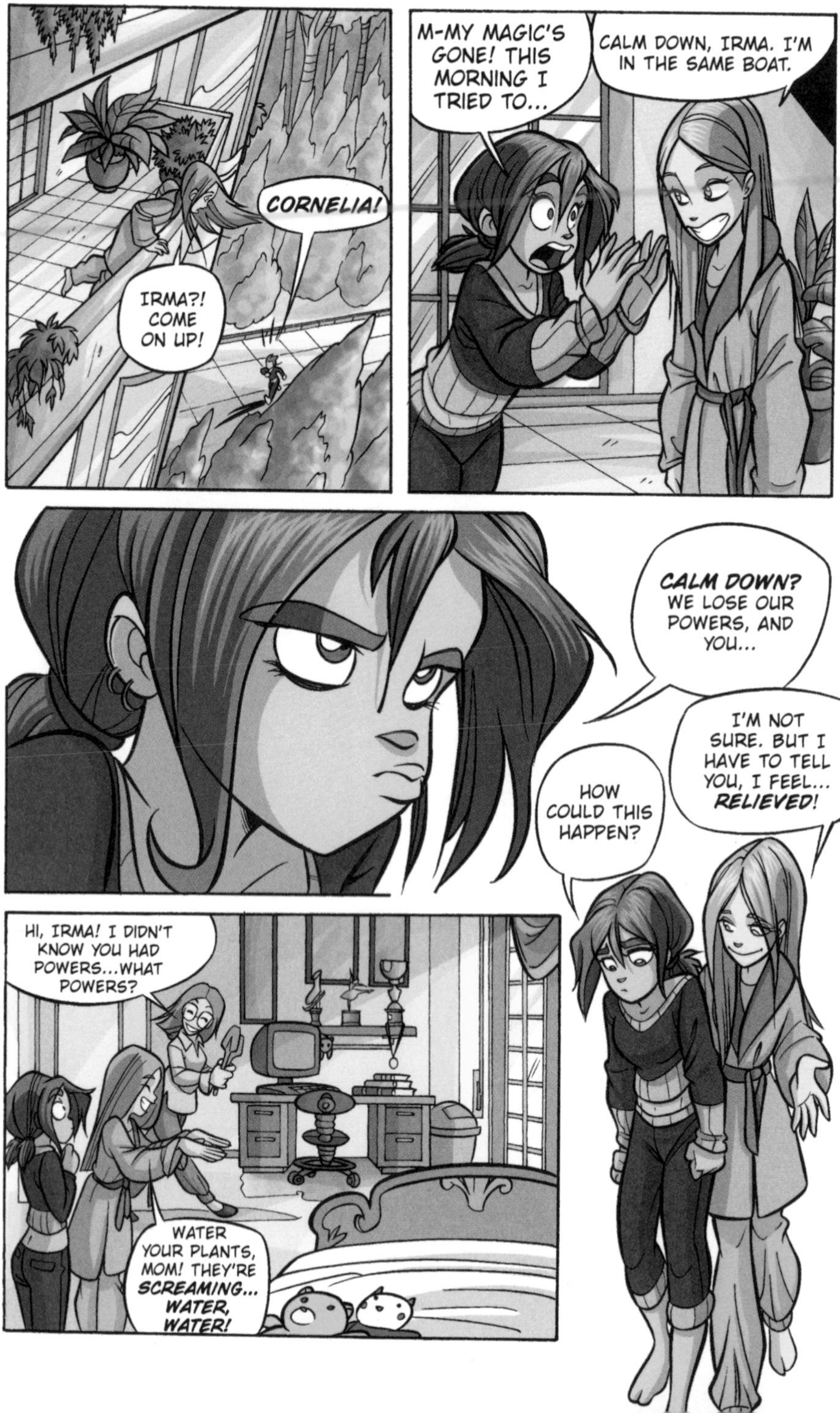
CORNELIA!
IRMA?! COME ON UP!
M-MY MAGIC'S GONE! THIS MORNING I TRIED TO...
CALM DOWN, IRMA. I'M IN THE SAME BOAT.
CALM DOWN? WE LOSE OUR POWERS, AND YOU...
HOW COULD THIS HAPPEN?
I'M NOT SURE. BUT I HAVE TO TELL YOU, I FEEL... *RELIEVED!*
HI, IRMA! I DIDN'T KNOW YOU HAD POWERS...WHAT POWERS?
WATER YOUR PLANTS, MOM! THEY'RE *SCREAMING... WATER, WATER!*

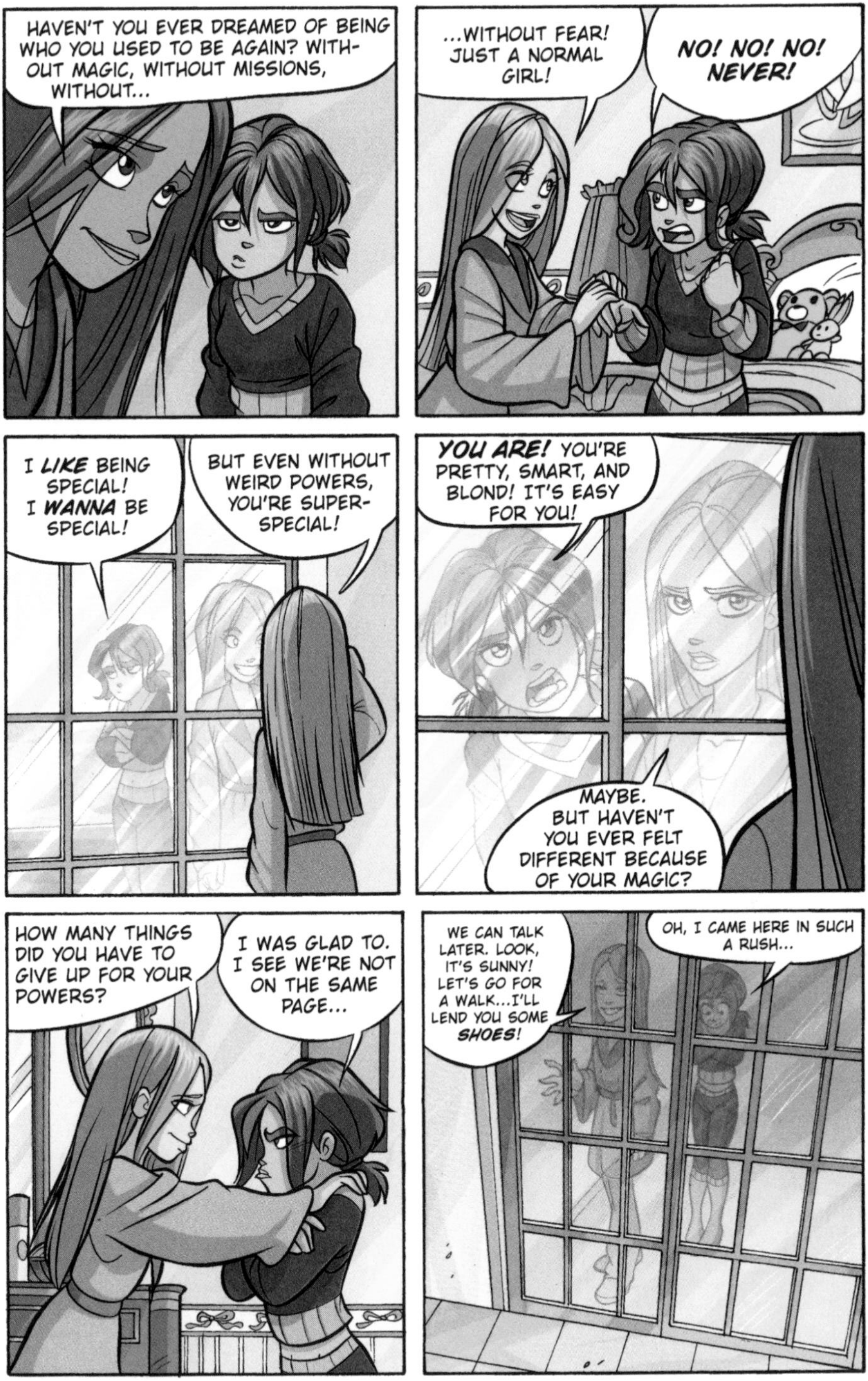
HAVEN'T YOU EVER DREAMED OF BEING WHO YOU USED TO BE AGAIN? WITHOUT MAGIC, WITHOUT MISSIONS, WITHOUT...
...WITHOUT FEAR! JUST A NORMAL GIRL!
NO! NO! NO! NEVER!
I LIKE BEING SPECIAL! I WANNA BE SPECIAL!
BUT EVEN WITHOUT WEIRD POWERS, YOU'RE SUPER-SPECIAL!
YOU ARE! YOU'RE PRETTY, SMART, AND BLOND! IT'S EASY FOR YOU!
MAYBE. BUT HAVEN'T YOU EVER FELT DIFFERENT BECAUSE OF YOUR MAGIC?
HOW MANY THINGS DID YOU HAVE TO GIVE UP FOR YOUR POWERS?
I WAS GLAD TO. I SEE WE'RE NOT ON THE SAME PAGE...
WE CAN TALK LATER. LOOK, IT'S SUNNY! LET'S GO FOR A WALK...I'LL LEND YOU SOME SHOES!
OH, I CAME HERE IN SUCH A RUSH...

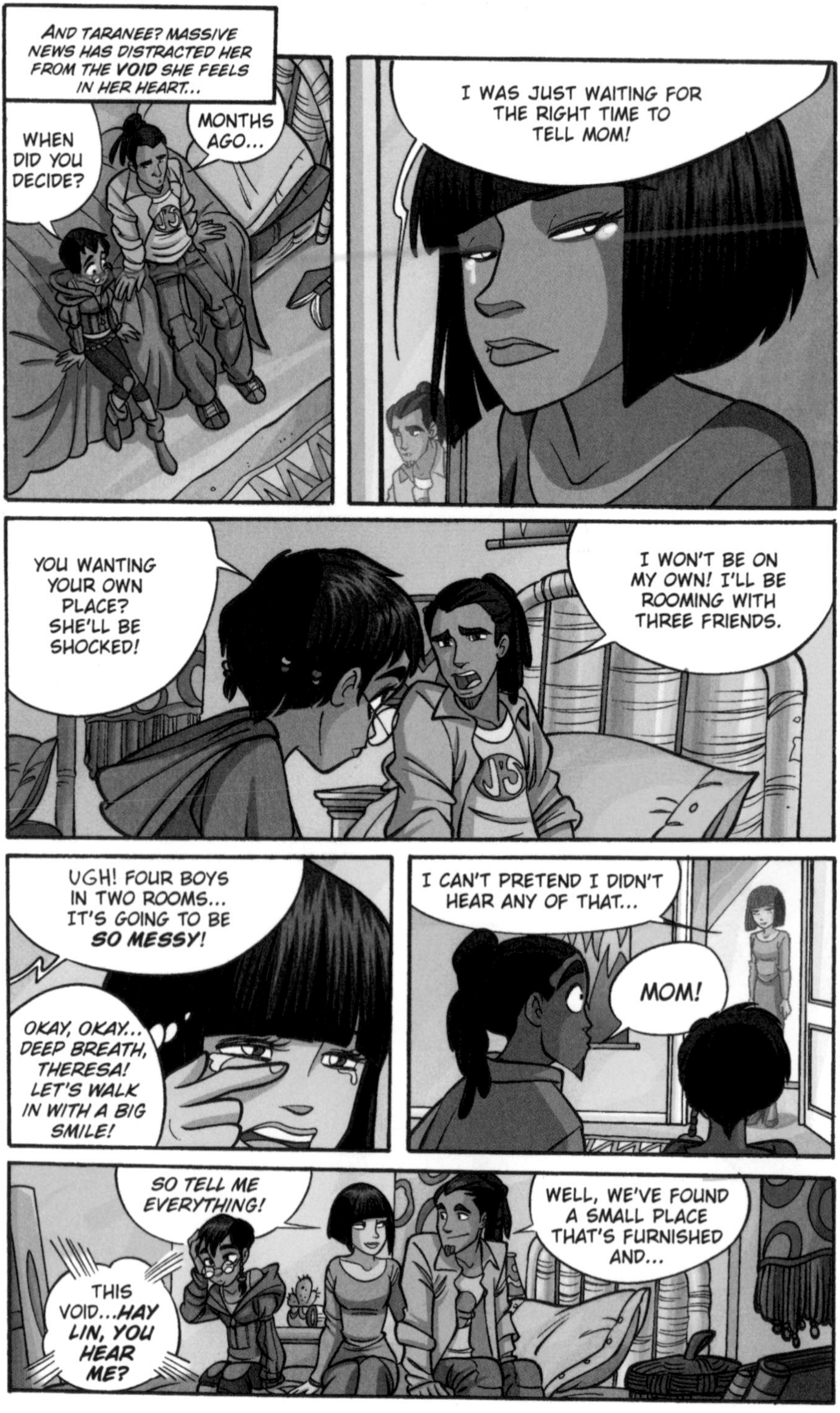

AND TARANEE? MASSIVE NEWS HAS DISTRACTED HER FROM THE VOID SHE FEELS IN HER HEART...
WHEN DID YOU DECIDE?
MONTHS AGO...
I WAS JUST WAITING FOR THE RIGHT TIME TO TELL MOM!
YOU WANTING YOUR OWN PLACE? SHE'LL BE SHOCKED!
I WON'T BE ON MY OWN! I'LL BE ROOMING WITH THREE FRIENDS.
UGH! FOUR BOYS IN TWO ROOMS... IT'S GOING TO BE SO MESSY!
OKAY, OKAY... DEEP BREATH, THERESA! LET'S WALK IN WITH A BIG SMILE!
I CAN'T PRETEND I DIDN'T HEAR ANY OF THAT...
MOM!
SO TELL ME EVERYTHING!
WELL, WE'VE FOUND A SMALL PLACE THAT'S FURNISHED AND...
THIS VOID...HAY LIN, YOU HEAR ME?

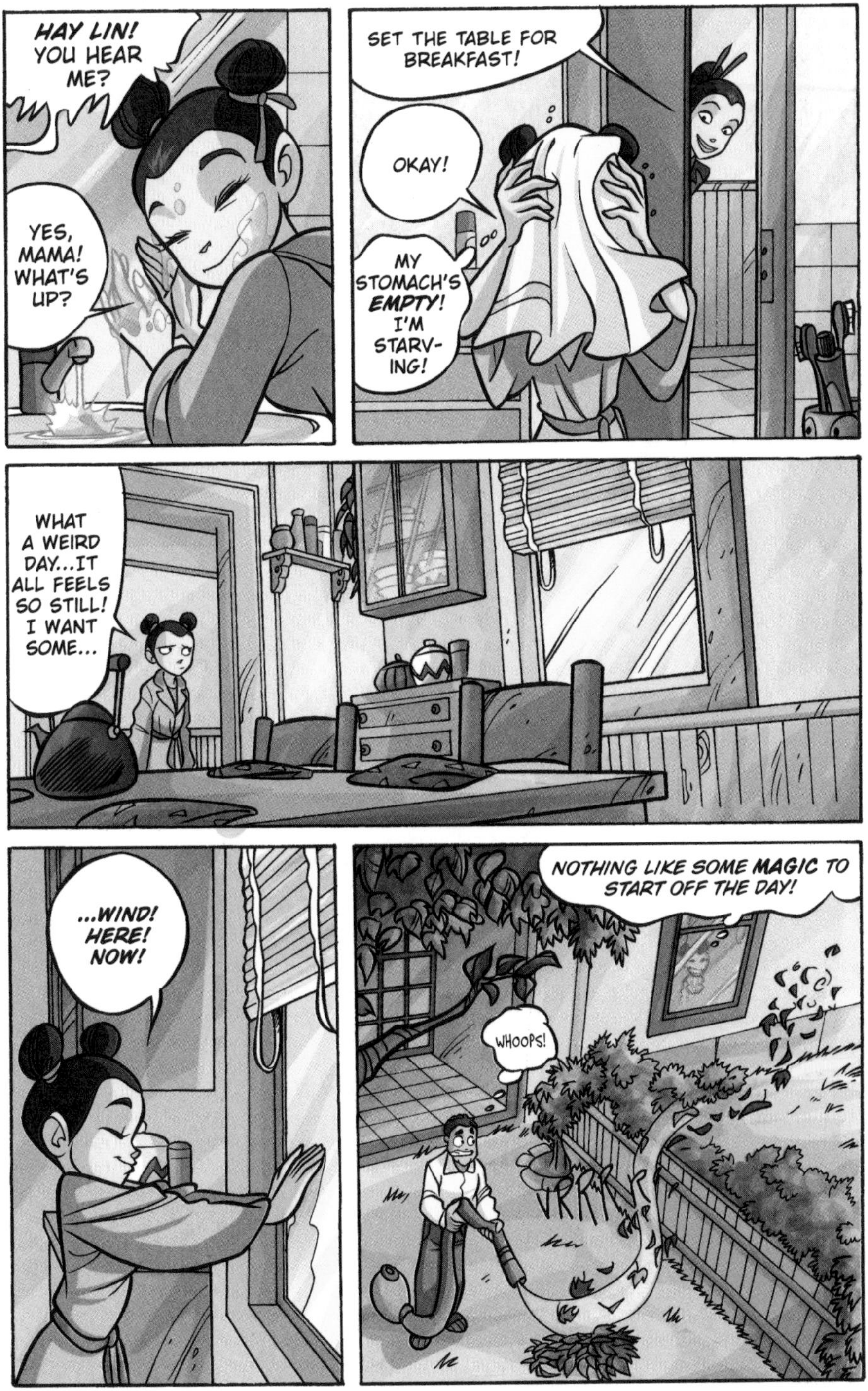
HAY LIN! YOU HEAR ME?
YES, MAMA! WHAT'S UP?
SET THE TABLE FOR BREAKFAST!
OKAY!
MY STOMACH'S EMPTY! I'M STARVING!
WHAT A WEIRD DAY...IT ALL FEELS SO STILL! I WANT SOME...
...WIND! HERE! NOW!
NOTHING LIKE SOME MAGIC TO START OFF THE DAY!
WHOOPS!

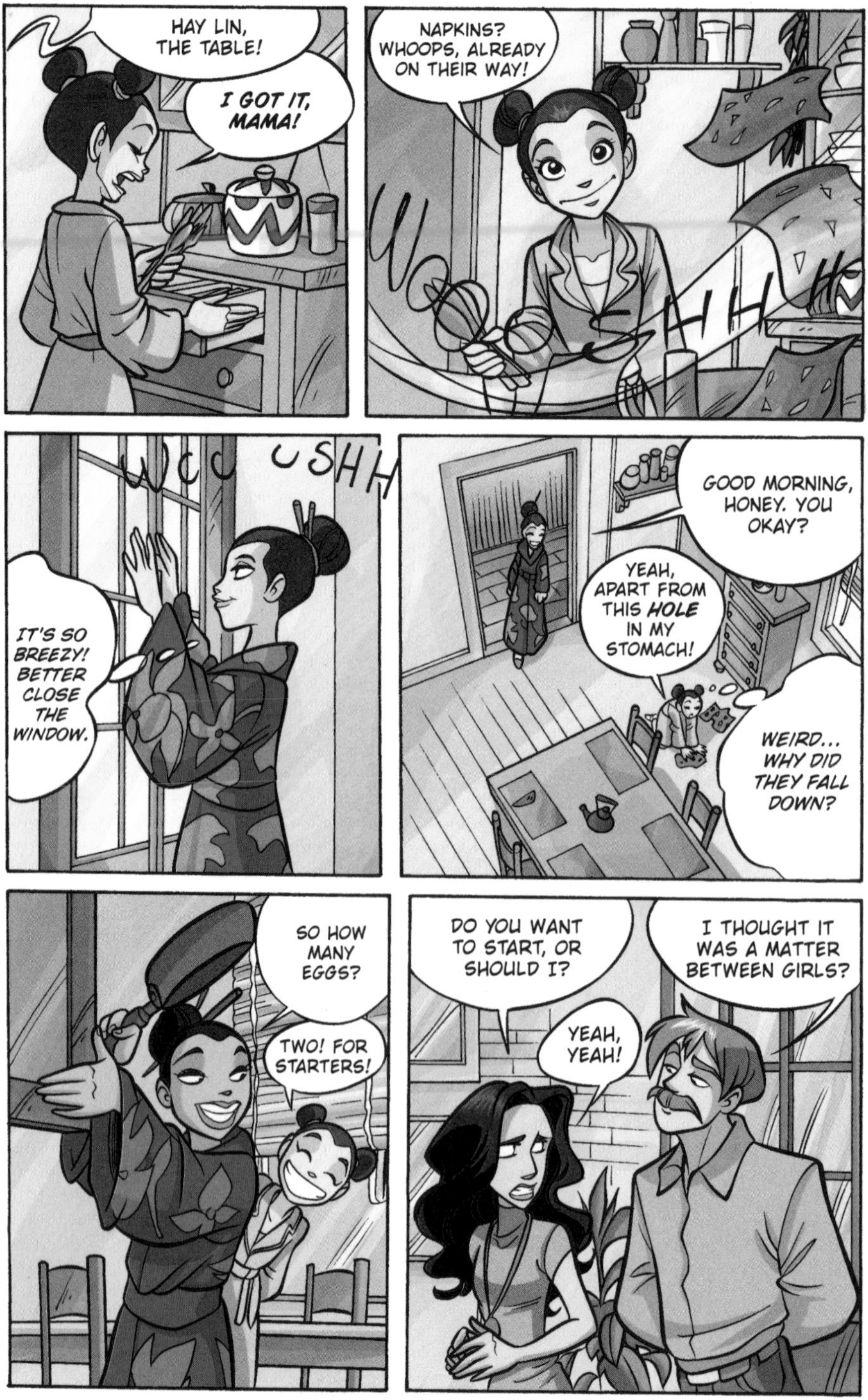
HAY LIN, THE TABLE!
I GOT IT, MAMA!
NAPKINS? WHOOPS, ALREADY ON THEIR WAY!
WOOOSHHH
WOOSHH
IT'S SO BREEZY! BETTER CLOSE THE WINDOW.
GOOD MORNING, HONEY. YOU OKAY?
YEAH, APART FROM THIS HOLE IN MY STOMACH!
WEIRD... WHY DID THEY FALL DOWN?
SO HOW MANY EGGS?
TWO! FOR STARTERS!
DO YOU WANT TO START, OR SHOULD I?
YEAH, YEAH!
I THOUGHT IT WAS A MATTER BETWEEN GIRLS?

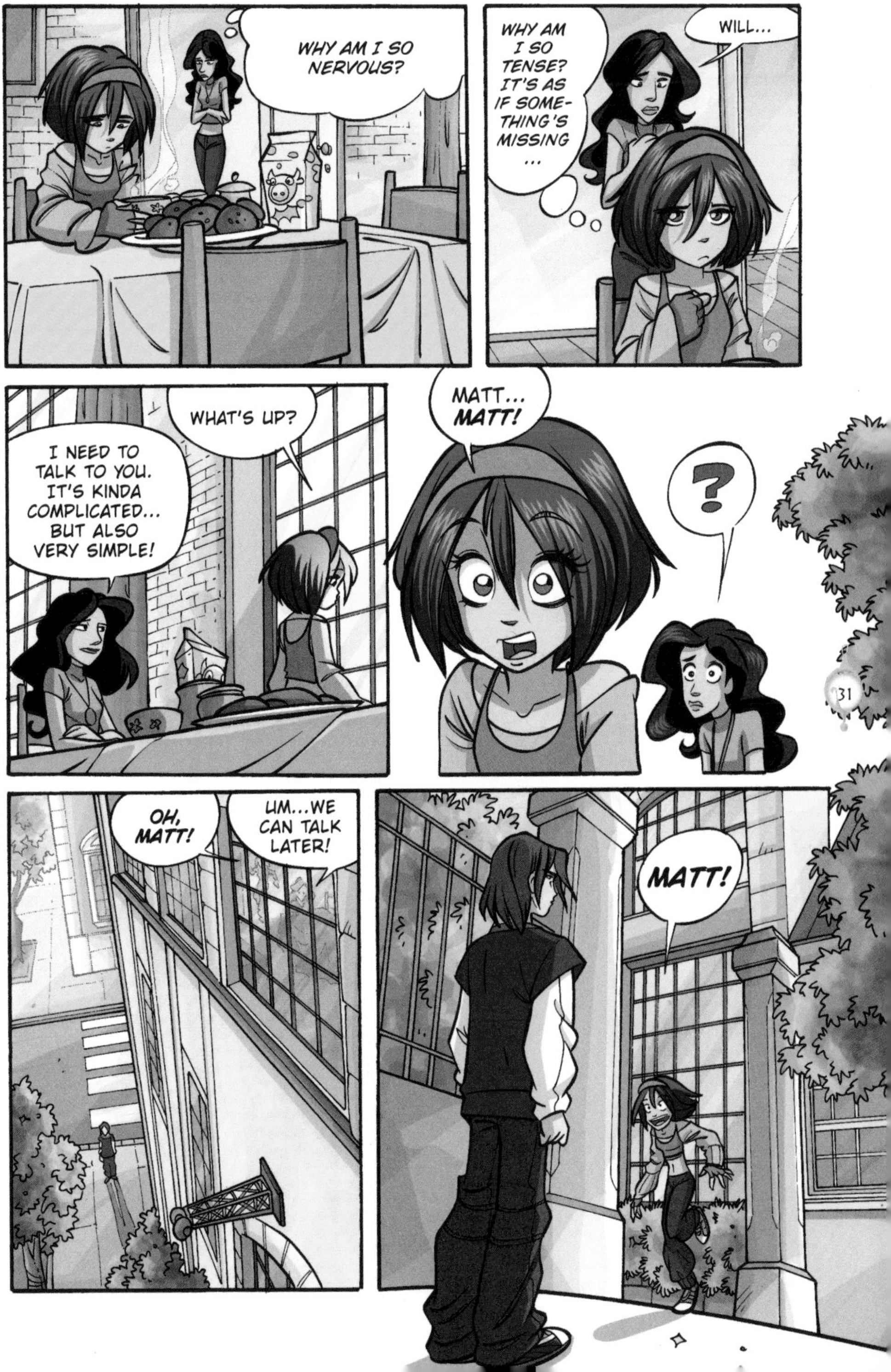
WHY AM I SO NERVOUS?
WHY AM I SO TENSE? IT'S AS IF SOME-THING'S MISSING ...
WILL...
WHAT'S UP?
I NEED TO TALK TO YOU. IT'S KINDA COMPLICATED... BUT ALSO VERY SIMPLE!
MATT... MATT!
?
OH, MATT!
UM...WE CAN TALK LATER!
MATT!

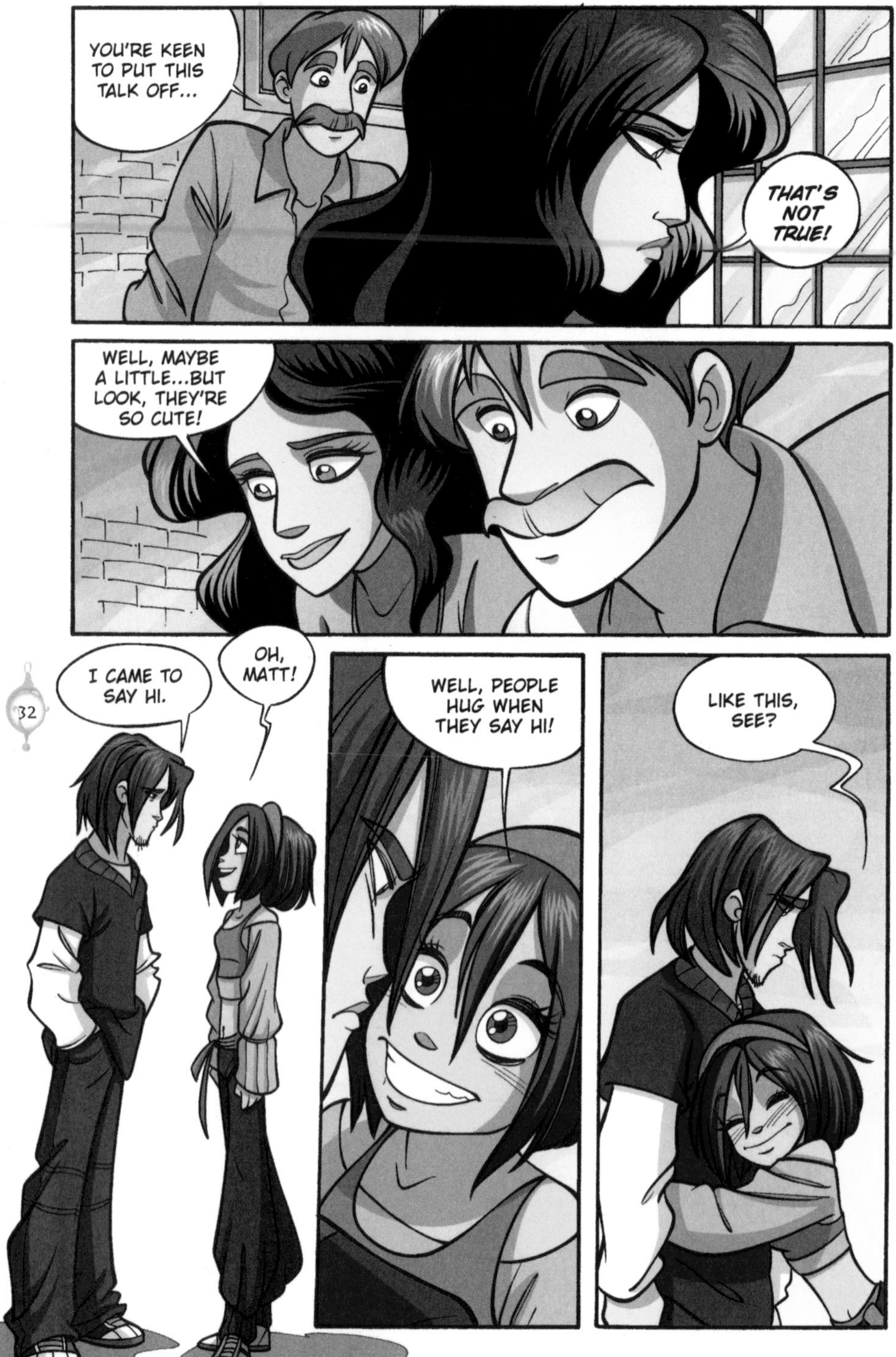
YOU'RE KEEN TO PUT THIS TALK OFF...
THAT'S NOT TRUE!
WELL, MAYBE A LITTLE...BUT LOOK, THEY'RE SO CUTE!
I CAME TO SAY HI.
OH, MATT!
WELL, PEOPLE HUG WHEN THEY SAY HI!
LIKE THIS, SEE?

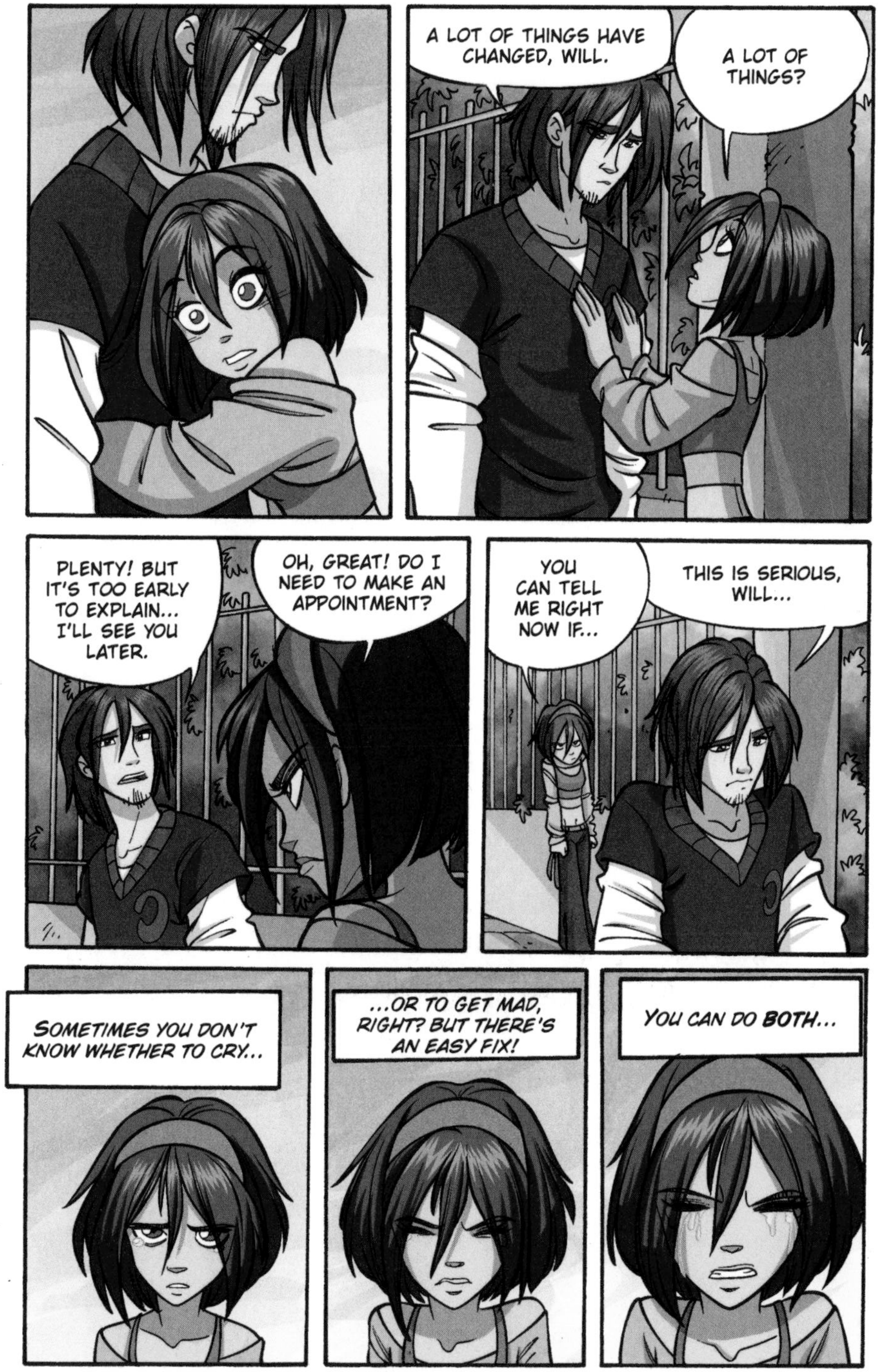

A LOT OF THINGS HAVE CHANGED, WILL.
A LOT OF THINGS?
PLENTY! BUT IT'S TOO EARLY TO EXPLAIN... I'LL SEE YOU LATER.
OH, GREAT! DO I NEED TO MAKE AN APPOINTMENT?
YOU CAN TELL ME RIGHT NOW IF...
THIS IS SERIOUS, WILL...
SOMETIMES YOU DON'T KNOW WHETHER TO CRY...
...OR TO GET MAD, RIGHT? BUT THERE'S AN EASY FIX!
YOU CAN DO BOTH...

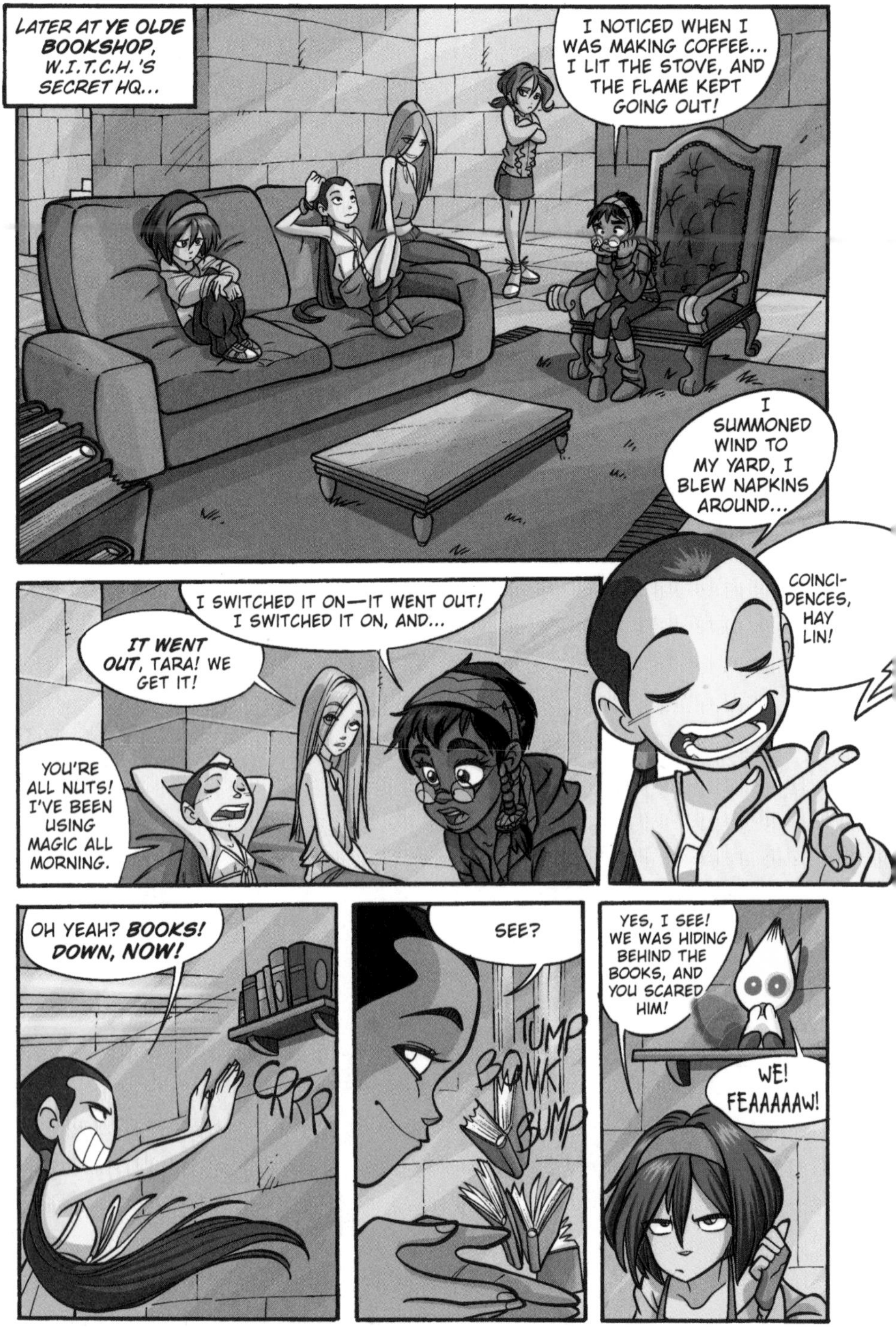
LATER AT **YE OLDE BOOKSHOP**, W.I.T.C.H.'S SECRET HQ...
I NOTICED WHEN I WAS MAKING COFFEE... I LIT THE STOVE, AND THE FLAME KEPT GOING OUT!
I SUMMONED WIND TO MY YARD, I BLEW NAPKINS AROUND...
I SWITCHED IT ON—IT WENT OUT! I SWITCHED IT ON, AND...
IT WENT OUT, TARA! WE GET IT!
YOU'RE ALL NUTS! I'VE BEEN USING MAGIC ALL MORNING.
COINCI-DENCES, HAY LIN!
OH YEAH? **BOOKS! DOWN, NOW!**
CRRR
SEE?
TUMP
BONK
BUMP
YES, I SEE! WE WAS HIDING BEHIND THE BOOKS, AND YOU SCARED HIM!
WE! FEAAAAAW!

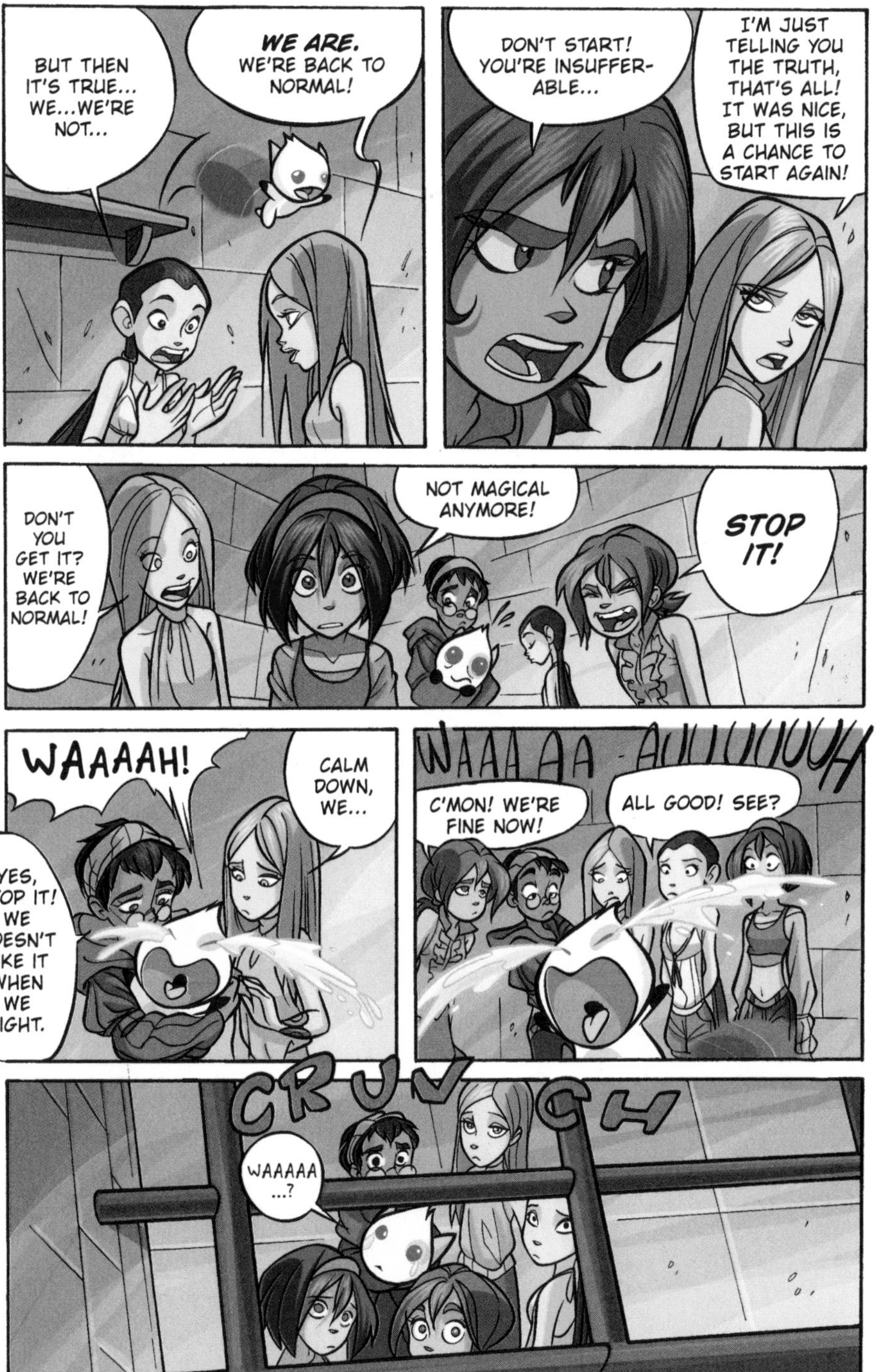

BUT THEN IT'S TRUE... WE...WE'RE NOT...
WE ARE. WE'RE BACK TO NORMAL!
DON'T START! YOU'RE INSUFFER-ABLE...
I'M JUST TELLING YOU THE TRUTH, THAT'S ALL! IT WAS NICE, BUT THIS IS A CHANCE TO START AGAIN!
DON'T YOU GET IT? WE'RE BACK TO NORMAL!
NOT MAGICAL ANYMORE!
STOP IT!
WAAAAH!
CALM DOWN, WE...
YES, STOP IT! WE DOESN'T LIKE IT WHEN WE FIGHT.
WAAA AA - AUUUUUUH
C'MON! WE'RE FINE NOW!
ALL GOOD! SEE?
CRUNCH
WAAAAA ...?

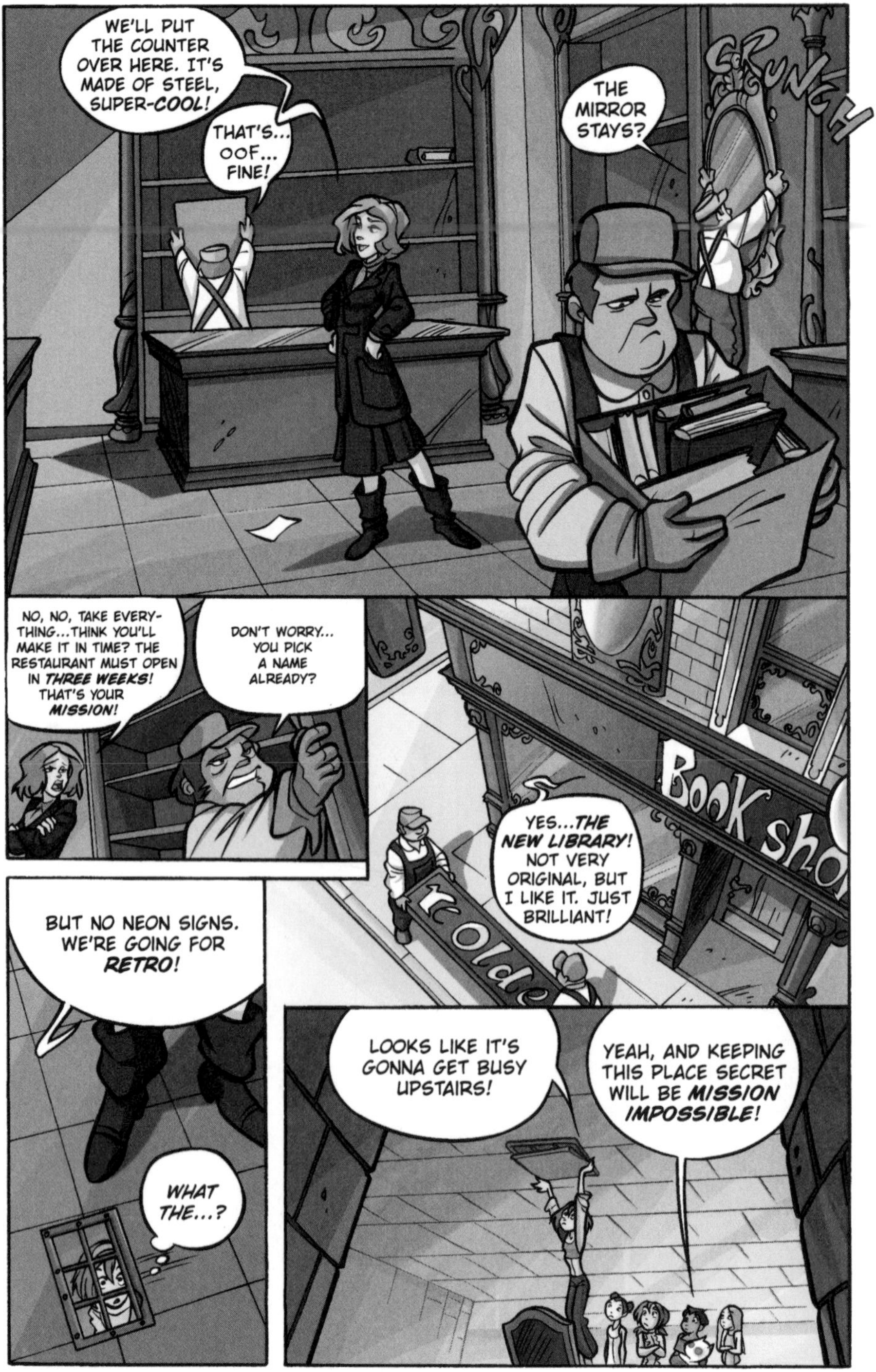
WE'LL PUT THE COUNTER OVER HERE. IT'S MADE OF STEEL, SUPER-COOL!
THAT'S... OOF... FINE!
THE MIRROR STAYS?
CRUNCH
NO, NO, TAKE EVERYTHING...THINK YOU'LL MAKE IT IN TIME? THE RESTAURANT MUST OPEN IN THREE WEEKS! THAT'S YOUR MISSION!
DON'T WORRY... YOU PICK A NAME ALREADY?
Book shop
YES...THE NEW LIBRARY! NOT VERY ORIGINAL, BUT I LIKE IT. JUST BRILLIANT!
BUT NO NEON SIGNS. WE'RE GOING FOR RETRO!
WHAT THE...?
LOOKS LIKE IT'S GONNA GET BUSY UPSTAIRS!
YEAH, AND KEEPING THIS PLACE SECRET WILL BE MISSION IMPOSSIBLE!

WELL, WE DON'T NEED A SECRET LAIR NOW! WE'RE CLEARLY NOT MAGICAL ANYMORE.

WAAAAAAH!

AAAAAAH!

PLEASE! I'M CONFUSED ENOUGH ALREADY!

YOU WERE SAYING ABOUT MATT... SO HE'S BACK!

I WOULDN'T SAY HE'S BACK. MORE LIKE... HE *CAME BY*!

MAYBE IT MADE HIM TOO EMOTIONAL TO SEE YOU AGAIN...

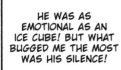

HE WAS AS EMOTIONAL AS AN ICE CUBE! BUT WHAT BUGGED ME THE MOST WAS HIS SILENCE!

I CAN'T STAND PEOPLE WHO'RE TOO CHICKEN TO TELL YOU WHAT'S WHAT!

MAYBE...

MAYBE I WAS A FOOL THINKING HE WAS SOMEONE HE'S NOT... AN HONEST, RELIABLE GUY!

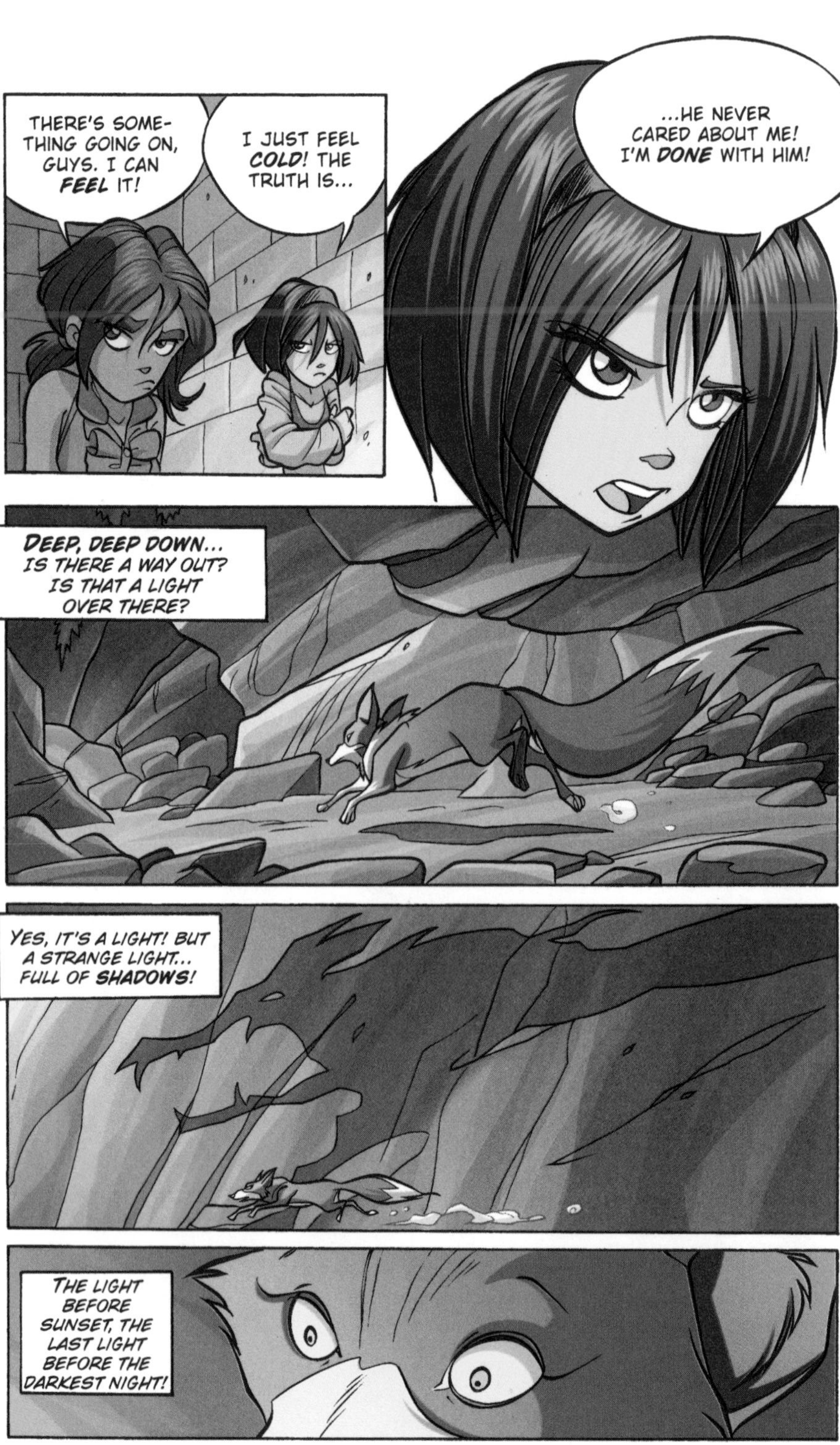
THERE'S SOME-THING GOING ON, GUYS. I CAN FEEL IT!
I JUST FEEL COLD! THE TRUTH IS...
...HE NEVER CARED ABOUT ME! I'M DONE WITH HIM!
DEEP, DEEP DOWN... IS THERE A WAY OUT? IS THAT A LIGHT OVER THERE?
YES, IT'S A LIGHT! BUT A STRANGE LIGHT... FULL OF SHADOWS!
THE LIGHT BEFORE SUNSET, THE LAST LIGHT BEFORE THE DARKEST NIGHT!

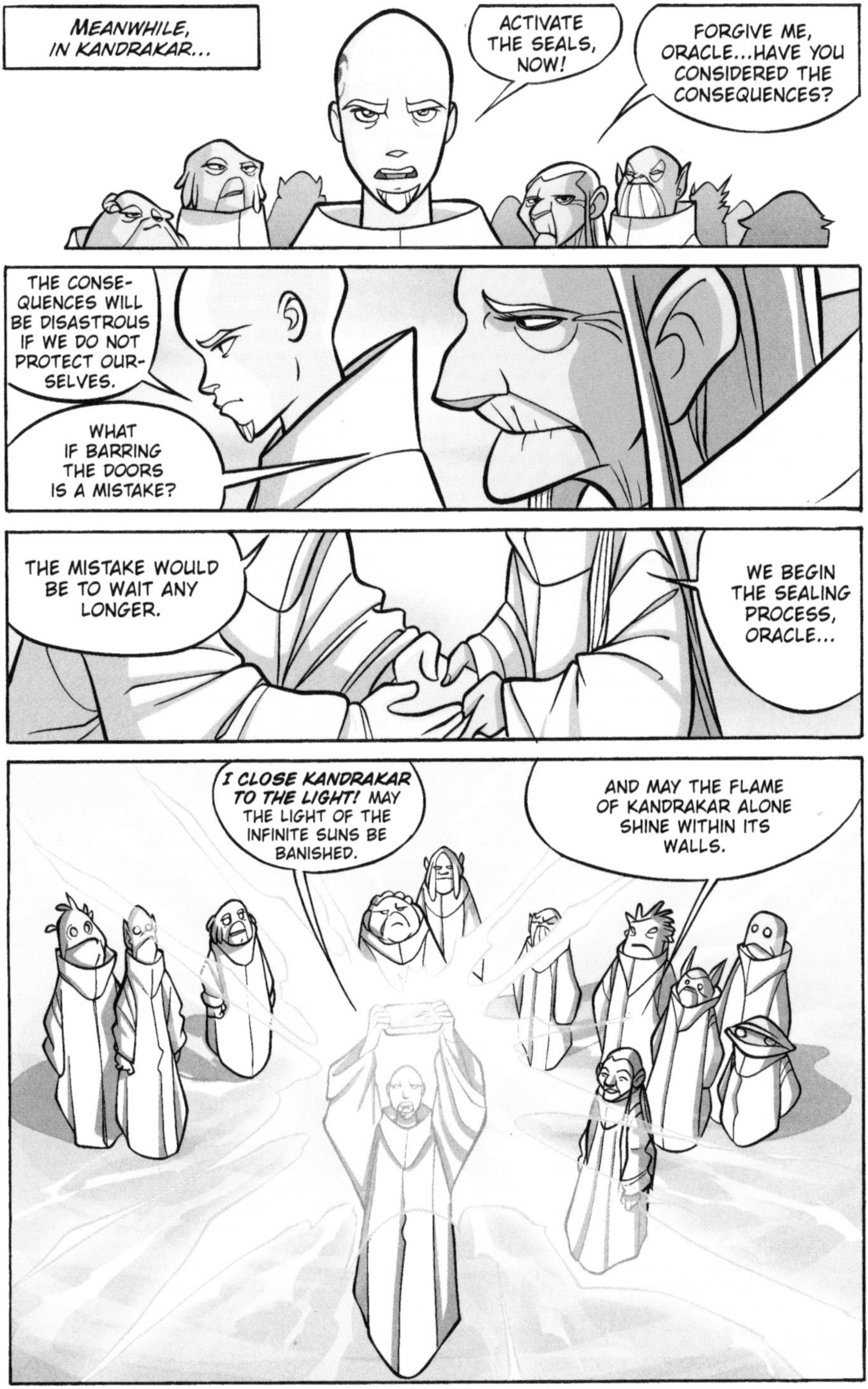
MEANWHILE, IN KANDRAKAR...
ACTIVATE THE SEALS, NOW!
FORGIVE ME, ORACLE...HAVE YOU CONSIDERED THE CONSEQUENCES?
THE CONSEQUENCES WILL BE DISASTROUS IF WE DO NOT PROTECT OURSELVES.
WHAT IF BARRING THE DOORS IS A MISTAKE?
THE MISTAKE WOULD BE TO WAIT ANY LONGER.
WE BEGIN THE SEALING PROCESS, ORACLE...
I CLOSE KANDRAKAR TO THE LIGHT! MAY THE LIGHT OF THE INFINITE SUNS BE BANISHED.
AND MAY THE FLAME OF KANDRAKAR ALONE SHINE WITHIN ITS WALLS.

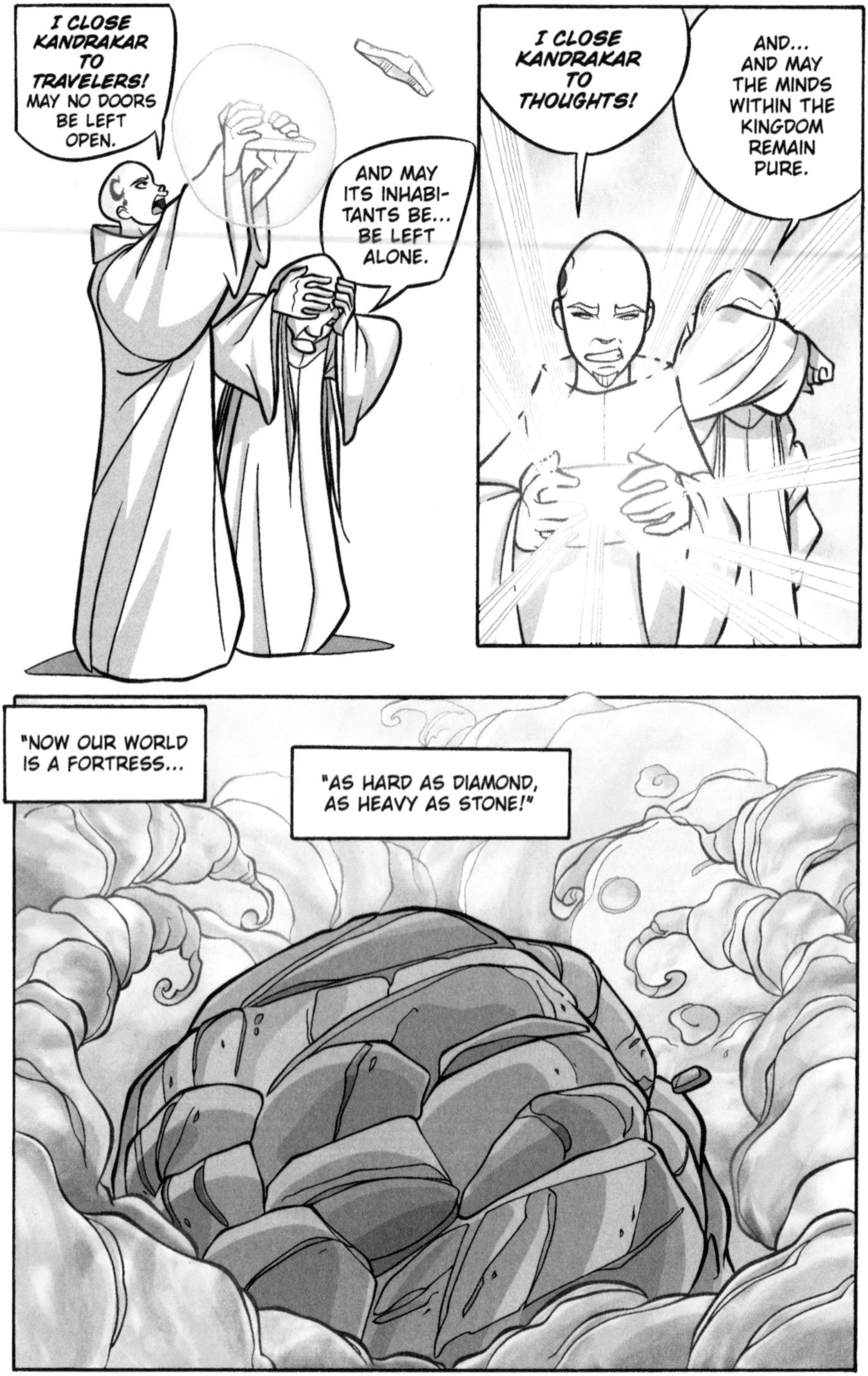
I CLOSE KANDRAKAR TO TRAVELERS! MAY NO DOORS BE LEFT OPEN.
AND MAY ITS INHABITANTS BE... BE LEFT ALONE.
I CLOSE KANDRAKAR TO THOUGHTS!
AND... AND MAY THE MINDS WITHIN THE KINGDOM REMAIN PURE.
"NOW OUR WORLD IS A FORTRESS...
"AS HARD AS DIAMOND, AS HEAVY AS STONE!"

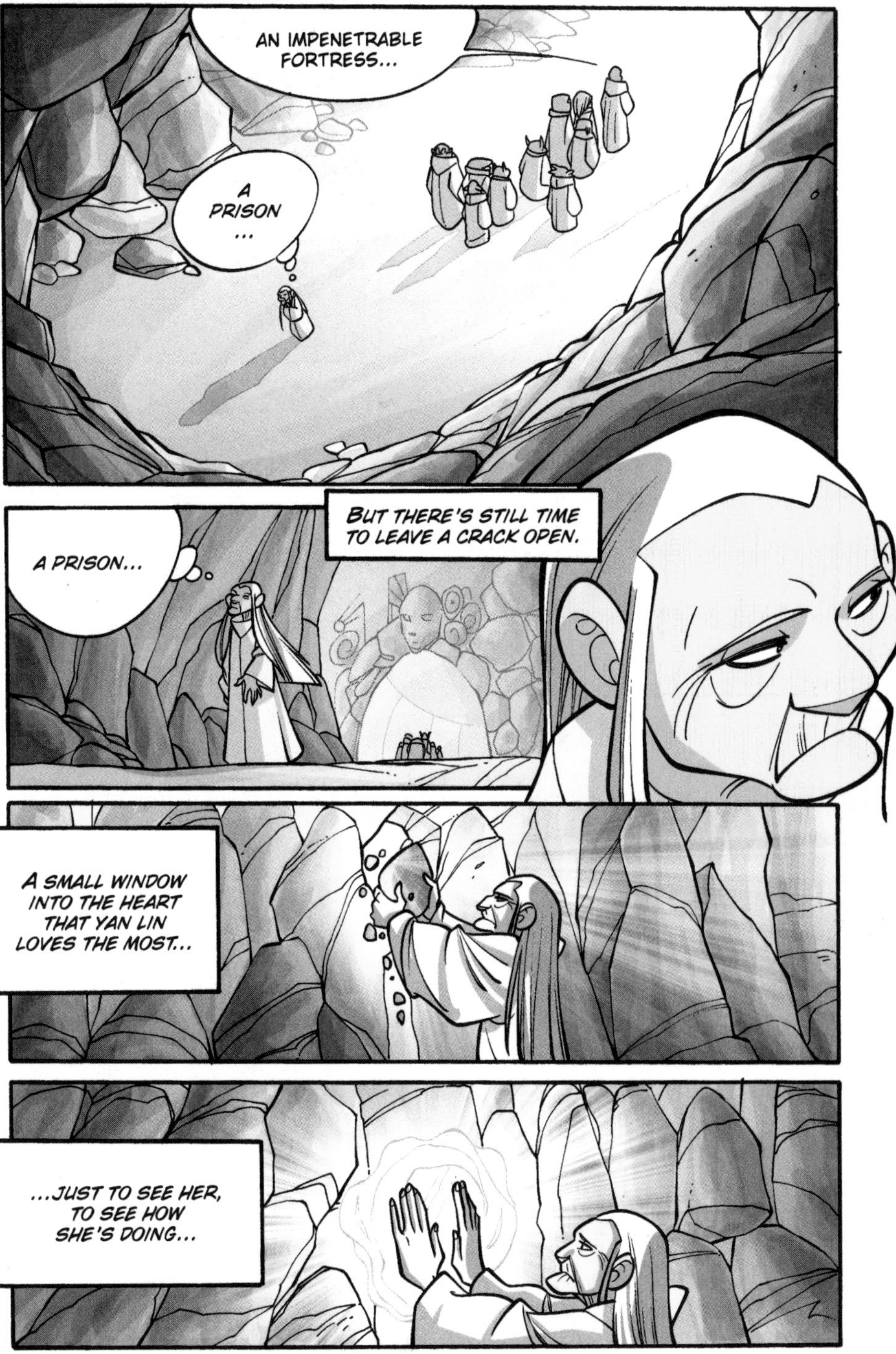
AN IMPENETRABLE FORTRESS...
A PRISON ...
A PRISON...
BUT THERE'S STILL TIME TO LEAVE A CRACK OPEN.
A SMALL WINDOW INTO THE HEART THAT YAN LIN LOVES THE MOST...
...JUST TO SEE HER, TO SEE HOW SHE'S DOING...

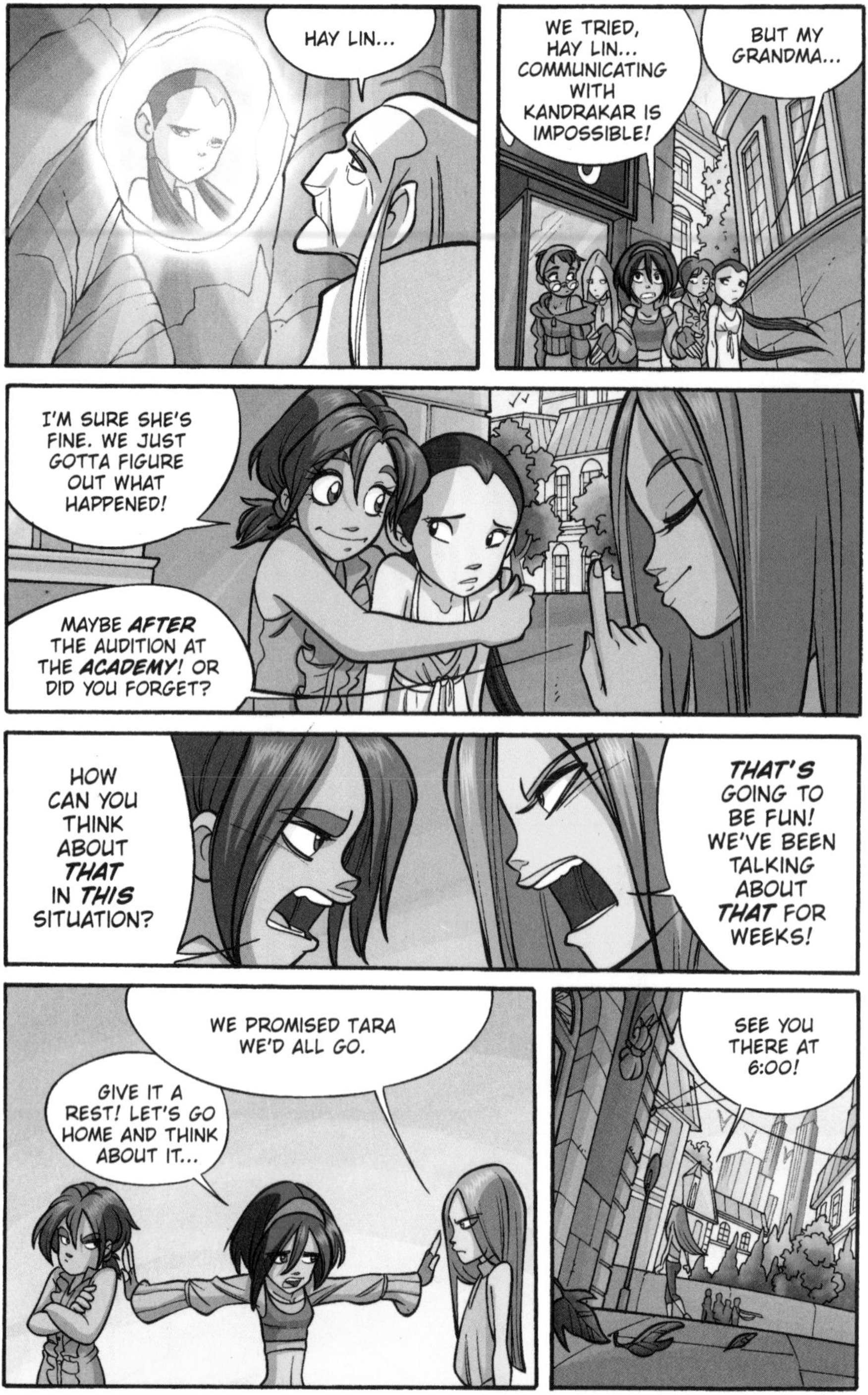
HAY LIN...
WE TRIED, HAY LIN... COMMUNICATING WITH KANDRAKAR IS IMPOSSIBLE!
BUT MY GRANDMA...
I'M SURE SHE'S FINE. WE JUST GOTTA FIGURE OUT WHAT HAPPENED!
MAYBE ***AFTER*** THE AUDITION AT THE ***ACADEMY!*** OR DID YOU FORGET?
HOW CAN YOU THINK ABOUT ***THAT*** IN ***THIS*** SITUATION?
THAT'S GOING TO BE FUN! WE'VE BEEN TALKING ABOUT ***THAT*** FOR WEEKS!
WE PROMISED TARA WE'D ALL GO.
GIVE IT A REST! LET'S GO HOME AND THINK ABOUT IT...
SEE YOU THERE AT 6:00!

LATER, AT WILL'S PLACE...

I HAVE TO TALK TO YOU...

NOT NOW, MOM. EVERYTHING'S A MESS...

IT'S IMPORTANT, WILL.

CAN WE TALK TONIGHT?

I'M GONNA HAVE A BABY.

OR MAYBE TOMORROW, WHEN I'M FEELING A BIT...

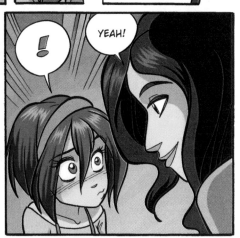

!

YEAH!

43

A BOY OR A GIRL... DEAN AND I DON'T WANT TO FIND OUT. NOT YET!

A BABY BROTHER OR SISTER! ...WILL?

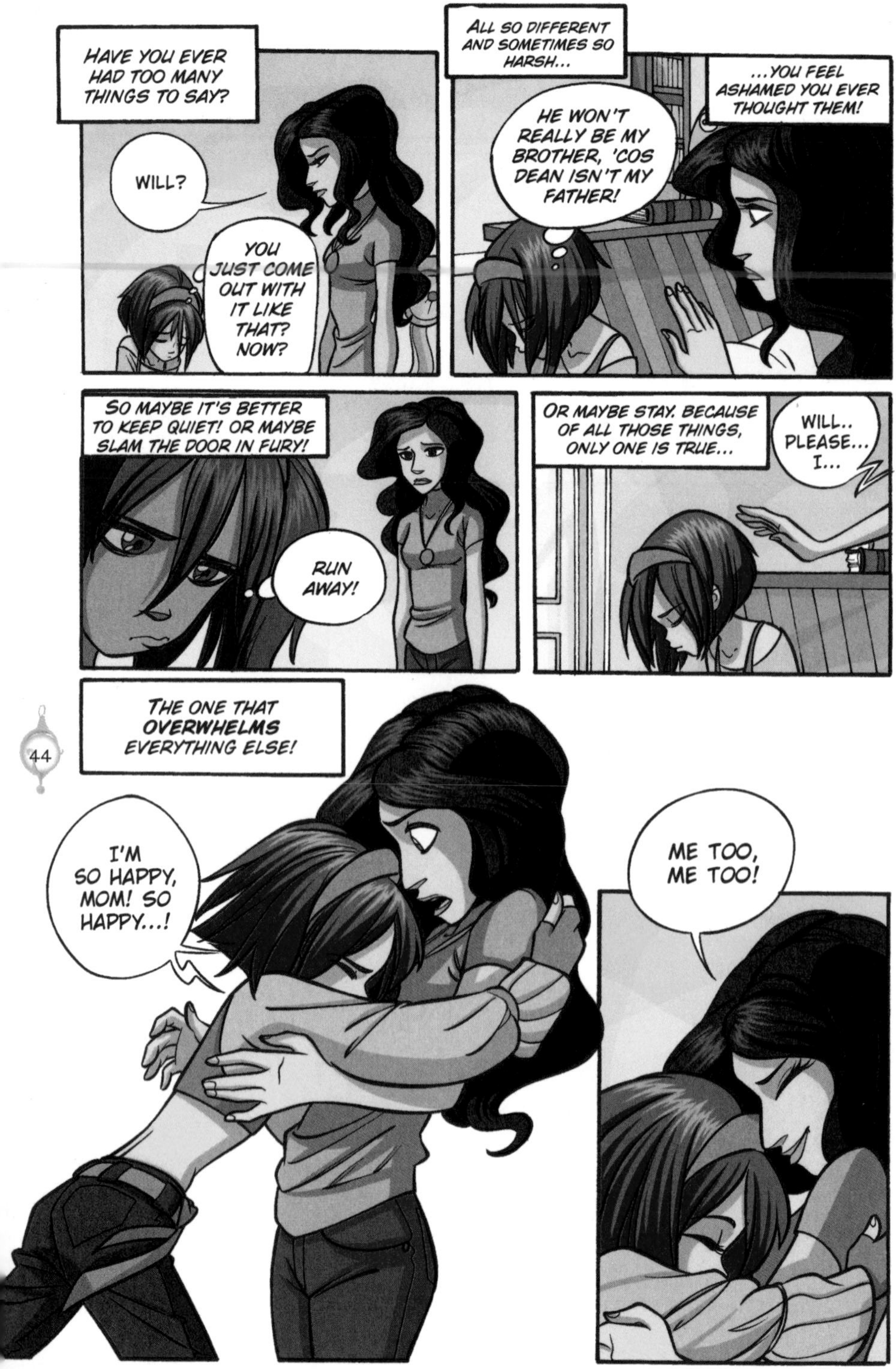
HAVE YOU EVER HAD TOO MANY THINGS TO SAY?
WILL?
YOU JUST COME OUT WITH IT LIKE THAT? NOW?
ALL SO DIFFERENT AND SOMETIMES SO HARSH...
HE WON'T REALLY BE MY BROTHER, 'COS DEAN ISN'T MY FATHER!
...YOU FEEL ASHAMED YOU EVER THOUGHT THEM!
SO MAYBE IT'S BETTER TO KEEP QUIET! OR MAYBE SLAM THE DOOR IN FURY!
RUN AWAY!
OR MAYBE STAY. BECAUSE OF ALL THOSE THINGS, ONLY ONE IS TRUE...
WILL.. PLEASE... I...
THE ONE THAT OVERWHELMS EVERYTHING ELSE!
I'M SO HAPPY, MOM! SO HAPPY...!
ME TOO, ME TOO!

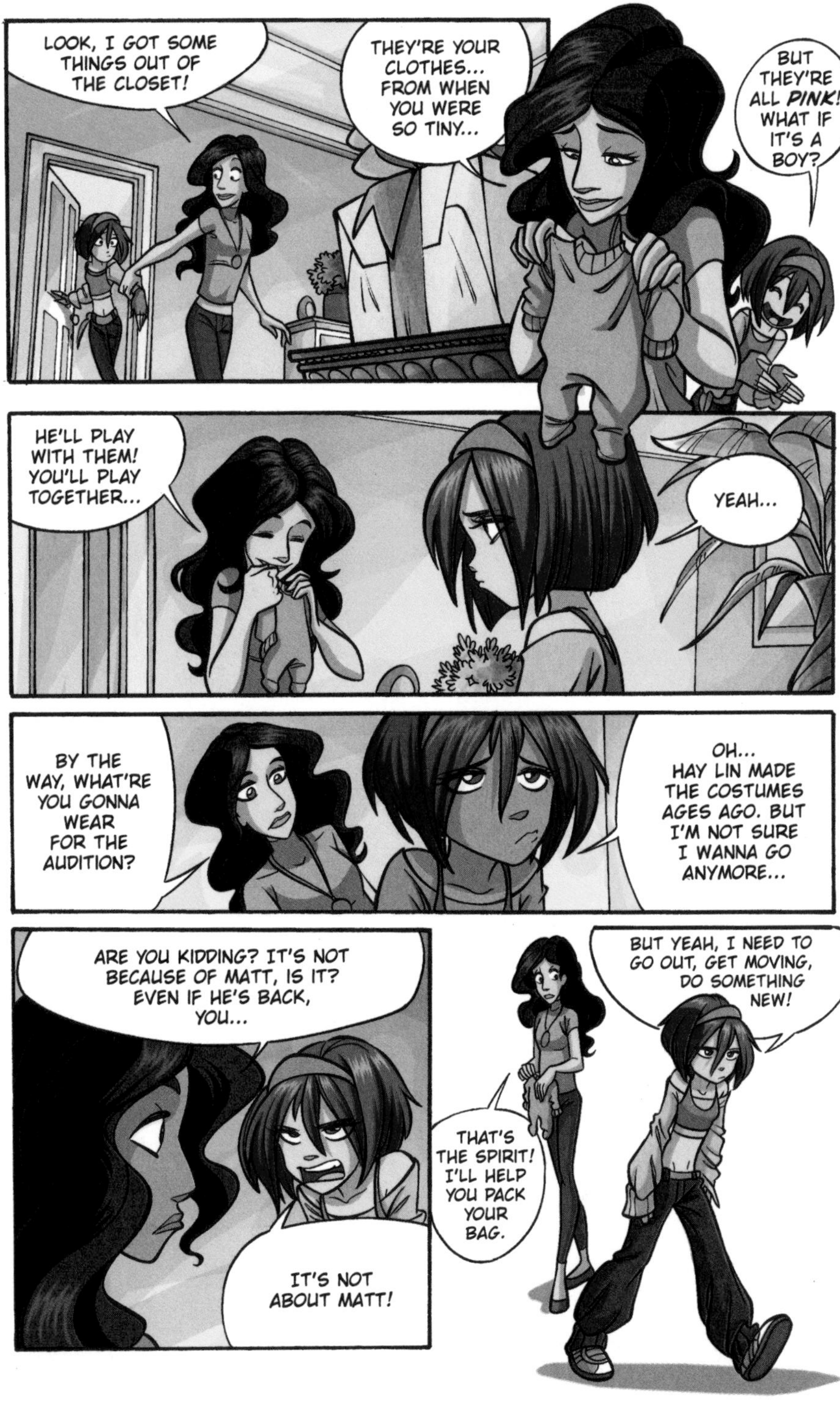
LOOK, I GOT SOME THINGS OUT OF THE CLOSET!
THEY'RE YOUR CLOTHES... FROM WHEN YOU WERE SO TINY...
BUT THEY'RE ALL PINK! WHAT IF IT'S A BOY?
HE'LL PLAY WITH THEM! YOU'LL PLAY TOGETHER...
YEAH...
BY THE WAY, WHAT'RE YOU GONNA WEAR FOR THE AUDITION?
OH... HAY LIN MADE THE COSTUMES AGES AGO. BUT I'M NOT SURE I WANNA GO ANYMORE...
ARE YOU KIDDING? IT'S NOT BECAUSE OF MATT, IS IT? EVEN IF HE'S BACK, YOU...
IT'S NOT ABOUT MATT!
BUT YEAH, I NEED TO GO OUT, GET MOVING, DO SOMETHING NEW!
THAT'S THE SPIRIT! I'LL HELP YOU PACK YOUR BAG.

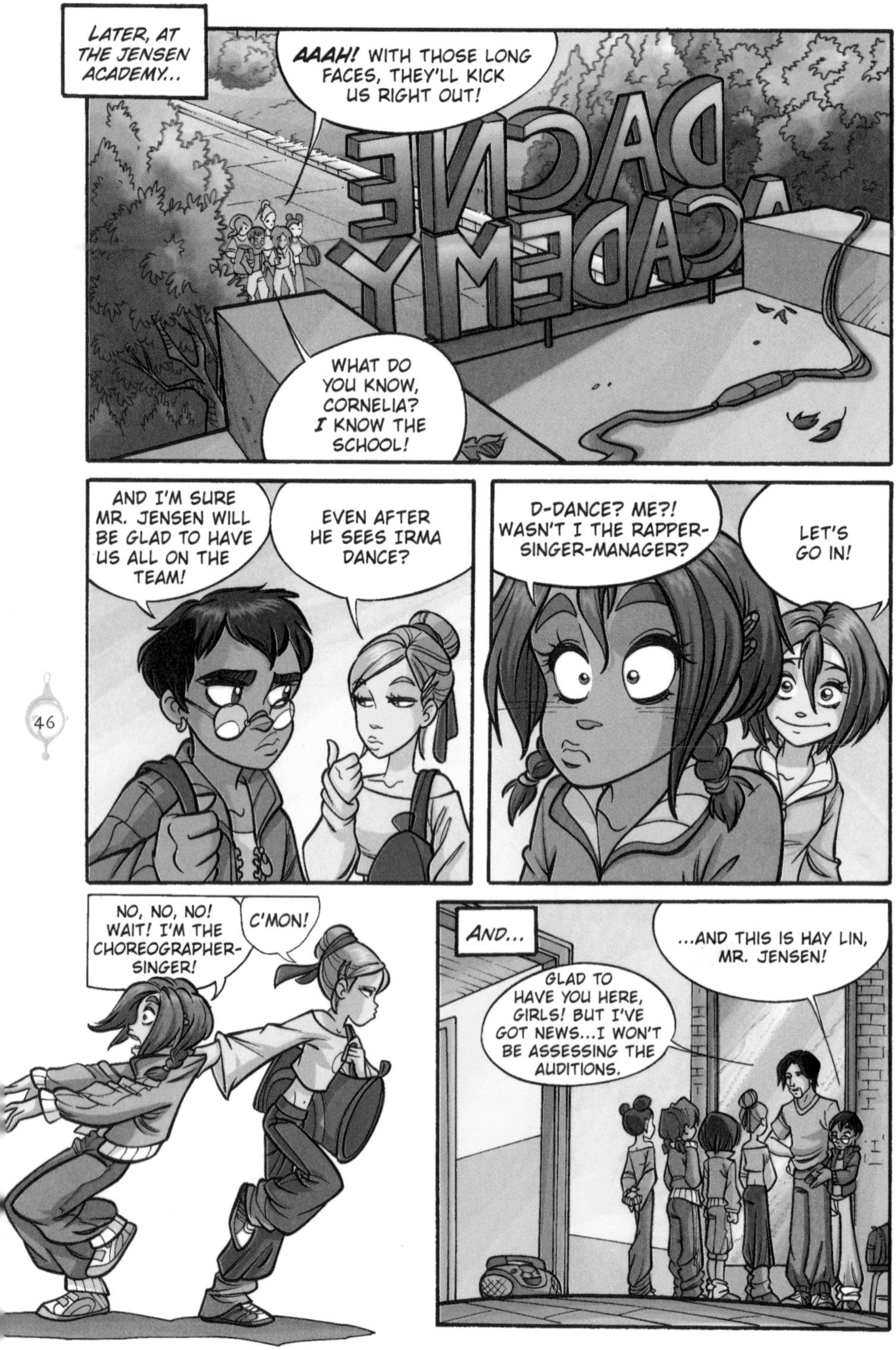
LATER, AT THE JENSEN ACADEMY...
AAAH! WITH THOSE LONG FACES, THEY'LL KICK US RIGHT OUT!
WHAT DO YOU KNOW, CORNELIA? I KNOW THE SCHOOL!
AND I'M SURE MR. JENSEN WILL BE GLAD TO HAVE US ALL ON THE TEAM!
EVEN AFTER HE SEES IRMA DANCE?
D-DANCE? ME?! WASN'T I THE RAPPER-SINGER-MANAGER?
LET'S GO IN!
NO, NO, NO! WAIT! I'M THE CHOREOGRAPHER-SINGER!
C'MON!
AND...
...AND THIS IS HAY LIN, MR. JENSEN!
GLAD TO HAVE YOU HERE, GIRLS! BUT I'VE GOT NEWS...I WON'T BE ASSESSING THE AUDITIONS.

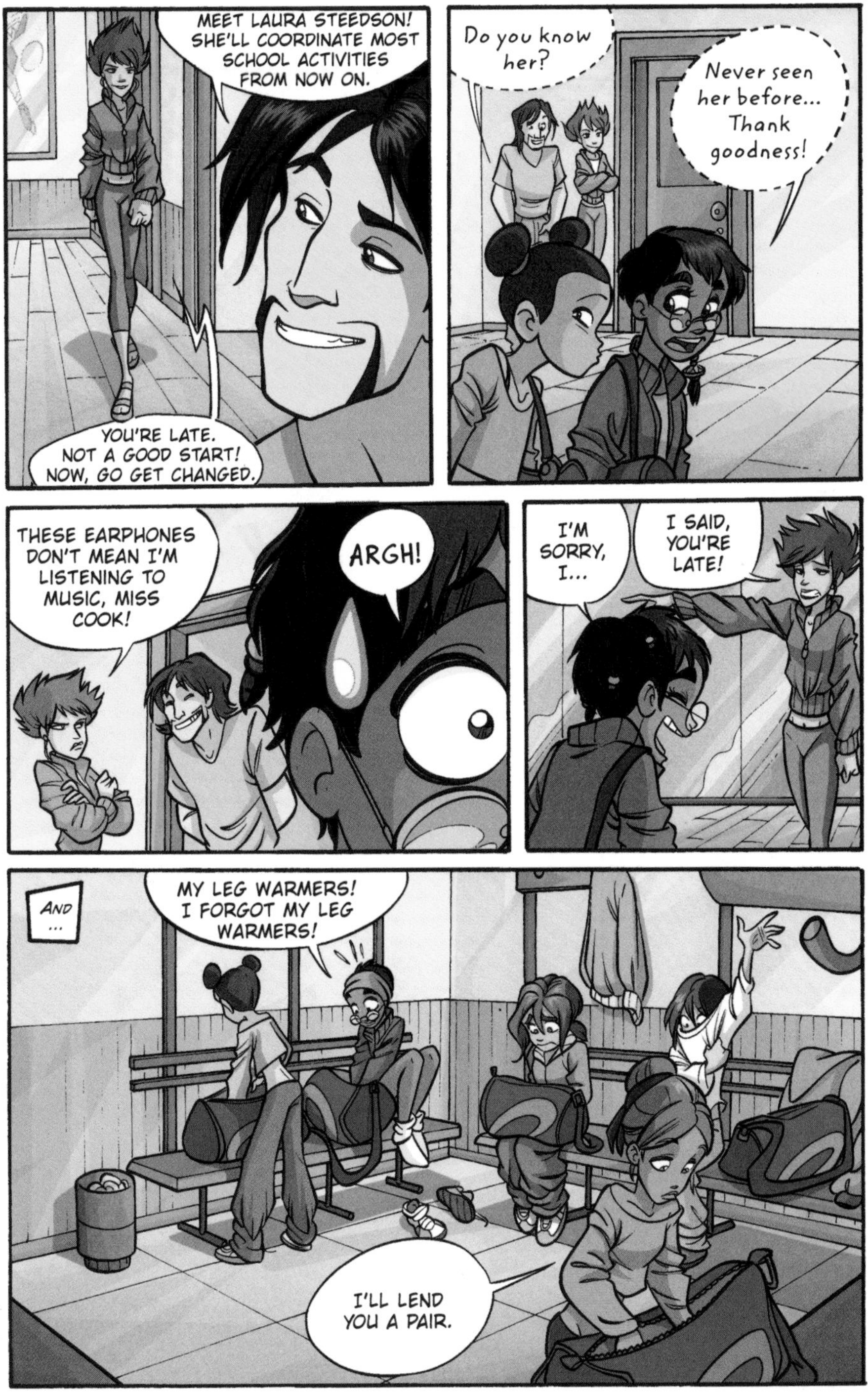
MEET LAURA STEEDSON! SHE'LL COORDINATE MOST SCHOOL ACTIVITIES FROM NOW ON.
YOU'RE LATE. NOT A GOOD START! NOW, GO GET CHANGED.
Do you know her?
Never seen her before... Thank goodness!
THESE EARPHONES DON'T MEAN I'M LISTENING TO MUSIC, MISS COOK!
ARGH!
I'M SORRY, I...
I SAID, YOU'RE LATE!
AND ...
MY LEG WARMERS! I FORGOT MY LEG WARMERS!
I'LL LEND YOU A PAIR.

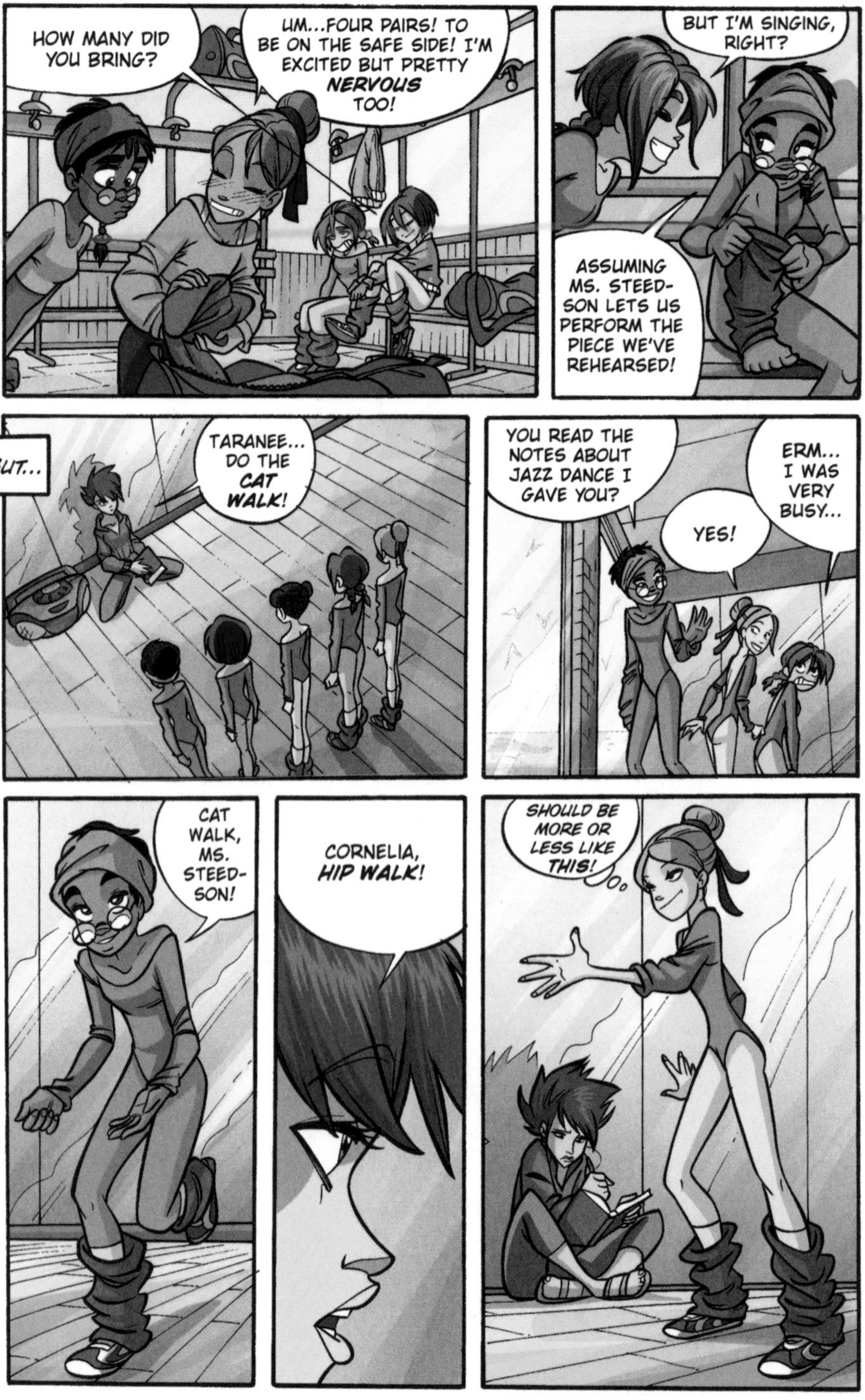
HOW MANY DID YOU BRING?
UM...FOUR PAIRS! TO BE ON THE SAFE SIDE! I'M EXCITED BUT PRETTY NERVOUS TOO!
BUT I'M SINGING, RIGHT?
ASSUMING MS. STEEDSON LETS US PERFORM THE PIECE WE'VE REHEARSED!
BUT...
TARANEE... DO THE CAT WALK!
YOU READ THE NOTES ABOUT JAZZ DANCE I GAVE YOU?
YES!
ERM... I WAS VERY BUSY...
CAT WALK, MS. STEEDSON!
CORNELIA, HIP WALK!
SHOULD BE MORE OR LESS LIKE THIS!

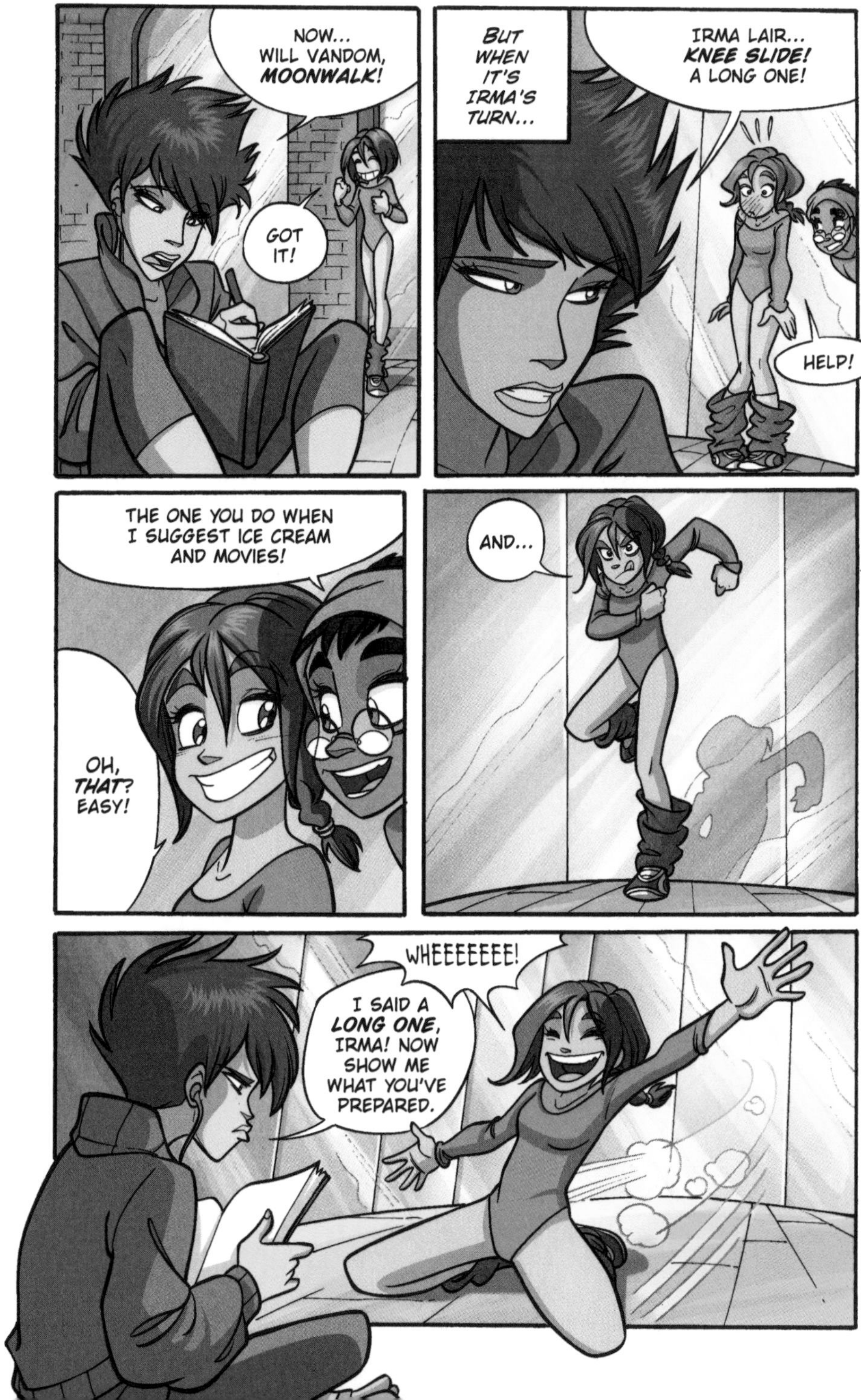
NOW... WILL VANDOM, MOONWALK!
GOT IT!
BUT WHEN IT'S IRMA'S TURN...
IRMA LAIR... KNEE SLIDE! A LONG ONE!
HELP!
THE ONE YOU DO WHEN I SUGGEST ICE CREAM AND MOVIES!
OH, THAT? EASY!
AND...
WHEEEEEEE!
I SAID A LONG ONE, IRMA! NOW SHOW ME WHAT YOU'VE PREPARED.

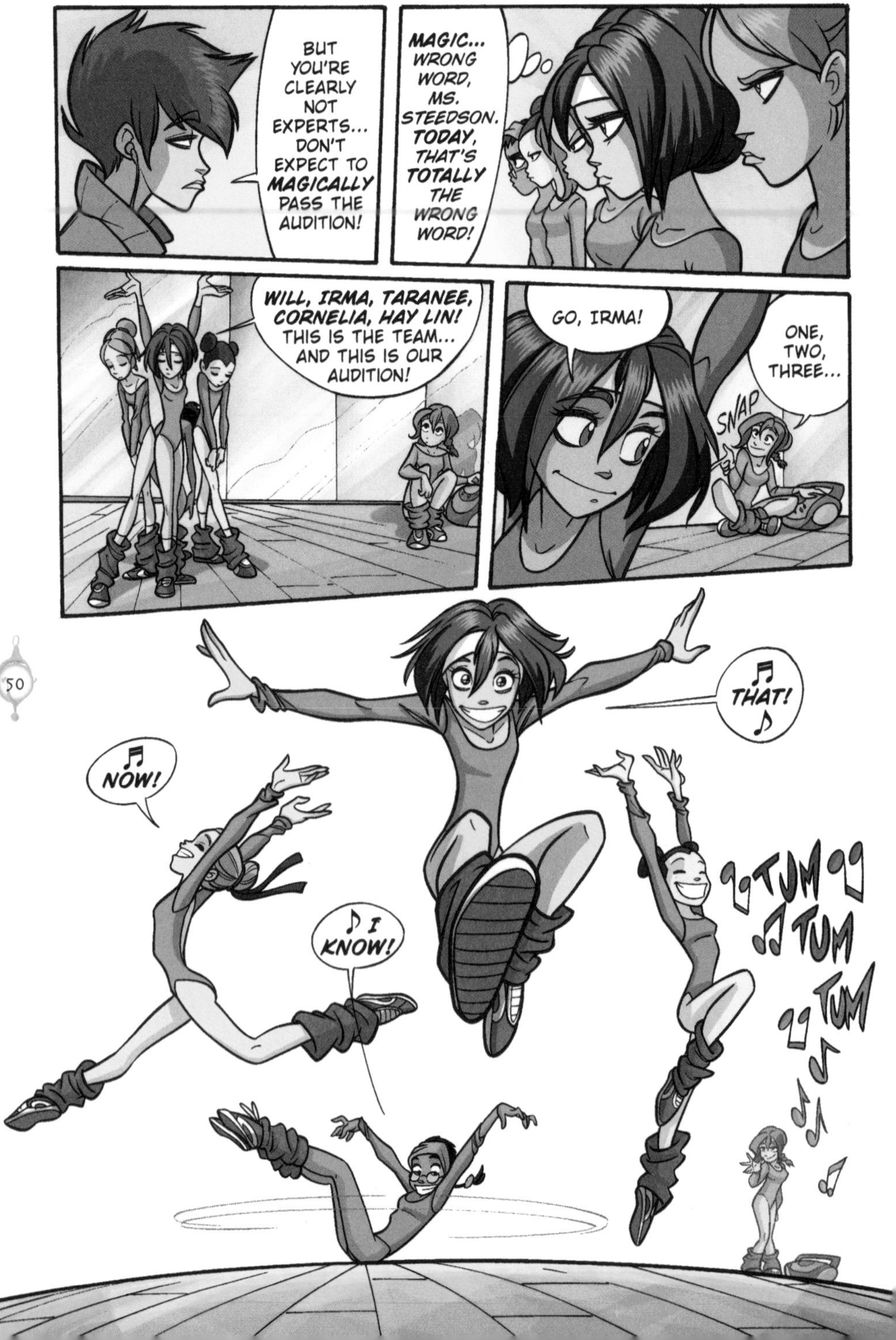
BUT YOU'RE CLEARLY NOT EXPERTS... DON'T EXPECT TO MAGICALLY PASS THE AUDITION!
MAGIC... WRONG WORD, MS. STEEDSON. TODAY, THAT'S TOTALLY THE WRONG WORD!
WILL, IRMA, TARANEE, CORNELIA, HAY LIN! THIS IS THE TEAM... AND THIS IS OUR AUDITION!
GO, IRMA!
ONE, TWO, THREE...
SNAP
♫ THAT! ♪
♫ NOW!
♪ I KNOW!
TUM
TUM
TUM

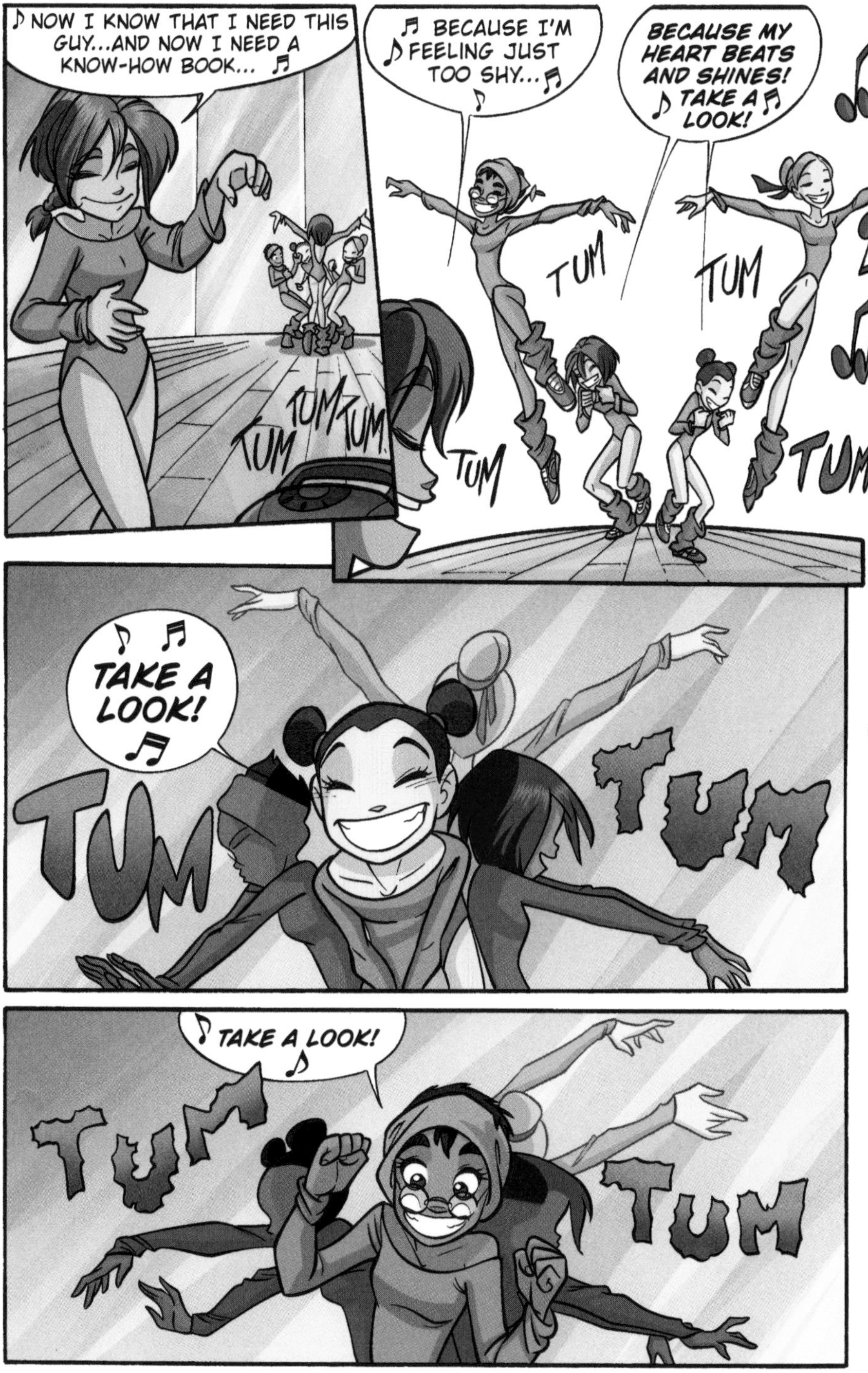
NOW I KNOW THAT I NEED THIS GUY...AND NOW I NEED A KNOW-HOW BOOK...
TUM TUM TUM
BECAUSE I'M FEELING JUST TOO SHY...
BECAUSE MY HEART BEATS AND SHINES! TAKE A LOOK!
TUM
TUM
TUM
TUM
TAKE A LOOK!
TUM
TUM
TAKE A LOOK!
TUM
TUM

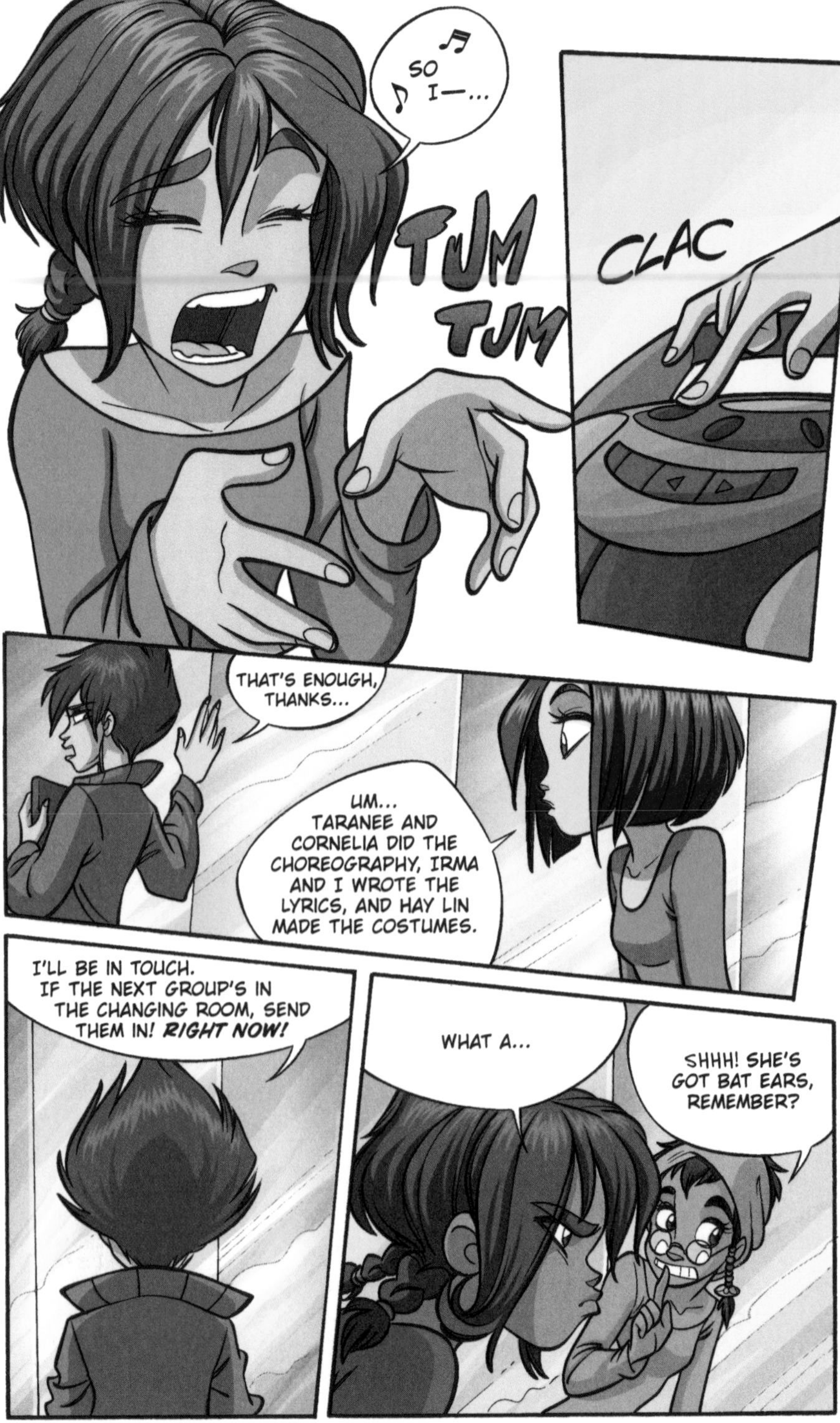

♪ SO I—... ♫
TUM TUM TUM
CLAC
THAT'S ENOUGH, THANKS...
UM... TARANEE AND CORNELIA DID THE CHOREOGRAPHY, IRMA AND I WROTE THE LYRICS, AND HAY LIN MADE THE COSTUMES.
I'LL BE IN TOUCH. IF THE NEXT GROUP'S IN THE CHANGING ROOM, SEND THEM IN! *RIGHT NOW!*
WHAT A...
SHHH! SHE'S GOT BAT EARS, REMEMBER?

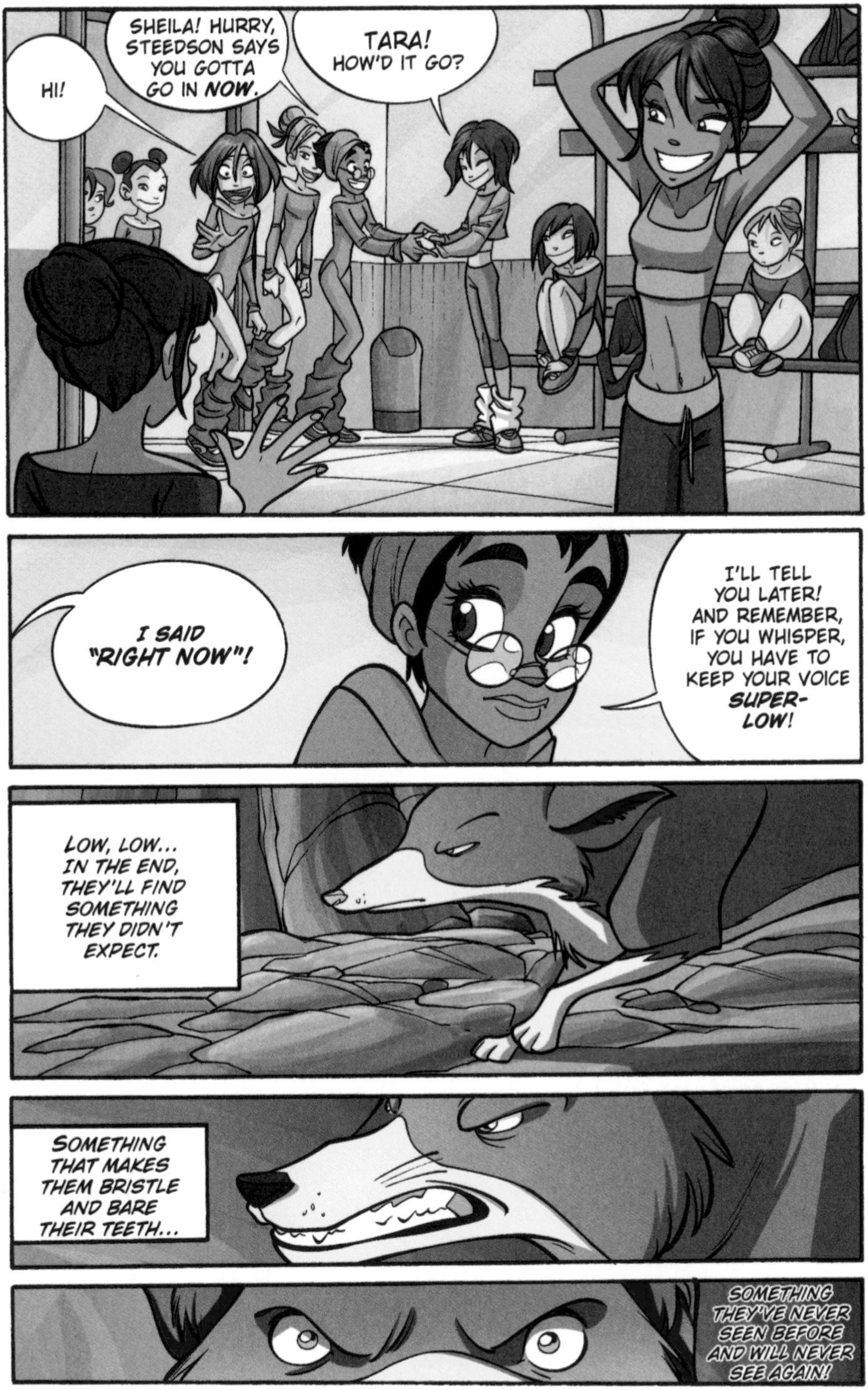
HI!
SHEILA! HURRY, STEEDSON SAYS YOU GOTTA GO IN NOW.
TARA! HOW'D IT GO?
I SAID "RIGHT NOW"!
I'LL TELL YOU LATER! AND REMEMBER, IF YOU WHISPER, YOU HAVE TO KEEP YOUR VOICE SUPER-LOW!
LOW, LOW... IN THE END, THEY'LL FIND SOMETHING THEY DIDN'T EXPECT.
SOMETHING THAT MAKES THEM BRISTLE AND BARE THEIR TEETH...
SOMETHING THEY'VE NEVER SEEN BEFORE AND WILL NEVER SEE AGAIN!

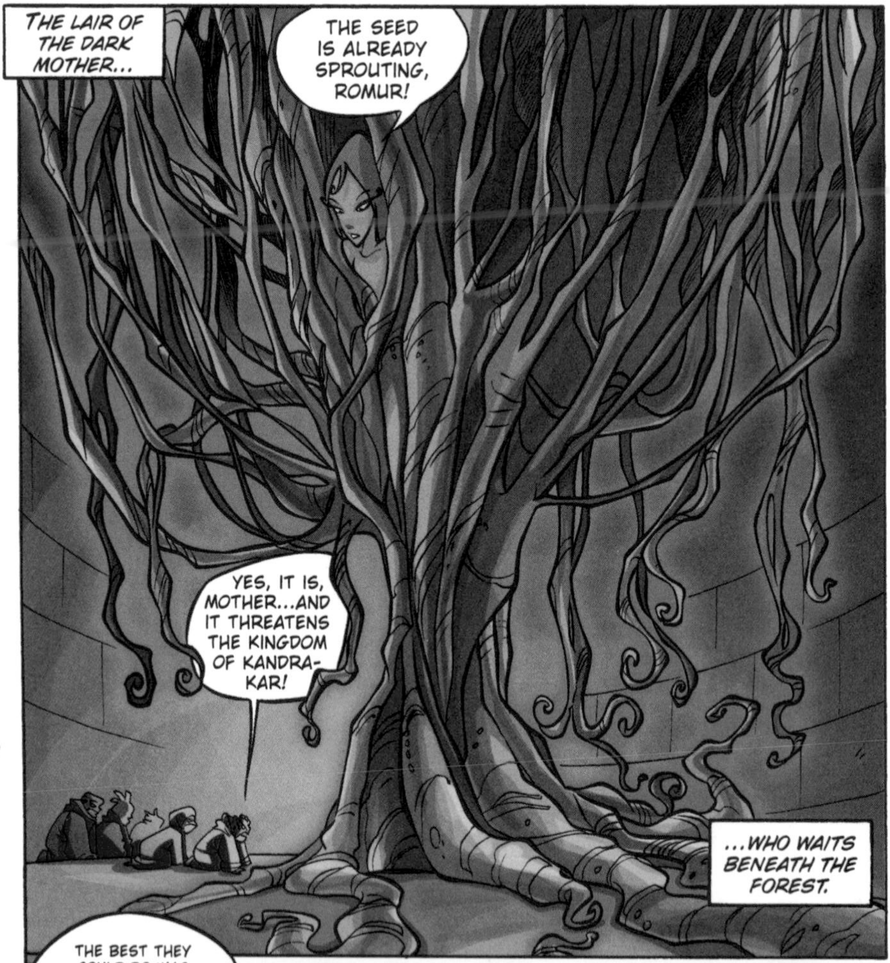
THE LAIR OF THE DARK MOTHER...
THE SEED IS ALREADY SPROUTING, ROMUR!
YES, IT IS, MOTHER...AND IT THREATENS THE KINGDOM OF KANDRA-KAR!
...WHO WAITS BENEATH THE FOREST.

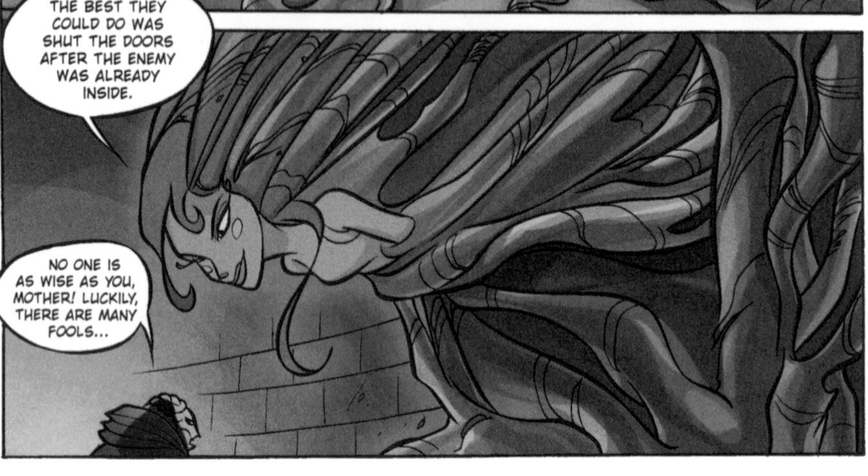
THE BEST THEY COULD DO WAS SHUT THE DOORS AFTER THE ENEMY WAS ALREADY INSIDE.
NO ONE IS AS WISE AS YOU, MOTHER! LUCKILY, THERE ARE MANY FOOLS...

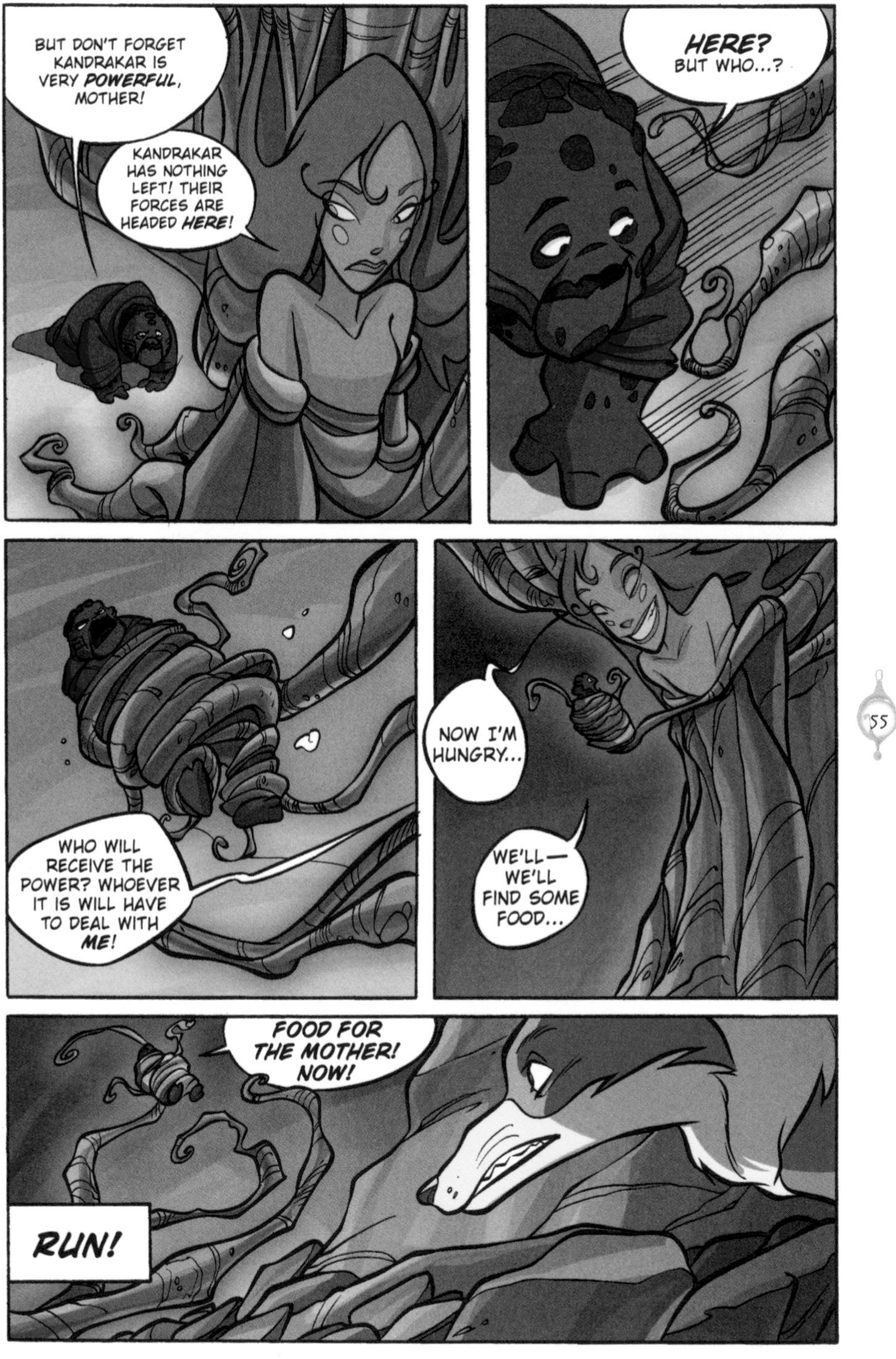
BUT DON'T FORGET KANDRAKAR IS VERY POWERFUL, MOTHER!
KANDRAKAR HAS NOTHING LEFT! THEIR FORCES ARE HEADED HERE!
HERE? BUT WHO...?
WHO WILL RECEIVE THE POWER? WHOEVER IT IS WILL HAVE TO DEAL WITH ME!
NOW I'M HUNGRY...
WE'LL— WE'LL FIND SOME FOOD...
FOOD FOR THE MOTHER! NOW!
RUN!

DO THEY REALLY NEED TO BE TOLD?

IF THE HORROR IS TOO MUCH, IF THEY *HAVE* TO FIND A WAY OUT...

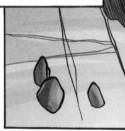

56

...THEY'LL FIND A WAY OUT, EVEN IF THEY HAVE TO RUN ALL NIGHT...

...EVEN BREATHLESS, THEY'LL FIND THE SKY AGAIN, THE REFRESHING EVENING BREEZE...

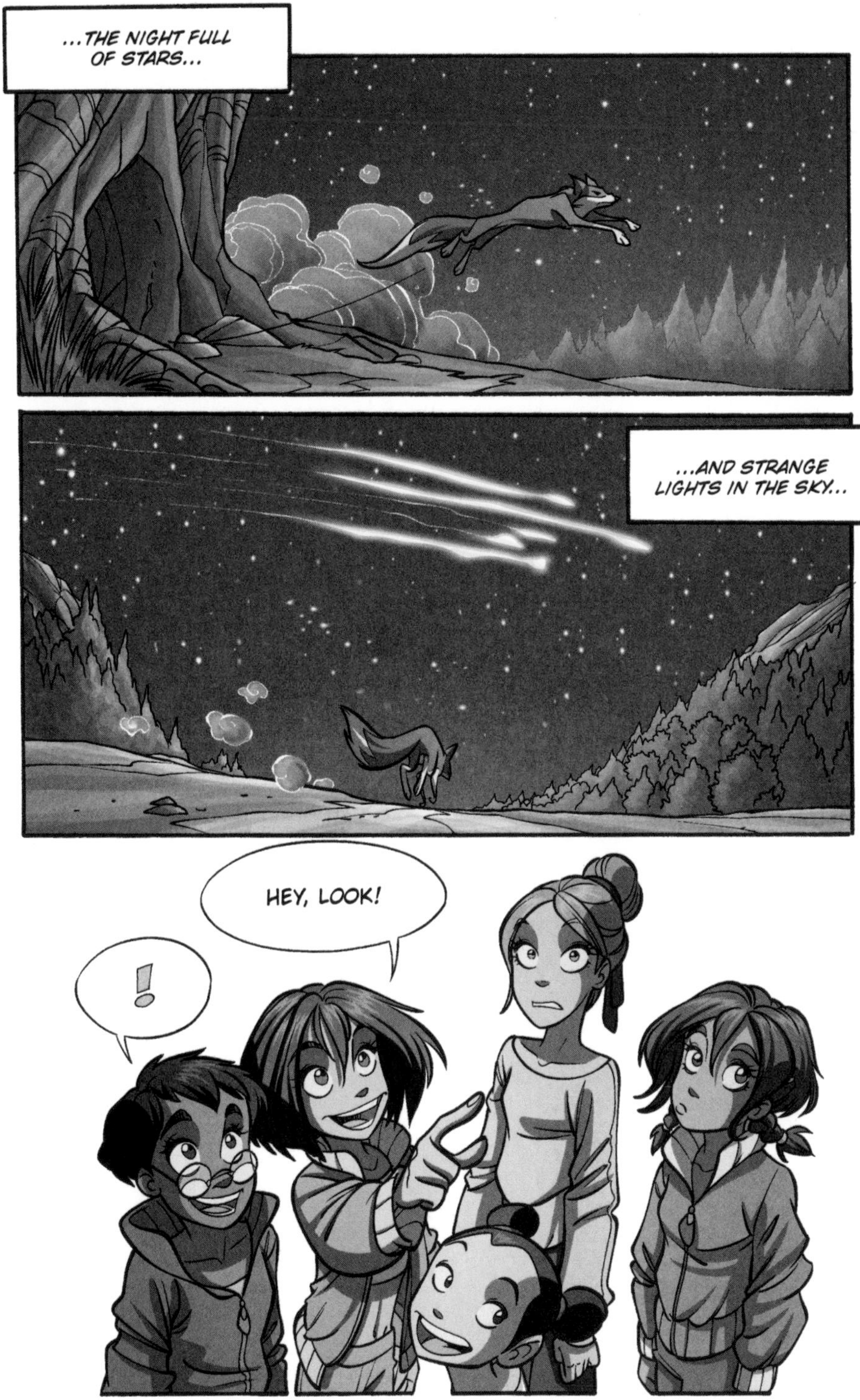
...THE NIGHT FULL OF STARS...
...AND STRANGE LIGHTS IN THE SKY...
!
HEY, LOOK!

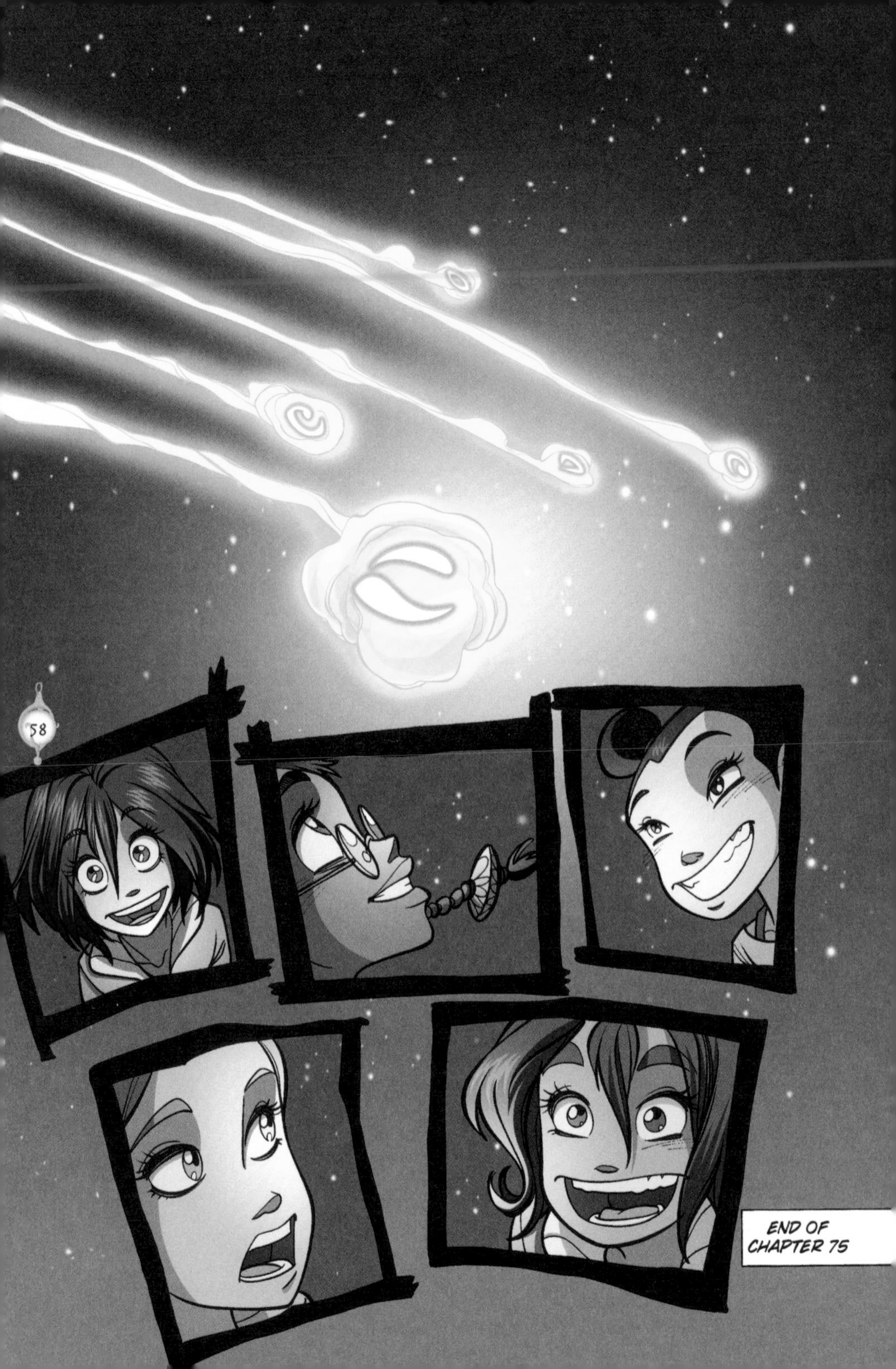
END OF
CHAPTER 75

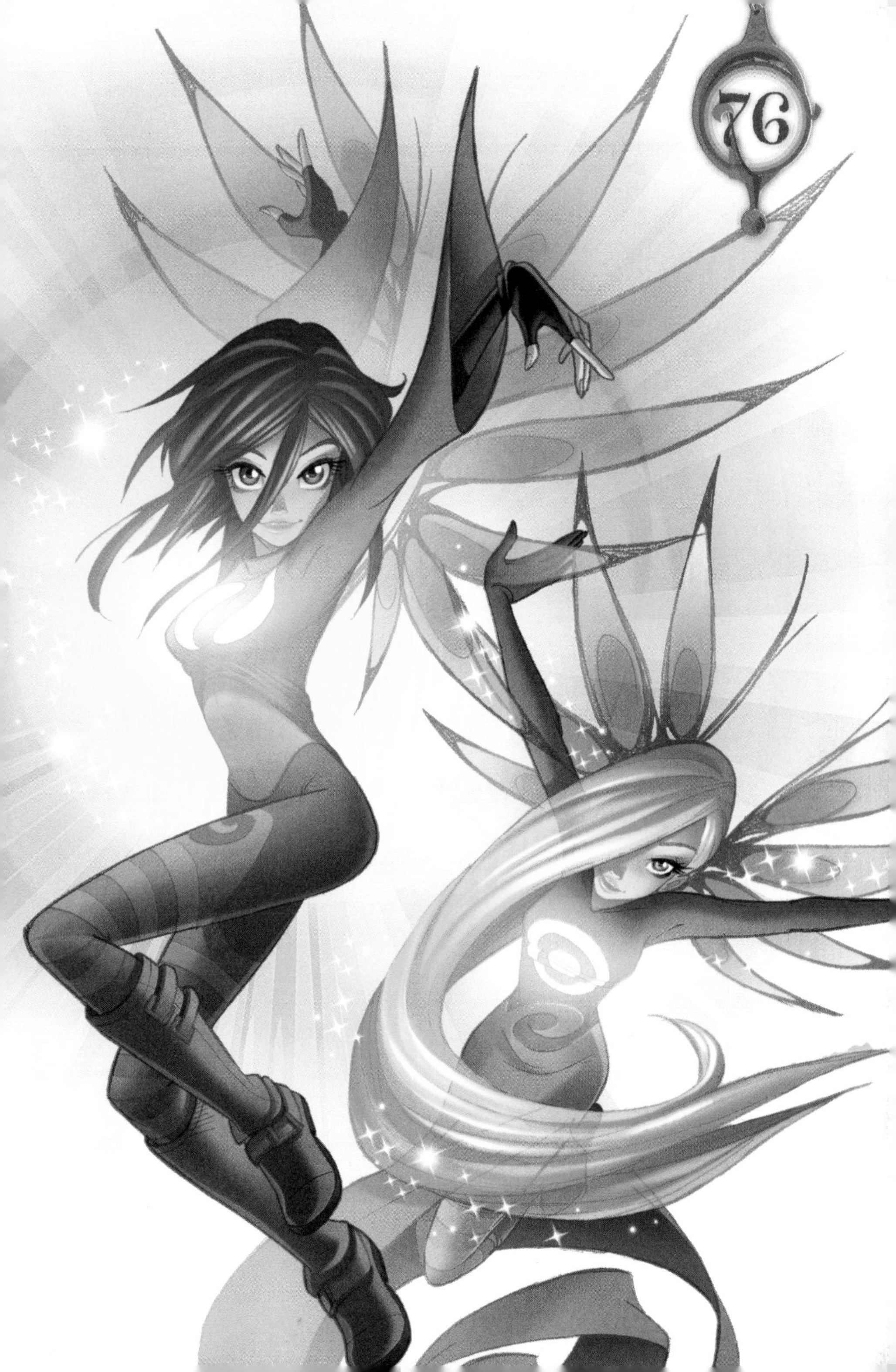
76

Earth

"What used to be will remain."

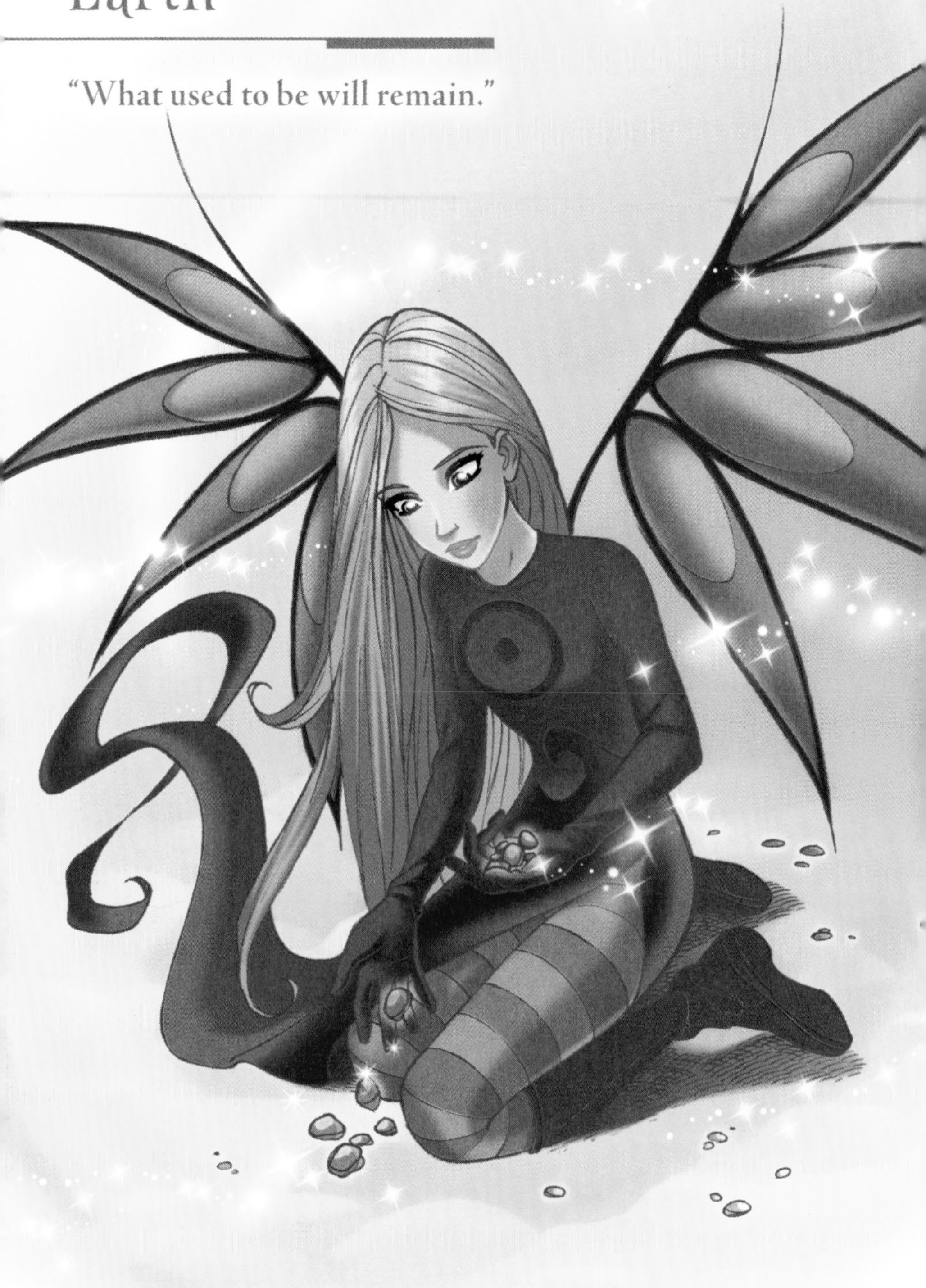

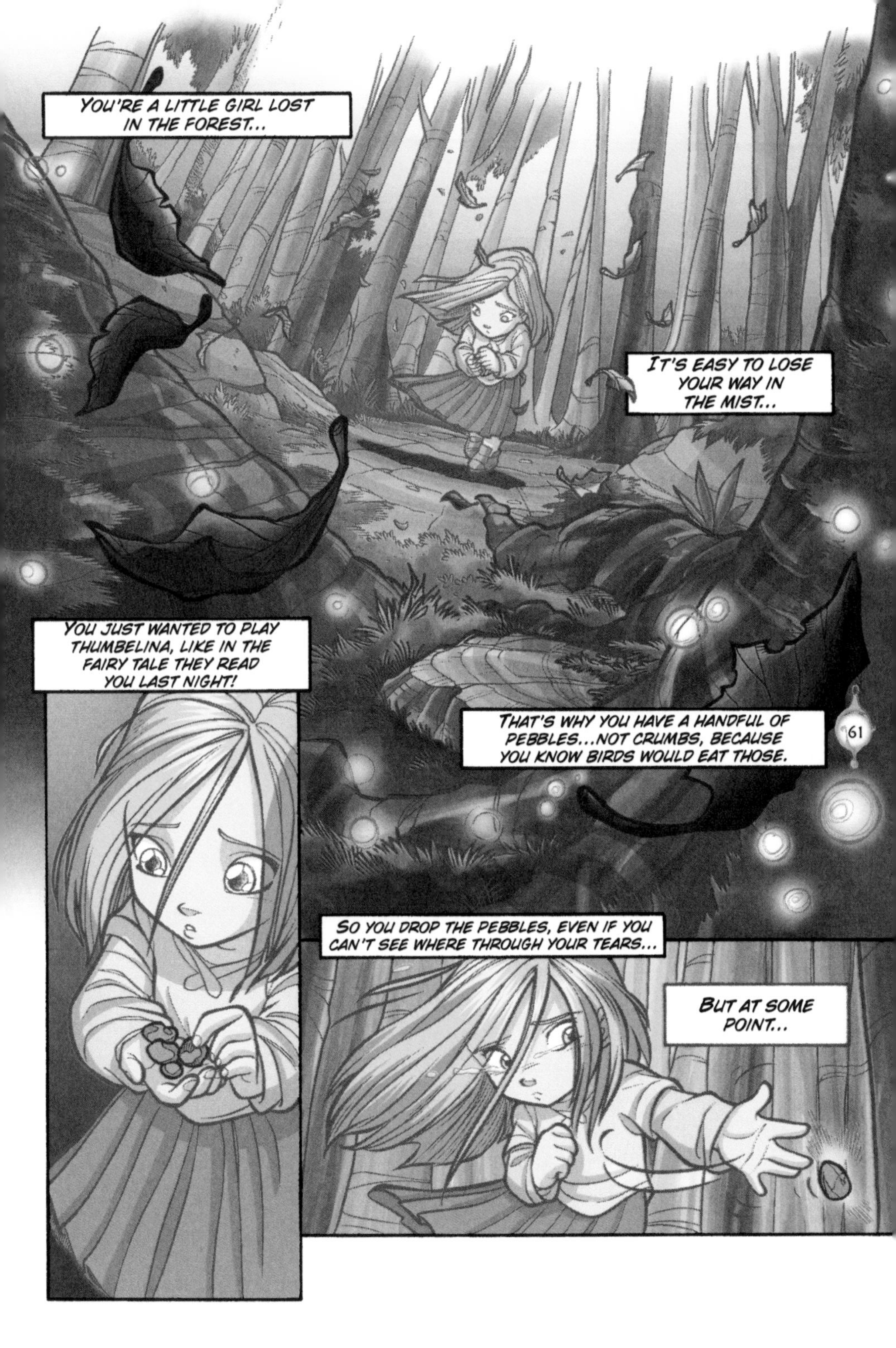
YOU'RE A LITTLE GIRL LOST IN THE FOREST...
IT'S EASY TO LOSE YOUR WAY IN THE MIST...
YOU JUST WANTED TO PLAY THUMBELINA, LIKE IN THE FAIRY TALE THEY READ YOU LAST NIGHT!
THAT'S WHY YOU HAVE A HANDFUL OF PEBBLES...NOT CRUMBS, BECAUSE YOU KNOW BIRDS WOULD EAT THOSE.
SO YOU DROP THE PEBBLES, EVEN IF YOU CAN'T SEE WHERE THROUGH YOUR TEARS...
BUT AT SOME POINT...

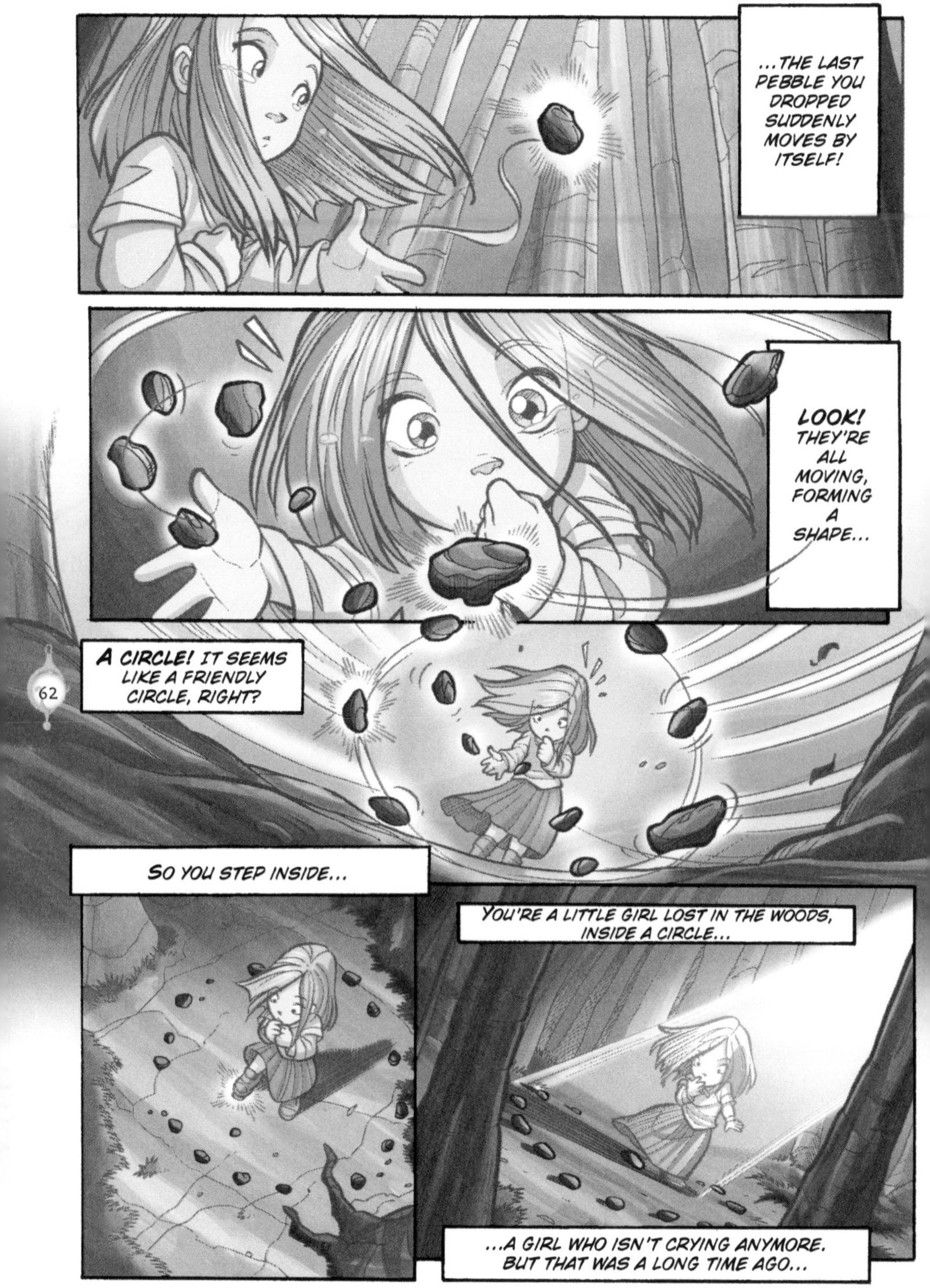
...THE LAST PEBBLE YOU DROPPED SUDDENLY MOVES BY ITSELF!
LOOK! THEY'RE ALL MOVING, FORMING A SHAPE...
A CIRCLE! IT SEEMS LIKE A FRIENDLY CIRCLE, RIGHT?
SO YOU STEP INSIDE...
YOU'RE A LITTLE GIRL LOST IN THE WOODS, INSIDE A CIRCLE...
...A GIRL WHO ISN'T CRYING ANYMORE. BUT THAT WAS A LONG TIME AGO...

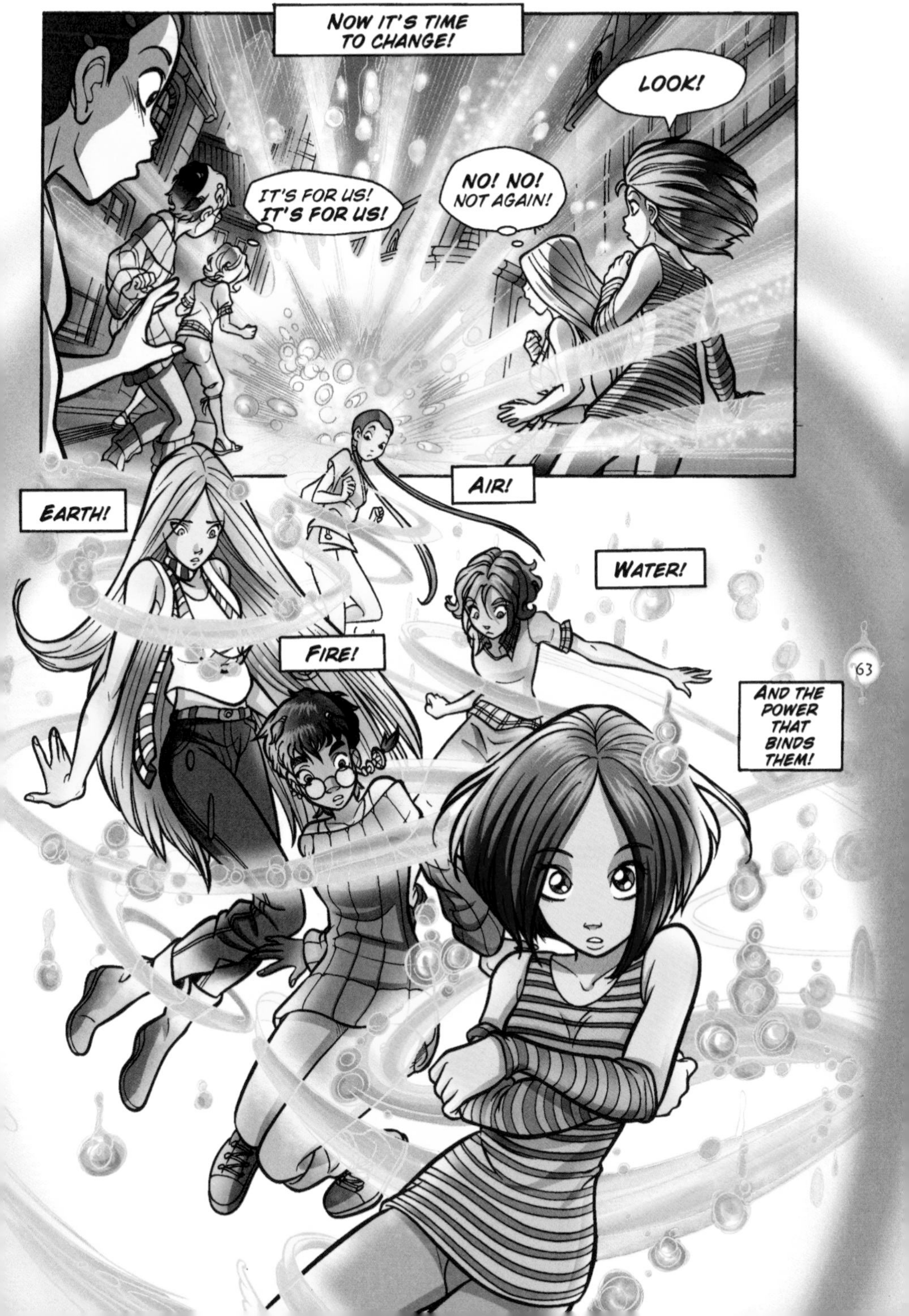
NOW IT'S TIME TO CHANGE!
IT'S FOR US! IT'S FOR US!
NO! NO! NOT AGAIN!
LOOK!
EARTH!
AIR!
WATER!
FIRE!
AND THE POWER THAT BINDS THEM!

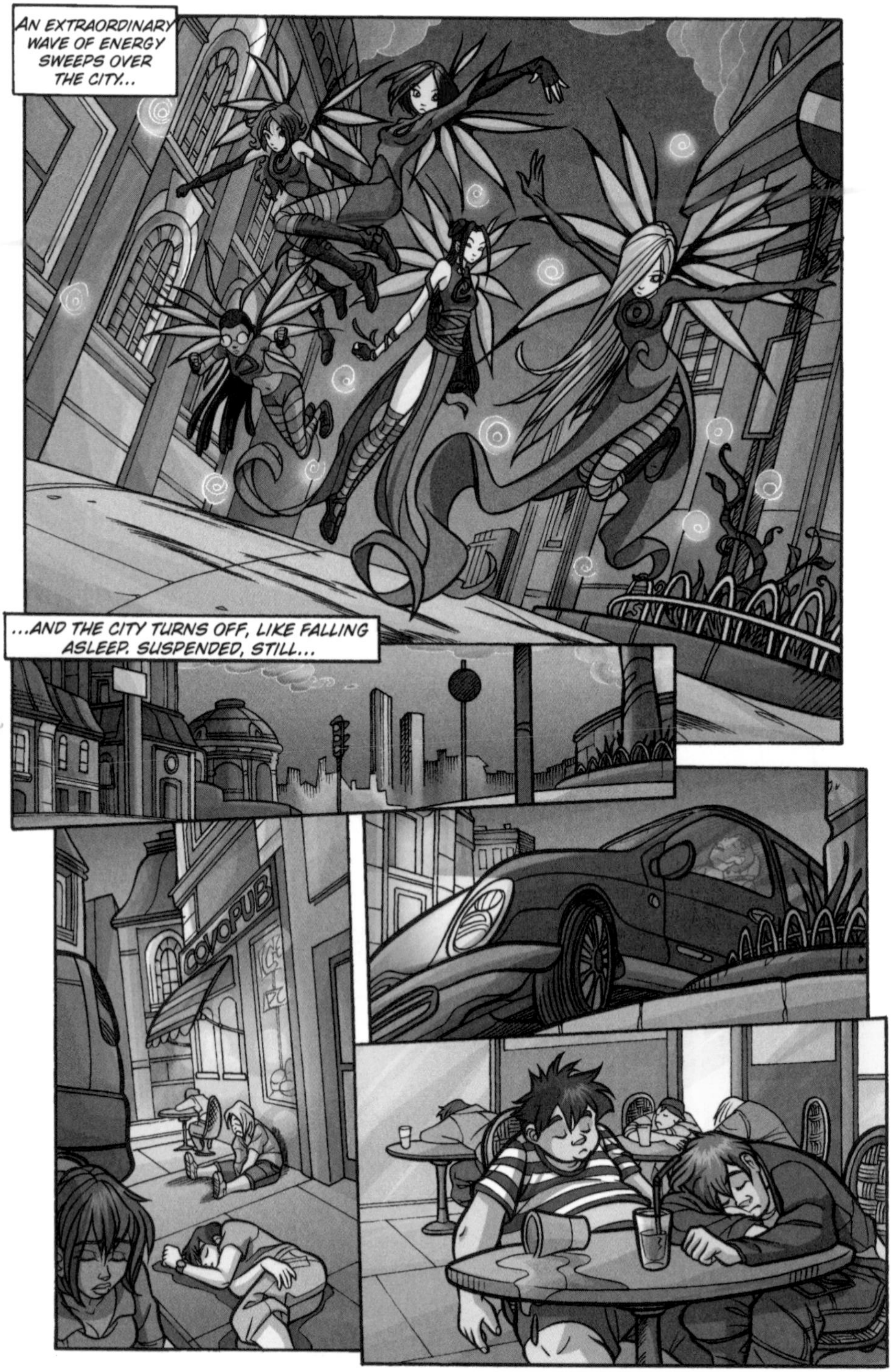
AN EXTRAORDINARY WAVE OF ENERGY SWEEPS OVER THE CITY...
...AND THE CITY TURNS OFF, LIKE FALLING ASLEEP. SUSPENDED, STILL...

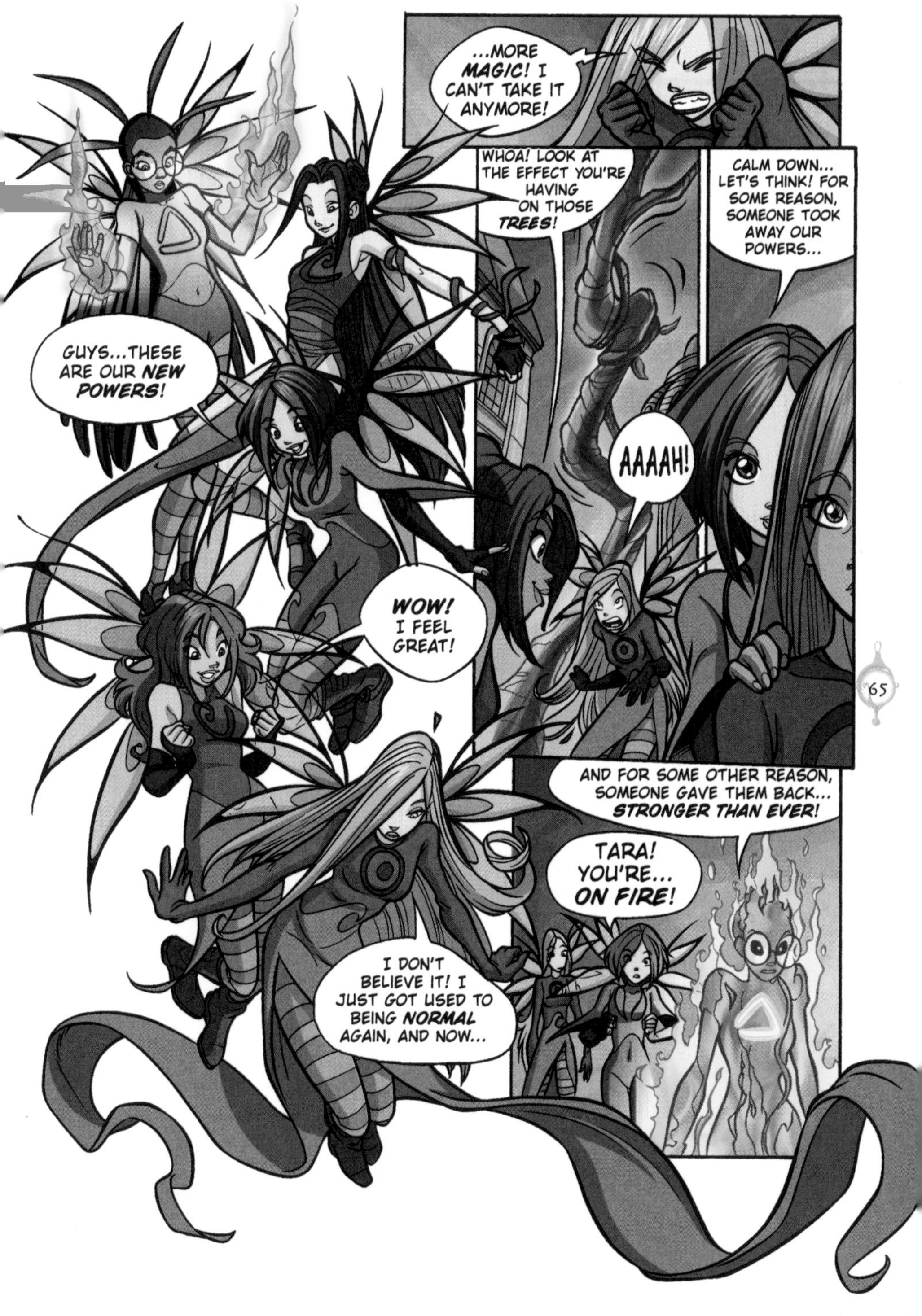

...MORE MAGIC! I CAN'T TAKE IT ANYMORE!
GUYS...THESE ARE OUR NEW POWERS!
WHOA! LOOK AT THE EFFECT YOU'RE HAVING ON THOSE TREES!
CALM DOWN... LET'S THINK! FOR SOME REASON, SOMEONE TOOK AWAY OUR POWERS...
AAAAH!
WOW! I FEEL GREAT!
AND FOR SOME OTHER REASON, SOMEONE GAVE THEM BACK... STRONGER THAN EVER!
TARA! YOU'RE... ON FIRE!
I DON'T BELIEVE IT! I JUST GOT USED TO BEING NORMAL AGAIN, AND NOW...

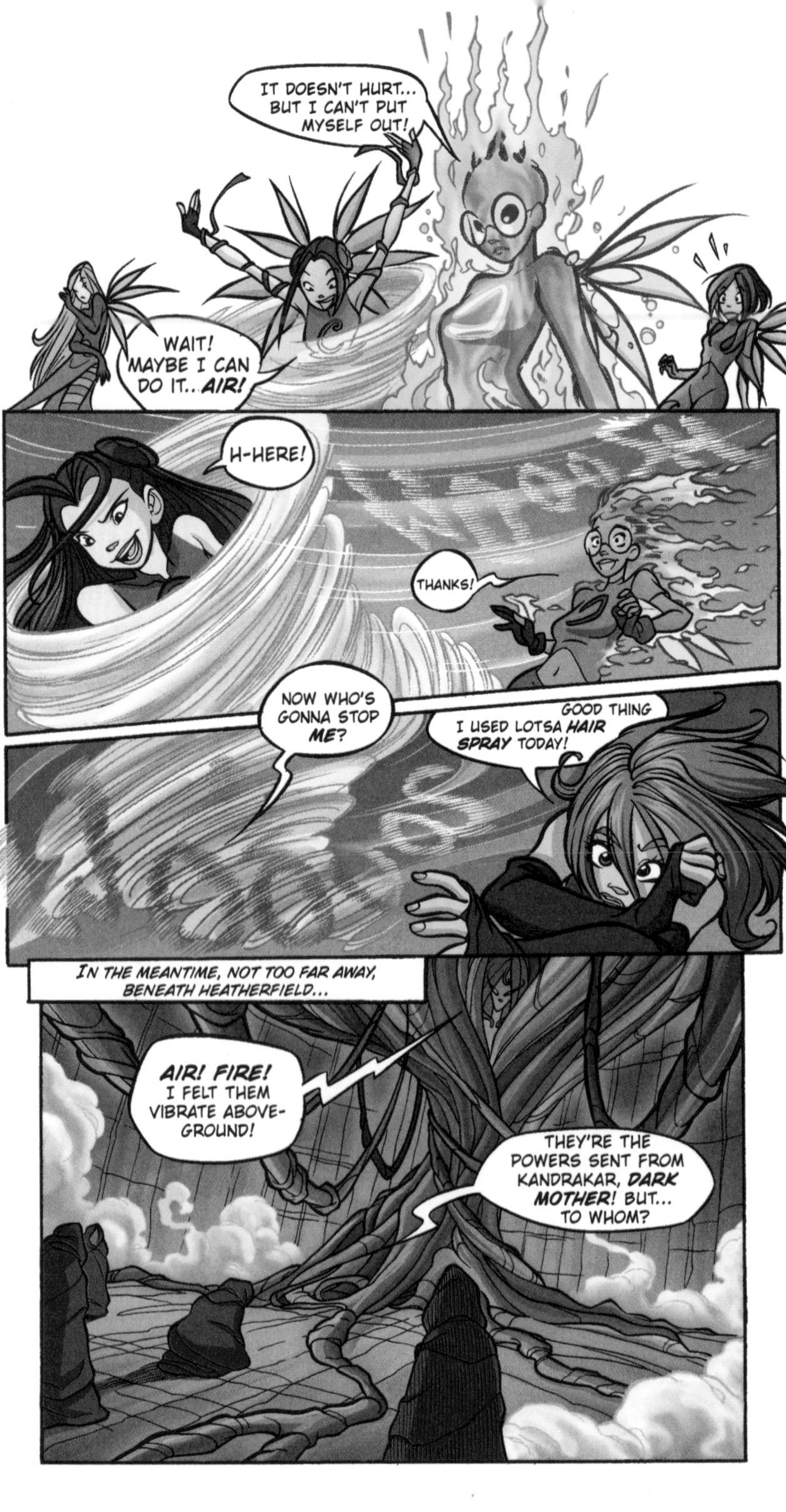
IT DOESN'T HURT... BUT I CAN'T PUT MYSELF OUT!
WAIT! MAYBE I CAN DO IT... AIR!
H-HERE!
THANKS!
NOW WHO'S GONNA STOP ME?
GOOD THING I USED LOTSA HAIR SPRAY TODAY!
IN THE MEANTIME, NOT TOO FAR AWAY, BENEATH HEATHERFIELD...
AIR! FIRE! I FELT THEM VIBRATE ABOVE-GROUND!
THEY'RE THE POWERS SENT FROM KANDRAKAR, DARK MOTHER! BUT... TO WHOM?

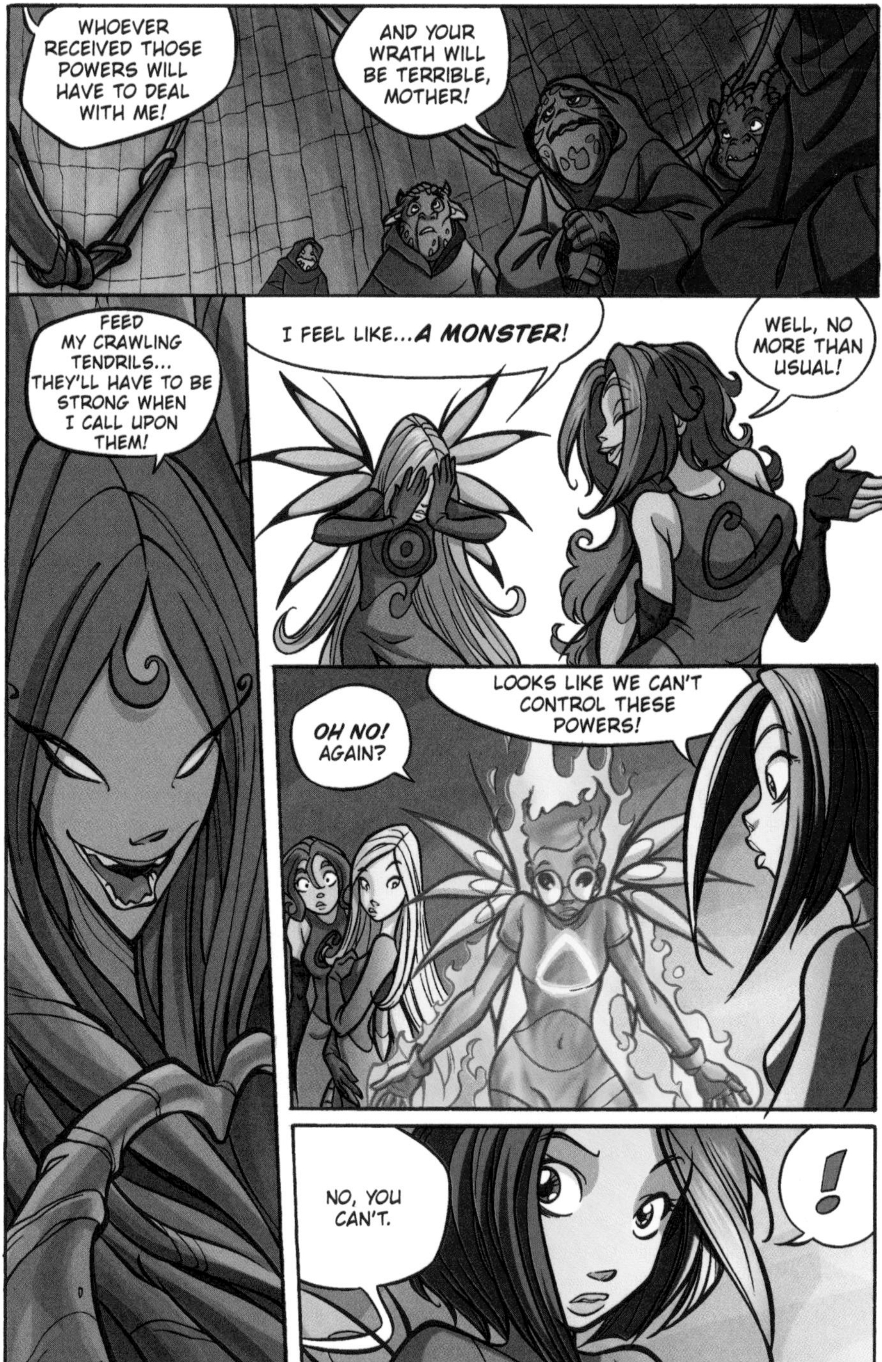
WHOEVER RECEIVED THOSE POWERS WILL HAVE TO DEAL WITH ME!
AND YOUR WRATH WILL BE TERRIBLE, MOTHER!
FEED MY CRAWLING TENDRILS... THEY'LL HAVE TO BE STRONG WHEN I CALL UPON THEM!
I FEEL LIKE...*A MONSTER*!
WELL, NO MORE THAN USUAL!
LOOKS LIKE WE CAN'T CONTROL THESE POWERS!
OH NO! AGAIN?
NO, YOU CAN'T.
!

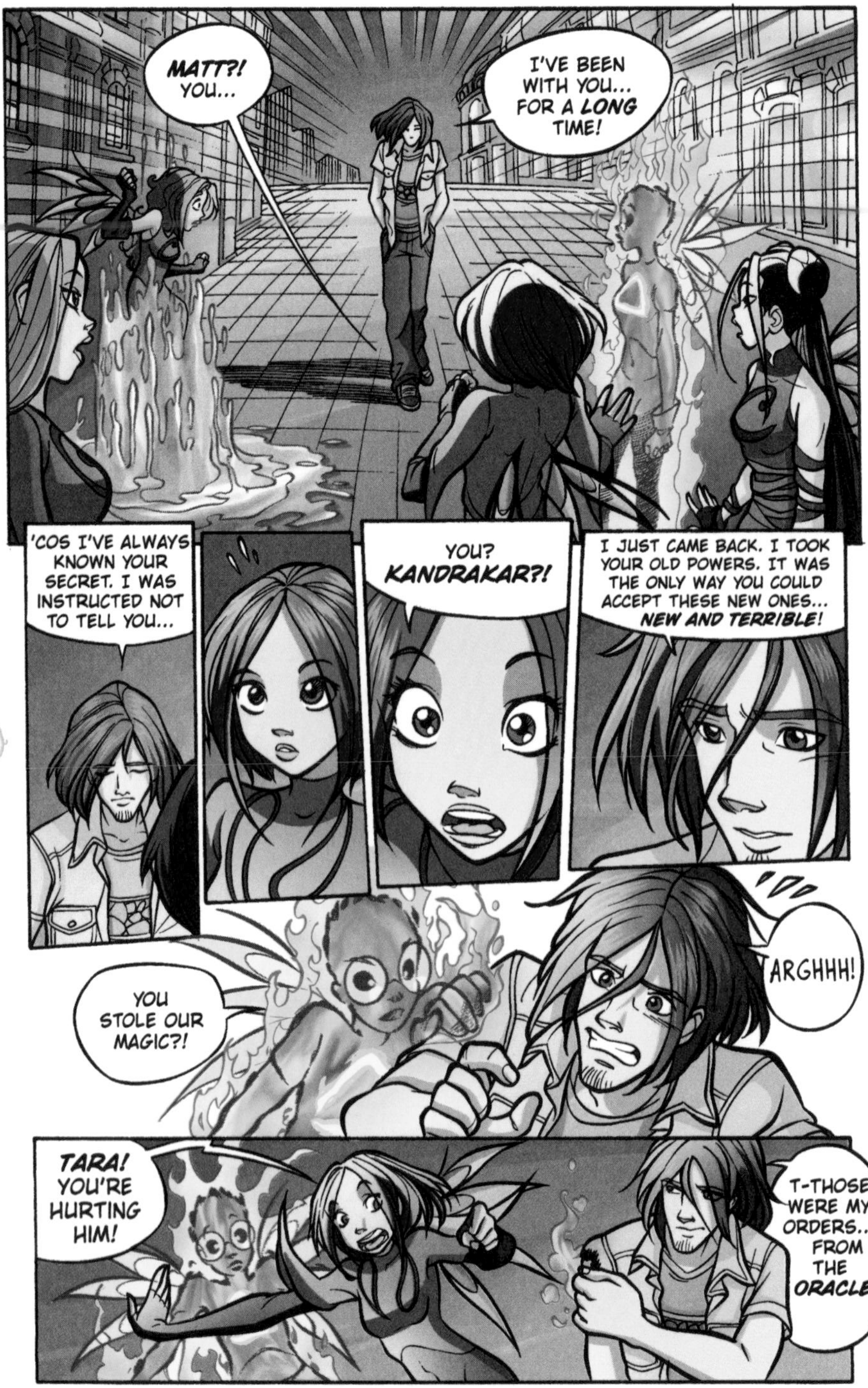
MATT?! YOU...
I'VE BEEN WITH YOU... FOR A LONG TIME!
'COS I'VE ALWAYS KNOWN YOUR SECRET. I WAS INSTRUCTED NOT TO TELL YOU...
YOU? KANDRAKAR?!
I JUST CAME BACK. I TOOK YOUR OLD POWERS. IT WAS THE ONLY WAY YOU COULD ACCEPT THESE NEW ONES... NEW AND TERRIBLE!
YOU STOLE OUR MAGIC?!
ARGHHH!
TARA! YOU'RE HURTING HIM!
T-THOSE WERE MY ORDERS... FROM THE ORACLE!

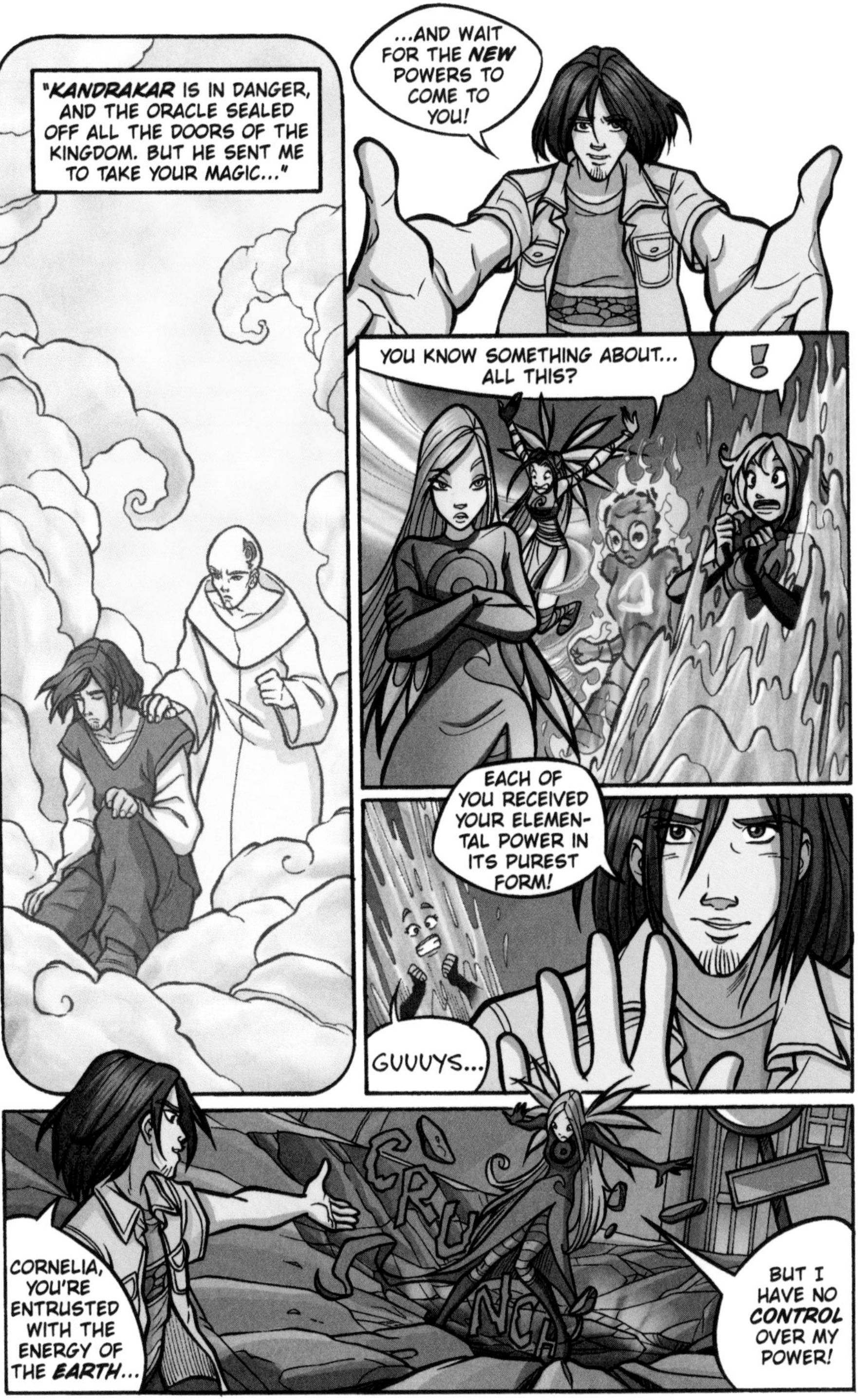
"KANDRAKAR IS IN DANGER, AND THE ORACLE SEALED OFF ALL THE DOORS OF THE KINGDOM. BUT HE SENT ME TO TAKE YOUR MAGIC..."
...AND WAIT FOR THE NEW POWERS TO COME TO YOU!
YOU KNOW SOMETHING ABOUT... ALL THIS?
!
EACH OF YOU RECEIVED YOUR ELEMENTAL POWER IN ITS PUREST FORM!
GUUUYS...
CRUNCH
CORNELIA, YOU'RE ENTRUSTED WITH THE ENERGY OF THE EARTH...
BUT I HAVE NO CONTROL OVER MY POWER!

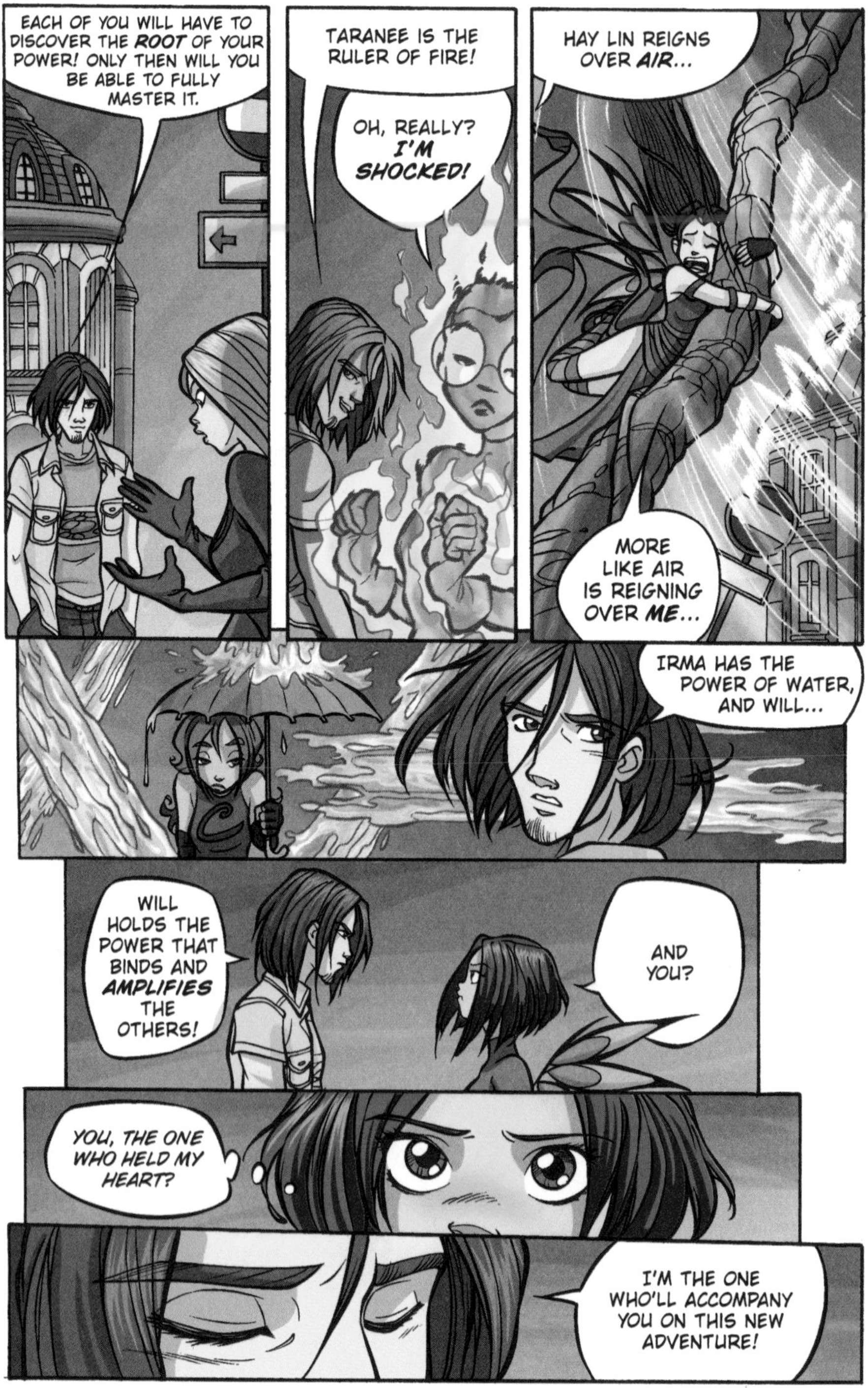
EACH OF YOU WILL HAVE TO DISCOVER THE ***ROOT*** OF YOUR POWER! ONLY THEN WILL YOU BE ABLE TO FULLY MASTER IT.
TARANEE IS THE RULER OF FIRE!
OH, REALLY? ***I'M SHOCKED!***
HAY LIN REIGNS OVER ***AIR***...
MORE LIKE AIR IS REIGNING OVER ***ME***...
IRMA HAS THE POWER OF WATER, AND WILL...
WILL HOLDS THE POWER THAT BINDS AND ***AMPLIFIES*** THE OTHERS!
AND YOU?
YOU, THE ONE WHO HELD MY HEART?
I'M THE ONE WHO'LL ACCOMPANY YOU ON THIS NEW ADVENTURE!

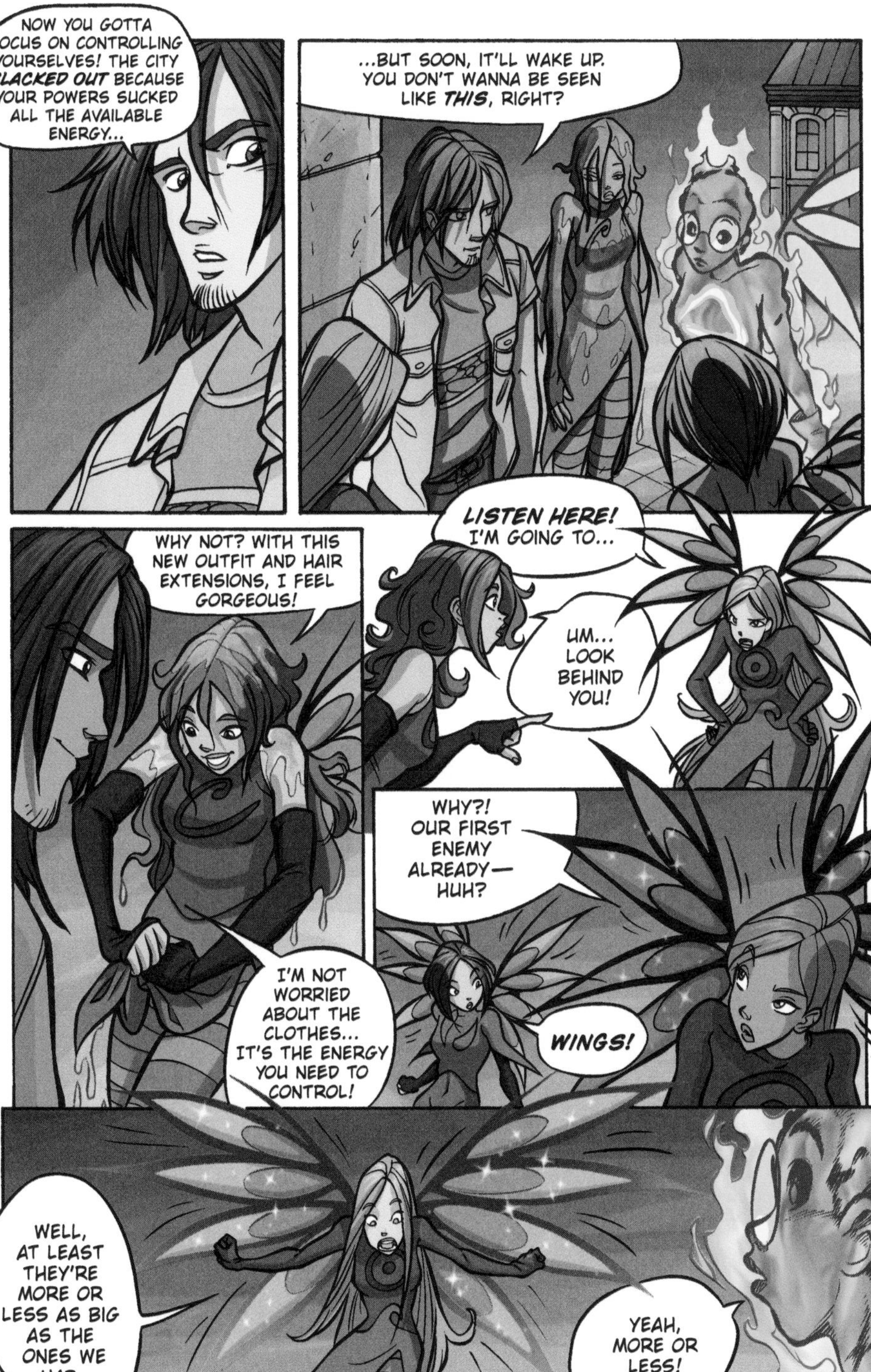
NOW YOU GOTTA FOCUS ON CONTROLLING YOURSELVES! THE CITY BLACKED OUT BECAUSE YOUR POWERS SUCKED ALL THE AVAILABLE ENERGY...
...BUT SOON, IT'LL WAKE UP. YOU DON'T WANNA BE SEEN LIKE THIS, RIGHT?
WHY NOT? WITH THIS NEW OUTFIT AND HAIR EXTENSIONS, I FEEL GORGEOUS!
I'M NOT WORRIED ABOUT THE CLOTHES... IT'S THE ENERGY YOU NEED TO CONTROL!
LISTEN HERE! I'M GOING TO...
UM... LOOK BEHIND YOU!
WHY?! OUR FIRST ENEMY ALREADY—HUH?
WINGS!
WELL, AT LEAST THEY'RE MORE OR LESS AS BIG AS THE ONES WE HAD...
YEAH, MORE OR LESS!

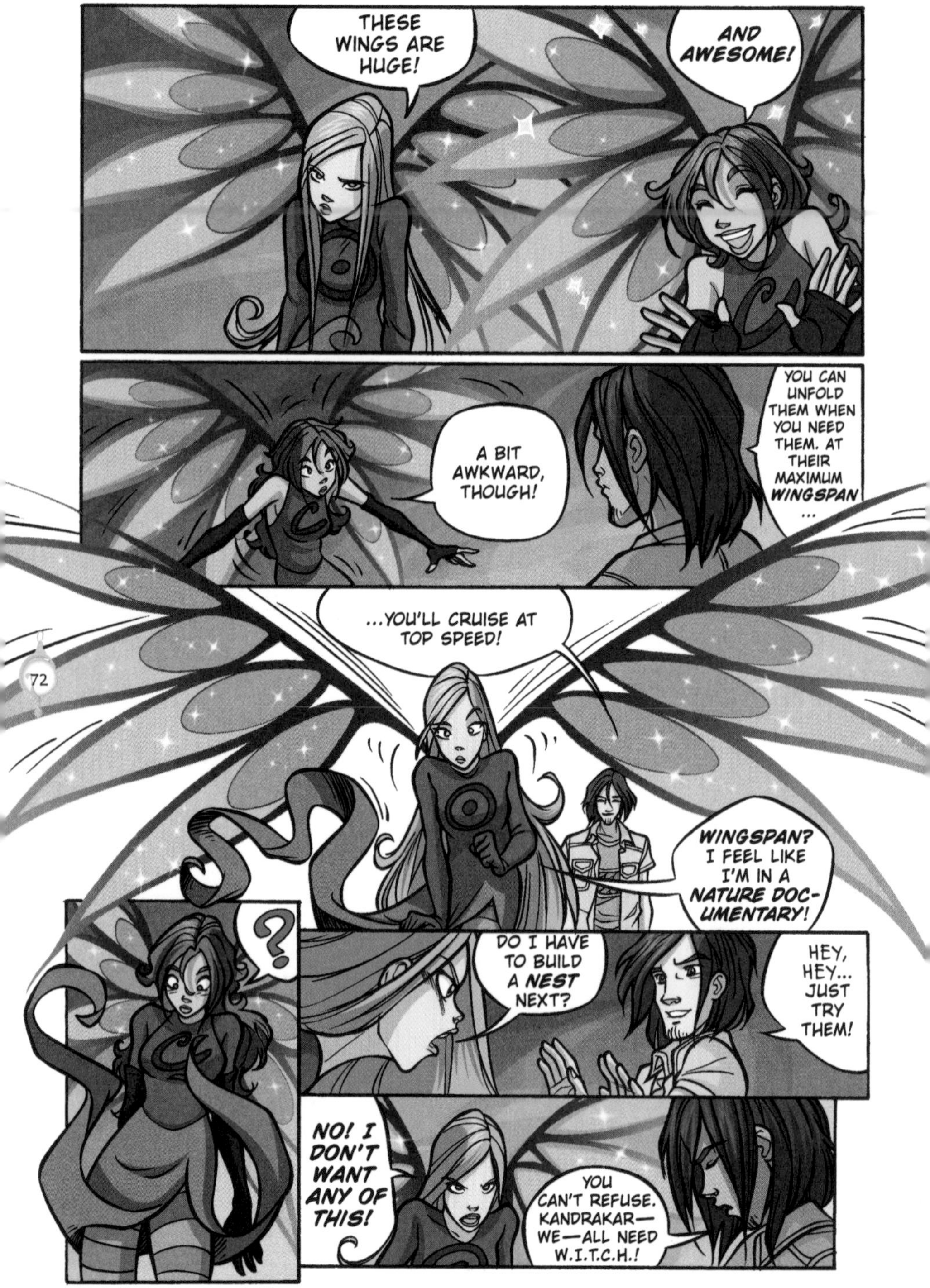
THESE WINGS ARE HUGE!
AND AWESOME!
A BIT AWKWARD, THOUGH!
YOU CAN UNFOLD THEM WHEN YOU NEED THEM. AT THEIR MAXIMUM WINGSPAN ...
...YOU'LL CRUISE AT TOP SPEED!
WINGSPAN? I FEEL LIKE I'M IN A NATURE DOC-UMENTARY!
?
DO I HAVE TO BUILD A NEST NEXT?
HEY, HEY... JUST TRY THEM!
NO! I DON'T WANT ANY OF THIS!
YOU CAN'T REFUSE. KANDRAKAR—WE—ALL NEED W.I.T.C.H.!

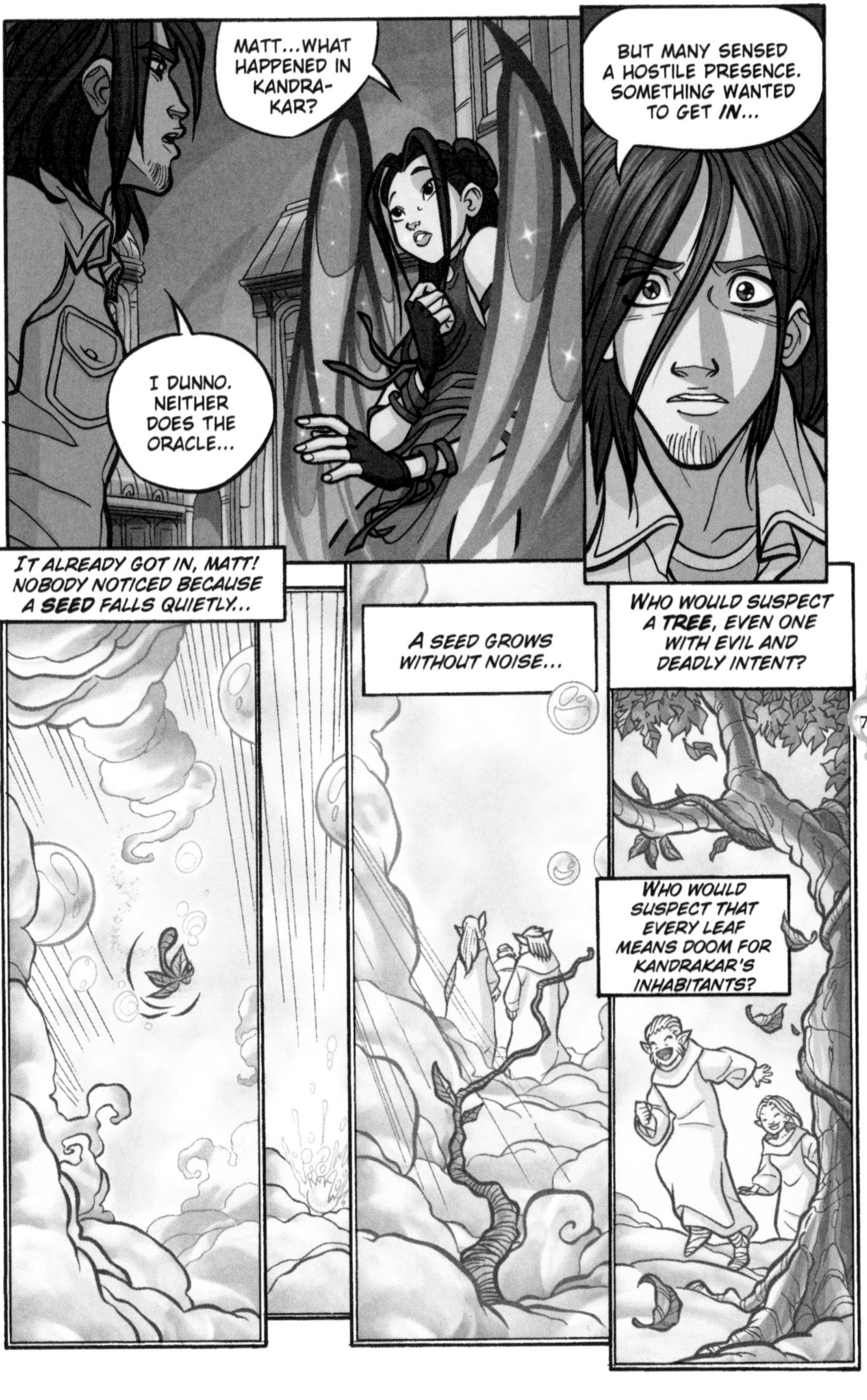
MATT...WHAT HAPPENED IN KANDRA-KAR?
I DUNNO. NEITHER DOES THE ORACLE...
BUT MANY SENSED A HOSTILE PRESENCE. SOMETHING WANTED TO GET *IN*...
IT ALREADY GOT IN, MATT! NOBODY NOTICED BECAUSE A ***SEED*** *FALLS QUIETLY...*
A SEED GROWS WITHOUT NOISE...
WHO WOULD SUSPECT A ***TREE****, EVEN ONE WITH EVIL AND DEADLY INTENT?*
WHO WOULD SUSPECT THAT EVERY LEAF MEANS DOOM FOR KANDRAKAR'S INHABITANTS?

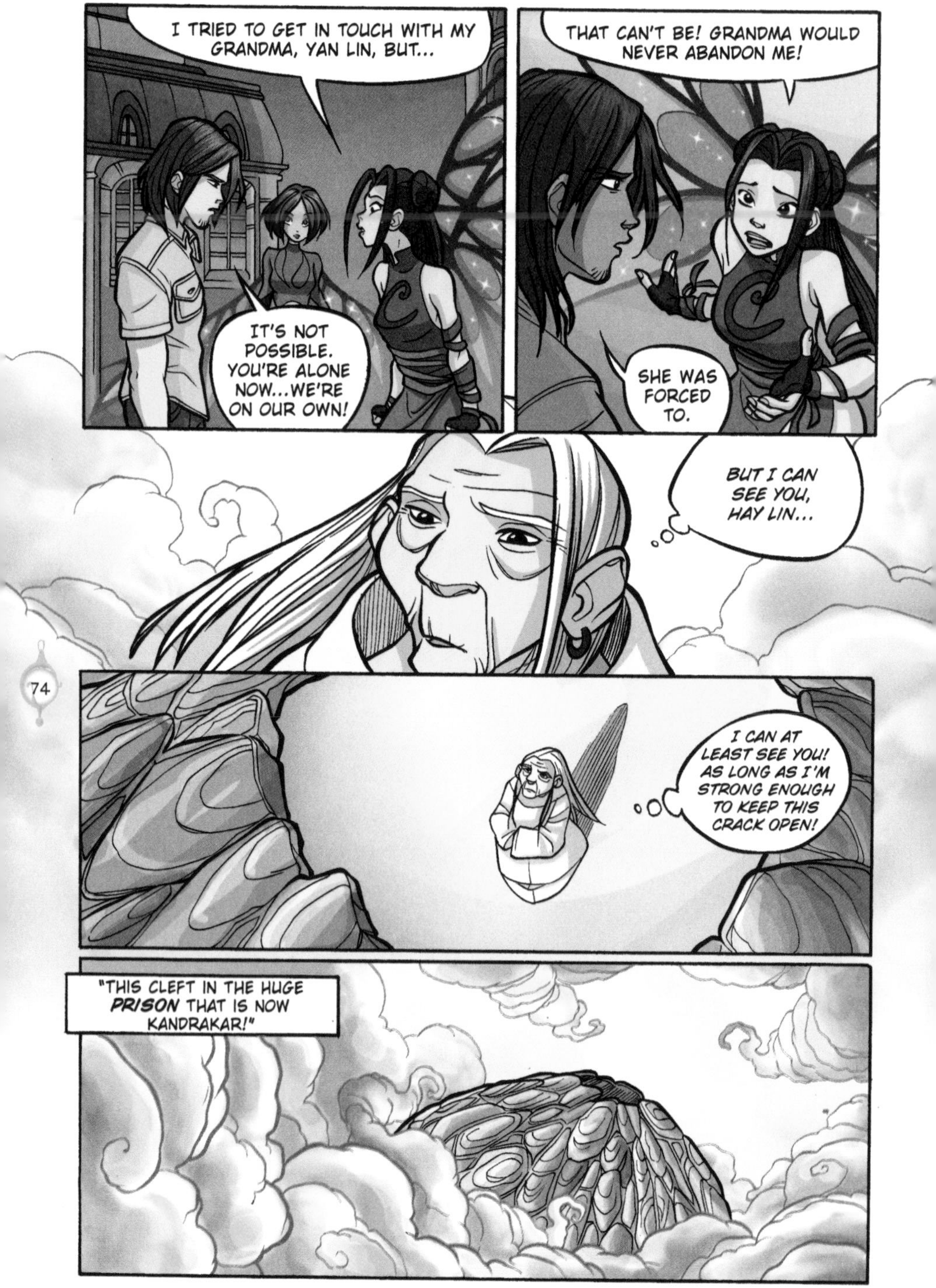
I TRIED TO GET IN TOUCH WITH MY GRANDMA, YAN LIN, BUT...
IT'S NOT POSSIBLE. YOU'RE ALONE NOW...WE'RE ON OUR OWN!
THAT CAN'T BE! GRANDMA WOULD NEVER ABANDON ME!
SHE WAS FORCED TO.
BUT I CAN SEE YOU, HAY LIN...
I CAN AT LEAST SEE YOU! AS LONG AS I'M STRONG ENOUGH TO KEEP THIS CRACK OPEN!
"THIS CLEFT IN THE HUGE PRISON THAT IS NOW KANDRAKAR!"

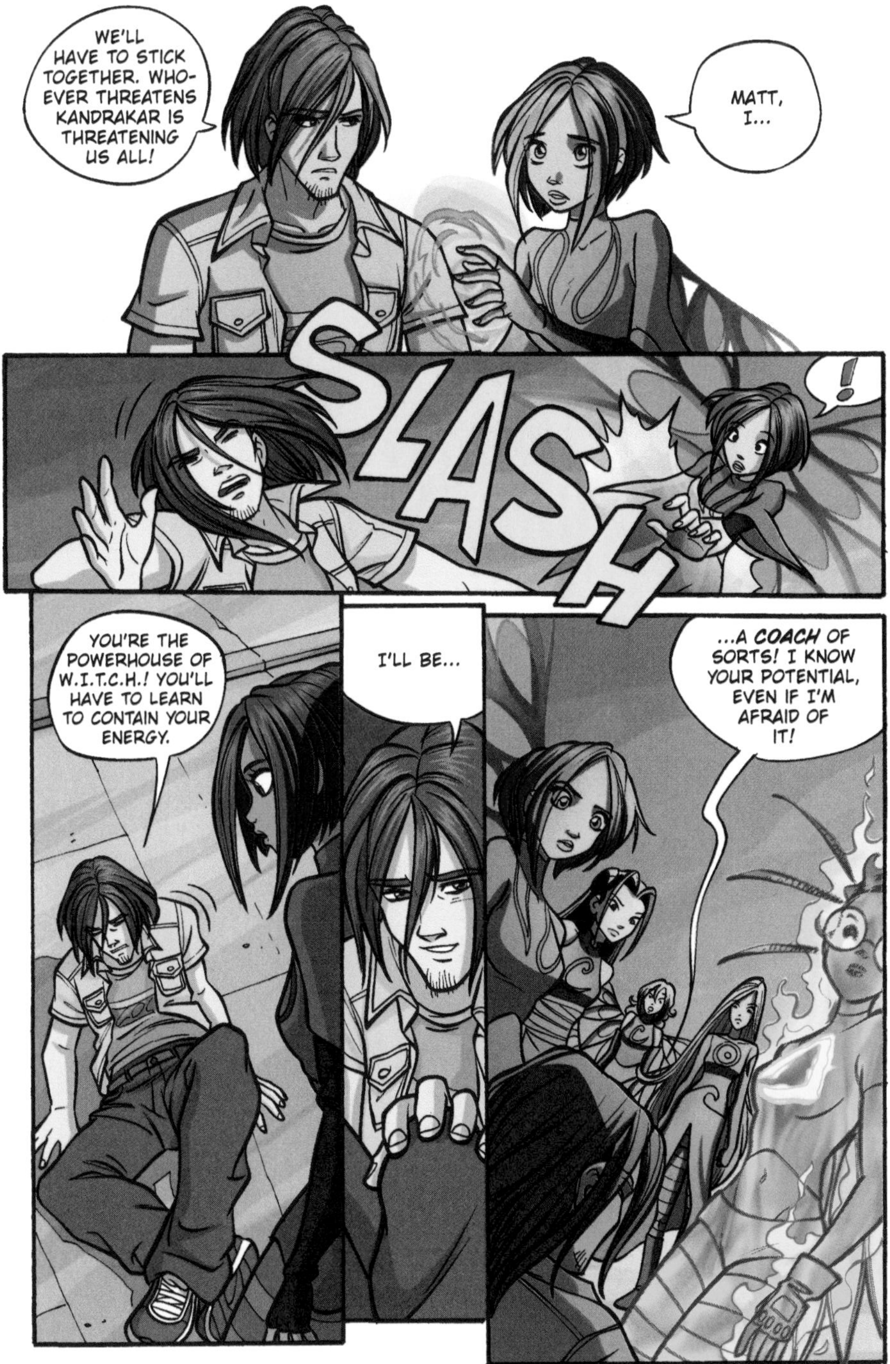
WE'LL HAVE TO STICK TOGETHER. WHO-EVER THREATENS KANDRAKAR IS THREATENING US ALL!
MATT, I...
SLASH
!
YOU'RE THE POWERHOUSE OF W.I.T.C.H.! YOU'LL HAVE TO LEARN TO CONTAIN YOUR ENERGY.
I'LL BE...
...A COACH OF SORTS! I KNOW YOUR POTENTIAL, EVEN IF I'M AFRAID OF IT!

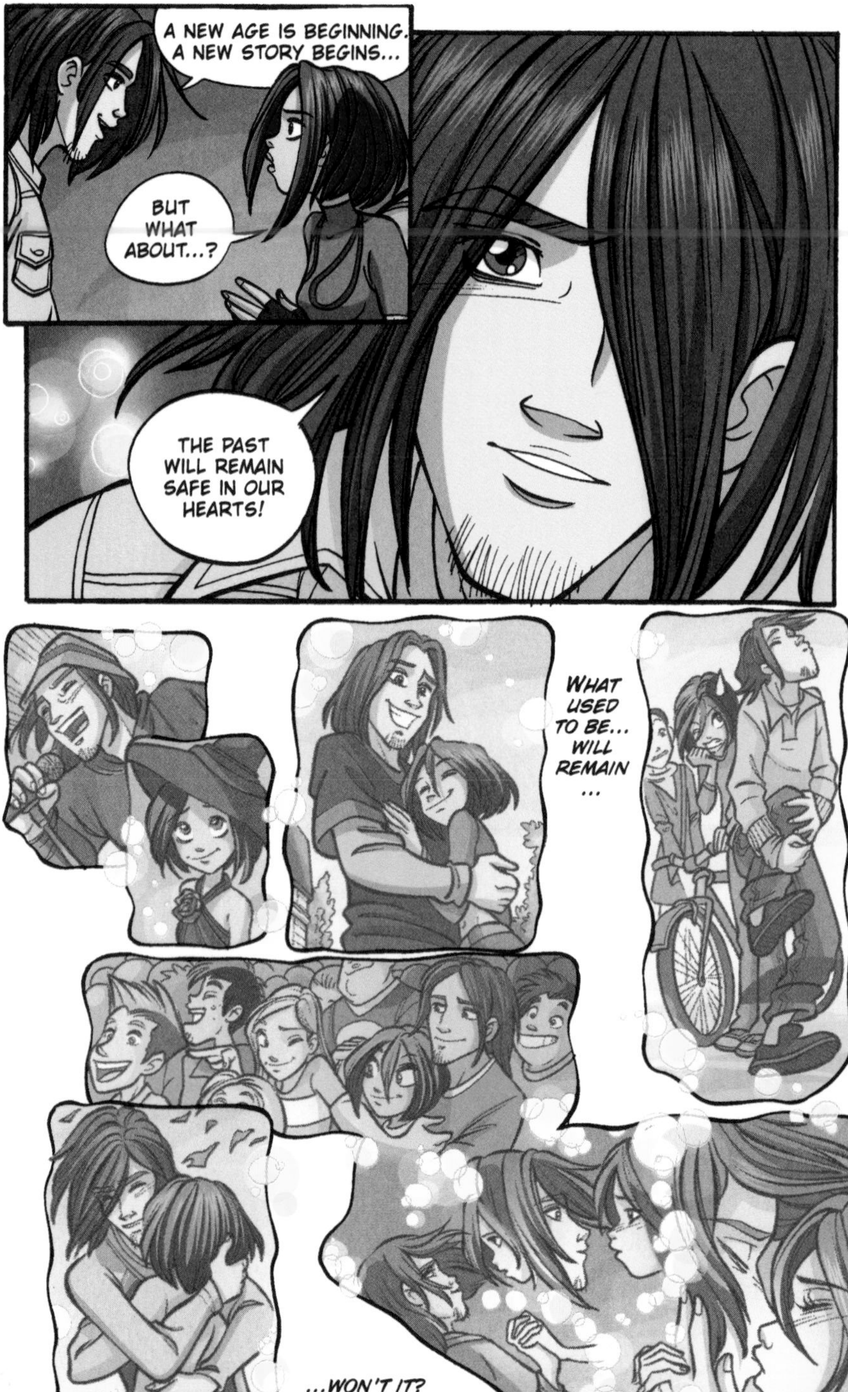

A NEW AGE IS BEGINNING. A NEW STORY BEGINS...
BUT WHAT ABOUT...?
THE PAST WILL REMAIN SAFE IN OUR HEARTS!
WHAT USED TO BE... WILL REMAIN ...
...WON'T IT?

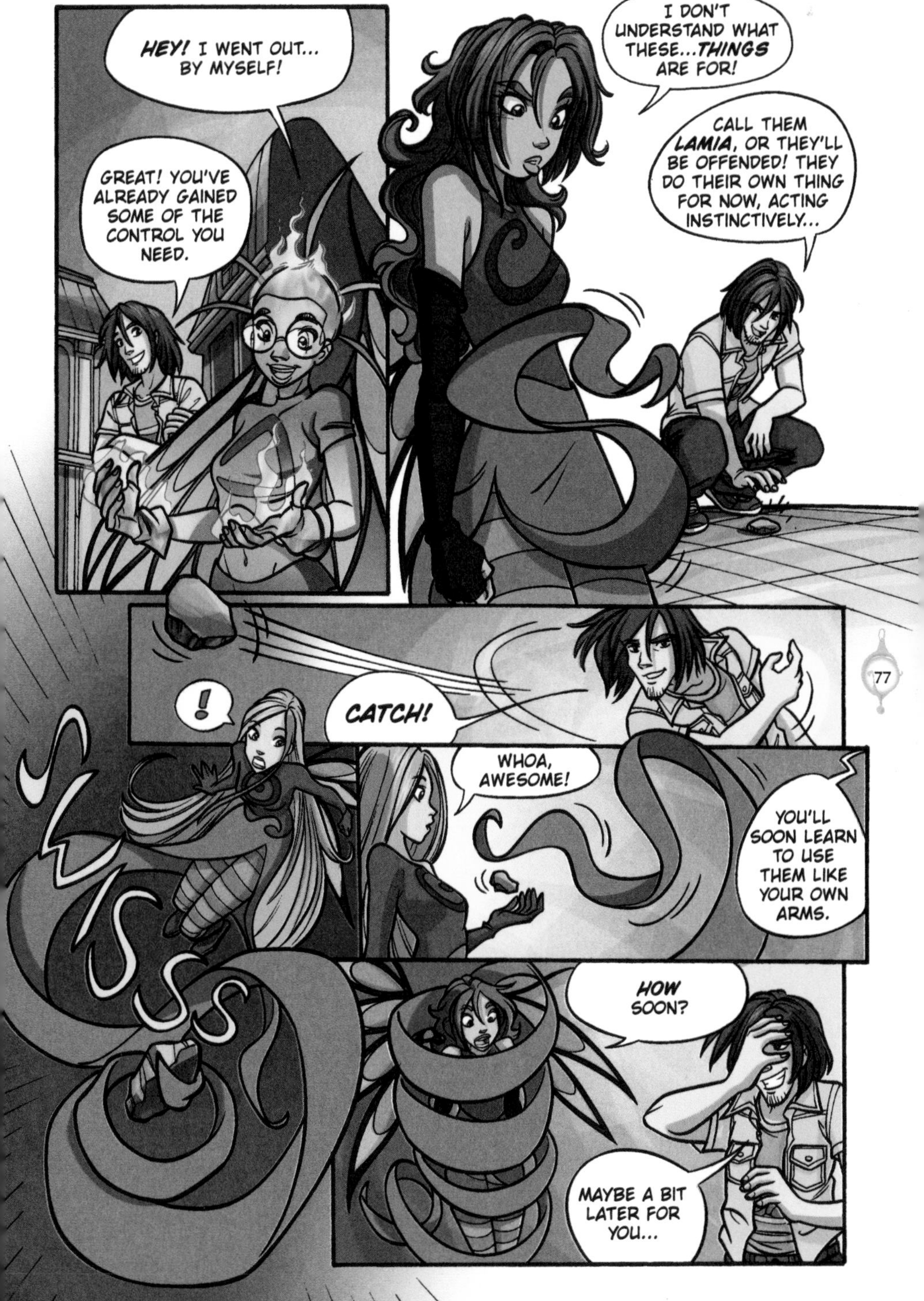
HEY! I WENT OUT... BY MYSELF!
GREAT! YOU'VE ALREADY GAINED SOME OF THE CONTROL YOU NEED.
I DON'T UNDERSTAND WHAT THESE...THINGS ARE FOR!
CALL THEM LAMIA, OR THEY'LL BE OFFENDED! THEY DO THEIR OWN THING FOR NOW, ACTING INSTINCTIVELY...
CATCH!
!
WHOA, AWESOME!
YOU'LL SOON LEARN TO USE THEM LIKE YOUR OWN ARMS.
HOW SOON?
MAYBE A BIT LATER FOR YOU...

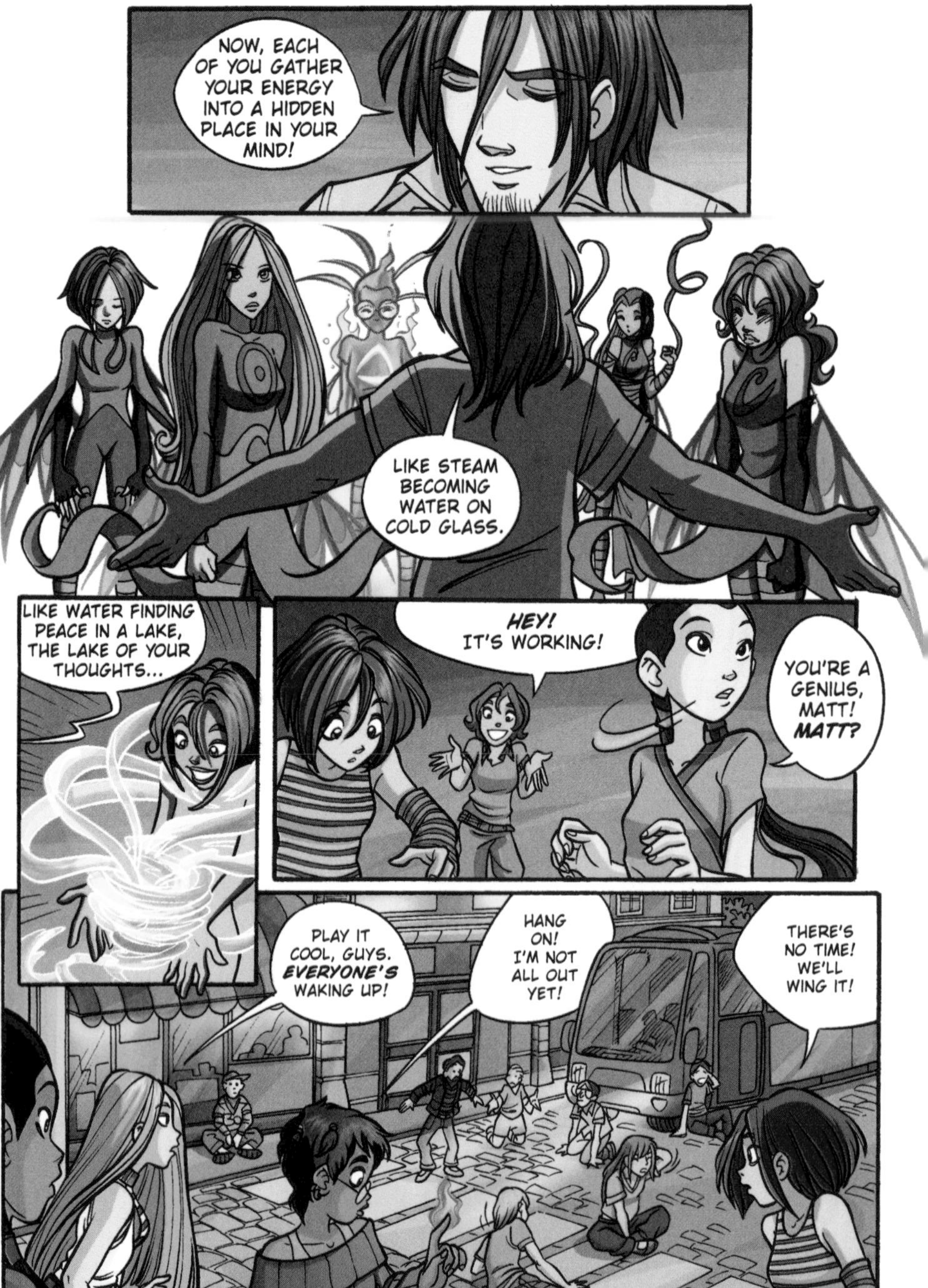
NOW, EACH OF YOU GATHER YOUR ENERGY INTO A HIDDEN PLACE IN YOUR MIND!
LIKE STEAM BECOMING WATER ON COLD GLASS.
LIKE WATER FINDING PEACE IN A LAKE, THE LAKE OF YOUR THOUGHTS...
HEY! IT'S WORKING!
YOU'RE A GENIUS, MATT! MATT?
PLAY IT COOL, GUYS. EVERYONE'S WAKING UP!
HANG ON! I'M NOT ALL OUT YET!
THERE'S NO TIME! WE'LL WING IT!

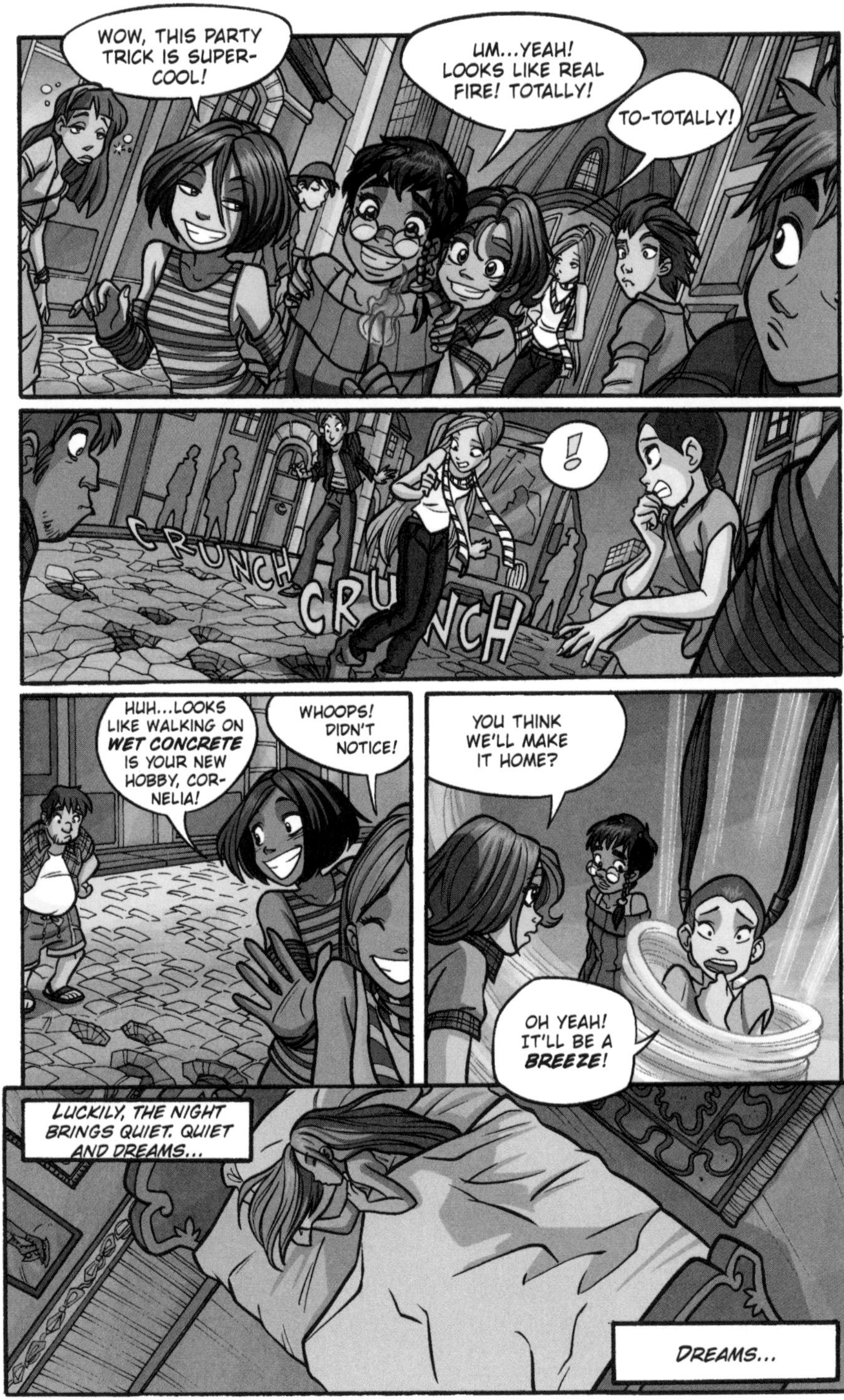
WOW, THIS PARTY TRICK IS SUPER-COOL!
UM...YEAH! LOOKS LIKE REAL FIRE! TOTALLY!
TO-TOTALLY!
!
CRUNCH
CRUNCH
HUH...LOOKS LIKE WALKING ON WET CONCRETE IS YOUR NEW HOBBY, COR-NELIA!
WHOOPS! DIDN'T NOTICE!
YOU THINK WE'LL MAKE IT HOME?
OH YEAH! IT'LL BE A BREEZE!
LUCKILY, THE NIGHT BRINGS QUIET. QUIET AND DREAMS...
DREAMS...

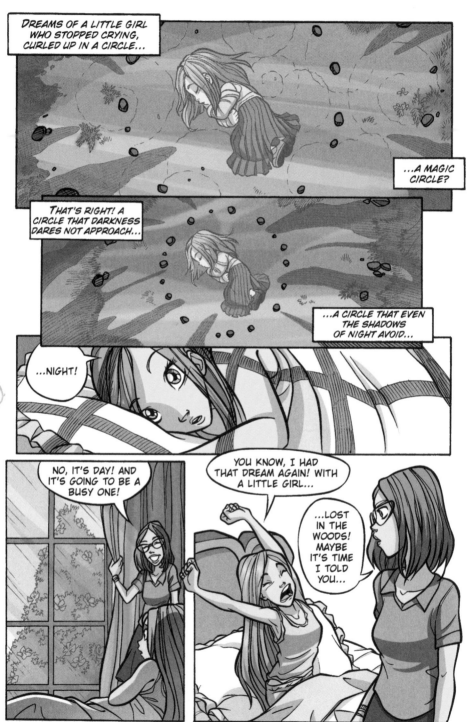

DREAMS OF A LITTLE GIRL WHO STOPPED CRYING, CURLED UP IN A CIRCLE...

...A MAGIC CIRCLE?

THAT'S RIGHT! A CIRCLE THAT DARKNESS DARES NOT APPROACH...

...A CIRCLE THAT EVEN THE SHADOWS OF NIGHT AVOID...

...NIGHT!

80

NO, IT'S DAY! AND IT'S GOING TO BE A BUSY ONE!

YOU KNOW, I HAD THAT DREAM AGAIN! WITH A LITTLE GIRL...

...LOST IN THE WOODS! MAYBE IT'S TIME I TOLD YOU...

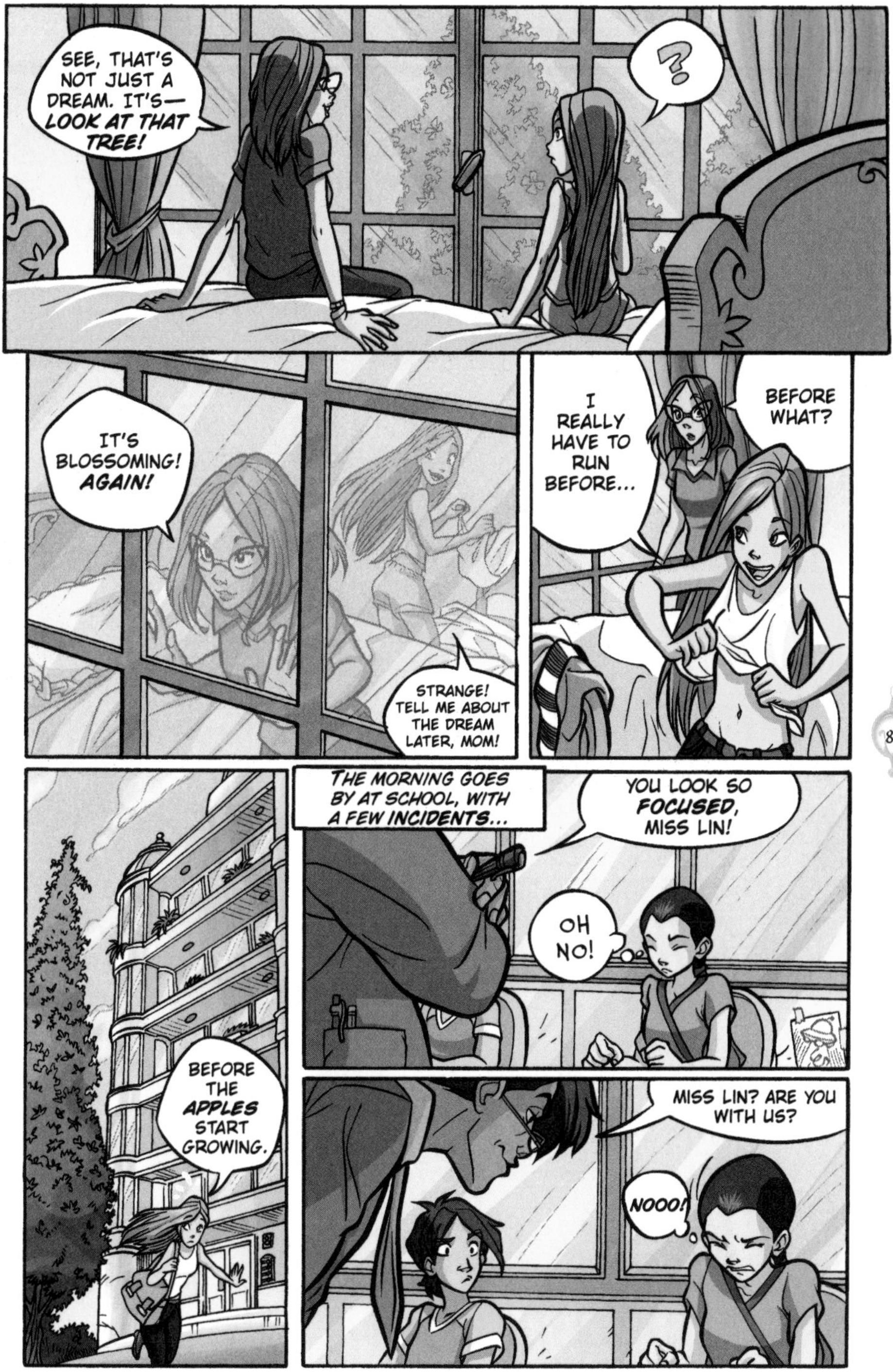
SEE, THAT'S NOT JUST A DREAM. IT'S— LOOK AT THAT TREE!
?
IT'S BLOSSOMING! AGAIN!
STRANGE! TELL ME ABOUT THE DREAM LATER, MOM!
I REALLY HAVE TO RUN BEFORE...
BEFORE WHAT?
BEFORE THE APPLES START GROWING.
THE MORNING GOES BY AT SCHOOL, WITH A FEW INCIDENTS...
YOU LOOK SO FOCUSED, MISS LIN!
OH NO!
MISS LIN? ARE YOU WITH US?
NOOO!

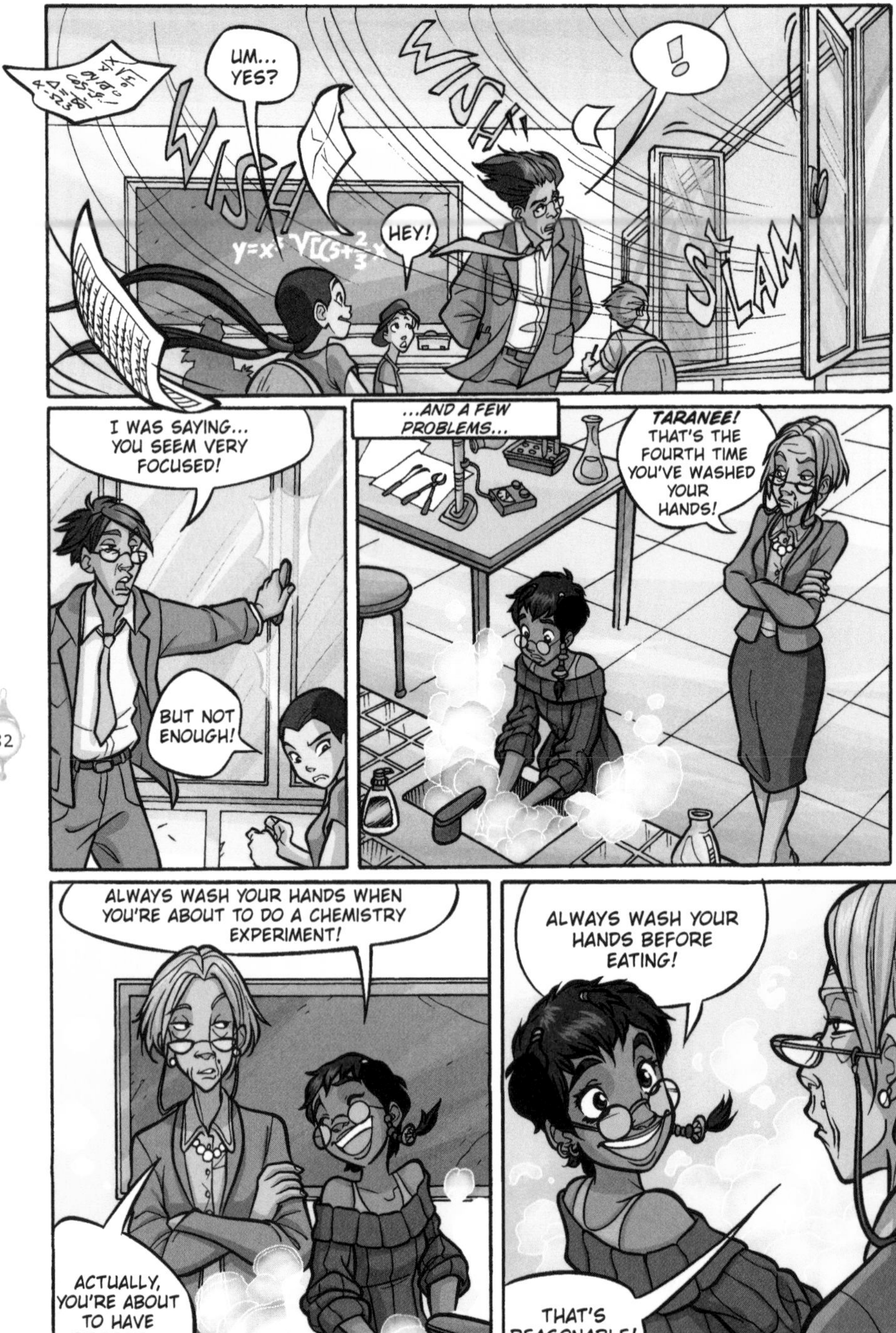
UM... YES?
WISH
WISH
!
HEY!
SLAM
I WAS SAYING... YOU SEEM VERY FOCUSED!
BUT NOT ENOUGH!
...AND A FEW PROBLEMS...
TARANEE! THAT'S THE FOURTH TIME YOU'VE WASHED YOUR HANDS!
ALWAYS WASH YOUR HANDS WHEN YOU'RE ABOUT TO DO A CHEMISTRY EXPERIMENT!
ACTUALLY, YOU'RE ABOUT TO HAVE RECESS...
ALWAYS WASH YOUR HANDS BEFORE EATING!
THAT'S REASONABLE!

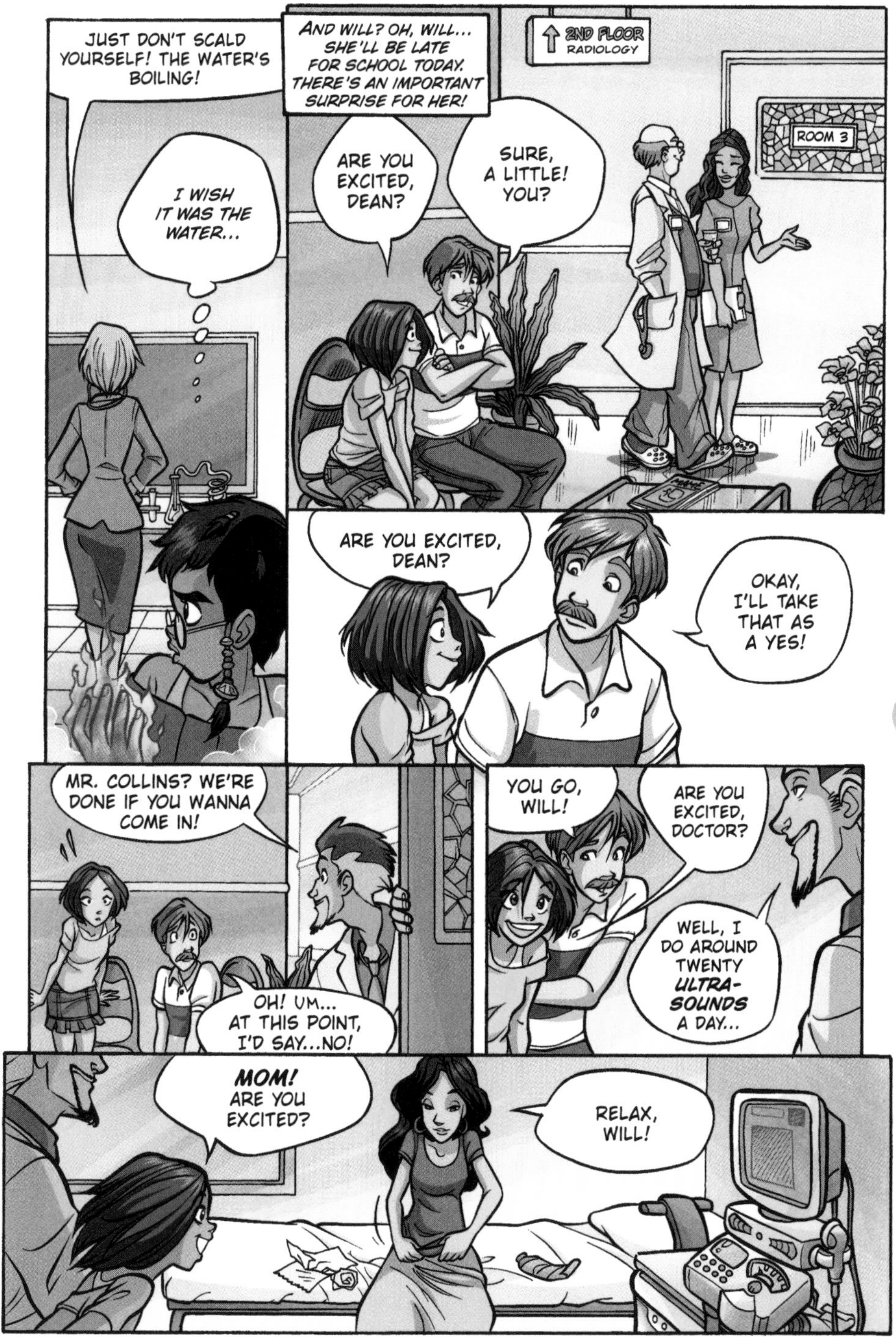

JUST DON'T SCALD YOURSELF! THE WATER'S BOILING!
I WISH IT WAS THE WATER...
AND WILL? OH, WILL... SHE'LL BE LATE FOR SCHOOL TODAY. THERE'S AN IMPORTANT SURPRISE FOR HER!
2ND FLOOR
RADIOLOGY
ROOM 3
ARE YOU EXCITED, DEAN?
SURE, A LITTLE! YOU?
ARE YOU EXCITED, DEAN?
OKAY, I'LL TAKE THAT AS A YES!
MR. COLLINS? WE'RE DONE IF YOU WANNA COME IN!
OH! UM... AT THIS POINT, I'D SAY...NO!
YOU GO, WILL!
ARE YOU EXCITED, DOCTOR?
WELL, I DO AROUND TWENTY ULTRA-SOUNDS A DAY...
MOM! ARE YOU EXCITED?
RELAX, WILL!

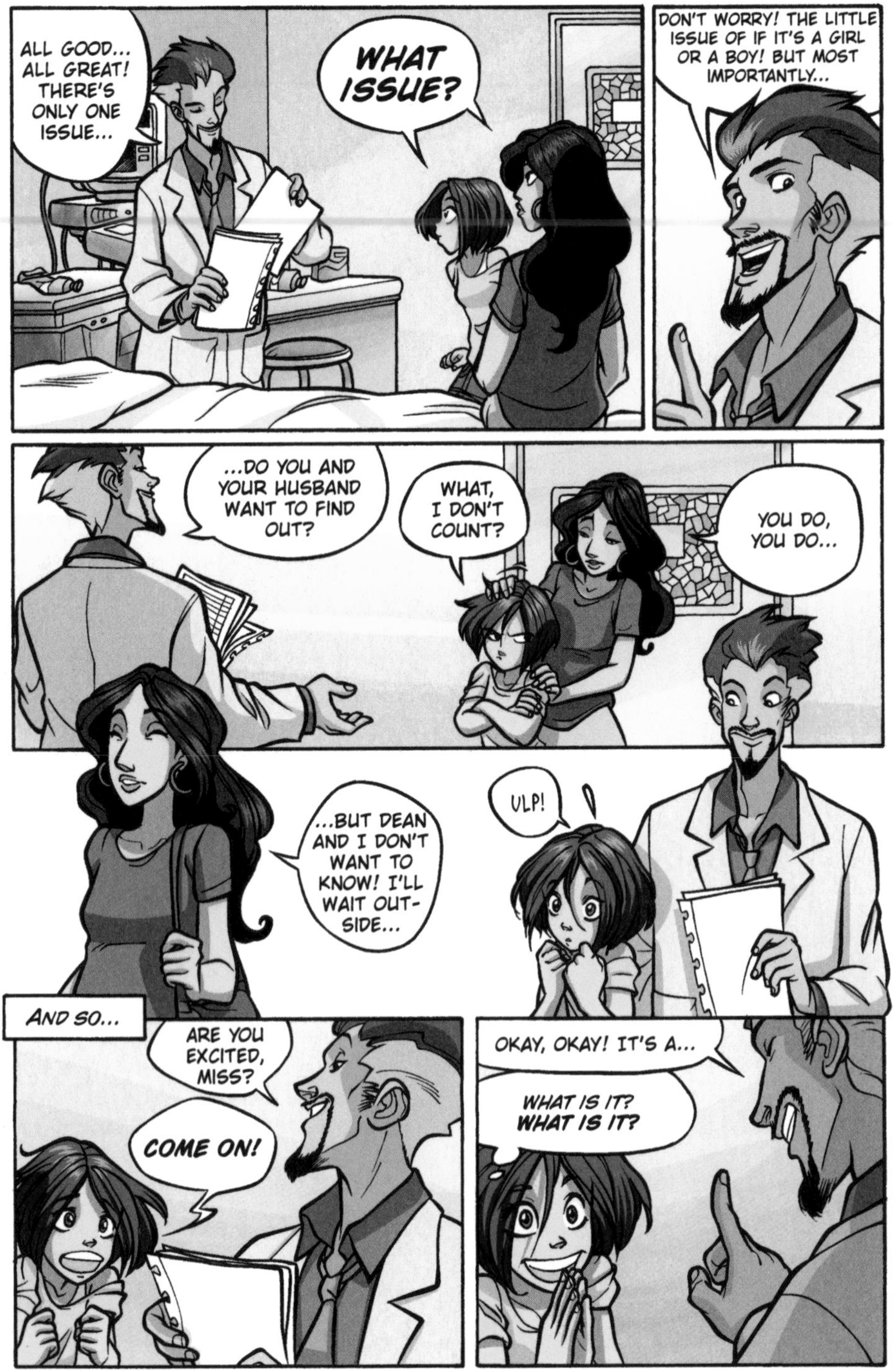
ALL GOOD... ALL GREAT! THERE'S ONLY ONE ISSUE...
WHAT ISSUE?
DON'T WORRY! THE LITTLE ISSUE OF IF IT'S A GIRL OR A BOY! BUT MOST IMPORTANTLY...
...DO YOU AND YOUR HUSBAND WANT TO FIND OUT?
WHAT, I DON'T COUNT?
YOU DO, YOU DO...
...BUT DEAN AND I DON'T WANT TO KNOW! I'LL WAIT OUT-SIDE...
ULP!
AND SO...
ARE YOU EXCITED, MISS?
COME ON!
OKAY, OKAY! IT'S A...
WHAT IS IT? WHAT IS IT?

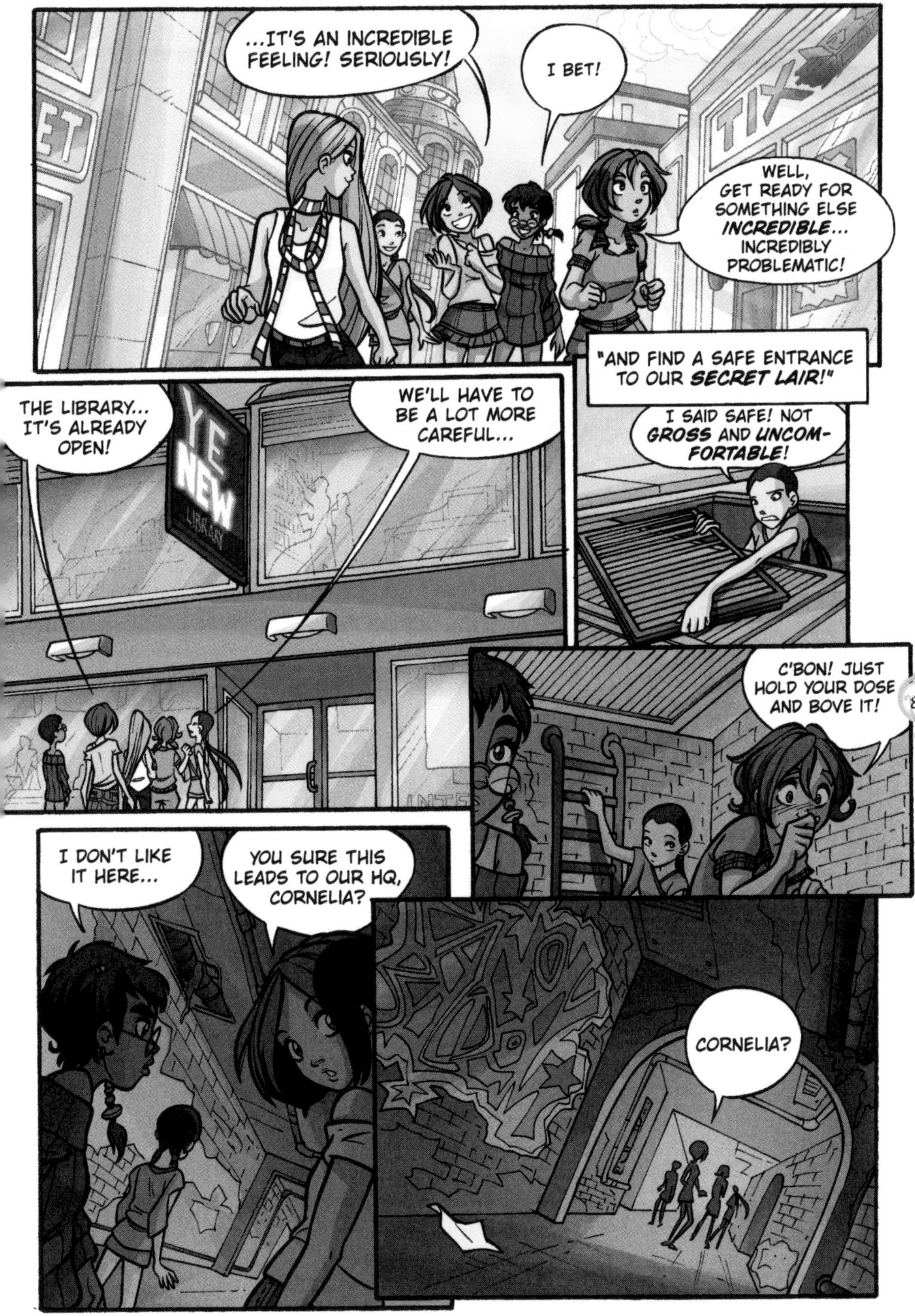
...IT'S AN INCREDIBLE FEELING! SERIOUSLY!
I BET!
WELL, GET READY FOR SOMETHING ELSE *INCREDIBLE*... INCREDIBLY PROBLEMATIC!
THE LIBRARY... IT'S ALREADY OPEN!
YE NEW LIBRARY
WE'LL HAVE TO BE A LOT MORE CAREFUL...
"AND FIND A SAFE ENTRANCE TO OUR *SECRET LAIR!*"
I SAID SAFE! NOT *GROSS* AND *UNCOMFORTABLE*!
C'BON! JUST HOLD YOUR DOSE AND BOVE IT!
I DON'T LIKE IT HERE...
YOU SURE THIS LEADS TO OUR HQ, CORNELIA?
CORNELIA?

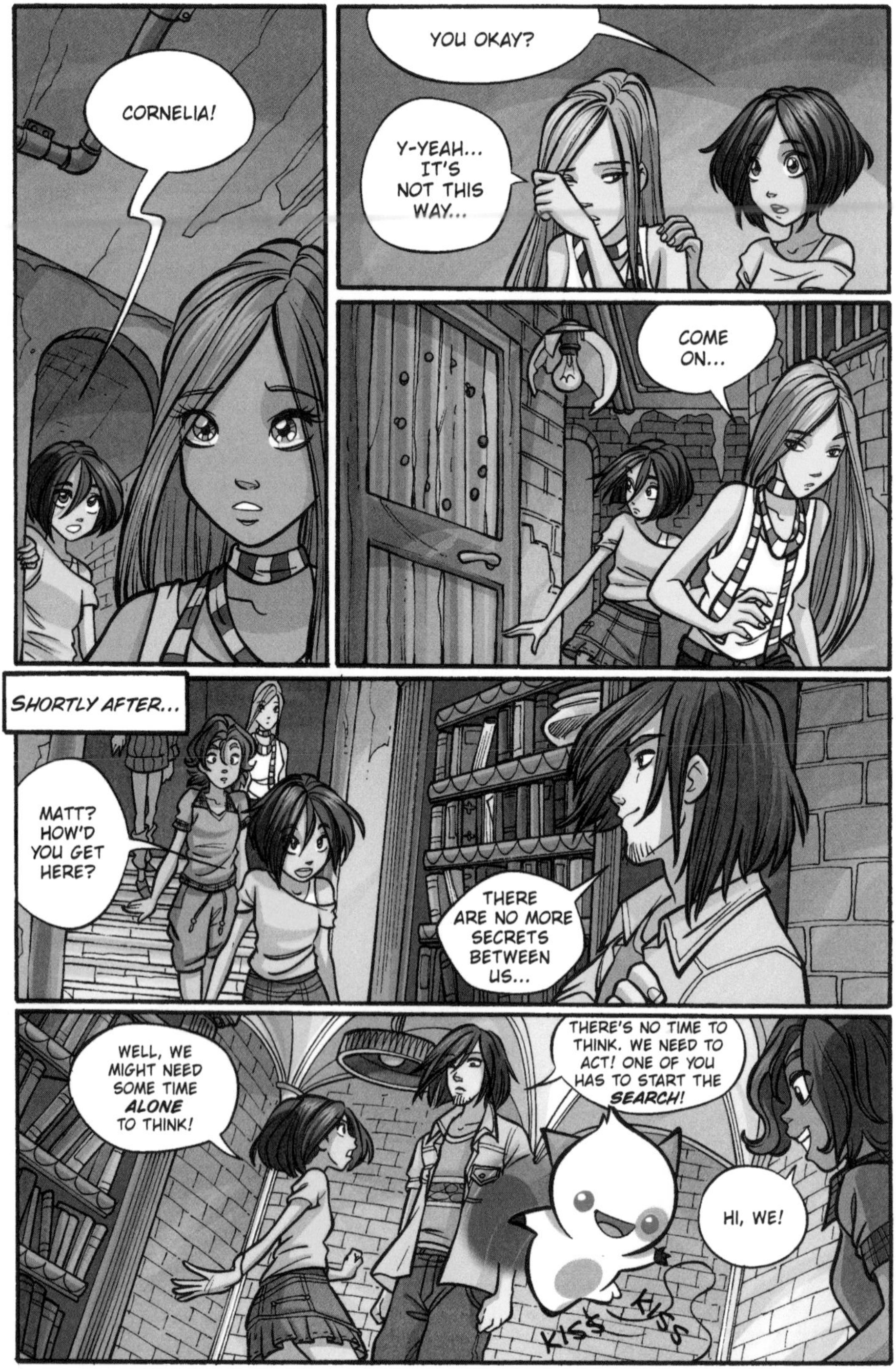
CORNELIA!
YOU OKAY?
Y-YEAH... IT'S NOT THIS WAY...
COME ON...
SHORTLY AFTER...
MATT? HOW'D YOU GET HERE?
THERE ARE NO MORE SECRETS BETWEEN US...
WELL, WE MIGHT NEED SOME TIME ALONE TO THINK!
THERE'S NO TIME TO THINK. WE NEED TO ACT! ONE OF YOU HAS TO START THE SEARCH!
HI, WE!
KISS KISS

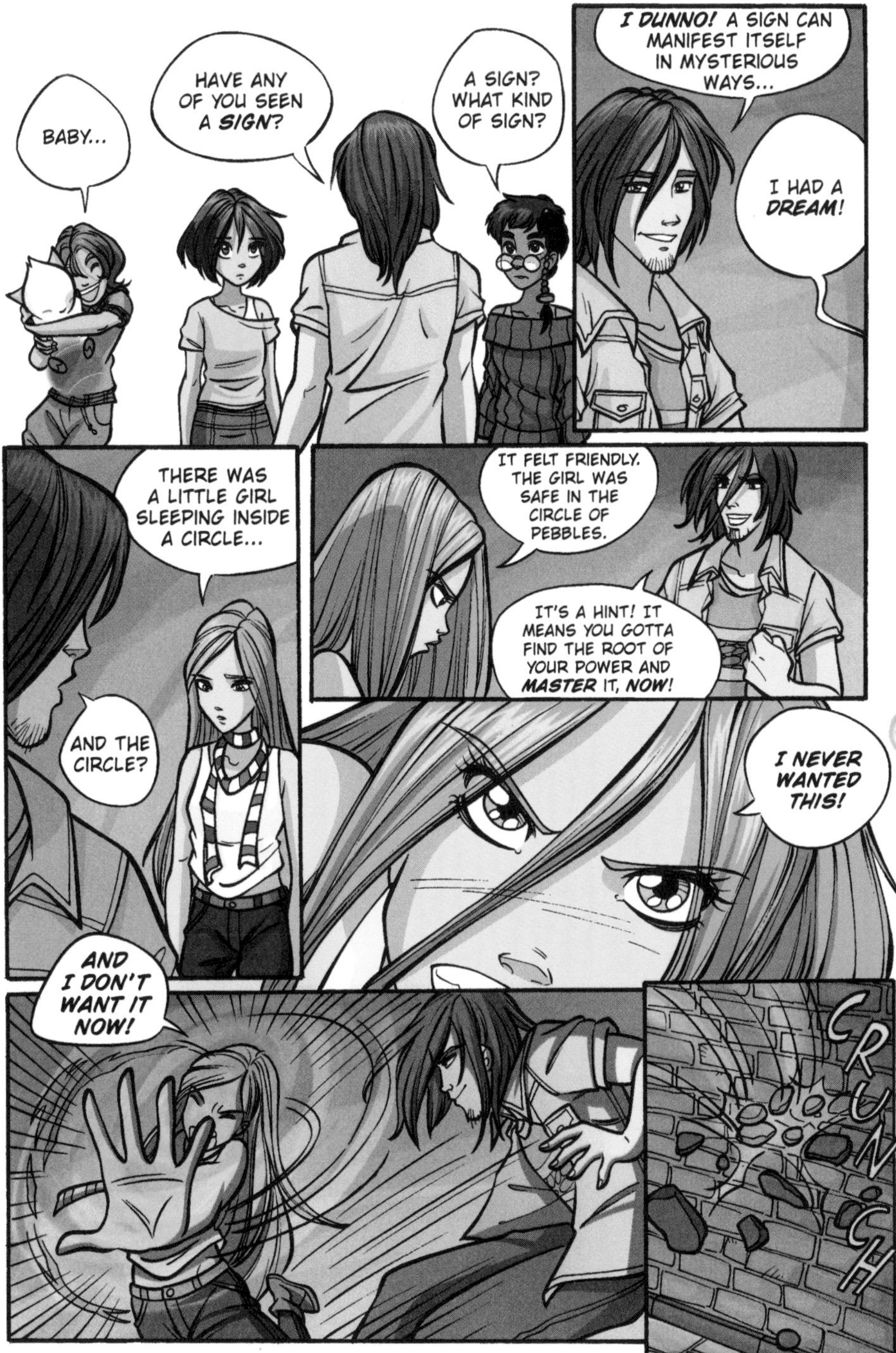
BABY...
HAVE ANY OF YOU SEEN A *SIGN*?
A SIGN? WHAT KIND OF SIGN?
I DUNNO! A SIGN CAN MANIFEST ITSELF IN MYSTERIOUS WAYS...
I HAD A *DREAM*!
THERE WAS A LITTLE GIRL SLEEPING INSIDE A CIRCLE...
AND THE CIRCLE?
IT FELT FRIENDLY. THE GIRL WAS SAFE IN THE CIRCLE OF PEBBLES.
IT'S A HINT! IT MEANS YOU GOTTA FIND THE ROOT OF YOUR POWER AND *MASTER* IT, *NOW*!
I NEVER WANTED THIS!
AND I DON'T WANT IT NOW!
CRUNCH

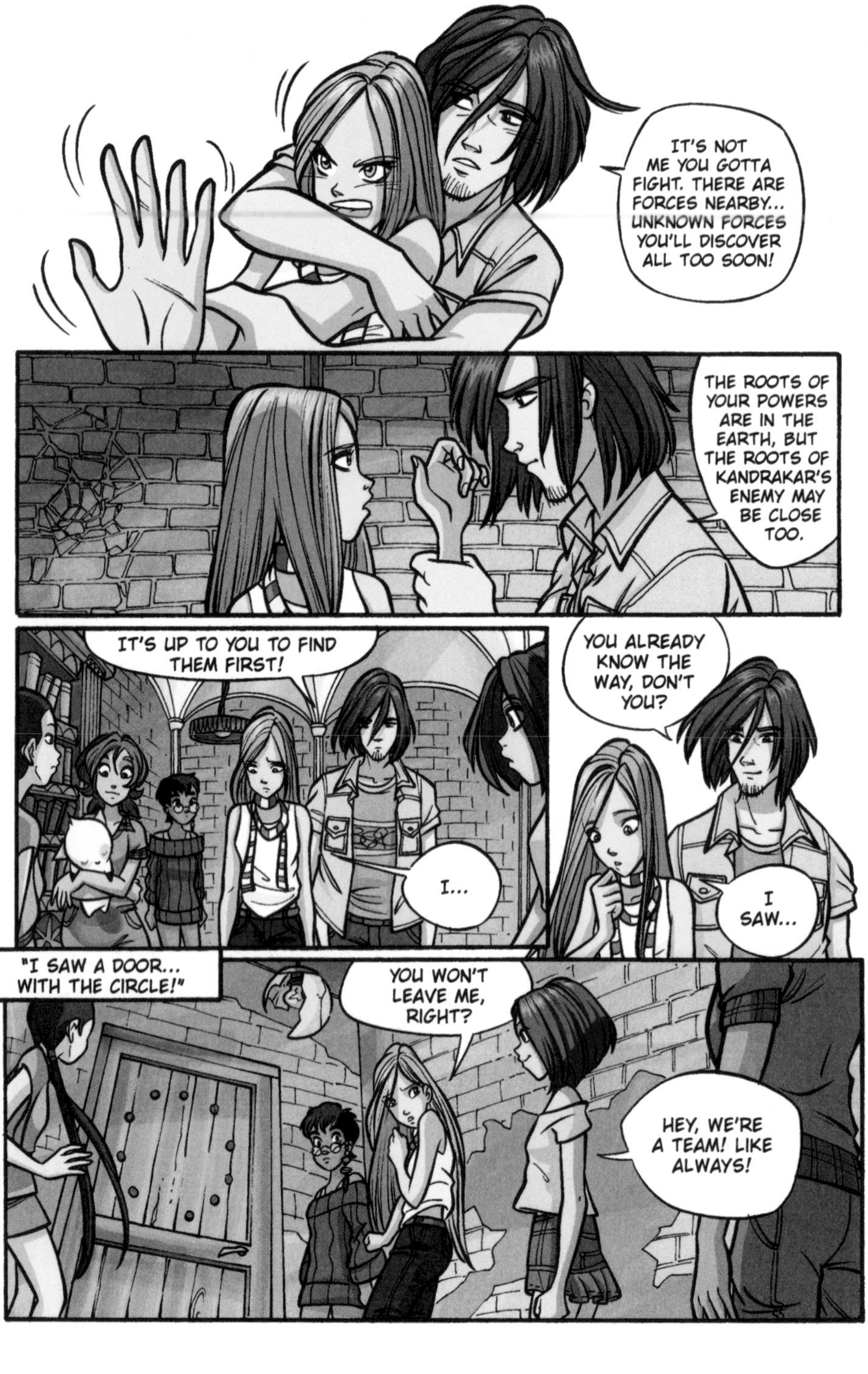
IT'S NOT ME YOU GOTTA FIGHT. THERE ARE FORCES NEARBY... UNKNOWN FORCES YOU'LL DISCOVER ALL TOO SOON!
THE ROOTS OF YOUR POWERS ARE IN THE EARTH, BUT THE ROOTS OF KANDRAKAR'S ENEMY MAY BE CLOSE TOO.
IT'S UP TO YOU TO FIND THEM FIRST!
I...
YOU ALREADY KNOW THE WAY, DON'T YOU?
I SAW...
"I SAW A DOOR... WITH THE CIRCLE!"
YOU WON'T LEAVE ME, RIGHT?
HEY, WE'RE A TEAM! LIKE ALWAYS!

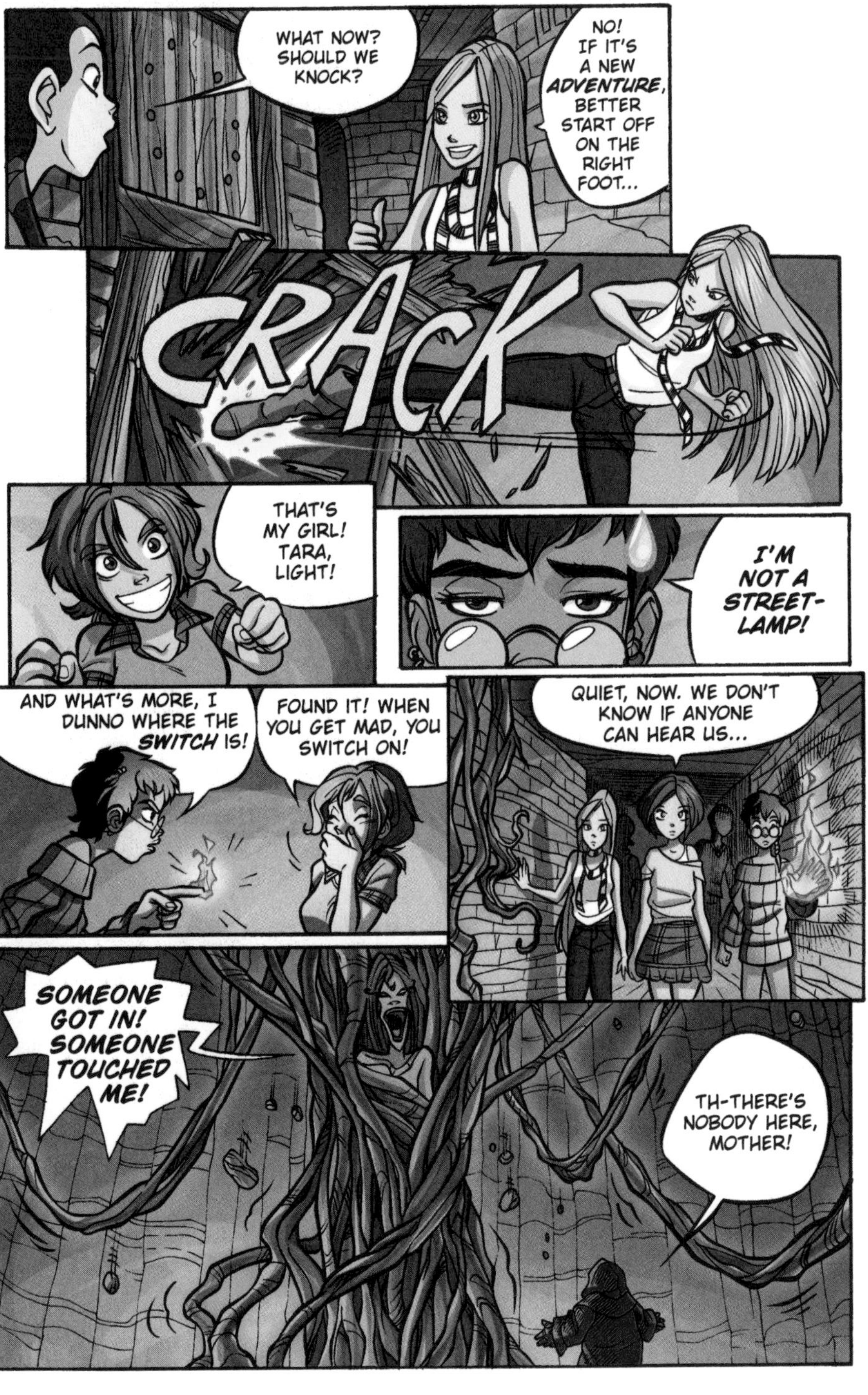
WHAT NOW? SHOULD WE KNOCK?
NO! IF IT'S A NEW ADVENTURE, BETTER START OFF ON THE RIGHT FOOT...
CRACK
THAT'S MY GIRL! TARA, LIGHT!
I'M NOT A STREET-LAMP!
AND WHAT'S MORE, I DUNNO WHERE THE SWITCH IS!
FOUND IT! WHEN YOU GET MAD, YOU SWITCH ON!
QUIET, NOW. WE DON'T KNOW IF ANYONE CAN HEAR US...
SOMEONE GOT IN! SOMEONE TOUCHED ME!
TH-THERE'S NOBODY HERE, MOTHER!

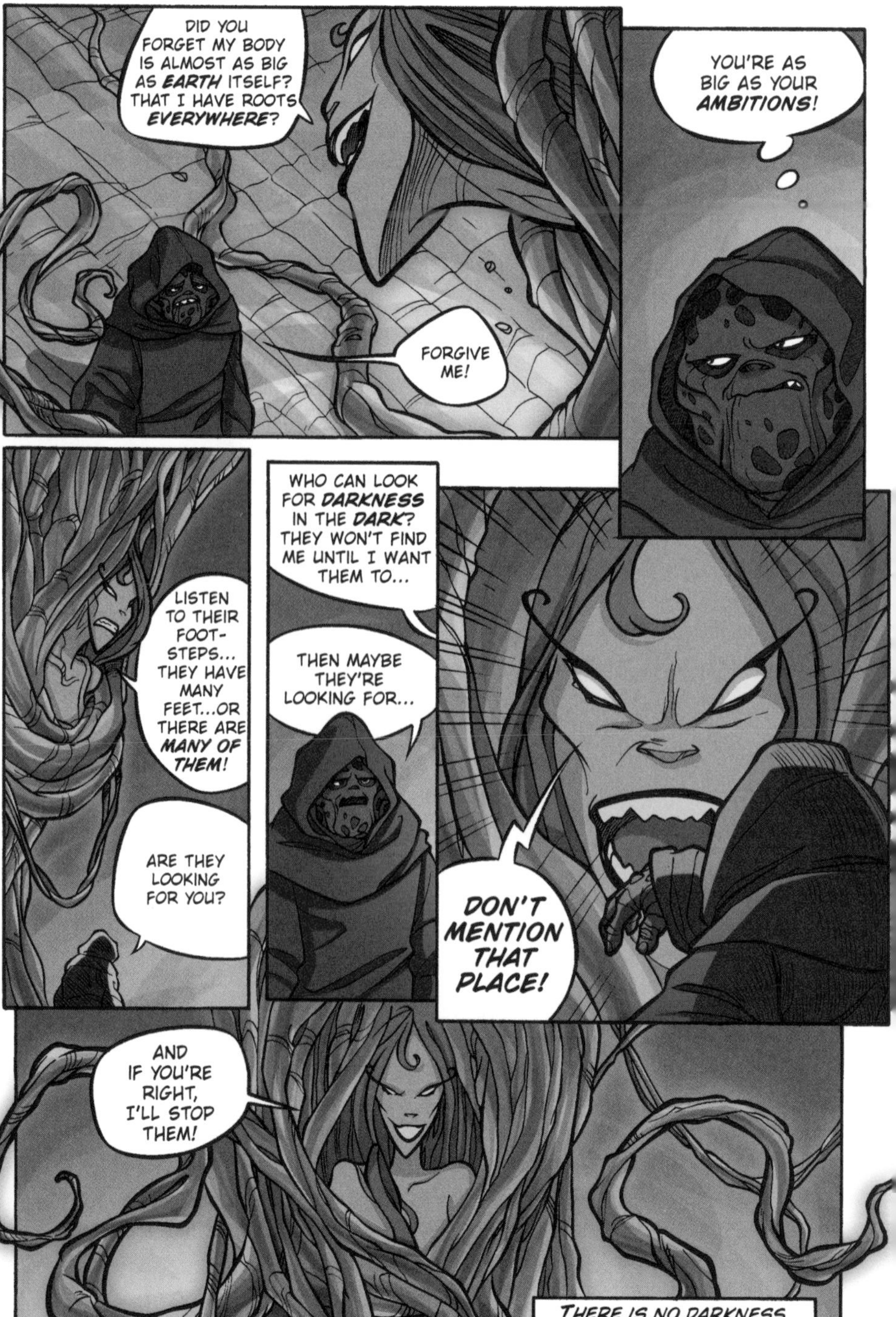

DID YOU FORGET MY BODY IS ALMOST AS BIG AS EARTH ITSELF? THAT I HAVE ROOTS EVERYWHERE?
FORGIVE ME!
YOU'RE AS BIG AS YOUR AMBITIONS!
LISTEN TO THEIR FOOT-STEPS... THEY HAVE MANY FEET...OR THERE ARE MANY OF THEM!
ARE THEY LOOKING FOR YOU?
WHO CAN LOOK FOR DARKNESS IN THE DARK? THEY WON'T FIND ME UNTIL I WANT THEM TO...
THEN MAYBE THEY'RE LOOKING FOR...
DON'T MENTION THAT PLACE!
AND IF YOU'RE RIGHT, I'LL STOP THEM!
THERE IS NO DARKNESS WITHOUT LIGHT...

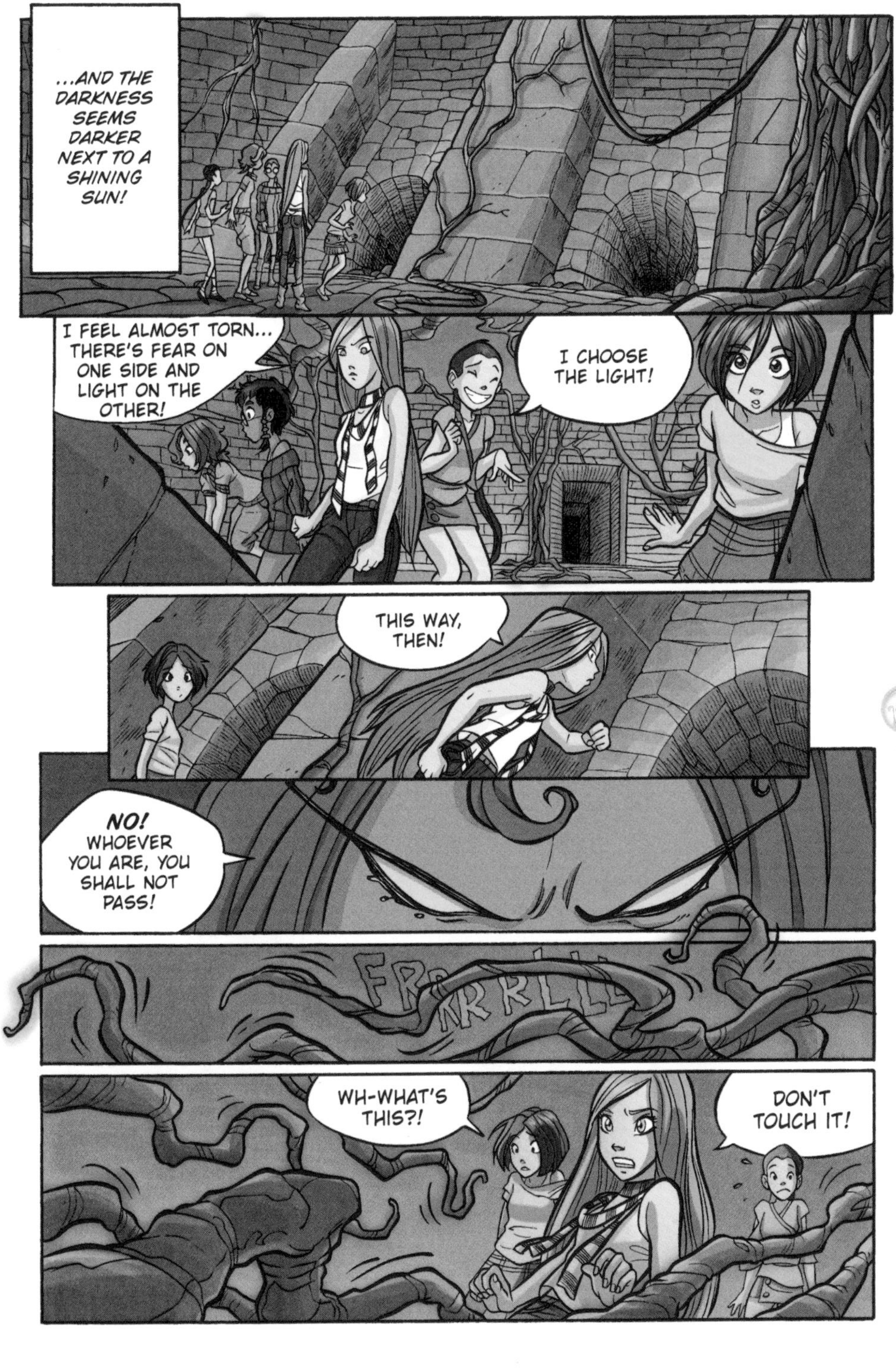
...AND THE DARKNESS SEEMS DARKER NEXT TO A SHINING SUN!
I FEEL ALMOST TORN... THERE'S FEAR ON ONE SIDE AND LIGHT ON THE OTHER!
I CHOOSE THE LIGHT!
THIS WAY, THEN!
NO! WHOEVER YOU ARE, YOU SHALL NOT PASS!
WH-WHAT'S THIS?!
DON'T TOUCH IT!

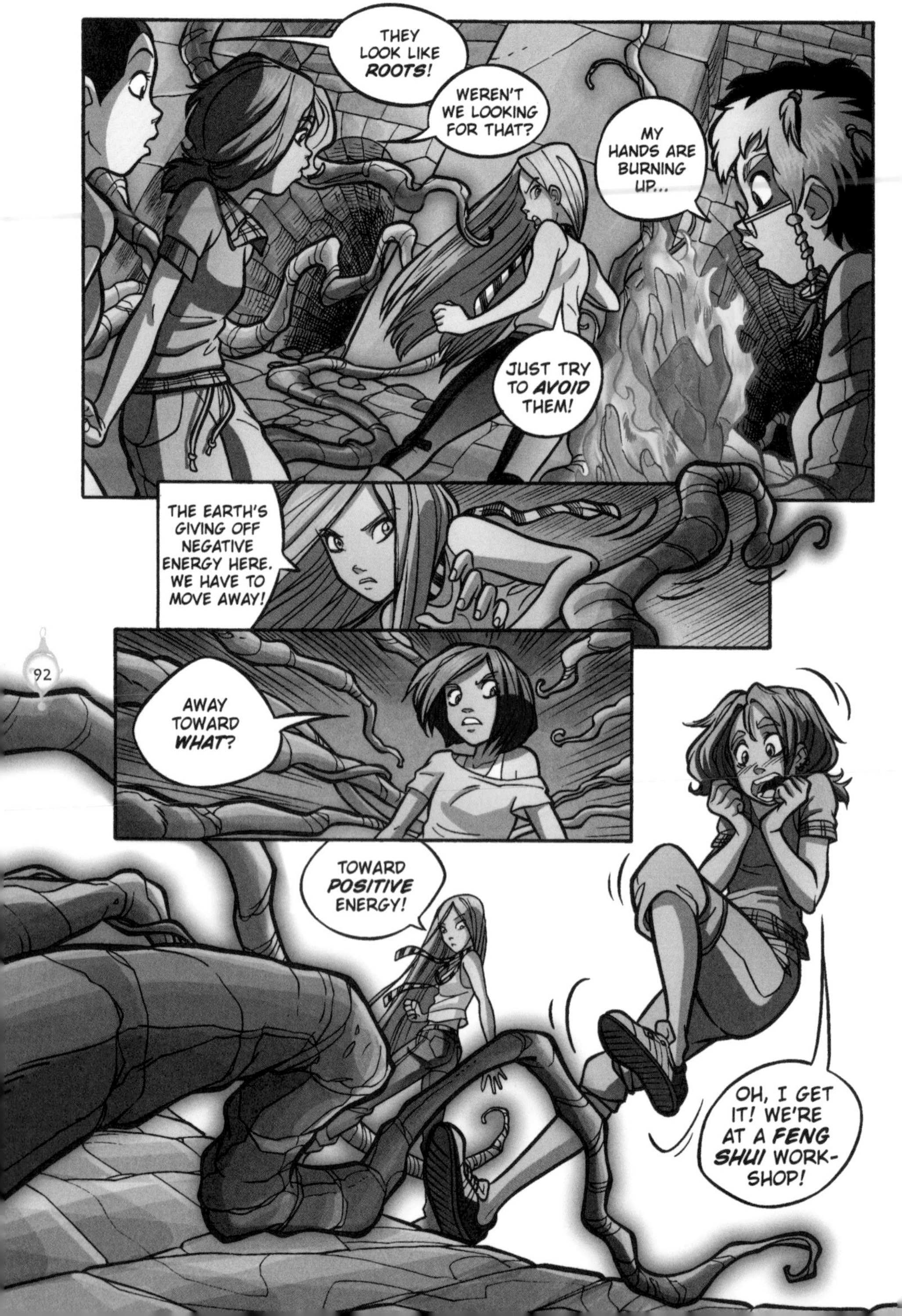
THEY LOOK LIKE ROOTS!
WEREN'T WE LOOKING FOR THAT?
MY HANDS ARE BURNING UP...
JUST TRY TO AVOID THEM!
THE EARTH'S GIVING OFF NEGATIVE ENERGY HERE. WE HAVE TO MOVE AWAY!
AWAY TOWARD WHAT?
TOWARD POSITIVE ENERGY!
OH, I GET IT! WE'RE AT A FENG SHUI WORK-SHOP!

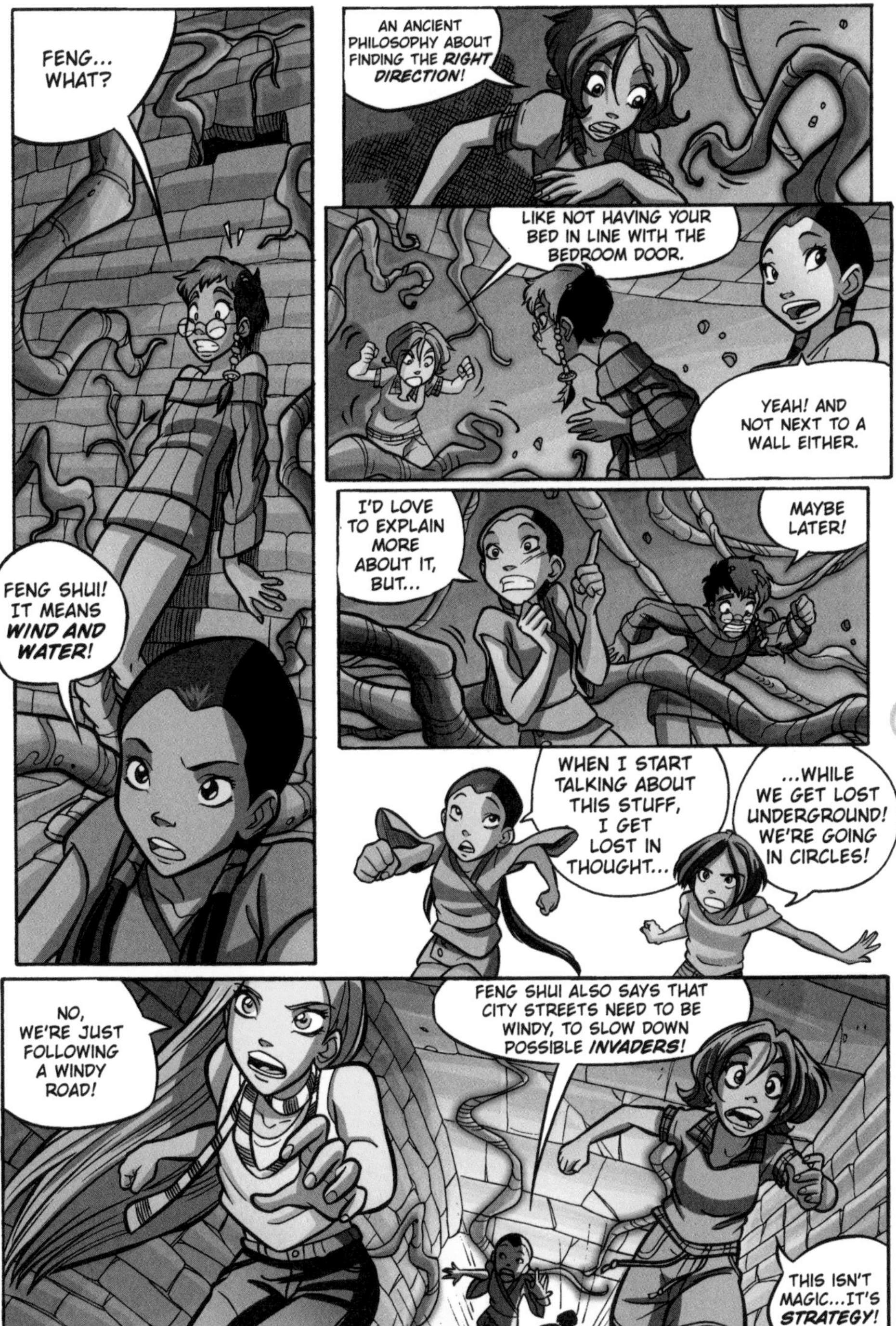
FENG... WHAT?
AN ANCIENT PHILOSOPHY ABOUT FINDING THE *RIGHT DIRECTION*!
LIKE NOT HAVING YOUR BED IN LINE WITH THE BEDROOM DOOR.
YEAH! AND NOT NEXT TO A WALL EITHER.
FENG SHUI! IT MEANS ***WIND AND WATER***!
I'D LOVE TO EXPLAIN MORE ABOUT IT, BUT...
MAYBE LATER!
WHEN I START TALKING ABOUT THIS STUFF, I GET LOST IN THOUGHT...
...WHILE WE GET LOST UNDERGROUND! WE'RE GOING IN CIRCLES!
NO, WE'RE JUST FOLLOWING A WINDY ROAD!
FENG SHUI ALSO SAYS THAT CITY STREETS NEED TO BE WINDY, TO SLOW DOWN POSSIBLE *INVADERS*!
THIS ISN'T MAGIC...IT'S ***STRATEGY***!

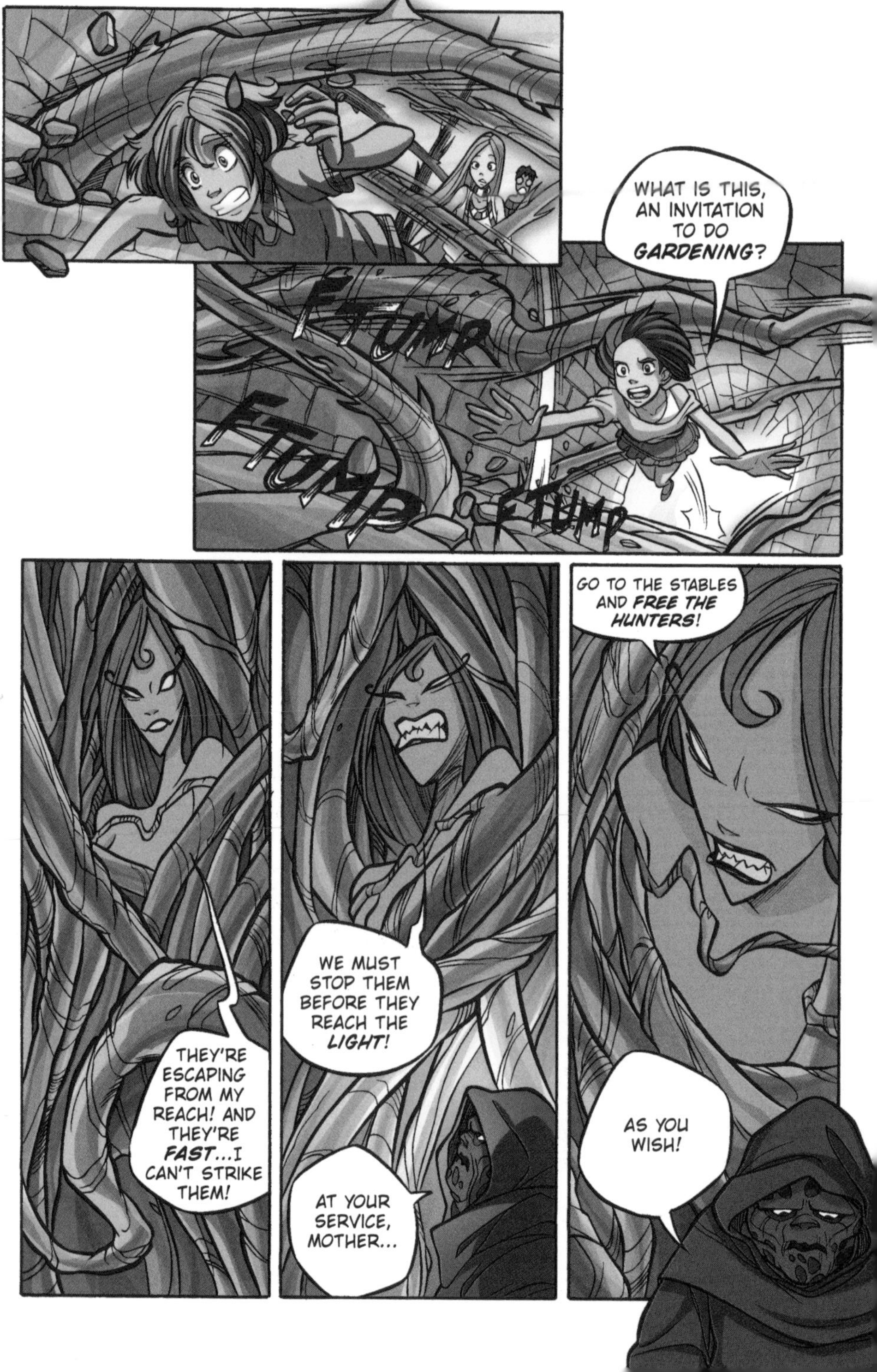
WHAT IS THIS, AN INVITATION TO DO GARDENING?
FTUMP
FTUMP
FTUMP
THEY'RE ESCAPING FROM MY REACH! AND THEY'RE FAST...I CAN'T STRIKE THEM!
WE MUST STOP THEM BEFORE THEY REACH THE LIGHT!
AT YOUR SERVICE, MOTHER...
GO TO THE STABLES AND FREE THE HUNTERS!
AS YOU WISH!

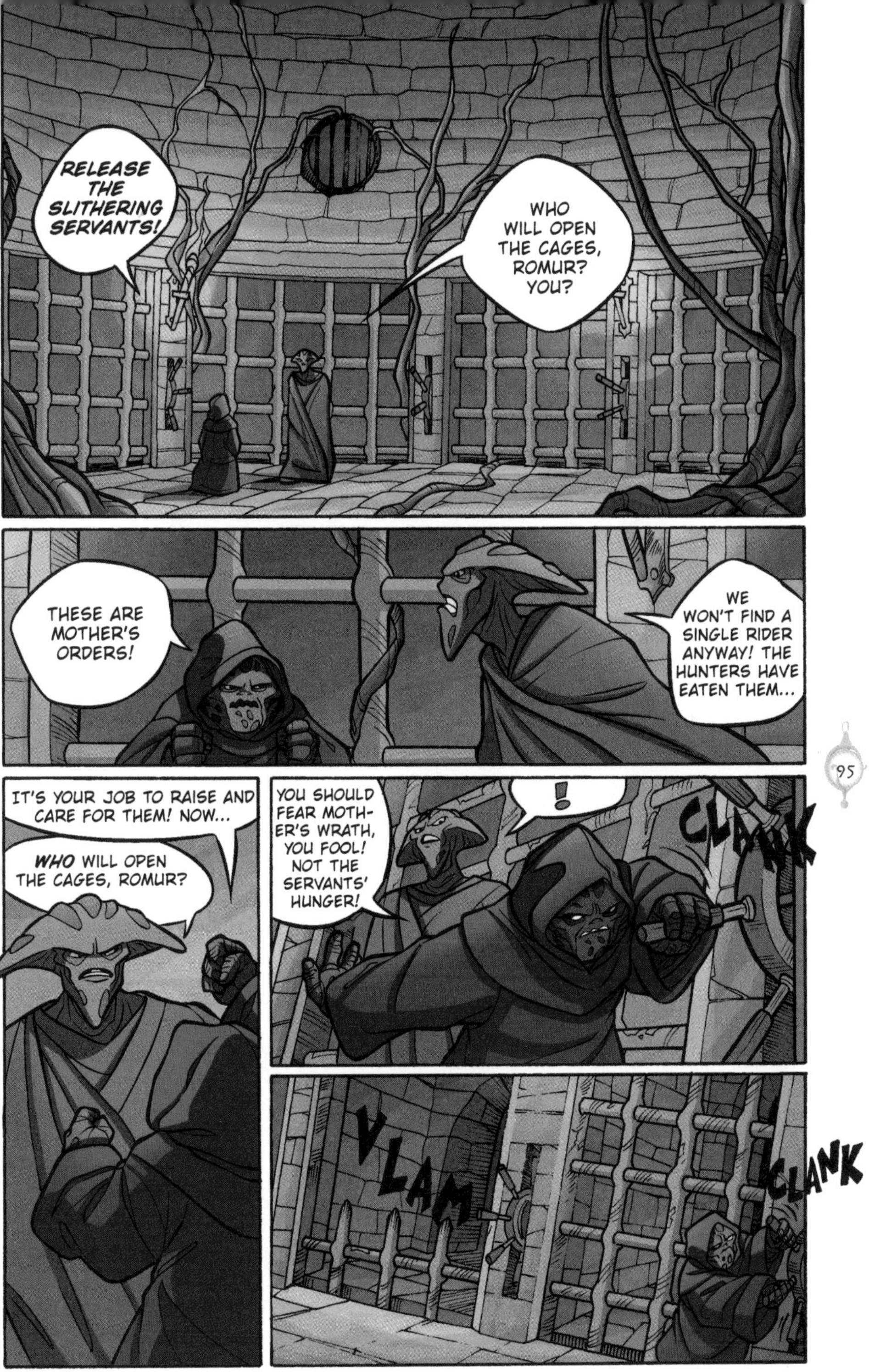
RELEASE THE SLITHERING SERVANTS!
WHO WILL OPEN THE CAGES, ROMUR? YOU?
THESE ARE MOTHER'S ORDERS!
WE WON'T FIND A SINGLE RIDER ANYWAY! THE HUNTERS HAVE EATEN THEM...
IT'S YOUR JOB TO RAISE AND CARE FOR THEM! NOW...
WHO WILL OPEN THE CAGES, ROMUR?
YOU SHOULD FEAR MOTHER'S WRATH, YOU FOOL! NOT THE SERVANTS' HUNGER!
!
CLANK
VLAM
CLANK

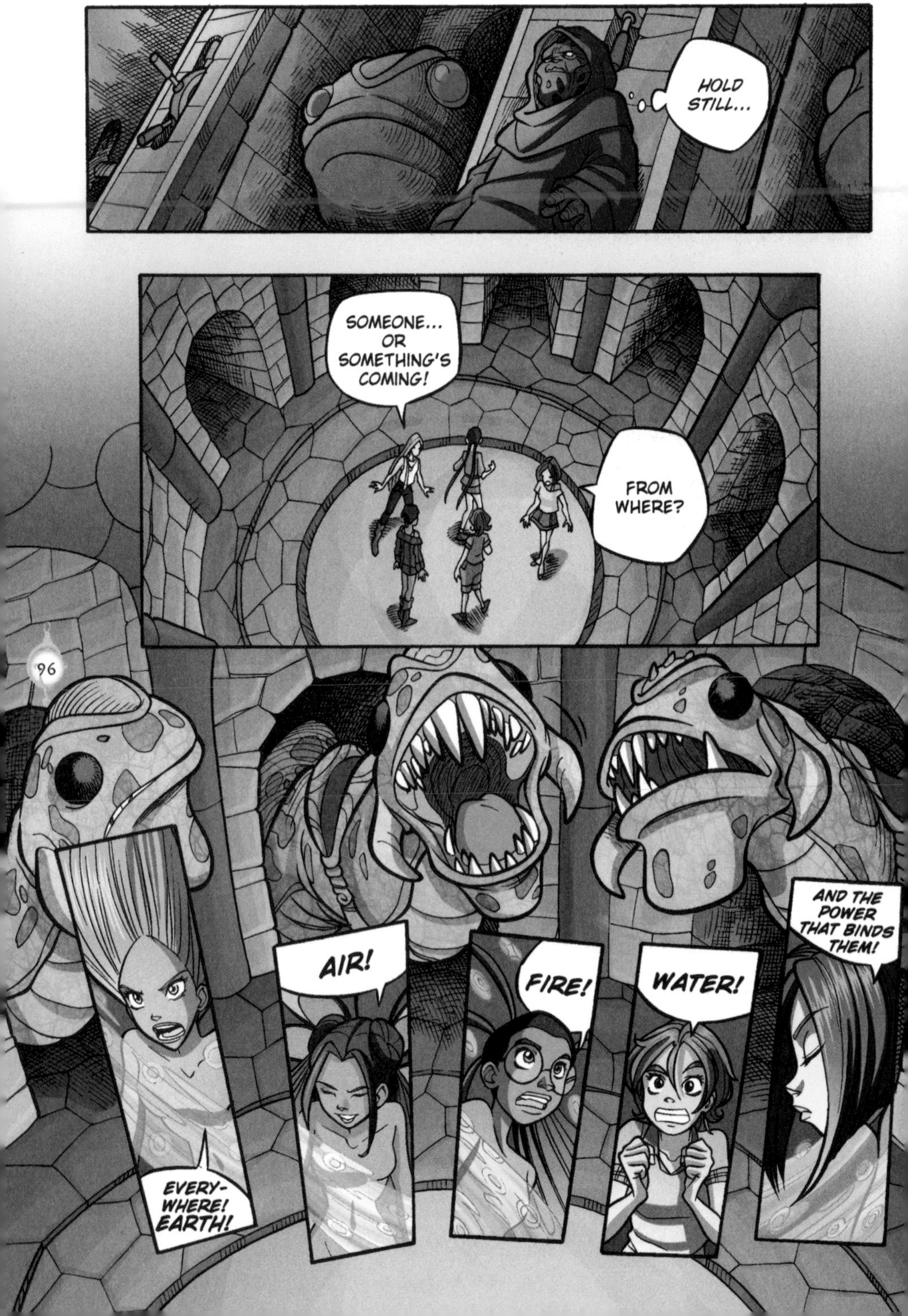
HOLD STILL...
SOMEONE... OR SOMETHING'S COMING!
FROM WHERE?
EVERY-WHERE! EARTH!
AIR!
FIRE!
WATER!
AND THE POWER THAT BINDS THEM!

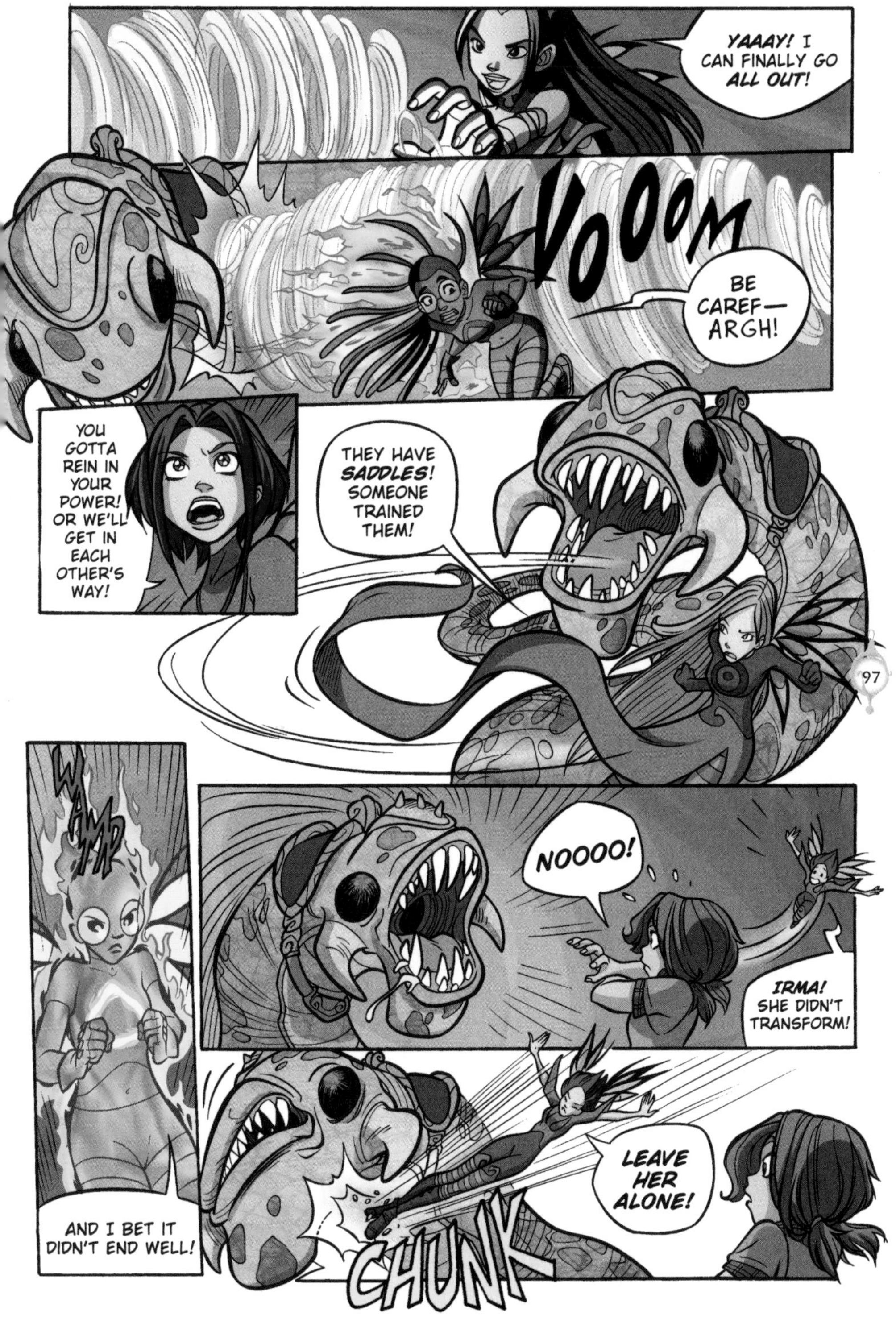
YAAAY! I CAN FINALLY GO ALL OUT!
VOOOM
BE CAREF— ARGH!
YOU GOTTA REIN IN YOUR POWER! OR WE'LL GET IN EACH OTHER'S WAY!
THEY HAVE SADDLES! SOMEONE TRAINED THEM!
WAMP
NOOOO!
IRMA! SHE DIDN'T TRANSFORM!
AND I BET IT DIDN'T END WELL!
LEAVE HER ALONE!
CHUNK

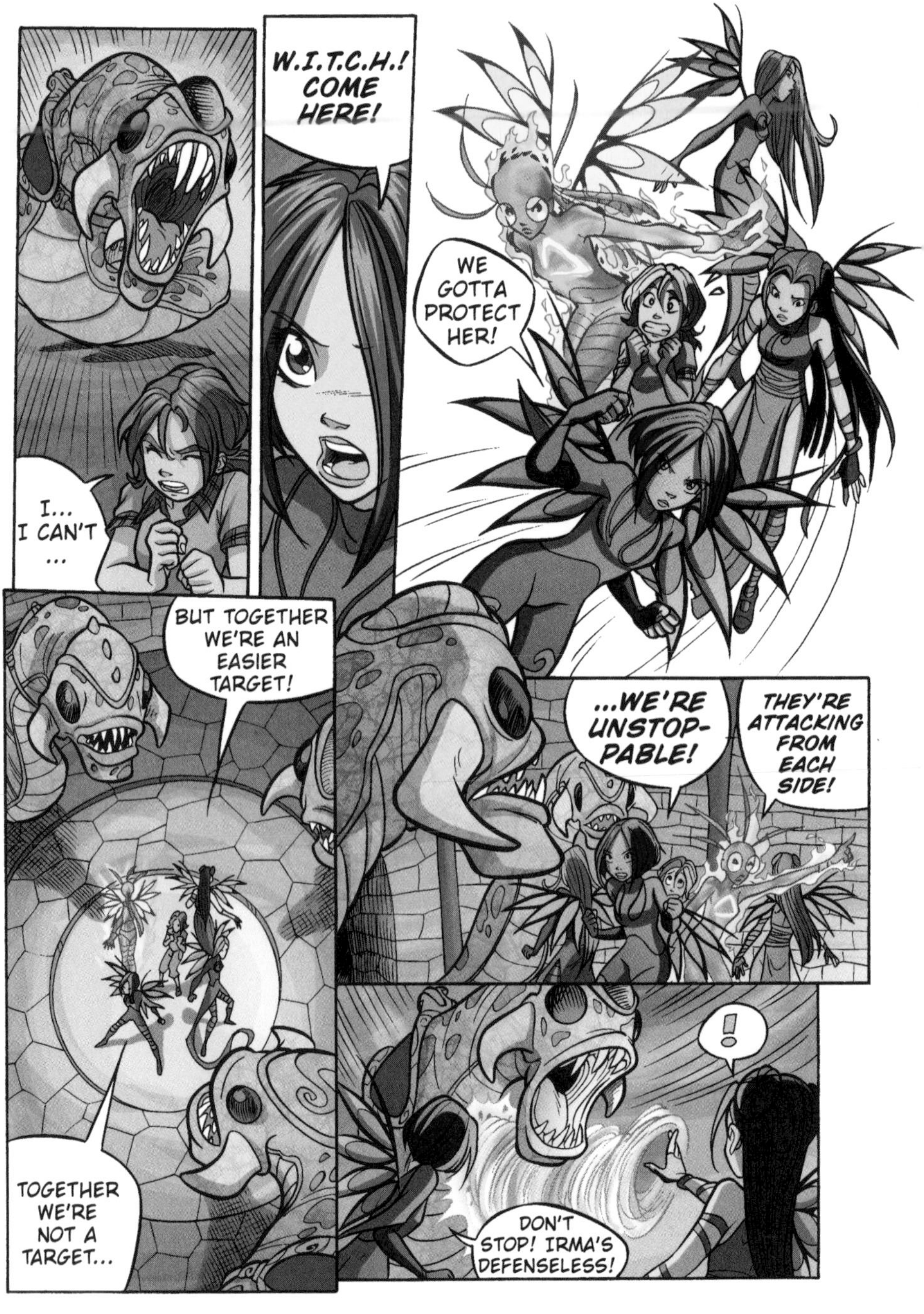
I... I CAN'T ...
W.I.T.C.H.! COME HERE!
WE GOTTA PROTECT HER!
BUT TOGETHER WE'RE AN EASIER TARGET!
TOGETHER WE'RE NOT A TARGET...
...WE'RE UNSTOP-PABLE!
THEY'RE ATTACKING FROM EACH SIDE!
!
DON'T STOP! IRMA'S DEFENSELESS!

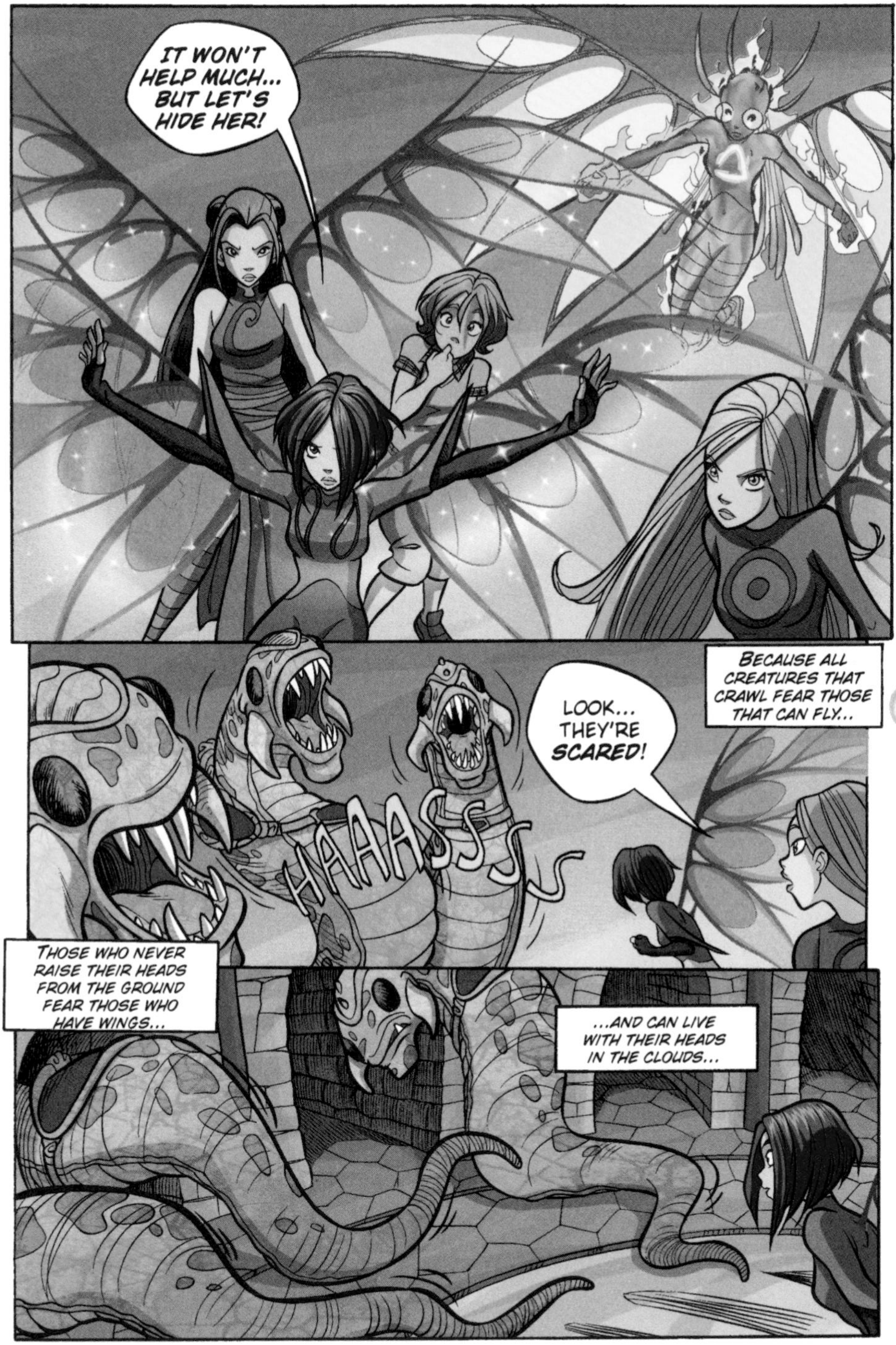
IT WON'T HELP MUCH... BUT LET'S HIDE HER!
BECAUSE ALL CREATURES THAT CRAWL FEAR THOSE THAT CAN FLY...
LOOK... THEY'RE SCARED!
HAAAASSS
THOSE WHO NEVER RAISE THEIR HEADS FROM THE GROUND FEAR THOSE WHO HAVE WINGS...
...AND CAN LIVE WITH THEIR HEADS IN THE CLOUDS...

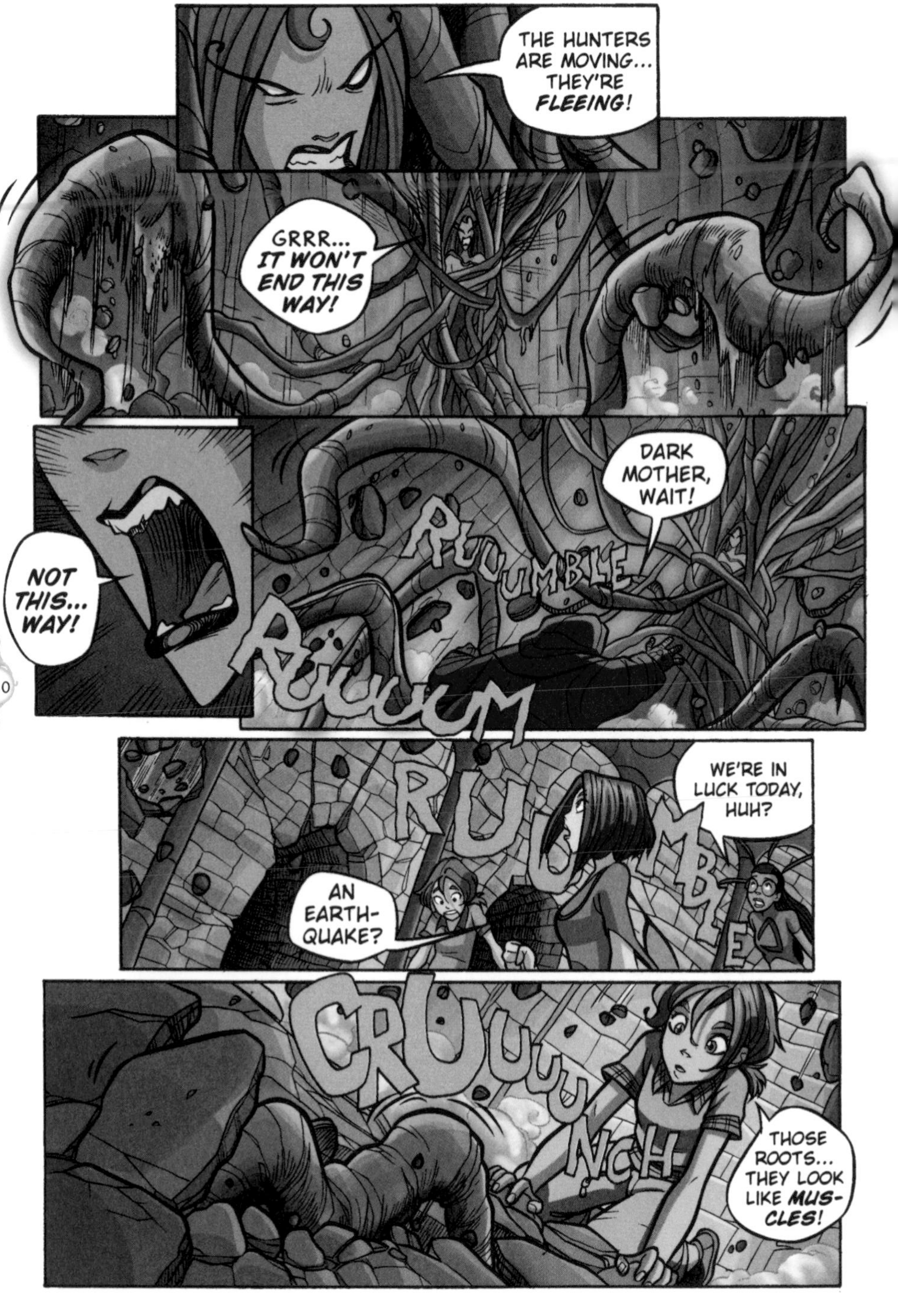
THE HUNTERS ARE MOVING... THEY'RE *FLEEING*!
GRRR... *IT WON'T END THIS WAY!*
NOT THIS... WAY!
DARK MOTHER, WAIT!
RUUUMBLE
RUUUUM
RUUUMBLE
WE'RE IN LUCK TODAY, HUH?
AN EARTH-QUAKE?
CRUUUUNCH
THOSE ROOTS... THEY LOOK LIKE *MUS-CLES*!

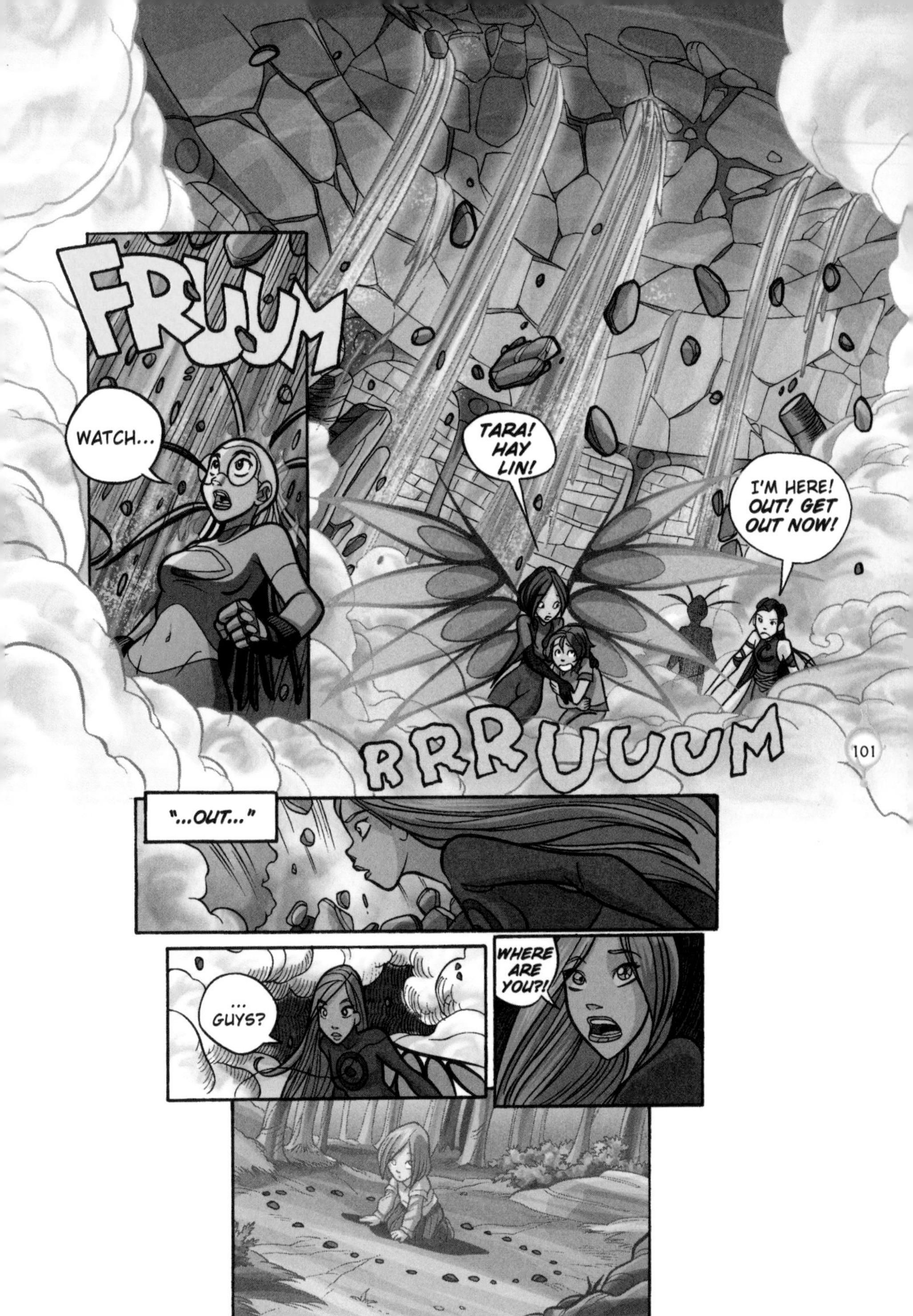
FRUUM
WATCH...
TARA! HAY LIN!
I'M HERE! OUT! GET OUT NOW!
RRRUUUM
"...OUT..."
... GUYS?
WHERE ARE YOU?!

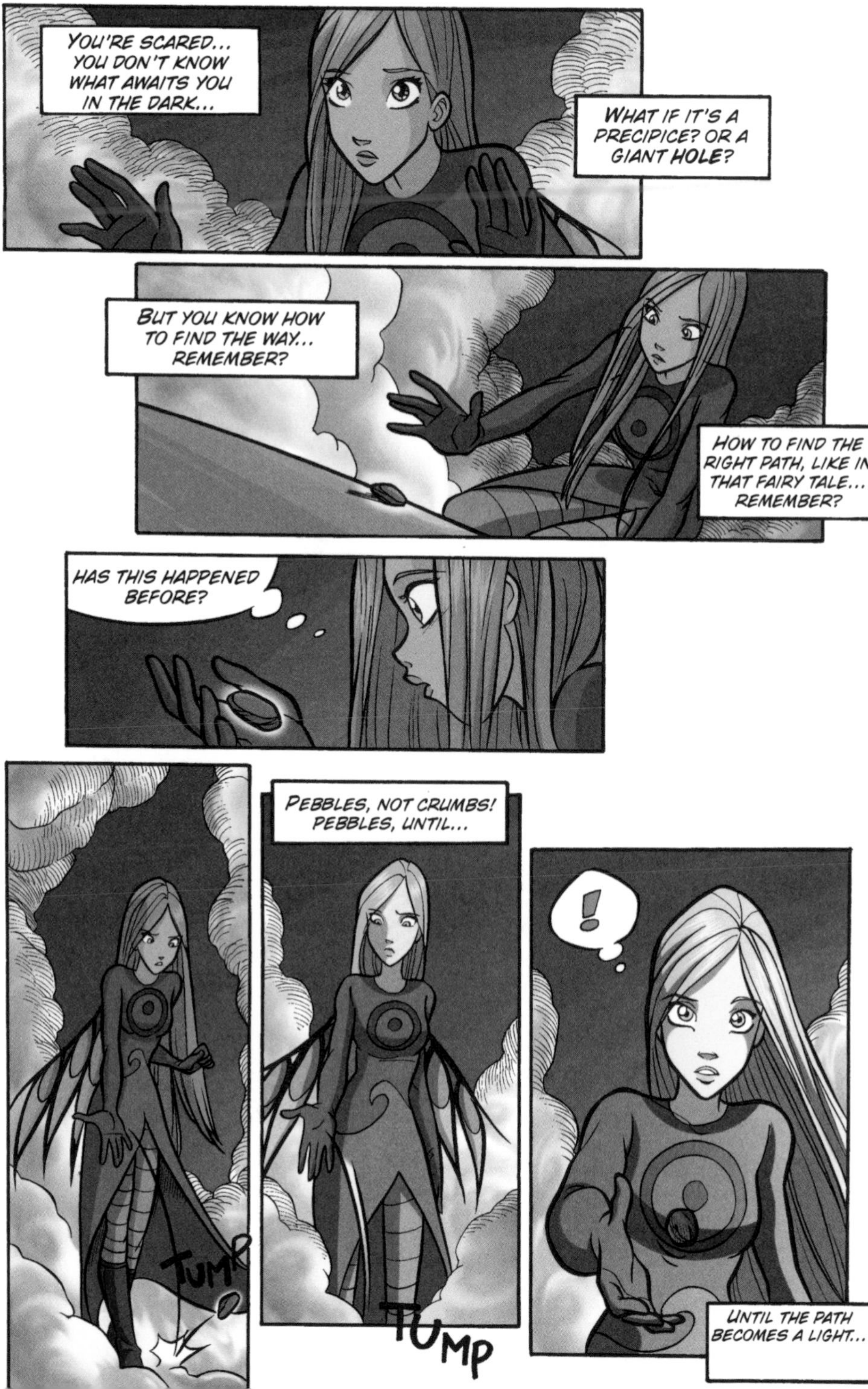

YOU'RE SCARED... YOU DON'T KNOW WHAT AWAITS YOU IN THE DARK...
WHAT IF IT'S A PRECIPICE? OR A GIANT HOLE?
BUT YOU KNOW HOW TO FIND THE WAY... REMEMBER?
HOW TO FIND THE RIGHT PATH, LIKE IN THAT FAIRY TALE... REMEMBER?
HAS THIS HAPPENED BEFORE?
TUMP
PEBBLES, NOT CRUMBS! PEBBLES, UNTIL...
TUMP
!
UNTIL THE PATH BECOMES A LIGHT...

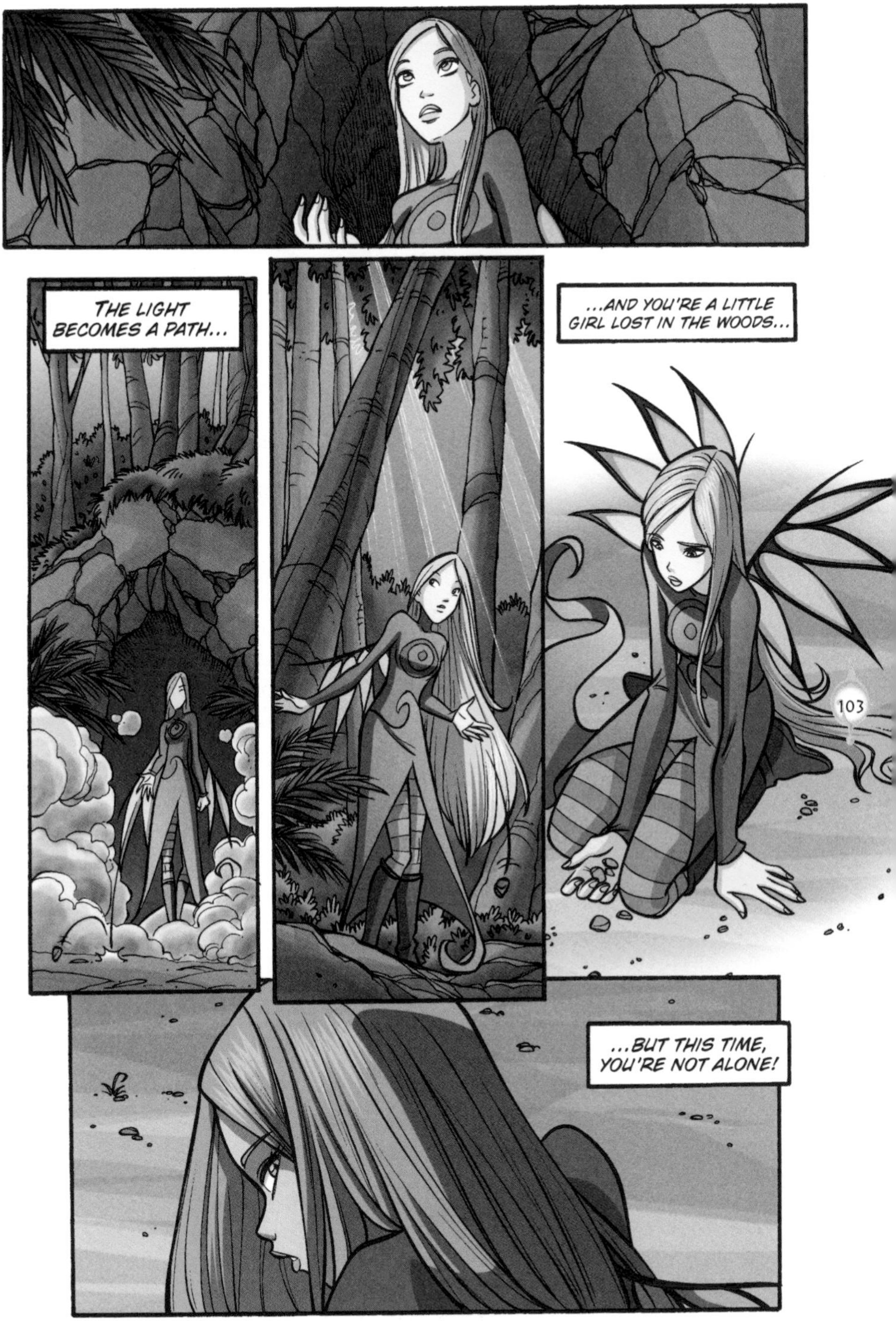
THE LIGHT BECOMES A PATH...
...AND YOU'RE A LITTLE GIRL LOST IN THE WOODS...
...BUT THIS TIME, YOU'RE NOT ALONE!

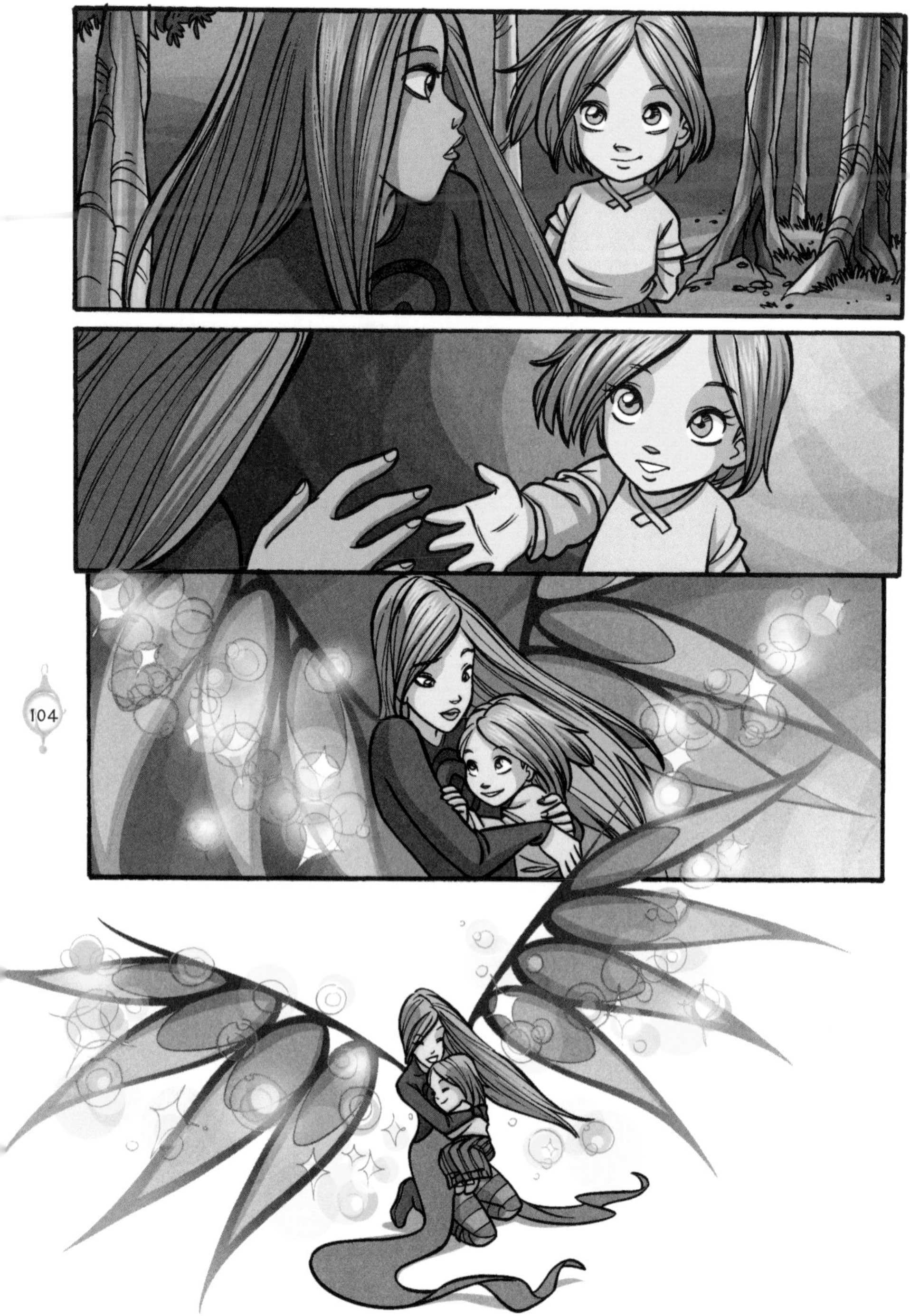

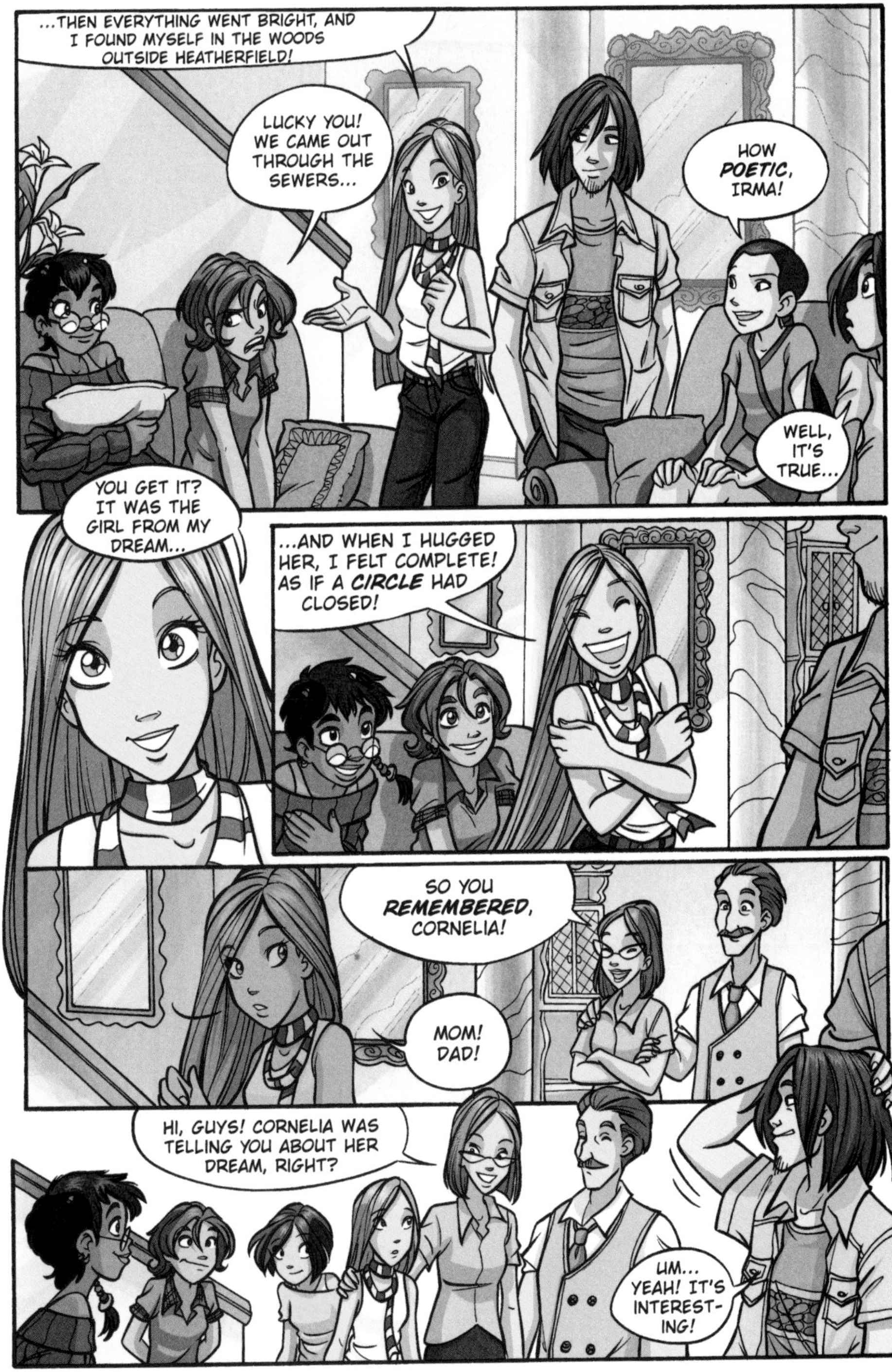

...THEN EVERYTHING WENT BRIGHT, AND I FOUND MYSELF IN THE WOODS OUTSIDE HEATHERFIELD!
LUCKY YOU! WE CAME OUT THROUGH THE SEWERS...
HOW *POETIC*, IRMA!
WELL, IT'S TRUE...
YOU GET IT? IT WAS THE GIRL FROM MY DREAM...
...AND WHEN I HUGGED HER, I FELT COMPLETE! AS IF A *CIRCLE* HAD CLOSED!
SO YOU *REMEMBERED*, CORNELIA!
MOM! DAD!
HI, GUYS! CORNELIA WAS TELLING YOU ABOUT HER DREAM, RIGHT?
UM... YEAH! IT'S INTEREST-ING!

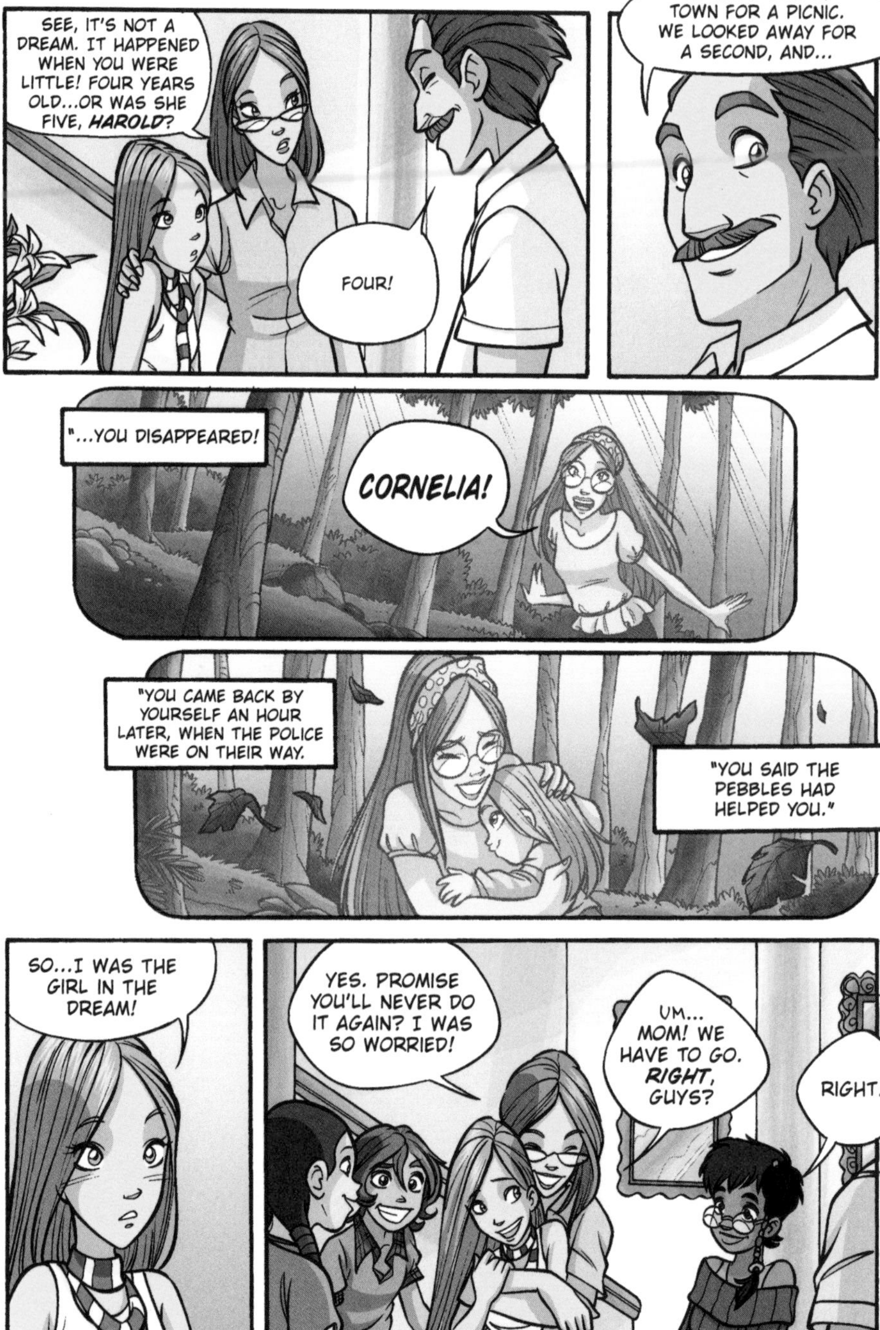
SEE, IT'S NOT A DREAM. IT HAPPENED WHEN YOU WERE LITTLE! FOUR YEARS OLD...OR WAS SHE FIVE, ***HAROLD***?
FOUR!
WE WERE OUT OF TOWN FOR A PICNIC. WE LOOKED AWAY FOR A SECOND, AND...
"...YOU DISAPPEARED!
CORNELIA!
"YOU CAME BACK BY YOURSELF AN HOUR LATER, WHEN THE POLICE WERE ON THEIR WAY.
"YOU SAID THE PEBBLES HAD HELPED YOU."
SO...I WAS THE GIRL IN THE DREAM!
YES. PROMISE YOU'LL NEVER DO IT AGAIN? I WAS SO WORRIED!
UM... MOM! WE HAVE TO GO. ***RIGHT***, GUYS?
RIGHT!

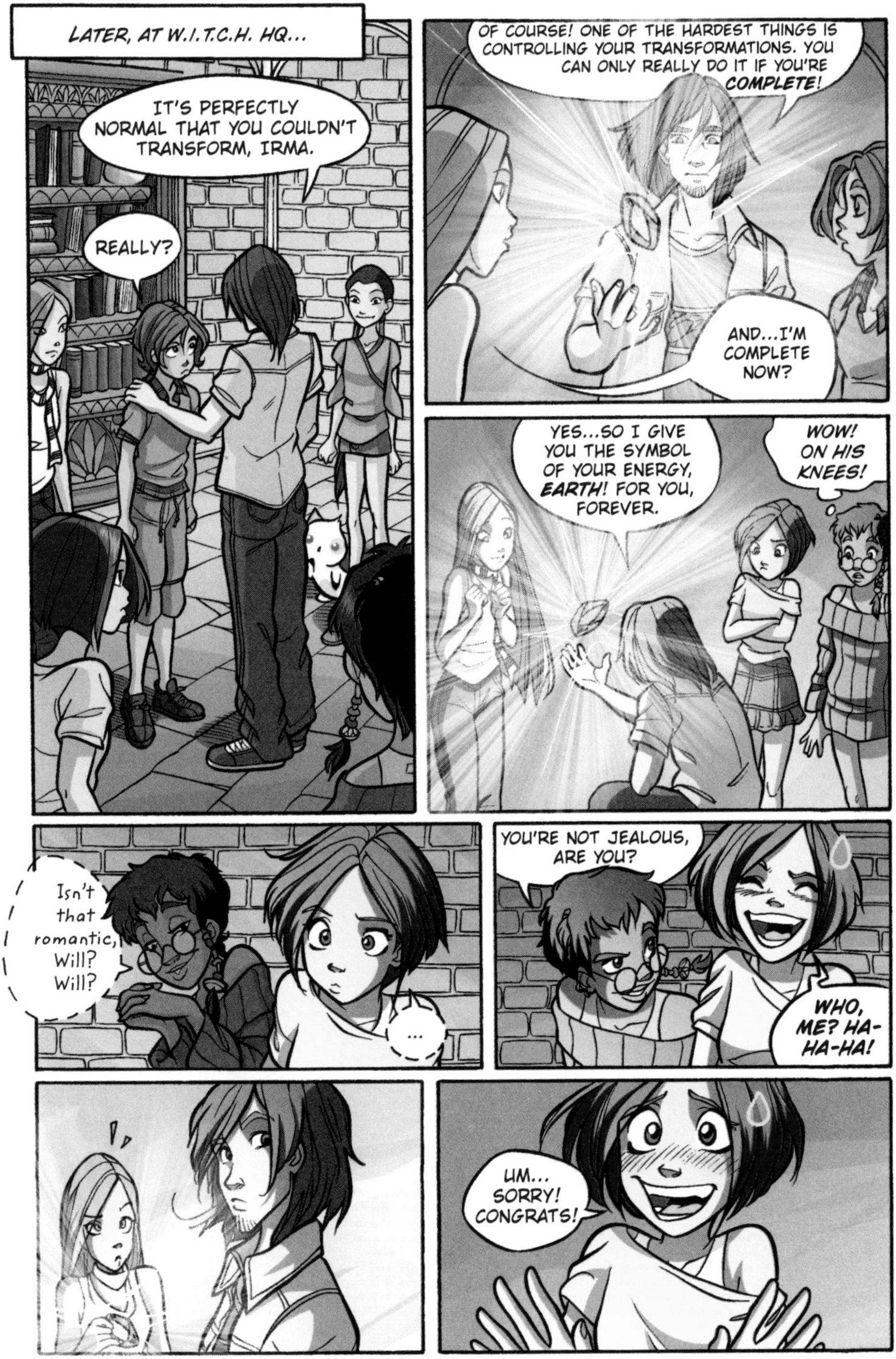
LATER, AT W.I.T.C.H. HQ...
IT'S PERFECTLY NORMAL THAT YOU COULDN'T TRANSFORM, IRMA.
REALLY?
OF COURSE! ONE OF THE HARDEST THINGS IS CONTROLLING YOUR TRANSFORMATIONS. YOU CAN ONLY REALLY DO IT IF YOU'RE COMPLETE!
AND...I'M COMPLETE NOW?
YES...SO I GIVE YOU THE SYMBOL OF YOUR ENERGY, EARTH! FOR YOU, FOREVER.
WOW! ON HIS KNEES!
Isn't that romantic, Will? Will?
...
YOU'RE NOT JEALOUS, ARE YOU?
WHO, ME? HA-HA-HA!
UM... SORRY! CONGRATS!

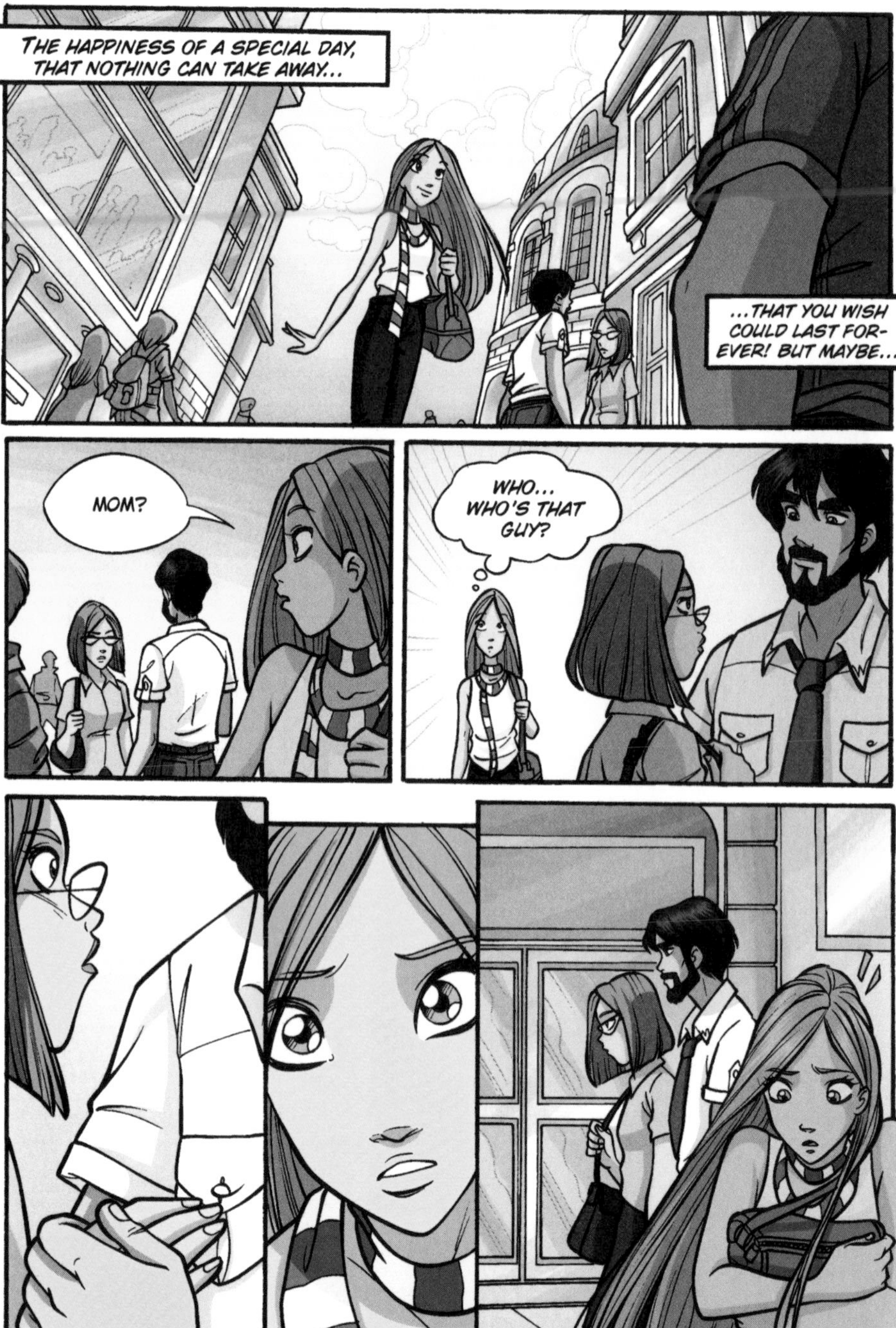
THE HAPPINESS OF A SPECIAL DAY, THAT NOTHING CAN TAKE AWAY...
...THAT YOU WISH COULD LAST FOR-EVER! BUT MAYBE...
MOM?
WHO... WHO'S THAT GUY?

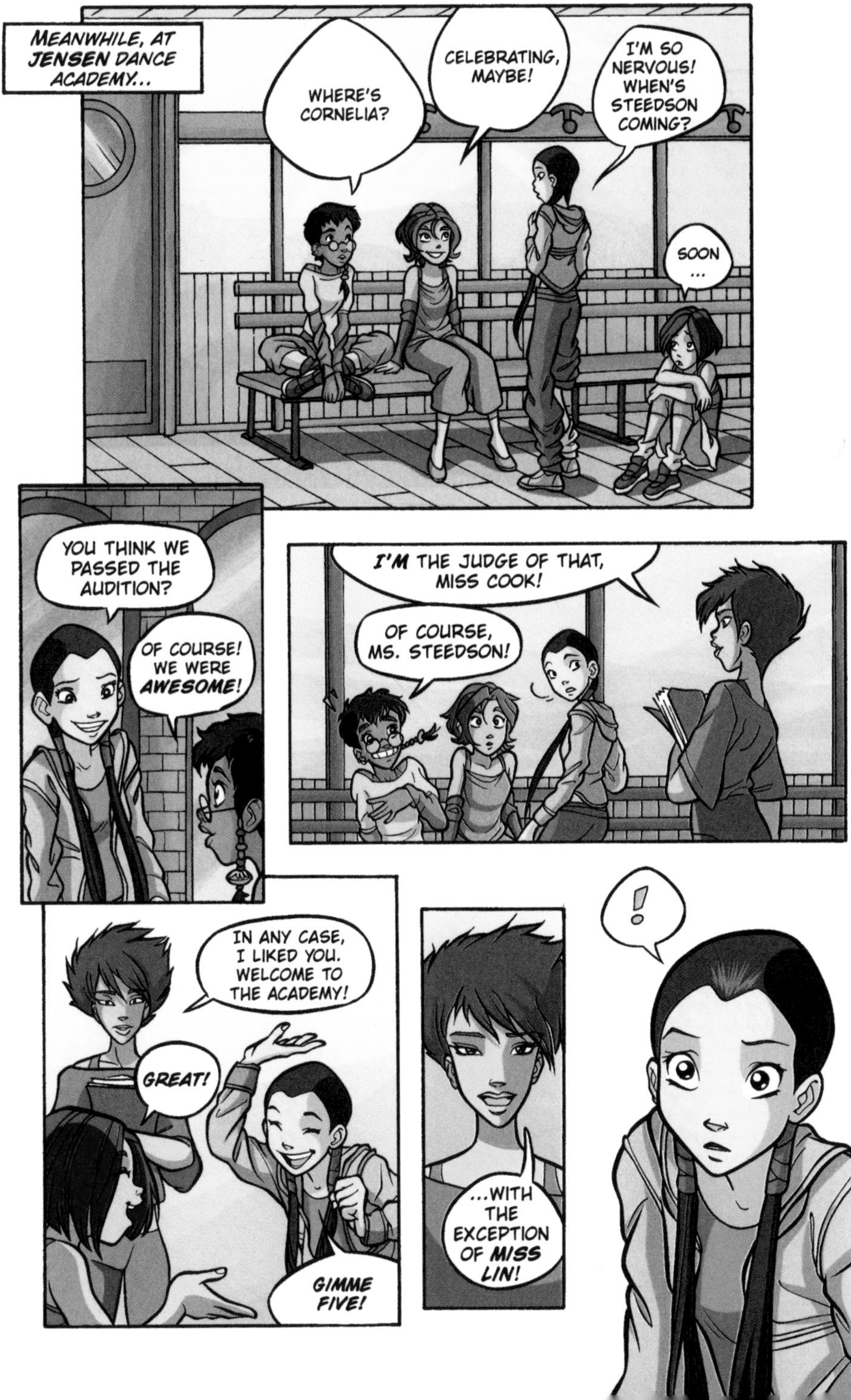
MEANWHILE, AT JENSEN DANCE ACADEMY...
WHERE'S CORNELIA?
CELEBRATING, MAYBE!
I'M SO NERVOUS! WHEN'S STEEDSON COMING?
SOON ...
YOU THINK WE PASSED THE AUDITION?
OF COURSE! WE WERE AWESOME!
I'M THE JUDGE OF THAT, MISS COOK!
OF COURSE, MS. STEEDSON!
IN ANY CASE, I LIKED YOU. WELCOME TO THE ACADEMY!
GREAT!
GIMME FIVE!
...WITH THE EXCEPTION OF MISS LIN!
!

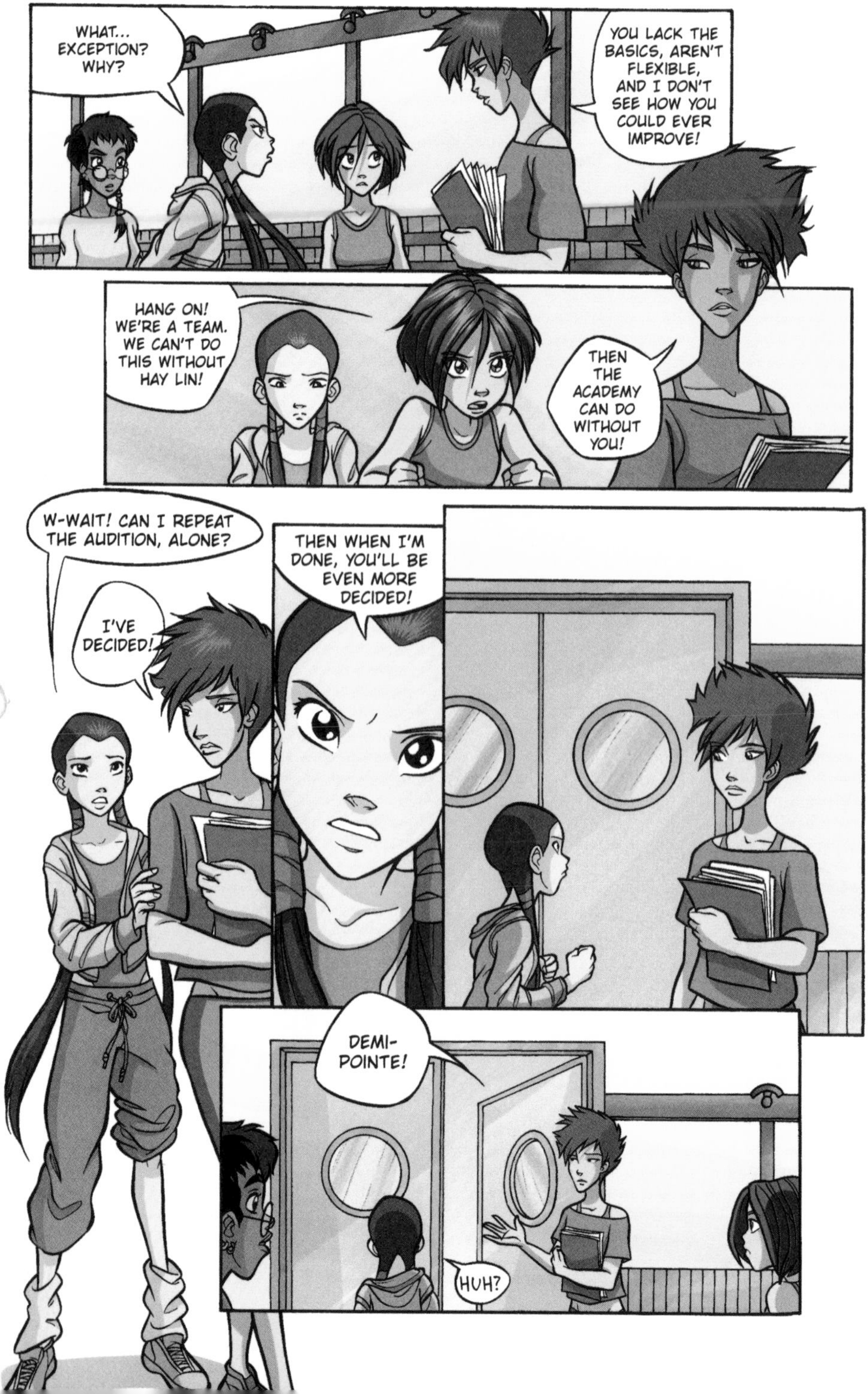
WHAT... EXCEPTION? WHY?
YOU LACK THE BASICS, AREN'T FLEXIBLE, AND I DON'T SEE HOW YOU COULD EVER IMPROVE!
HANG ON! WE'RE A TEAM. WE CAN'T DO THIS WITHOUT HAY LIN!
THEN THE ACADEMY CAN DO WITHOUT YOU!
W-WAIT! CAN I REPEAT THE AUDITION, ALONE?
I'VE DECIDED!
THEN WHEN I'M DONE, YOU'LL BE EVEN MORE DECIDED!
DEMI-POINTE!
HUH?

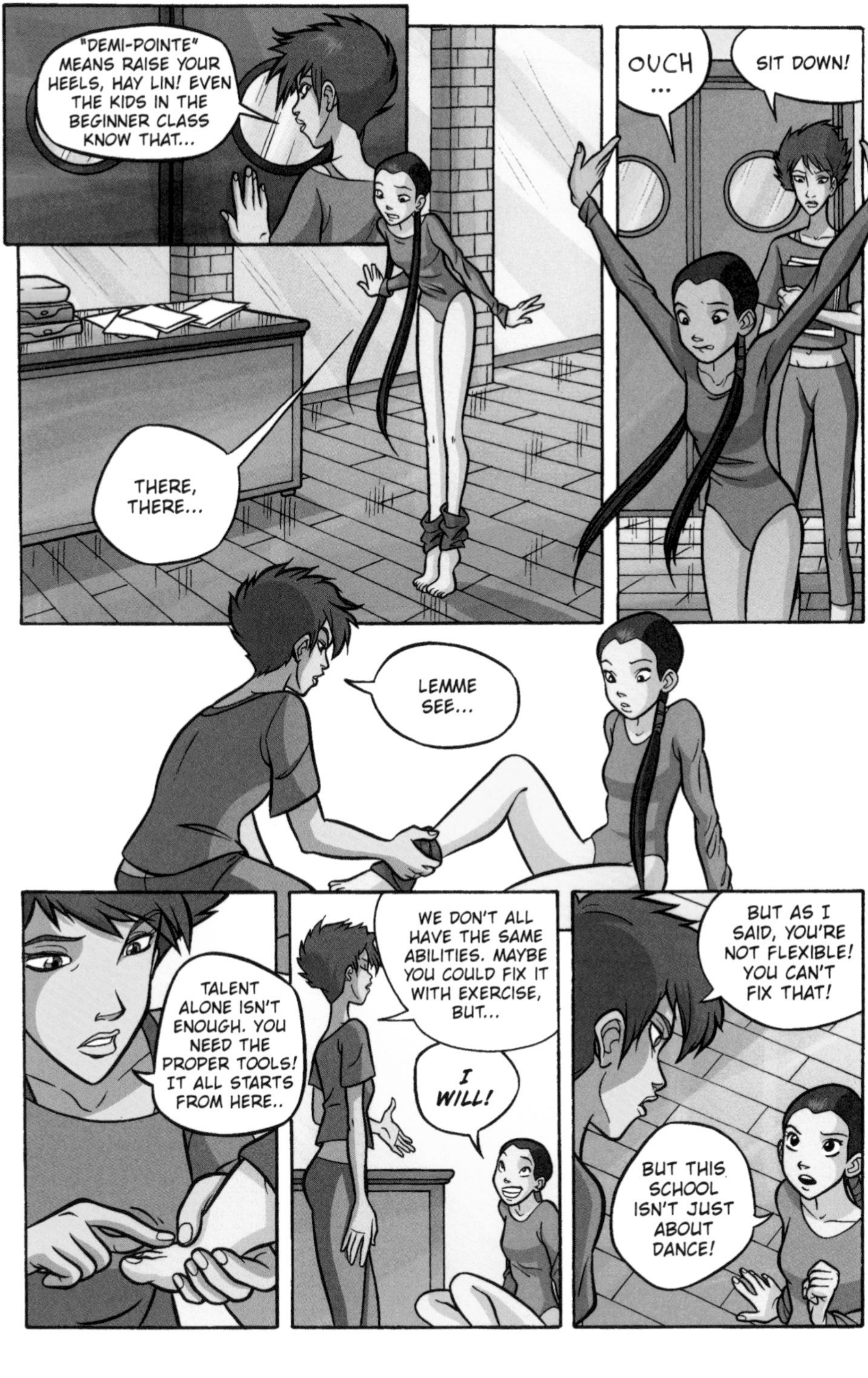
"DEMI-POINTE" MEANS RAISE YOUR HEELS, HAY LIN! EVEN THE KIDS IN THE BEGINNER CLASS KNOW THAT...
THERE, THERE...
OUCH ...
SIT DOWN!
LEMME SEE...
TALENT ALONE ISN'T ENOUGH. YOU NEED THE PROPER TOOLS! IT ALL STARTS FROM HERE..
WE DON'T ALL HAVE THE SAME ABILITIES. MAYBE YOU COULD FIX IT WITH EXERCISE, BUT...
I WILL!
BUT AS I SAID, YOU'RE NOT FLEXIBLE! YOU CAN'T FIX THAT!
BUT THIS SCHOOL ISN'T JUST ABOUT DANCE!

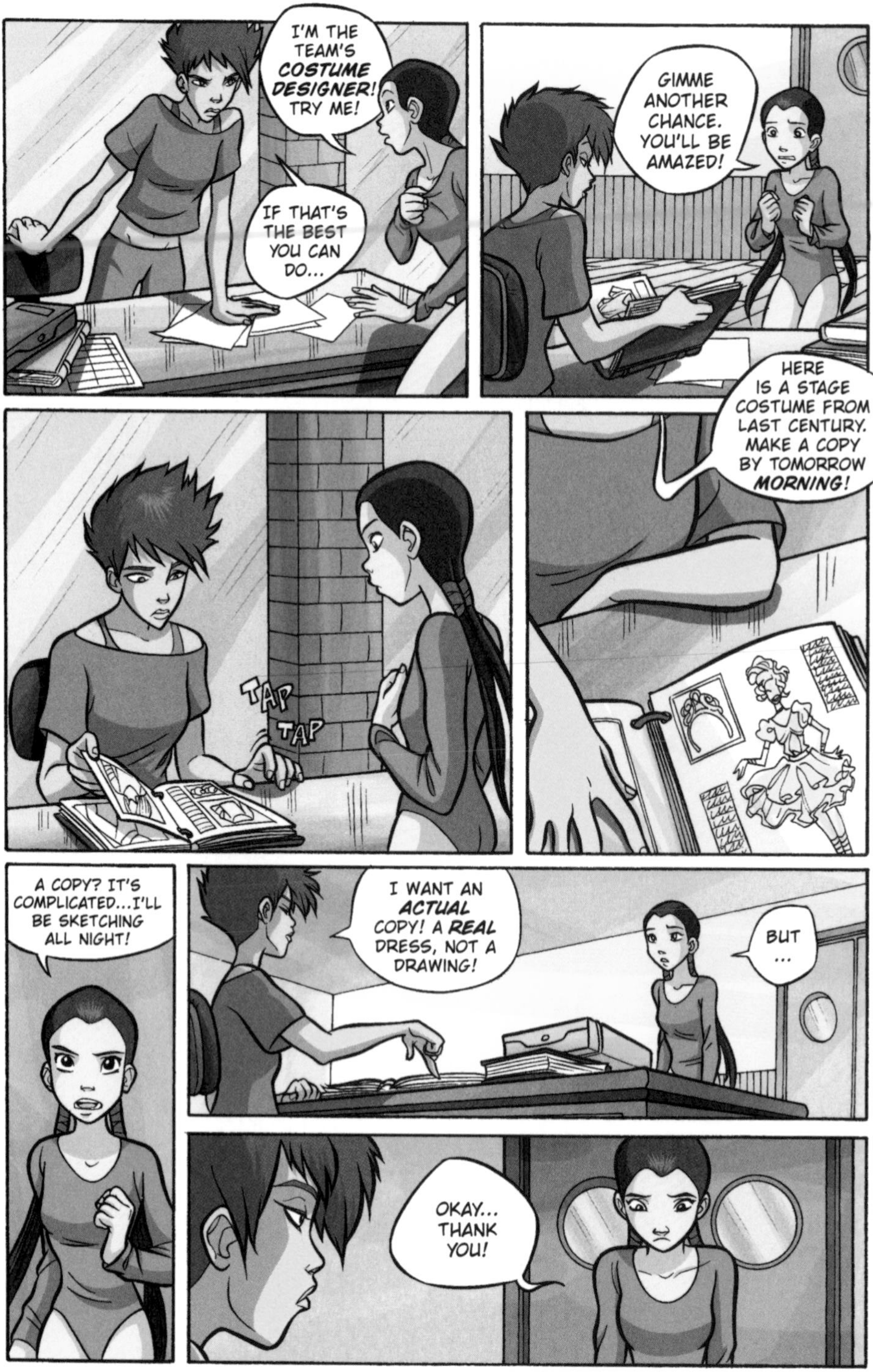
I'M THE TEAM'S *COSTUME DESIGNER*! TRY ME!
IF THAT'S THE BEST YOU CAN DO...
GIMME ANOTHER CHANCE. YOU'LL BE AMAZED!
TAP
TAP
HERE IS A STAGE COSTUME FROM LAST CENTURY. MAKE A COPY BY TOMORROW *MORNING*!
A COPY? IT'S COMPLICATED...I'LL BE SKETCHING ALL NIGHT!
I WANT AN *ACTUAL* COPY! A *REAL* DRESS, NOT A DRAWING!
BUT ...
OKAY... THANK YOU!

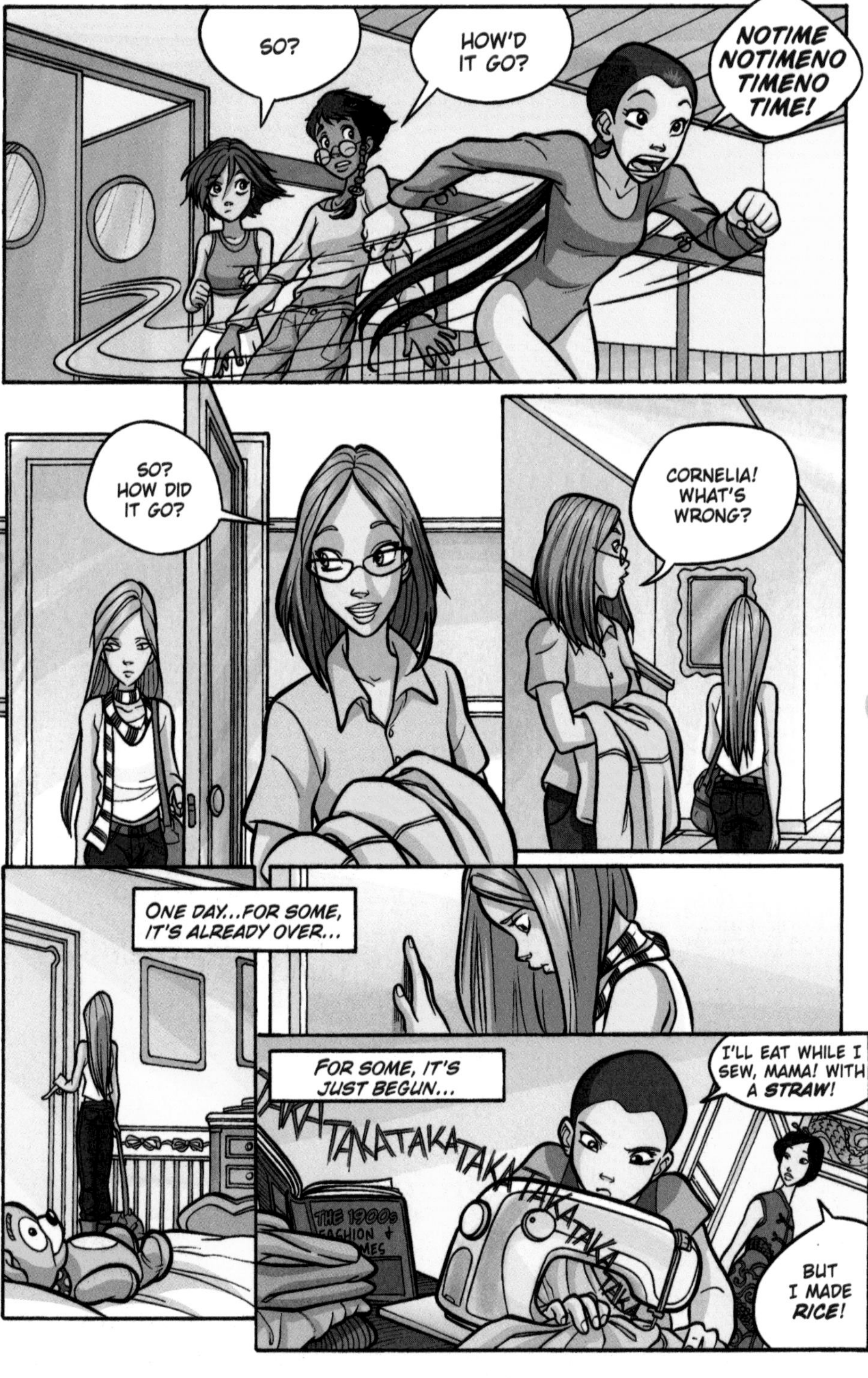
SO?
HOW'D IT GO?
NOTIME NOTIMENO TIMENO TIME!
SO? HOW DID IT GO?
CORNELIA! WHAT'S WRONG?
ONE DAY...FOR SOME, IT'S ALREADY OVER...
FOR SOME, IT'S JUST BEGUN...
I'LL EAT WHILE I SEW, MAMA! WITH A STRAW!
TAKATAKATAKATAKATAKATAKATAKATAKA
THE 1900s FASHION +
BUT I MADE RICE!

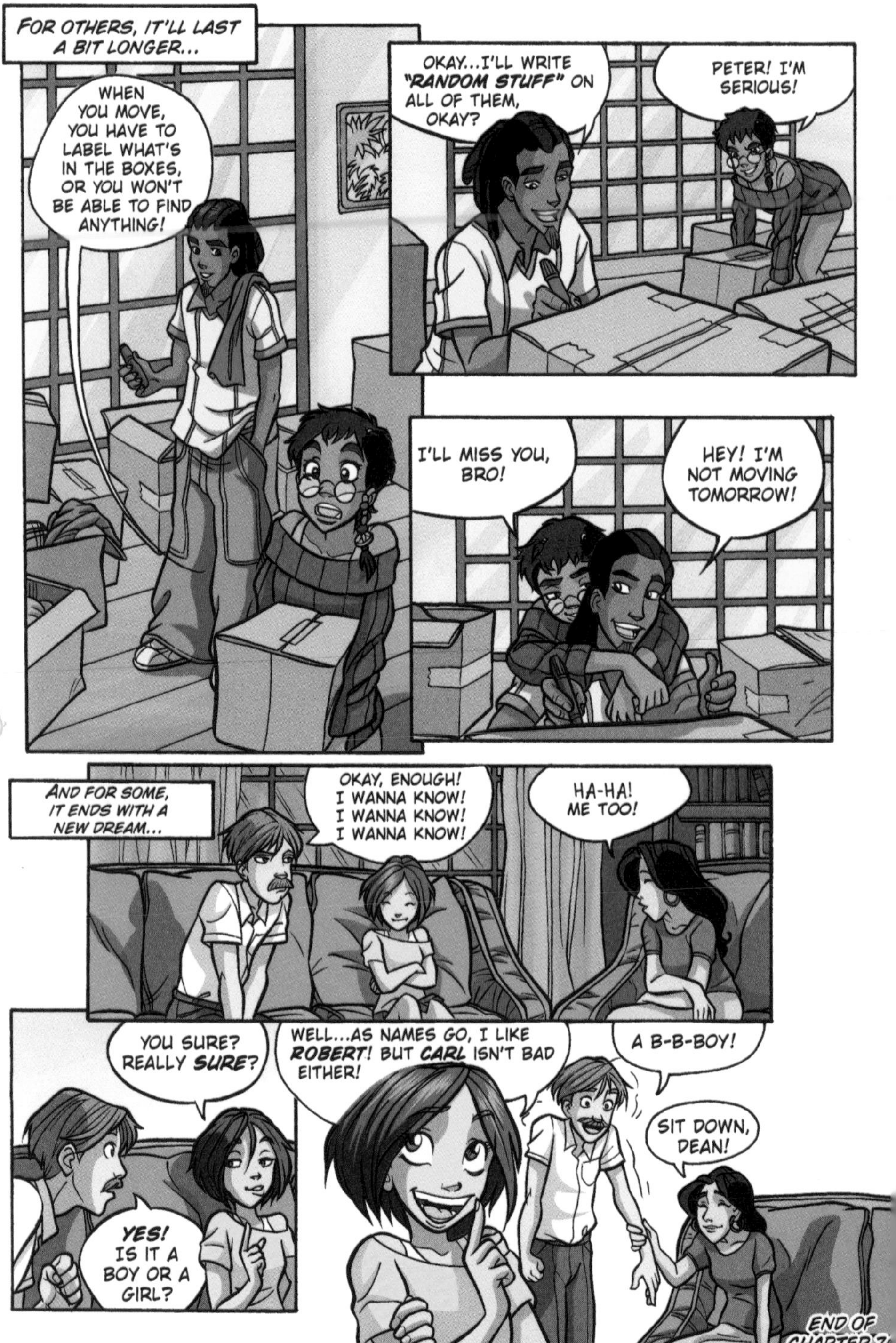
FOR OTHERS, IT'LL LAST A BIT LONGER...
WHEN YOU MOVE, YOU HAVE TO LABEL WHAT'S IN THE BOXES, OR YOU WON'T BE ABLE TO FIND ANYTHING!
OKAY...I'LL WRITE "RANDOM STUFF" ON ALL OF THEM, OKAY?
PETER! I'M SERIOUS!
I'LL MISS YOU, BRO!
HEY! I'M NOT MOVING TOMORROW!
AND FOR SOME, IT ENDS WITH A NEW DREAM...
OKAY, ENOUGH! I WANNA KNOW! I WANNA KNOW! I WANNA KNOW!
HA-HA! ME TOO!
YOU SURE? REALLY SURE?
YES! IS IT A BOY OR A GIRL?
WELL...AS NAMES GO, I LIKE ROBERT! BUT CARL ISN'T BAD EITHER!
A B-B-BOY!
SIT DOWN, DEAN!
END OF CHAPTER 7

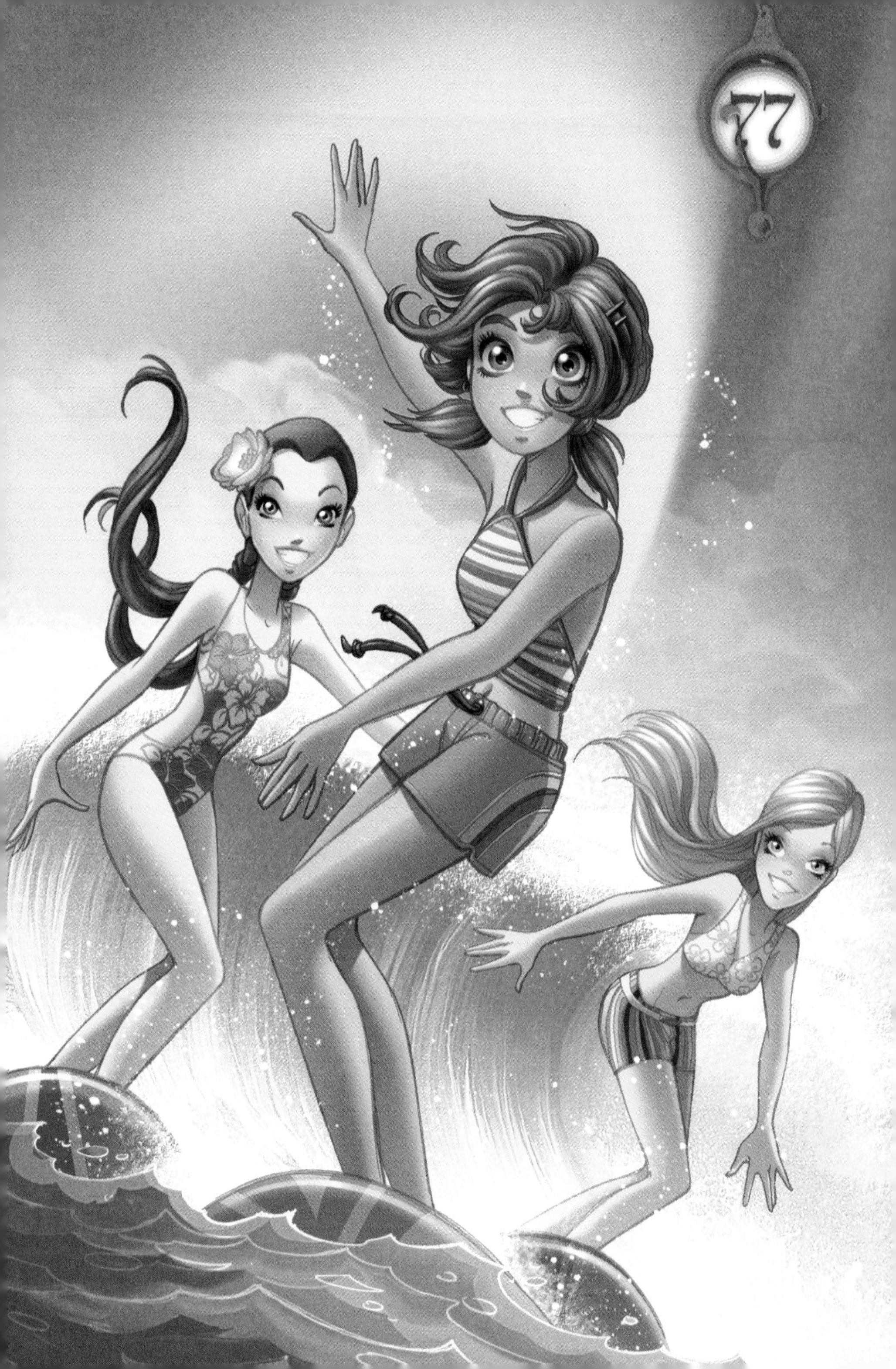
77

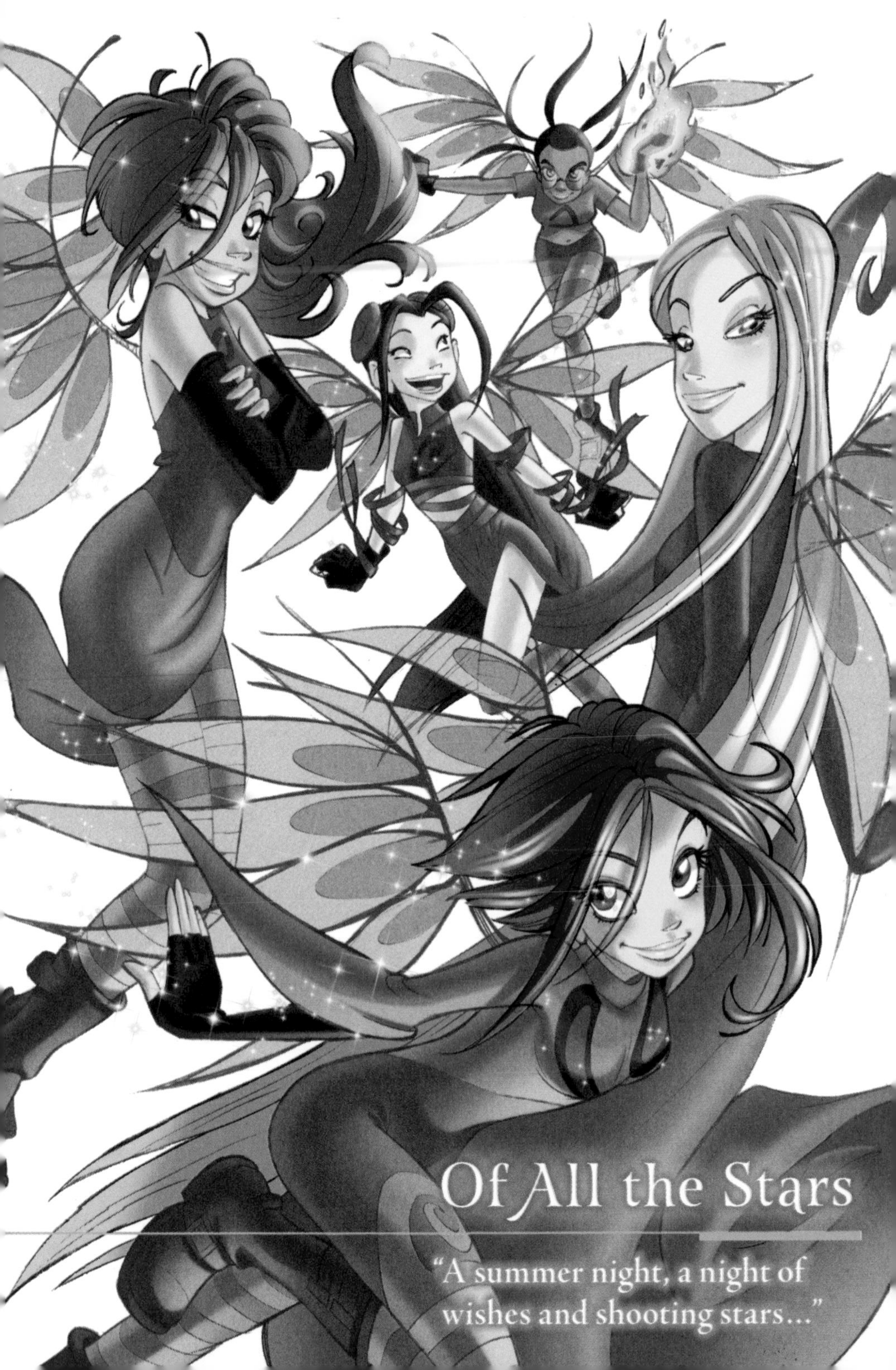

Of All the Stars

"A summer night, a night of
wishes and shooting stars..."

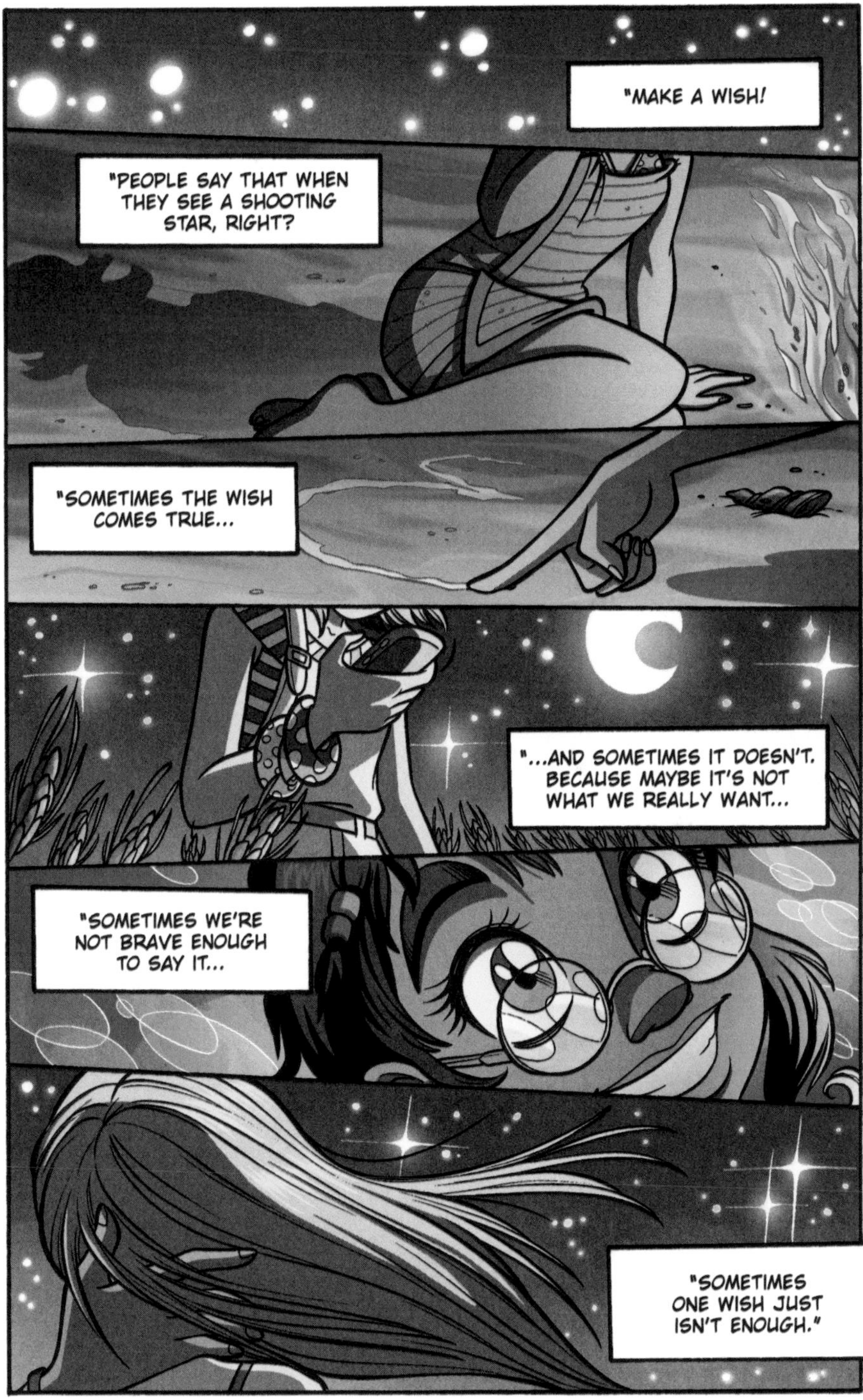
"MAKE A WISH!
"PEOPLE SAY THAT WHEN THEY SEE A SHOOTING STAR, RIGHT?
"SOMETIMES THE WISH COMES TRUE...
"...AND SOMETIMES IT DOESN'T. BECAUSE MAYBE IT'S NOT WHAT WE REALLY WANT...
"SOMETIMES WE'RE NOT BRAVE ENOUGH TO SAY IT...
"SOMETIMES ONE WISH JUST ISN'T ENOUGH."

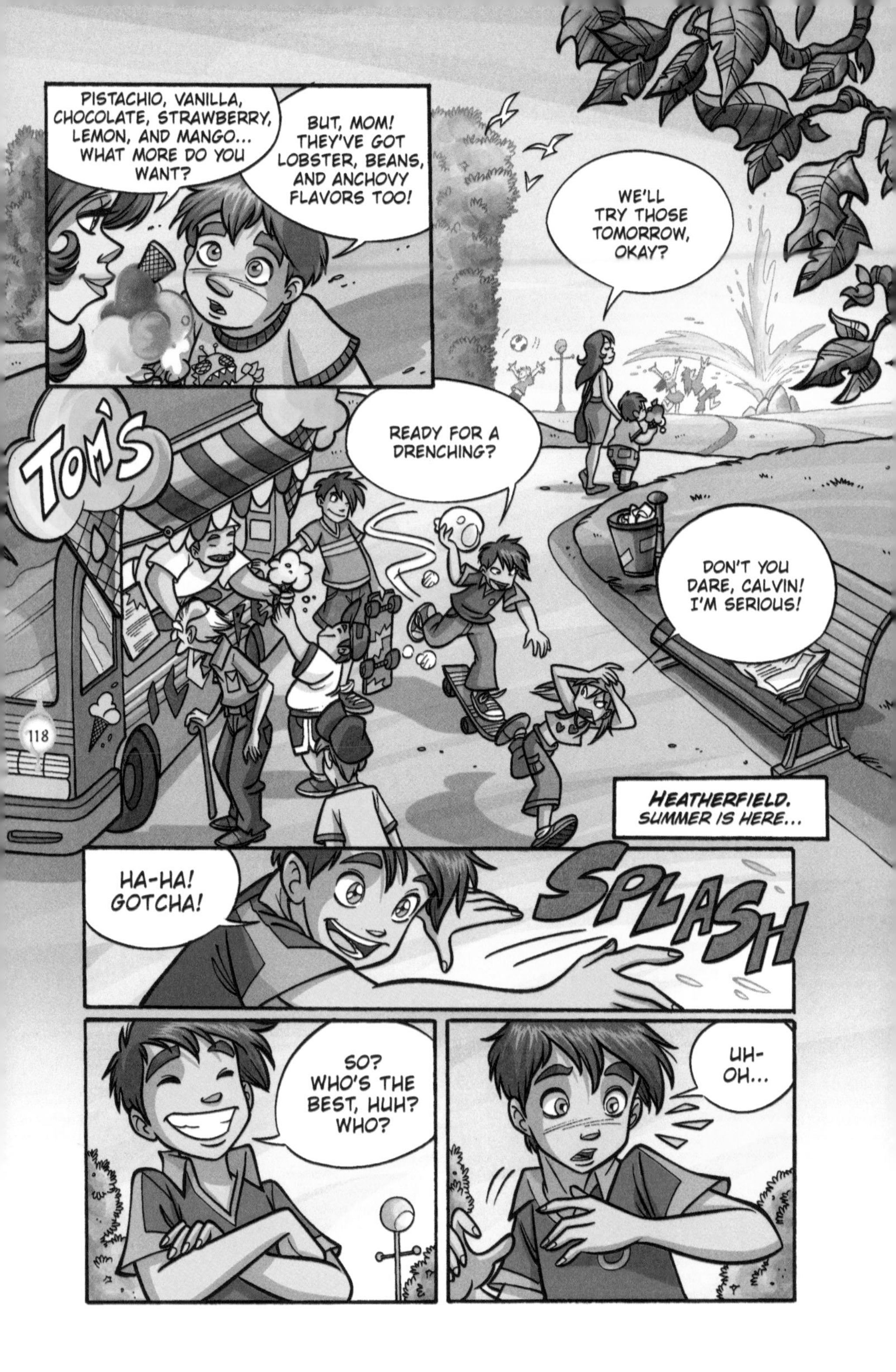
PISTACHIO, VANILLA, CHOCOLATE, STRAWBERRY, LEMON, AND MANGO... WHAT MORE DO YOU WANT?
BUT, MOM! THEY'VE GOT LOBSTER, BEANS, AND ANCHOVY FLAVORS TOO!
WE'LL TRY THOSE TOMORROW, OKAY?
TOM'S
READY FOR A DRENCHING?
DON'T YOU DARE, CALVIN! I'M SERIOUS!
HEATHERFIELD. SUMMER IS HERE...
HA-HA! GOTCHA!
SPLASH
SO? WHO'S THE BEST, HUH? WHO?
UH-OH...

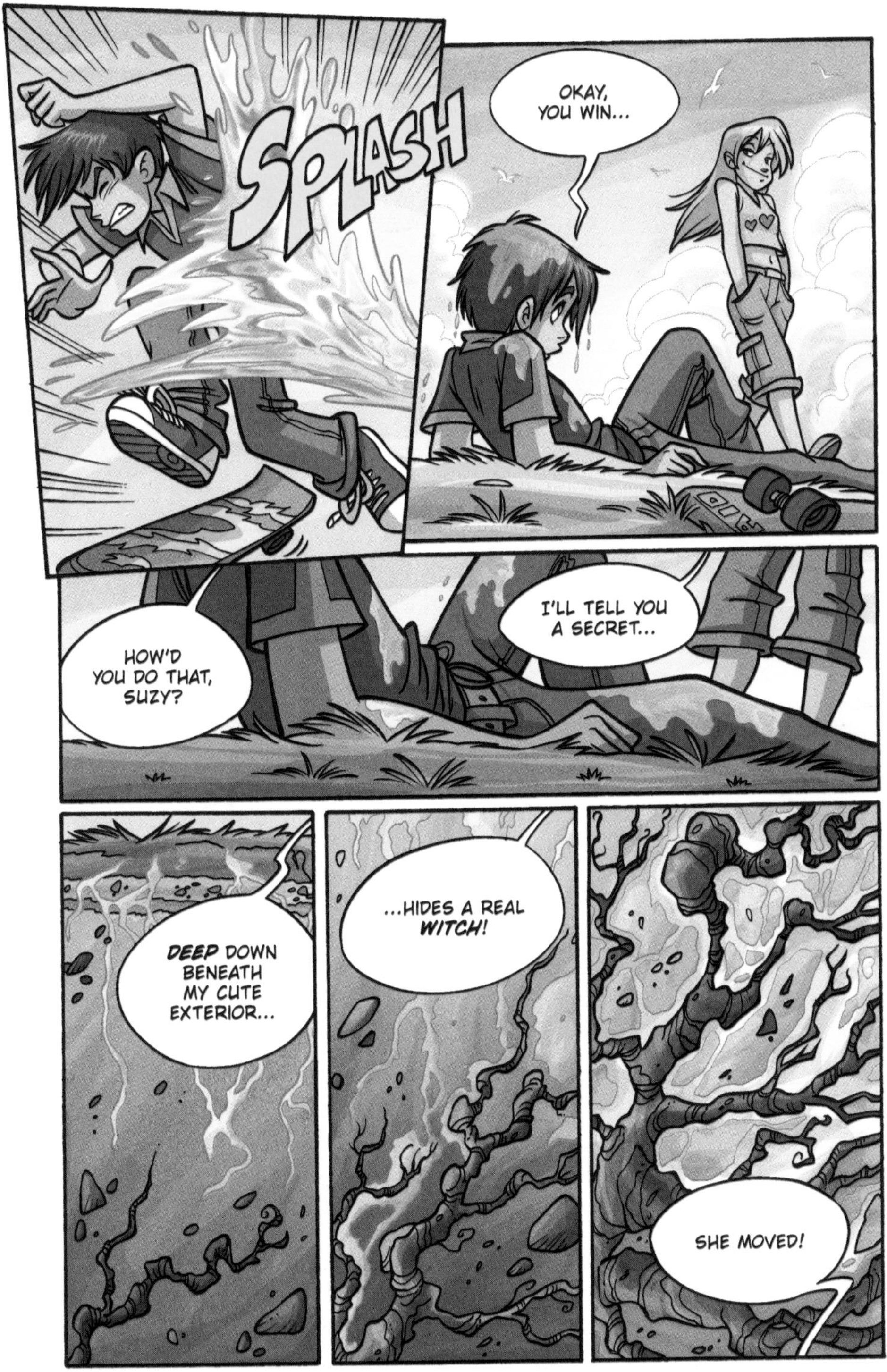
SPLASH
OKAY, YOU WIN...
HOW'D YOU DO THAT, SUZY?
I'LL TELL YOU A SECRET...
DEEP DOWN BENEATH MY CUTE EXTERIOR...
...HIDES A REAL **WITCH**!
SHE MOVED!

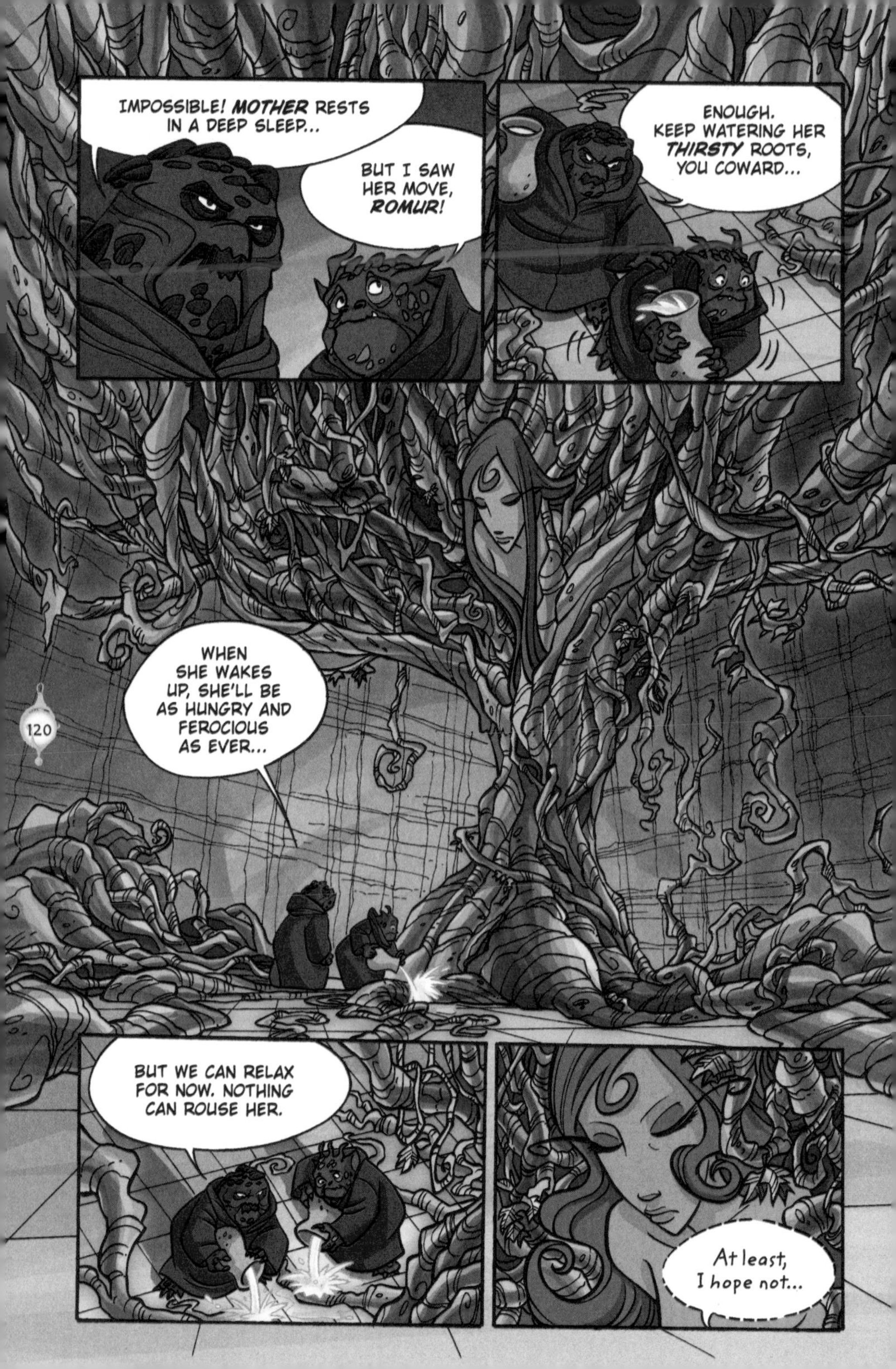
IMPOSSIBLE! MOTHER RESTS IN A DEEP SLEEP...
BUT I SAW HER MOVE, ROMUR!
ENOUGH. KEEP WATERING HER THIRSTY ROOTS, YOU COWARD...
WHEN SHE WAKES UP, SHE'LL BE AS HUNGRY AND FEROCIOUS AS EVER...
BUT WE CAN RELAX FOR NOW. NOTHING CAN ROUSE HER.
At least, I hope not...

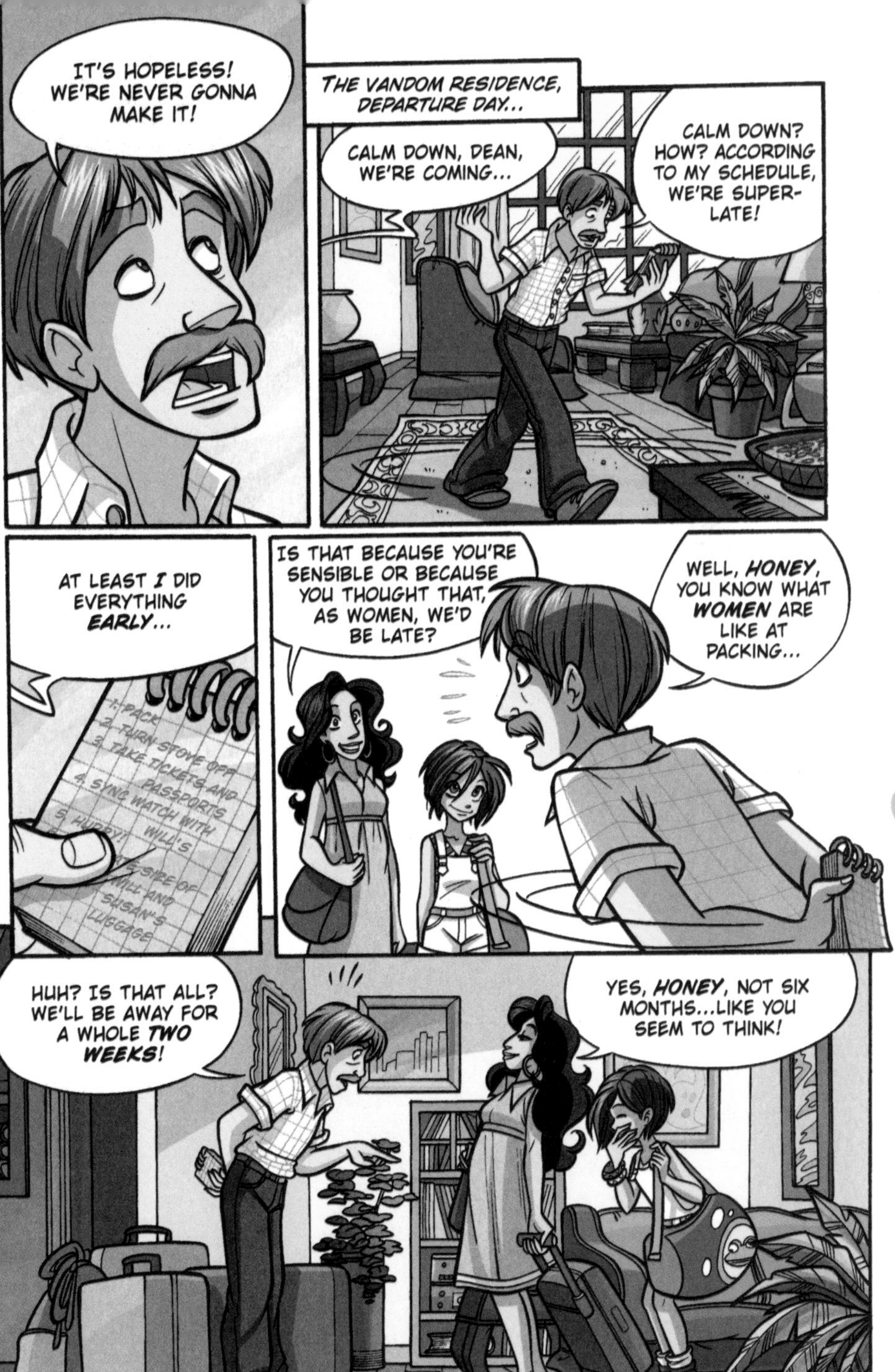

IT'S HOPELESS! WE'RE NEVER GONNA MAKE IT!
THE VANDOM RESIDENCE, DEPARTURE DAY...
CALM DOWN, DEAN, WE'RE COMING...
CALM DOWN? HOW? ACCORDING TO MY SCHEDULE, WE'RE SUPER-LATE!
AT LEAST I DID EVERYTHING EARLY...
1. PACK
2. TURN STOVE OFF
3. TAKE TICKETS AND PASSPORTS
4. SYNC WATCH WITH WILL'S
5. HURRY!
SIZE OF WILL AND SUSAN'S LUGGAGE
IS THAT BECAUSE YOU'RE SENSIBLE OR BECAUSE YOU THOUGHT THAT, AS WOMEN, WE'D BE LATE?
WELL, HONEY, YOU KNOW WHAT WOMEN ARE LIKE AT PACKING...
HUH? IS THAT ALL? WE'LL BE AWAY FOR A WHOLE TWO WEEKS!
YES, HONEY, NOT SIX MONTHS...LIKE YOU SEEM TO THINK!

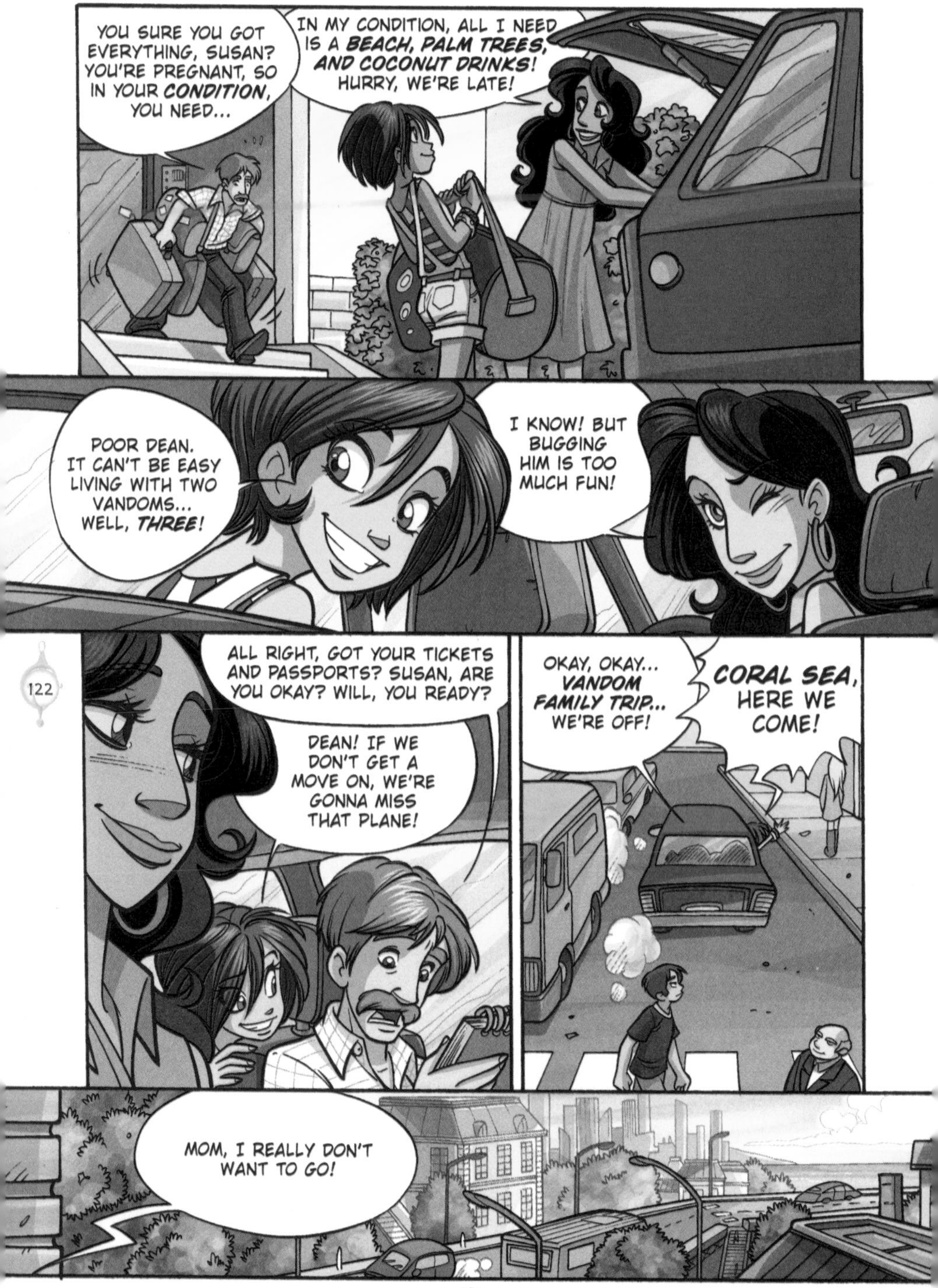
YOU SURE YOU GOT EVERYTHING, SUSAN? YOU'RE PREGNANT, SO IN YOUR CONDITION, YOU NEED...
IN MY CONDITION, ALL I NEED IS A BEACH, PALM TREES, AND COCONUT DRINKS! HURRY, WE'RE LATE!
POOR DEAN. IT CAN'T BE EASY LIVING WITH TWO VANDOMS... WELL, THREE!
I KNOW! BUT BUGGING HIM IS TOO MUCH FUN!
ALL RIGHT, GOT YOUR TICKETS AND PASSPORTS? SUSAN, ARE YOU OKAY? WILL, YOU READY?
DEAN! IF WE DON'T GET A MOVE ON, WE'RE GONNA MISS THAT PLANE!
OKAY, OKAY... VANDOM FAMILY TRIP... WE'RE OFF!
CORAL SEA, HERE WE COME!
MOM, I REALLY DON'T WANT TO GO!

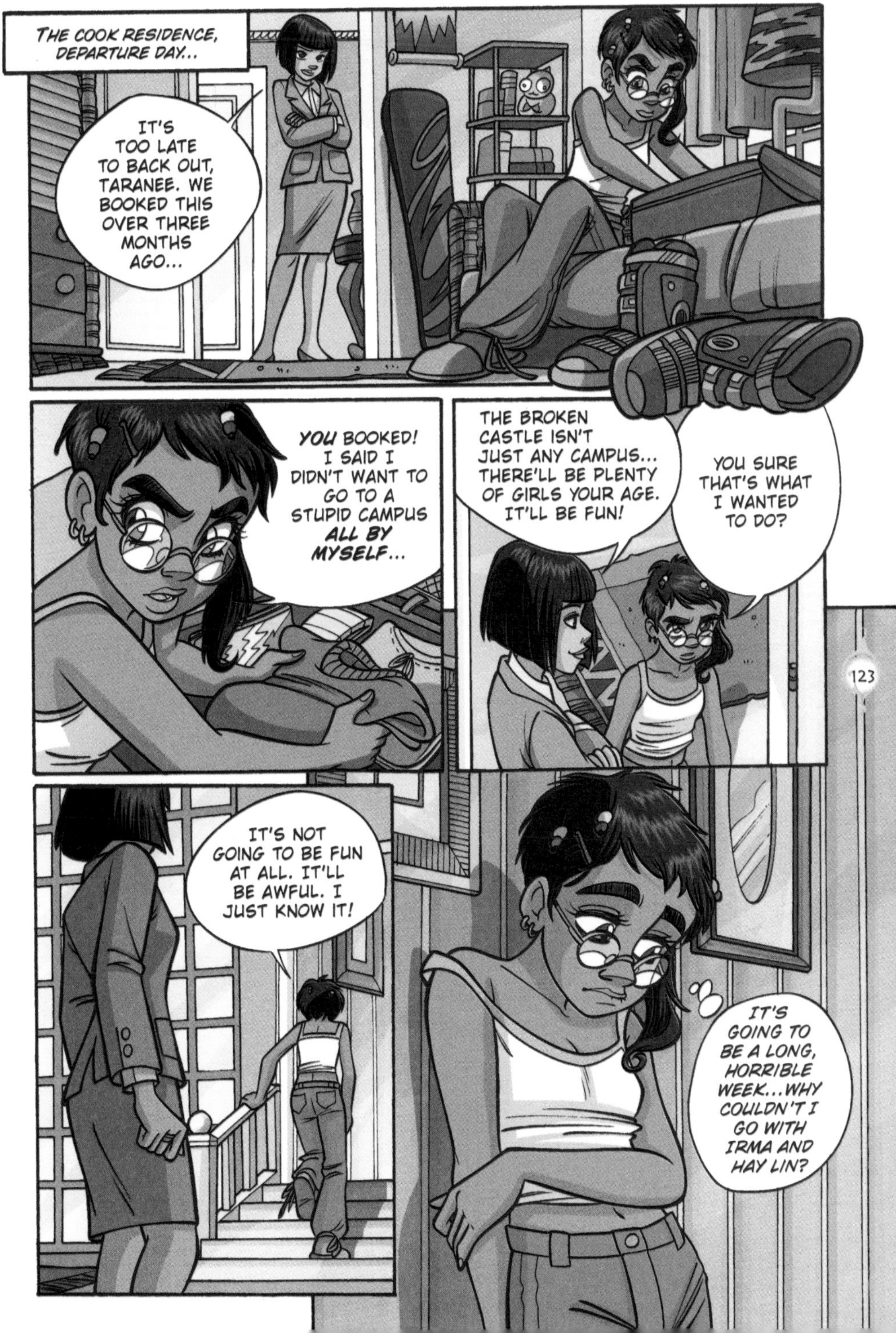
THE COOK RESIDENCE, DEPARTURE DAY...
IT'S TOO LATE TO BACK OUT, TARANEE. WE BOOKED THIS OVER THREE MONTHS AGO...
YOU BOOKED! I SAID I DIDN'T WANT TO GO TO A STUPID CAMPUS ***ALL BY MYSELF***...
THE BROKEN CASTLE ISN'T JUST ANY CAMPUS... THERE'LL BE PLENTY OF GIRLS YOUR AGE. IT'LL BE FUN!
YOU SURE THAT'S WHAT I WANTED TO DO?
IT'S NOT GOING TO BE FUN AT ALL. IT'LL BE AWFUL. I JUST KNOW IT!
IT'S GOING TO BE A LONG, HORRIBLE WEEK...WHY COULDN'T I GO WITH IRMA AND HAY LIN?

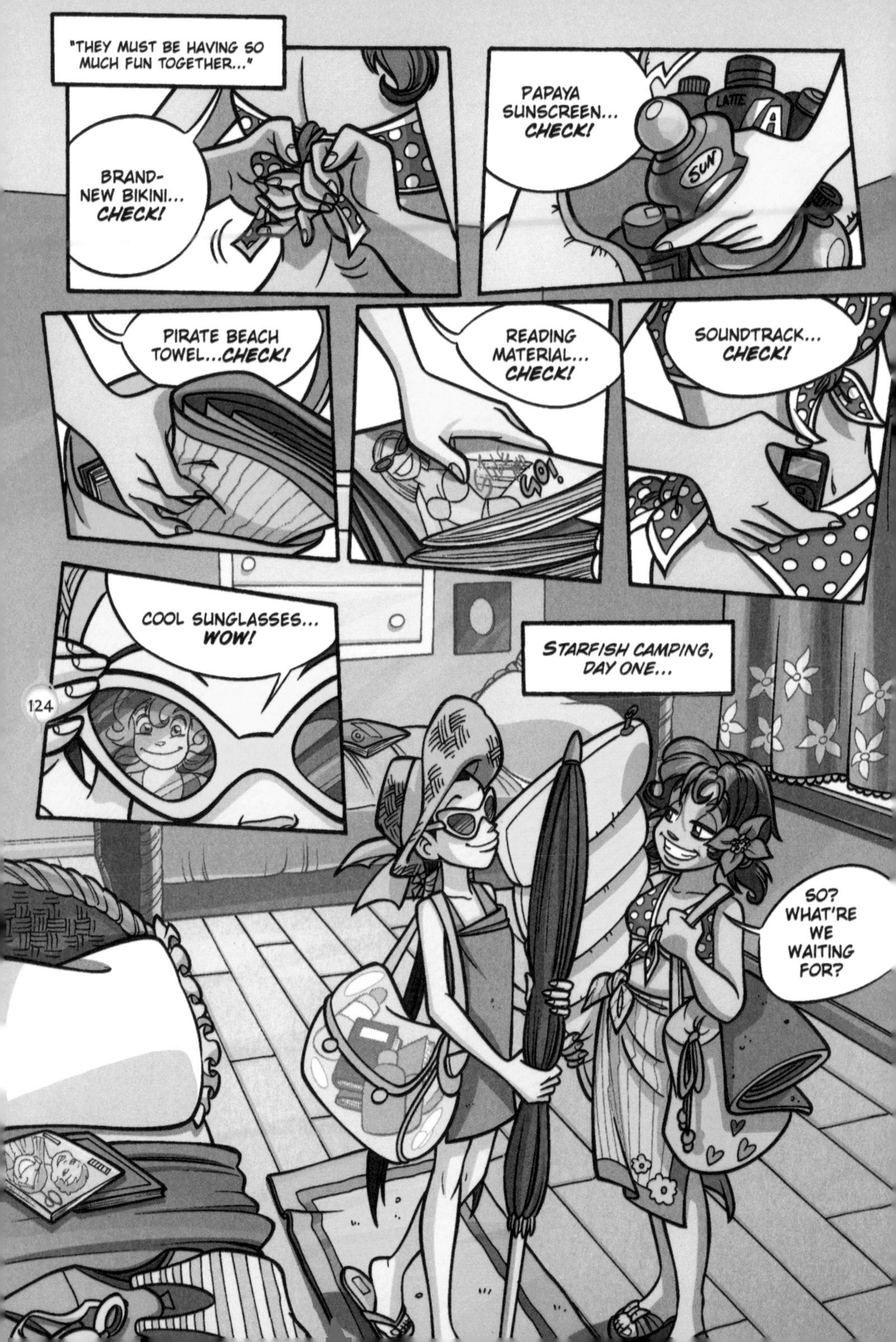
"THEY MUST BE HAVING SO MUCH FUN TOGETHER..."
BRAND-NEW BIKINI... CHECK!
PAPAYA SUNSCREEN... CHECK!
PIRATE BEACH TOWEL...CHECK!
READING MATERIAL... CHECK!
SOUNDTRACK... CHECK!
COOL SUNGLASSES... WOW!
STARFISH CAMPING, DAY ONE...
SO? WHAT'RE WE WAITING FOR?

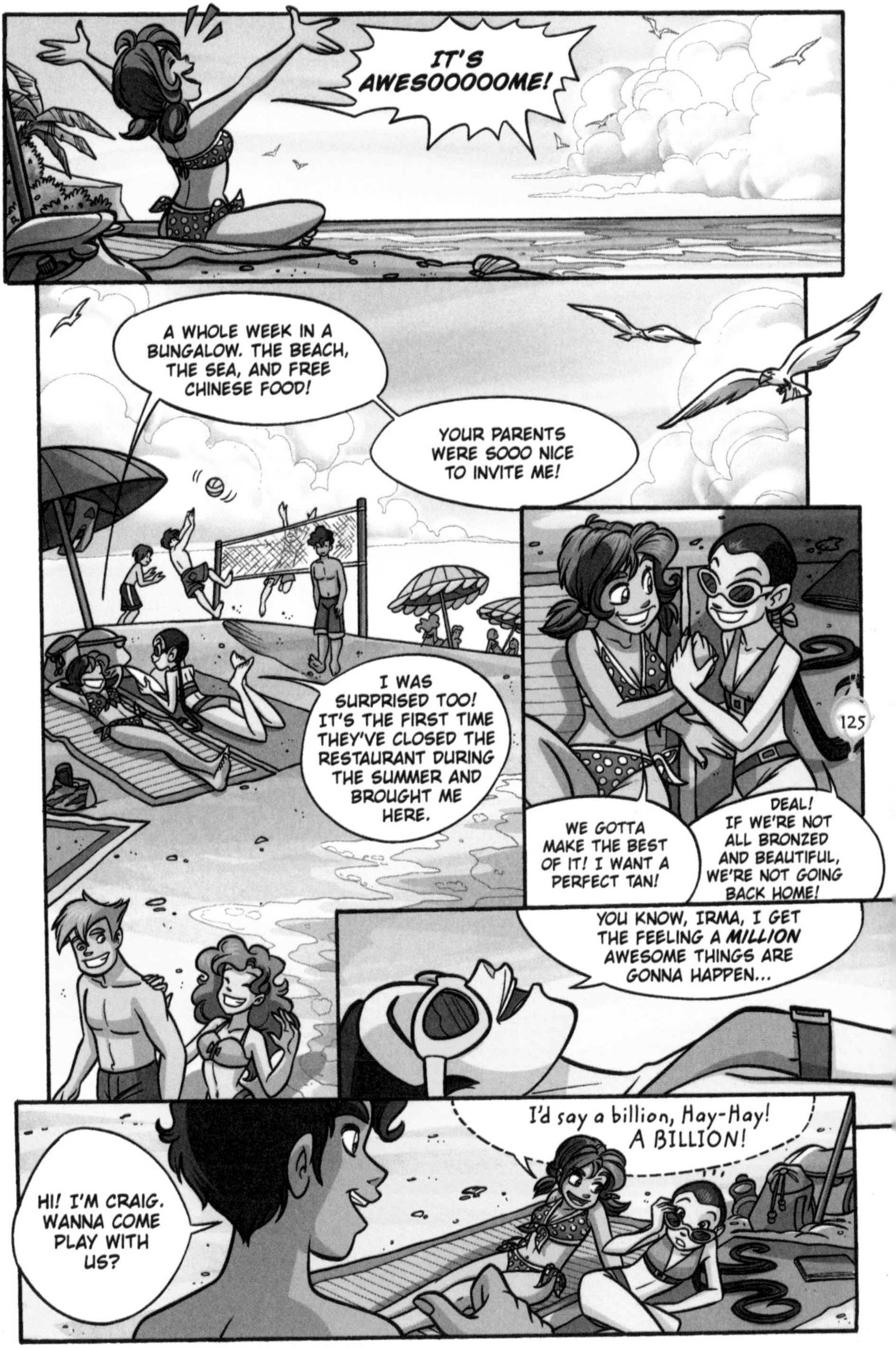
IT'S AWESOOOOOME!
A WHOLE WEEK IN A BUNGALOW. THE BEACH, THE SEA, AND FREE CHINESE FOOD!
YOUR PARENTS WERE SOOO NICE TO INVITE ME!
I WAS SURPRISED TOO! IT'S THE FIRST TIME THEY'VE CLOSED THE RESTAURANT DURING THE SUMMER AND BROUGHT ME HERE.
WE GOTTA MAKE THE BEST OF IT! I WANT A PERFECT TAN!
DEAL! IF WE'RE NOT ALL BRONZED AND BEAUTIFUL, WE'RE NOT GOING BACK HOME!
YOU KNOW, IRMA, I GET THE FEELING A MILLION AWESOME THINGS ARE GONNA HAPPEN...
I'd say a billion, Hay-Hay! A BILLION!
HI! I'M CRAIG. WANNA COME PLAY WITH US?

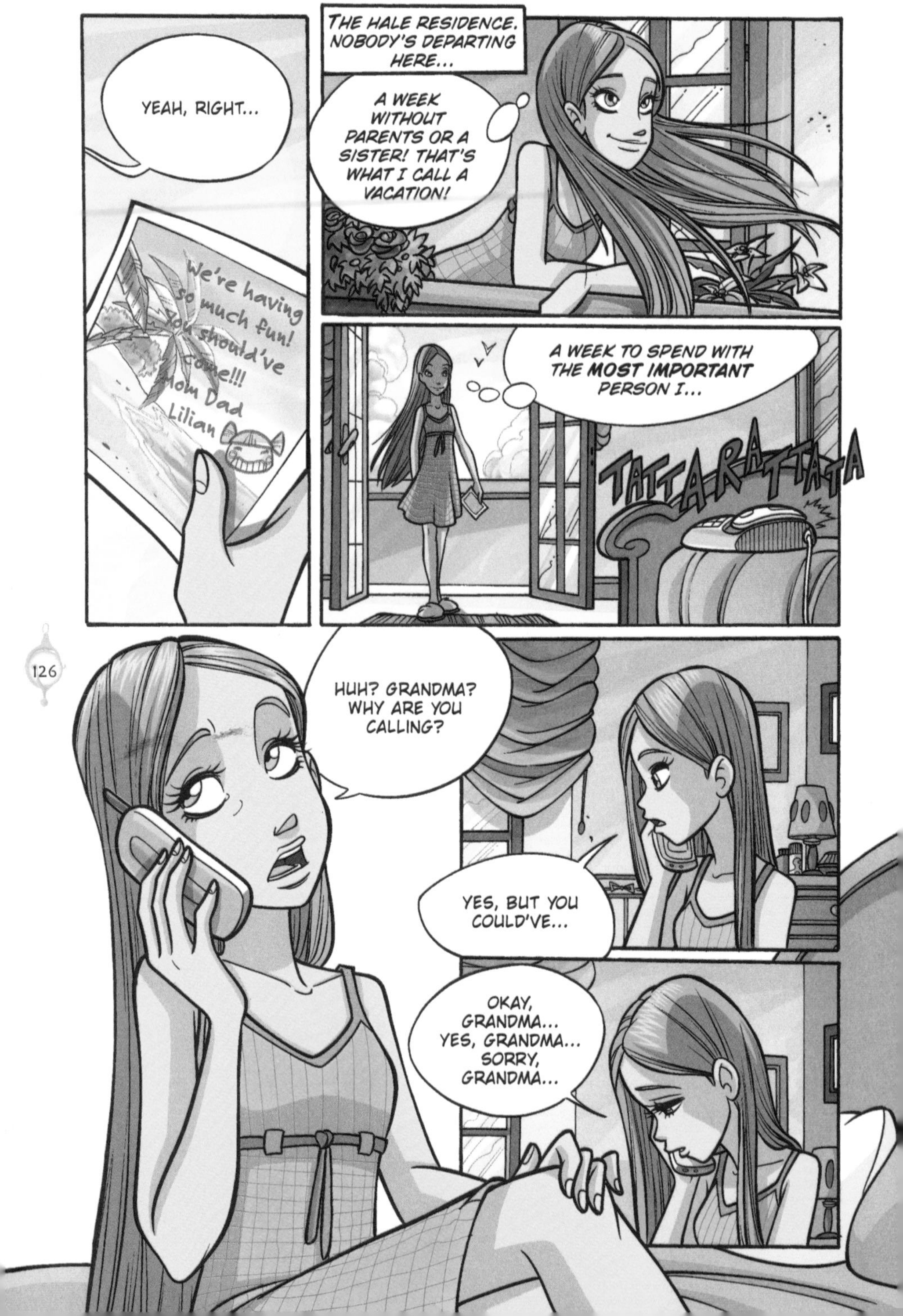
YEAH, RIGHT...
We're having so much fun! You should've come!!! Mom Dad Lilian
THE HALE RESIDENCE. NOBODY'S DEPARTING HERE...
A WEEK WITHOUT PARENTS OR A SISTER! THAT'S WHAT I CALL A VACATION!
A WEEK TO SPEND WITH THE MOST IMPORTANT PERSON I...
TATTARATTATA
HUH? GRANDMA? WHY ARE YOU CALLING?
YES, BUT YOU COULD'VE...
OKAY, GRANDMA... YES, GRANDMA... SORRY, GRANDMA...

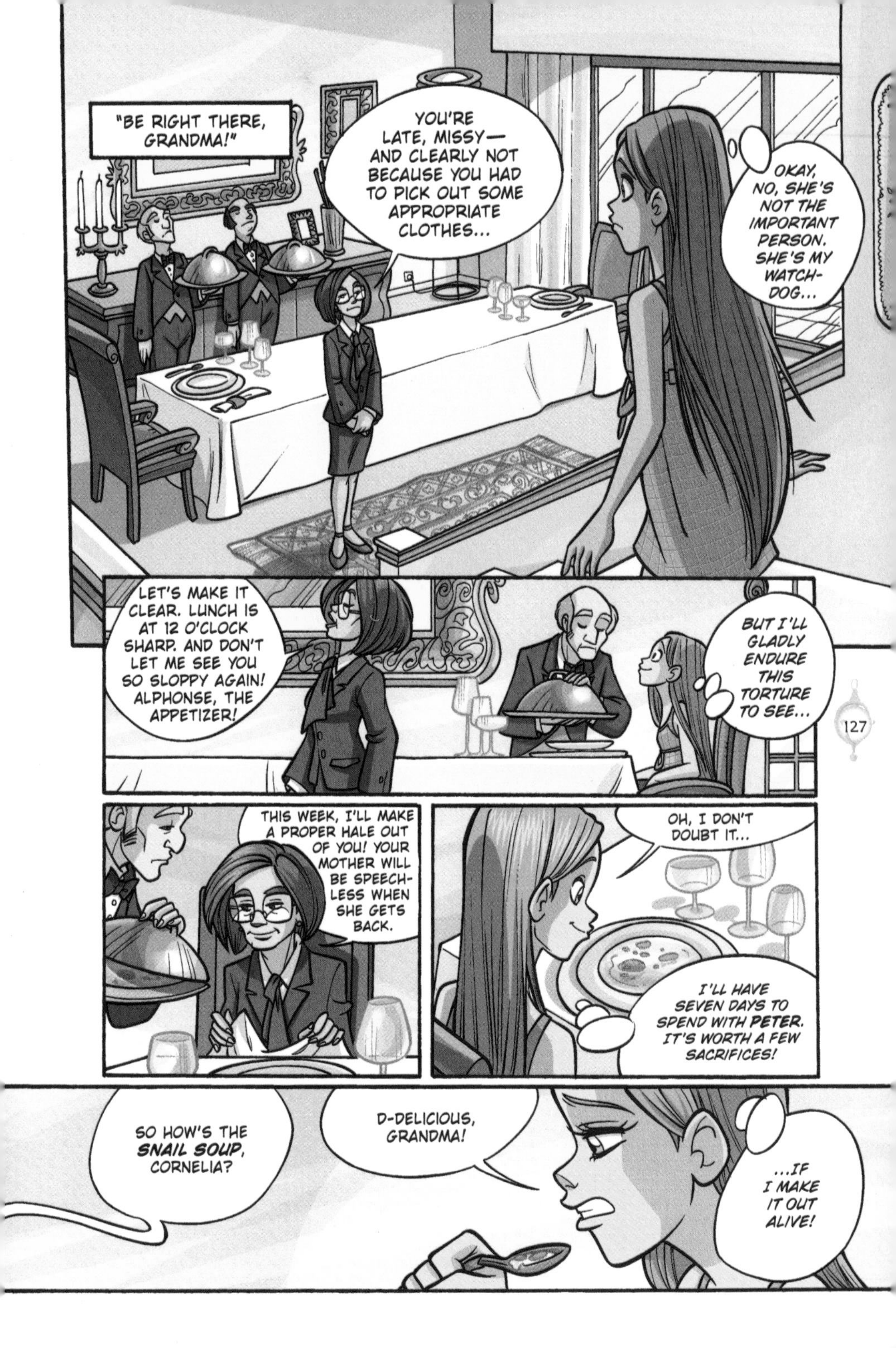

"BE RIGHT THERE, GRANDMA!"
YOU'RE LATE, MISSY—AND CLEARLY NOT BECAUSE YOU HAD TO PICK OUT SOME APPROPRIATE CLOTHES...
OKAY, NO, SHE'S NOT THE IMPORTANT PERSON. SHE'S MY WATCH-DOG...
LET'S MAKE IT CLEAR. LUNCH IS AT 12 O'CLOCK SHARP. AND DON'T LET ME SEE YOU SO SLOPPY AGAIN! ALPHONSE, THE APPETIZER!
BUT I'LL GLADLY ENDURE THIS TORTURE TO SEE...
THIS WEEK, I'LL MAKE A PROPER HALE OUT OF YOU! YOUR MOTHER WILL BE SPEECH-LESS WHEN SHE GETS BACK.
OH, I DON'T DOUBT IT...
I'LL HAVE SEVEN DAYS TO SPEND WITH **PETER**. IT'S WORTH A FEW SACRIFICES!
SO HOW'S THE **SNAIL SOUP**, CORNELIA?
D-DELICIOUS, GRANDMA!
...IF I MAKE IT OUT ALIVE!

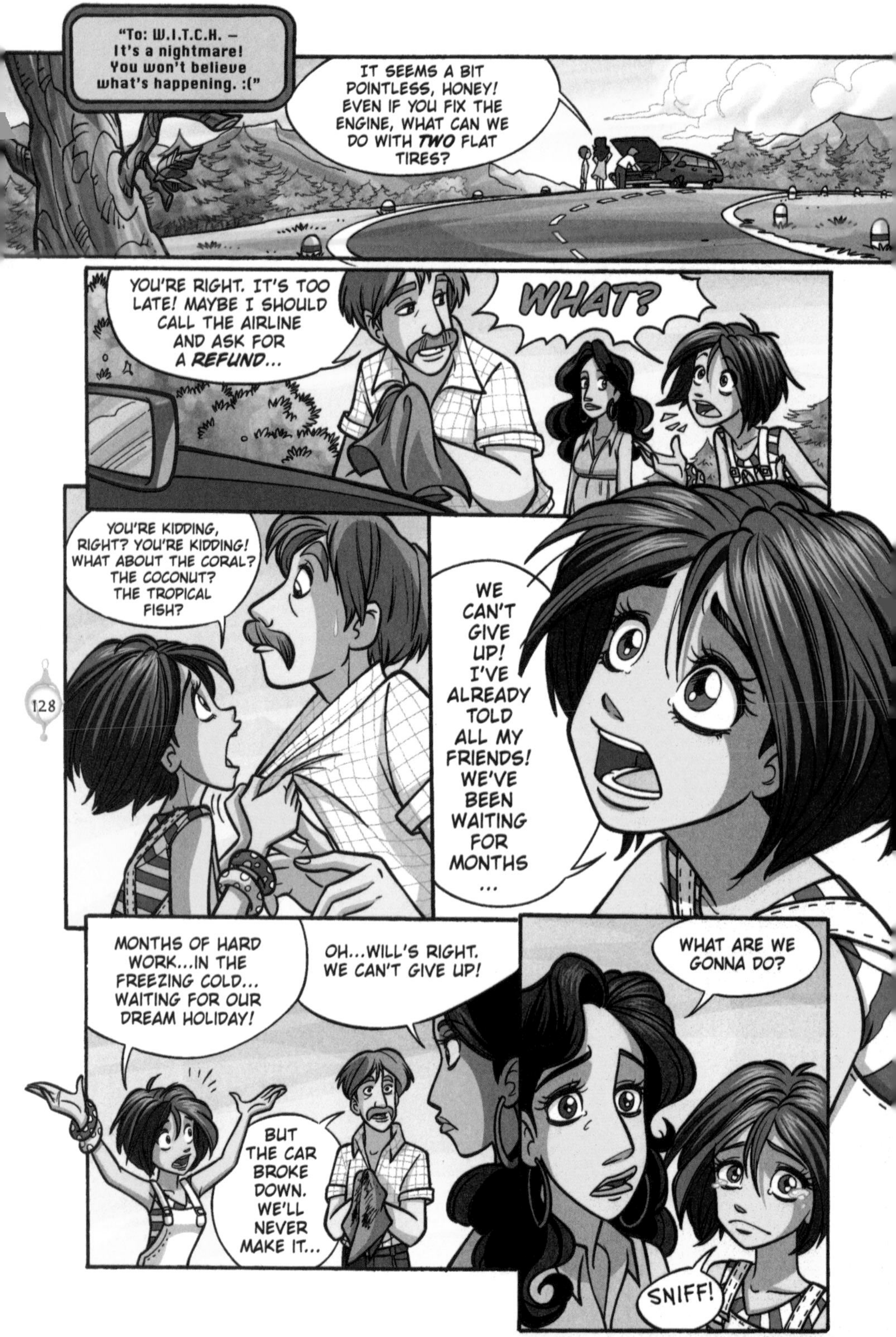
"To: W.I.T.C.H. – It's a nightmare! You won't believe what's happening. :("
IT SEEMS A BIT POINTLESS, HONEY! EVEN IF YOU FIX THE ENGINE, WHAT CAN WE DO WITH TWO FLAT TIRES?
YOU'RE RIGHT. IT'S TOO LATE! MAYBE I SHOULD CALL THE AIRLINE AND ASK FOR A REFUND...
WHAT?
YOU'RE KIDDING, RIGHT? YOU'RE KIDDING! WHAT ABOUT THE CORAL? THE COCONUT? THE TROPICAL FISH?
WE CAN'T GIVE UP! I'VE ALREADY TOLD ALL MY FRIENDS! WE'VE BEEN WAITING FOR MONTHS...
MONTHS OF HARD WORK...IN THE FREEZING COLD... WAITING FOR OUR DREAM HOLIDAY!
OH...WILL'S RIGHT. WE CAN'T GIVE UP!
BUT THE CAR BROKE DOWN. WE'LL NEVER MAKE IT...
WHAT ARE WE GONNA DO?
SNIFF!

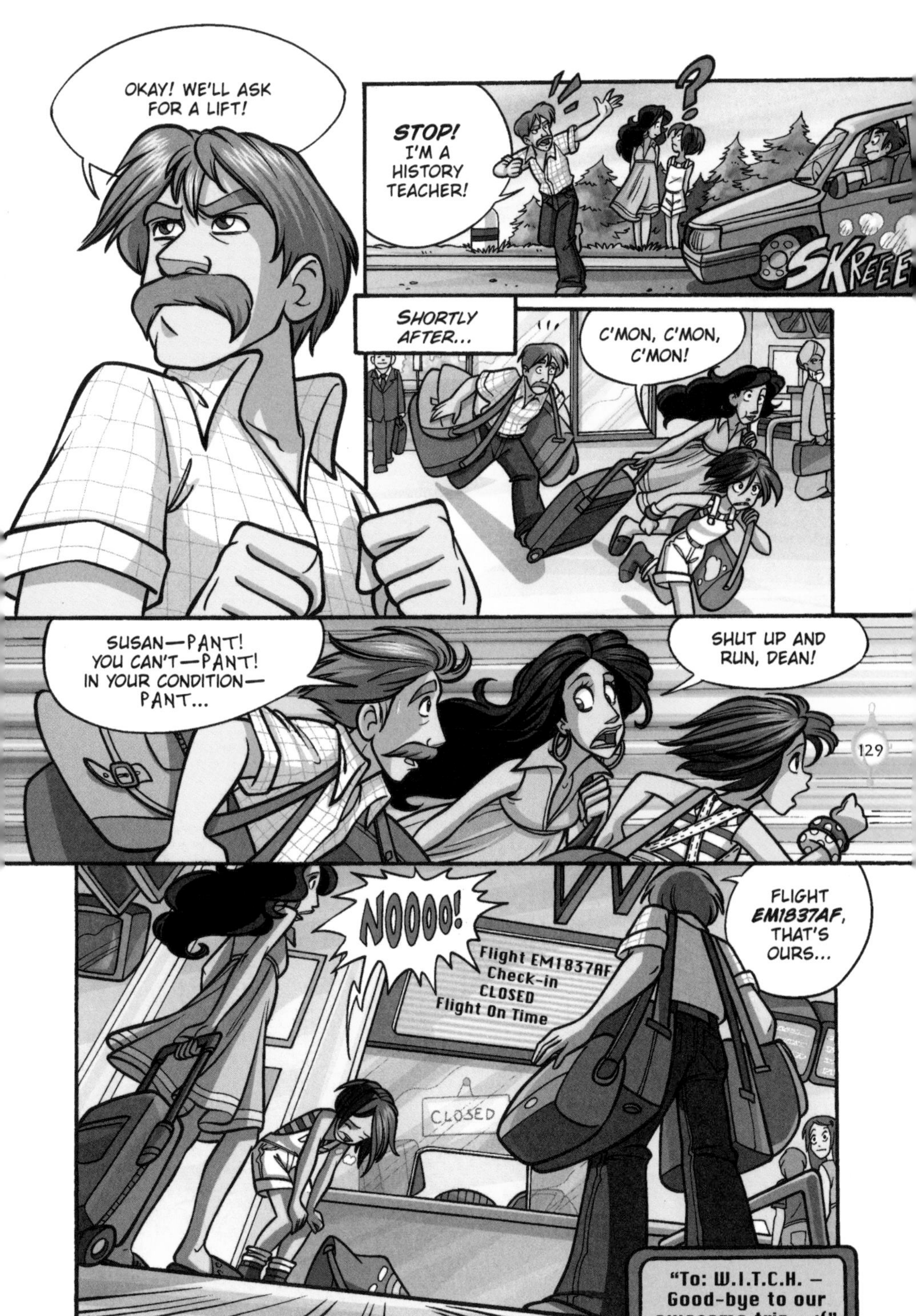
OKAY! WE'LL ASK FOR A LIFT!
STOP! I'M A HISTORY TEACHER!
SKREEE
SHORTLY AFTER...
C'MON, C'MON, C'MON!
SUSAN—PANT! YOU CAN'T—PANT! IN YOUR CONDITION—PANT...
SHUT UP AND RUN, DEAN!
NOOOO!
Flight EM1837AF Check-in CLOSED Flight On Time
FLIGHT EM1837AF, THAT'S OURS...
CLOSED
"To: W.I.T.C.H. – Good-bye to our awesome trip... :("

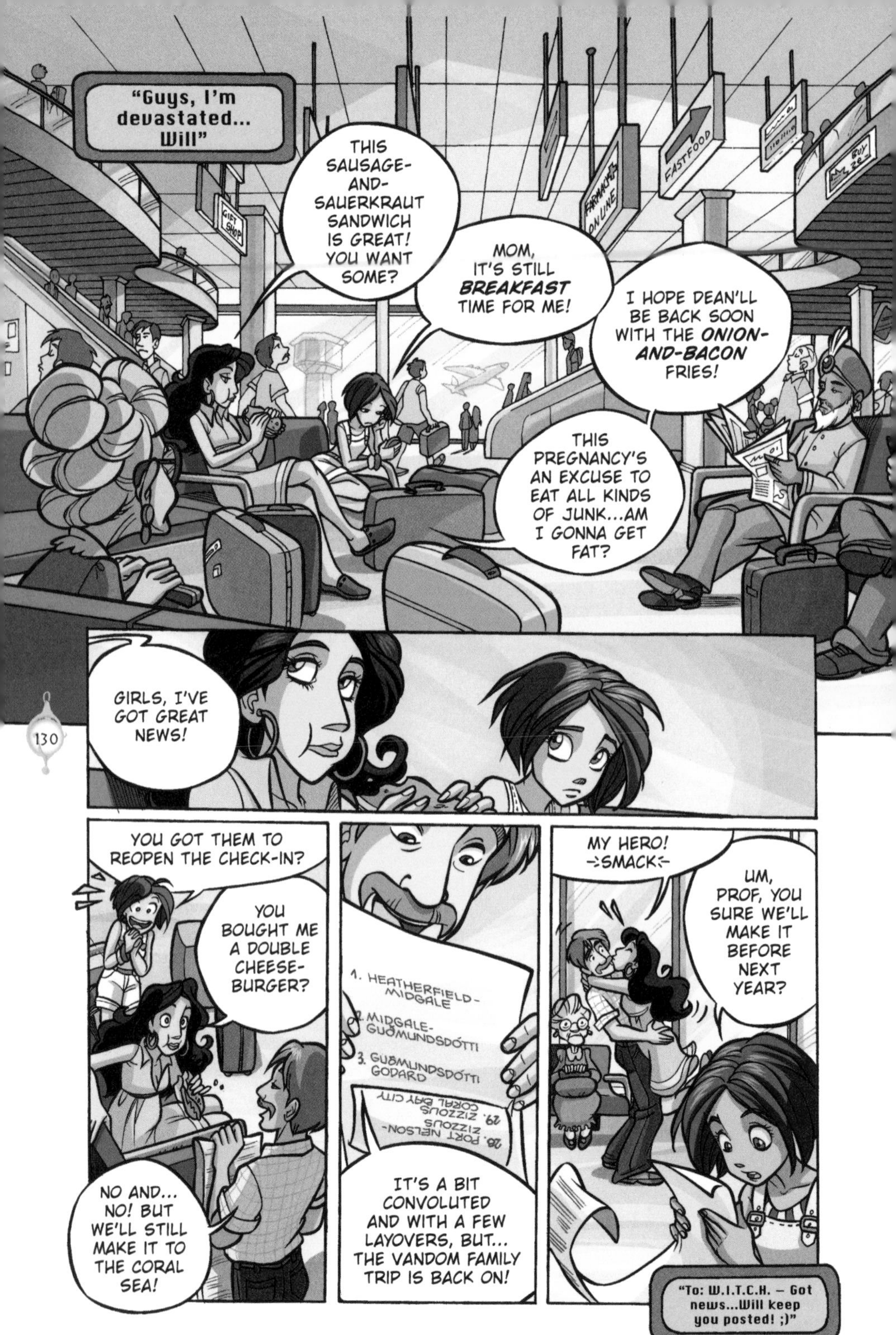

"Guys, I'm devastated... Will"
GIFT SHOP
FASTFOOD
THIS SAUSAGE-AND-SAUERKRAUT SANDWICH IS GREAT! YOU WANT SOME?
MOM, IT'S STILL ***BREAKFAST*** TIME FOR ME!
I HOPE DEAN'LL BE BACK SOON WITH THE ***ONION-AND-BACON*** FRIES!
THIS PREGNANCY'S AN EXCUSE TO EAT ALL KINDS OF JUNK...AM I GONNA GET FAT?
GIRLS, I'VE GOT GREAT NEWS!
YOU GOT THEM TO REOPEN THE CHECK-IN?
YOU BOUGHT ME A DOUBLE CHEESE-BURGER?
NO AND... NO! BUT WE'LL STILL MAKE IT TO THE CORAL SEA!
1. HEATHERFIELD-MIDGALE
2. MIDGALE-GUÐMUNDSDÓTTI
3. GUÐMUNDSDÓTTI GODARD
28. PORT NELSON-ZIZZOUS
29. ZIZZOUS CORAL BAY CITY
IT'S A BIT CONVOLUTED AND WITH A FEW LAYOVERS, BUT... THE VANDOM FAMILY TRIP IS BACK ON!
MY HERO! -SMACK-
UM, PROF, YOU SURE WE'LL MAKE IT BEFORE NEXT YEAR?
"To: W.I.T.C.H. – Got news...Will keep you posted! ;)"

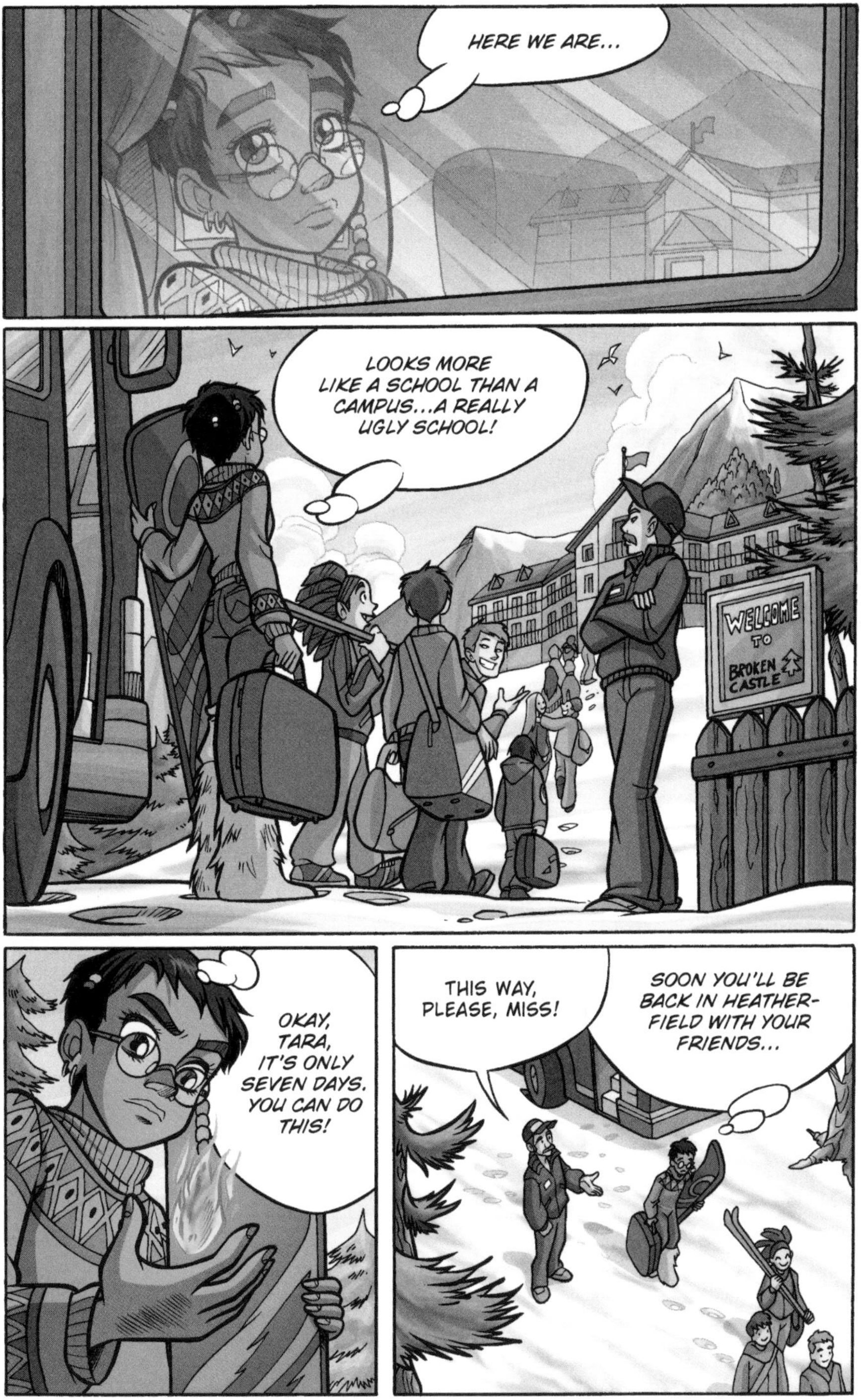
HERE WE ARE...
LOOKS MORE LIKE A SCHOOL THAN A CAMPUS...A REALLY UGLY SCHOOL!
WELCOME TO BROKEN CASTLE
OKAY, TARA, IT'S ONLY SEVEN DAYS. YOU CAN DO THIS!
THIS WAY, PLEASE, MISS!
SOON YOU'LL BE BACK IN HEATHER-FIELD WITH YOUR FRIENDS...

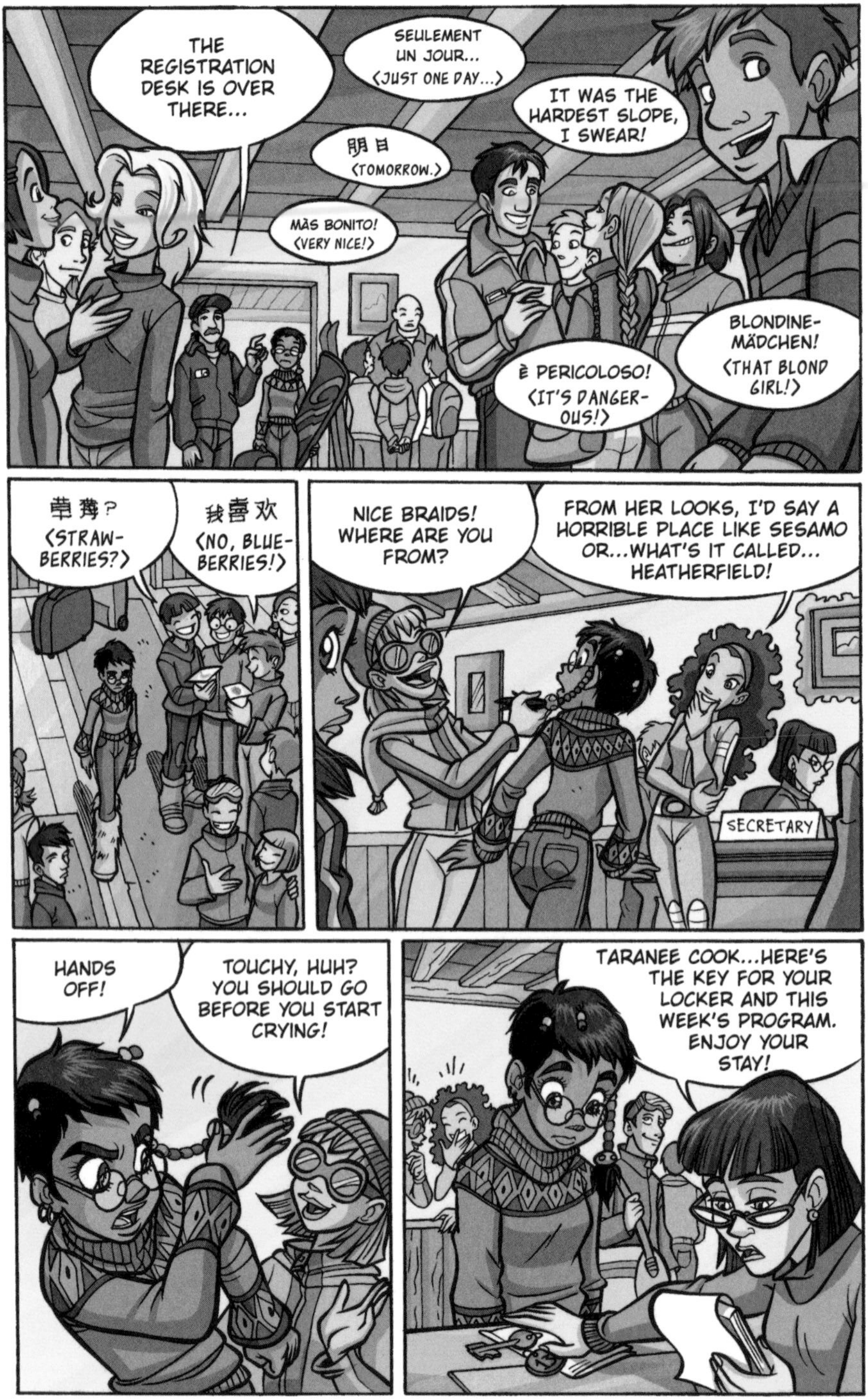

THE REGISTRATION DESK IS OVER THERE...
SEULEMENT UN JOUR... <JUST ONE DAY...>
IT WAS THE HARDEST SLOPE, I SWEAR!
朋日 <TOMORROW.>
MÀS BONITO! <VERY NICE!>
BLONDINE-MÄDCHEN! <THAT BLOND GIRL!>
È PERICOLOSO! <IT'S DANGER-OUS!>
草莓? <STRAW-BERRIES?>
我喜欢 <NO, BLUE-BERRIES!>
NICE BRAIDS! WHERE ARE YOU FROM?
FROM HER LOOKS, I'D SAY A HORRIBLE PLACE LIKE SESAMO OR...WHAT'S IT CALLED... HEATHERFIELD!
SECRETARY
HANDS OFF!
TOUCHY, HUH? YOU SHOULD GO BEFORE YOU START CRYING!
TARANEE COOK...HERE'S THE KEY FOR YOUR LOCKER AND THIS WEEK'S PROGRAM. ENJOY YOUR STAY!

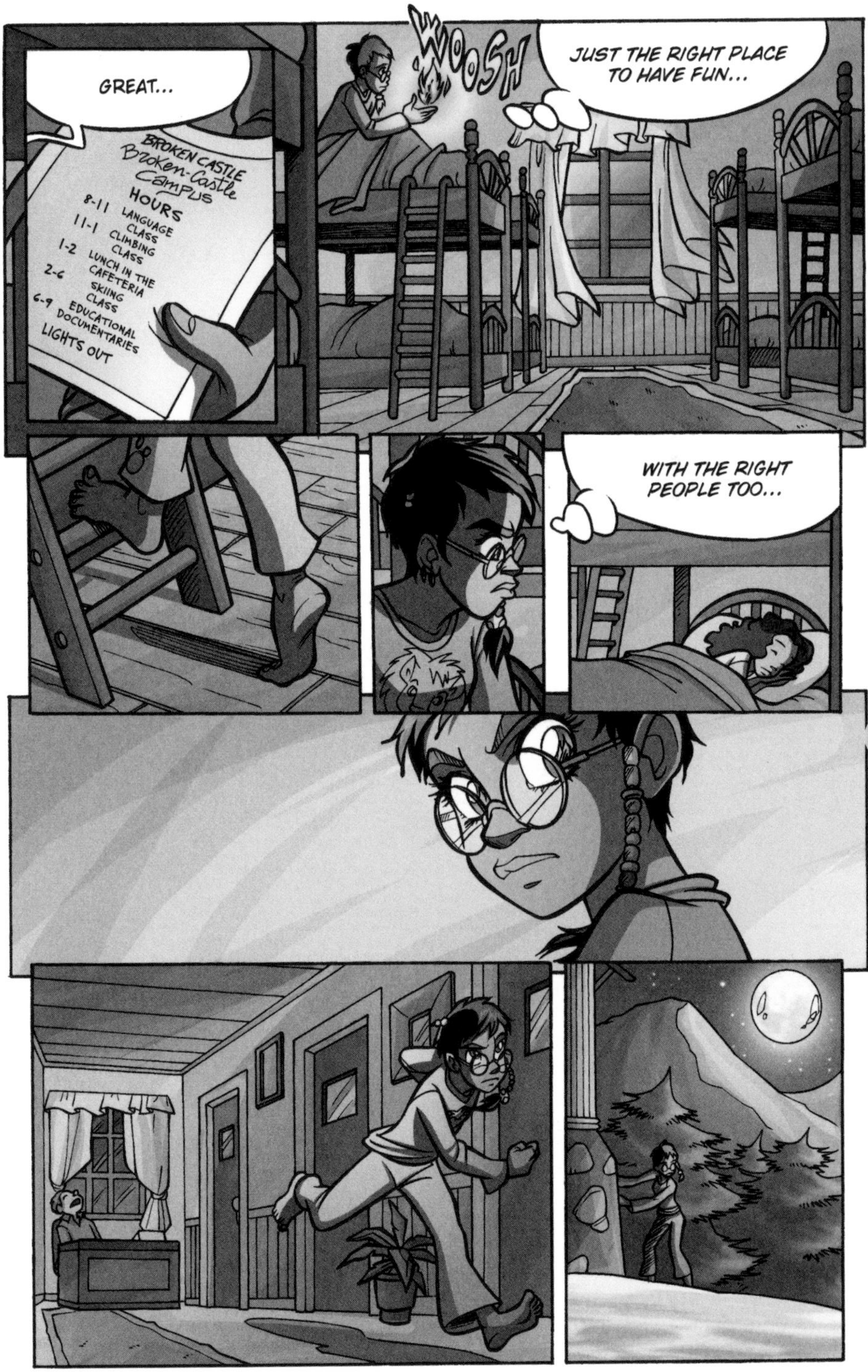
GREAT...
BROKEN CASTLE
Broken-Castle Campus
HOURS
8-11 LANGUAGE CLASS
11-1 CLIMBING CLASS
1-2 LUNCH IN THE CAFETERIA
2-6 SKIING CLASS
6-9 EDUCATIONAL DOCUMENTARIES
LIGHTS OUT
WOOSH
JUST THE RIGHT PLACE TO HAVE FUN...
WITH THE RIGHT PEOPLE TOO...

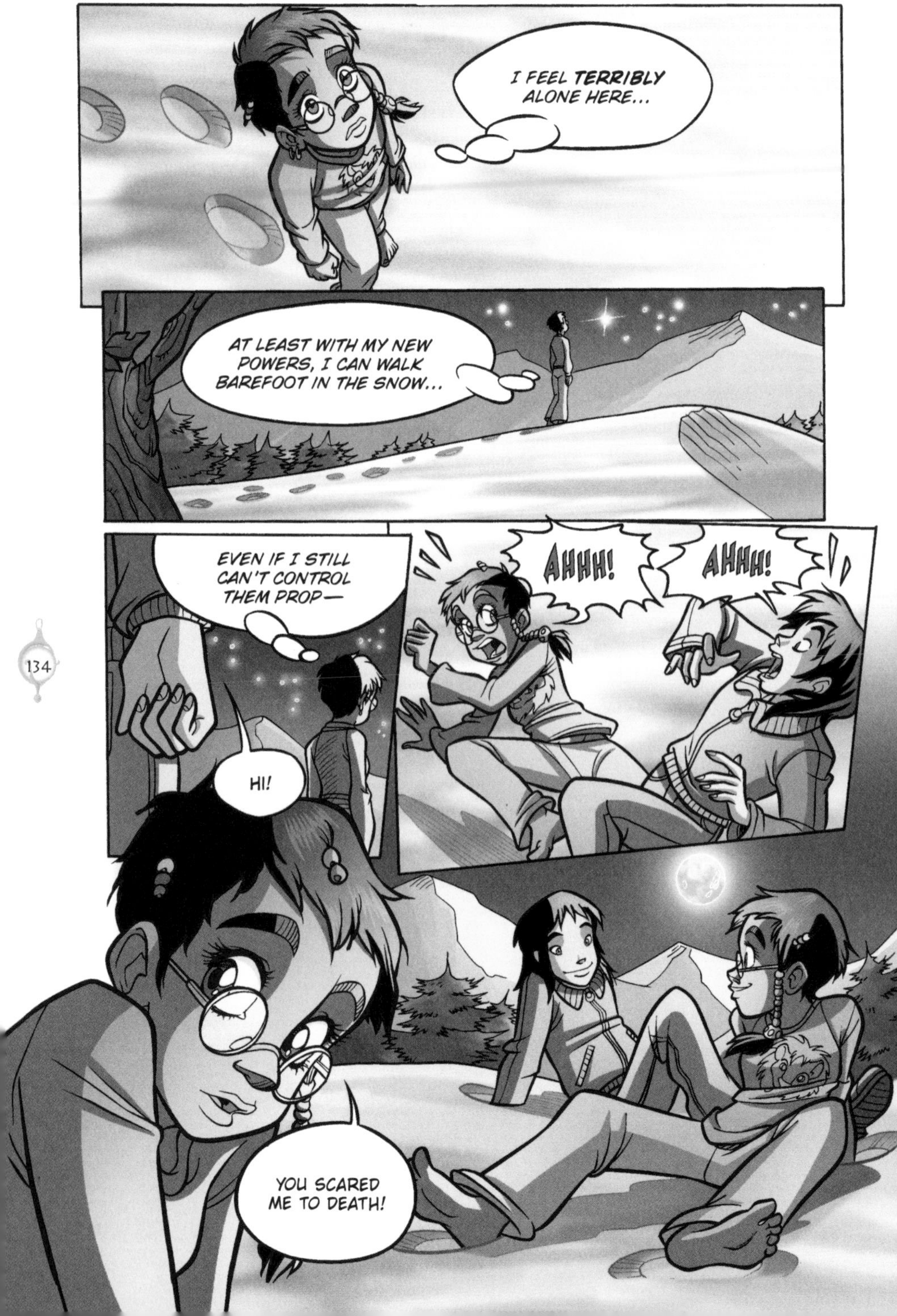
I FEEL TERRIBLY ALONE HERE...
AT LEAST WITH MY NEW POWERS, I CAN WALK BAREFOOT IN THE SNOW...
EVEN IF I STILL CAN'T CONTROL THEM PROP—
HI!
AHHH!
AHHH!
YOU SCARED ME TO DEATH!

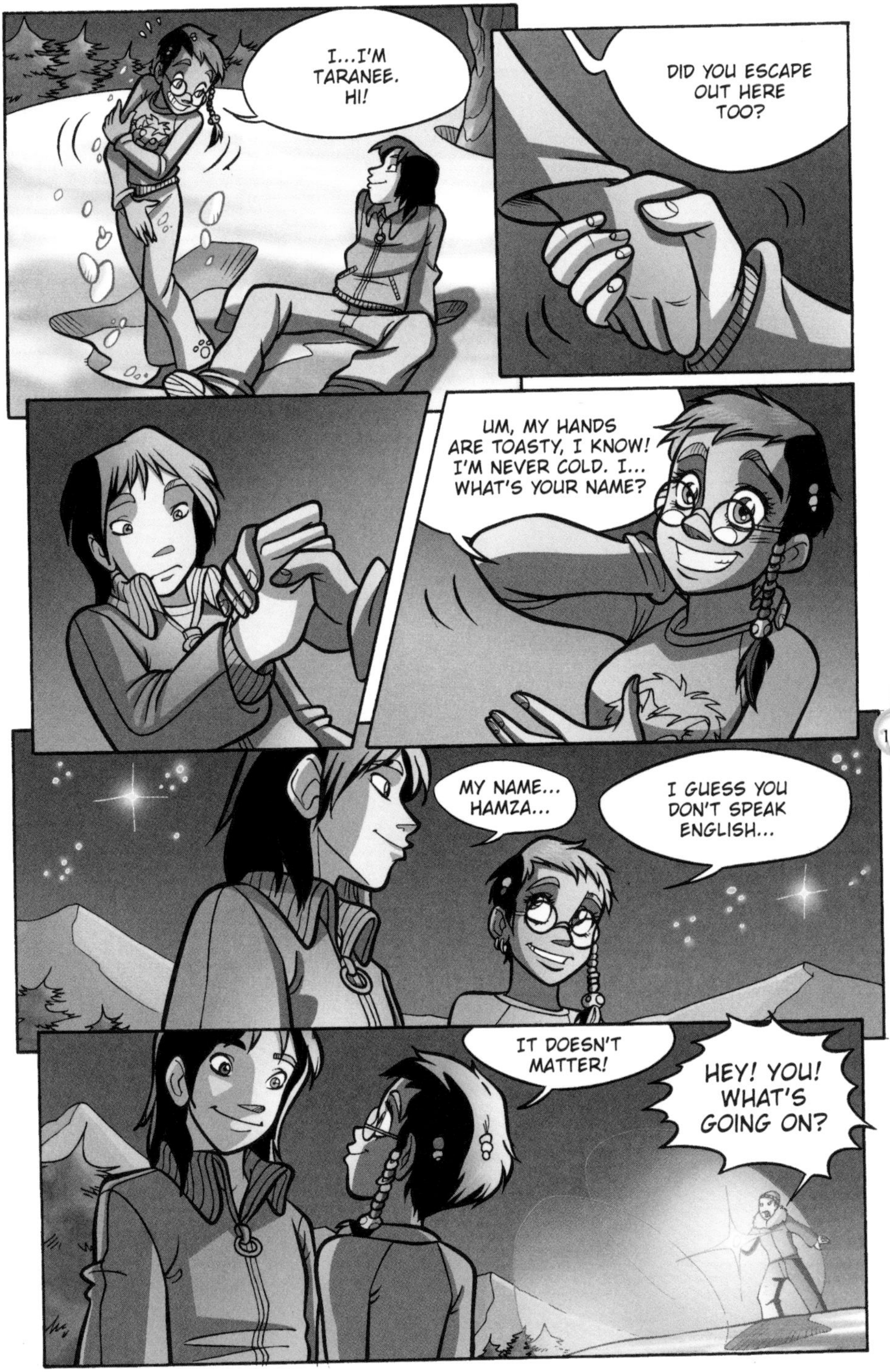
I...I'M TARANEE. HI!
DID YOU ESCAPE OUT HERE TOO?
UM, MY HANDS ARE TOASTY, I KNOW! I'M NEVER COLD. I... WHAT'S YOUR NAME?
MY NAME... HAMZA...
I GUESS YOU DON'T SPEAK ENGLISH...
IT DOESN'T MATTER!
HEY! YOU! WHAT'S GOING ON?

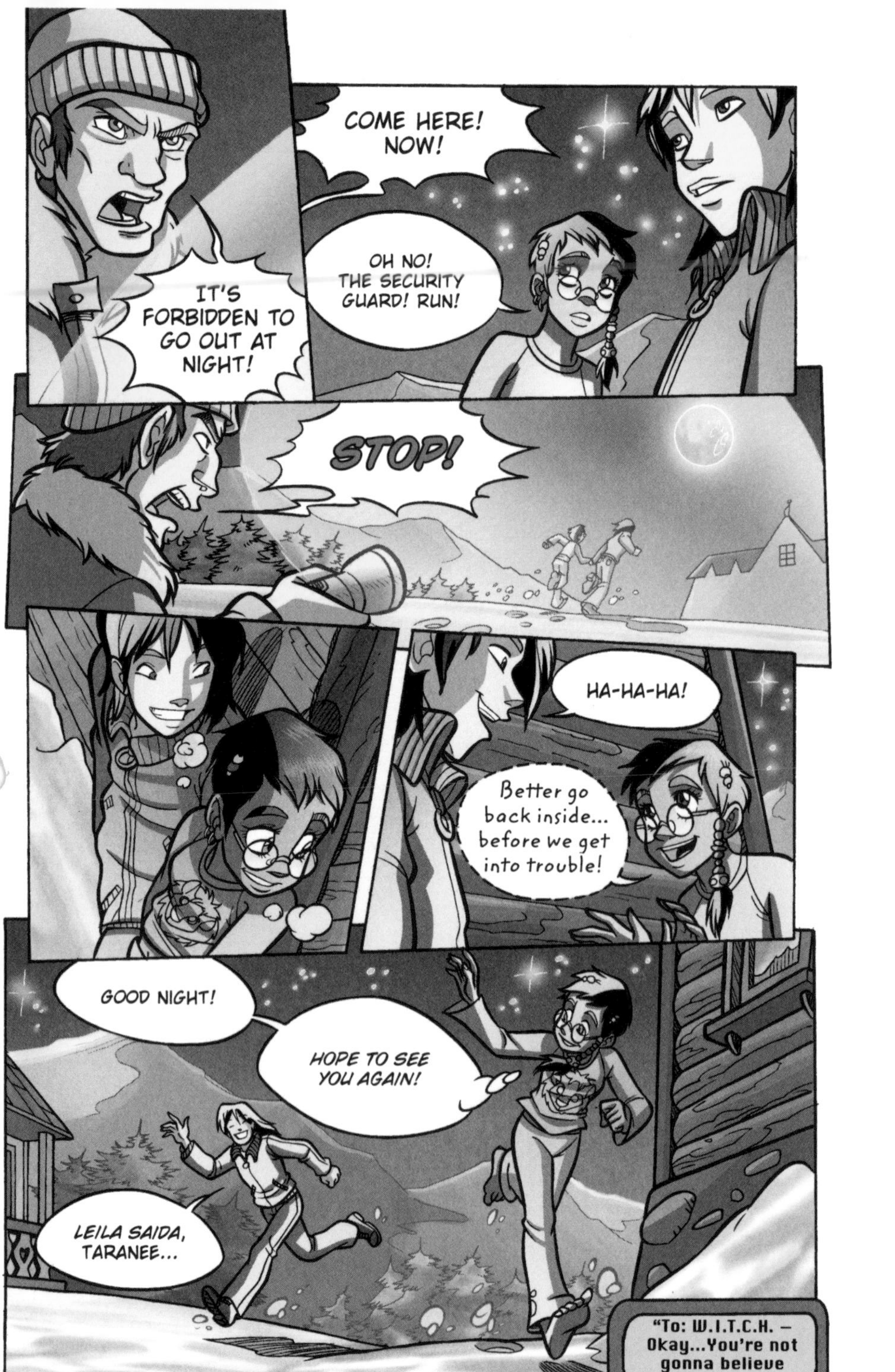
COME HERE! NOW!
IT'S FORBIDDEN TO GO OUT AT NIGHT!
OH NO! THE SECURITY GUARD! RUN!
STOP!
HA-HA-HA!
Better go back inside... before we get into trouble!
GOOD NIGHT!
HOPE TO SEE YOU AGAIN!
LEILA SAIDA, TARANEE...
"To: W.I.T.C.H. – Okay...You're not gonna believe this...

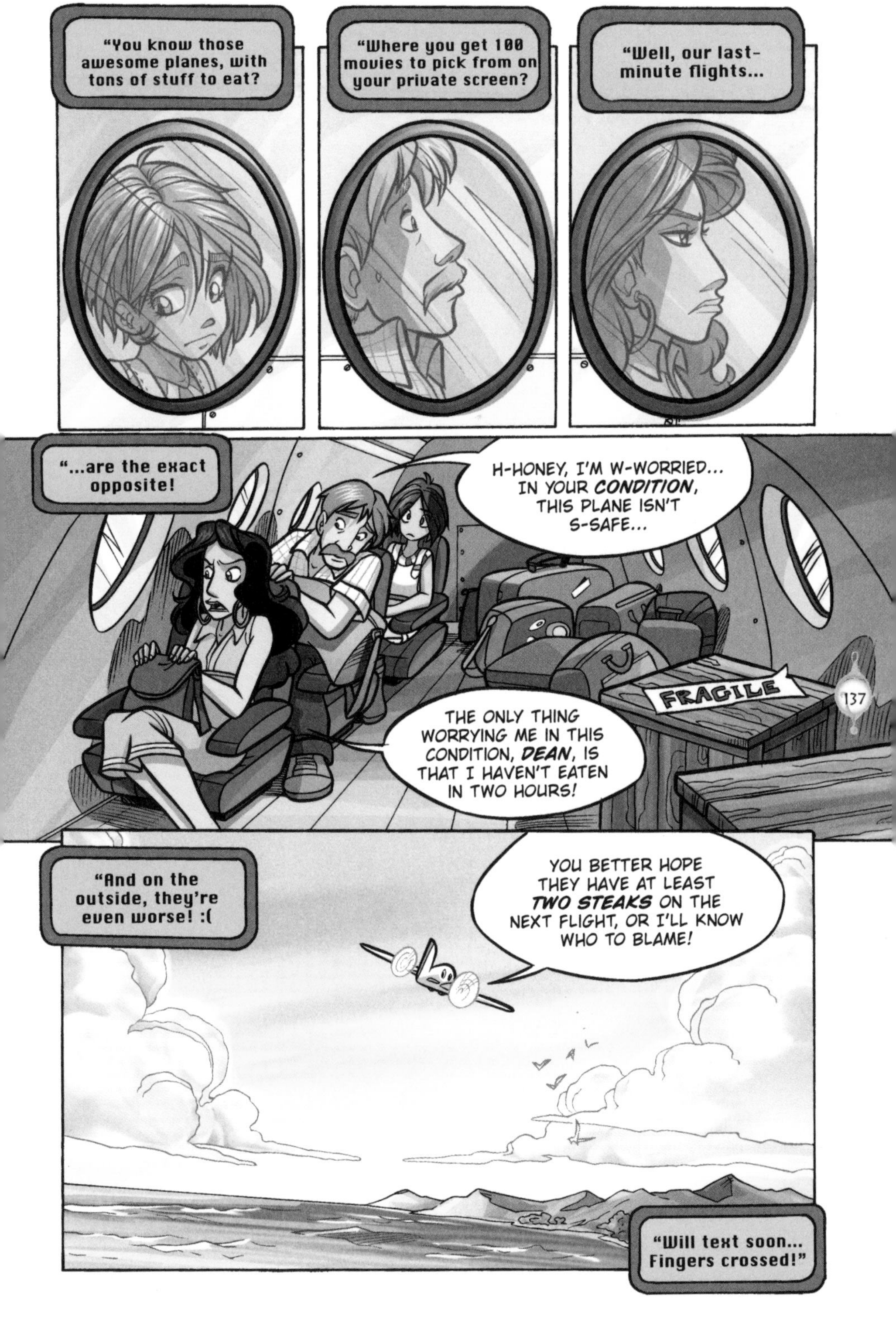
"You know those awesome planes, with tons of stuff to eat?
"Where you get 100 movies to pick from on your private screen?
"Well, our last-minute flights...
"...are the exact opposite!
H-HONEY, I'M W-WORRIED... IN YOUR CONDITION, THIS PLANE ISN'T S-SAFE...
FRAGILE
THE ONLY THING WORRYING ME IN THIS CONDITION, DEAN, IS THAT I HAVEN'T EATEN IN TWO HOURS!
"And on the outside, they're even worse! :(
YOU BETTER HOPE THEY HAVE AT LEAST TWO STEAKS ON THE NEXT FLIGHT, OR I'LL KNOW WHO TO BLAME!
"Will text soon... Fingers crossed!"

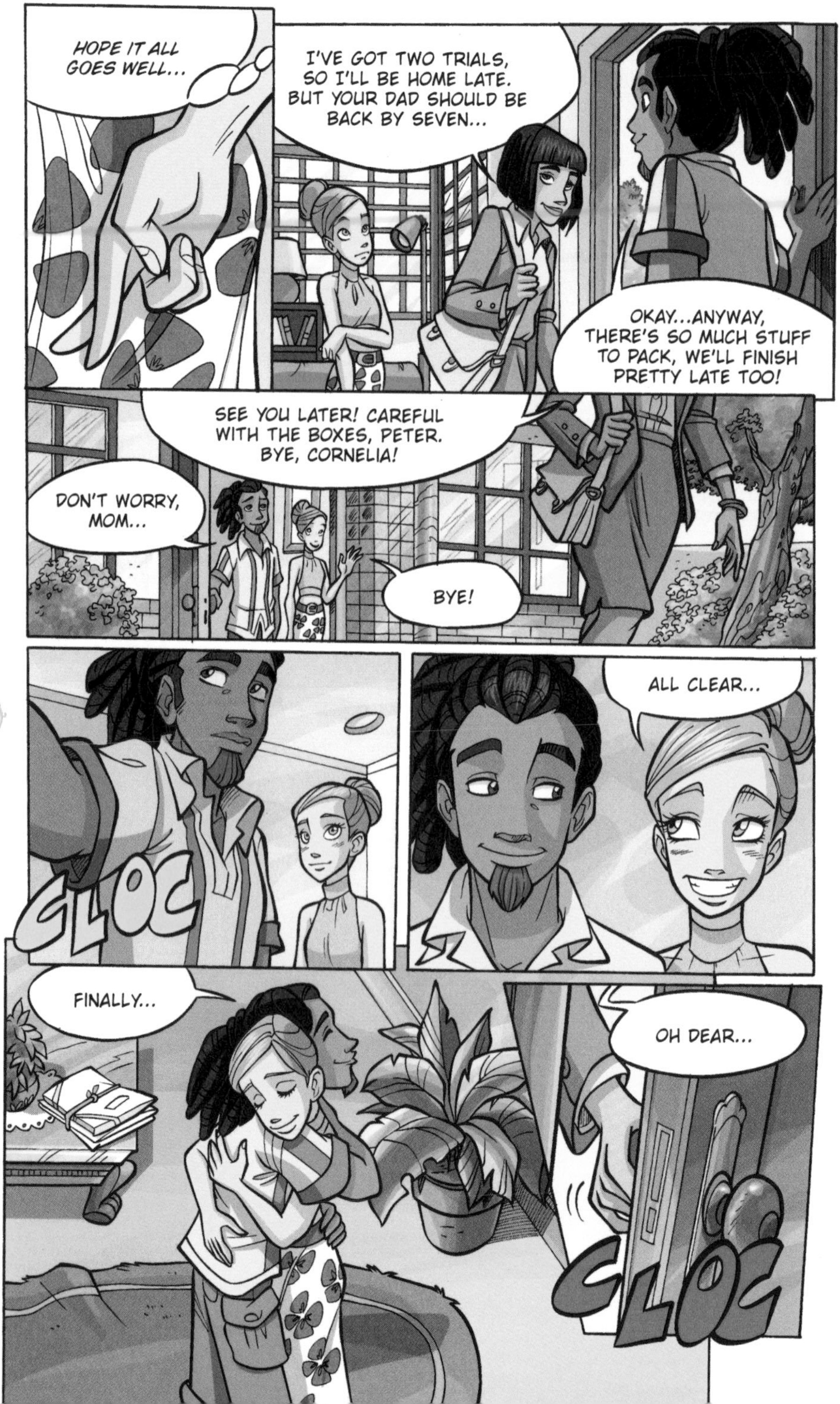

HOPE IT ALL GOES WELL...
I'VE GOT TWO TRIALS, SO I'LL BE HOME LATE. BUT YOUR DAD SHOULD BE BACK BY SEVEN...
OKAY...ANYWAY, THERE'S SO MUCH STUFF TO PACK, WE'LL FINISH PRETTY LATE TOO!
SEE YOU LATER! CAREFUL WITH THE BOXES, PETER. BYE, CORNELIA!
DON'T WORRY, MOM...
BYE!
CLOC
ALL CLEAR...
FINALLY...
OH DEAR...
CLOC

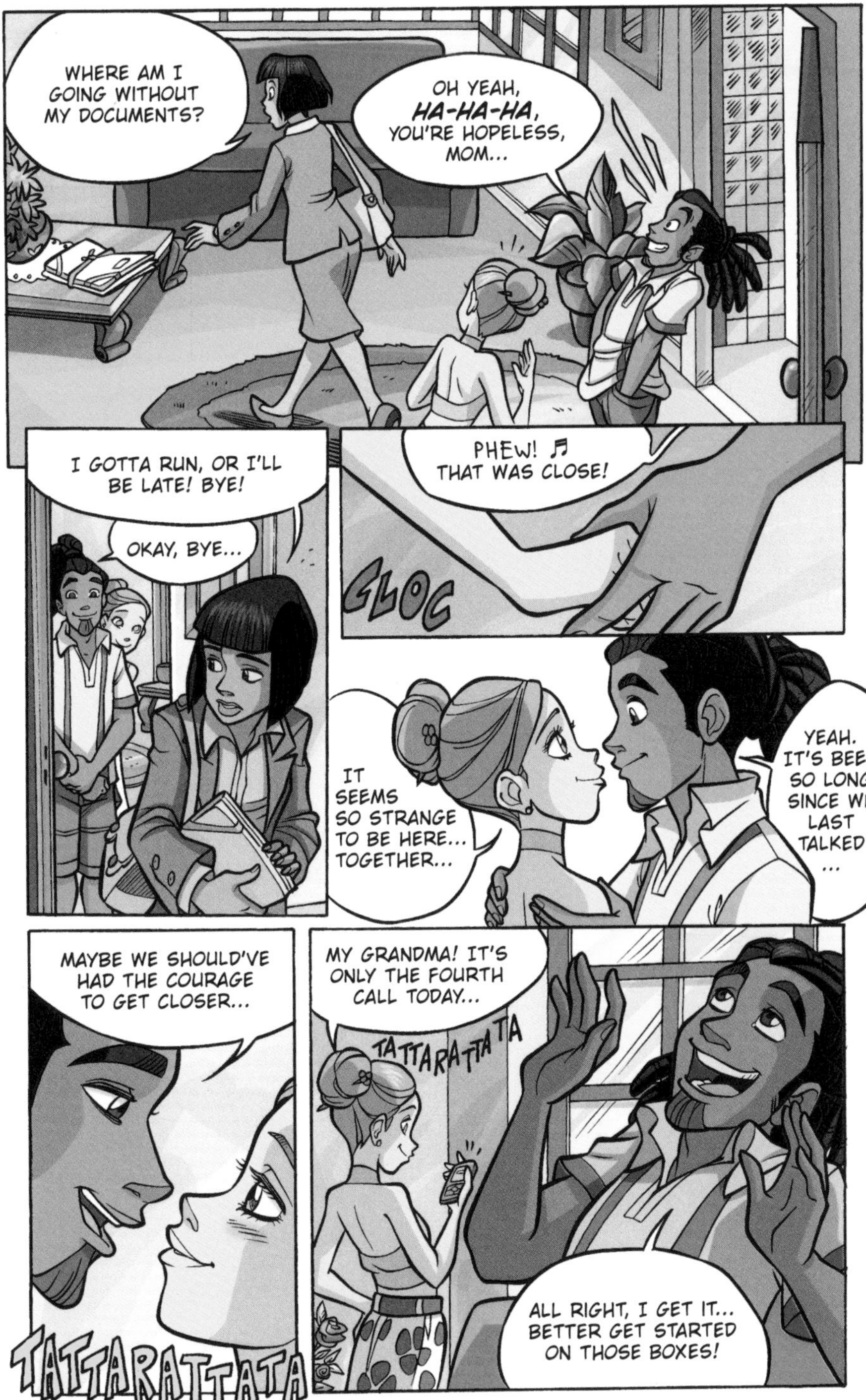
WHERE AM I GOING WITHOUT MY DOCUMENTS?
OH YEAH, HA-HA-HA, YOU'RE HOPELESS, MOM...
I GOTTA RUN, OR I'LL BE LATE! BYE!
OKAY, BYE...
PHEW! ♫ THAT WAS CLOSE!
CLOC
IT SEEMS SO STRANGE TO BE HERE... TOGETHER...
YEAH. IT'S BEEN SO LONG SINCE WE LAST TALKED ...
MAYBE WE SHOULD'VE HAD THE COURAGE TO GET CLOSER...
TATTARATTATA
MY GRANDMA! IT'S ONLY THE FOURTH CALL TODAY...
TATTARATTATA
ALL RIGHT, I GET IT... BETTER GET STARTED ON THOSE BOXES!

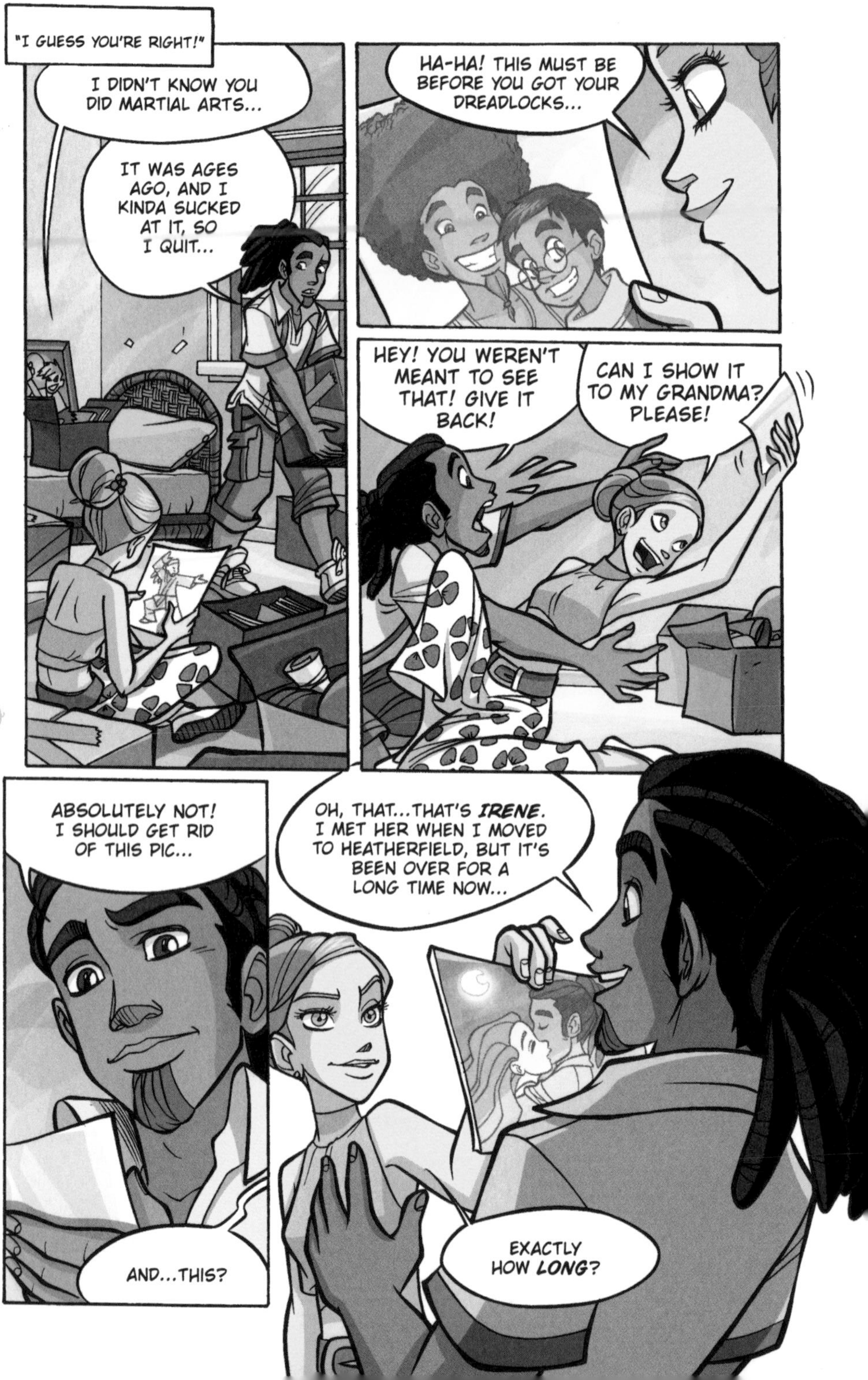

"I GUESS YOU'RE RIGHT!"
I DIDN'T KNOW YOU DID MARTIAL ARTS...
IT WAS AGES AGO, AND I KINDA SUCKED AT IT, SO I QUIT...
HA-HA! THIS MUST BE BEFORE YOU GOT YOUR DREADLOCKS...
HEY! YOU WEREN'T MEANT TO SEE THAT! GIVE IT BACK!
CAN I SHOW IT TO MY GRANDMA? PLEASE!
ABSOLUTELY NOT! I SHOULD GET RID OF THIS PIC...
AND...THIS?
OH, THAT...THAT'S *IRENE*. I MET HER WHEN I MOVED TO HEATHERFIELD, BUT IT'S BEEN OVER FOR A LONG TIME NOW...
EXACTLY HOW *LONG*?

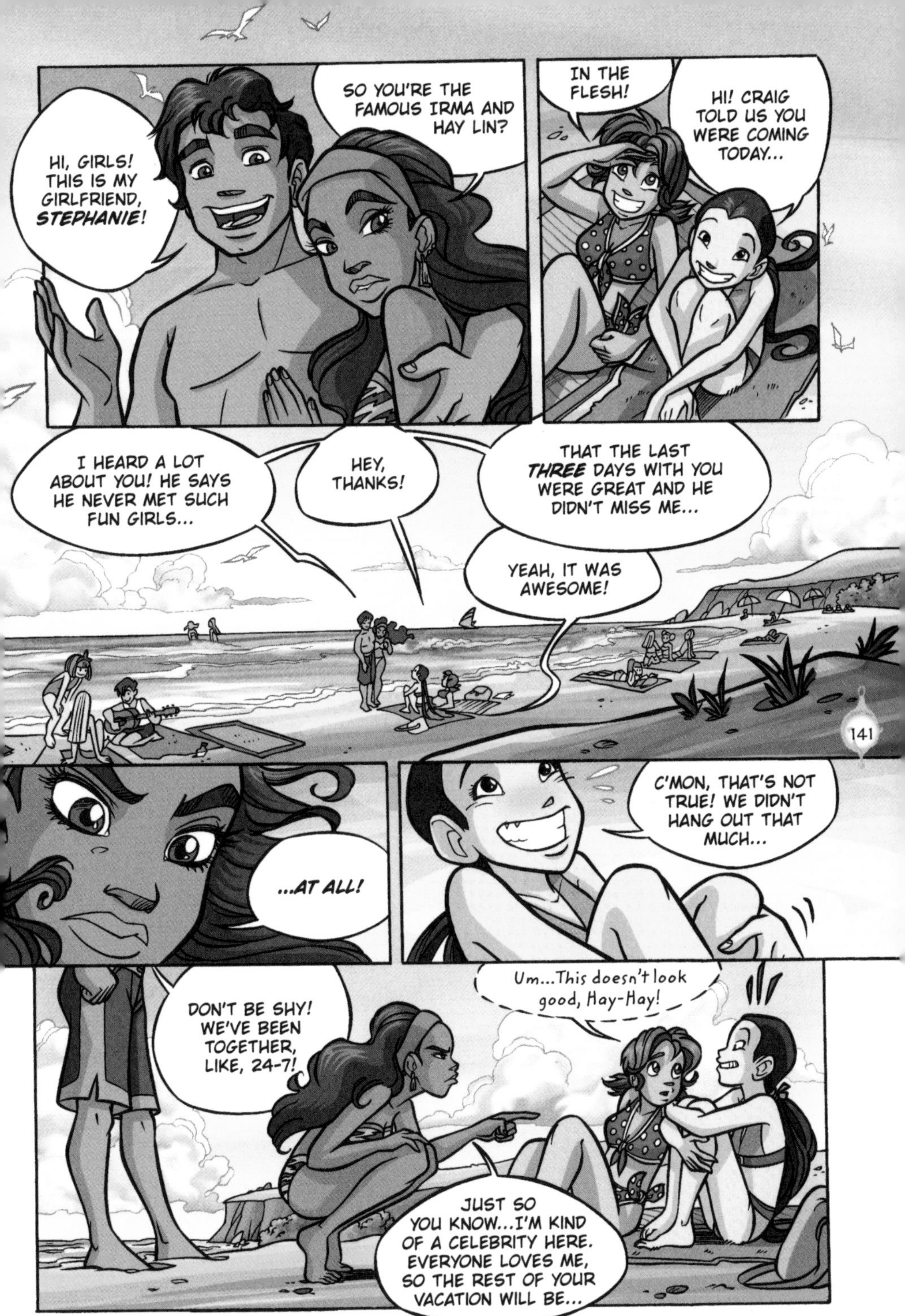
HI, GIRLS! THIS IS MY GIRLFRIEND, STEPHANIE!
SO YOU'RE THE FAMOUS IRMA AND HAY LIN?
IN THE FLESH!
HI! CRAIG TOLD US YOU WERE COMING TODAY...
I HEARD A LOT ABOUT YOU! HE SAYS HE NEVER MET SUCH FUN GIRLS...
HEY, THANKS!
THAT THE LAST THREE DAYS WITH YOU WERE GREAT AND HE DIDN'T MISS ME...
YEAH, IT WAS AWESOME!
...AT ALL!
C'MON, THAT'S NOT TRUE! WE DIDN'T HANG OUT THAT MUCH...
DON'T BE SHY! WE'VE BEEN TOGETHER, LIKE, 24-7!
Um...This doesn't look good, Hay-Hay!
JUST SO YOU KNOW...I'M KIND OF A CELEBRITY HERE. EVERYONE LOVES ME, SO THE REST OF YOUR VACATION WILL BE...

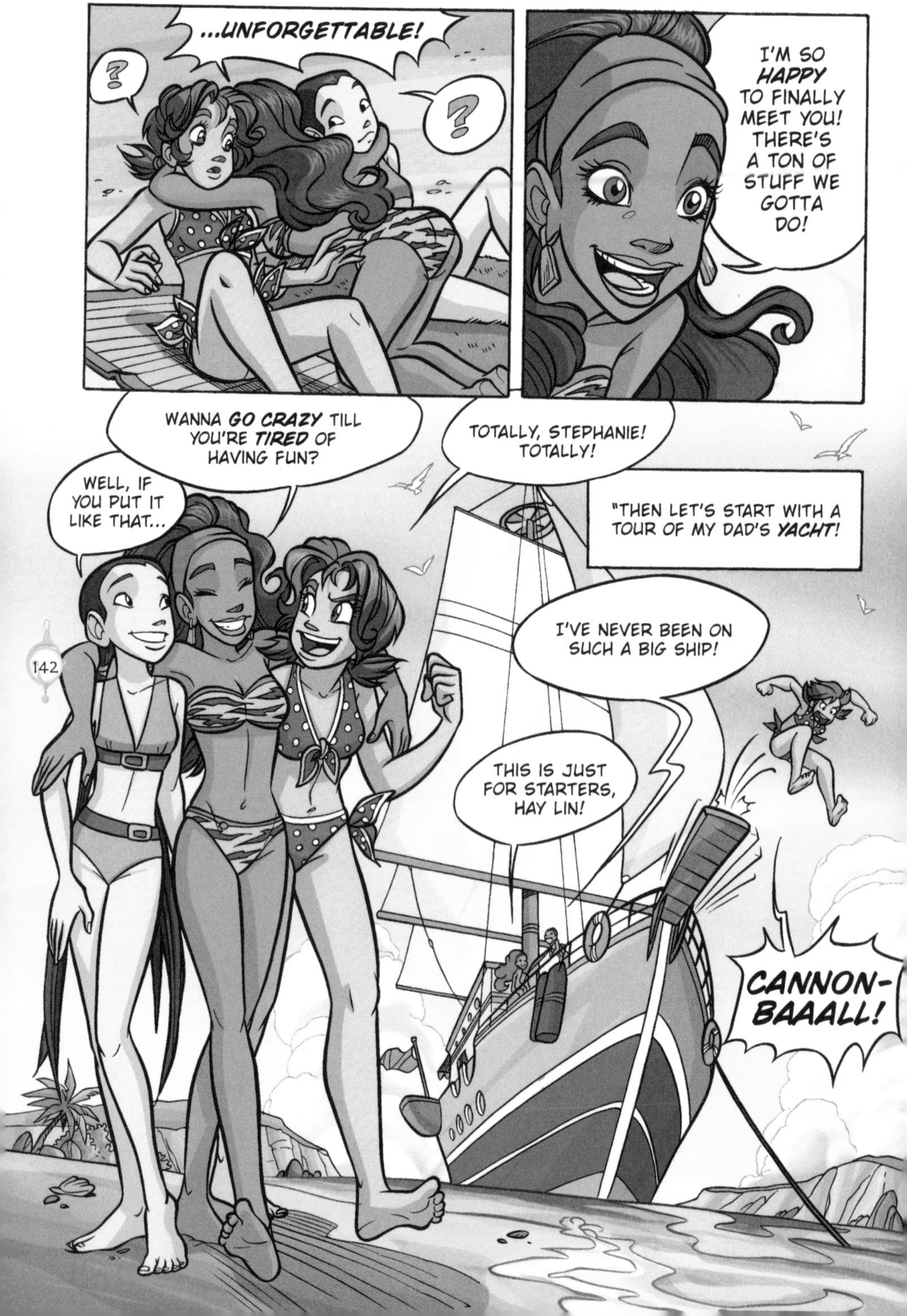

...UNFORGETTABLE!
?
?
I'M SO HAPPY TO FINALLY MEET YOU! THERE'S A TON OF STUFF WE GOTTA DO!
WANNA GO CRAZY TILL YOU'RE TIRED OF HAVING FUN?
TOTALLY, STEPHANIE! TOTALLY!
WELL, IF YOU PUT IT LIKE THAT...
"THEN LET'S START WITH A TOUR OF MY DAD'S YACHT!
I'VE NEVER BEEN ON SUCH A BIG SHIP!
THIS IS JUST FOR STARTERS, HAY LIN!
CANNON-BAAALL!

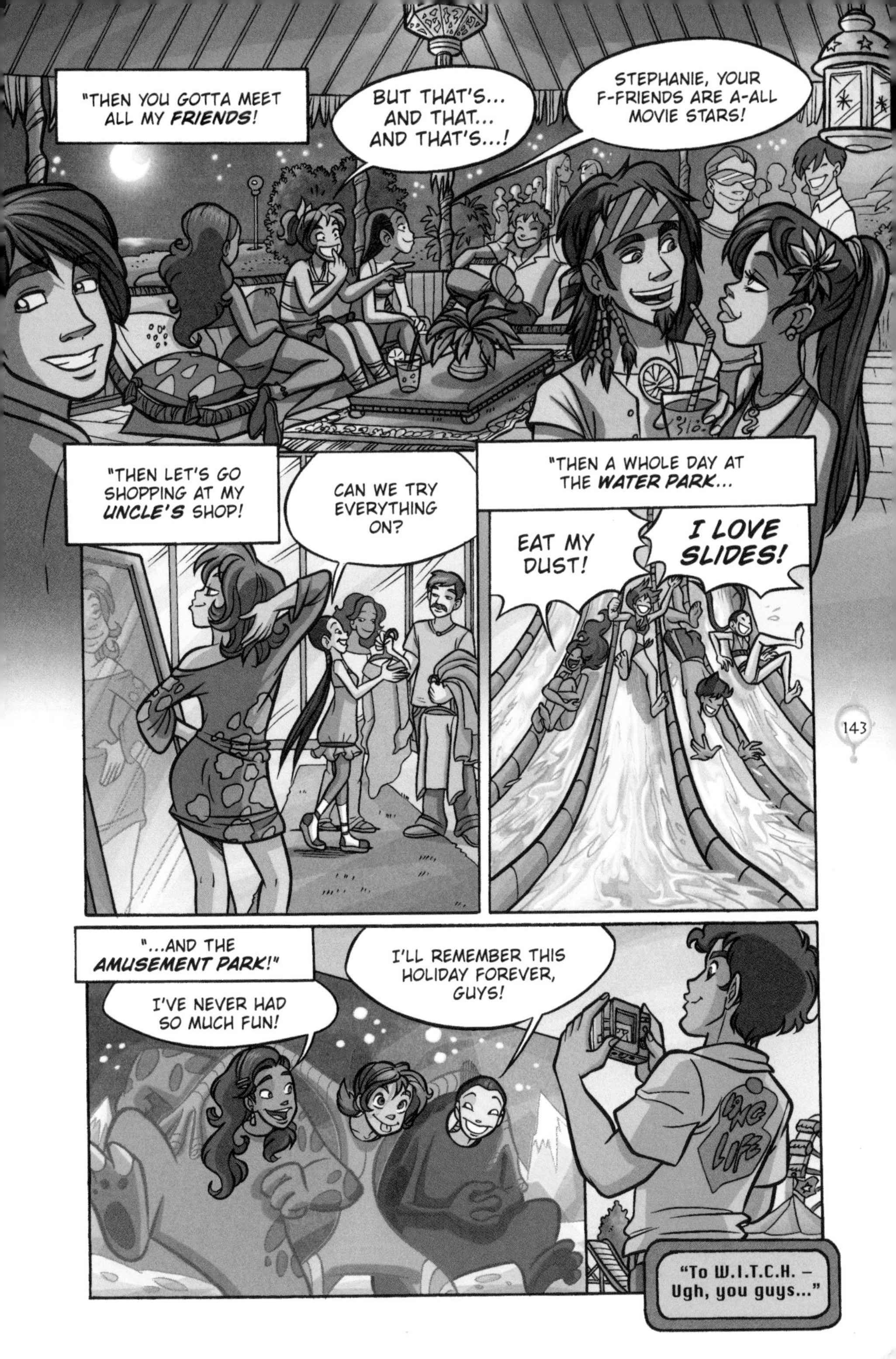
"THEN YOU GOTTA MEET ALL MY FRIENDS!
BUT THAT'S... AND THAT... AND THAT'S...!
STEPHANIE, YOUR F-FRIENDS ARE A-ALL MOVIE STARS!
"THEN LET'S GO SHOPPING AT MY UNCLE'S SHOP!
CAN WE TRY EVERYTHING ON?
"THEN A WHOLE DAY AT THE WATER PARK...
EAT MY DUST!
I LOVE SLIDES!
"...AND THE AMUSEMENT PARK!"
I'VE NEVER HAD SO MUCH FUN!
I'LL REMEMBER THIS HOLIDAY FOREVER, GUYS!
"To W.I.T.C.H. – Ugh, you guys..."

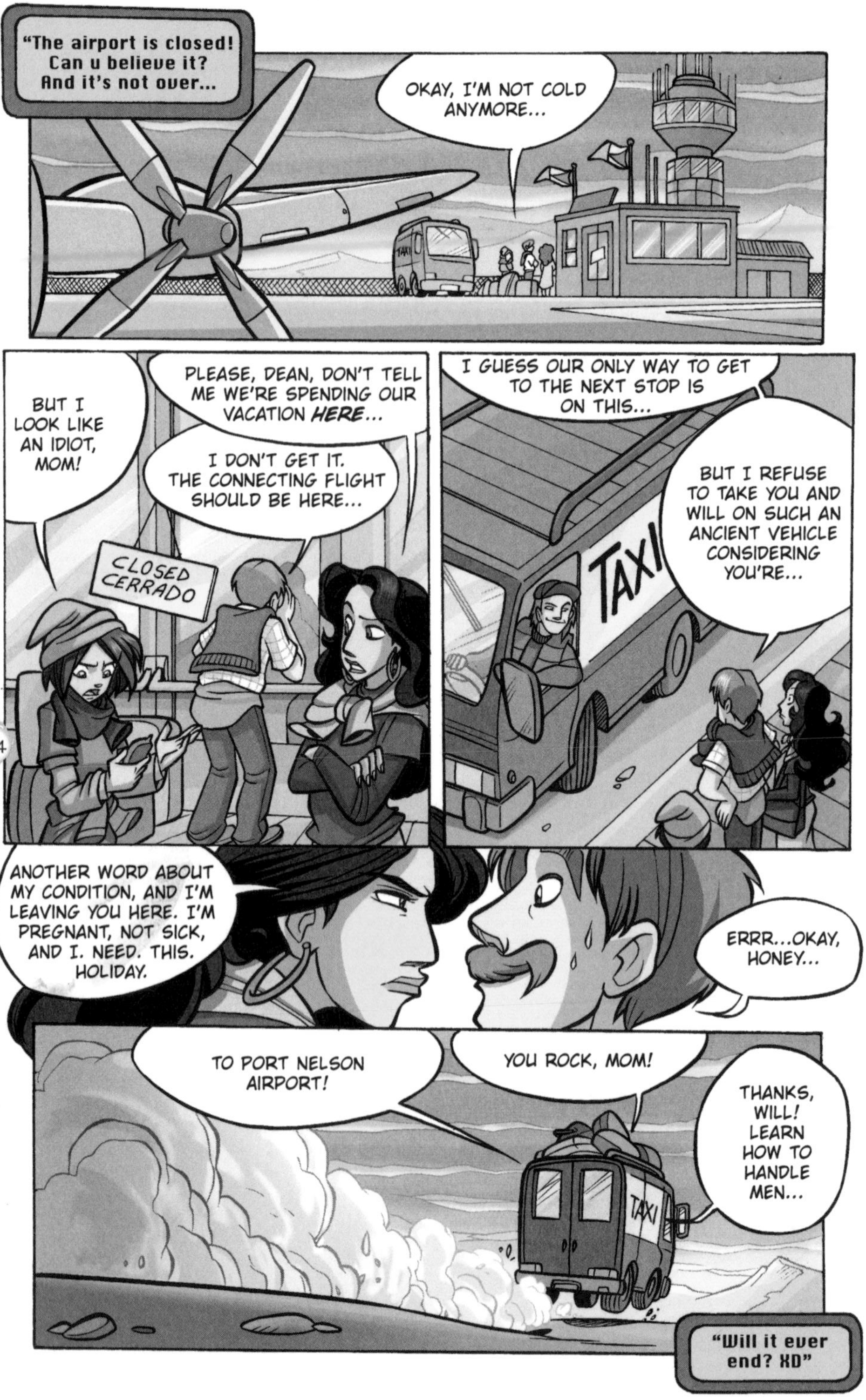
"The airport is closed! Can u believe it? And it's not over...
OKAY, I'M NOT COLD ANYMORE...
BUT I LOOK LIKE AN IDIOT, MOM!
PLEASE, DEAN, DON'T TELL ME WE'RE SPENDING OUR VACATION HERE...
I DON'T GET IT. THE CONNECTING FLIGHT SHOULD BE HERE...
CLOSED CERRADO
I GUESS OUR ONLY WAY TO GET TO THE NEXT STOP IS ON THIS...
BUT I REFUSE TO TAKE YOU AND WILL ON SUCH AN ANCIENT VEHICLE CONSIDERING YOU'RE...
TAXI
ANOTHER WORD ABOUT MY CONDITION, AND I'M LEAVING YOU HERE. I'M PREGNANT, NOT SICK, AND I. NEED. THIS. HOLIDAY.
ERRR...OKAY, HONEY...
TO PORT NELSON AIRPORT!
YOU ROCK, MOM!
THANKS, WILL! LEARN HOW TO HANDLE MEN...
TAXI
"Will it ever end? XD"

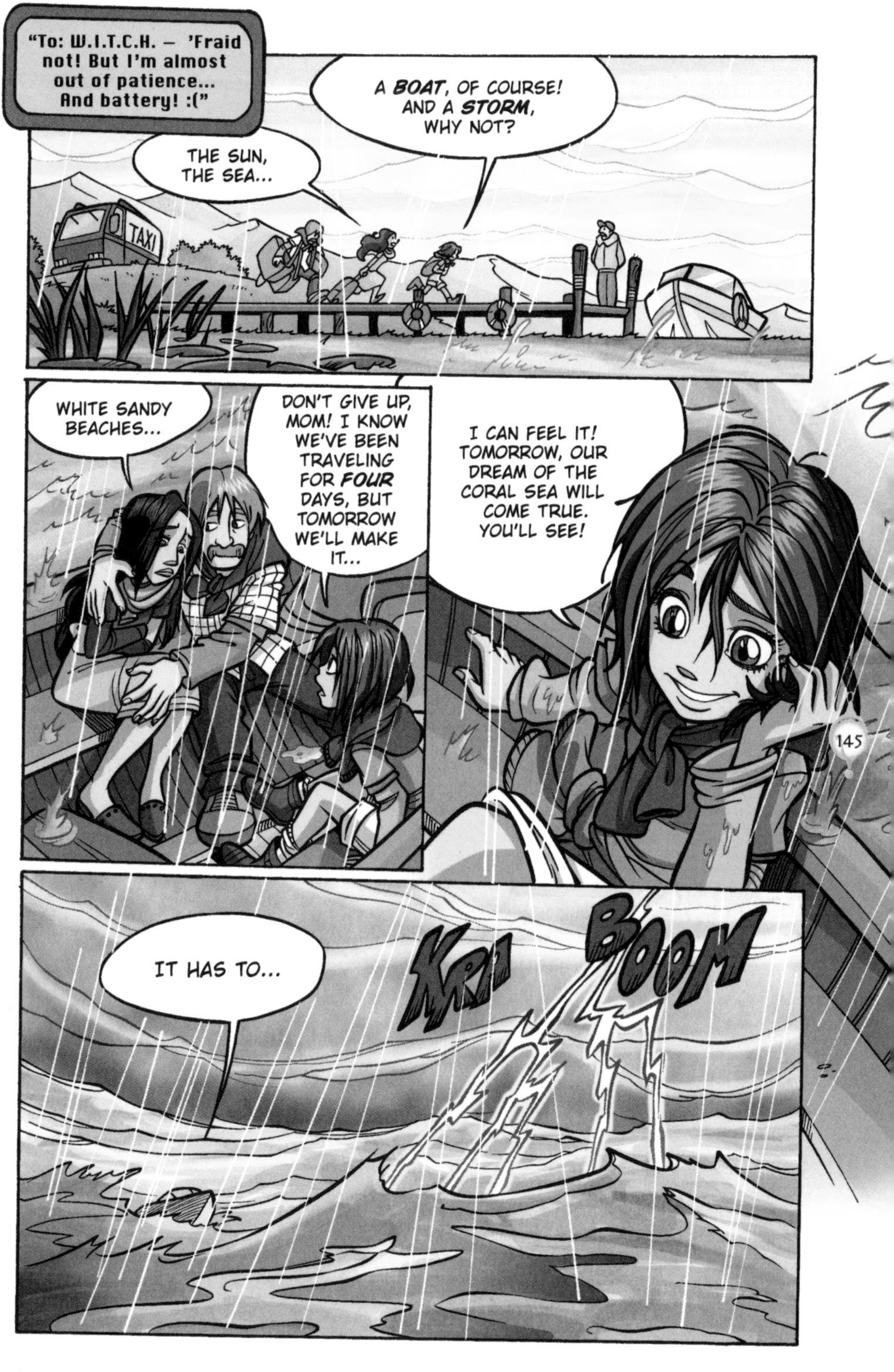
"To: W.I.T.C.H. — 'Fraid not! But I'm almost out of patience... And battery! :("
THE SUN, THE SEA...
A BOAT, OF COURSE! AND A STORM, WHY NOT?
TAXI
WHITE SANDY BEACHES...
DON'T GIVE UP, MOM! I KNOW WE'VE BEEN TRAVELING FOR FOUR DAYS, BUT TOMORROW WE'LL MAKE IT...
I CAN FEEL IT! TOMORROW, OUR DREAM OF THE CORAL SEA WILL COME TRUE. YOU'LL SEE!
IT HAS TO...
KRA BOOM

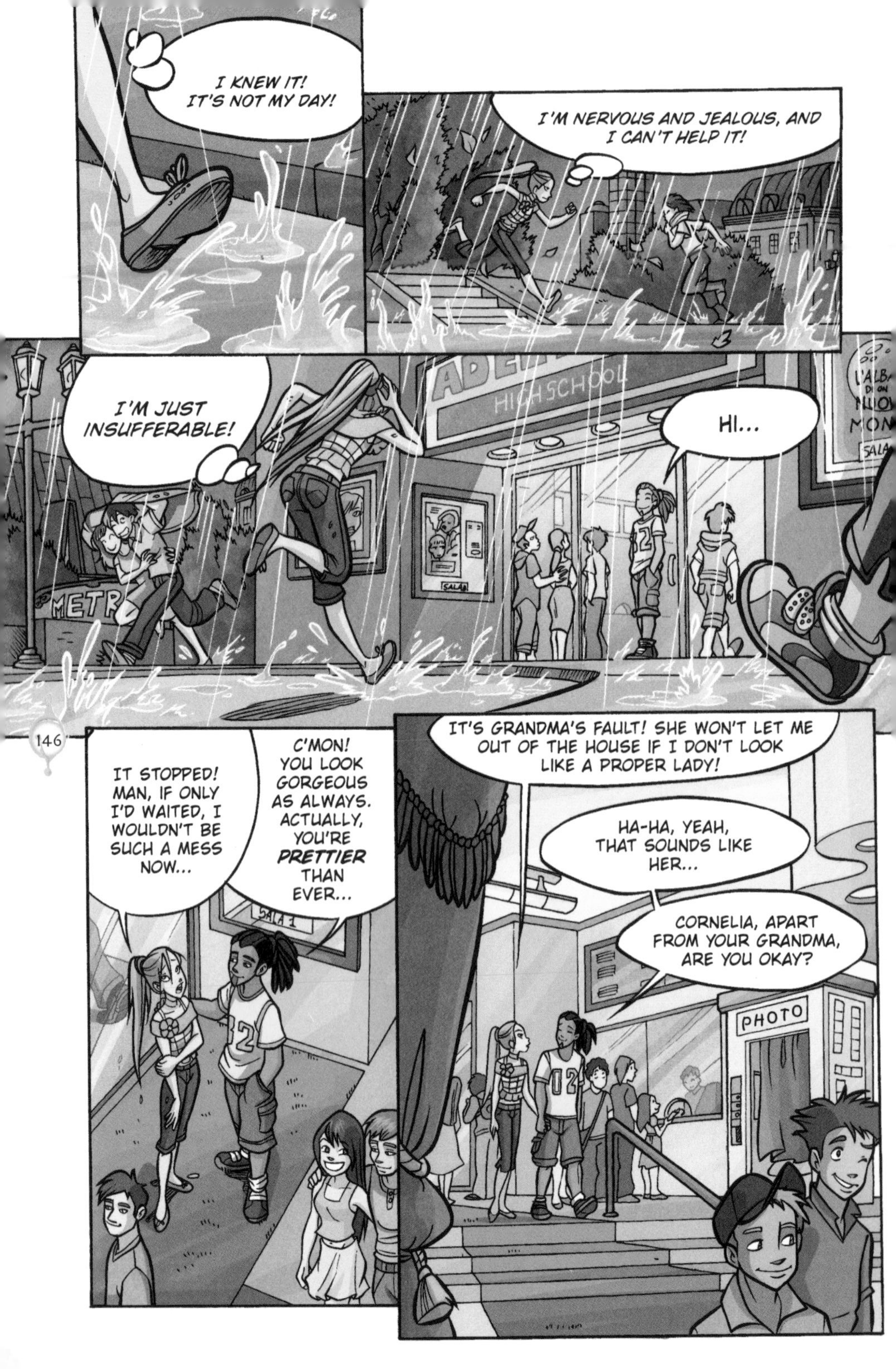

I KNEW IT! IT'S NOT MY DAY!
I'M NERVOUS AND JEALOUS, AND I CAN'T HELP IT!
I'M JUST INSUFFERABLE!
METR
HIGH SCHOOL
SALA
HI...
IT STOPPED! MAN, IF ONLY I'D WAITED, I WOULDN'T BE SUCH A MESS NOW...
C'MON! YOU LOOK GORGEOUS AS ALWAYS. ACTUALLY, YOU'RE ***PRETTIER*** THAN EVER...
SALA 1
IT'S GRANDMA'S FAULT! SHE WON'T LET ME OUT OF THE HOUSE IF I DON'T LOOK LIKE A PROPER LADY!
HA-HA, YEAH, THAT SOUNDS LIKE HER...
CORNELIA, APART FROM YOUR GRANDMA, ARE YOU OKAY?
PHOTO

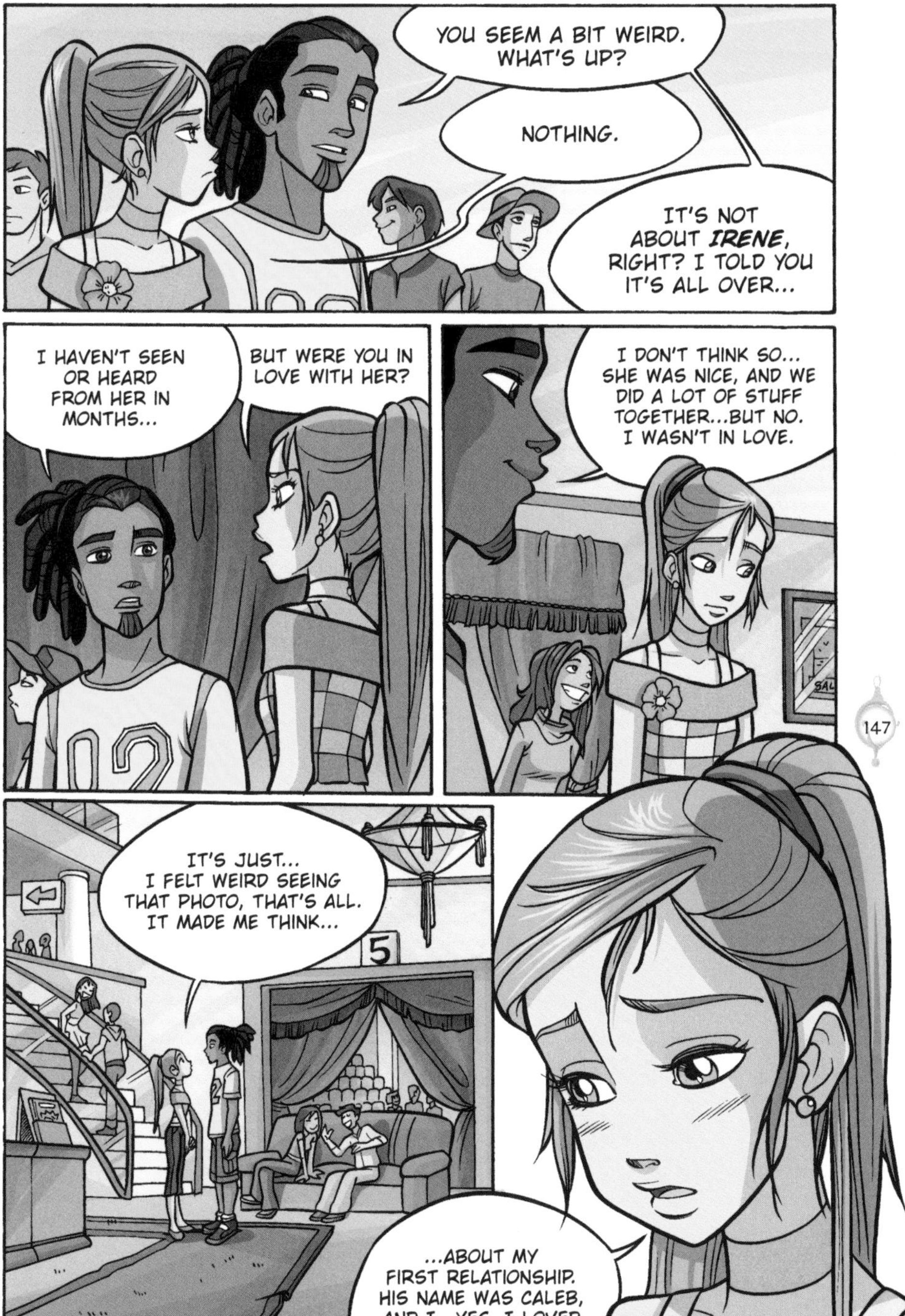
YOU SEEM A BIT WEIRD. WHAT'S UP?
NOTHING.
IT'S NOT ABOUT *IRENE*, RIGHT? I TOLD YOU IT'S ALL OVER...
I HAVEN'T SEEN OR HEARD FROM HER IN MONTHS...
BUT WERE YOU IN LOVE WITH HER?
I DON'T THINK SO... SHE WAS NICE, AND WE DID A LOT OF STUFF TOGETHER...BUT NO. I WASN'T IN LOVE.
IT'S JUST... I FELT WEIRD SEEING THAT PHOTO, THAT'S ALL. IT MADE ME THINK...
5
...ABOUT MY FIRST RELATIONSHIP. HIS NAME WAS CALEB, AND I...YES, I LOVED HIM. VERY MUCH...

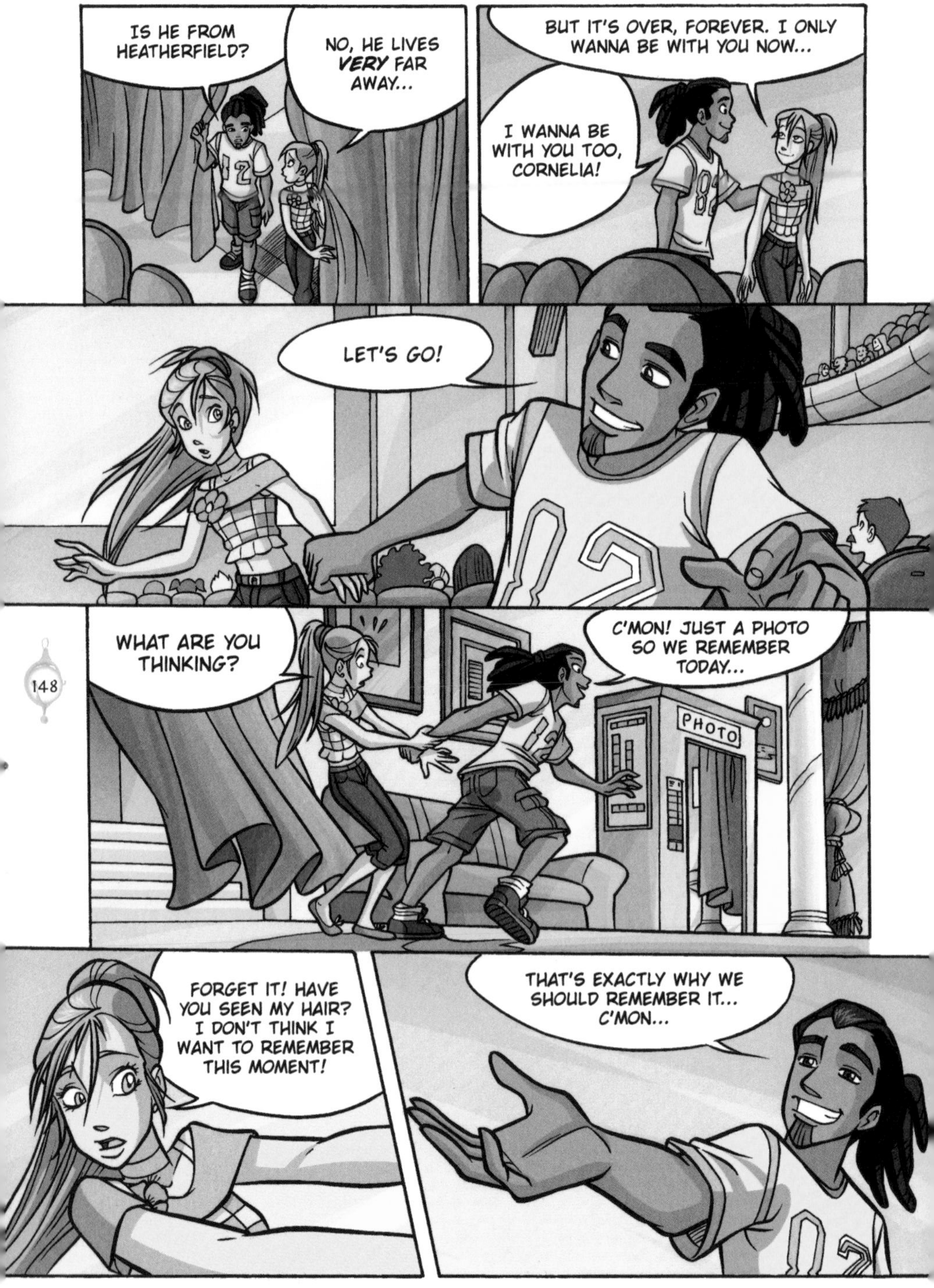

IS HE FROM HEATHERFIELD?
NO, HE LIVES *VERY* FAR AWAY...
BUT IT'S OVER, FOREVER. I ONLY WANNA BE WITH YOU NOW...
I WANNA BE WITH YOU TOO, CORNELIA!
LET'S GO!
WHAT ARE YOU THINKING?
C'MON! JUST A PHOTO SO WE REMEMBER TODAY...
PHOTO
FORGET IT! HAVE YOU SEEN MY HAIR? I DON'T THINK I WANT TO REMEMBER THIS MOMENT!
THAT'S EXACTLY WHY WE SHOULD REMEMBER IT... C'MON...

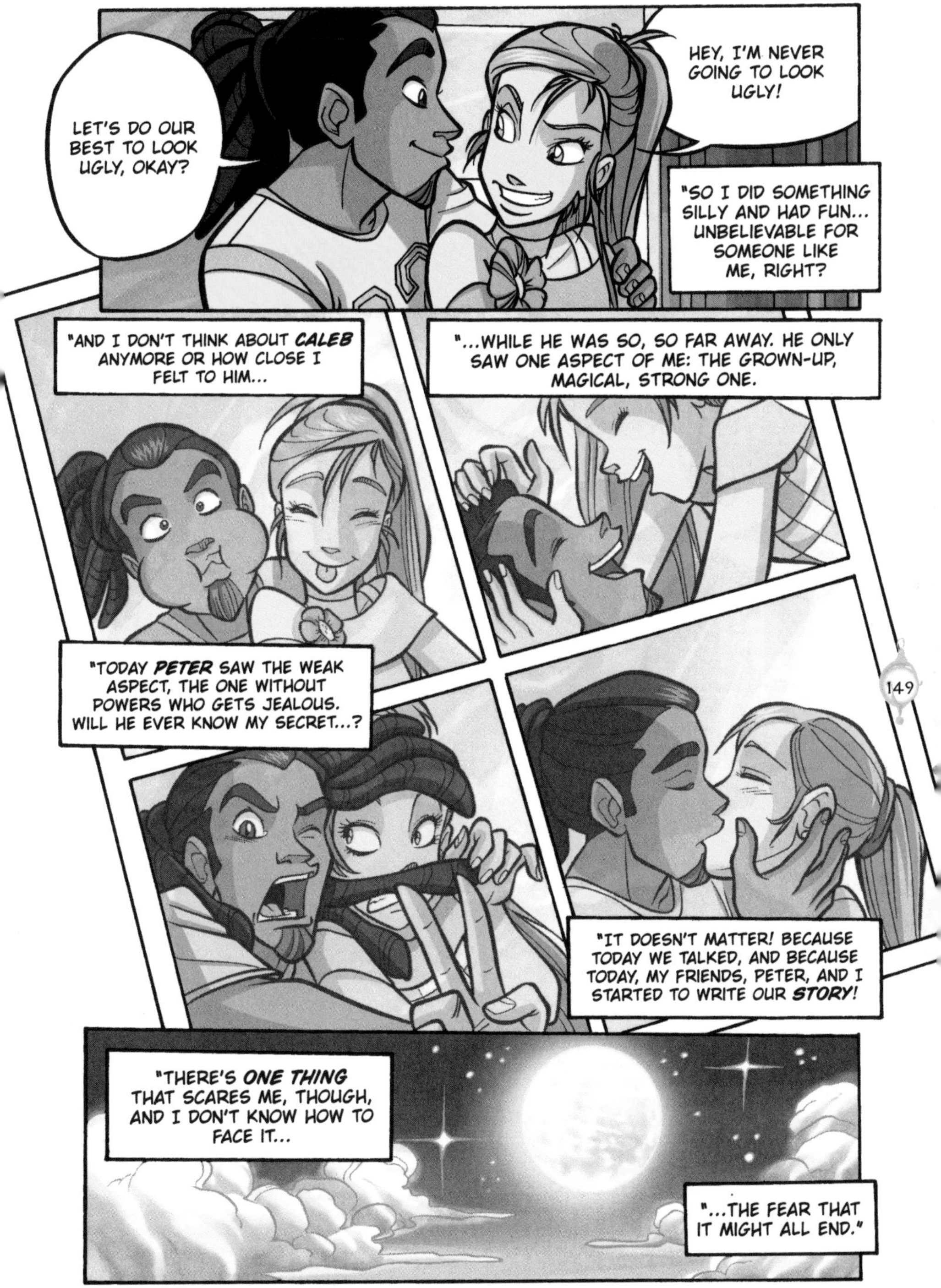
LET'S DO OUR BEST TO LOOK UGLY, OKAY?
HEY, I'M NEVER GOING TO LOOK UGLY!
"SO I DID SOMETHING SILLY AND HAD FUN... UNBELIEVABLE FOR SOMEONE LIKE ME, RIGHT?
"AND I DON'T THINK ABOUT CALEB ANYMORE OR HOW CLOSE I FELT TO HIM...
"...WHILE HE WAS SO, SO FAR AWAY. HE ONLY SAW ONE ASPECT OF ME: THE GROWN-UP, MAGICAL, STRONG ONE.
"TODAY PETER SAW THE WEAK ASPECT, THE ONE WITHOUT POWERS WHO GETS JEALOUS. WILL HE EVER KNOW MY SECRET...?
"IT DOESN'T MATTER! BECAUSE TODAY WE TALKED, AND BECAUSE TODAY, MY FRIENDS, PETER, AND I STARTED TO WRITE OUR STORY!
"THERE'S ONE THING THAT SCARES ME, THOUGH, AND I DON'T KNOW HOW TO FACE IT...
"...THE FEAR THAT IT MIGHT ALL END."

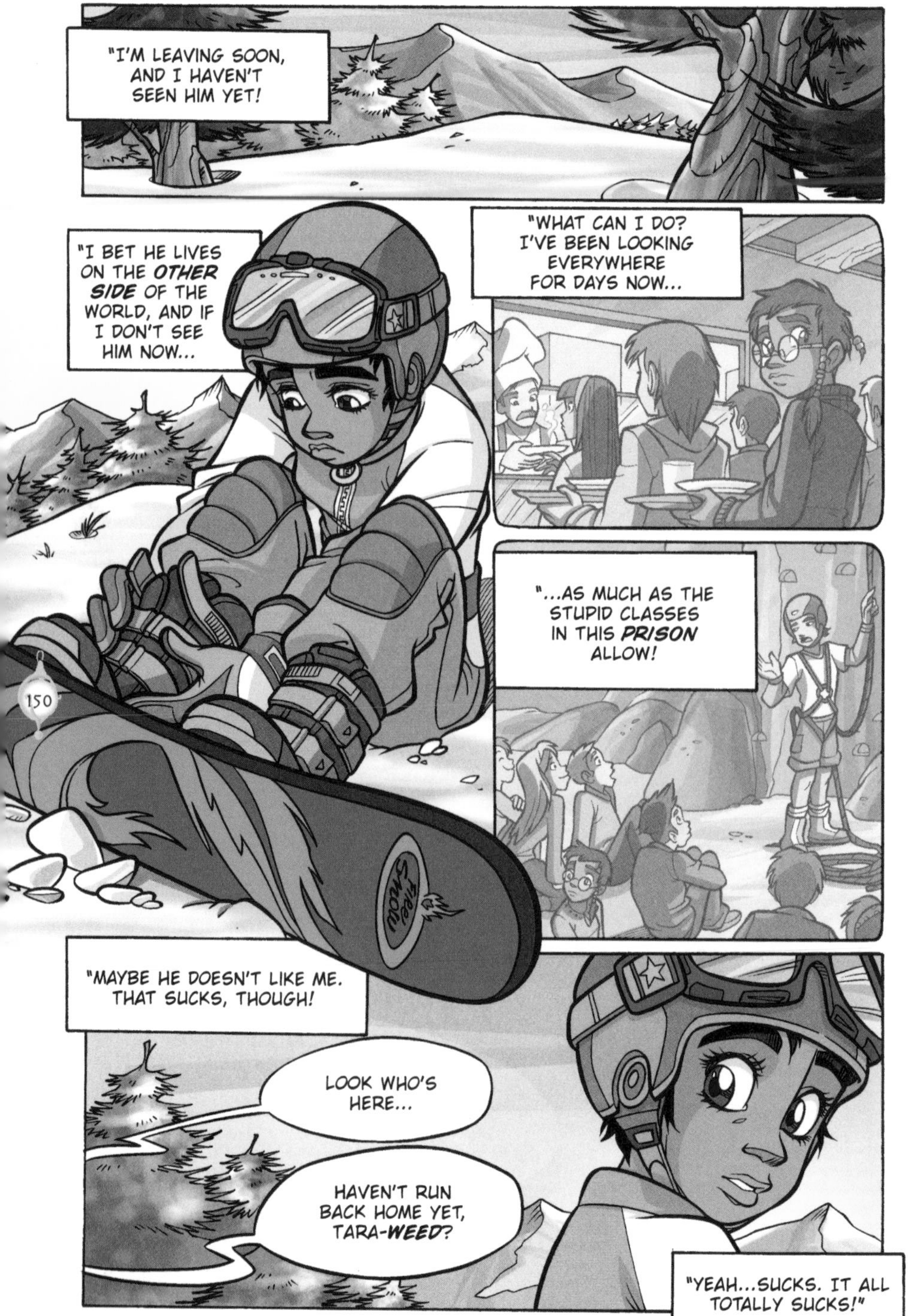
"I'M LEAVING SOON, AND I HAVEN'T SEEN HIM YET!
"I BET HE LIVES ON THE OTHER SIDE OF THE WORLD, AND IF I DON'T SEE HIM NOW...
"WHAT CAN I DO? I'VE BEEN LOOKING EVERYWHERE FOR DAYS NOW...
"...AS MUCH AS THE STUPID CLASSES IN THIS PRISON ALLOW!
"MAYBE HE DOESN'T LIKE ME. THAT SUCKS, THOUGH!
LOOK WHO'S HERE...
HAVEN'T RUN BACK HOME YET, TARA-WEED?
"YEAH...SUCKS. IT ALL TOTALLY SUCKS!"

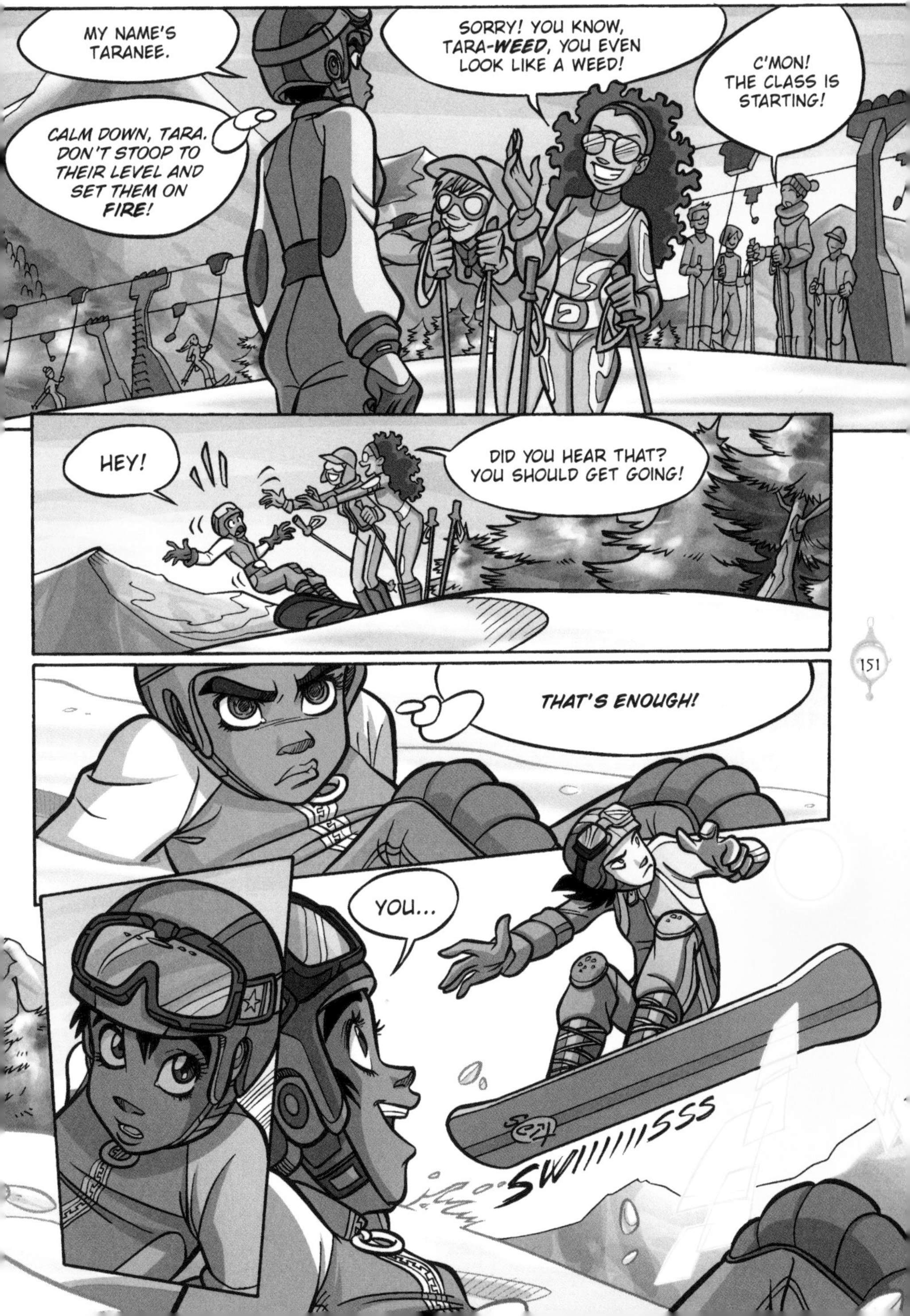
MY NAME'S TARANEE.
CALM DOWN, TARA. DON'T STOOP TO THEIR LEVEL AND SET THEM ON FIRE!
SORRY! YOU KNOW, TARA-WEED, YOU EVEN LOOK LIKE A WEED!
C'MON! THE CLASS IS STARTING!
HEY!
DID YOU HEAR THAT? YOU SHOULD GET GOING!
THAT'S ENOUGH!
YOU...
SWIIIIIISSS

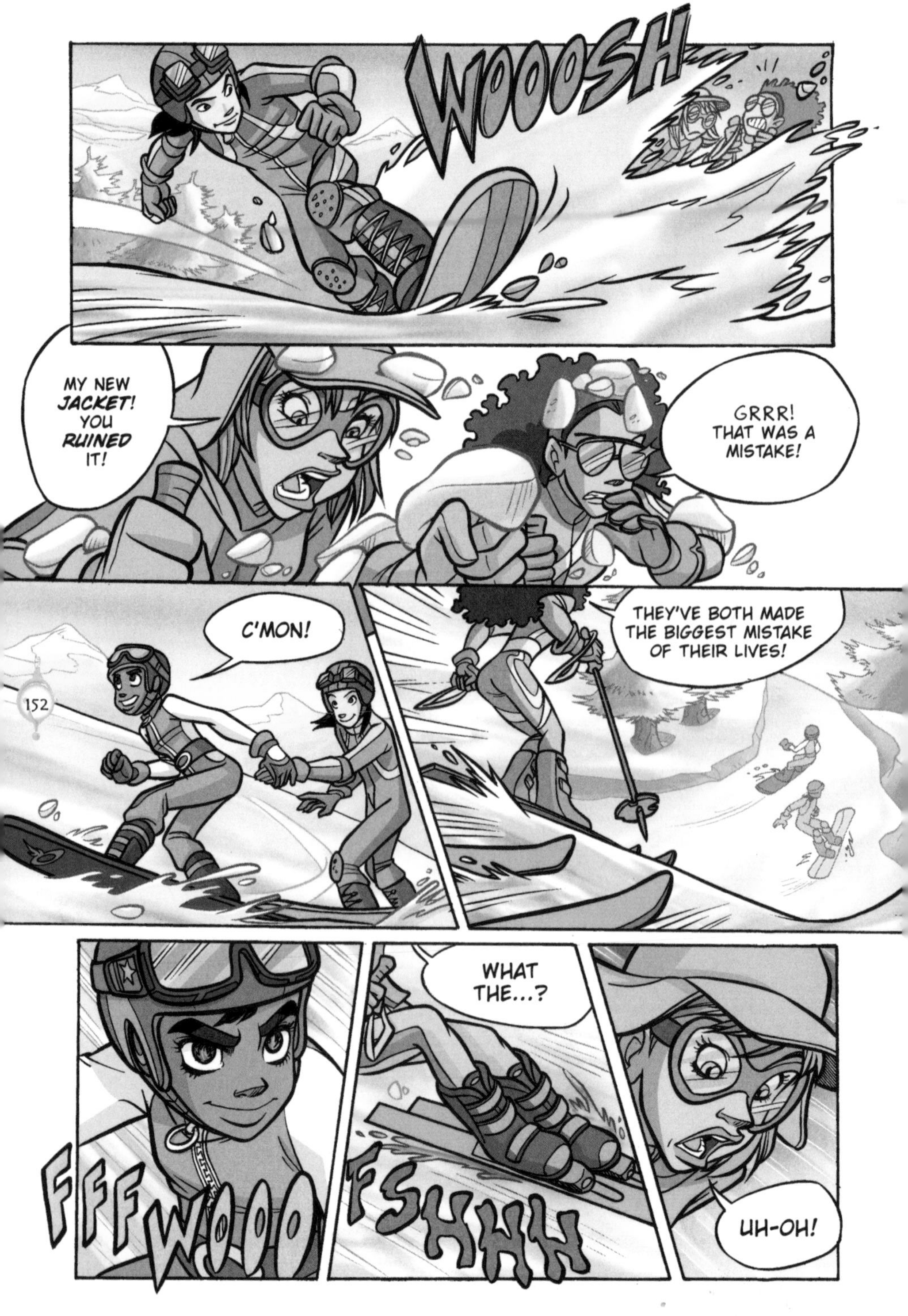
WOOOSH
MY NEW JACKET! YOU RUINED IT!
GRRR! THAT WAS A MISTAKE!
C'MON!
THEY'VE BOTH MADE THE BIGGEST MISTAKE OF THEIR LIVES!
FFFWOOO
WHAT THE...?
FSHHH
UH-OH!

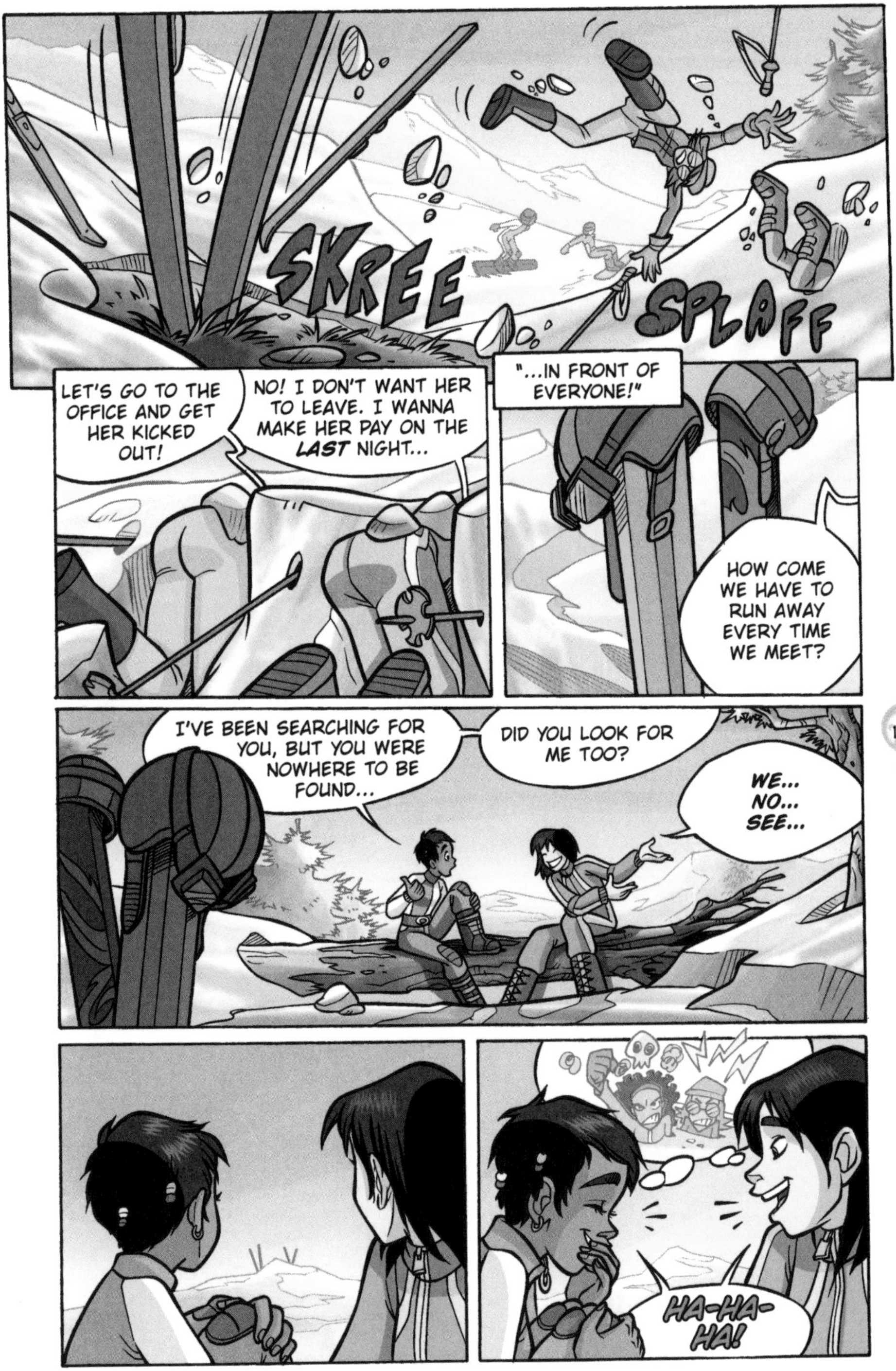
SKREE
SPLAFF
LET'S GO TO THE OFFICE AND GET HER KICKED OUT!
NO! I DON'T WANT HER TO LEAVE. I WANNA MAKE HER PAY ON THE LAST NIGHT...
"...IN FRONT OF EVERYONE!"
HOW COME WE HAVE TO RUN AWAY EVERY TIME WE MEET?
I'VE BEEN SEARCHING FOR YOU, BUT YOU WERE NOWHERE TO BE FOUND...
DID YOU LOOK FOR ME TOO?
WE... NO... SEE...
HA-HA-HA!

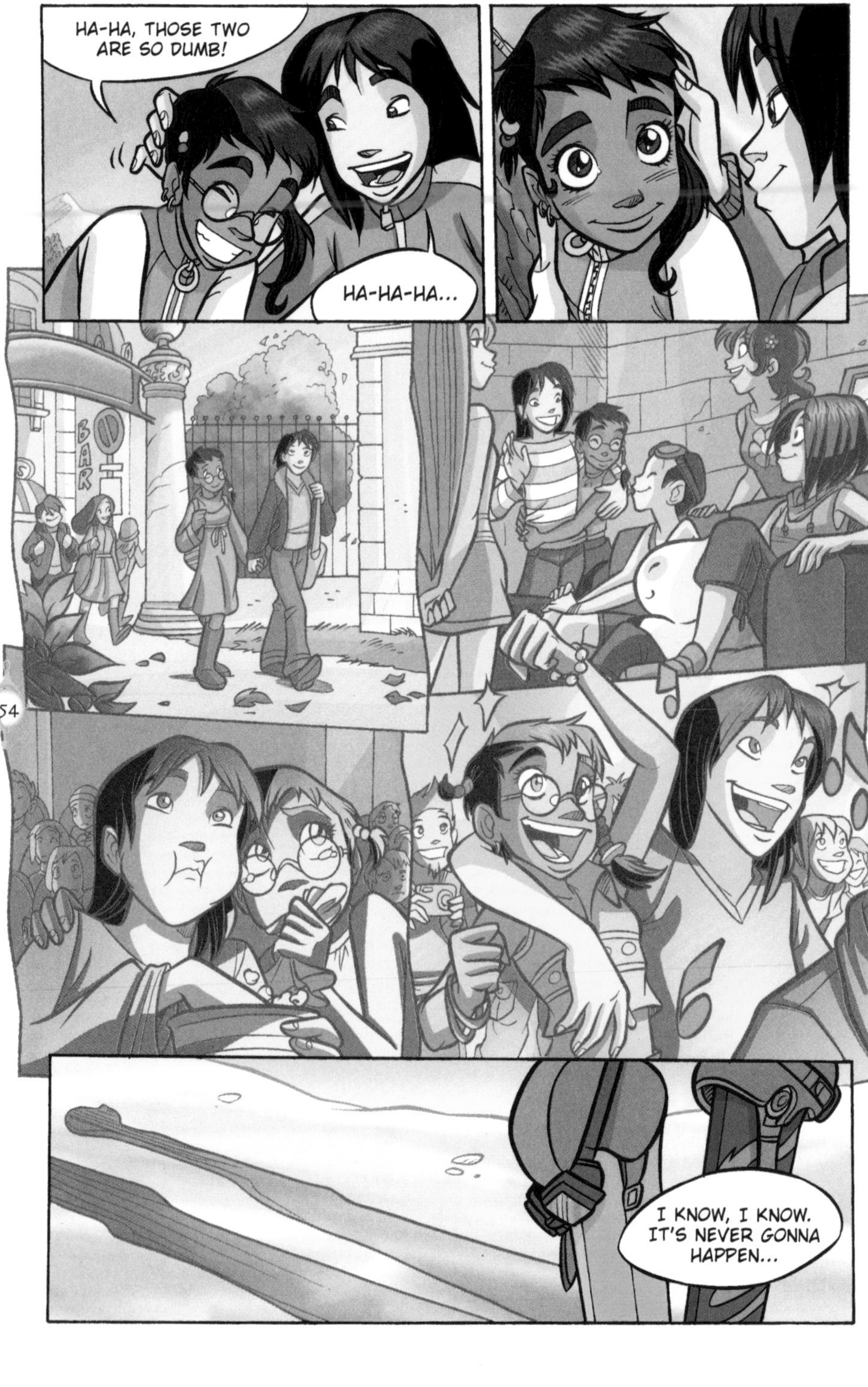
HA-HA, THOSE TWO ARE SO DUMB!
HA-HA-HA...
BAR
I KNOW, I KNOW. IT'S NEVER GONNA HAPPEN...

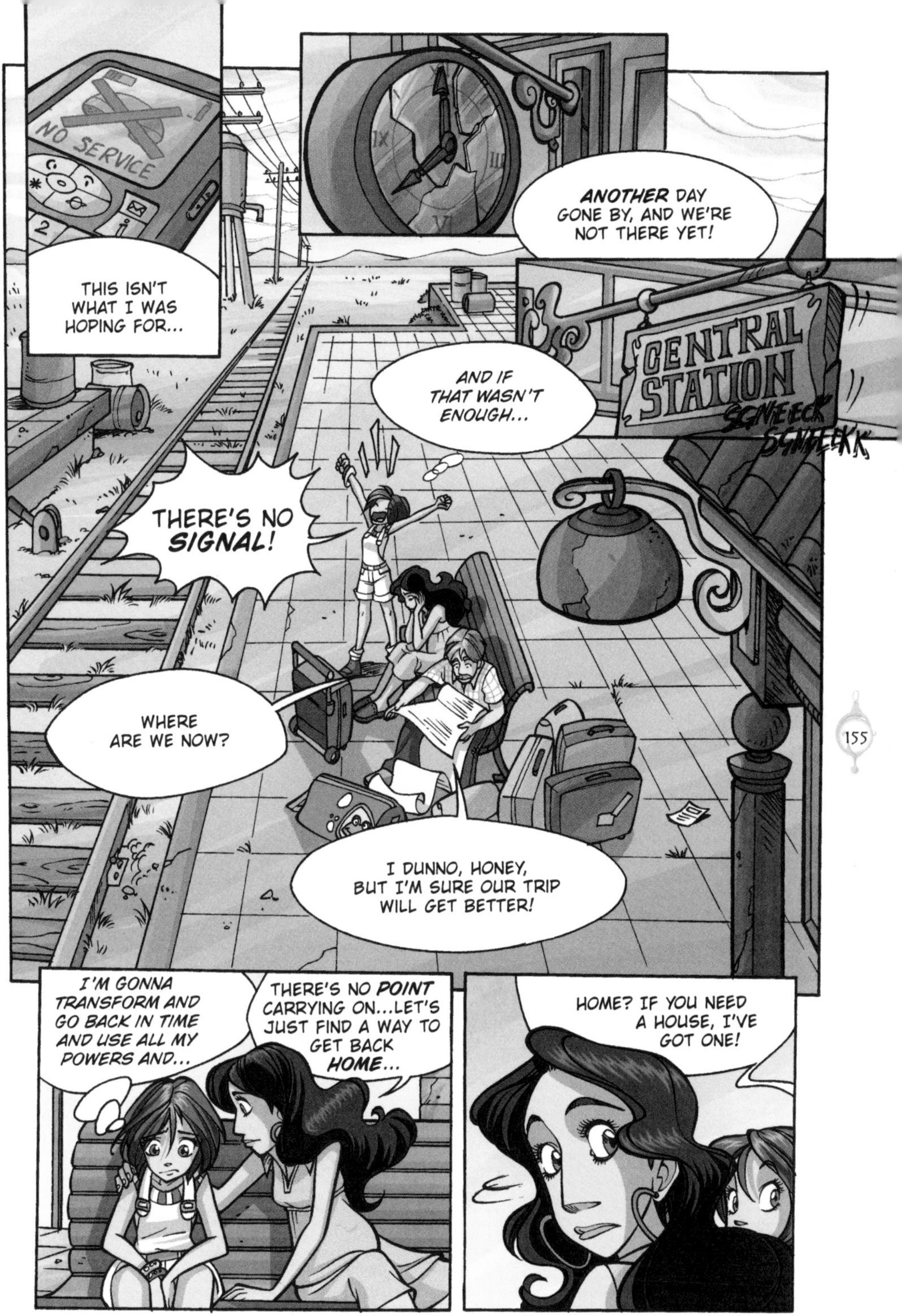
NO SERVICE
THIS ISN'T WHAT I WAS HOPING FOR...
ANOTHER DAY GONE BY, AND WE'RE NOT THERE YET!
CENTRAL STATION
AND IF THAT WASN'T ENOUGH...
THERE'S NO SIGNAL!
WHERE ARE WE NOW?
I DUNNO, HONEY, BUT I'M SURE OUR TRIP WILL GET BETTER!
I'M GONNA TRANSFORM AND GO BACK IN TIME AND USE ALL MY POWERS AND...
THERE'S NO POINT CARRYING ON...LET'S JUST FIND A WAY TO GET BACK HOME...
HOME? IF YOU NEED A HOUSE, I'VE GOT ONE!

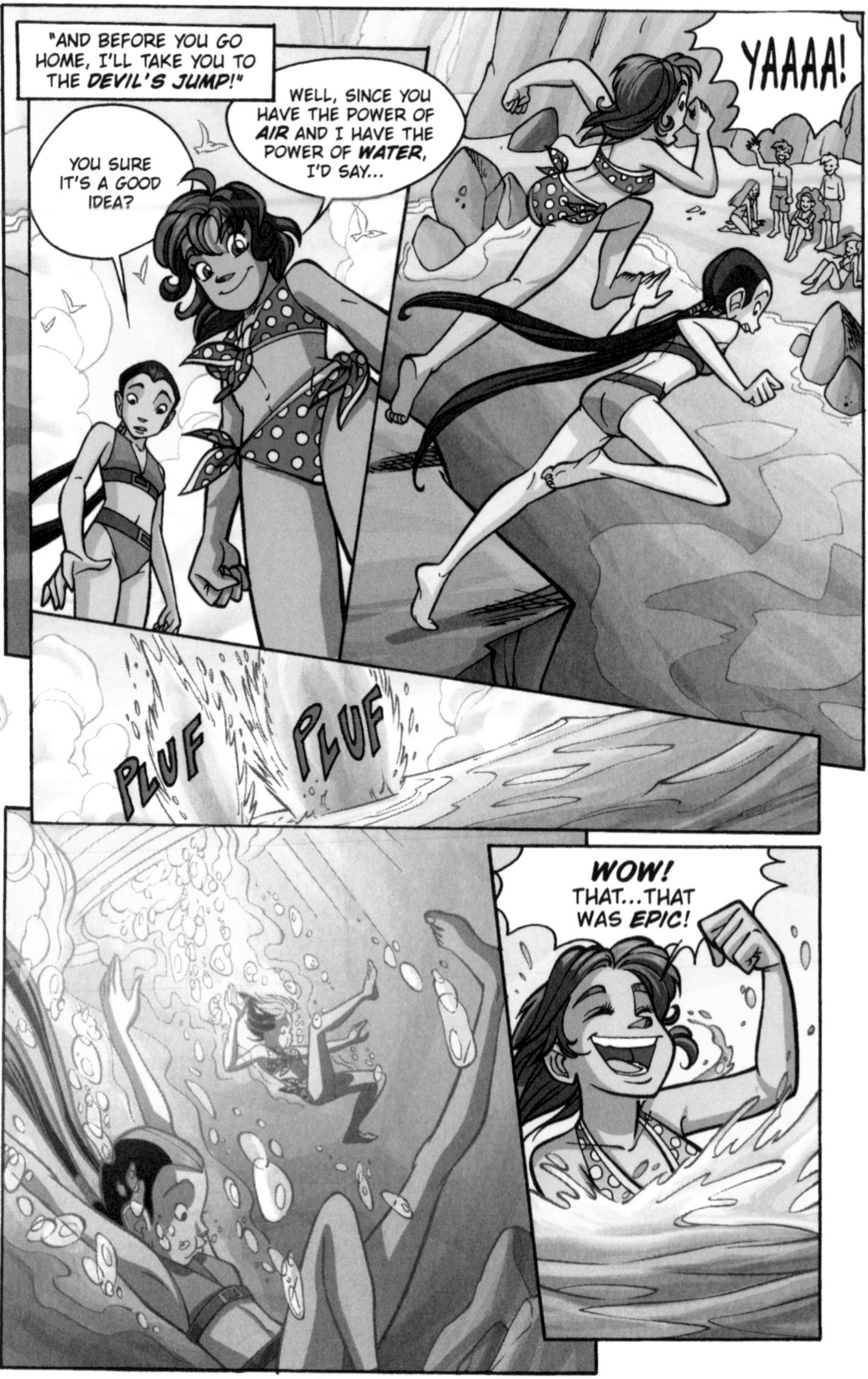

"AND BEFORE YOU GO HOME, I'LL TAKE YOU TO THE DEVIL'S JUMP!"
YOU SURE IT'S A GOOD IDEA?
WELL, SINCE YOU HAVE THE POWER OF AIR AND I HAVE THE POWER OF WATER, I'D SAY...
YAAAA!
PLUF
PLUF
WOW! THAT...THAT WAS EPIC!

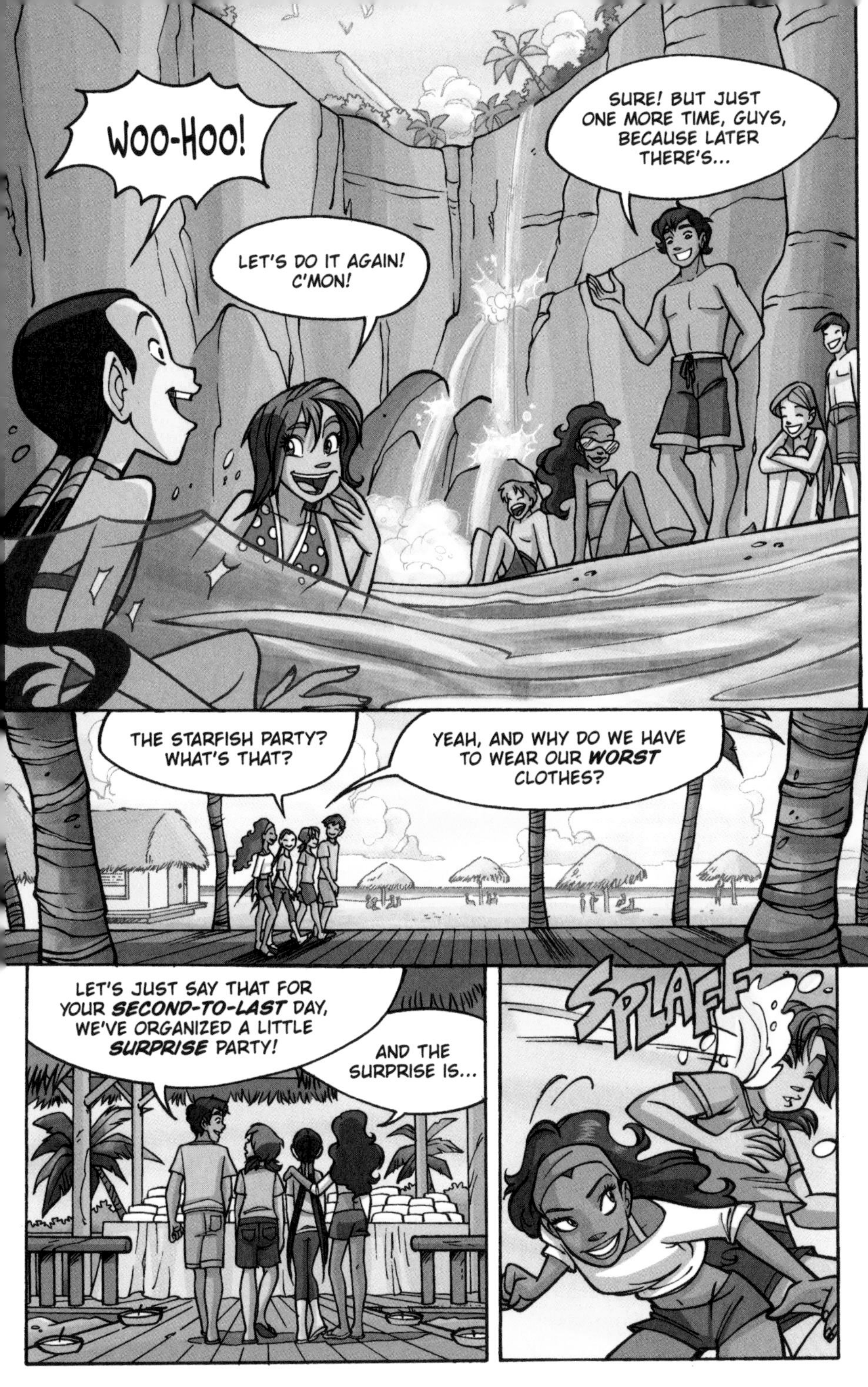
WOO-HOO!
LET'S DO IT AGAIN! C'MON!
SURE! BUT JUST ONE MORE TIME, GUYS, BECAUSE LATER THERE'S...
THE STARFISH PARTY? WHAT'S THAT?
YEAH, AND WHY DO WE HAVE TO WEAR OUR **WORST** CLOTHES?
LET'S JUST SAY THAT FOR YOUR **SECOND-TO-LAST** DAY, WE'VE ORGANIZED A LITTLE **SURPRISE** PARTY!
AND THE SURPRISE IS...
SPLAFF

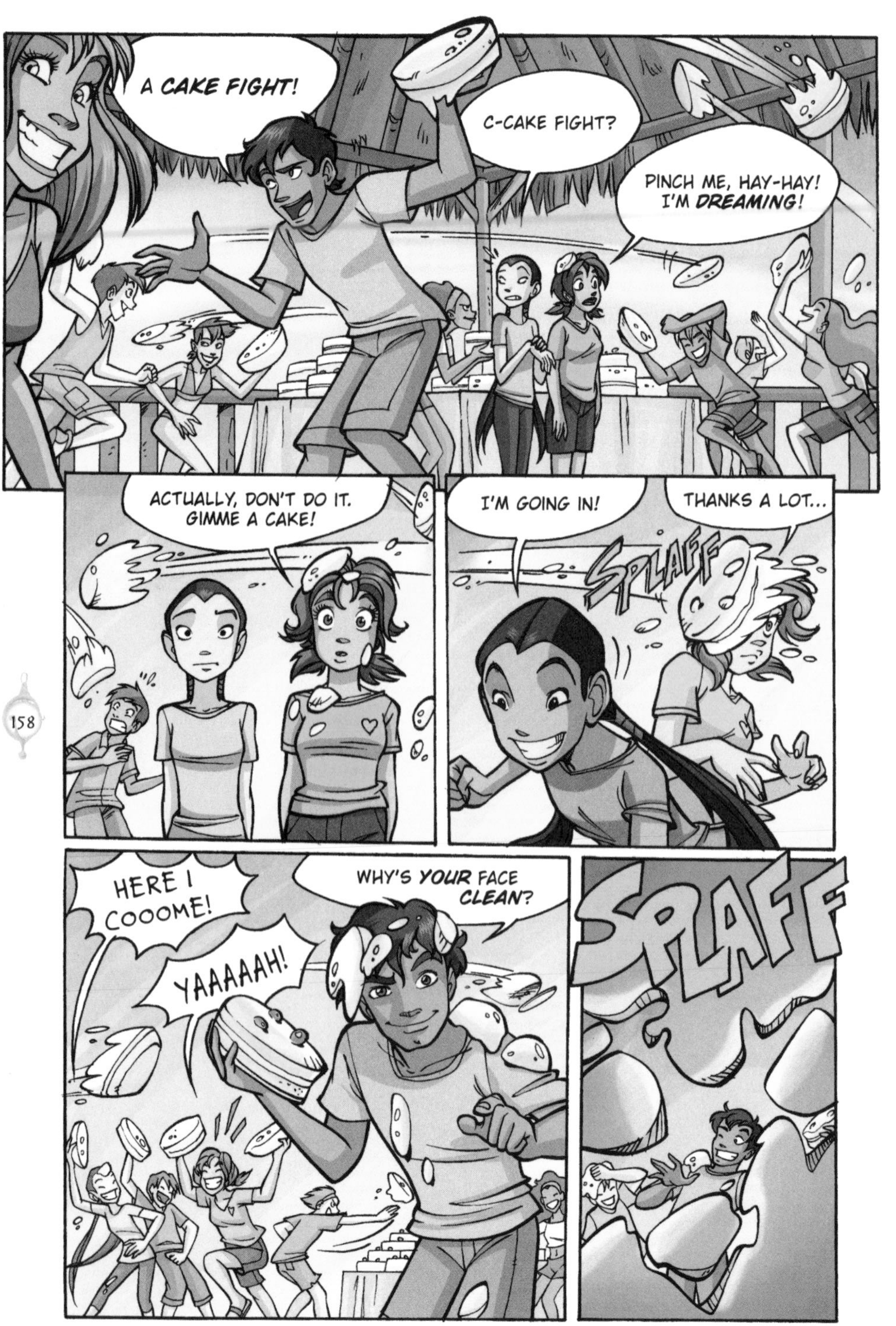
A CAKE FIGHT!
C-CAKE FIGHT?
PINCH ME, HAY-HAY! I'M DREAMING!
ACTUALLY, DON'T DO IT. GIMME A CAKE!
I'M GOING IN!
THANKS A LOT...
SPLAFF
HERE I COOOME!
WHY'S YOUR FACE CLEAN?
YAAAAAH!
SPLAFF

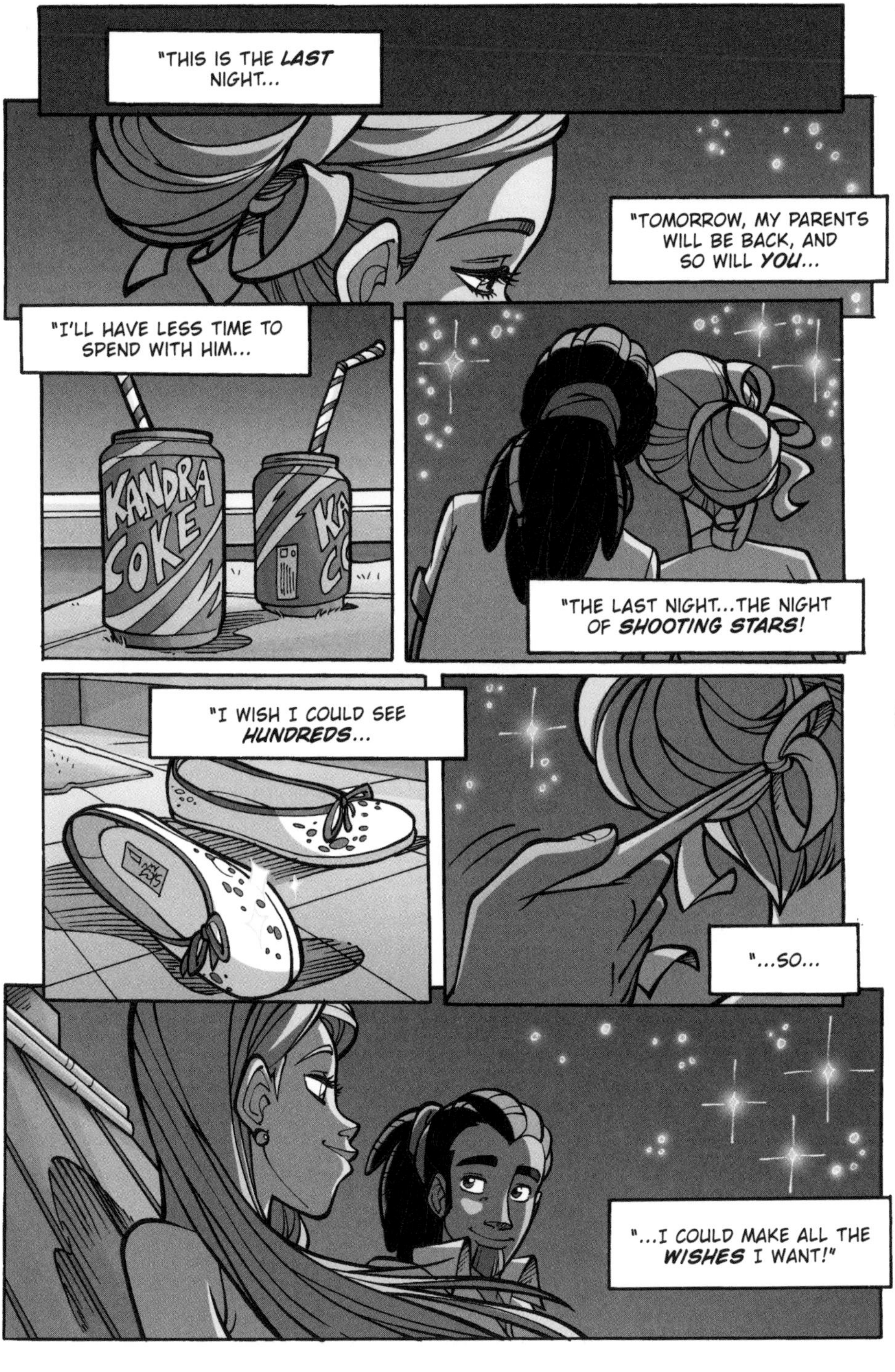
"THIS IS THE LAST NIGHT...
"TOMORROW, MY PARENTS WILL BE BACK, AND SO WILL YOU...
"I'LL HAVE LESS TIME TO SPEND WITH HIM...
KANDRA COKE
"THE LAST NIGHT...THE NIGHT OF SHOOTING STARS!
"I WISH I COULD SEE HUNDREDS...
"...SO...
"...I COULD MAKE ALL THE WISHES I WANT!"

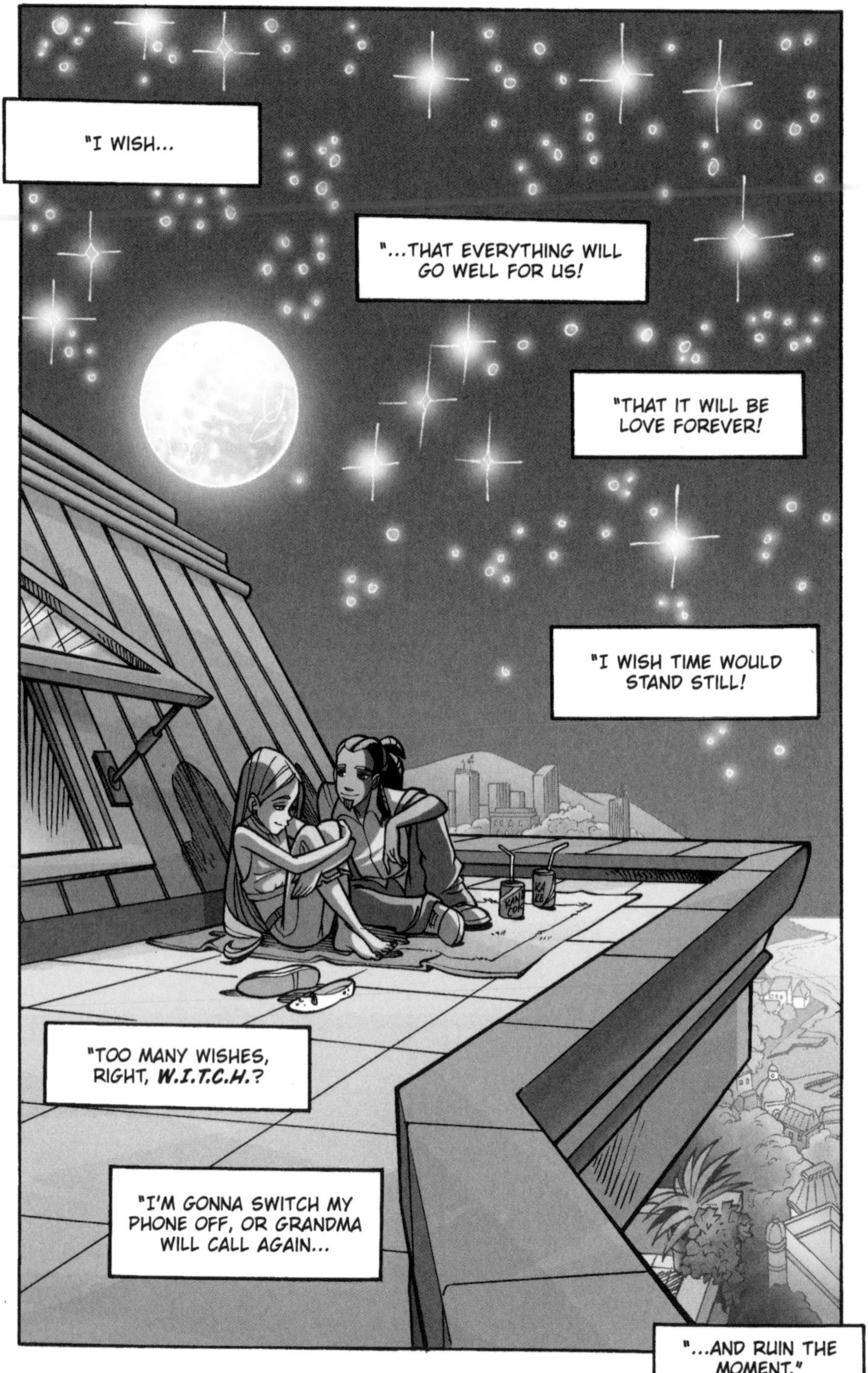
"I WISH...
"...THAT EVERYTHING WILL GO WELL FOR US!
"THAT IT WILL BE LOVE FOREVER!
"I WISH TIME WOULD STAND STILL!
"TOO MANY WISHES, RIGHT, W.I.T.C.H.?
"I'M GONNA SWITCH MY PHONE OFF, OR GRANDMA WILL CALL AGAIN...
"...AND RUIN THE MOMENT."

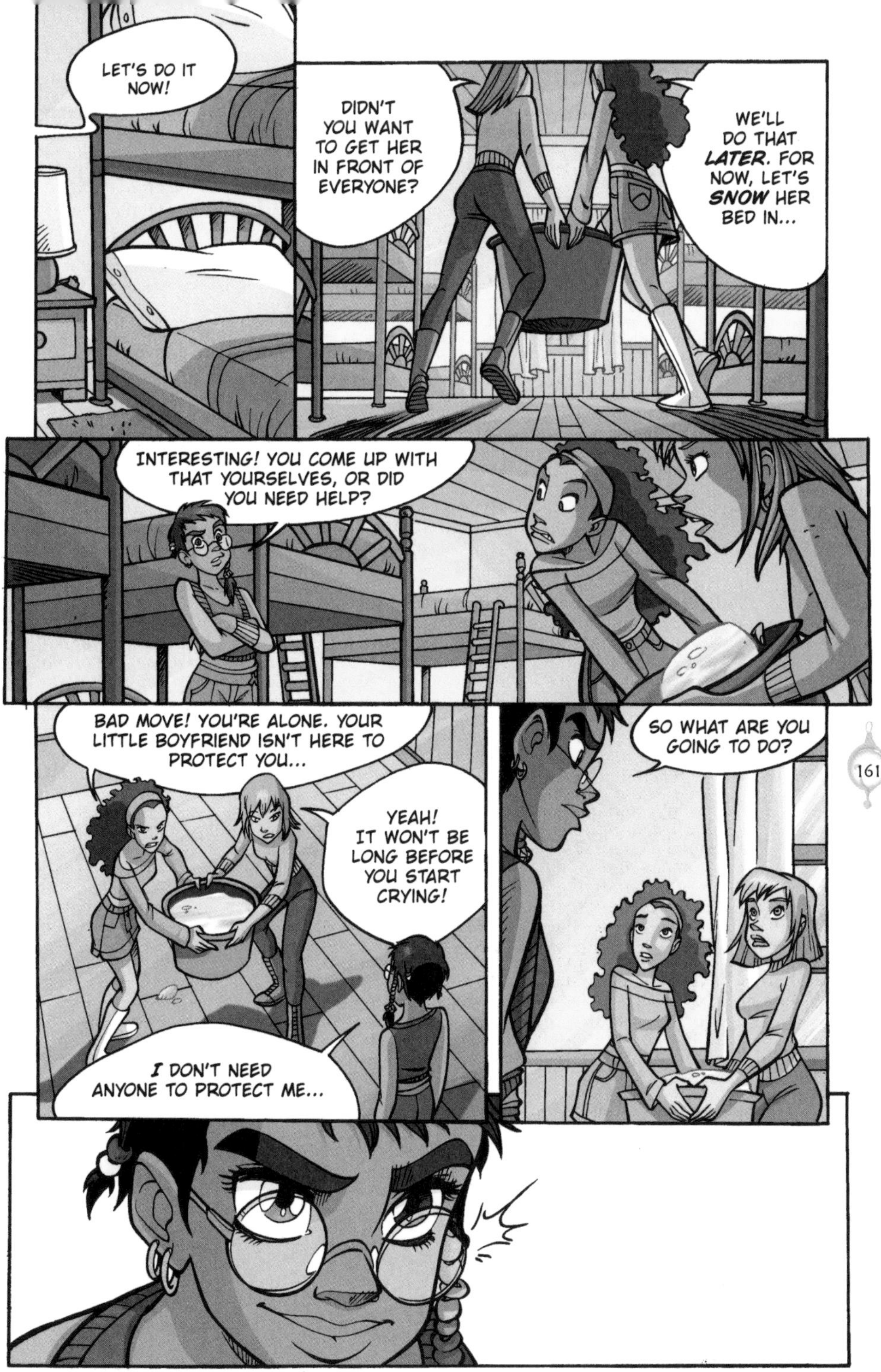
LET'S DO IT NOW!
DIDN'T YOU WANT TO GET HER IN FRONT OF EVERYONE?
WE'LL DO THAT LATER. FOR NOW, LET'S SNOW HER BED IN...
INTERESTING! YOU COME UP WITH THAT YOURSELVES, OR DID YOU NEED HELP?
BAD MOVE! YOU'RE ALONE. YOUR LITTLE BOYFRIEND ISN'T HERE TO PROTECT YOU...
YEAH! IT WON'T BE LONG BEFORE YOU START CRYING!
I DON'T NEED ANYONE TO PROTECT ME...
SO WHAT ARE YOU GOING TO DO?

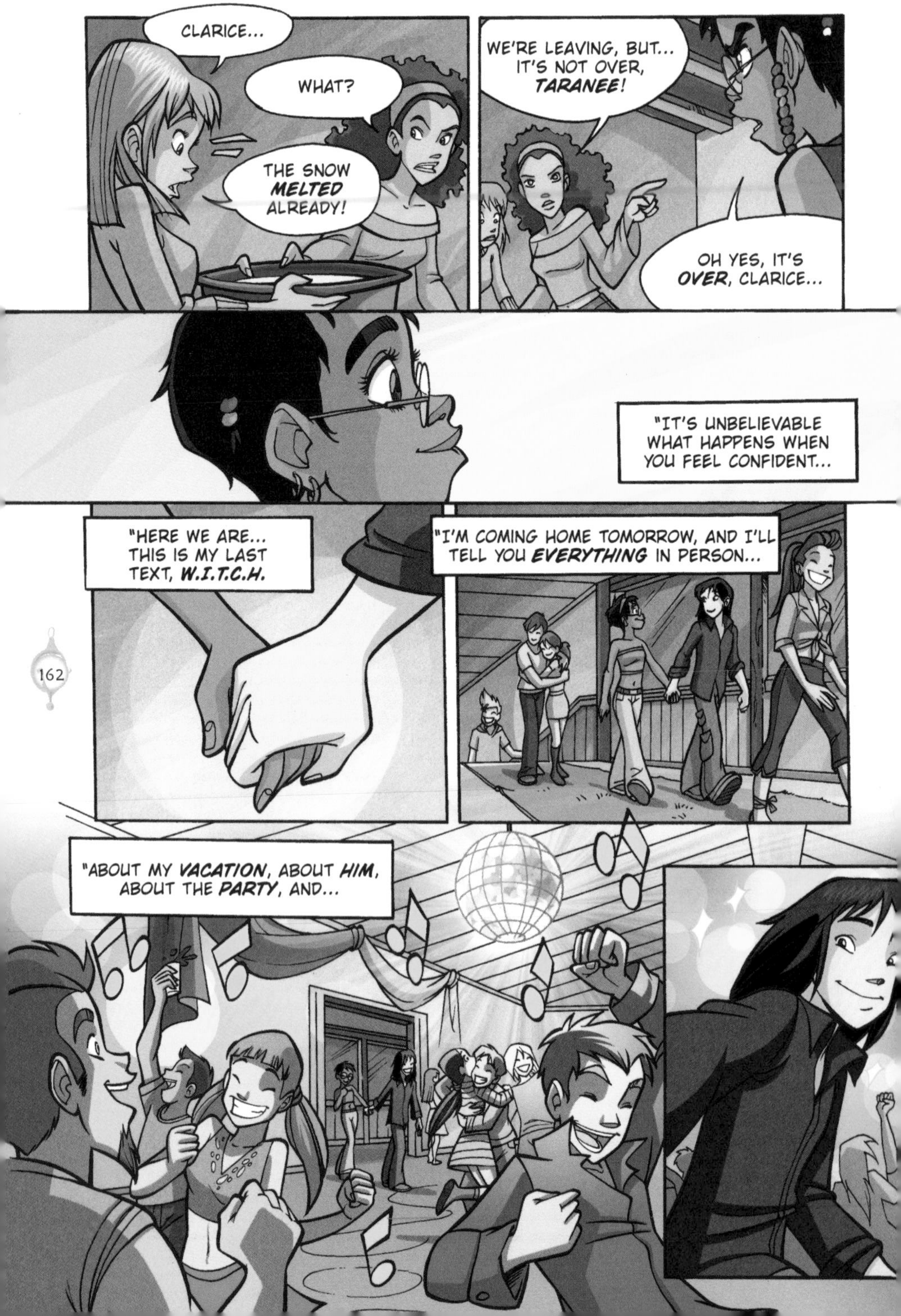
CLARICE...
WHAT?
THE SNOW MELTED ALREADY!
WE'RE LEAVING, BUT... IT'S NOT OVER, TARANEE!
OH YES, IT'S OVER, CLARICE...
"IT'S UNBELIEVABLE WHAT HAPPENS WHEN YOU FEEL CONFIDENT...
"HERE WE ARE... THIS IS MY LAST TEXT, W.I.T.C.H.
"I'M COMING HOME TOMORROW, AND I'LL TELL YOU EVERYTHING IN PERSON...
"ABOUT MY VACATION, ABOUT HIM, ABOUT THE PARTY, AND...

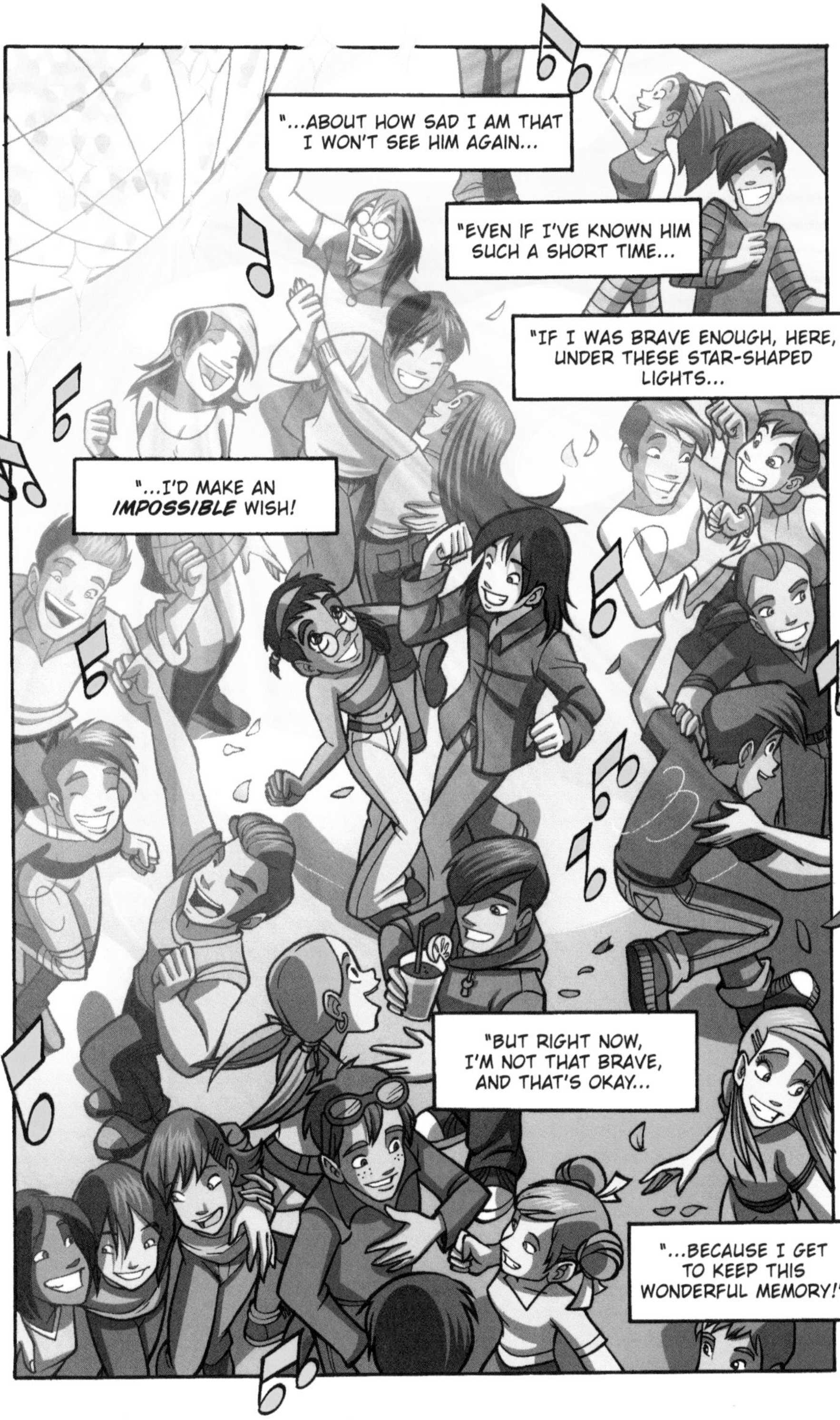
"...ABOUT HOW SAD I AM THAT I WON'T SEE HIM AGAIN...
"EVEN IF I'VE KNOWN HIM SUCH A SHORT TIME...
"IF I WAS BRAVE ENOUGH, HERE, UNDER THESE STAR-SHAPED LIGHTS...
"...I'D MAKE AN *IMPOSSIBLE* WISH!
"BUT RIGHT NOW, I'M NOT THAT BRAVE, AND THAT'S OKAY...
"...BECAUSE I GET TO KEEP THIS WONDERFUL MEMORY!"

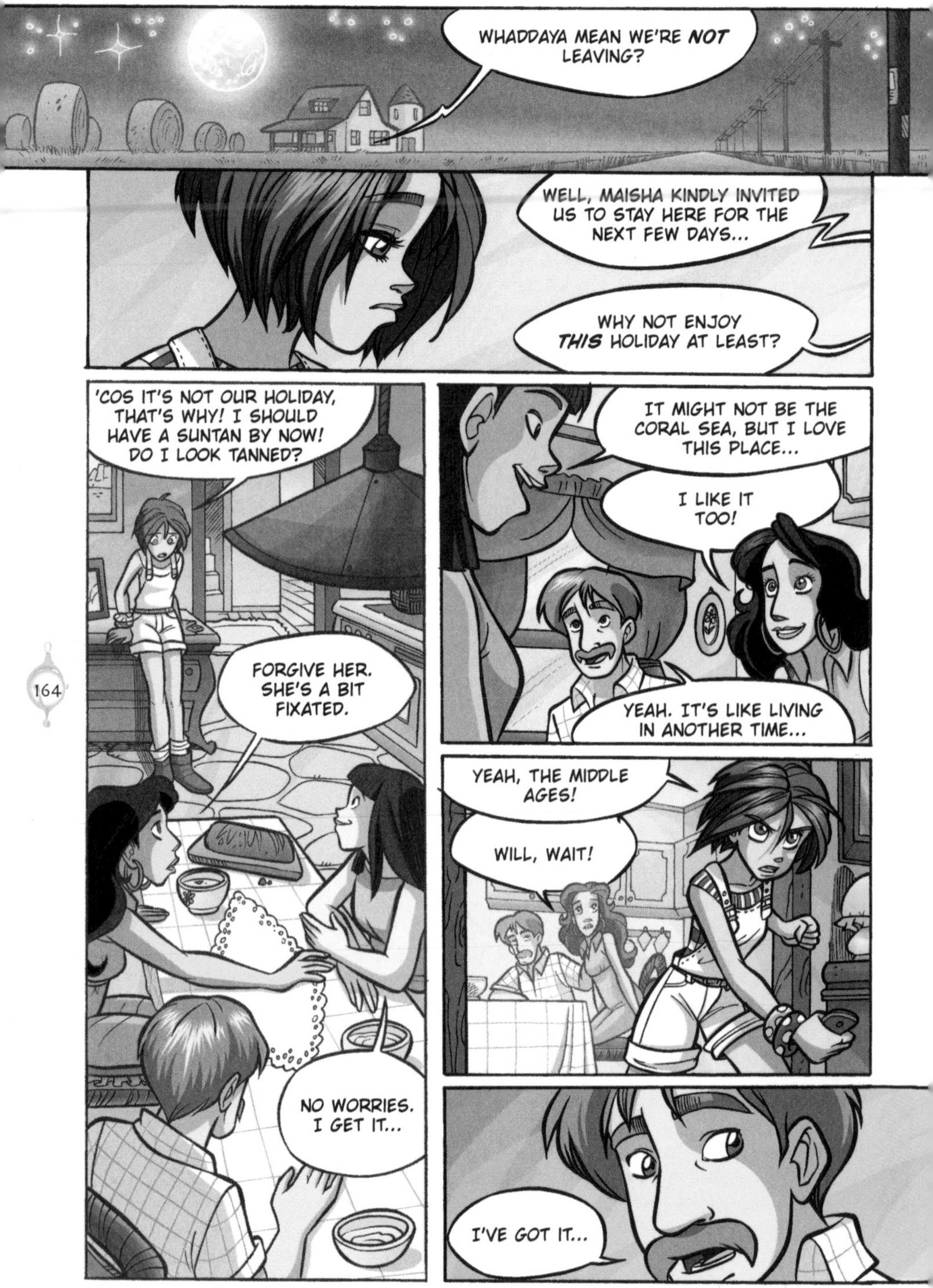
WHADDAYA MEAN WE'RE *NOT* LEAVING?
WELL, MAISHA KINDLY INVITED US TO STAY HERE FOR THE NEXT FEW DAYS...
WHY NOT ENJOY *THIS* HOLIDAY AT LEAST?
'COS IT'S NOT OUR HOLIDAY, THAT'S WHY! I SHOULD HAVE A SUNTAN BY NOW! DO I LOOK TANNED?
FORGIVE HER. SHE'S A BIT FIXATED.
NO WORRIES. I GET IT...
IT MIGHT NOT BE THE CORAL SEA, BUT I LOVE THIS PLACE...
I LIKE IT TOO!
YEAH. IT'S LIKE LIVING IN ANOTHER TIME...
YEAH, THE MIDDLE AGES!
WILL, WAIT!
I'VE GOT IT...

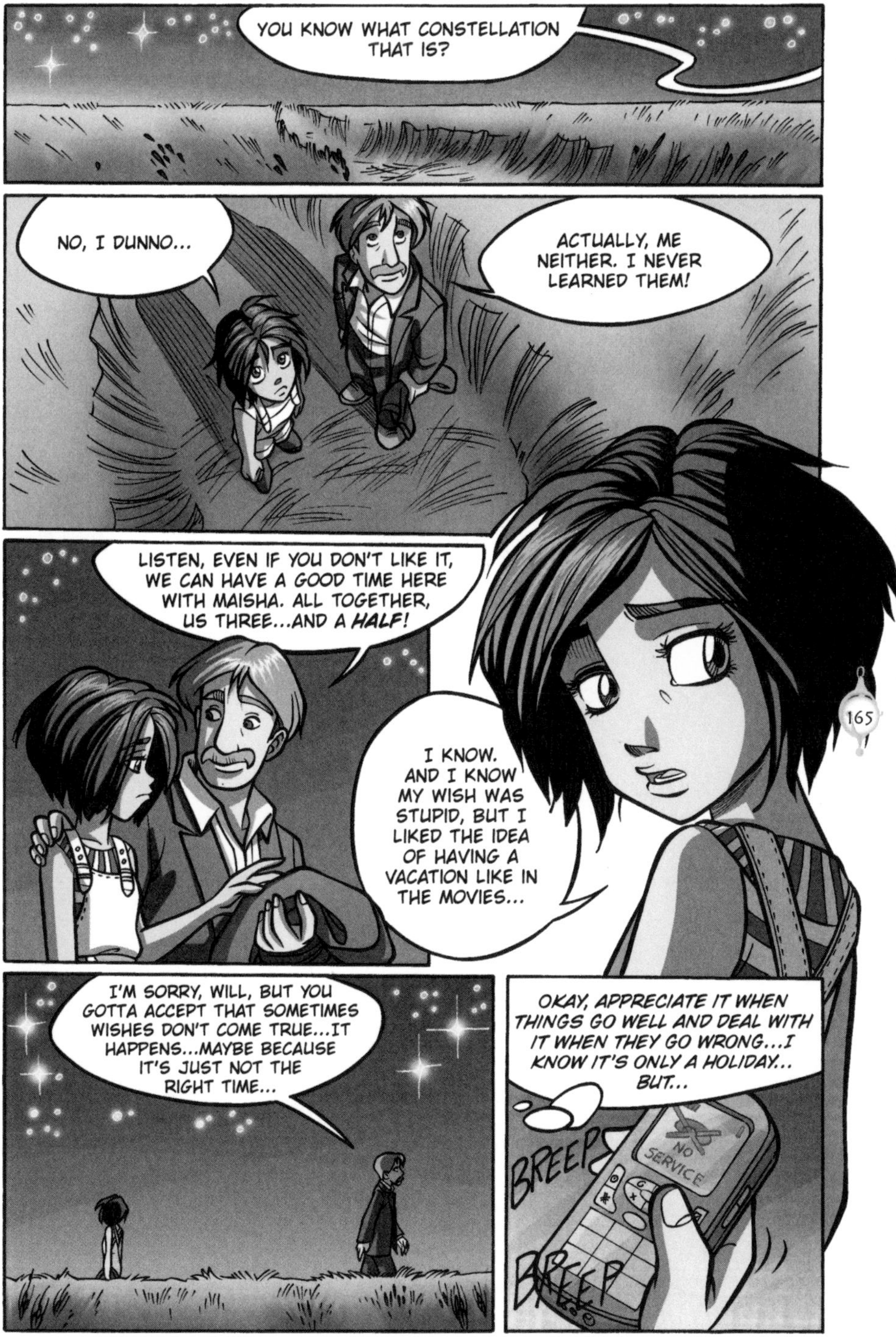
YOU KNOW WHAT CONSTELLATION THAT IS?
NO, I DUNNO...
ACTUALLY, ME NEITHER. I NEVER LEARNED THEM!
LISTEN, EVEN IF YOU DON'T LIKE IT, WE CAN HAVE A GOOD TIME HERE WITH MAISHA. ALL TOGETHER, US THREE...AND A *HALF*!
I KNOW. AND I KNOW MY WISH WAS STUPID, BUT I LIKED THE IDEA OF HAVING A VACATION LIKE IN THE MOVIES...
I'M SORRY, WILL, BUT YOU GOTTA ACCEPT THAT SOMETIMES WISHES DON'T COME TRUE...IT HAPPENS...MAYBE BECAUSE IT'S JUST NOT THE RIGHT TIME...
OKAY, APPRECIATE IT WHEN THINGS GO WELL AND DEAL WITH IT WHEN THEY GO WRONG...I KNOW IT'S ONLY A HOLIDAY... BUT...
BREEP
NO SERVICE
BREEP

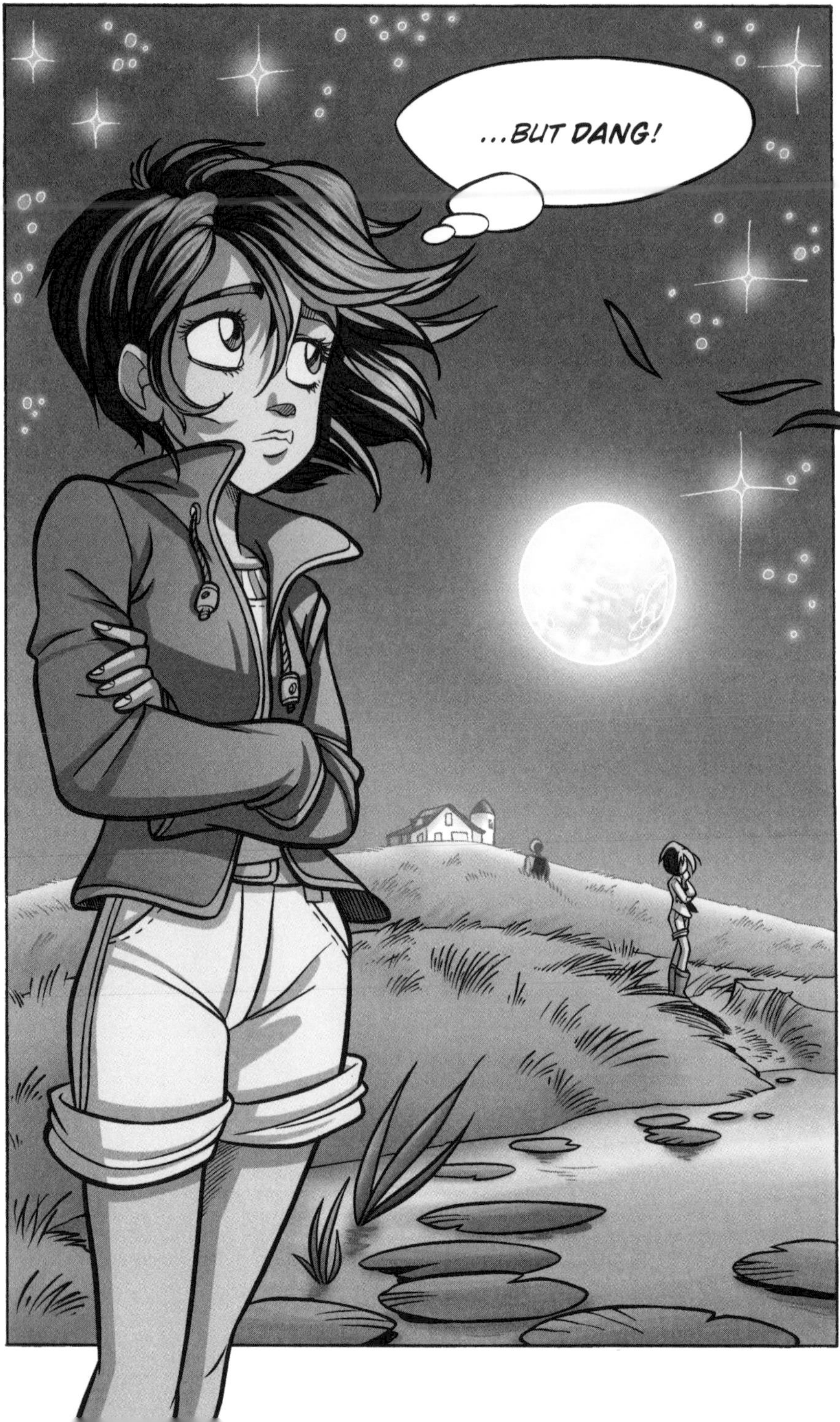
...BUT DANG!

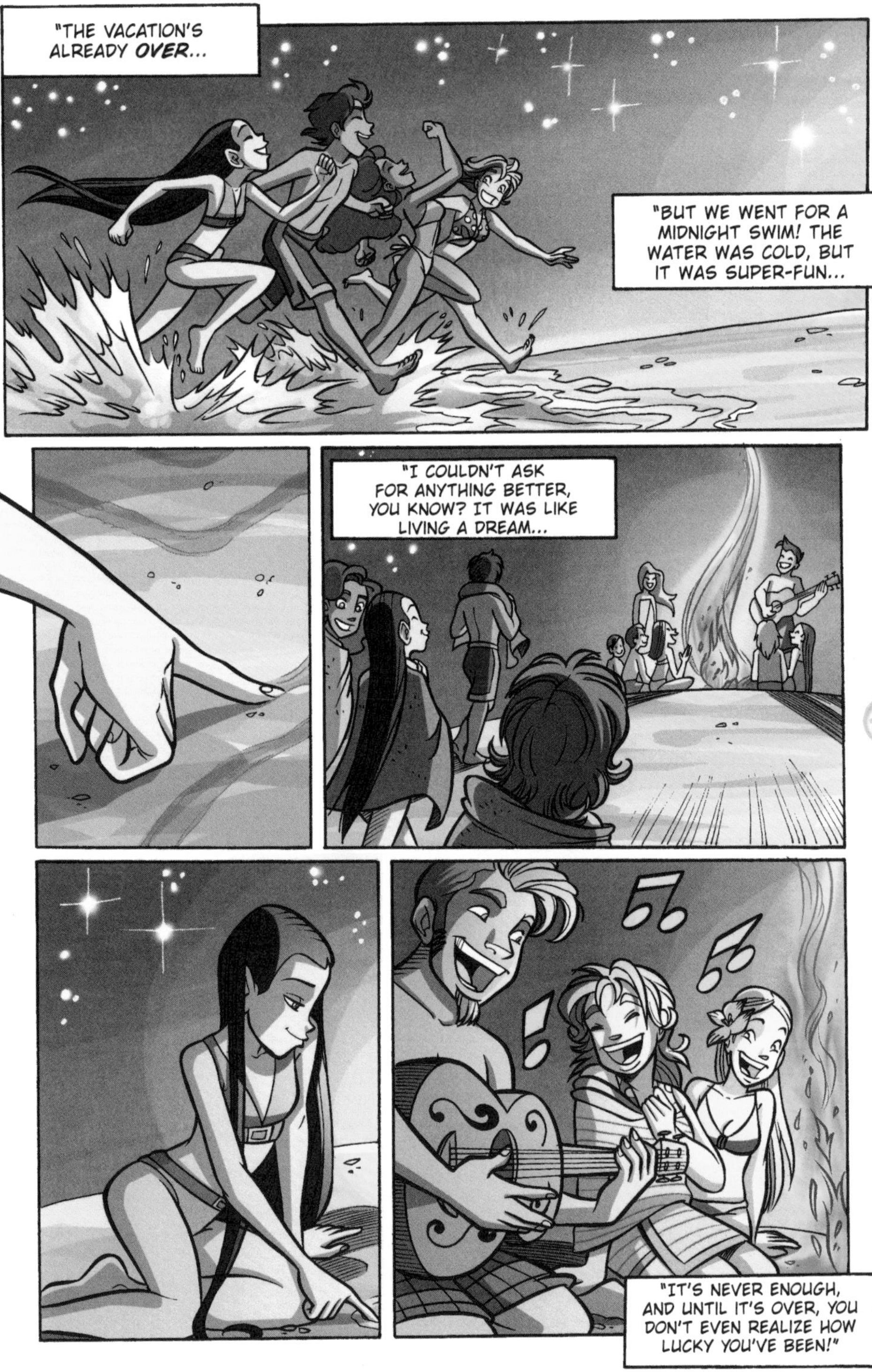
"THE VACATION'S ALREADY OVER...
"BUT WE WENT FOR A MIDNIGHT SWIM! THE WATER WAS COLD, BUT IT WAS SUPER-FUN...
"I COULDN'T ASK FOR ANYTHING BETTER, YOU KNOW? IT WAS LIKE LIVING A DREAM...
"IT'S NEVER ENOUGH, AND UNTIL IT'S OVER, YOU DON'T EVEN REALIZE HOW LUCKY YOU'VE BEEN!"

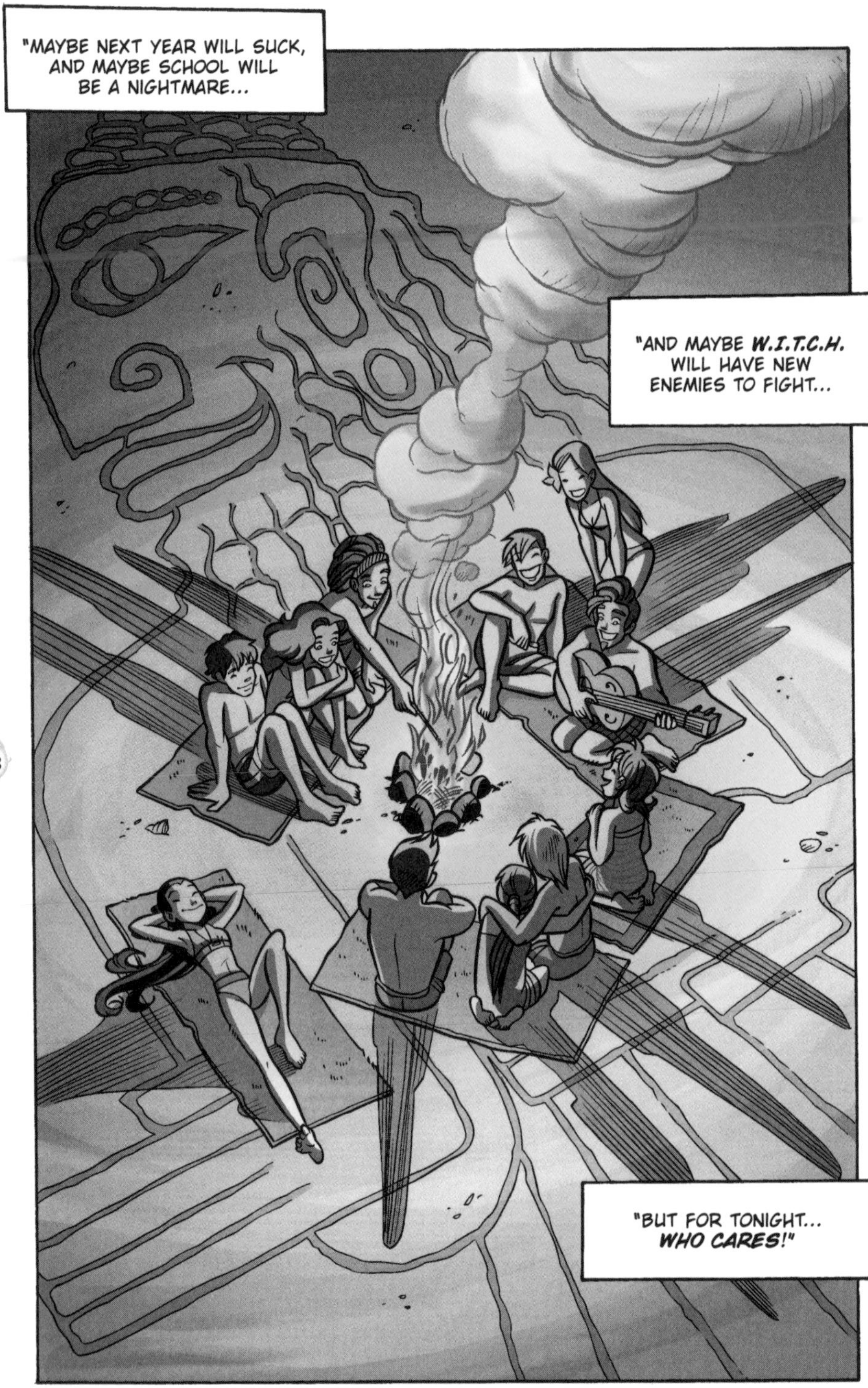
"MAYBE NEXT YEAR WILL SUCK, AND MAYBE SCHOOL WILL BE A NIGHTMARE...
"AND MAYBE W.I.T.C.H. WILL HAVE NEW ENEMIES TO FIGHT...
"BUT FOR TONIGHT... WHO CARES!"

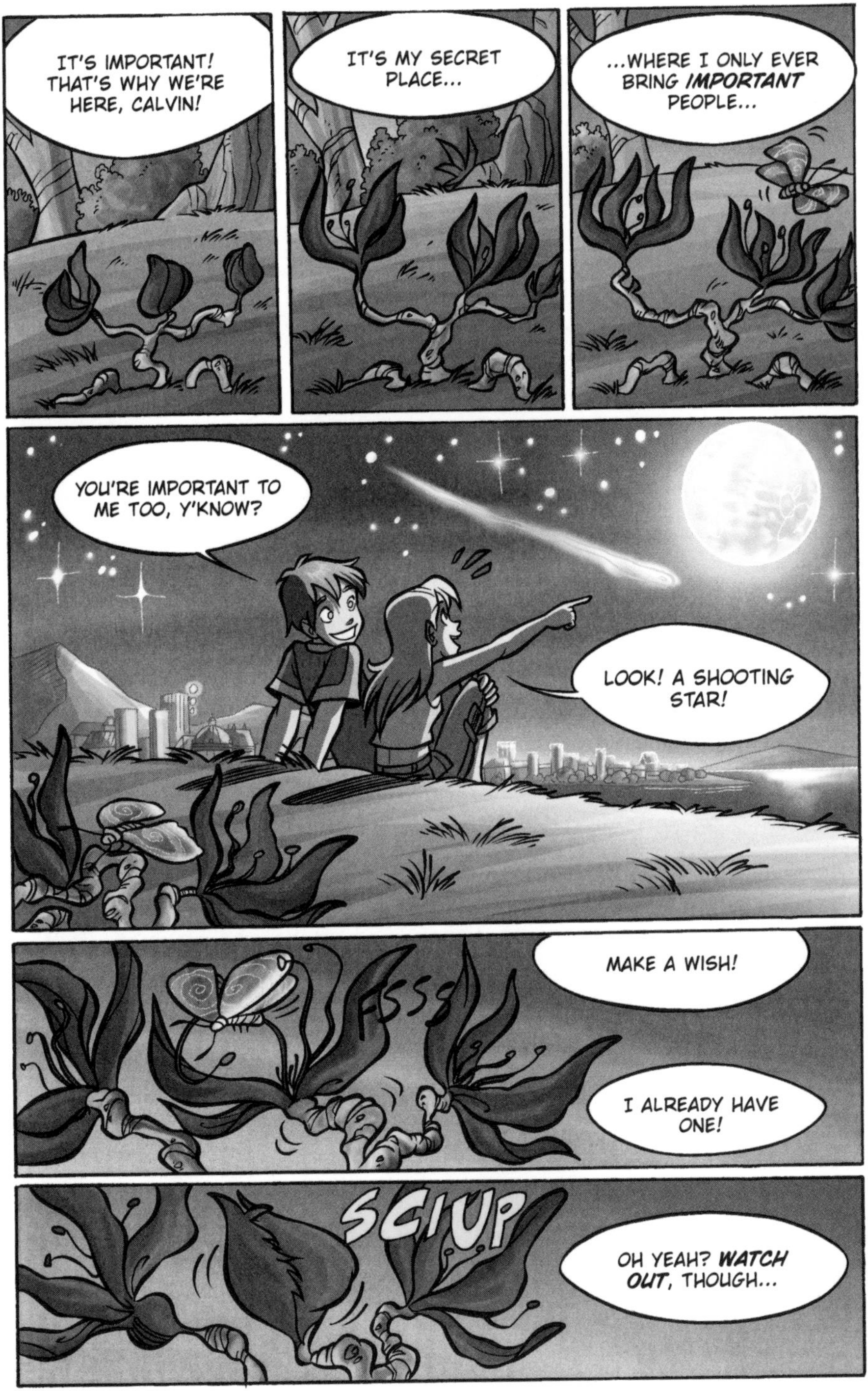

IT'S IMPORTANT! THAT'S WHY WE'RE HERE, CALVIN!
IT'S MY SECRET PLACE...
...WHERE I ONLY EVER BRING *IMPORTANT* PEOPLE...
YOU'RE IMPORTANT TO ME TOO, Y'KNOW?
LOOK! A SHOOTING STAR!
MAKE A WISH!
FSSS
I ALREADY HAVE ONE!
SCIUP
OH YEAH? *WATCH OUT*, THOUGH...

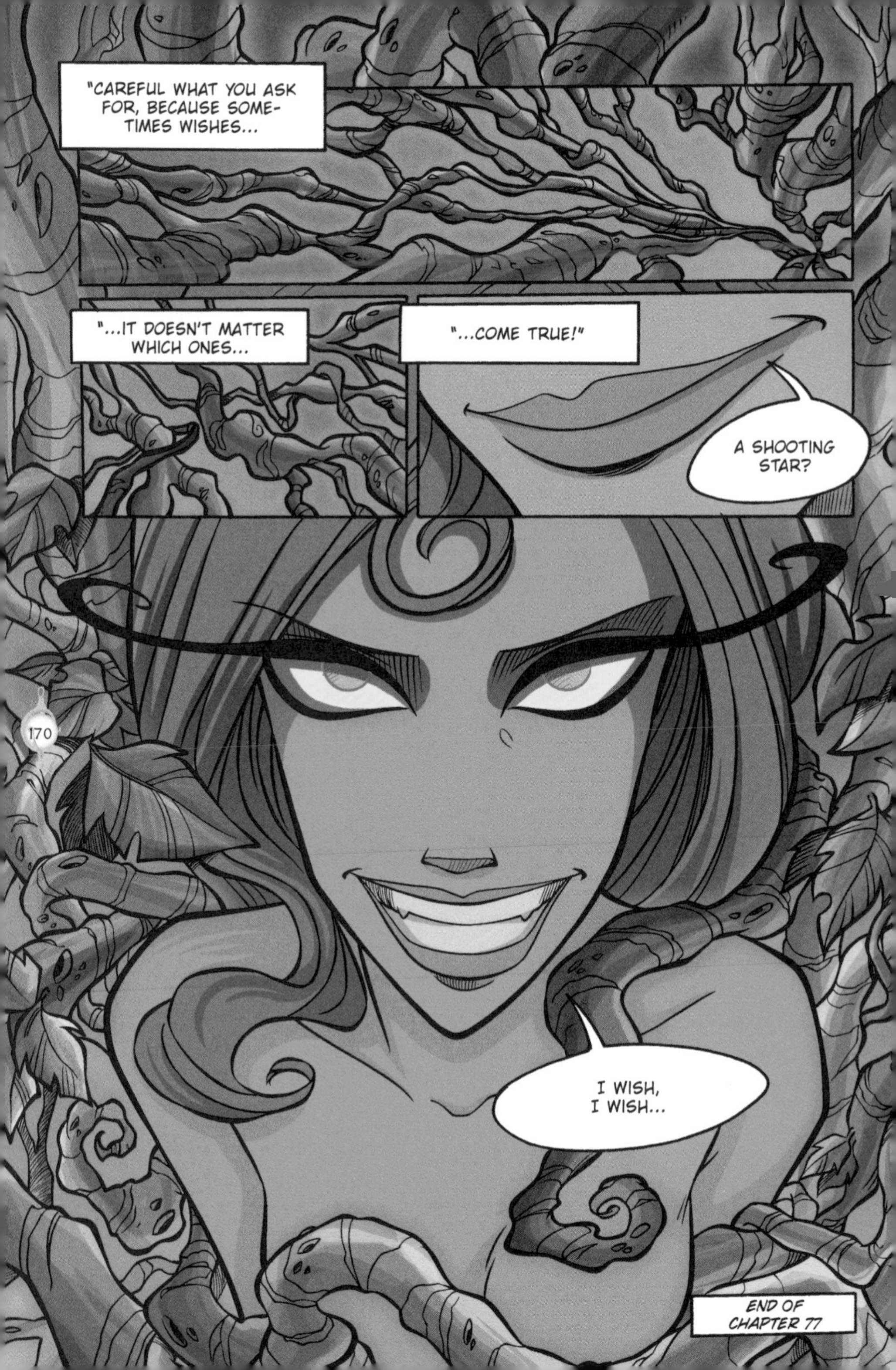

"CAREFUL WHAT YOU ASK FOR, BECAUSE SOME-TIMES WISHES...
"...IT DOESN'T MATTER WHICH ONES...
"...COME TRUE!"
A SHOOTING STAR?
I WISH, I WISH...
END OF CHAPTER 77

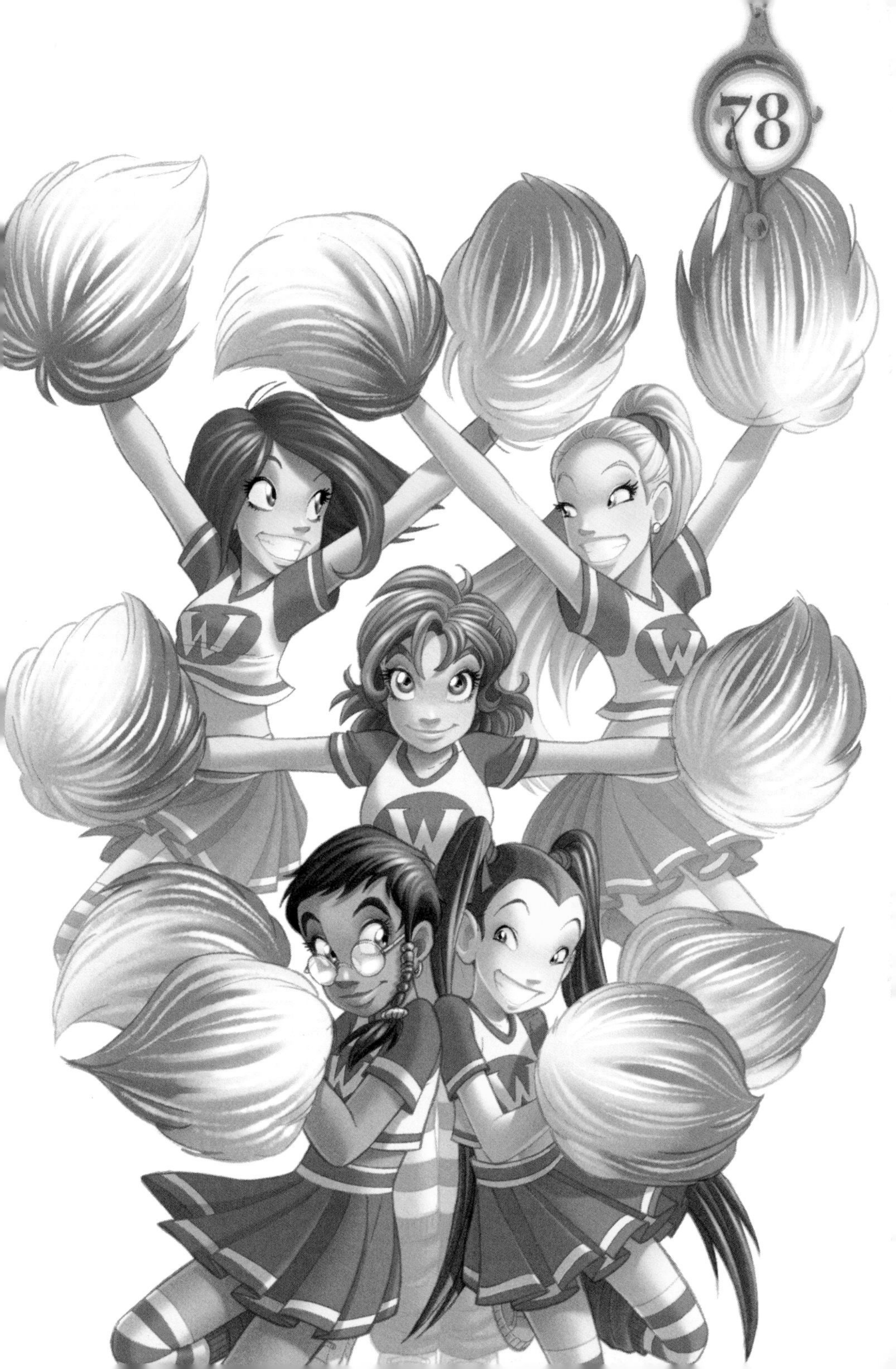
78

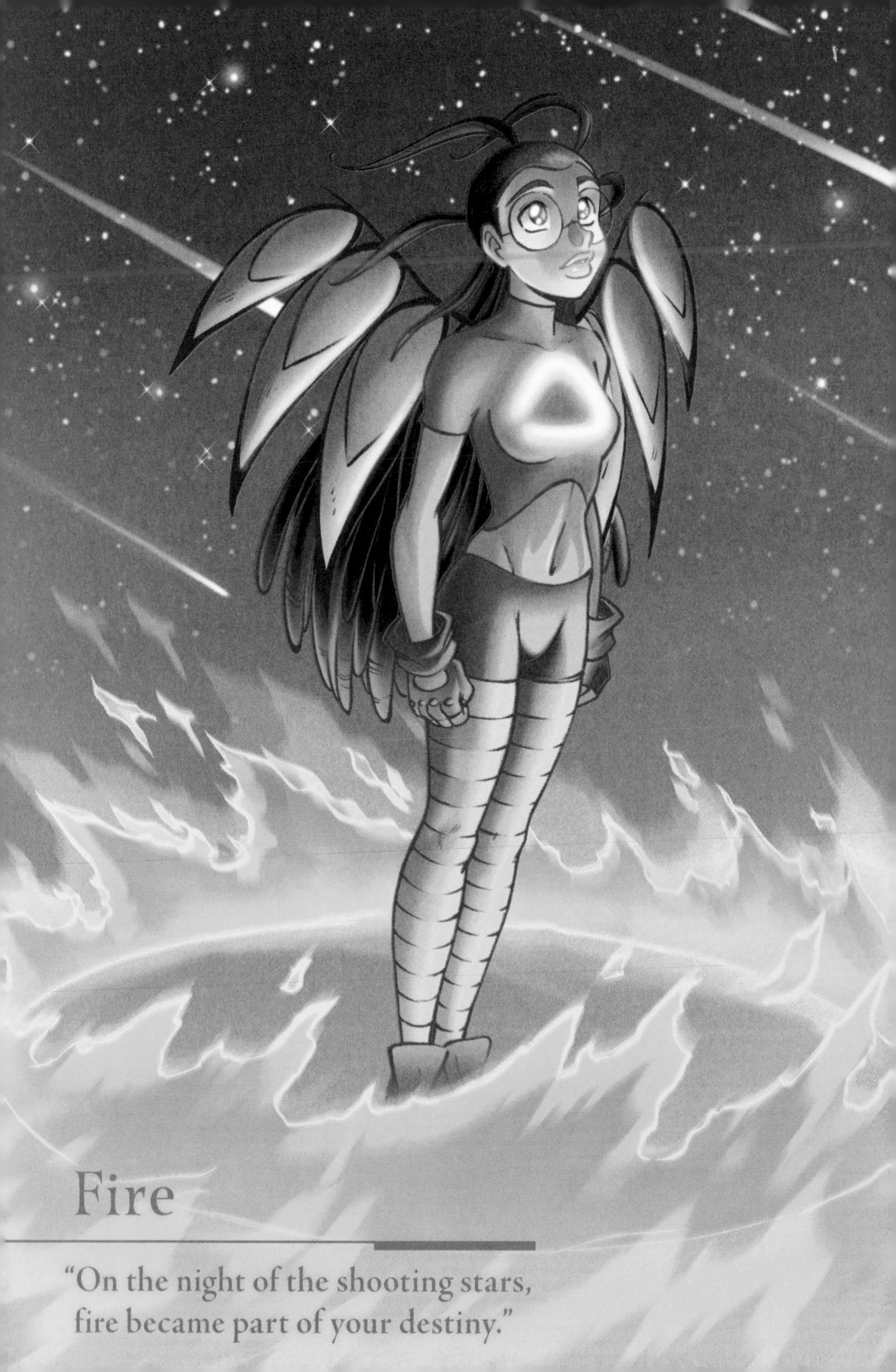

Fire

"On the night of the shooting stars,
fire became part of your destiny."

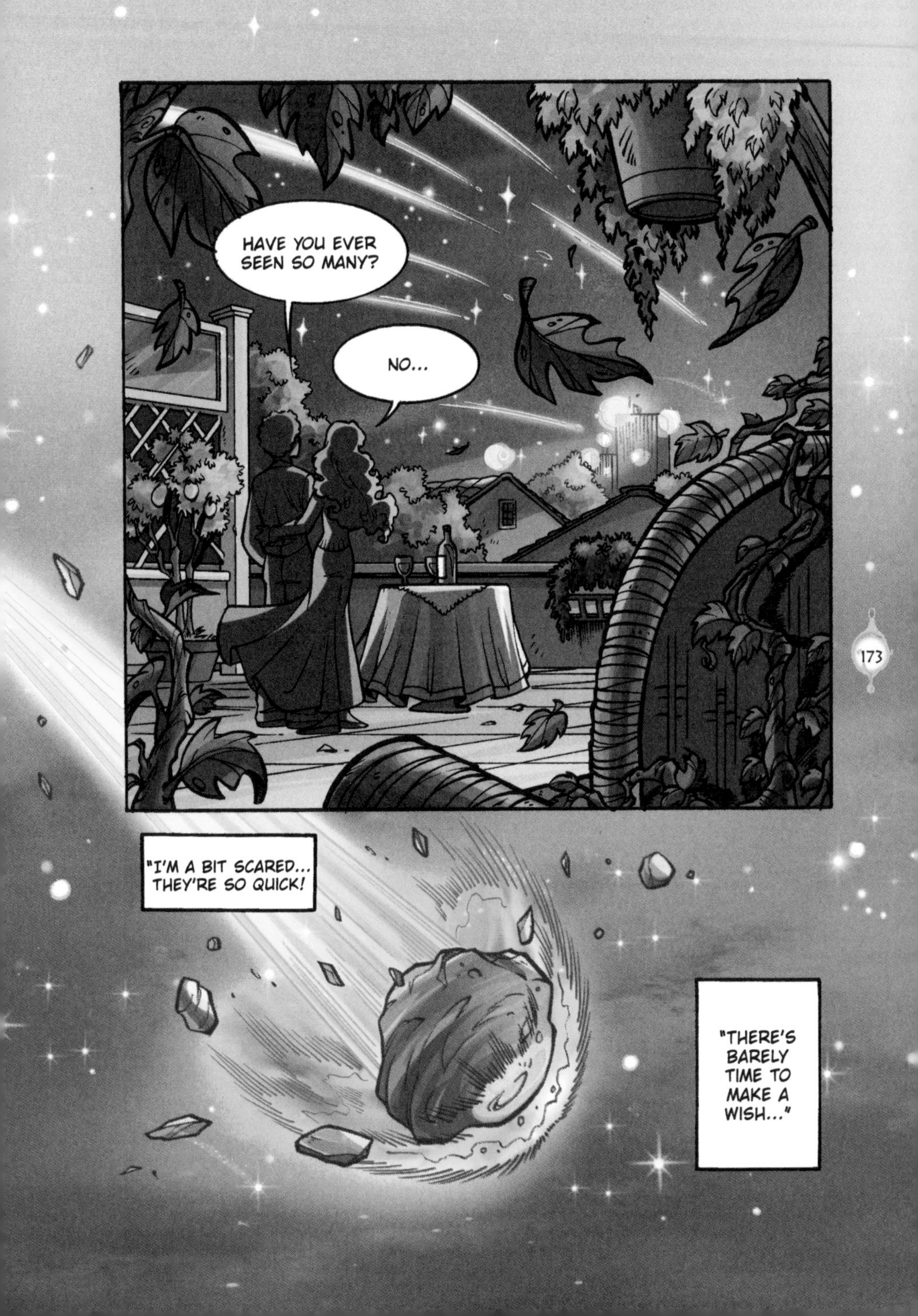
HAVE YOU EVER SEEN SO MANY?
NO...
"I'M A BIT SCARED... THEY'RE SO QUICK!
"THERE'S BARELY TIME TO MAKE A WISH..."

173

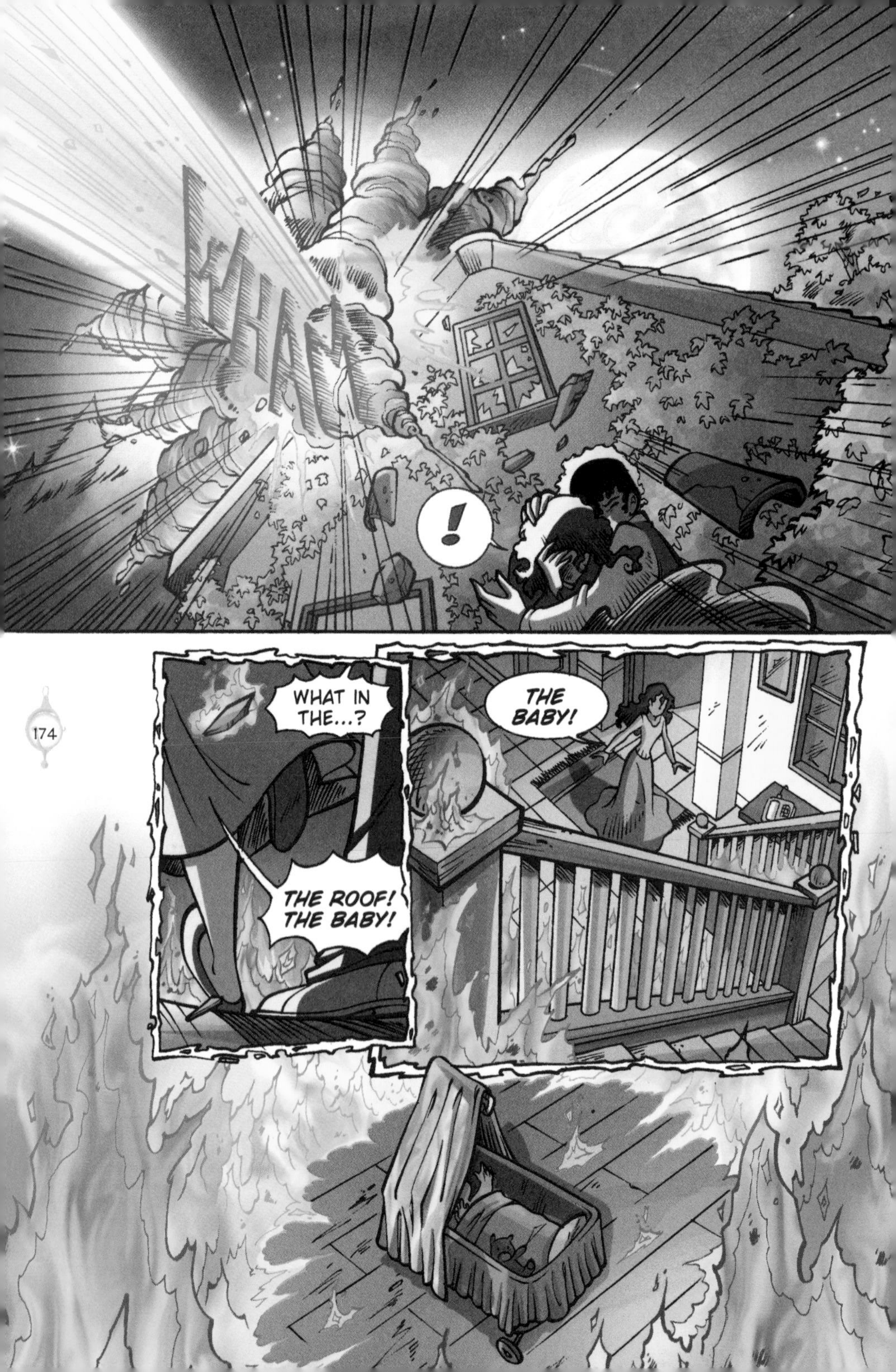
WHAM
!
WHAT IN THE...?
THE ROOF! THE BABY!
THE BABY!

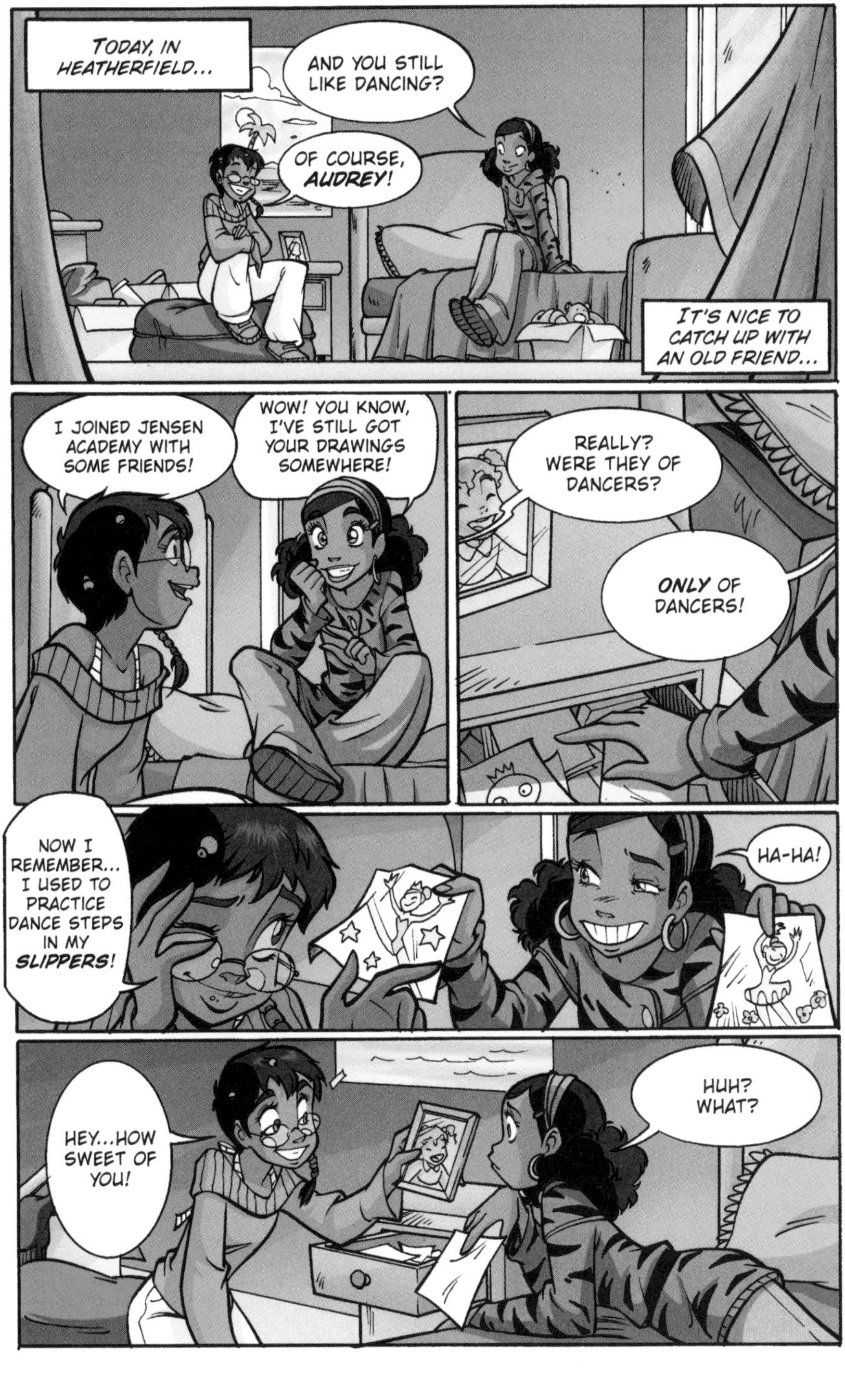
TODAY, IN HEATHERFIELD...
AND YOU STILL LIKE DANCING?
OF COURSE, AUDREY!
IT'S NICE TO CATCH UP WITH AN OLD FRIEND...
I JOINED JENSEN ACADEMY WITH SOME FRIENDS!
WOW! YOU KNOW, I'VE STILL GOT YOUR DRAWINGS SOMEWHERE!
REALLY? WERE THEY OF DANCERS?
ONLY OF DANCERS!
NOW I REMEMBER... I USED TO PRACTICE DANCE STEPS IN MY SLIPPERS!
HA-HA!
HEY...HOW SWEET OF YOU!
HUH? WHAT?

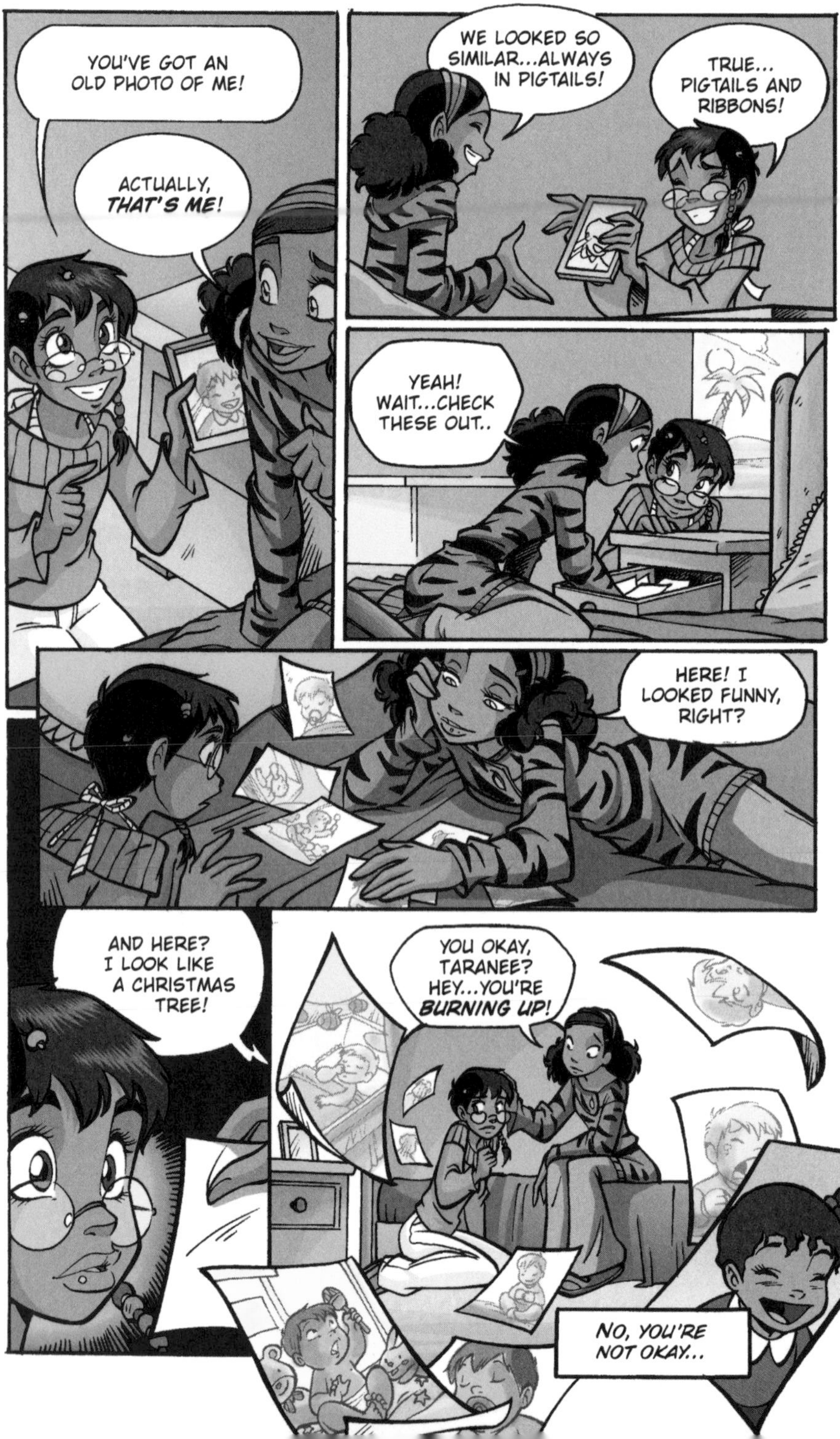
YOU'VE GOT AN OLD PHOTO OF ME!
ACTUALLY, *THAT'S ME*!
WE LOOKED SO SIMILAR...ALWAYS IN PIGTAILS!
TRUE... PIGTAILS AND RIBBONS!
YEAH! WAIT...CHECK THESE OUT..
HERE! I LOOKED FUNNY, RIGHT?
AND HERE? I LOOK LIKE A CHRISTMAS TREE!
YOU OKAY, TARANEE? HEY...YOU'RE *BURNING UP*!
NO, YOU'RE NOT OKAY...

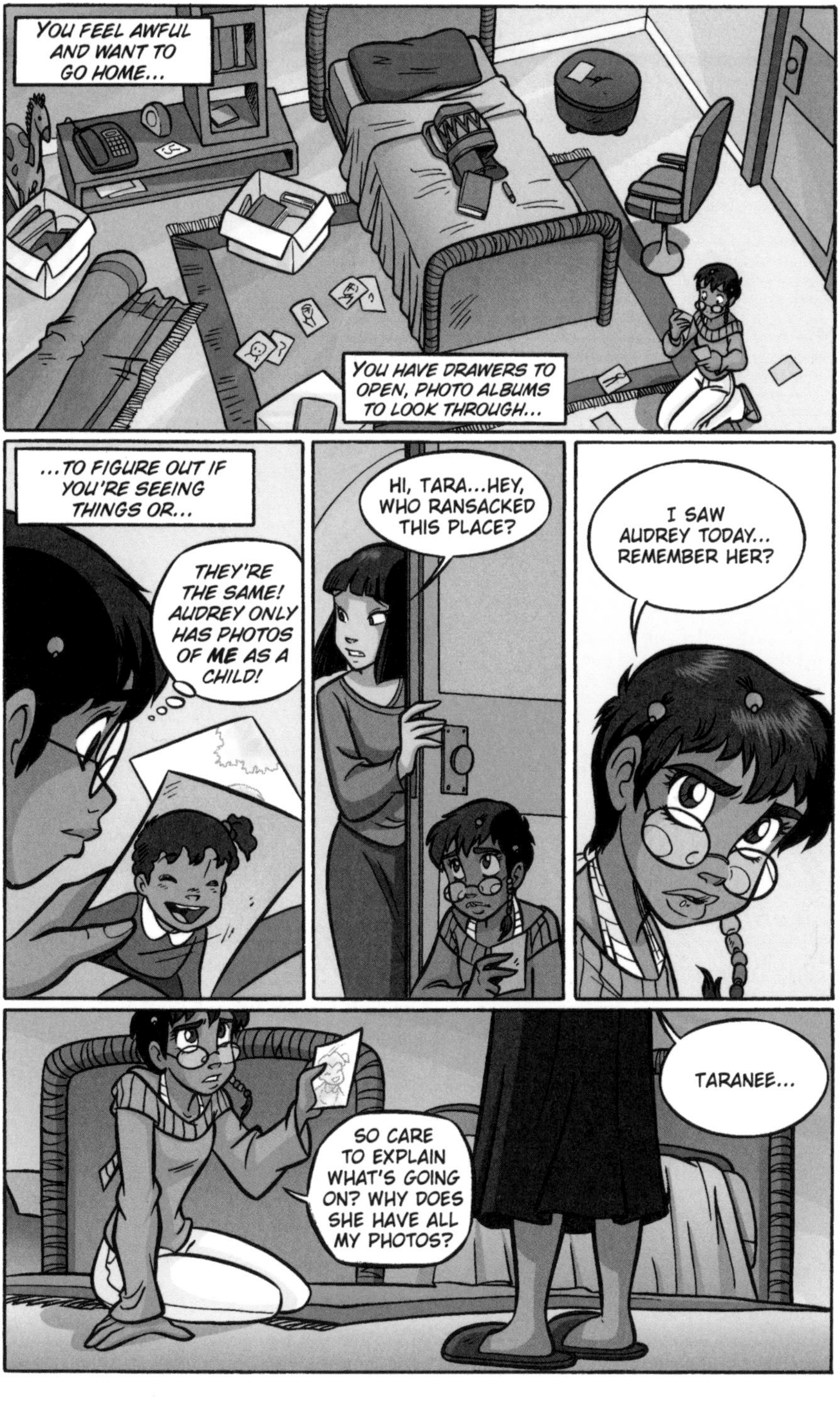
YOU FEEL AWFUL AND WANT TO GO HOME...
YOU HAVE DRAWERS TO OPEN, PHOTO ALBUMS TO LOOK THROUGH...
...TO FIGURE OUT IF YOU'RE SEEING THINGS OR...
THEY'RE THE SAME! AUDREY ONLY HAS PHOTOS OF ME AS A CHILD!
HI, TARA...HEY, WHO RANSACKED THIS PLACE?
I SAW AUDREY TODAY... REMEMBER HER?
SO CARE TO EXPLAIN WHAT'S GOING ON? WHY DOES SHE HAVE ALL MY PHOTOS?
TARANEE...

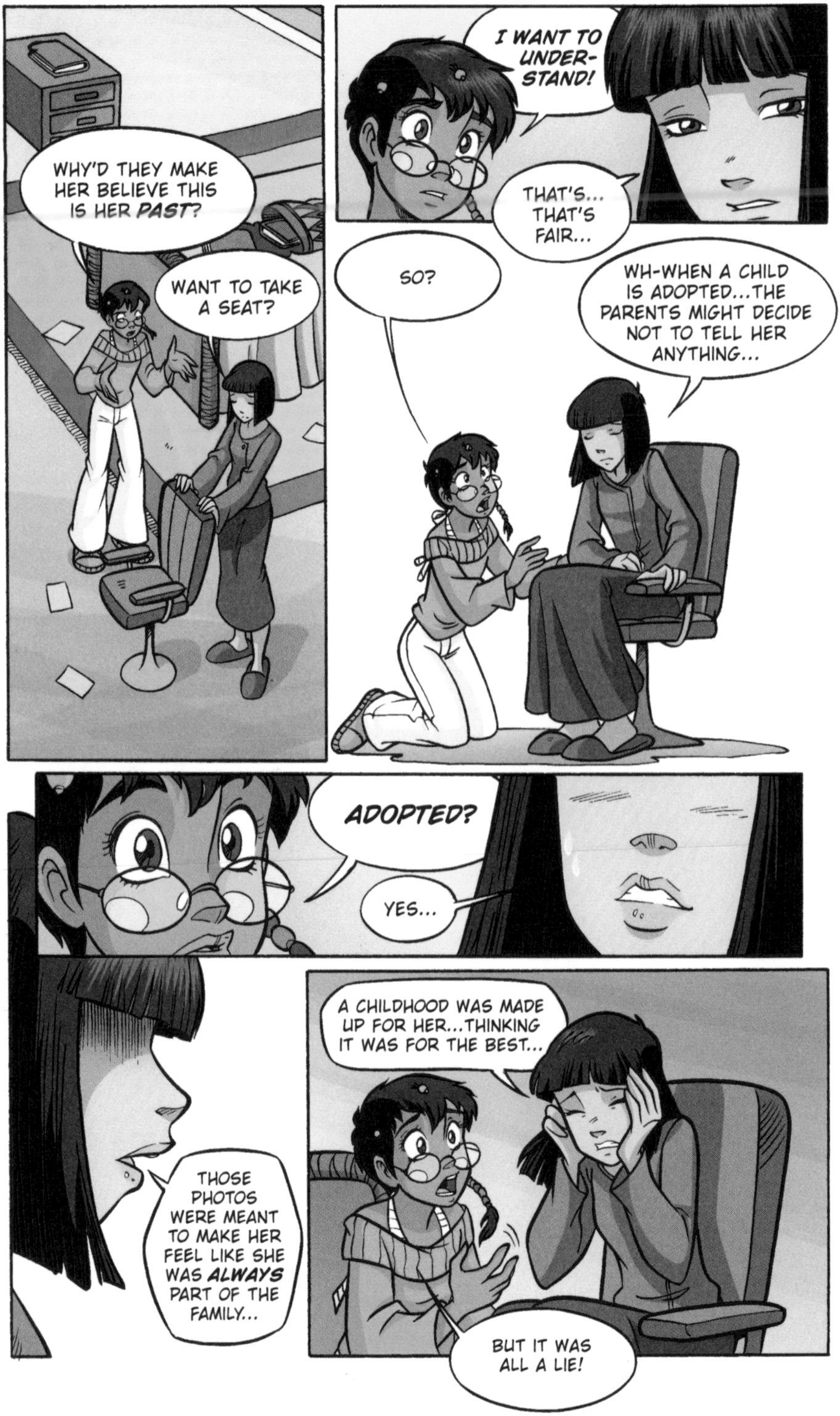

WHY'D THEY MAKE HER BELIEVE THIS IS HER *PAST*?
WANT TO TAKE A SEAT?
I WANT TO UNDER-STAND!
THAT'S... THAT'S FAIR...
SO?
WH-WHEN A CHILD IS ADOPTED...THE PARENTS MIGHT DECIDE NOT TO TELL HER ANYTHING...
ADOPTED?
YES...
A CHILDHOOD WAS MADE UP FOR HER...THINKING IT WAS FOR THE BEST...
THOSE PHOTOS WERE MEANT TO MAKE HER FEEL LIKE SHE WAS *ALWAYS* PART OF THE FAMILY...
BUT IT WAS ALL A LIE!

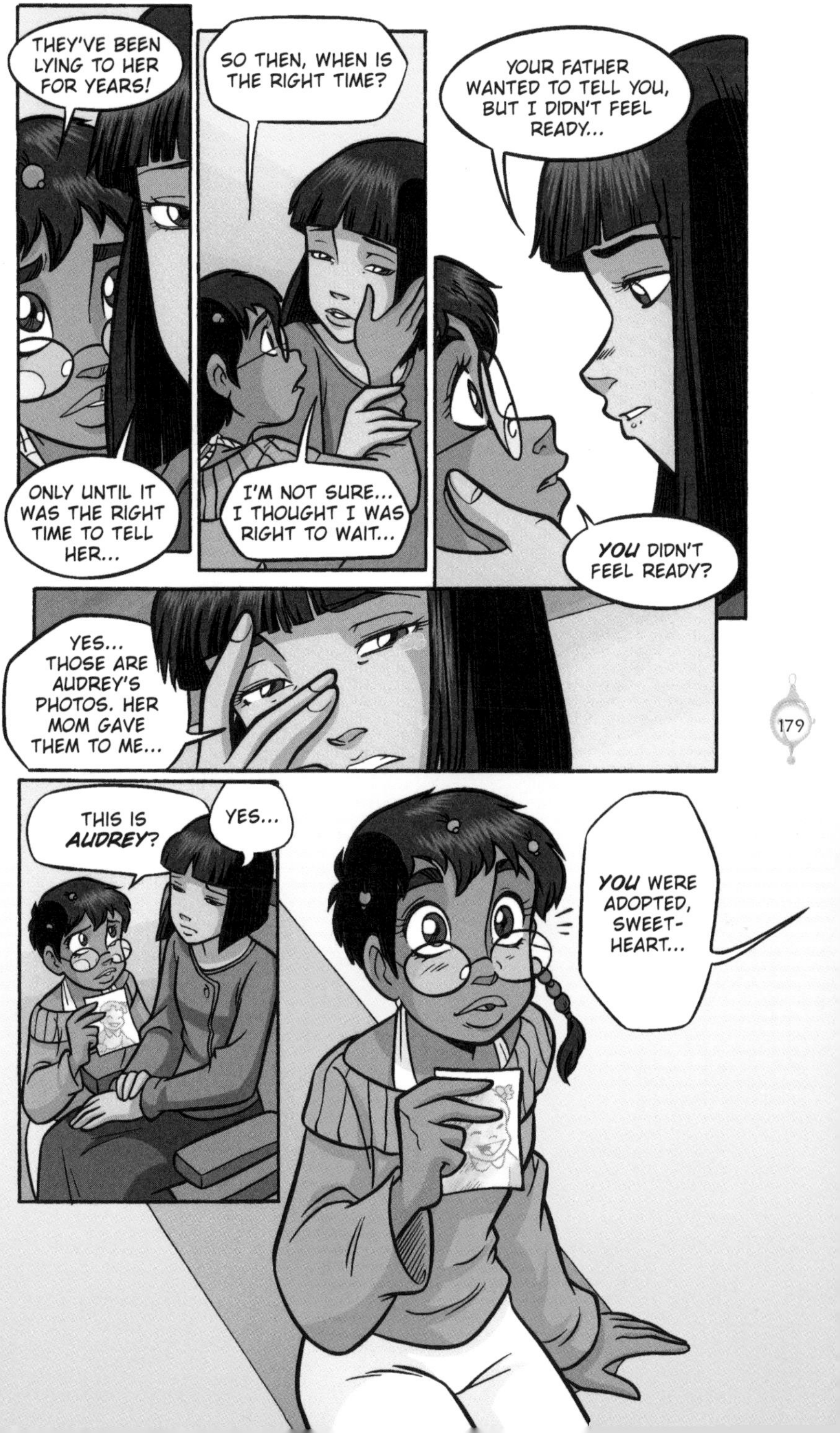
THEY'VE BEEN LYING TO HER FOR YEARS!
ONLY UNTIL IT WAS THE RIGHT TIME TO TELL HER...
SO THEN, WHEN IS THE RIGHT TIME?
I'M NOT SURE... I THOUGHT I WAS RIGHT TO WAIT...
YOUR FATHER WANTED TO TELL YOU, BUT I DIDN'T FEEL READY...
YOU DIDN'T FEEL READY?
YES... THOSE ARE AUDREY'S PHOTOS. HER MOM GAVE THEM TO ME...
THIS IS AUDREY?
YES...
YOU WERE ADOPTED, SWEET-HEART...

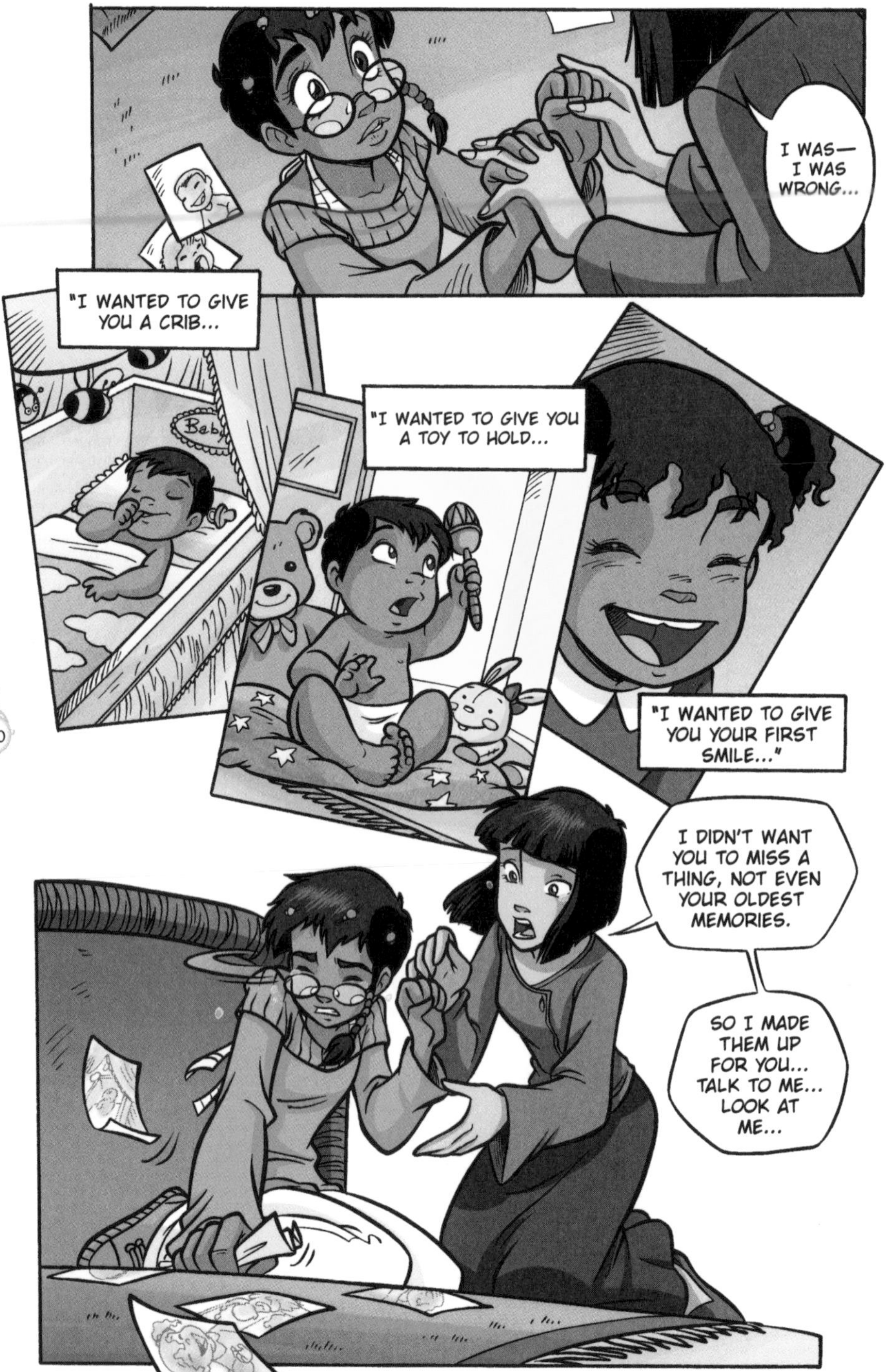

I WAS—
I WAS
WRONG...
"I WANTED TO GIVE
YOU A CRIB...
Baby
"I WANTED TO GIVE YOU
A TOY TO HOLD...
"I WANTED TO GIVE
YOU YOUR FIRST
SMILE..."
I DIDN'T WANT
YOU TO MISS A
THING, NOT EVEN
YOUR OLDEST
MEMORIES.
SO I MADE
THEM UP
FOR YOU...
TALK TO ME...
LOOK AT
ME...

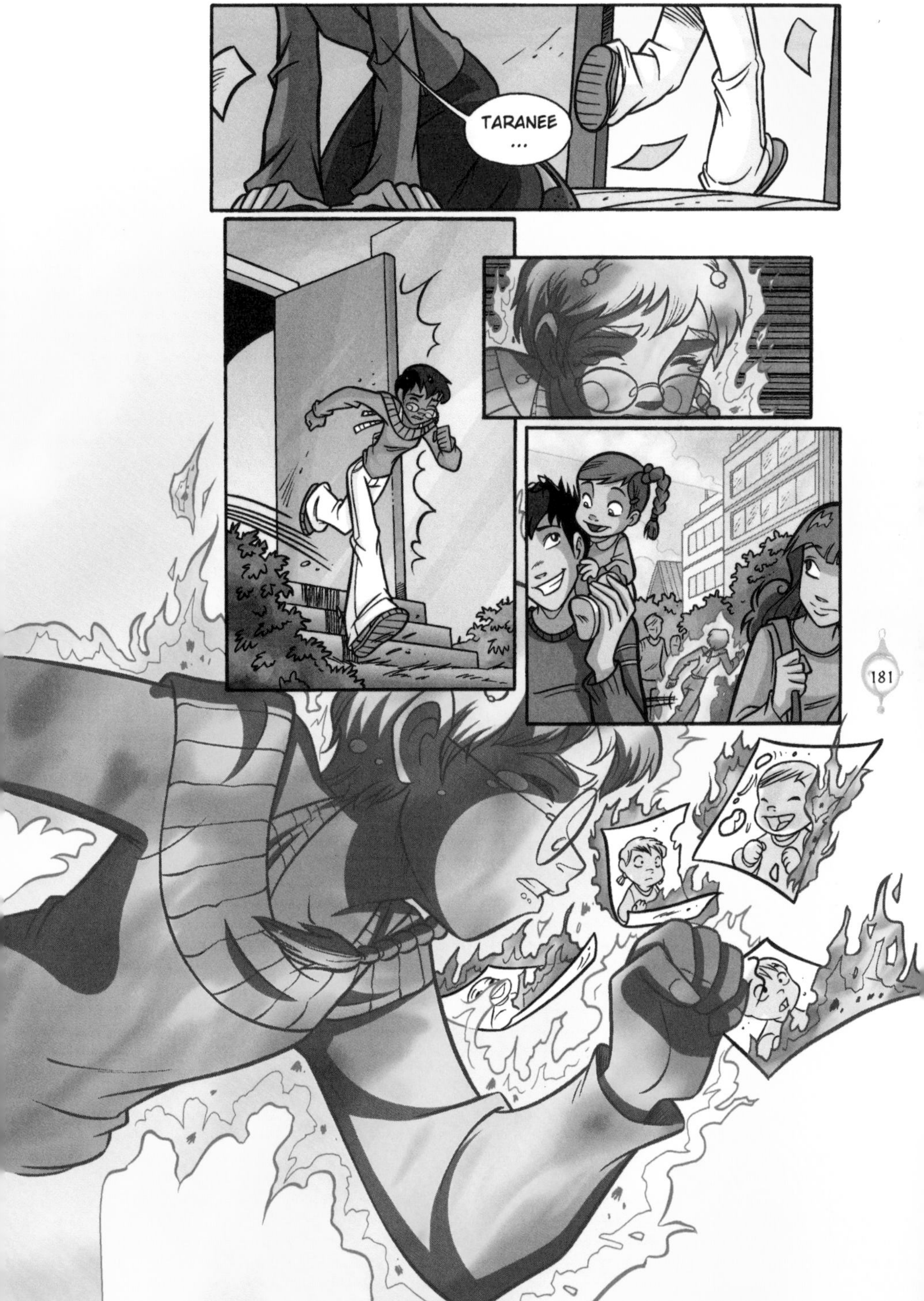
TARANEE
...

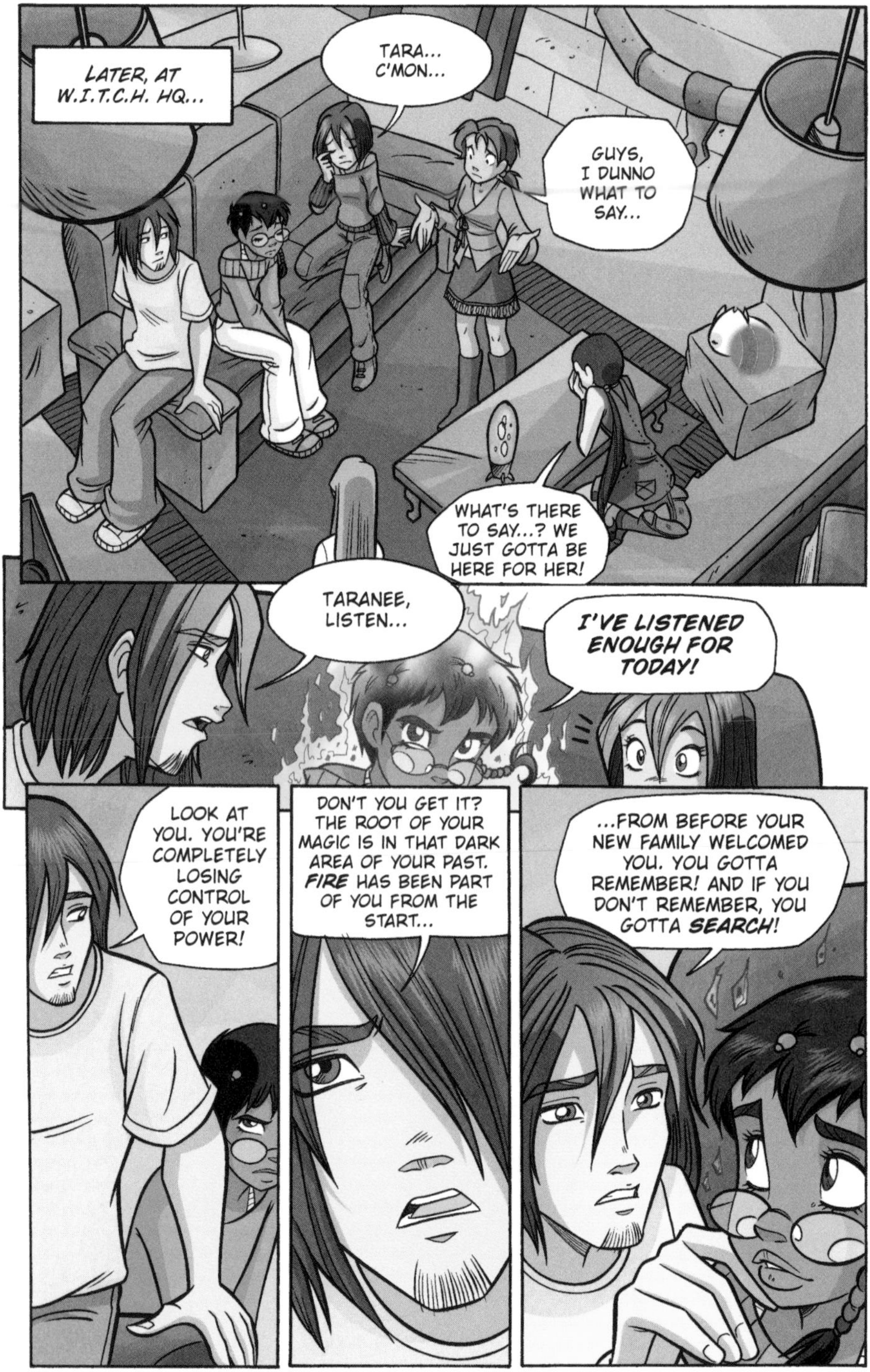
LATER, AT W.I.T.C.H. HQ...
TARA... C'MON...
GUYS, I DUNNO WHAT TO SAY...
WHAT'S THERE TO SAY...? WE JUST GOTTA BE HERE FOR HER!
TARANEE, LISTEN...
I'VE LISTENED ENOUGH FOR TODAY!
LOOK AT YOU. YOU'RE COMPLETELY LOSING CONTROL OF YOUR POWER!
DON'T YOU GET IT? THE ROOT OF YOUR MAGIC IS IN THAT DARK AREA OF YOUR PAST. FIRE HAS BEEN PART OF YOU FROM THE START...
...FROM BEFORE YOUR NEW FAMILY WELCOMED YOU. YOU GOTTA REMEMBER! AND IF YOU DON'T REMEMBER, YOU GOTTA SEARCH!

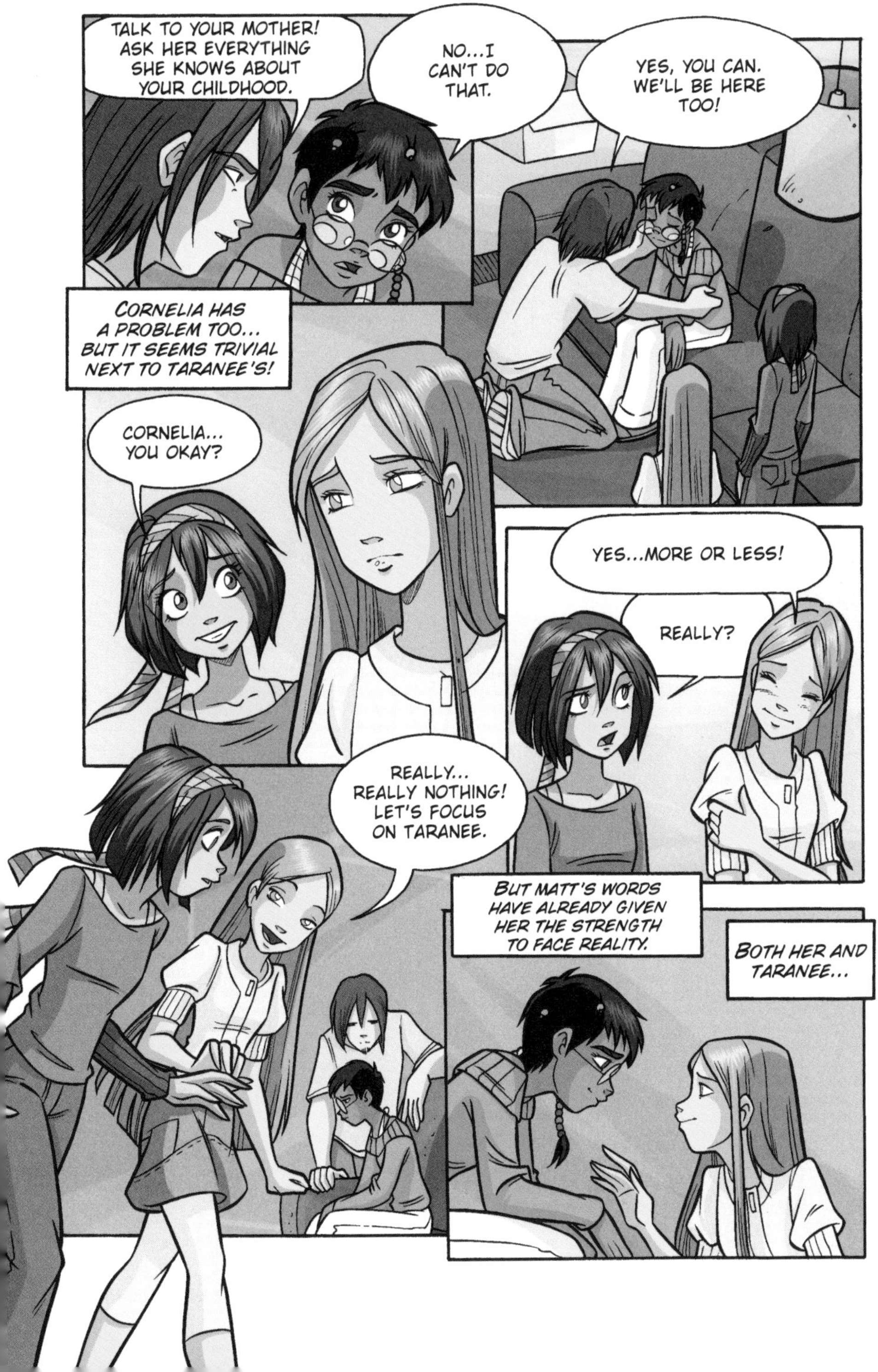
TALK TO YOUR MOTHER! ASK HER EVERYTHING SHE KNOWS ABOUT YOUR CHILDHOOD.
NO...I CAN'T DO THAT.
YES, YOU CAN. WE'LL BE HERE TOO!
CORNELIA HAS A PROBLEM TOO... BUT IT SEEMS TRIVIAL NEXT TO TARANEE'S!
CORNELIA... YOU OKAY?
YES...MORE OR LESS!
REALLY?
REALLY... REALLY NOTHING! LET'S FOCUS ON TARANEE.
BUT MATT'S WORDS HAVE ALREADY GIVEN HER THE STRENGTH TO FACE REALITY.
BOTH HER AND TARANEE...

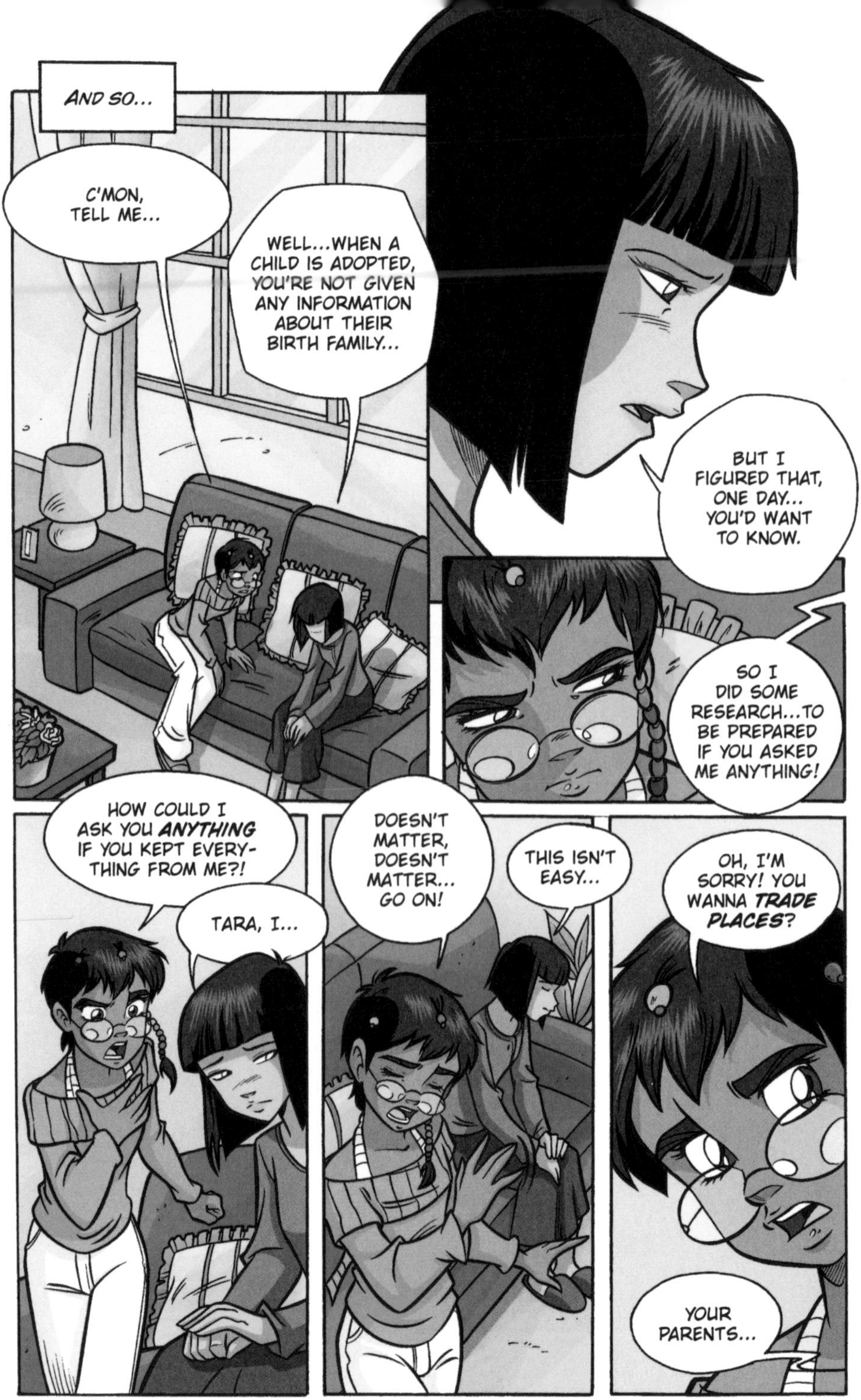
AND SO...
C'MON, TELL ME...
WELL...WHEN A CHILD IS ADOPTED, YOU'RE NOT GIVEN ANY INFORMATION ABOUT THEIR BIRTH FAMILY...
BUT I FIGURED THAT, ONE DAY... YOU'D WANT TO KNOW.
SO I DID SOME RESEARCH...TO BE PREPARED IF YOU ASKED ME ANYTHING!
HOW COULD I ASK YOU ***ANYTHING*** IF YOU KEPT EVERY-THING FROM ME?!
TARA, I...
DOESN'T MATTER, DOESN'T MATTER... GO ON!
THIS ISN'T EASY...
OH, I'M SORRY! YOU WANNA ***TRADE PLACES***?
YOUR PARENTS...

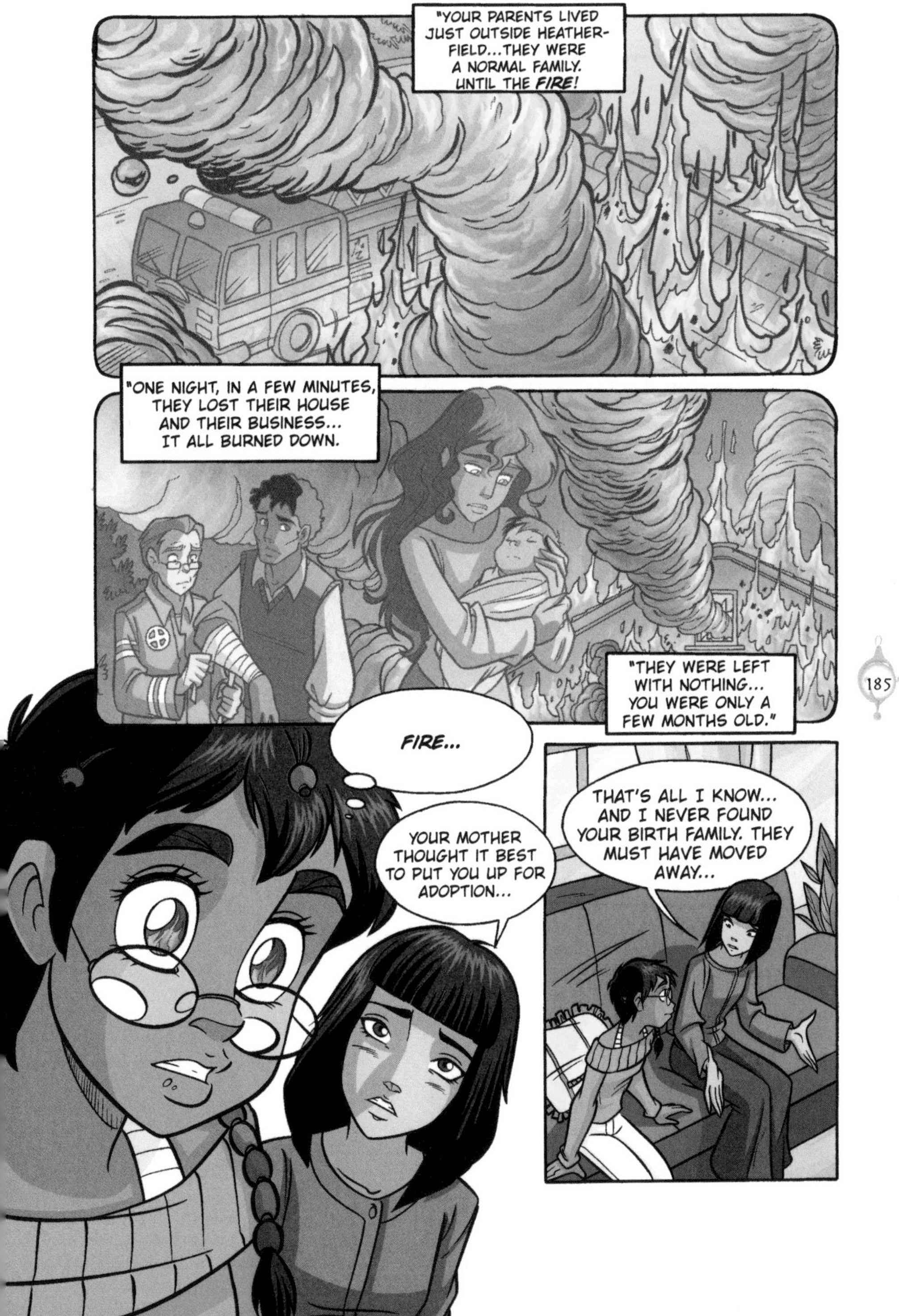
"YOUR PARENTS LIVED JUST OUTSIDE HEATHER-FIELD...THEY WERE A NORMAL FAMILY. UNTIL THE *FIRE*!
"ONE NIGHT, IN A FEW MINUTES, THEY LOST THEIR HOUSE AND THEIR BUSINESS... IT ALL BURNED DOWN.
"THEY WERE LEFT WITH NOTHING... YOU WERE ONLY A FEW MONTHS OLD."
FIRE...
YOUR MOTHER THOUGHT IT BEST TO PUT YOU UP FOR ADOPTION...
THAT'S ALL I KNOW... AND I NEVER FOUND YOUR BIRTH FAMILY. THEY MUST HAVE MOVED AWAY...

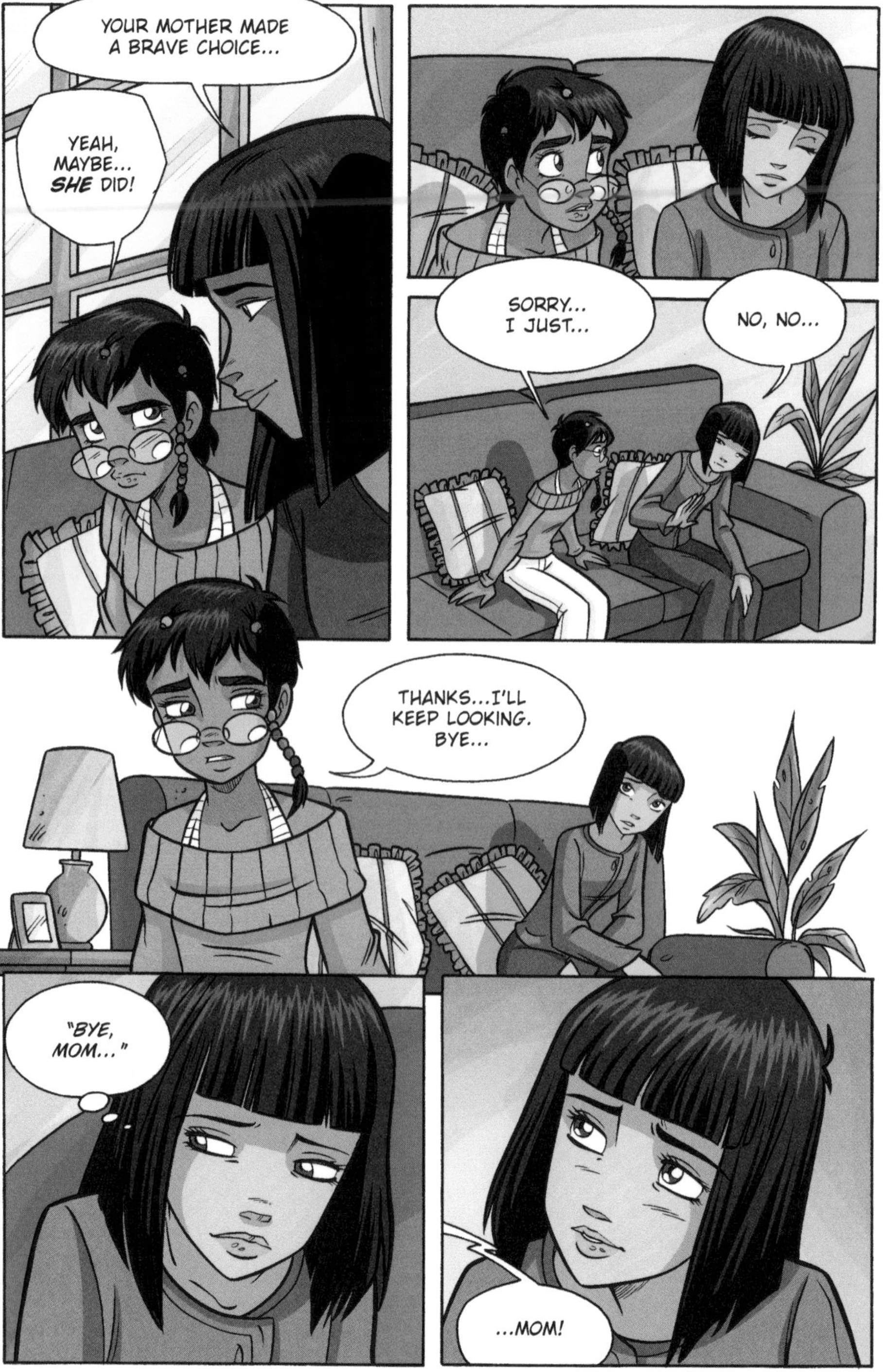
YOUR MOTHER MADE A BRAVE CHOICE...
YEAH, MAYBE... **SHE** DID!
SORRY... I JUST...
NO, NO...
THANKS...I'LL KEEP LOOKING. BYE...
"BYE, MOM..."
...MOM!

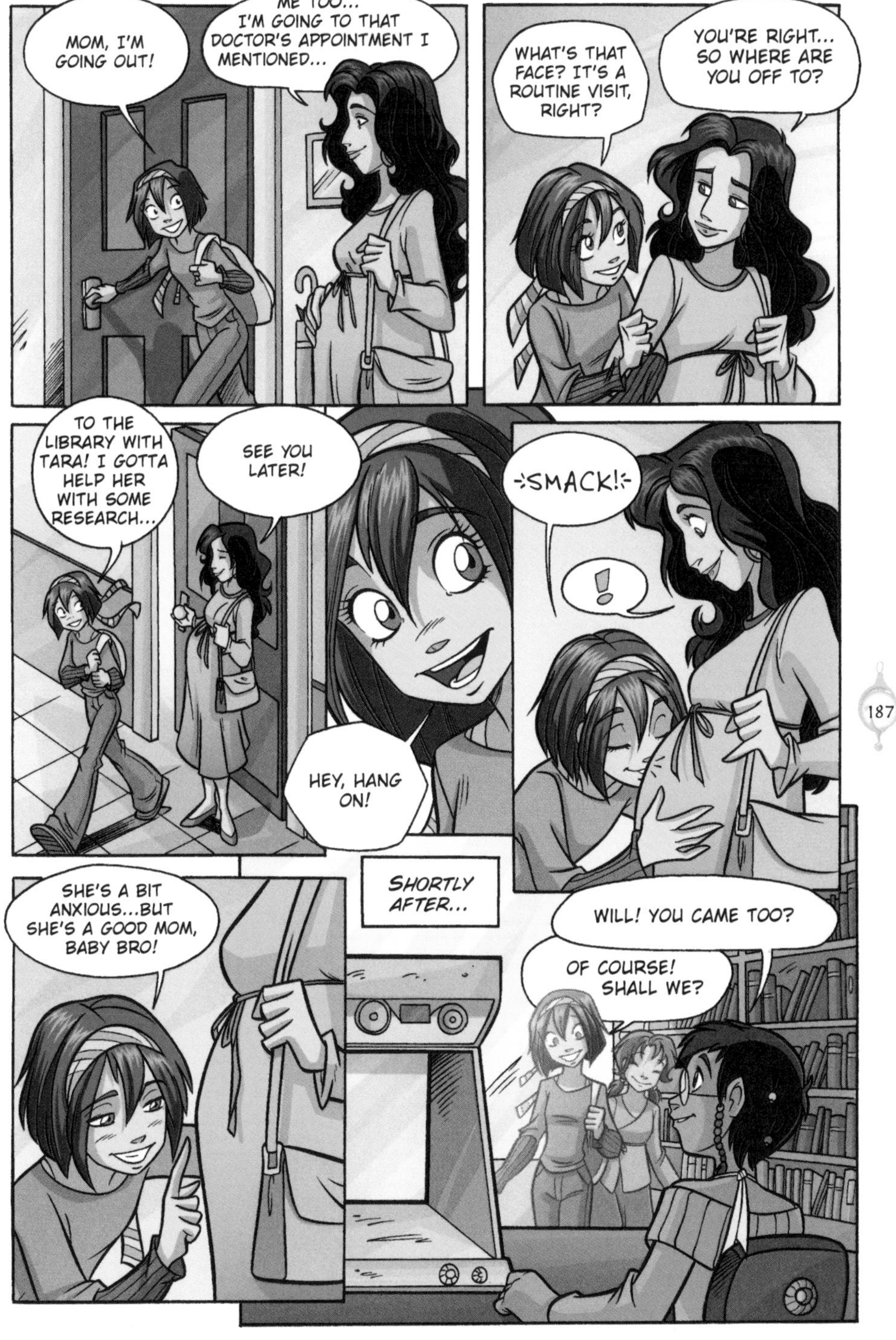
MOM, I'M GOING OUT!
ME TOO... I'M GOING TO THAT DOCTOR'S APPOINTMENT I MENTIONED...
WHAT'S THAT FACE? IT'S A ROUTINE VISIT, RIGHT?
YOU'RE RIGHT... SO WHERE ARE YOU OFF TO?
TO THE LIBRARY WITH TARA! I GOTTA HELP HER WITH SOME RESEARCH...
SEE YOU LATER!
HEY, HANG ON!
SMACK!
!
SHE'S A BIT ANXIOUS...BUT SHE'S A GOOD MOM, BABY BRO!
SHORTLY AFTER...
WILL! YOU CAME TOO?
OF COURSE! SHALL WE?

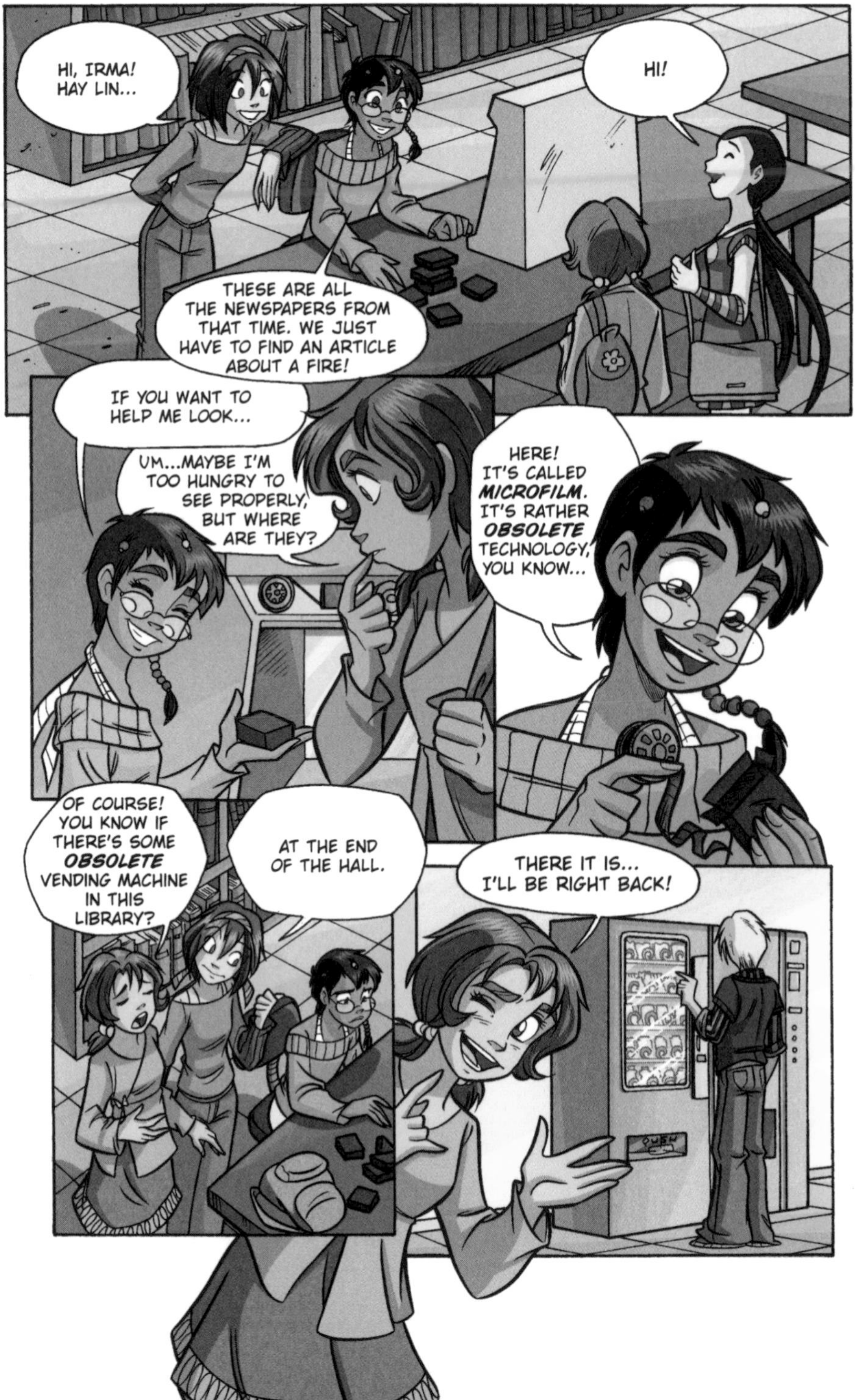
HI, IRMA! HAY LIN...
HI!
THESE ARE ALL THE NEWSPAPERS FROM THAT TIME. WE JUST HAVE TO FIND AN ARTICLE ABOUT A FIRE!
IF YOU WANT TO HELP ME LOOK...
UM...MAYBE I'M TOO HUNGRY TO SEE PROPERLY, BUT WHERE ARE THEY?
HERE! IT'S CALLED MICROFILM. IT'S RATHER OBSOLETE TECHNOLOGY, YOU KNOW...
OF COURSE! YOU KNOW IF THERE'S SOME OBSOLETE VENDING MACHINE IN THIS LIBRARY?
AT THE END OF THE HALL.
THERE IT IS... I'LL BE RIGHT BACK!

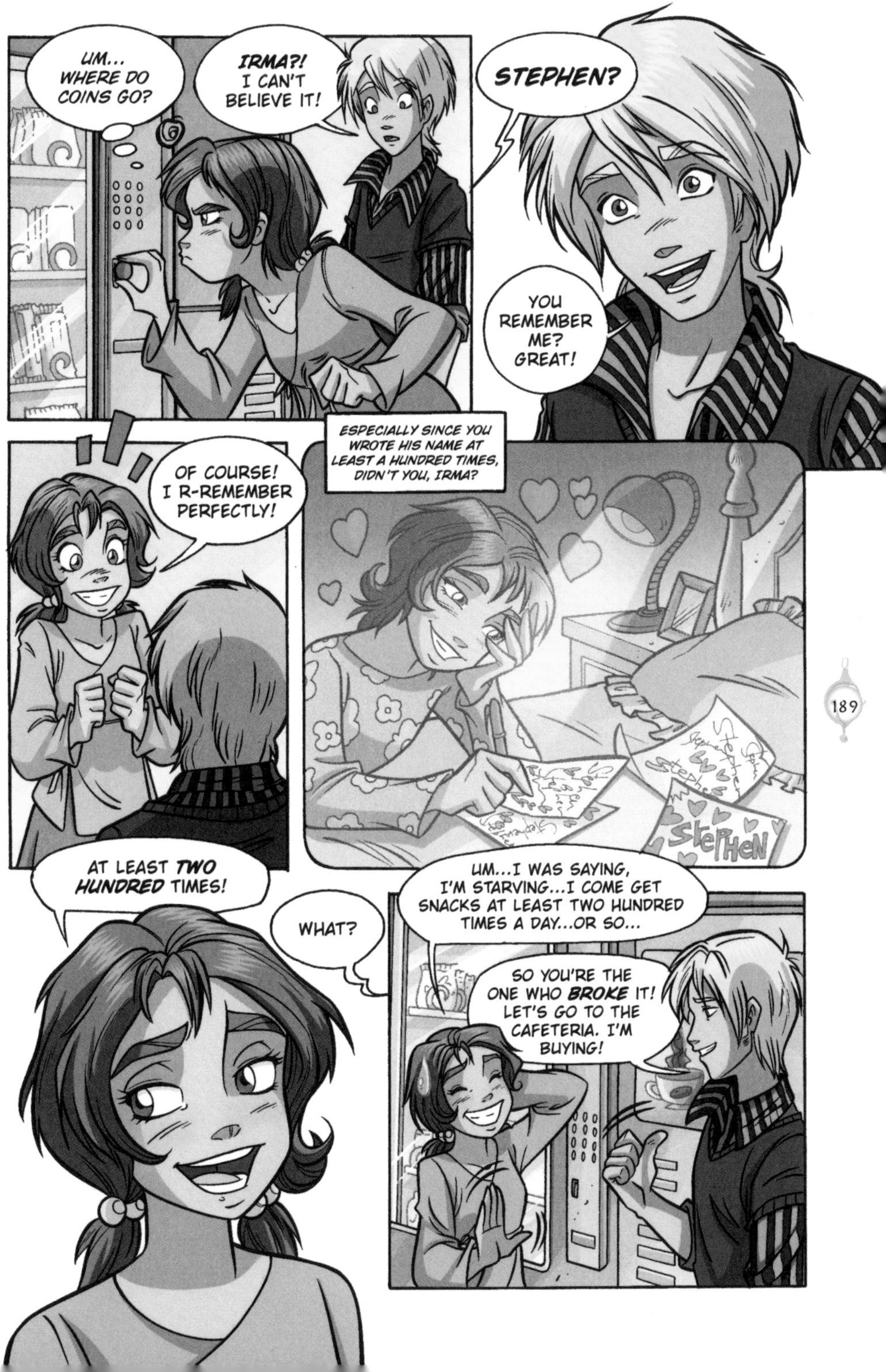
UM... WHERE DO COINS GO?
IRMA?! I CAN'T BELIEVE IT!
STEPHEN?
YOU REMEMBER ME? GREAT!
ESPECIALLY SINCE YOU WROTE HIS NAME AT LEAST A HUNDRED TIMES, DIDN'T YOU, IRMA?
OF COURSE! I R-REMEMBER PERFECTLY!
STEPHEN
AT LEAST TWO HUNDRED TIMES!
WHAT?
UM...I WAS SAYING, I'M STARVING...I COME GET SNACKS AT LEAST TWO HUNDRED TIMES A DAY...OR SO...
SO YOU'RE THE ONE WHO BROKE IT! LET'S GO TO THE CAFETERIA. I'M BUYING!

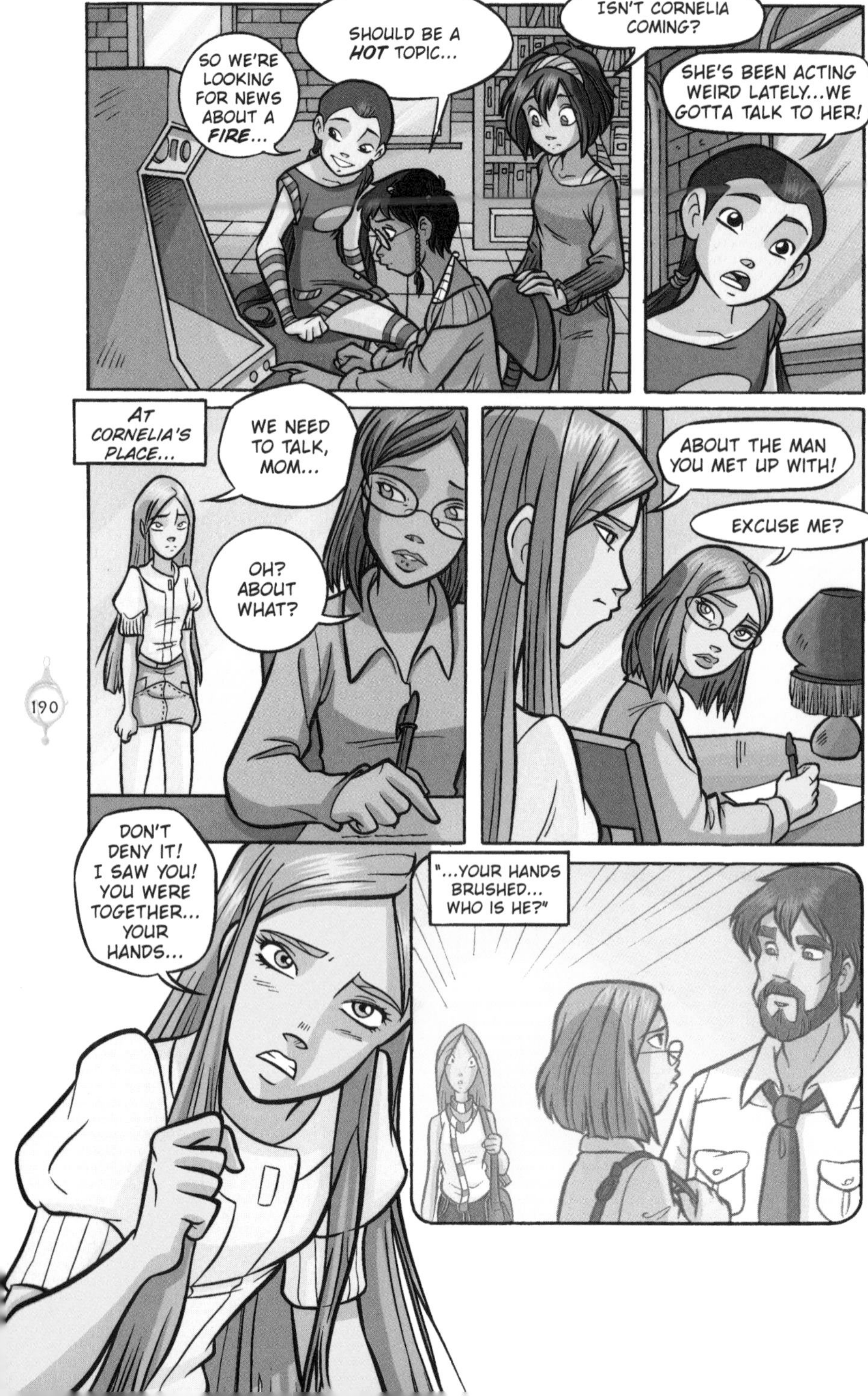
SO WE'RE LOOKING FOR NEWS ABOUT A FIRE...
SHOULD BE A HOT TOPIC...
ISN'T CORNELIA COMING?
SHE'S BEEN ACTING WEIRD LATELY...WE GOTTA TALK TO HER!
AT CORNELIA'S PLACE...
WE NEED TO TALK, MOM...
OH? ABOUT WHAT?
ABOUT THE MAN YOU MET UP WITH!
EXCUSE ME?
DON'T DENY IT! I SAW YOU! YOU WERE TOGETHER... YOUR HANDS...
"...YOUR HANDS BRUSHED... WHO IS HE?"

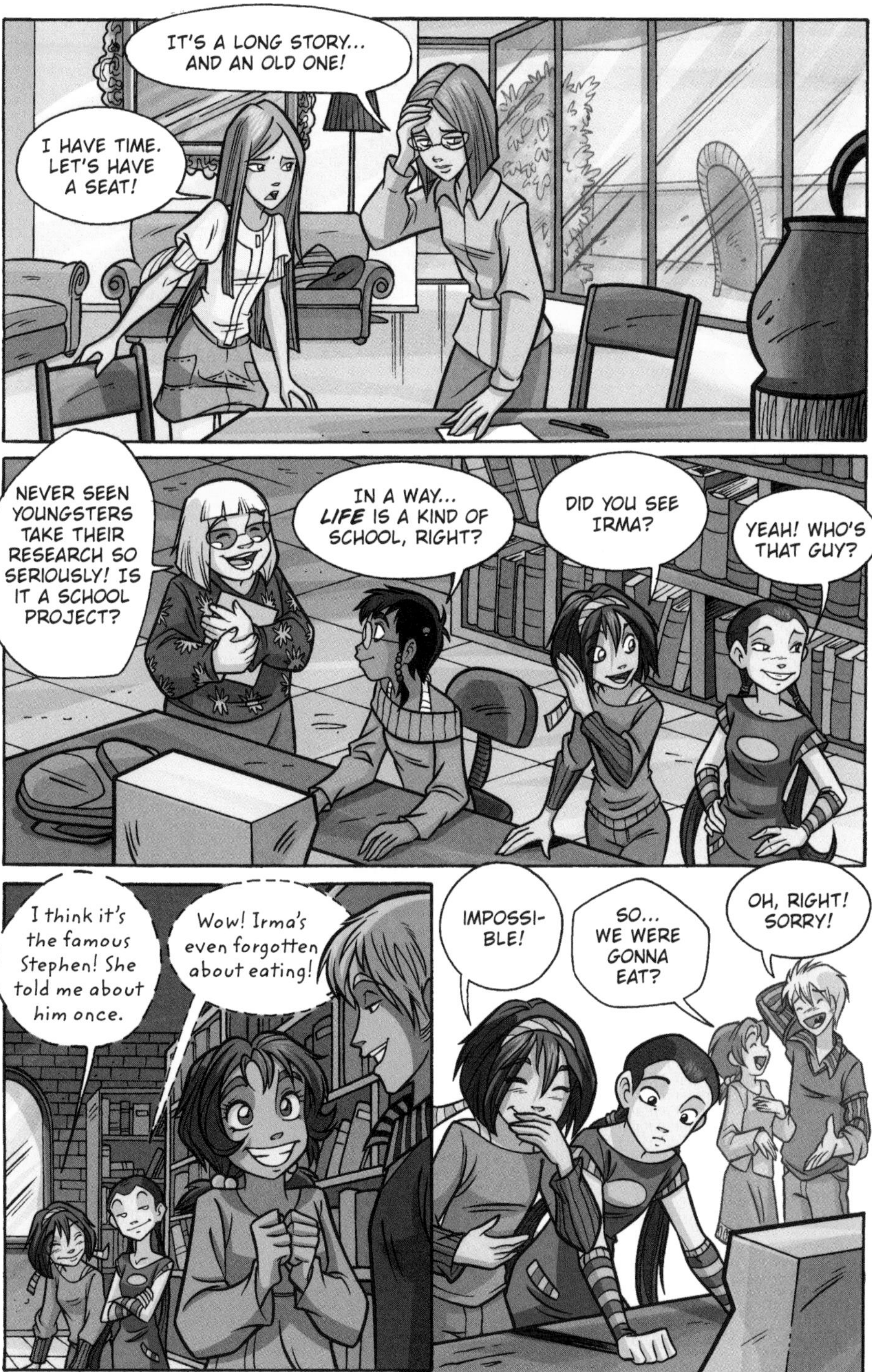

IT'S A LONG STORY... AND AN OLD ONE!
I HAVE TIME. LET'S HAVE A SEAT!
NEVER SEEN YOUNGSTERS TAKE THEIR RESEARCH SO SERIOUSLY! IS IT A SCHOOL PROJECT?
IN A WAY... *LIFE* IS A KIND OF SCHOOL, RIGHT?
DID YOU SEE IRMA?
YEAH! WHO'S THAT GUY?
I think it's the famous Stephen! She told me about him once.
Wow! Irma's even forgotten about eating!
IMPOSSI-BLE!
SO... WE WERE GONNA EAT?
OH, RIGHT! SORRY!

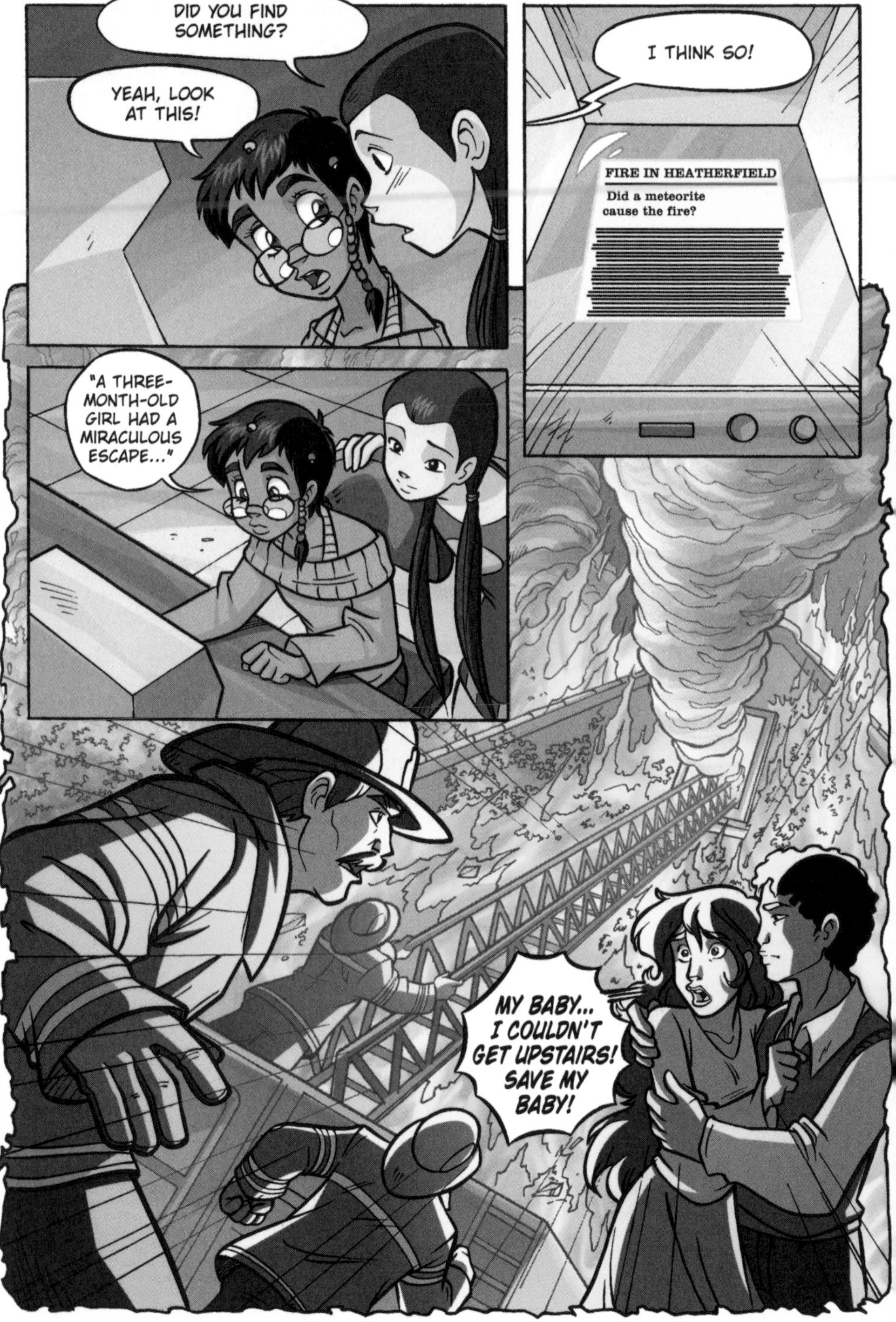
DID YOU FIND SOMETHING?
YEAH, LOOK AT THIS!
I THINK SO!
FIRE IN HEATHERFIELD
Did a meteorite cause the fire?
"A THREE-MONTH-OLD GIRL HAD A MIRACULOUS ESCAPE..."
MY BABY... I COULDN'T GET UPSTAIRS! SAVE MY BABY!

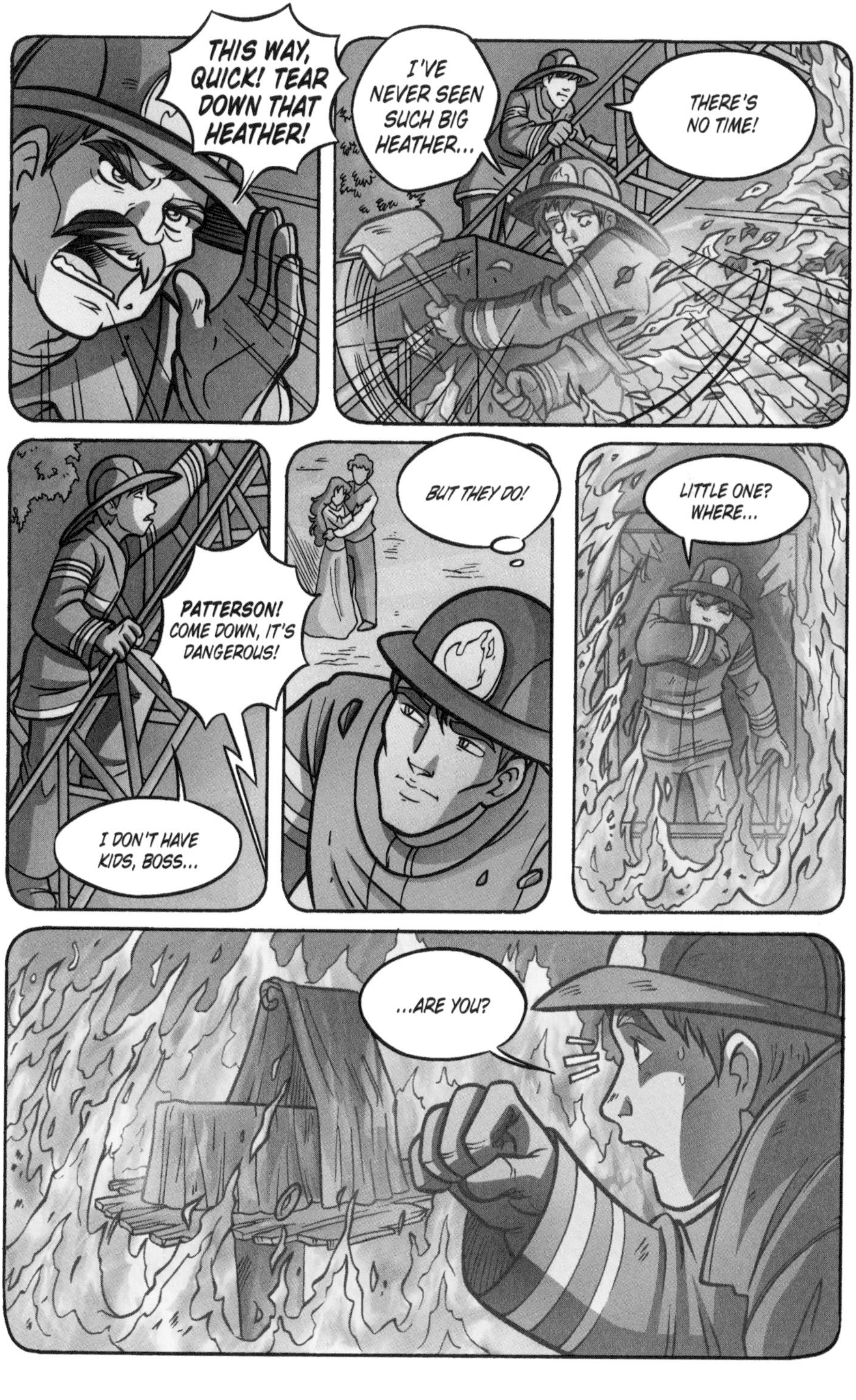

THIS WAY, QUICK! TEAR DOWN THAT HEATHER!
I'VE NEVER SEEN SUCH BIG HEATHER...
THERE'S NO TIME!
PATTERSON! COME DOWN, IT'S DANGEROUS!
I DON'T HAVE KIDS, BOSS...
BUT THEY DO!
LITTLE ONE? WHERE...
...ARE YOU?

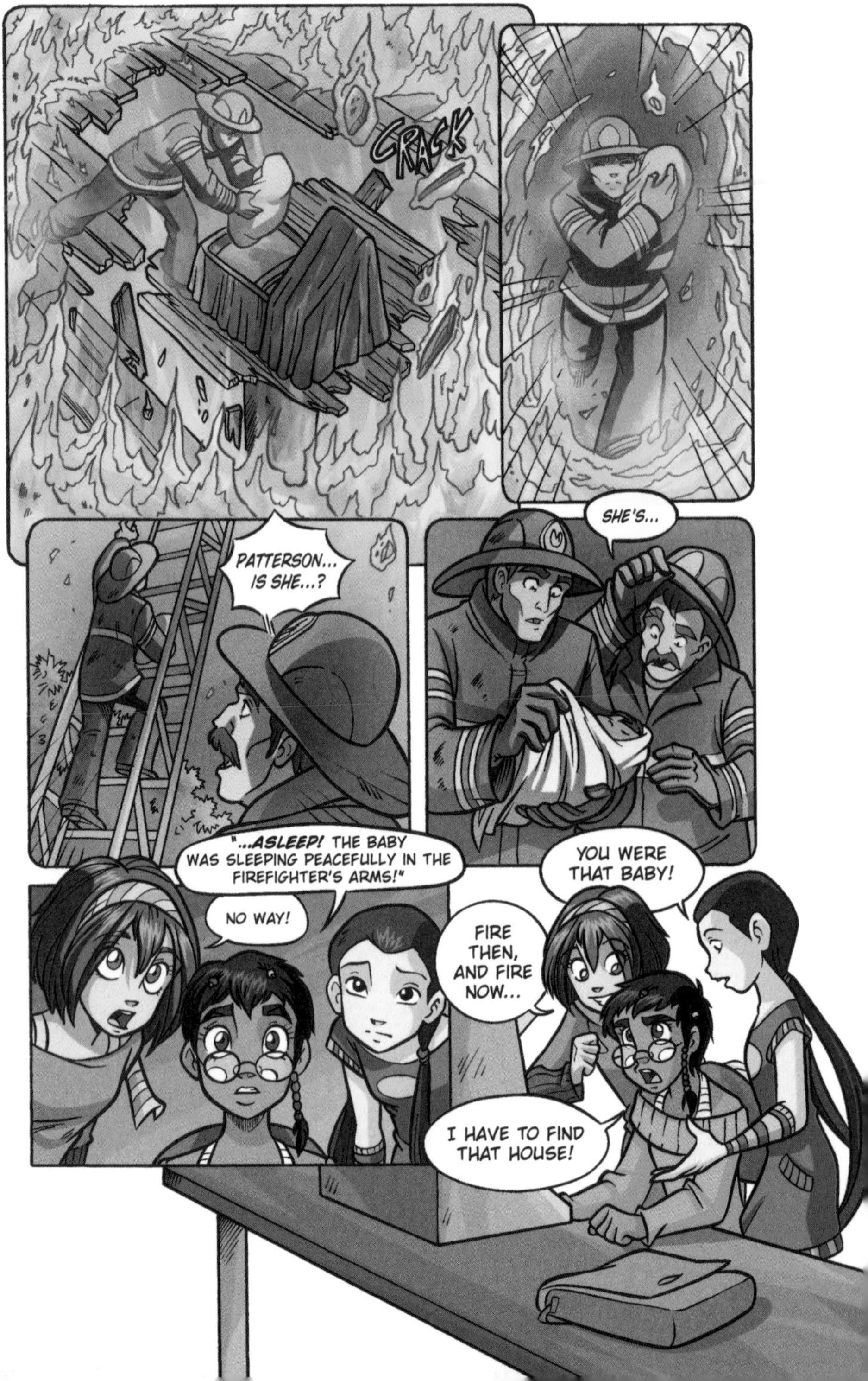
CRACK
PATTERSON... IS SHE...?
SHE'S...
"...ASLEEP! THE BABY WAS SLEEPING PEACEFULLY IN THE FIREFIGHTER'S ARMS!"
NO WAY!
YOU WERE THAT BABY!
FIRE THEN, AND FIRE NOW...
I HAVE TO FIND THAT HOUSE!

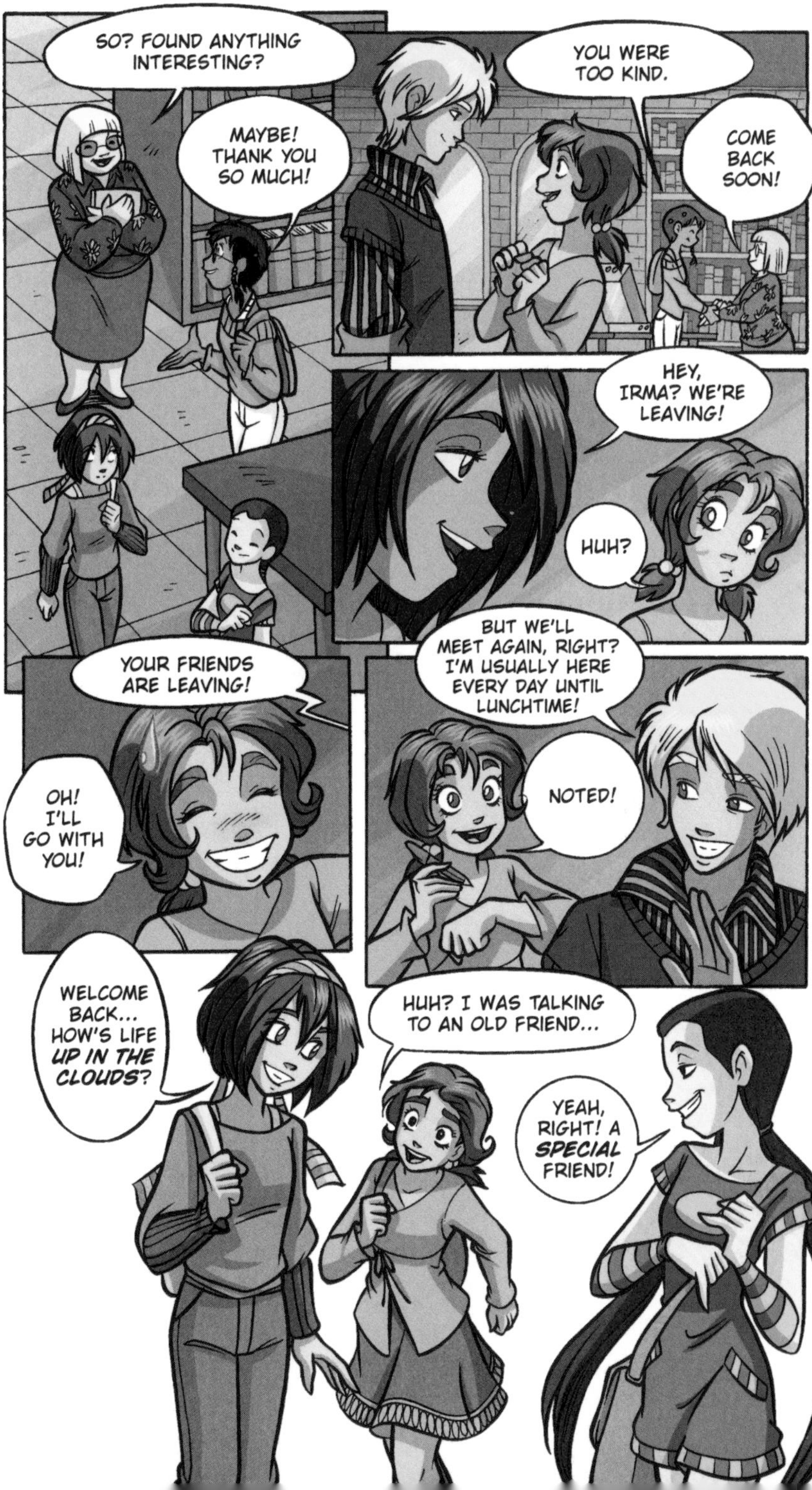
SO? FOUND ANYTHING INTERESTING?
MAYBE! THANK YOU SO MUCH!
YOU WERE TOO KIND.
COME BACK SOON!
HEY, IRMA? WE'RE LEAVING!
HUH?
YOUR FRIENDS ARE LEAVING!
OH! I'LL GO WITH YOU!
BUT WE'LL MEET AGAIN, RIGHT? I'M USUALLY HERE EVERY DAY UNTIL LUNCHTIME!
NOTED!
WELCOME BACK... HOW'S LIFE *UP IN THE CLOUDS*?
HUH? I WAS TALKING TO AN OLD FRIEND...
YEAH, RIGHT! A *SPECIAL* FRIEND!

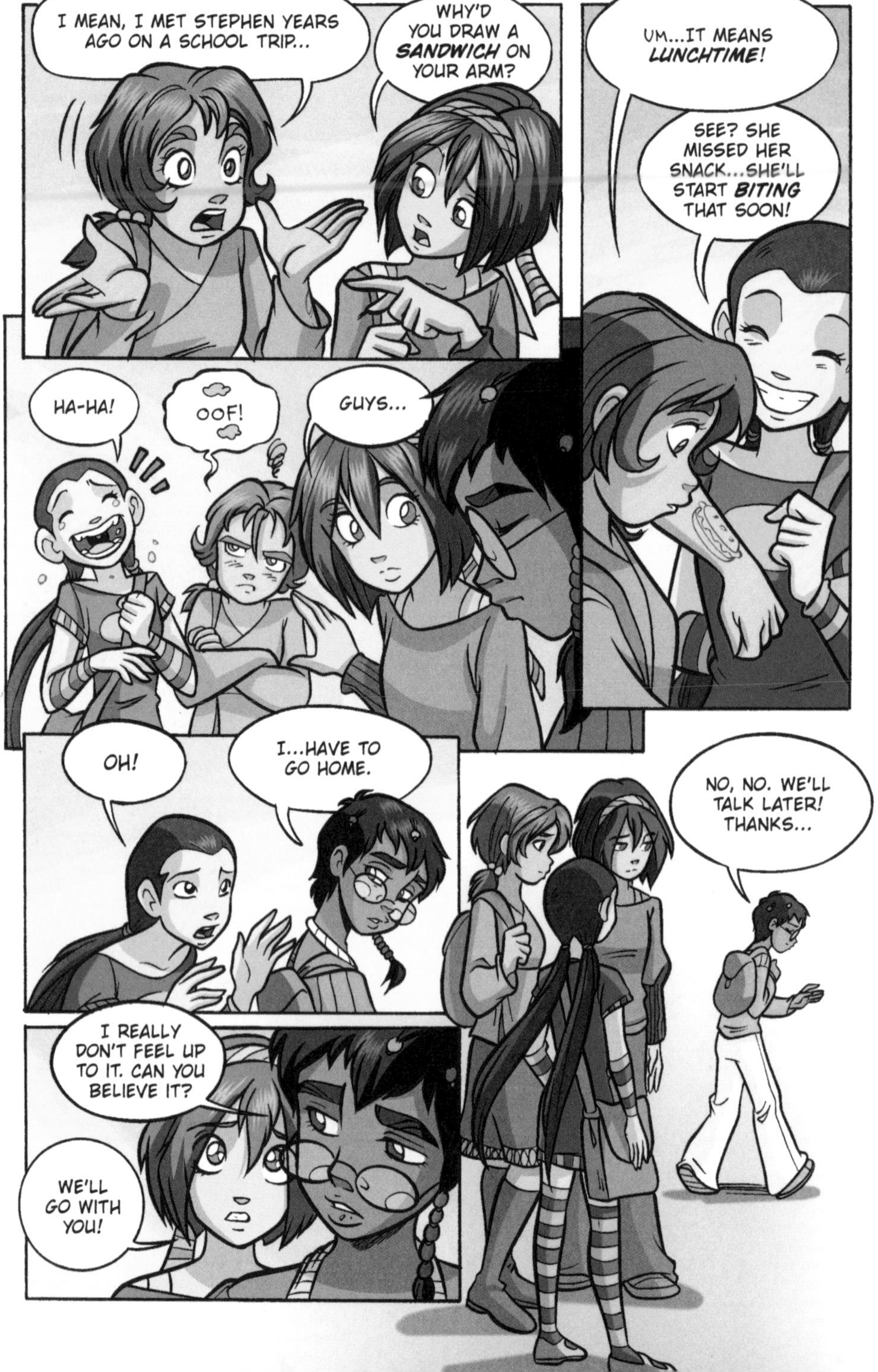

I MEAN, I MET STEPHEN YEARS AGO ON A SCHOOL TRIP...
WHY'D YOU DRAW A SANDWICH ON YOUR ARM?
UM...IT MEANS LUNCHTIME!
SEE? SHE MISSED HER SNACK...SHE'LL START BITING THAT SOON!
HA-HA!
OOF!
GUYS...
OH!
I...HAVE TO GO HOME.
NO, NO. WE'LL TALK LATER! THANKS...
I REALLY DON'T FEEL UP TO IT. CAN YOU BELIEVE IT?
WE'LL GO WITH YOU!

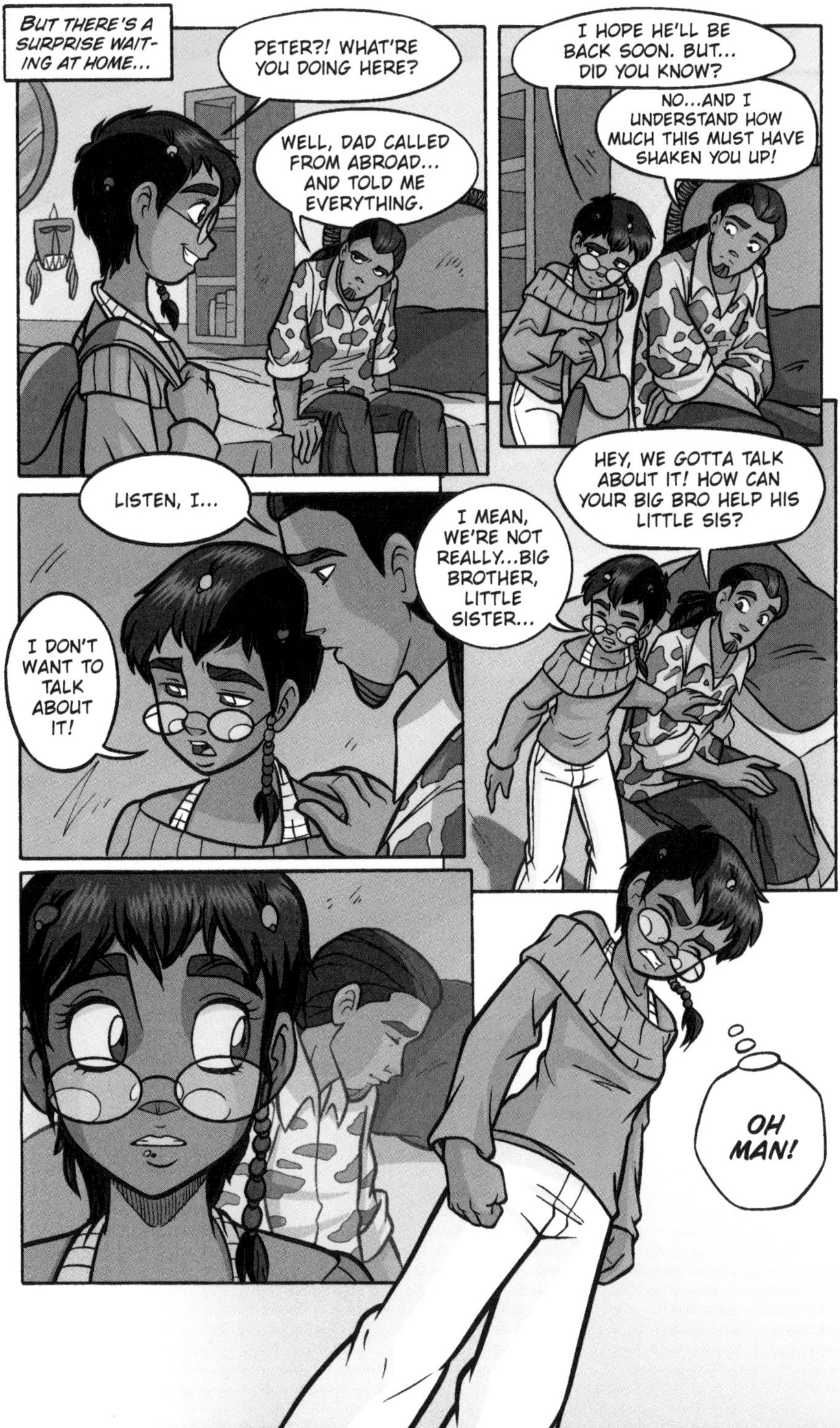
BUT THERE'S A SURPRISE WAITING AT HOME...
PETER?! WHAT'RE YOU DOING HERE?
WELL, DAD CALLED FROM ABROAD... AND TOLD ME EVERYTHING.
I HOPE HE'LL BE BACK SOON. BUT... DID YOU KNOW?
NO...AND I UNDERSTAND HOW MUCH THIS MUST HAVE SHAKEN YOU UP!
LISTEN, I...
I DON'T WANT TO TALK ABOUT IT!
HEY, WE GOTTA TALK ABOUT IT! HOW CAN YOUR BIG BRO HELP HIS LITTLE SIS?
I MEAN, WE'RE NOT REALLY...BIG BROTHER, LITTLE SISTER...
OH MAN!

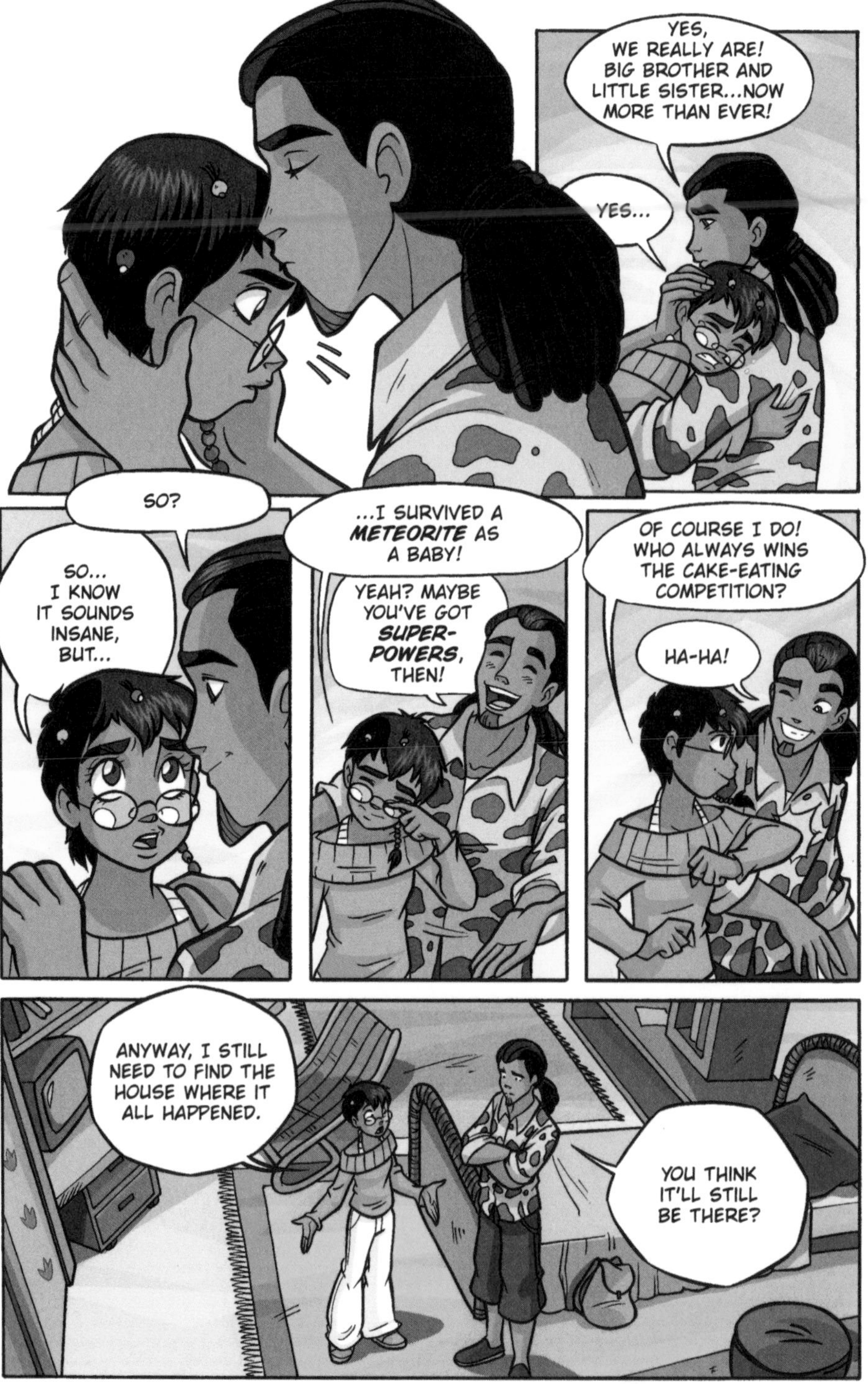
YES, WE REALLY ARE! BIG BROTHER AND LITTLE SISTER...NOW MORE THAN EVER!
YES...
SO?
SO... I KNOW IT SOUNDS INSANE, BUT...
...I SURVIVED A METEORITE AS A BABY!
YEAH? MAYBE YOU'VE GOT SUPER-POWERS, THEN!
OF COURSE I DO! WHO ALWAYS WINS THE CAKE-EATING COMPETITION?
HA-HA!
ANYWAY, I STILL NEED TO FIND THE HOUSE WHERE IT ALL HAPPENED.
YOU THINK IT'LL STILL BE THERE?

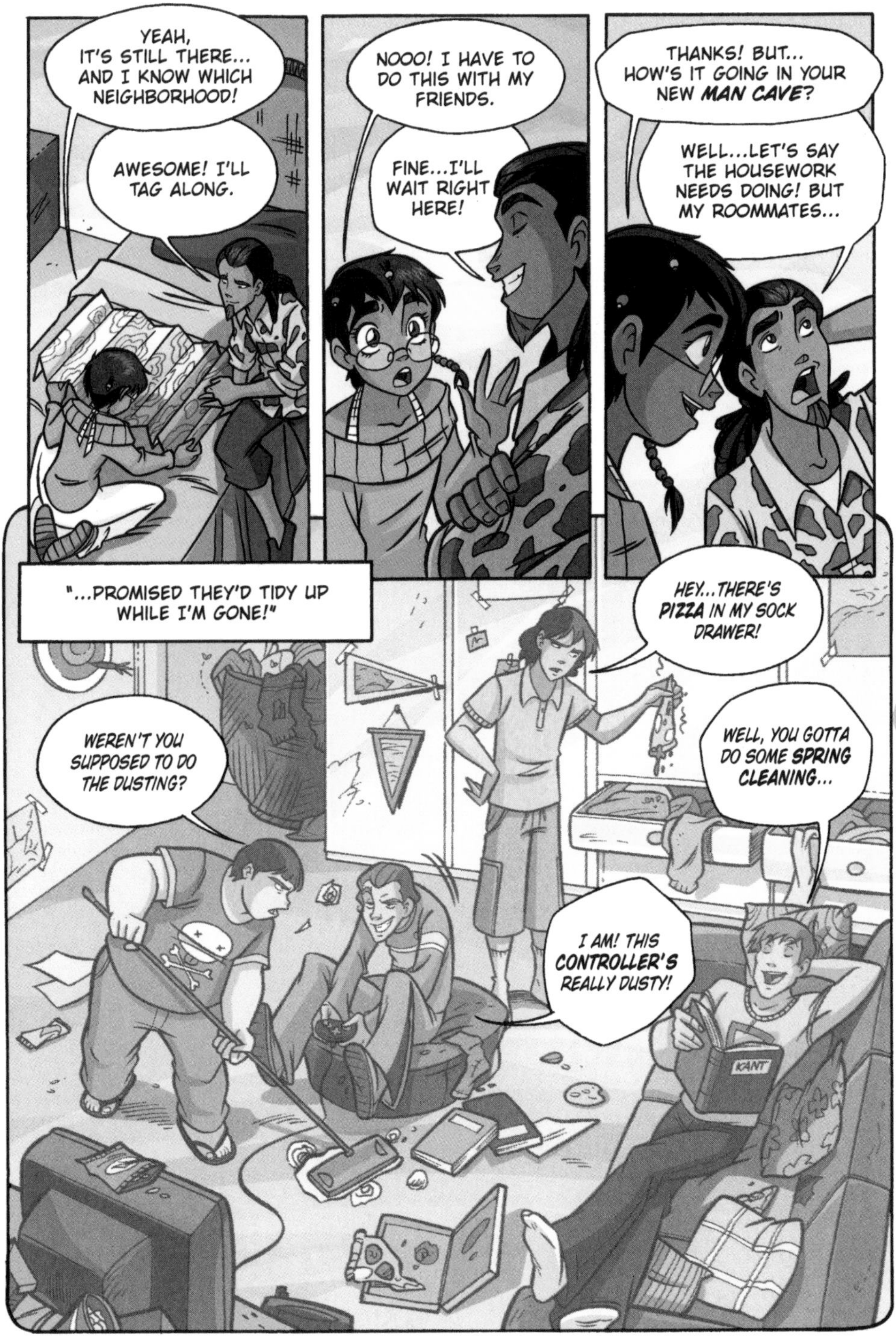

YEAH, IT'S STILL THERE... AND I KNOW WHICH NEIGHBORHOOD!
AWESOME! I'LL TAG ALONG.
NOOO! I HAVE TO DO THIS WITH MY FRIENDS.
FINE...I'LL WAIT RIGHT HERE!
THANKS! BUT... HOW'S IT GOING IN YOUR NEW **MAN CAVE**?
WELL...LET'S SAY THE HOUSEWORK NEEDS DOING! BUT MY ROOMMATES...
"...PROMISED THEY'D TIDY UP WHILE I'M GONE!"
HEY...THERE'S **PIZZA** IN MY SOCK DRAWER!
WEREN'T YOU SUPPOSED TO DO THE DUSTING?
WELL, YOU GOTTA DO SOME **SPRING CLEANING**...
I AM! THIS **CONTROLLER'S** REALLY DUSTY!
KANT

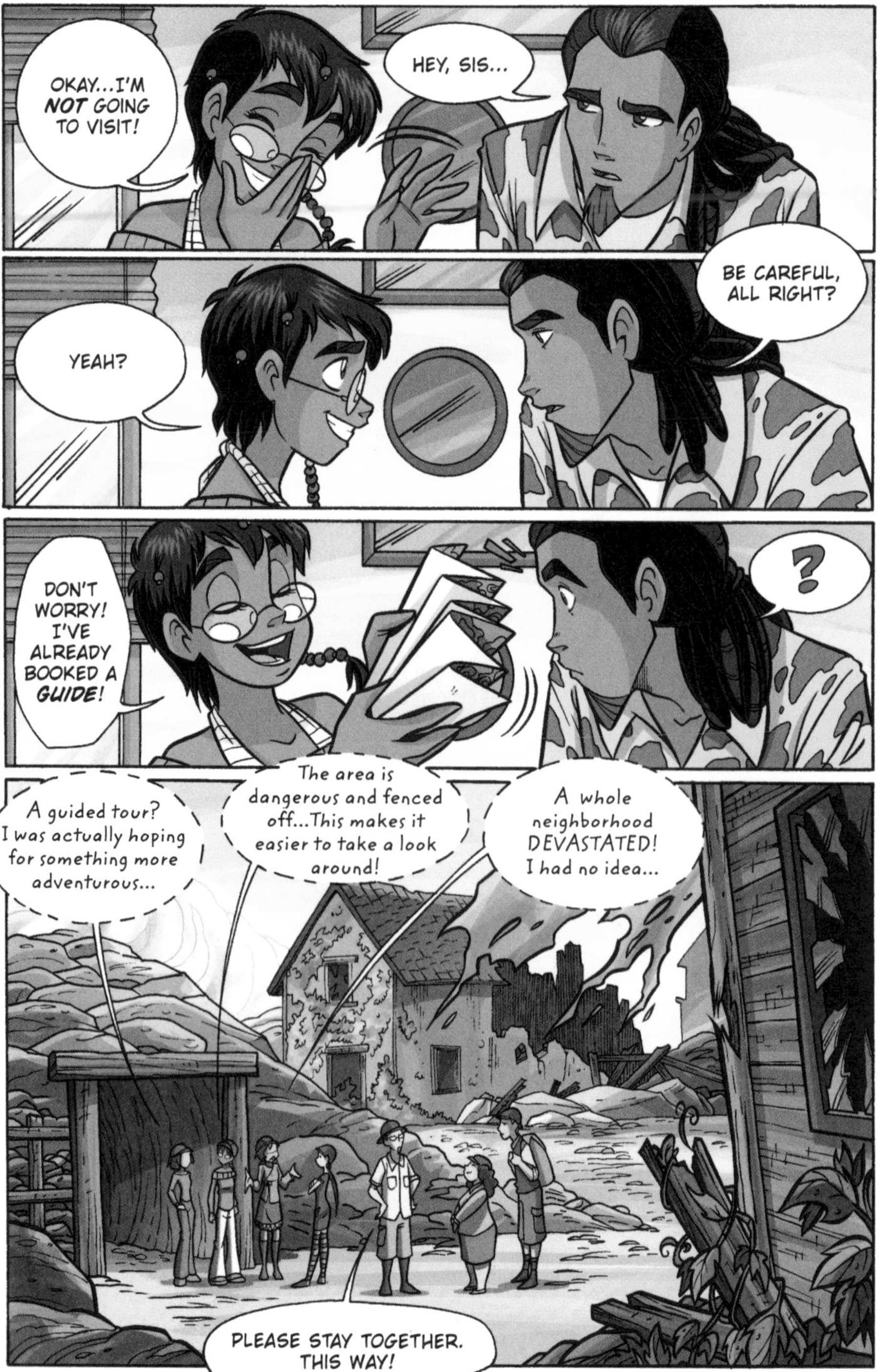

OKAY...I'M **NOT** GOING TO VISIT!
HEY, SIS...
YEAH?
BE CAREFUL, ALL RIGHT?
DON'T WORRY! I'VE ALREADY BOOKED A **GUIDE**!
?
A guided tour? I was actually hoping for something more adventurous...
The area is dangerous and fenced off...This makes it easier to take a look around!
A whole neighborhood DEVASTATED! I had no idea...
PLEASE STAY TOGETHER. THIS WAY!

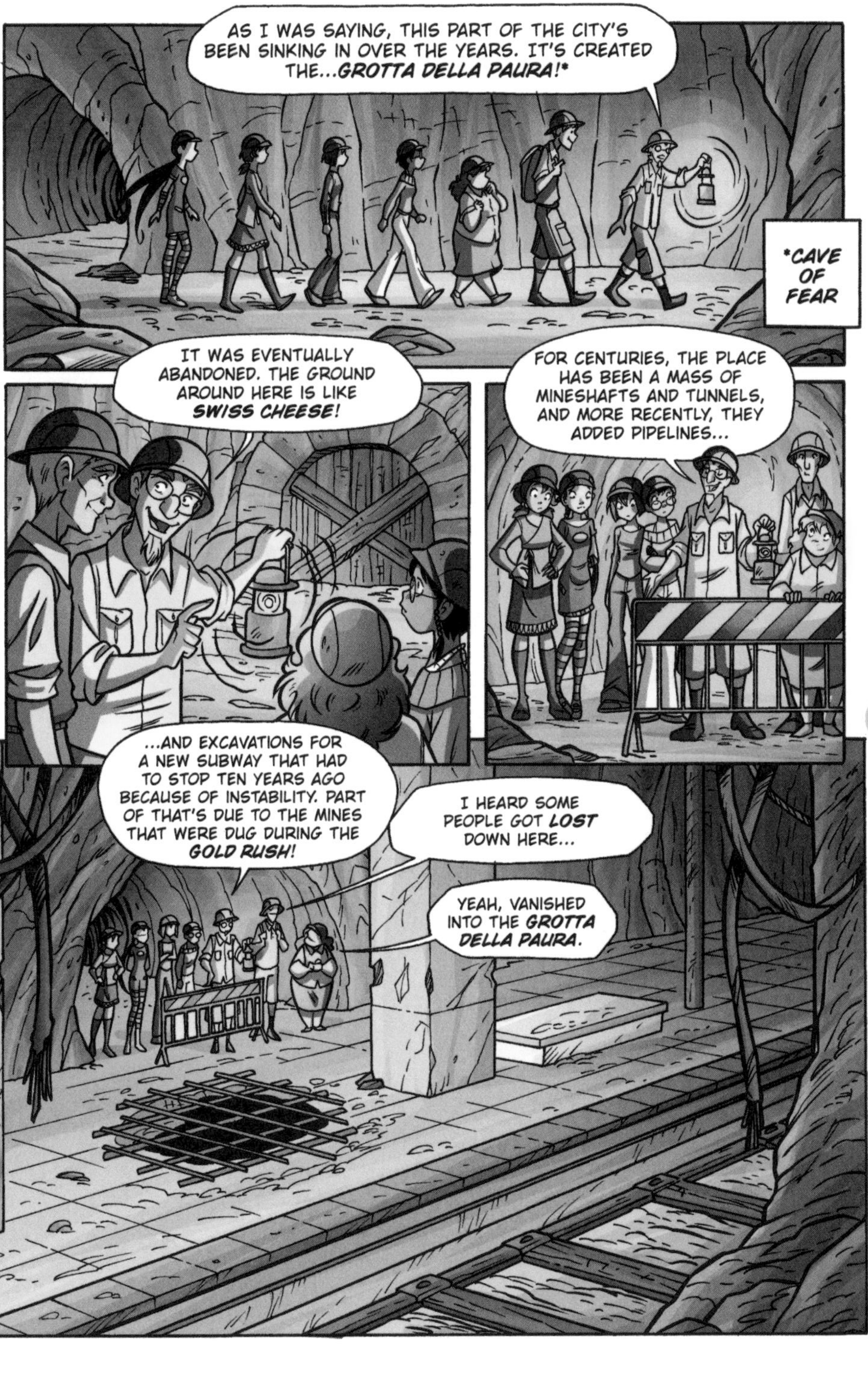
AS I WAS SAYING, THIS PART OF THE CITY'S BEEN SINKING IN OVER THE YEARS. IT'S CREATED THE...GROTTA DELLA PAURA!*
*CAVE OF FEAR
IT WAS EVENTUALLY ABANDONED. THE GROUND AROUND HERE IS LIKE SWISS CHEESE!
FOR CENTURIES, THE PLACE HAS BEEN A MASS OF MINESHAFTS AND TUNNELS, AND MORE RECENTLY, THEY ADDED PIPELINES...
...AND EXCAVATIONS FOR A NEW SUBWAY THAT HAD TO STOP TEN YEARS AGO BECAUSE OF INSTABILITY. PART OF THAT'S DUE TO THE MINES THAT WERE DUG DURING THE GOLD RUSH!
I HEARD SOME PEOPLE GOT LOST DOWN HERE...
YEAH, VANISHED INTO THE GROTTA DELLA PAURA.

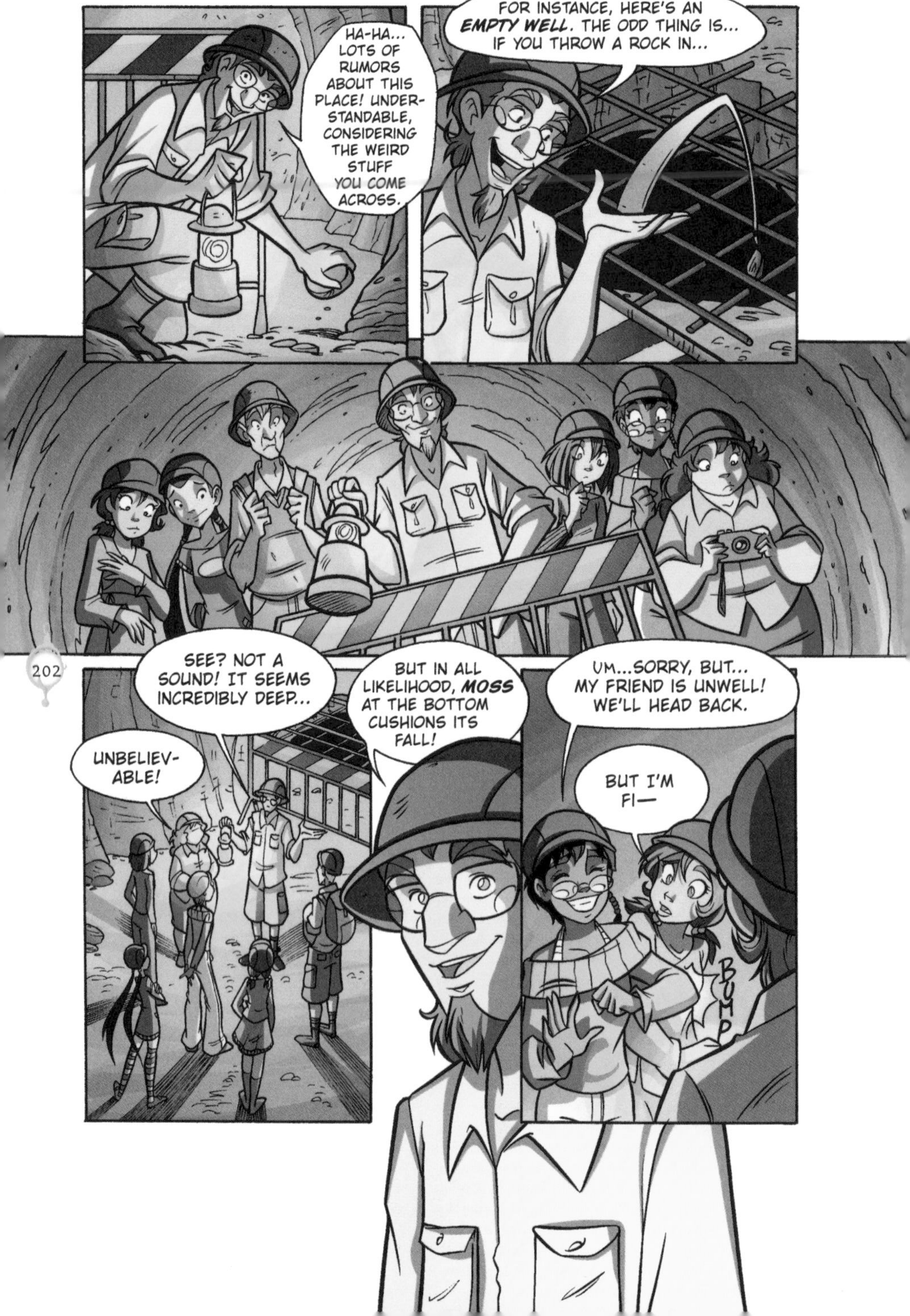
HA-HA... LOTS OF RUMORS ABOUT THIS PLACE! UNDERSTANDABLE, CONSIDERING THE WEIRD STUFF YOU COME ACROSS.
FOR INSTANCE, HERE'S AN **EMPTY WELL**. THE ODD THING IS... IF YOU THROW A ROCK IN...
SEE? NOT A SOUND! IT SEEMS INCREDIBLY DEEP...
UNBELIEVABLE!
BUT IN ALL LIKELIHOOD, **MOSS** AT THE BOTTOM CUSHIONS ITS FALL!
UM...SORRY, BUT... MY FRIEND IS UNWELL! WE'LL HEAD BACK.
BUT I'M FI—
BUMP

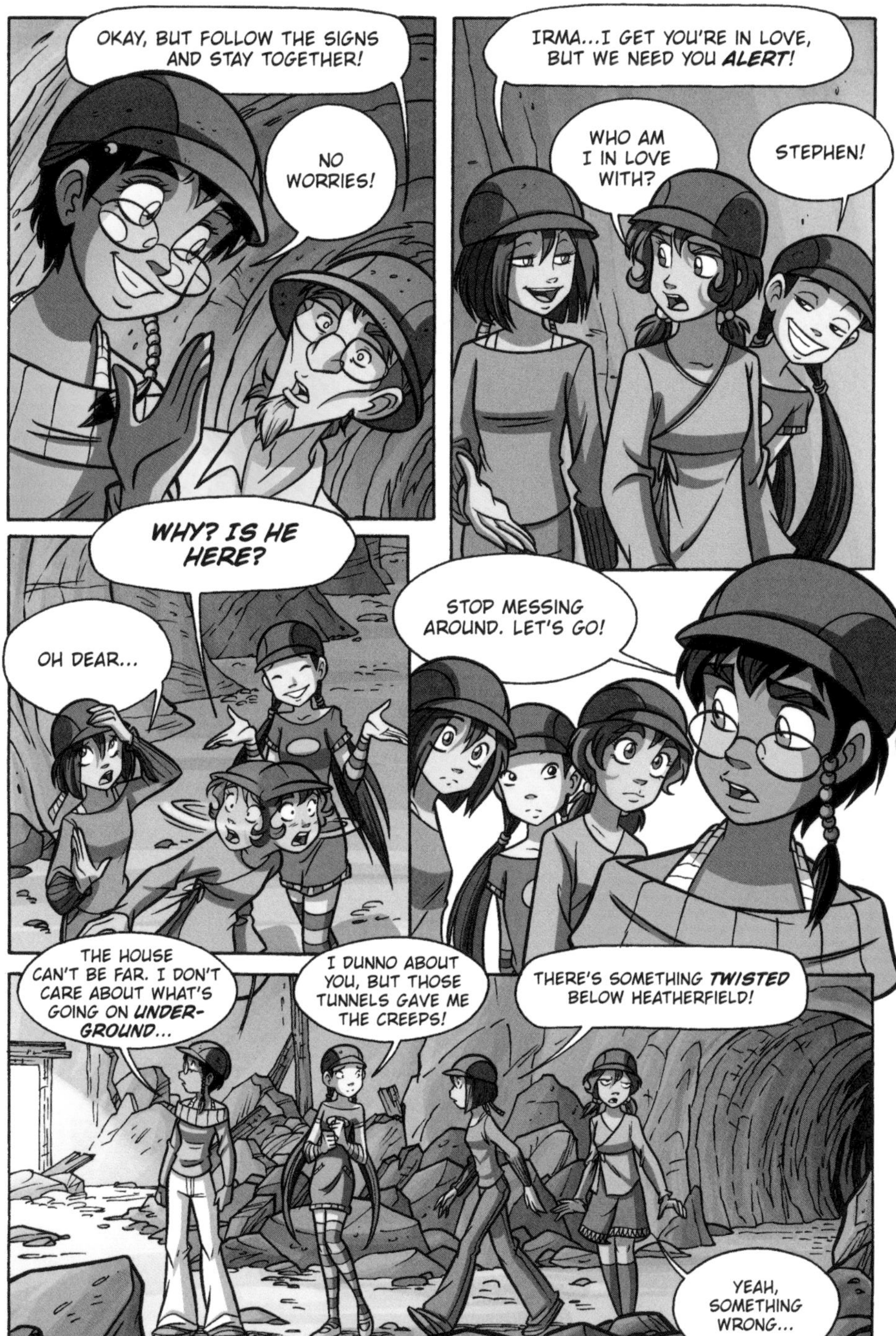
OKAY, BUT FOLLOW THE SIGNS AND STAY TOGETHER!
NO WORRIES!
IRMA...I GET YOU'RE IN LOVE, BUT WE NEED YOU ALERT!
WHO AM I IN LOVE WITH?
STEPHEN!
WHY? IS HE HERE?
OH DEAR...
STOP MESSING AROUND. LET'S GO!
THE HOUSE CAN'T BE FAR. I DON'T CARE ABOUT WHAT'S GOING ON UNDER-GROUND...
I DUNNO ABOUT YOU, BUT THOSE TUNNELS GAVE ME THE CREEPS!
THERE'S SOMETHING TWISTED BELOW HEATHERFIELD!
YEAH, SOMETHING WRONG...

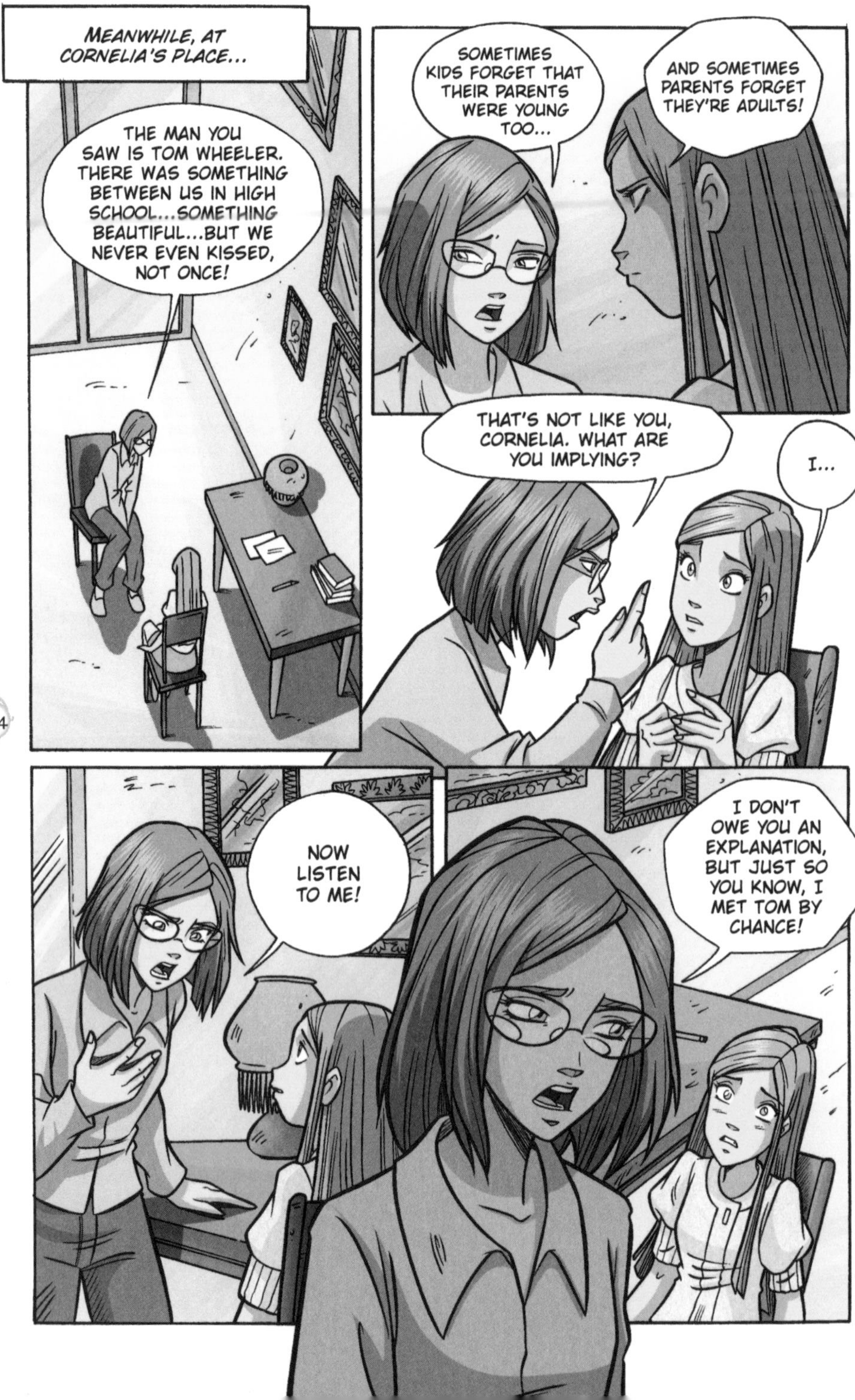
MEANWHILE, AT CORNELIA'S PLACE...
THE MAN YOU SAW IS TOM WHEELER. THERE WAS SOMETHING BETWEEN US IN HIGH SCHOOL...SOMETHING BEAUTIFUL...BUT WE NEVER EVEN KISSED, NOT ONCE!
SOMETIMES KIDS FORGET THAT THEIR PARENTS WERE YOUNG TOO...
AND SOMETIMES PARENTS FORGET THEY'RE ADULTS!
THAT'S NOT LIKE YOU, CORNELIA. WHAT ARE YOU IMPLYING?
I...
NOW LISTEN TO ME!
I DON'T OWE YOU AN EXPLANATION, BUT JUST SO YOU KNOW, I MET TOM BY CHANCE!

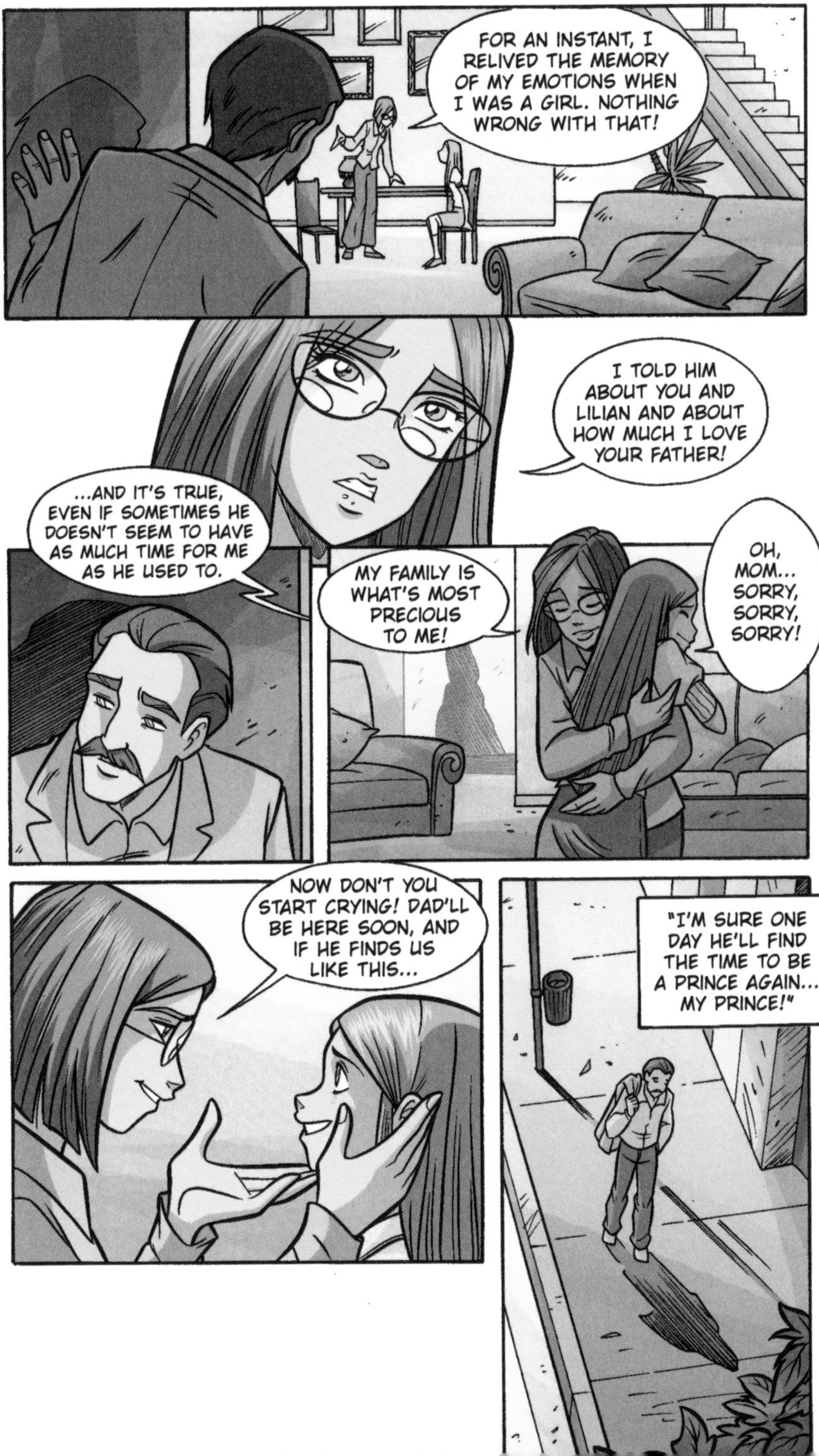
FOR AN INSTANT, I RELIVED THE MEMORY OF MY EMOTIONS WHEN I WAS A GIRL. NOTHING WRONG WITH THAT!
I TOLD HIM ABOUT YOU AND LILIAN AND ABOUT HOW MUCH I LOVE YOUR FATHER!
...AND IT'S TRUE, EVEN IF SOMETIMES HE DOESN'T SEEM TO HAVE AS MUCH TIME FOR ME AS HE USED TO.
MY FAMILY IS WHAT'S MOST PRECIOUS TO ME!
OH, MOM... SORRY, SORRY, SORRY!
NOW DON'T YOU START CRYING! DAD'LL BE HERE SOON, AND IF HE FINDS US LIKE THIS...
"I'M SURE ONE DAY HE'LL FIND THE TIME TO BE A PRINCE AGAIN... MY PRINCE!"

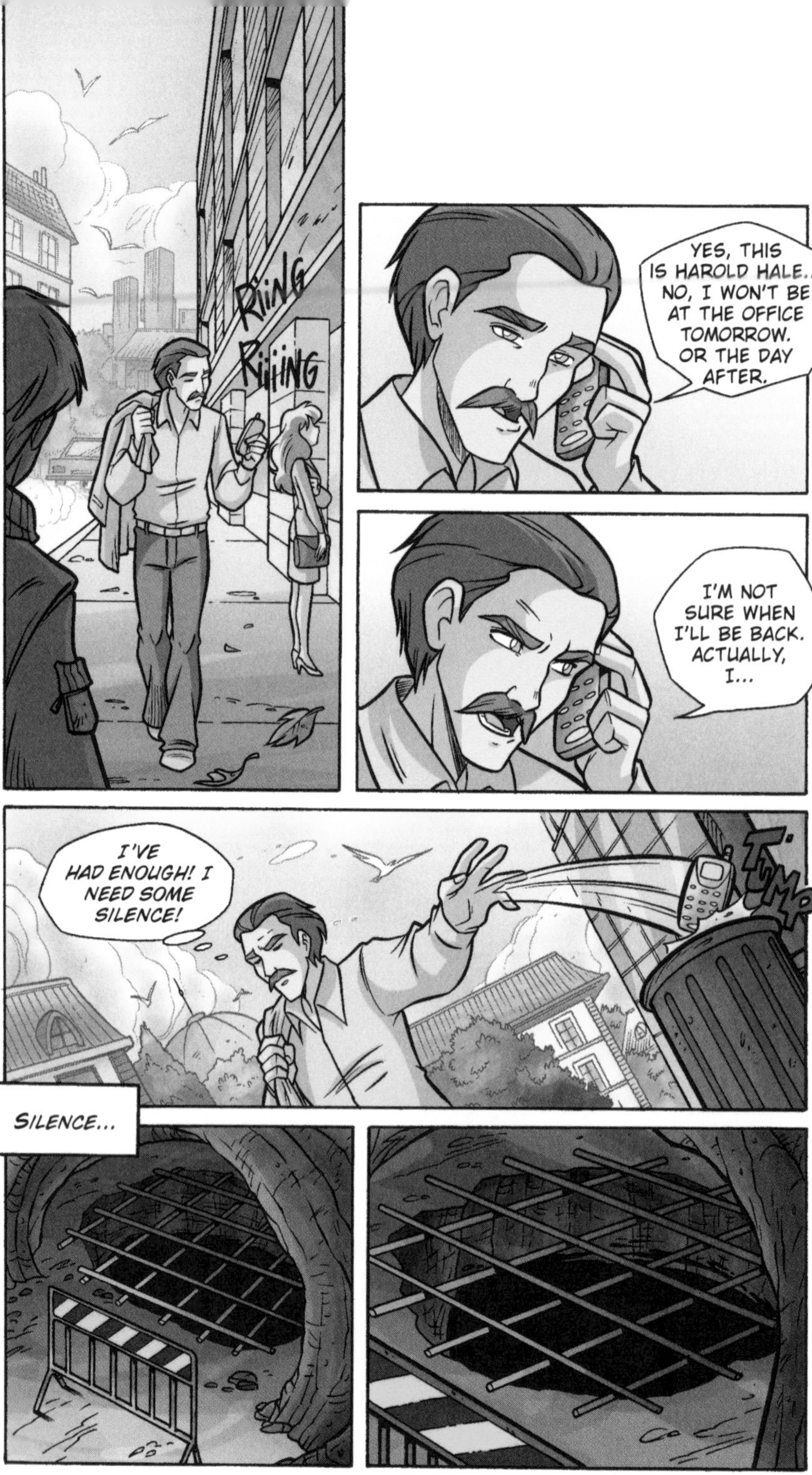
RIING
RIIING
YES, THIS IS HAROLD HALE... NO, I WON'T BE AT THE OFFICE TOMORROW. OR THE DAY AFTER.
I'M NOT SURE WHEN I'LL BE BACK. ACTUALLY, I...
I'VE HAD ENOUGH! I NEED SOME SILENCE!
TUMP
SILENCE...

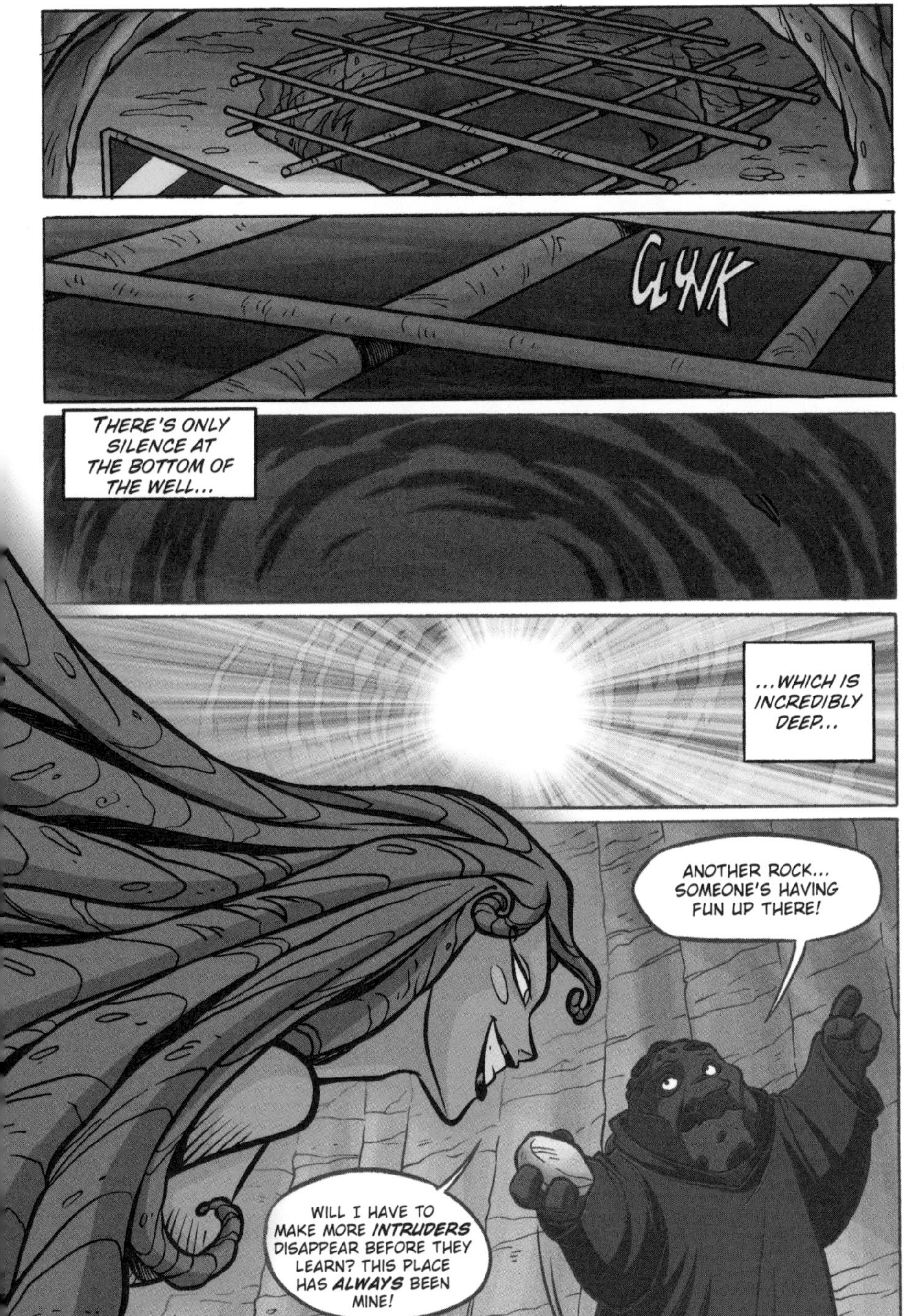
CLUNK
THERE'S ONLY SILENCE AT THE BOTTOM OF THE WELL...
...WHICH IS INCREDIBLY DEEP...
ANOTHER ROCK... SOMEONE'S HAVING FUN UP THERE!
WILL I HAVE TO MAKE MORE *INTRUDERS* DISAPPEAR BEFORE THEY LEARN? THIS PLACE HAS *ALWAYS* BEEN MINE!

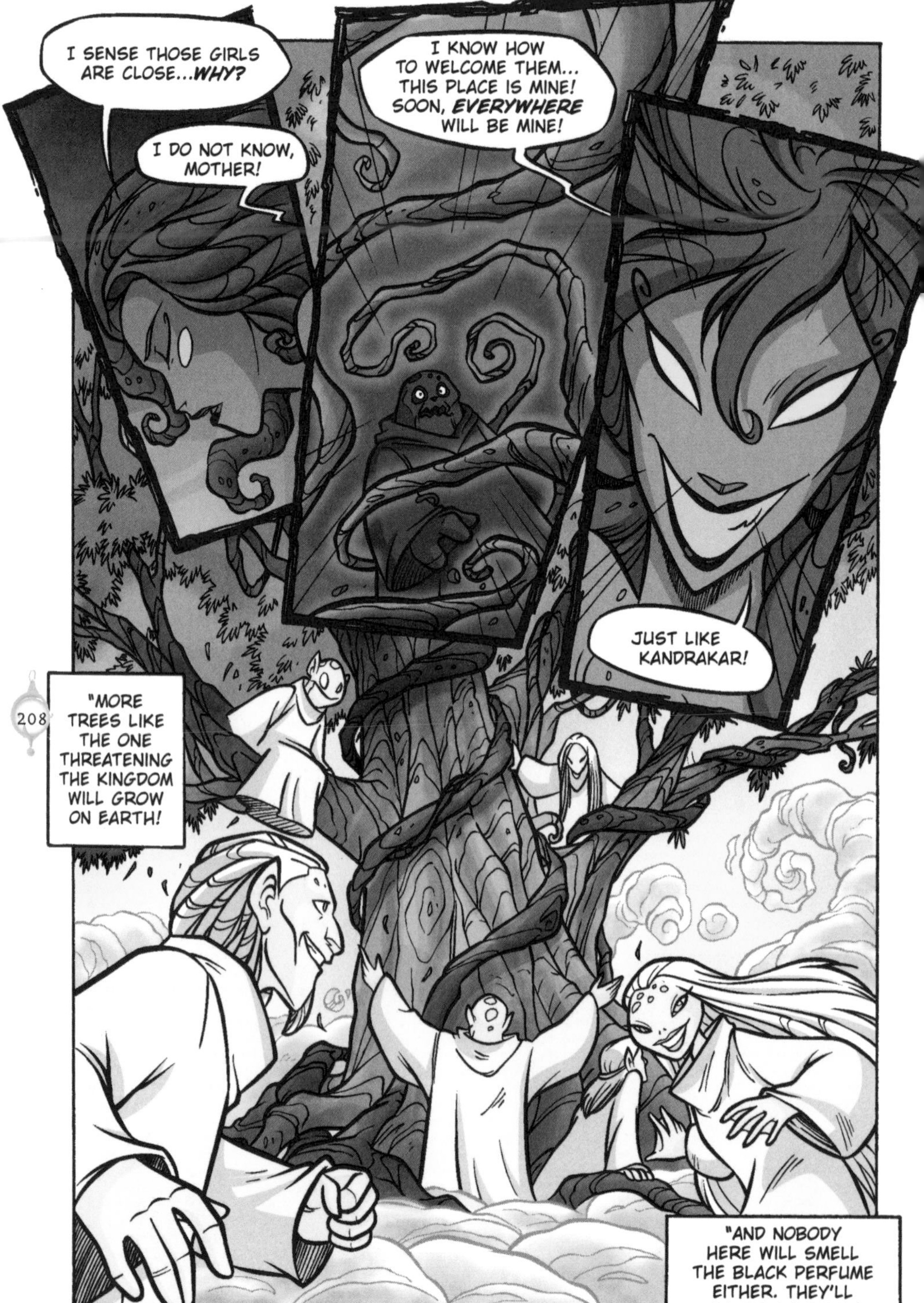

I SENSE THOSE GIRLS ARE CLOSE...WHY?
I DO NOT KNOW, MOTHER!
I KNOW HOW TO WELCOME THEM... THIS PLACE IS MINE! SOON, EVERYWHERE WILL BE MINE!
JUST LIKE KANDRAKAR!
"MORE TREES LIKE THE ONE THREATENING THE KINGDOM WILL GROW ON EARTH!
"AND NOBODY HERE WILL SMELL THE BLACK PERFUME EITHER. THEY'LL ALL BE CHARMED!

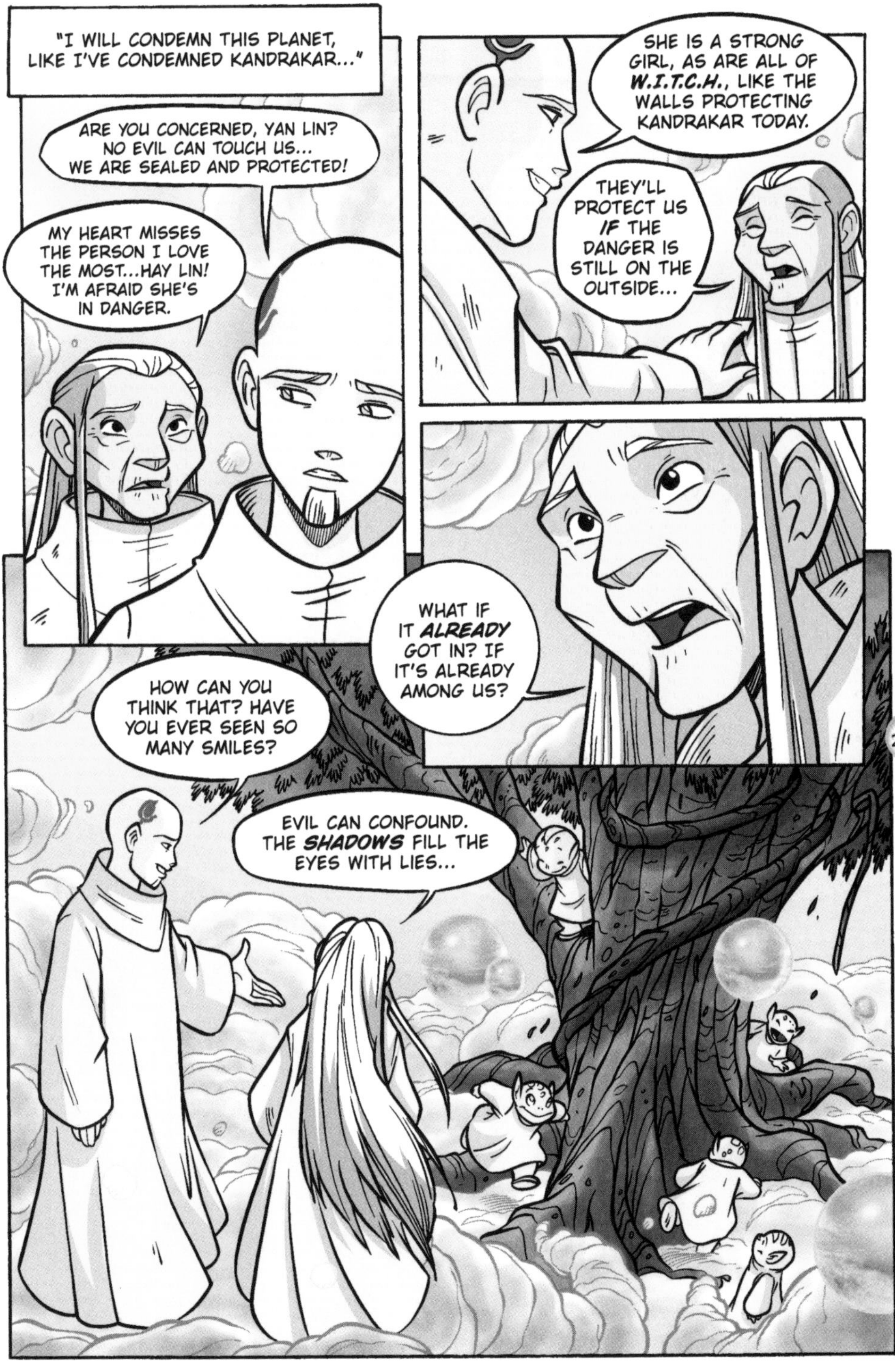
"I WILL CONDEMN THIS PLANET, LIKE I'VE CONDEMNED KANDRAKAR..."
ARE YOU CONCERNED, YAN LIN? NO EVIL CAN TOUCH US... WE ARE SEALED AND PROTECTED!
MY HEART MISSES THE PERSON I LOVE THE MOST...HAY LIN! I'M AFRAID SHE'S IN DANGER.
SHE IS A STRONG GIRL, AS ARE ALL OF W.I.T.C.H., LIKE THE WALLS PROTECTING KANDRAKAR TODAY.
THEY'LL PROTECT US IF THE DANGER IS STILL ON THE OUTSIDE...
WHAT IF IT ALREADY GOT IN? IF IT'S ALREADY AMONG US?
HOW CAN YOU THINK THAT? HAVE YOU EVER SEEN SO MANY SMILES?
EVIL CAN CONFOUND. THE SHADOWS FILL THE EYES WITH LIES...

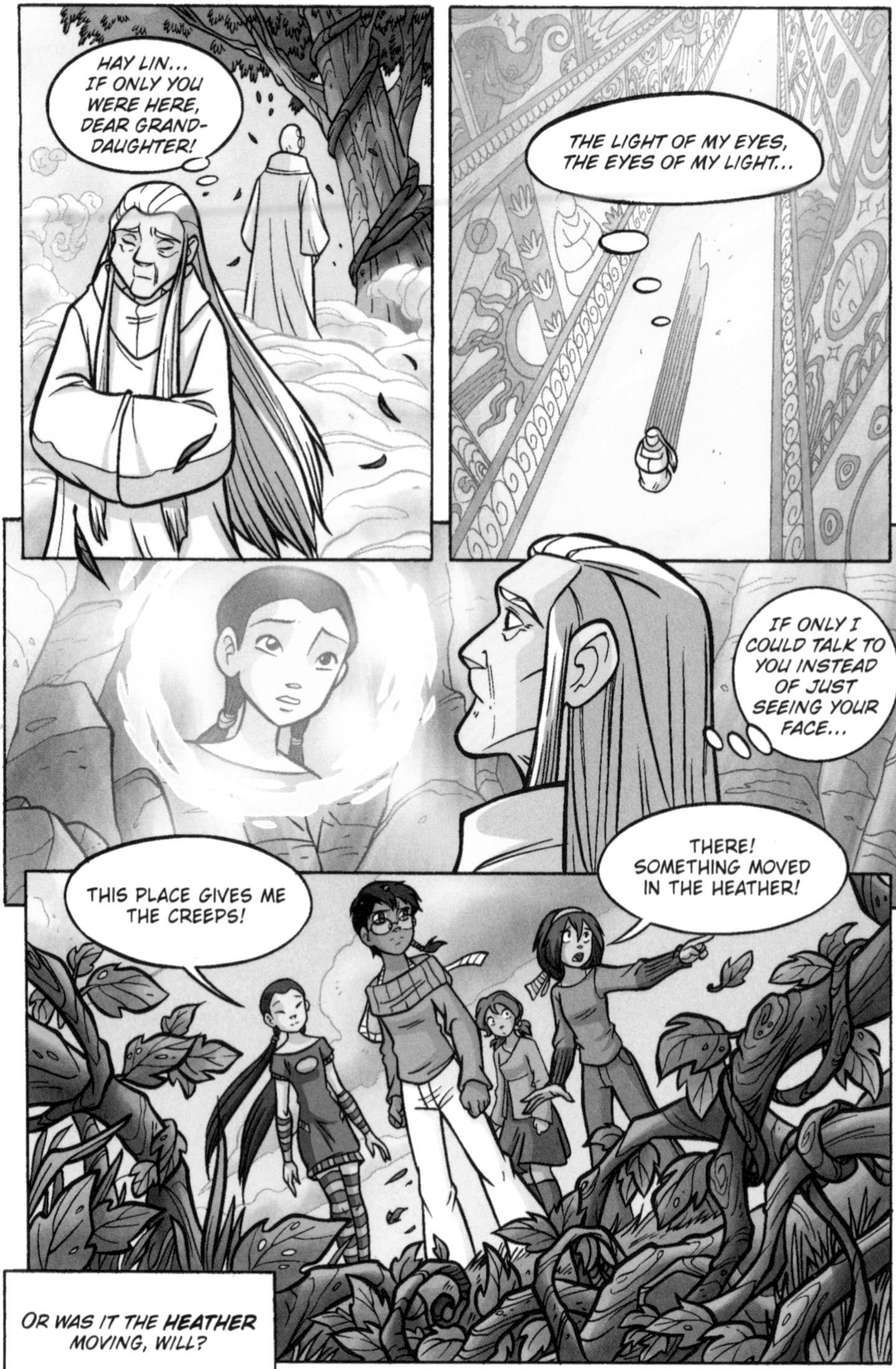
HAY LIN... IF ONLY YOU WERE HERE, DEAR GRAND-DAUGHTER!
THE LIGHT OF MY EYES, THE EYES OF MY LIGHT...
IF ONLY I COULD TALK TO YOU INSTEAD OF JUST SEEING YOUR FACE...
THIS PLACE GIVES ME THE CREEPS!
THERE! SOMETHING MOVED IN THE HEATHER!
OR WAS IT THE **HEATHER** MOVING, WILL?

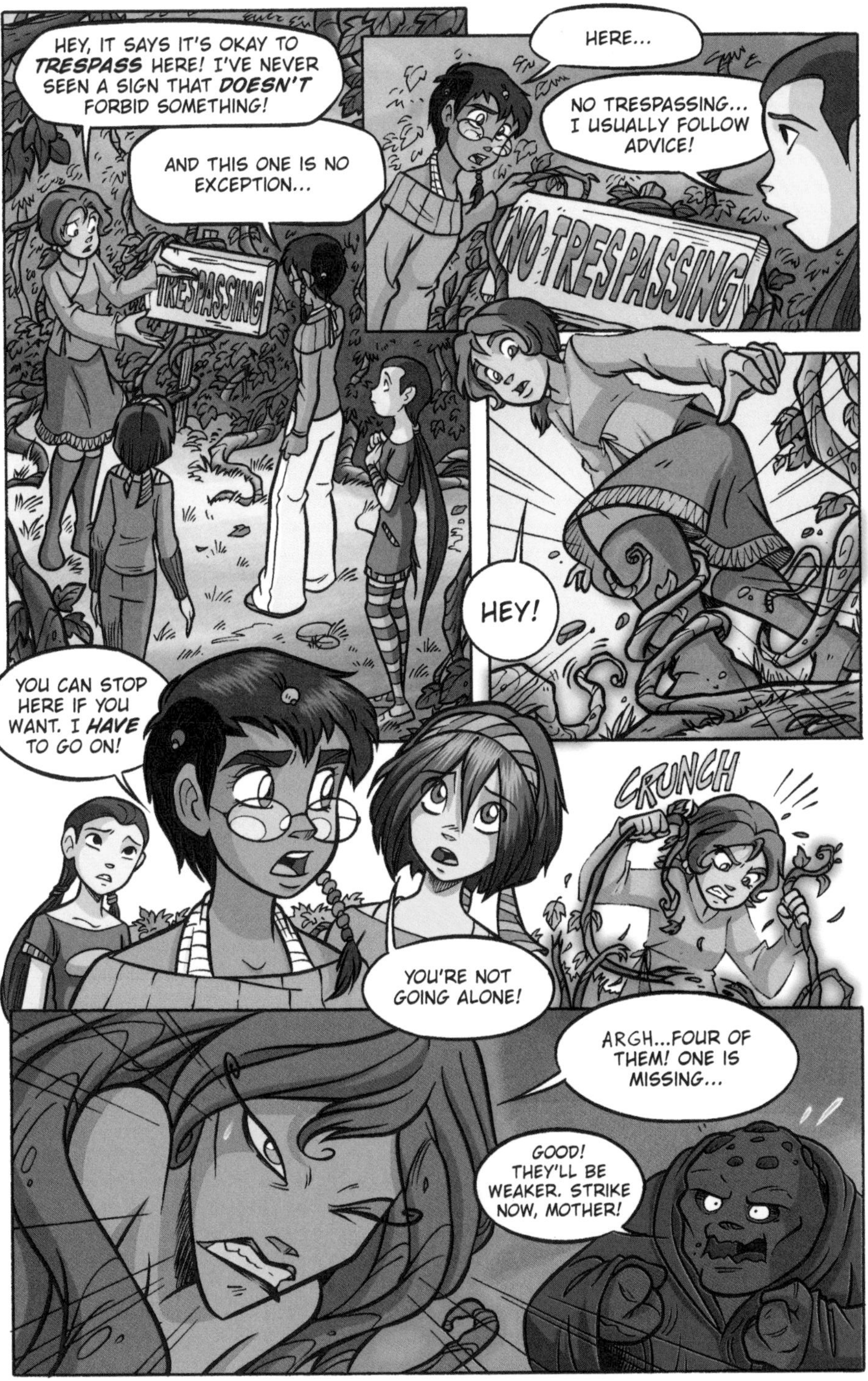
HEY, IT SAYS IT'S OKAY TO *TRESPASS* HERE! I'VE NEVER SEEN A SIGN THAT *DOESN'T* FORBID SOMETHING!
AND THIS ONE IS NO EXCEPTION...
TRESPASSING
HERE...
NO TRESPASSING... I USUALLY FOLLOW ADVICE!
NO TRESPASSING
HEY!
YOU CAN STOP HERE IF YOU WANT. I *HAVE* TO GO ON!
YOU'RE NOT GOING ALONE!
CRUNCH
ARGH...FOUR OF THEM! ONE IS MISSING...
GOOD! THEY'LL BE WEAKER. STRIKE NOW, MOTHER!

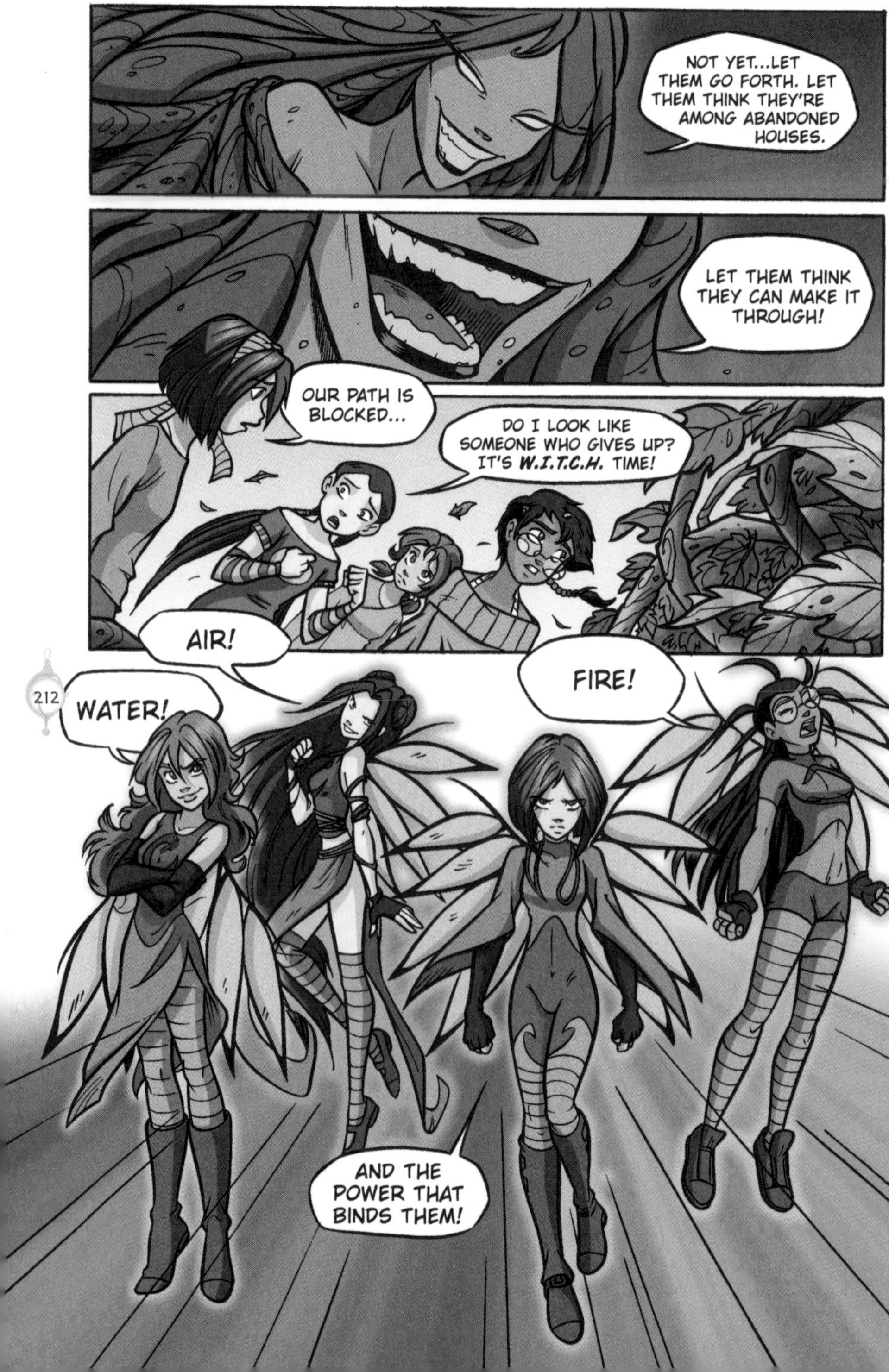

NOT YET...LET THEM GO FORTH. LET THEM THINK THEY'RE AMONG ABANDONED HOUSES.
LET THEM THINK THEY CAN MAKE IT THROUGH!
OUR PATH IS BLOCKED...
DO I LOOK LIKE SOMEONE WHO GIVES UP? IT'S W.I.T.C.H. TIME!
AIR!
WATER!
FIRE!
AND THE POWER THAT BINDS THEM!

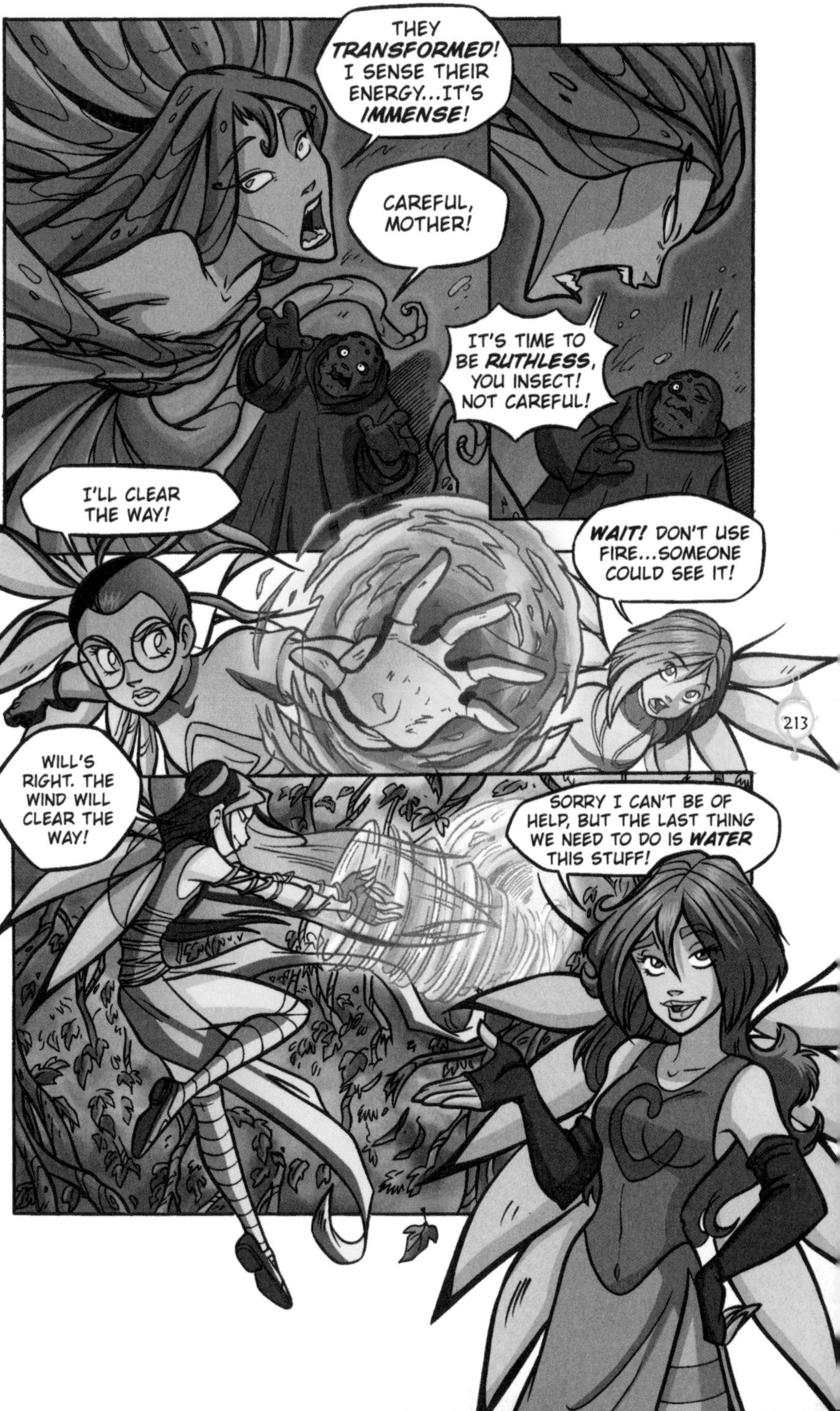
THEY TRANSFORMED! I SENSE THEIR ENERGY...IT'S IMMENSE!
CAREFUL, MOTHER!
IT'S TIME TO BE RUTHLESS, YOU INSECT! NOT CAREFUL!
I'LL CLEAR THE WAY!
WAIT! DON'T USE FIRE...SOMEONE COULD SEE IT!
WILL'S RIGHT. THE WIND WILL CLEAR THE WAY!
SORRY I CAN'T BE OF HELP, BUT THE LAST THING WE NEED TO DO IS WATER THIS STUFF!

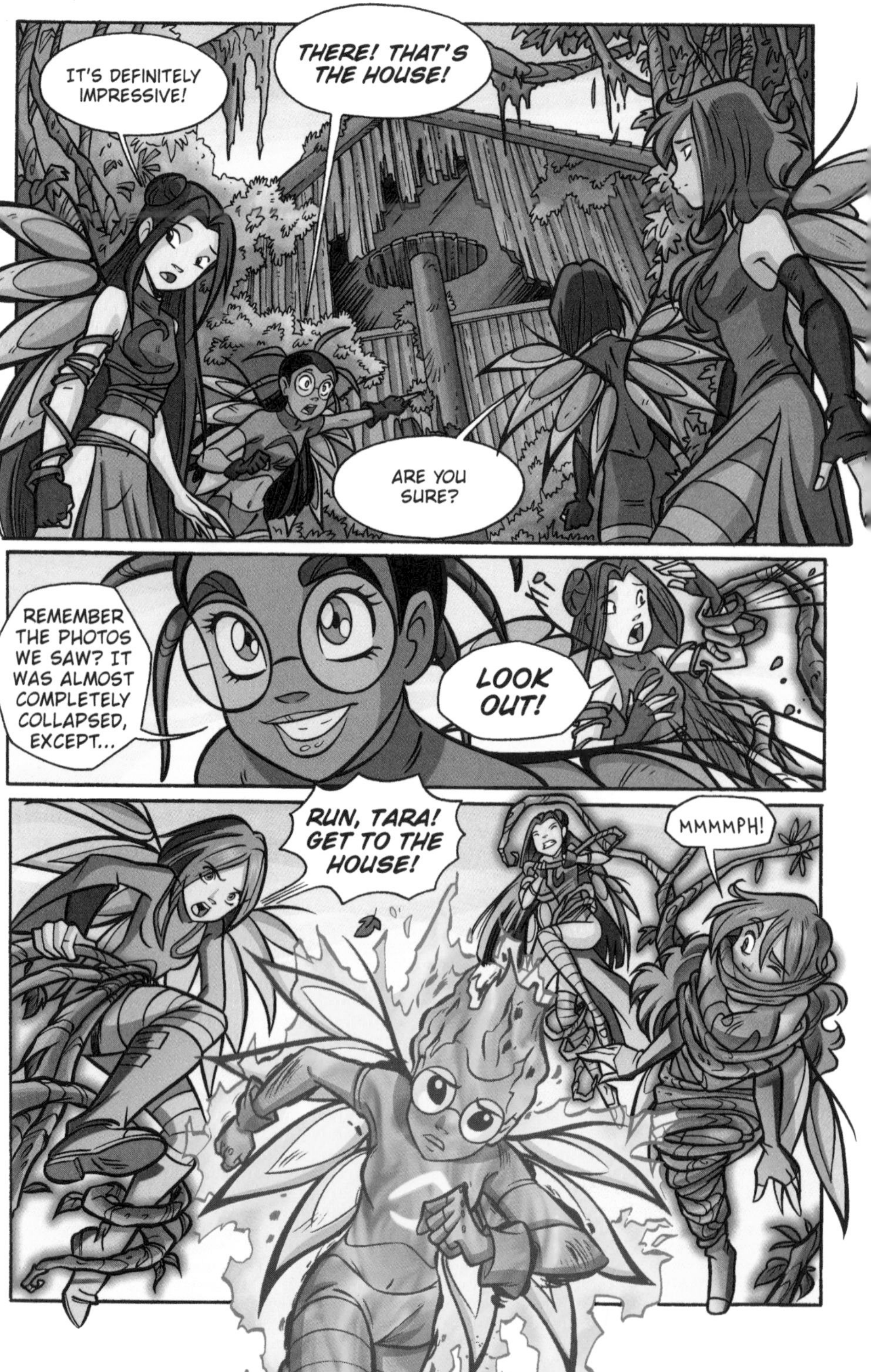

IT'S DEFINITELY IMPRESSIVE!
THERE! THAT'S THE HOUSE!
ARE YOU SURE?
REMEMBER THE PHOTOS WE SAW? IT WAS ALMOST COMPLETELY COLLAPSED, EXCEPT...
LOOK OUT!
RUN, TARA! GET TO THE HOUSE!
MMMMPH!

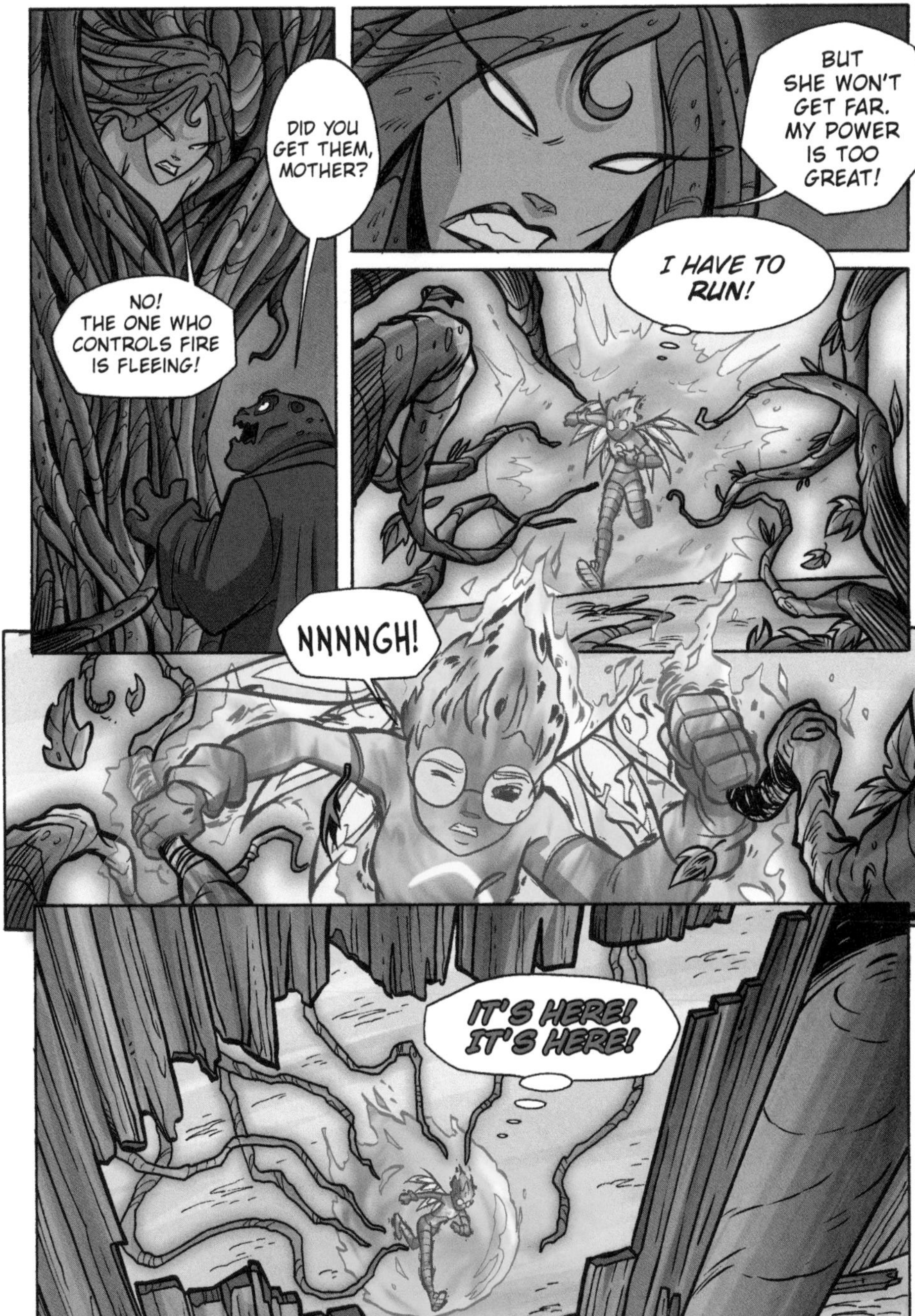
DID YOU GET THEM, MOTHER?
NO! THE ONE WHO CONTROLS FIRE IS FLEEING!
BUT SHE WON'T GET FAR. MY POWER IS TOO GREAT!
I HAVE TO RUN!
NNNNGH!
IT'S HERE! IT'S HERE!

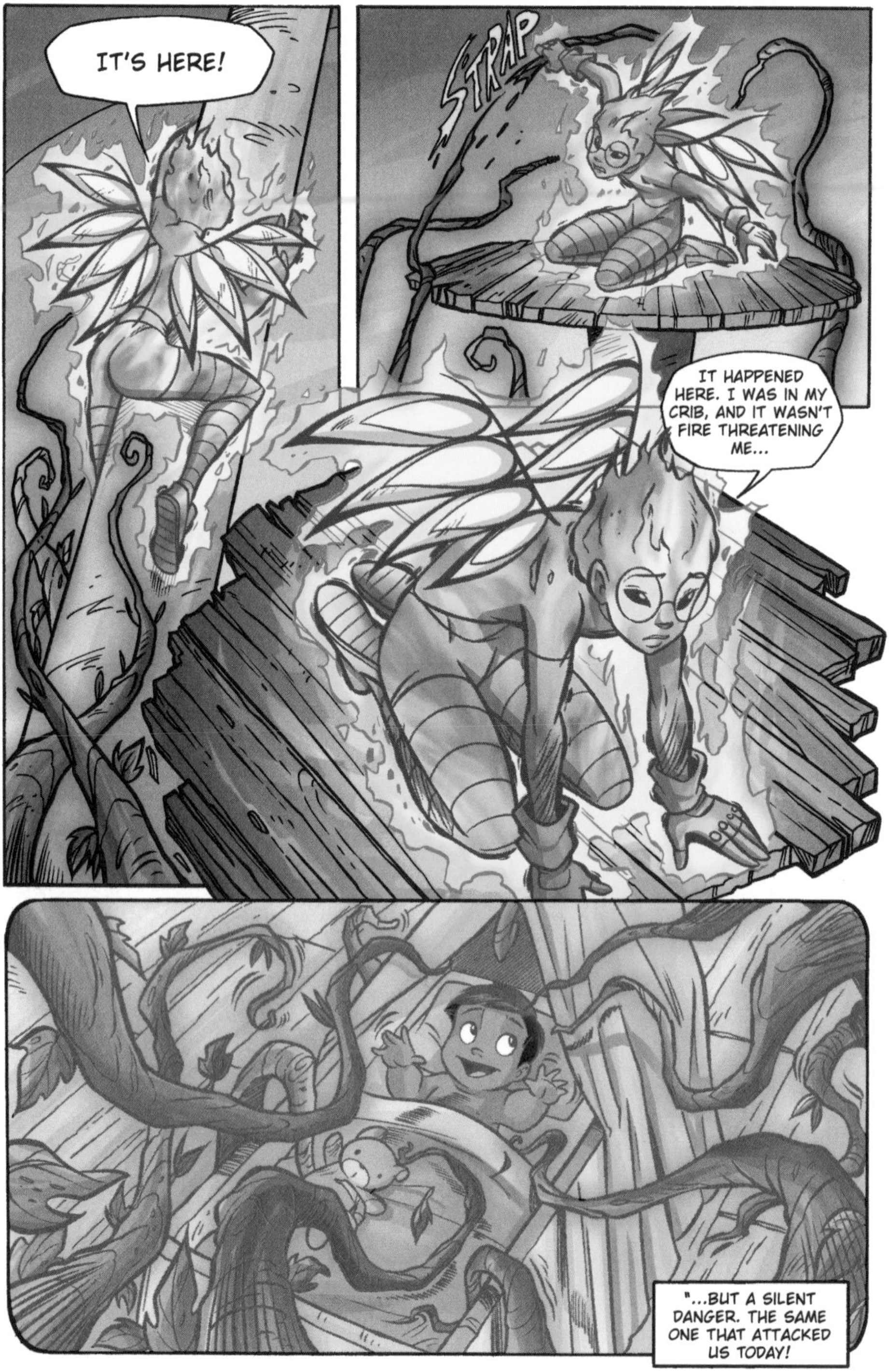
IT'S HERE!
STRAP
IT HAPPENED HERE. I WAS IN MY CRIB, AND IT WASN'T FIRE THREATENING ME...
"...BUT A SILENT DANGER. THE SAME ONE THAT ATTACKED US TODAY!

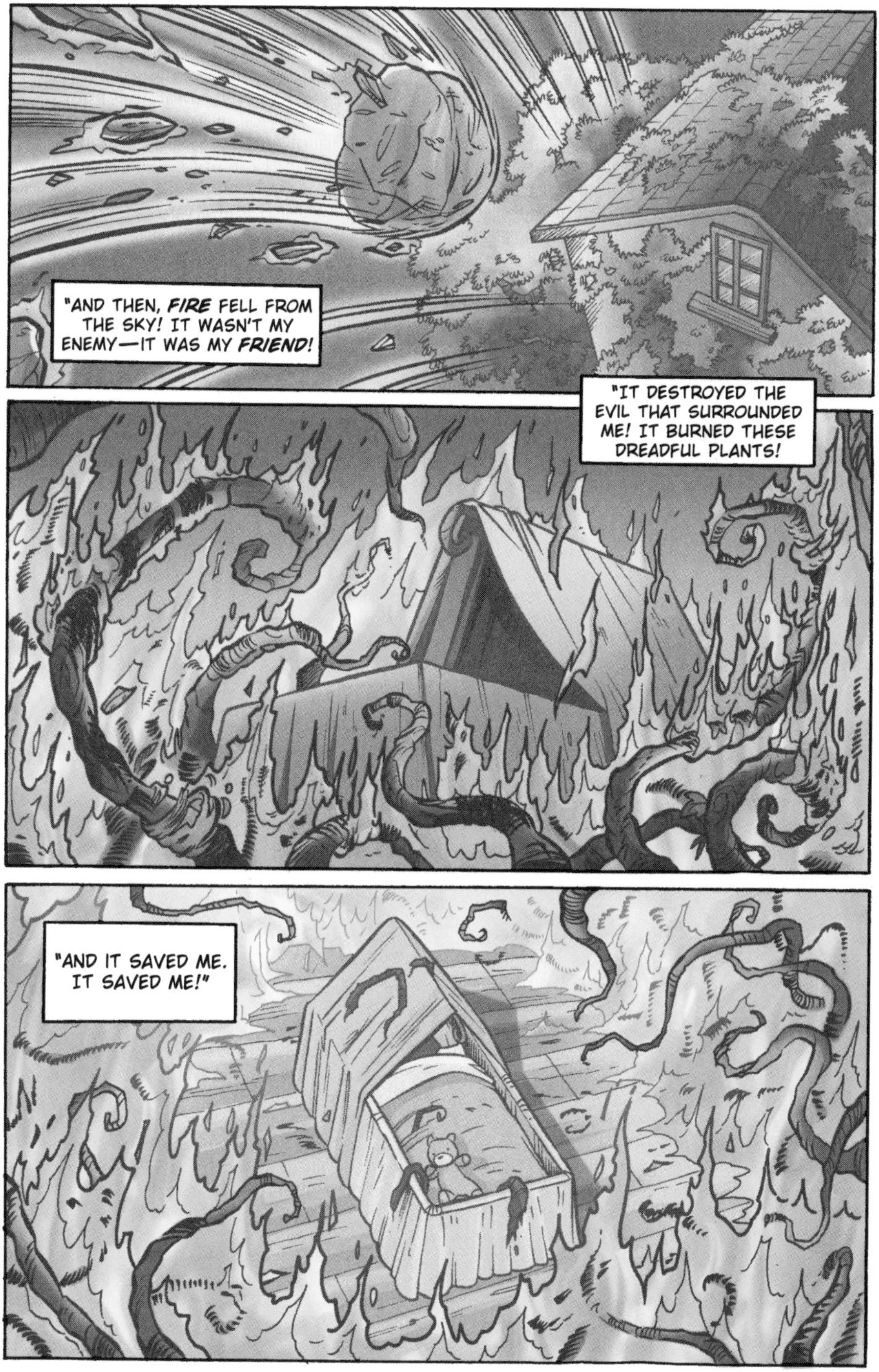
"AND THEN, FIRE FELL FROM THE SKY! IT WASN'T MY ENEMY—IT WAS MY FRIEND!
"IT DESTROYED THE EVIL THAT SURROUNDED ME! IT BURNED THESE DREADFUL PLANTS!
"AND IT SAVED ME. IT SAVED ME!"

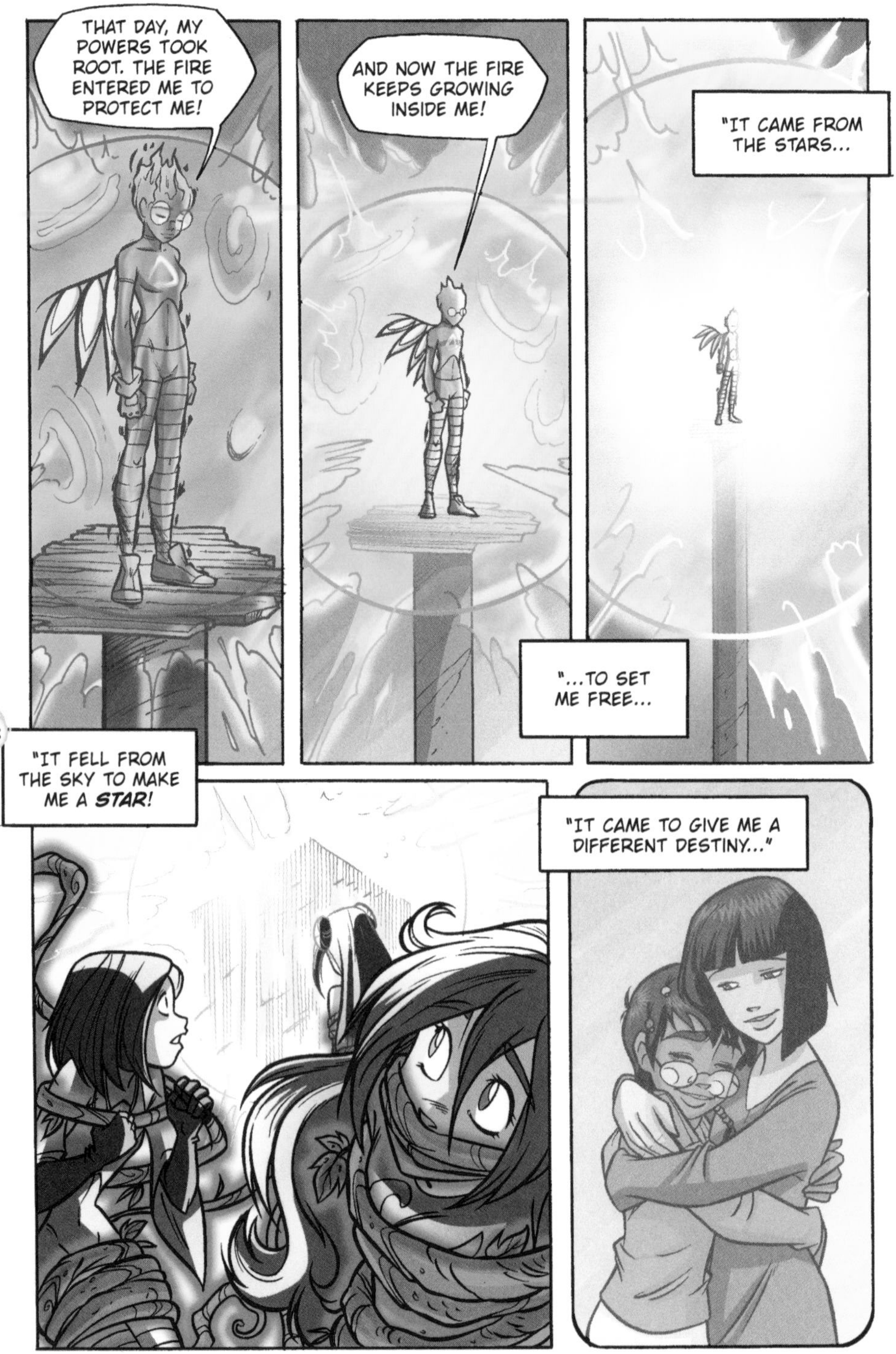

THAT DAY, MY POWERS TOOK ROOT. THE FIRE ENTERED ME TO PROTECT ME!
AND NOW THE FIRE KEEPS GROWING INSIDE ME!
"IT CAME FROM THE STARS...
"...TO SET ME FREE...
"IT FELL FROM THE SKY TO MAKE ME A STAR!
"IT CAME TO GIVE ME A DIFFERENT DESTINY..."

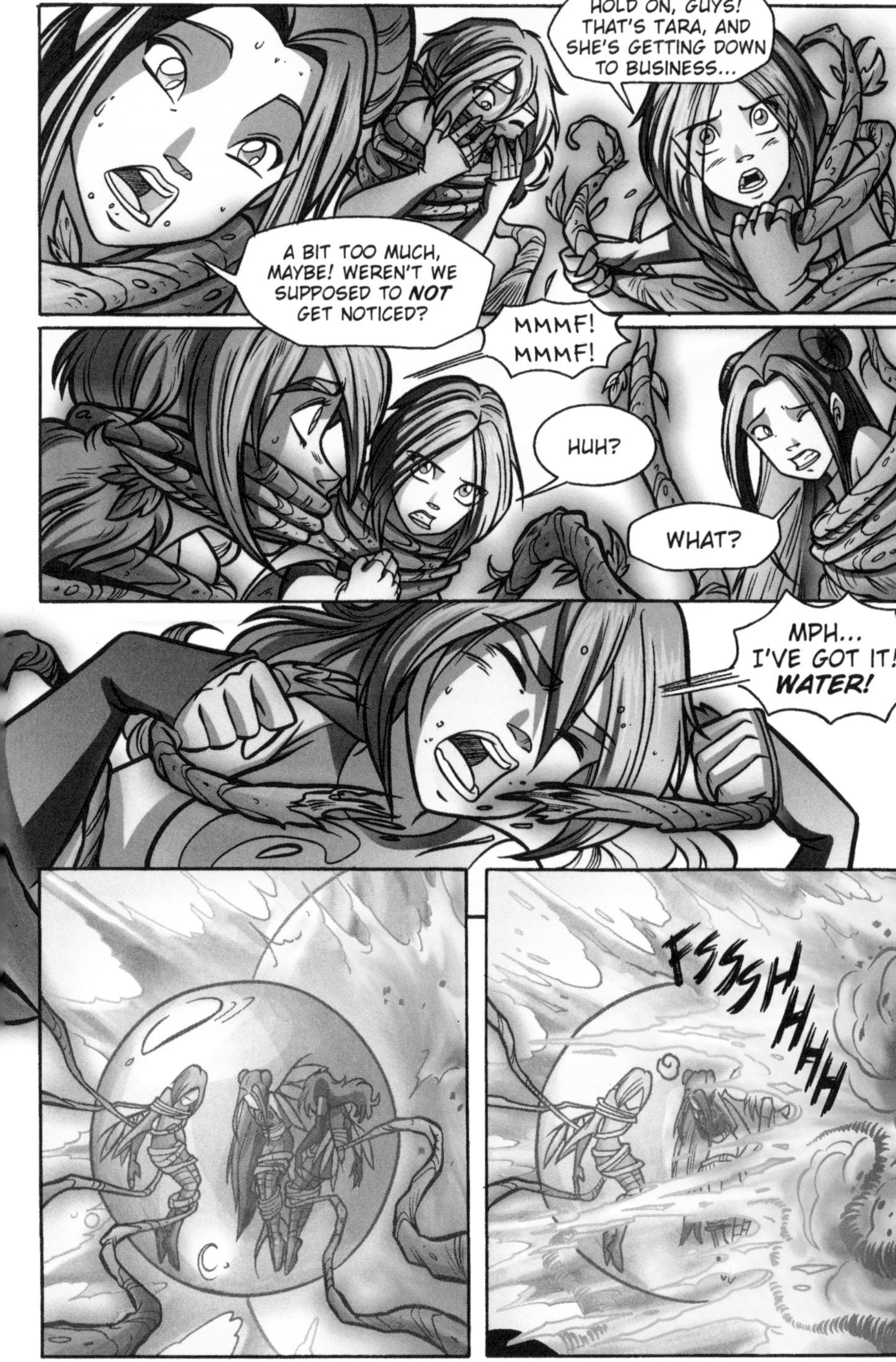
HOLD ON, GUYS! THAT'S TARA, AND SHE'S GETTING DOWN TO BUSINESS...
A BIT TOO MUCH, MAYBE! WEREN'T WE SUPPOSED TO **NOT** GET NOTICED?
MMMF! MMMF!
HUH?
WHAT?
MPH... I'VE GOT IT! ***WATER!***
FSSSHHHHH

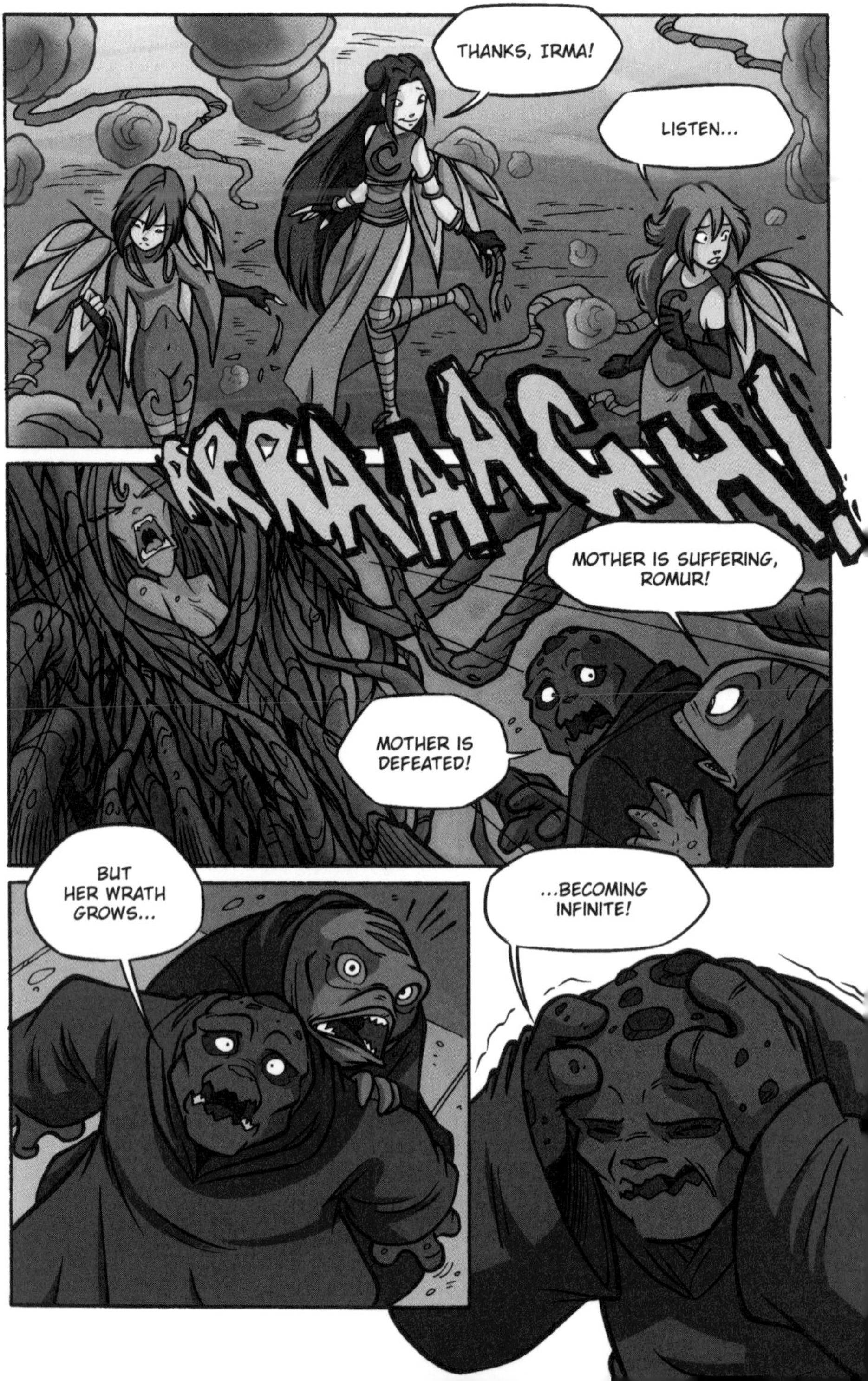
THANKS, IRMA!
LISTEN...
RRRAAAGH!
MOTHER IS SUFFERING, ROMUR!
MOTHER IS DEFEATED!
BUT HER WRATH GROWS...
...BECOMING INFINITE!

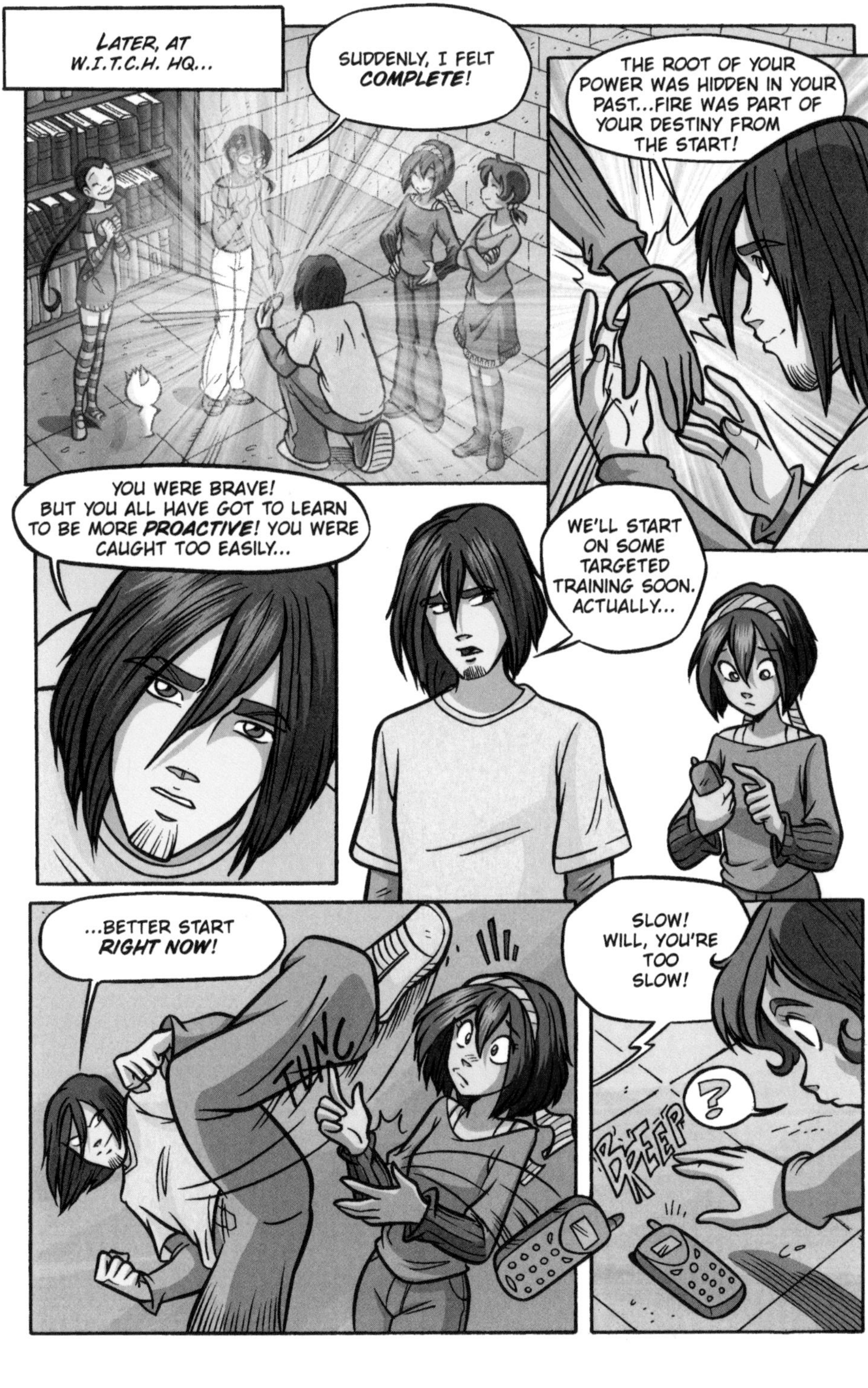
LATER, AT W.I.T.C.H. HQ...
SUDDENLY, I FELT COMPLETE!
THE ROOT OF YOUR POWER WAS HIDDEN IN YOUR PAST...FIRE WAS PART OF YOUR DESTINY FROM THE START!
YOU WERE BRAVE! BUT YOU ALL HAVE GOT TO LEARN TO BE MORE PROACTIVE! YOU WERE CAUGHT TOO EASILY...
WE'LL START ON SOME TARGETED TRAINING SOON. ACTUALLY...
...BETTER START RIGHT NOW!
FUNC
SLOW! WILL, YOU'RE TOO SLOW!
?
BEEEP

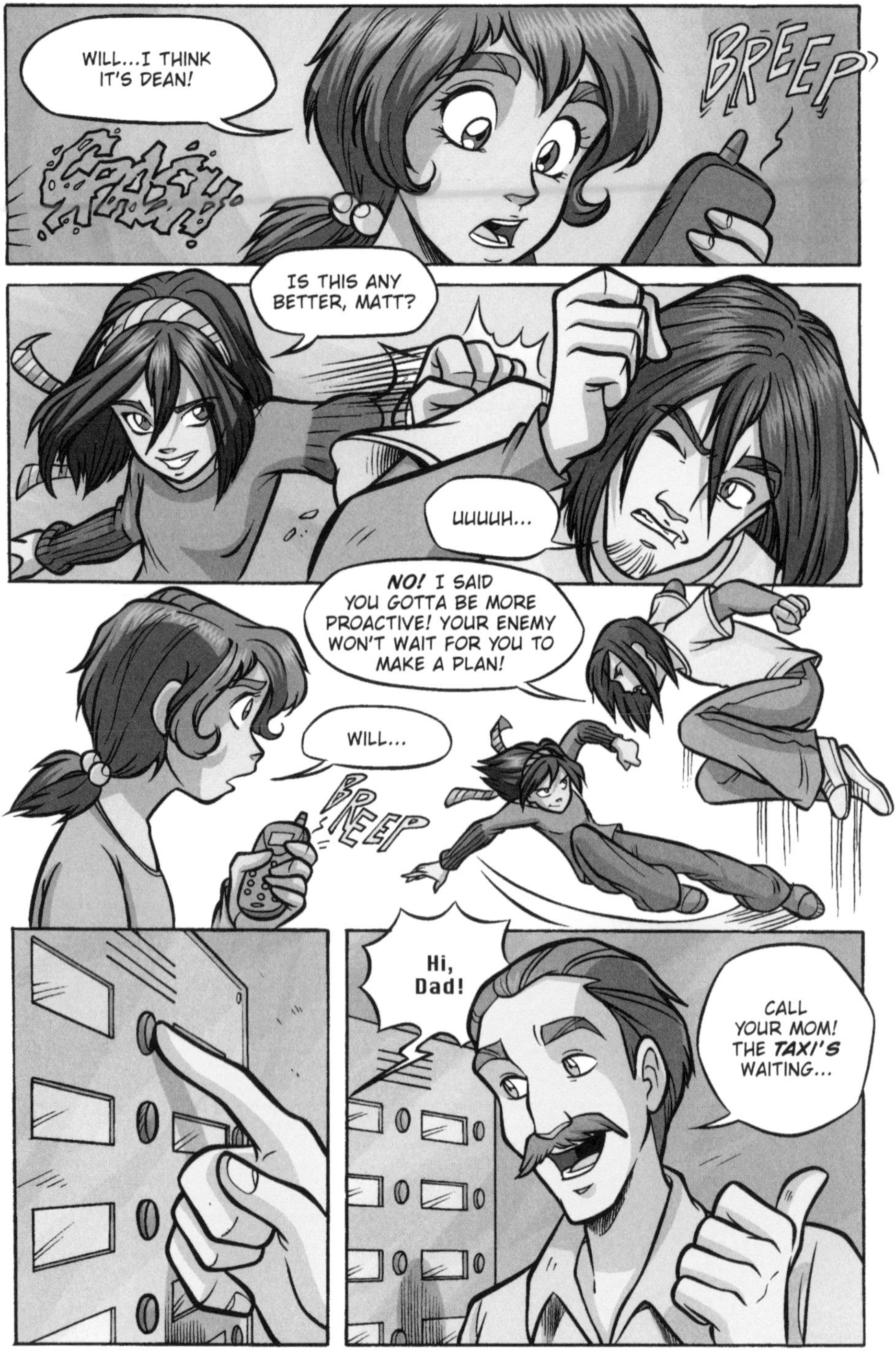
WILL...I THINK IT'S DEAN!
BREEP
IS THIS ANY BETTER, MATT?
UUUUH...
NO! I SAID YOU GOTTA BE MORE PROACTIVE! YOUR ENEMY WON'T WAIT FOR YOU TO MAKE A PLAN!
WILL...
BREEP
Hi, Dad!
CALL YOUR MOM! THE TAXI'S WAITING...

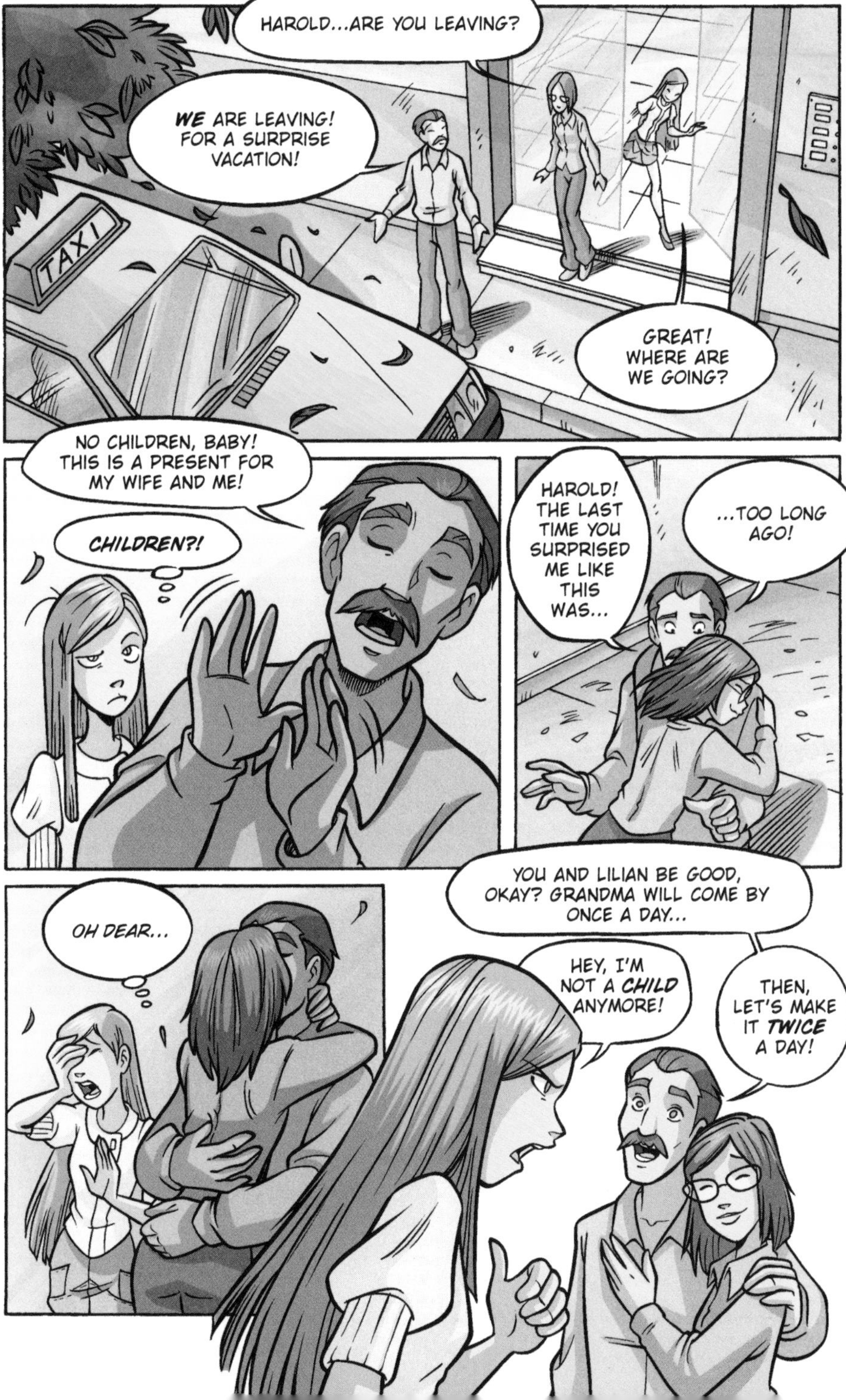
HAROLD...ARE YOU LEAVING?
WE ARE LEAVING! FOR A SURPRISE VACATION!
GREAT! WHERE ARE WE GOING?
TAXI
NO CHILDREN, BABY! THIS IS A PRESENT FOR MY WIFE AND ME!
CHILDREN?!
HAROLD! THE LAST TIME YOU SURPRISED ME LIKE THIS WAS...
...TOO LONG AGO!
OH DEAR...
YOU AND LILIAN BE GOOD, OKAY? GRANDMA WILL COME BY ONCE A DAY...
HEY, I'M NOT A CHILD ANYMORE!
THEN, LET'S MAKE IT TWICE A DAY!

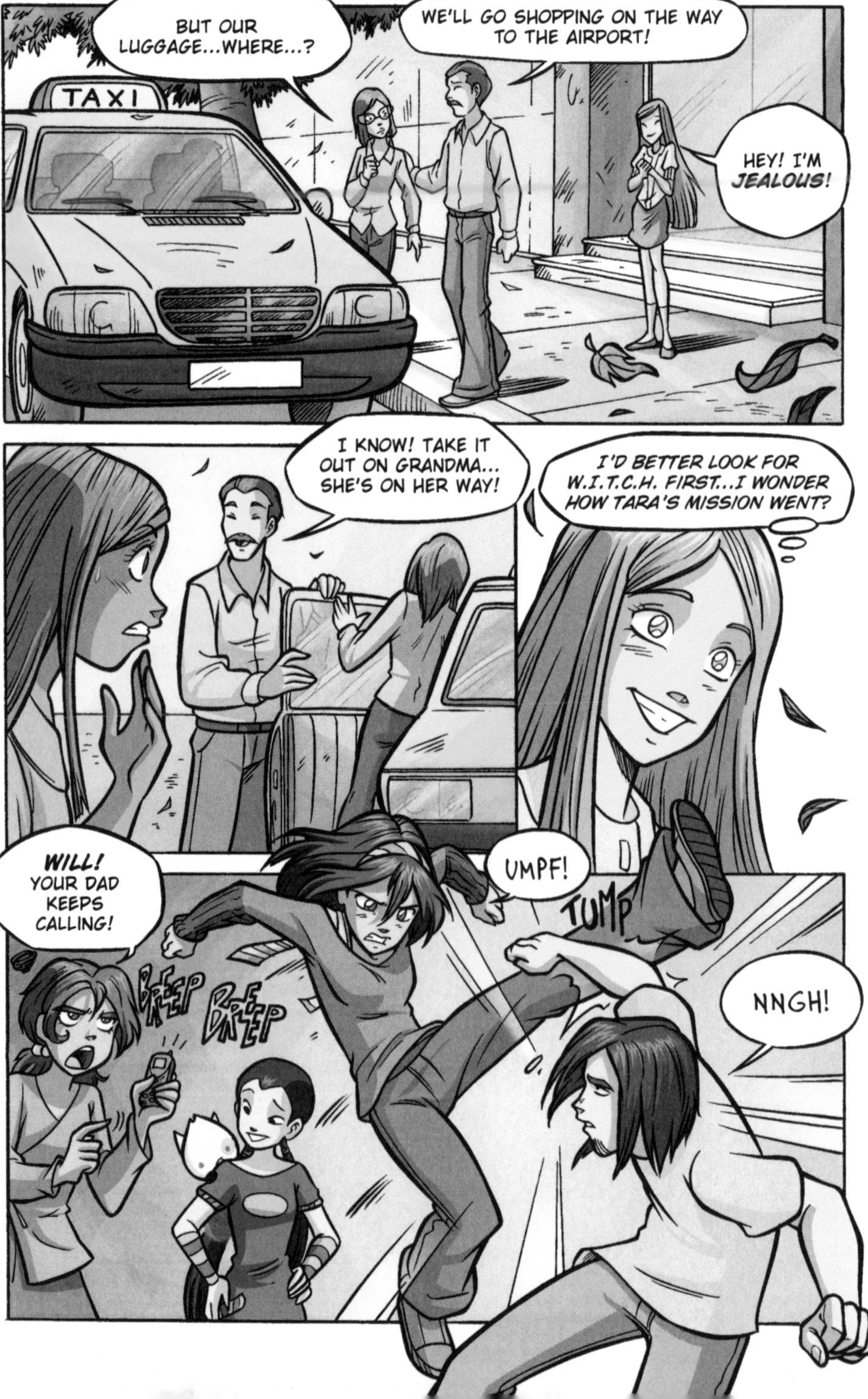
BUT OUR LUGGAGE...WHERE...?
WE'LL GO SHOPPING ON THE WAY TO THE AIRPORT!
TAXI
HEY! I'M *JEALOUS*!
I KNOW! TAKE IT OUT ON GRANDMA... SHE'S ON HER WAY!
I'D BETTER LOOK FOR W.I.T.C.H. FIRST...I WONDER HOW TARA'S MISSION WENT?
WILL! YOUR DAD KEEPS CALLING!
BREEP BREEP
UMPF!
TUMP
NNGH!

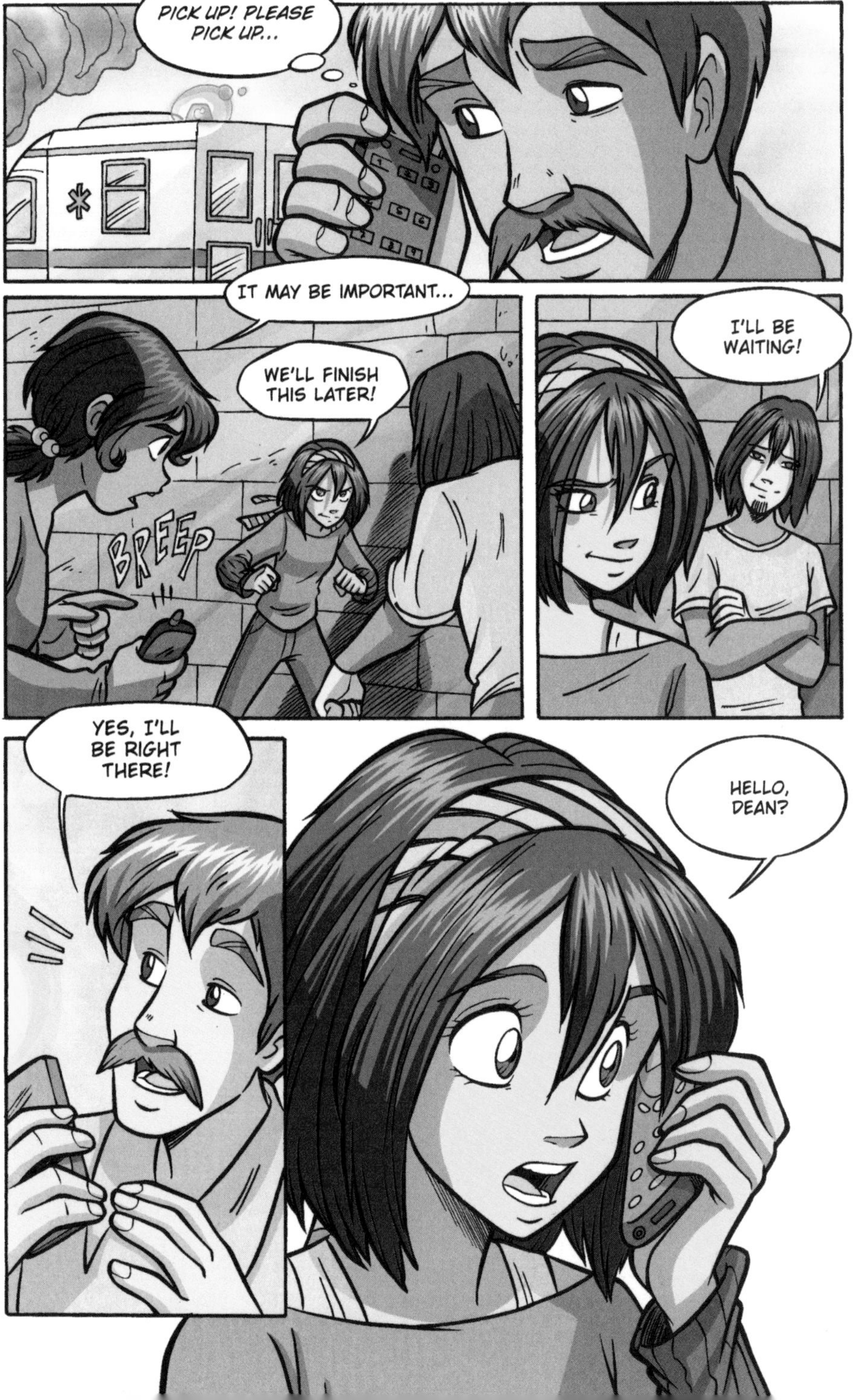
PICK UP! PLEASE PICK UP...
IT MAY BE IMPORTANT...
WE'LL FINISH THIS LATER!
BREEP
I'LL BE WAITING!
YES, I'LL BE RIGHT THERE!
HELLO, DEAN?

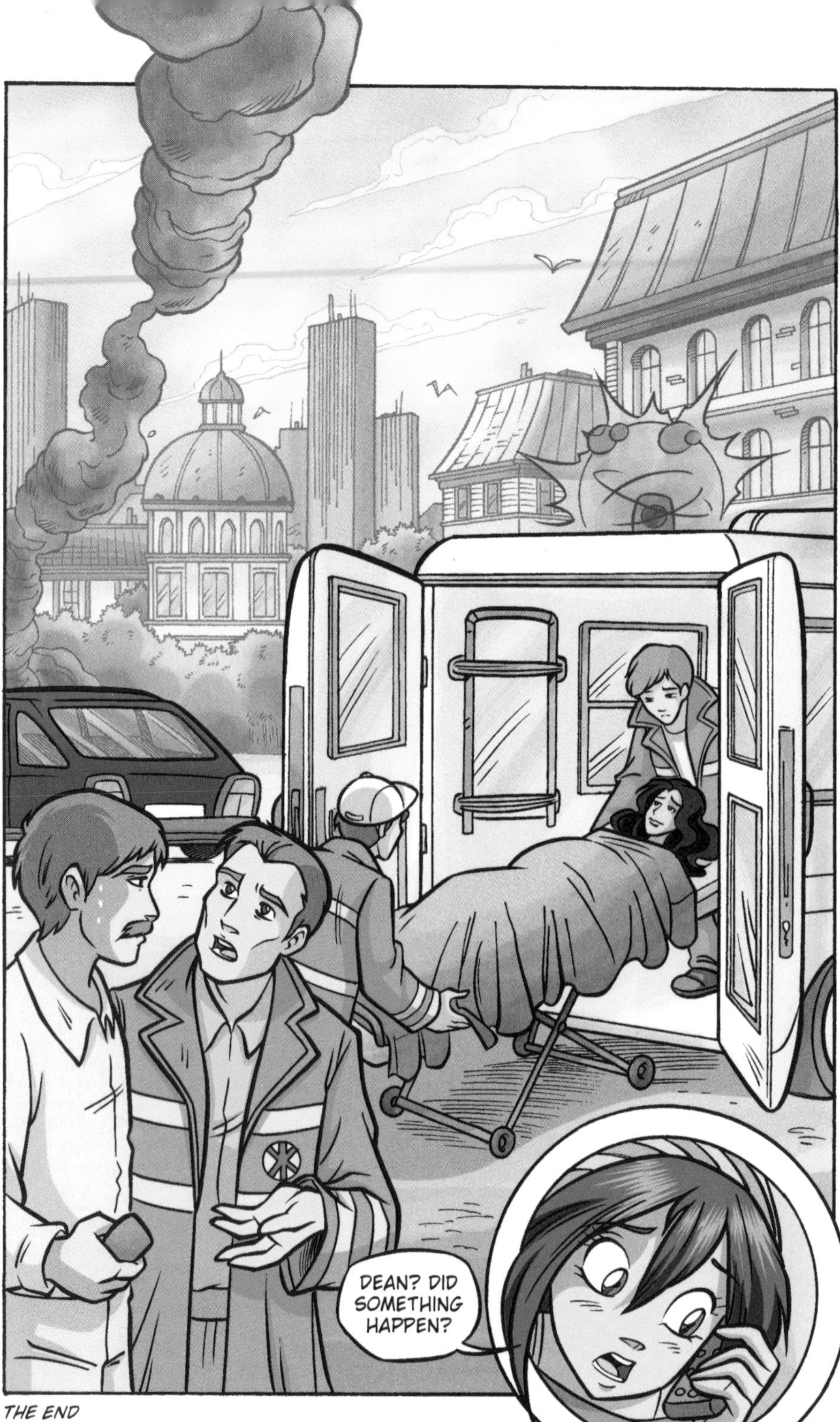
DEAN? DID SOMETHING HAPPEN?

THE END